The Keeper's Daughter

Susan X Meagher

The Keeper's Daughter
© 2019 BY SUSAN X MEAGHER

THIS TRADE PAPERBACK ORIGINAL IS PUBLISHED BY BRISK PRESS, WAPPINGERS FALLS, NY 12590.

EDITED BY: CATRIONA BENNINGTON
COVER DESIGN AND LAYOUT BY: CAROLYN NORMAN

FIRST PRINTING: FEBRUARY 2019

ISBN-13: 978-0-9987907-7-0

By Susan X Meagher

Novels

Arbor Vitae
All That Matters
Cherry Grove
Girl Meets Girl
The Lies That Bind
The Legacy
Doublecrossed
Smooth Sailing
How To Wrangle a Woman
Almost Heaven
The Crush
The Reunion
Inside Out
Out of Whack
Homecoming
The Right Time
Summer of Love
Chef's Special
Fame
Vacationland
Wait For Me
The Keeper's Daughter

Serial Novel

I Found My Heart In San Francisco

Anthologies

Acknowledgments

About five years ago, I visited Greenwich, England to take in the excellent National Maritime Museum. One of the exhibits was on lighthouses, and I was fascinated by the story of a retained lighthouse keeper who maintained all of the houses in a very large area, just making sure the automatic systems were in good shape.

I was taken by the thought of having a job that took you to such isolated, solitary places, and started thinking about how that would be a good profession for a character. Over time, and many different iterations, my character became Scottish, mostly because I had fallen in love with Scotland, and wanted a good excuse to visit more often.

Since then, I've traveled far and wide in Scotland, visiting every lighthouse I could find. But despite doing all of the leg-work I could manage, I am by no means an expert in the place or its people. So I put out a call for volunteers to help me purge the more blatant errors I'd made. Thankfully, five people jumped in to help.

Anne Maguire, Cheryl & Anne Hunter, Rachael Byrne, and Wendy Temple all graciously and generously donated their time and their sharp eyes to helping me make my Scottish characters sound as Scottish as I'm capable of. I'm certain some blunders remain, but they are wholly my fault.

For the portions of the book that take place in Columbus, I was confident of my English knowledge, but much less so of the city. I'm very grateful Brenda Barton was able to spend the evening with me discussing some fine points and taking a spin around town.

Finally, I owe a large debt of gratitude to Catherine Lane, who has once again helped me hone the story into what I hope is a pleasing shape.

Dedication

To the kind, caring, compassionate, and skillful medical professionals of the Dr. Mackinnon Memorial Hospital, Broadford, Skye.

Through the years, I have availed myself of the services of some of the largest, most respected medical centers in the US. I was under the belief that you needed billion-dollar facilities to insure a good outcome in an emergency. I learned how mistaken I was while visiting the Isle of Skye. When you need an empathetic person to hold your trembling hand and convince you that everything will be all right, it's only the size of the care-givers' hearts that matters.

Introduction

If you're lucky, you live in the place that best suits you. If you're slightly less lucky, you take a trip that reveals the place that speaks to you in ways other spots haven't.

I wish I had visited Scotland long before I first did, but I suppose that would have just left me pining away for it for a longer time period. I can't even say what combination of elements makes me love it, but love it I do.

Alba gu bràth!

CHAPTER ONE

A RAZOR-SHARP LETTER OPENER forcefully thrust between the ribs. The nib of her fountain pen swiftly and precisely drilled into his jugular. Actually, the enduring symbol of misogyny, the high heel, could get the job done. A lightly veiled message might add a nice frill to the grisly scene.

Gillian Lindsay peered beneath the conference room table, noting with regret that her heels weren't thin enough to break skin. She'd have to switch to stilettos for that plan to work.

Scanning the pleasant but anodyne space, she considered the possibility of luring her boss over to the window. The cord from the shade would work, but it would take more time, and someone might leap to his aid before she could effectively garrote him. She searched the room again, seeking anything heavy enough to bludgeon him with. There simply *had* to be a quick, yet painful way to rid the world of Ronald B. Hawkins.

"Gillian?"

Great. The Global President of Fabric Care, the head honcho, didn't recall how to pronounce her name. Correct him? If she did, she risked embarrassing him, or sounding persnickety. But if she didn't, he'd be embarrassed or annoyed —with *her*—when someone else said it properly. No way to win with this one.

"Yes, Gillian," Ron said, mimicking the incorrect pronunciation by stressing an annoyingly hard "G" even more, "we ought to hear your thoughts before we move forward. We don't want to be accused of ignoring the ladies."

He had that slick, smarmy smile on his face. The one she always wanted to slap right off him. But today, when he had the unmitigated gall to pass off her proposal as his own, even while she was sitting across from him, she had to clasp her hands together to stop herself from reaching across the table to punch him in the face.

"I would have spoken up if I didn't agree with the proposal," she said. "I hope I'm not overselling, but it's bordering on genius."

"I think so too," the big guy said, turning to give Ron a broad smile. "You just get better and better."

Steam was about to shoot from her ears, but she had to sit there and take it —again. Now Ron would spend a minute or two talking about how the brilliant idea had come to him, so she mentally checked out, allowing herself the small pleasure of continuing to plot his demise. As her imagination took flight, she got more and more into it, not coming back to earth until her teeth sank slightly into the surface of her pen. Jerking roughly, she yanked it out of her mouth to examine it, seeing faint dental imprints in the fourteen-carat gold. For seventeen years she'd treated her college graduation present with loving care, only to mar it with her own teeth. Disgusted with herself, she tossed it onto the conference room table, where it clattered noisily.

The nausea-inducing self-congratulation fest wrapped up quickly enough, and the big boss took off, leaving the North American Fabric Care Division Marketing Group to launch into their usual Friday afternoon wrap-up. The meeting Ron routinely called solely to make sure no one ever got a jump on the weekend. He couldn't bear to think of anyone having fun without him.

He kept blathering on, putting everyone but her to sleep. If she'd been a guy she might have tuned him out too. But she wasn't. She was the only woman VP in her division, which meant that everything she did—and didn't do—got a little more notice, a little more consideration, by both her boss and her co-workers.

To her great distress, Gillian—pronounced with a soft "G," thank you very much—had been taken in by this seemingly pleasant guy who'd slid into his position four years earlier. Ron had been hired by the Global President, who now had a vested interest in his success. She'd been with the company for eleven years at the time, and was maddeningly close to being ready to leapfrog two slots to nab the job herself. But she'd tended to agree that she'd needed just a little more seasoning, so she hadn't complained about being passed over.

Ron was a few years older than she was, had more experience managing a big staff, and had climbed up the ranks the same way she had, via marketing. That left her a clear shot at the job when he got his next promotion—which should have already happened. Ron's stagnation was the source of much gossip, but even Gillian had no idea why he hadn't been moved up. All she knew was that he was blocking her path to the corner office.

The only good news was that she'd been promoted when Ron was hired, and had secured the salary and other perks she thought she deserved. But the enhanced status didn't make up for suffering through the last four years with a guy who specialized in grand theft.

Every manager stole to some extent. That was to be expected. But Ron was a master, figuring out how to claim every bit of credit for any idea that flowed down the pipeline. He was actually so good at it that she had a certain grudging respect for him. But she also wanted to wring his neck with her bare hands. The fact that the Global President of her product line didn't know how to pronounce her name meant that Ron didn't talk her up. He was clearly trying to make sure she stayed right where she was—doing a great job while giving him all of the credit.

The worst part was that their success made everything worse. The better the division did, the more his star glittered. It was hard to complain about doing well, given her generous bonuses, but she'd begun to wish for a crash, just so the Global President took a closer look at Ron's weasel-like ways.

"Gillian," Ron said, giving her a quick look as he properly pronounced her name with a soft, almost delicate "G." "Find us a meeting room somewhere offsite. A hotel, a bar… We've got to celebrate this launch. About thirty people," he said thoughtfully. "Snacks, drinks, you know the drill." He opened his mouth again, adding, "Figure out a way to flag it as a division meeting. We've got money left in the budget for that."

"Wish I could," she said, not even trying to look regretful. "But I'm on vacation at close of business today." She was going to remind him that she was a full vice president, the manager of three senior directors, all of whom could dial a phone and ask for a room. But they had penises, which obviously got in the way of their doing any scut work.

"Oh, shit. I thought you had a week to go."

She sighed, resigned to spending the next half hour verbally recounting every point in the lengthy memo she'd sent the day before, in which she'd ticked off every project and initiative she had cooking.

"Hmm… Who can set this shindig up?"

She let her gaze travel around the room, pointedly staring at each and every man at or below her pay grade. "You have a lot of options. Draw straws?"

"I'll have my admin do it." He gave her a long look. "Why don't you postpone your trip? You should be here for the party, since you made a contribution, too."

She started to shake her head, but he just kept going. Ron paid rapt attention to an odd list of things, but he never caught clear signals that you weren't on board with whatever he was droning on about.

"Nonrefundable ticket," she said, the moment he paused for a breath. She made a show of looking at her watch. "I've got a call scheduled with my counterpart in London. Can't keep him waiting."

"Go, go," Ron said, shooing her from the table. "We're almost done."

Nodding, she got up and raced for the door, trying to get into the hall before he called her back for something stupid. *Too late.*

"Gillian? Make sure you wait for me," he said. "I'll swing by the minute I'm finished here."

After stopping in the break room for a cup of coffee, she raced to her office and called her counterpart in London. She'd just greeted him when Ron slithered into her office, sat on one of the side chairs, and leaned back until he could jam his heels onto the top of her desk.

Conducting a meeting with an audience was always a pain, but Ron obviously wanted to make sure she didn't get away without his noticing. While she spoke, he picked up and handled every single thing she had lying on her desk, playing with her stuff like a toddler. She rushed through her call, then swiveled her chair around to face her boss.

"Hey," he said quietly, giving her his hangdog look. The one that, perversely, must have at least once convinced someone to bend to his will. "I really did think you had a week left. No way you can delay, huh?"

"For...?" She'd have had to be physically restrained to keep her in the office for one more moment, much less a week, but she had to at least *act* like she'd stay if necessary.

"Nothing," he said. She had to hand it to him. He was a prize jerk, but almost always frank. "I just didn't remember you were leaving today, and I don't like surprises."

"Mmm." She started to put her things away, locking up anything she didn't want prying eyes to see. "I don't blame you. But you know I've got everything buttoned down. Each of my guys has his marching orders. They know exactly what I expect of them while I'm gone, and I'm completely confident they'll deliver."

"Yeah, yeah, I know," he said, pouting like a child. "But none of them can step in and handle things, you know? They can't guess what I need like you can."

"Well, if they were as competent as I was, you wouldn't need me, would you." She gave him her most superior smile, having found he was the type of guy who only wanted what he couldn't have. She could control him like a marionette when she was in the mood.

"I could..." His gaze traveled to her window, and grew unfocused. With a firm nod of his head, he looked at her again. "I've got some money left in my T&E budget that I can do without. I'll find a way to pay for every cent you're out. Just hang in for another week."

She snapped her briefcase closed after making a show of putting her computer in her bottom drawer and locking it. His eyes followed her as she stood, then slipped behind him to pause in the doorway. "Everything will be fine," she said, using her most soothing tone. "In two weeks, I'll be right here, celebrating our new marketing initiative. Just think of the fun we'll have!" She clapped him on the back as she grasped the handle of her suitcase and pulled it behind her. She was about ten feet away when he softly said, "Hey, Gillian?" but she kept on walking, hoping to make it clear that while he could steal her ideas, he couldn't steal her time.

Two rain-damp men sat on either side of the far curve of the bar, leaving a pair of empty stools between them—as men liked to do. It was almost impossible to think they'd known each other before tonight, but they were chatting away like a pair of magpies, both somewhat, but not exuberantly, blootered.

Neither of them was a regular, but one of them could have been. He had the form; a man who worked a trade, possibly, but probably not a seaman, fond of the drink, looking for a mate to while away the evening, or, just as likely, take a swing at if a cross word was uttered.

His neighbor should have been at The Royal Aberdeen Club, sipping port, but he was not. For reasons she couldn't imagine, he'd chosen to spend his night in a place far below his social status. "I'm afraid," he said, in a tone that made it clear he was being carefully polite, "that you're missing my point." He was English…or maybe Irish. Sometimes Torie had trouble picking out an accent if the person was of the lofty social order this fella was. Wherever he called home, he'd likely spent his formative years impressing the dons at Cambridge. Actually, he might have been a don. Expensive tweed jacket, well-worn, the tick in the weave helping hide the somewhat larger flakes of dandruff bedecking his shoulders. A starched white shirt collar poked out from a dark gray jumper. His hair was thick and gray on the sides, starting to thin upon the crown, topping a pale, unweathered face. Exactly the complexion thirty years spent in a chilly, gray office in a medieval building would give a man.

The young punter was over twenty years his junior, and significantly lower on both the status and wealth measures. Weather-beaten skin, limp brown hair, broad shoulders encased in a heavy wool shirt straining at the seams. He had no shame about his lower status, though, flapping his jaw so confidently that bits of spittle flew out. His ruddy face grew ruddier as he cut his conversational partner off with a wave of the hand.

"The Scots have lived on this land since people used stone tools. This has always been *Scot*-land. We don't *deserve* autonomy. We *are* autonomous. We've always been autonomous. Sharing an island doesn't mean we share a culture. We don't," he said, snapping his head down roughly, then pausing to drain his pint. His accent gave him away as a working-class Aberdonian, with lots of rounded vowels and a rising and falling tempo that reminded her of her late grandmother.

The older man sipped at his whisky with a thoughtful expression on his face. After a while, he cleared his throat, and said, "Our countries' interests have been identical for hundreds of years. It's madness to think you can go it alone. When the oil runs out, which it will, what will you have?" He answered for himself, showing an astounding amount of ignorance in just a few words. "Distilleries and hundreds of shops selling Harris tweed tea cozies. That's it."

Clearly, his earlier instinct to tip-toe around his point had disappeared, but the younger guy didn't seem upset. At his signal, Torie pulled a new pint for the autonomy side, accepted the damp note the man offered and quickly returned his change. Then she moved farther down the bar so she wouldn't be able to overhear any more of the conversation.

She didn't mind discussing politics—in fact, she delighted in it. And she loved talking about Scottish history as much as anyone in Scotland. But listening to people who didn't have their facts straight simply annoyed her. Anyone who dismissed the Picts or the Celts or the Britons didn't know what he was talking about, and to think Scotland was only whisky and tartan was equally daft.

She let out a sigh when she settled herself well away from any patrons, thankful for the space the long bar provided. Space she often used to snare a moment's peace. Some of her jobs required her to tolerate staggeringly ill-informed people, and she was easily able to go along. But this particular job only forced her to pull a proper pint or splash a wee dram of whisky into a glass. Conversation was optional. Since tips were modest, no matter how charming she tried to be, it made no sense to be overtly friendly. That only created more unwanted male interest than she could bear.

It had been slow all night, with an unsteady drip of patrons, each of them soaked from the icy rain that had been blowing about all day. But that gave her time to do a little housekeeping. They had over fifty bottles of whisky displayed on shelves in front of the mirrored back wall, and she liked to keep the bottles dust-free and facing forward like soldiers on parade. That took quite a while, but she was only interrupted twice for refills. The weather had slaked everyone's thirst.

After draining the bar mat and setting a tray full of clean pint glasses in their proper place, she leaned against the time-worn wood and did a physical assessment. Nothing hurt too badly, which was a relief, as well as a surprise. Checking the clock, she saw that it was only nine, leaving four more hours until the end of her shift. No wonder she didn't feel bad. She'd thought it was time to head home.

A straggler poked his head in, was not greeted by anyone, and quickly disappeared. Torie also didn't know anyone by name or face that night, but that wasn't too unusual. There were far more popular places to drink, many of them flashy and high end. But she refused to work at a pub with a three a.m. license, and she'd sworn off working at bars near one of their universities. Volume didn't correlate with tips, which were scant on the best of days. All she sought was a spot close to home, where she didn't work herself sick, run by an owner who didn't mind her trading shifts with the other bartenders. Given that she hadn't once worked her posted monthly schedule in the two years she'd been there, The Grampian Thistle was a perfect fit.

She started when her phone buzzed, signaling a text, and she quickly removed it from her back pocket.

Hmwrk dun/Off to Kirstys

Her eyes closed and stayed that way for a few seconds. How a boy not yet thirteen could create so much angst was a question she'd been pondering since Aiden had been born. He had a raft of good qualities. She was certain of that. She just couldn't recall any of them at the moment. Headstrong, self-involved, manipulative, sly, obstinate… Torie was sure she could run through a litany of disparaging adjectives long enough to keep herself busy until closing. But that wasn't fair to the boy.

Shivering as she imagined him riding his bike down the pitch-dark roads, she forced herself to give him permission—even though withholding it wouldn't have changed his plans. When you weren't at home to stop a child from leaving, you had to hope for the best.

"Have fun. I love you," she replied. Simple and heartfelt. Her love wasn't in doubt and she *did* want him to have fun. She just wished he hadn't taken off, alone, at his bedtime, to have it.

CHAPTER TWO

EVERYONE SAID THE BEST WAY to avoid jet lag was to stay up until bedtime, but Gillian was pretty sure everyone was wrong. She traveled often for business, but was lucky enough to generally stay in her own time zone. If she'd been forced to make frequent runs to Asia, she'd have been fired years ago.

After the overnight flight, she'd arrived at her hotel at seven that morning, with the cheerful reception clerk only able to hold her bags until check-in at three. For the last seven hours, she'd been wandering around aimlessly in an annoying mist just cold enough to make being outside unpleasant. It was a rare city that presented its best side on a gray day, and Edinburgh was no exception.

The buildings were as dark as the skies, and stuffed with tourists. The Royal Mile wasn't showing particularly well, not appearing to be a place any member of the royal family would have chosen to visit, unless they were running low on rented kilts or Scotch.

Edinburgh had to have a bustling business center, but all Gillian had seen so far were two and three story dark stone buildings. Now she was sitting in one of them, an impressive, but chilly church. She couldn't recall the last time she'd been in a church of her own volition, but it wasn't actively raining inside, which made it a lot more pleasant than the street. The little light the cloud-filled skies gave off filtered through a gorgeous stained-glass window, adding a spot of color to the otherwise uniformly gray interior. She hadn't expected pastel-painted buildings and scorching sunlight in Scotland, but Edinburgh had really gone big for gray.

She extended her foot, deciding her best leather flats were ruined. It was going to take days for the rest of her clothing to dry out, if she didn't freeze to death before then, a serious possibility. Her phone insisted it was forty-three degrees, but that must have been a system error. She'd been warmer in snow storms.

Besides being tired, damp, and wired from too much coffee, she'd discovered the caffeine was only working on her body, giving her the jitters. Her brain had been left in a mush-like state, almost like she had a bad hangover. Didn't that sound like the perfect time to take an expensive history tour? She'd made arrangements for the tour just after she'd decided to come, having read that the tour company was top-notch. But she was sure that even the best guide couldn't stuff any facts and figures into her sluggish synapses. The best she could hope for was enough stimulation to keep her awake. Too tired to think of any alternate plans, she slogged back up the street to stand under the narrow awning of an American coffee shop, sharing the space with four other souls trying to avoid the increasing rain, while she waited for her guide.

A tall, thin, nylon-encased person approached, her knee-high boots slapping happily through the puddles. Even though the hood of her yellow jacket obscured most of her face, Gillian could make out that the woman was looking right at her. A profusion of words came from her mouth, the last one possibly being "castle," but that was a wild guess.

"Pardon?"

This time the words came out in clear, measured, American-accented English. "Are you here for the Deep Dive Tour of the Royal Mile and the castle?"

"I am." She stuck her hand out. "I'm Gillian."

"Great. Just great. We'd best get out of this rain or we'll surely drown. Cup of tea?"

"I think I'd better." She followed the woman into the store and shrugged out of the cursed raincoat she'd recently bought in New York. It was obviously made exclusively for style, given that the shoulders of her sweater were sopping wet, with rivulets of cold rain skittering down her sides.

Her guide flipped off her hood, revealing hair colored not quite a classic red, but a little darker than strawberry blonde. It was cut in a short, spiky style, making her look perky and bright even on such a gloomy day. The big, expressive brown eyes that had locked onto Gillian added a welcome burst of warmth. The woman extended her hand, and they shook. "Torie Gunn," she said. "We're waiting for two more, then we can get right to it." She tilted her head toward the counter. "Let me fetch something for you. Tea? Coffee? Hot chocolate?"

"Hot chocolate, please," Gillian said, suddenly wanting a warm chocolate drink more than anything in the world. When she was stressed, or extra tired, she always craved sweets.

"Have a seat. The others should be along soon."

Gillian grabbed the table by the window when a shaggy-haired guy stood and packed up his laptop. When she sank into the nicely padded bench, she made a snap decision. She'd pay Torie for her time, drink her hot chocolate, and trudge back to the hotel. No matter how much it screwed up her system, she needed sleep more than historical information about Edinburgh.

While she waited in line, Torie removed her jacket, then grasped her dark gray rain pants near her hips and yanked—unsnapping them from her body in one motion. Then she removed a vibrant blue wool jacket and folded it over her arm, revealing a white blouse covered by a tartan plaid vest. Her clothing was so colorful and appropriate for the weather that it really made her stand out. Actually, she would have stood out just about anywhere. Cheerful. Bright. Attractive. Pretty, now that Gillian spent another moment assessing her. She wasn't Gillian's type, but she bet Torie would be right up most guys' alley. Who wouldn't go for a pretty woman who looked so friendly and approachable?

Torie grasped two mugs and carefully carried them over to the table, where she spoke once again. Gillian stared, sure her brain was playing tricks on her. But she was certain being tired had never destroyed her ability to decode speech. Could she have had a stroke?

Laughing, Torie sat down and took a sip of her drink. "I'm sorry," she said, again speaking slowly and clearly and Americanly. "Are you having trouble understanding me?"

"I am, but not consistently…"

"When I start a tour, I usually put on my fiercest Scottish accent and ask if the person's ready to hear a tale of intrigue, valor, bravery, and unbridled courage. But you're giving me that 'What in the world are you saying?' look I get from some Americans."

Blinking in confusion, Gillian said, "You can turn an accent on and off that quickly?"

"Of course," she said, nodding. "So can you. Tell me where you're from, but do it with a heavy Southern accent."

"Aahm certain ahh don't know what you mean," she said, chuckling along with Torie. "Okay. That was a dumb comment."

"No, not at all. I'll speak like I normally do." Her flat American accent disappeared, replaced with a relatively mild Scottish one. The kind of accent you'd hear from a Scottish actor who'd made it in America. Not too thick, not too fast. "You can understand me now, can't you?"

"Oh, sure," she said, giving her ears a second to catch up. Torie's accent was actually kind of fantastic, with just enough of a lilt to make it seem like it was caressing Gillian's ears. "Are you from Edinburgh?"

"Wait," she said, holding up a finger. "I can't let you go about embarrassing yourself like that. No matter what you do, you won't sound like a local, but try to pronounce it *Ed-in-burra*." Gillian gave it a try, drawing a pleased smile. "Lovely job," Torie said. "No one will have to cover their ears if you can keep that up."

"You're from Ed-in-burra?" she asked again, really trying to get it right.

"I am not," she said, with a sly smile. "I'm not certain I've ever spent the night in Edinburgh."

"But you're Scottish, right?"

"Aye," she said, giving Gillian a luminous smile. "They don't yet have DNA tests that will drill down as far as I'd like to go, but I think my ancestors were here before there was a Scotland. I probably have Pict, Gael, Briton, and Viking blood. More Pict and Viking, given where we lived. How about you?"

"Other than O negative, I have no idea what's in my blood."

Torie smiled warmly, shaking her head. "I was asking where you're from."

"Oh! Columbus, Ohio. Born and bred."

"O-hi-o," Torie said, testing it out. "I don't think I've met anyone from O-hi-o. That's in the middle west, isn't it?"

"It's just about the geographic center of the country. You've been to America?"

"I have not. But I'm willing to go—at once." She looked out at the street, where the rain had only grown in strength. "Your hot, dry, desert appeals to me in a visceral way after the rain we've had." She'd probably realized that wasn't a great thing for a tourist to hear. "We've been battered by a storm front that seems to be stuck, but surely that means it will move soon. We'll likely have nothing but sun for... How many days are you here?"

"Sixteen, including today."

"For sixteen days," she said, nodding confidently. Taking another look at people running to get under any form of shelter, she reached into her pocket and extracted her phone. "No messages from the others. Do you mind if we give them a few more minutes? The castle's open until five. Even if we don't get there until three, that will give us two hours, which will be plenty of time to stand in the rain while I pummel you with names and dates."

Gillian nodded, appreciating Torie's earnest enthusiasm. "How many tours of the castle have you done?"

Torie's eyebrows rose, and Gillian noticed they were a darker shade than her hair. "Are you asking if this is my first time?"

"No," she said, chuckling at her stunned expression. "I was asking a serious question. How many times?"

"It's not an insignificant number..." She seemed to think for a moment. "Three or four times a week in the summer, once a week if I'm lucky in the winter. Autumn and spring vary wildly. I've been doing this for ten years, so..."

Gillian put a hand on her arm and gave it a shake. "I bet you wouldn't mind skipping today."

Her eyes grew wide. "I don't have that option. I contract with Deep Dive—"

"I've already paid," Gillian interrupted. "But I'm too tired and wet to walk around any more. Bad planning on my part."

Still looking skittish, Torie said, "I don't feel right about charging for a service I haven't provided…"

"Well, I don't think you can carry me." She tried to boost the charm of her smile, pleased when Torie looked like she was beginning to relax. "If your other people show up, feel free to go. But if they don't, you can go home and put your feet up."

"Wouldn't that be nice," she said, flashing a smile that was just short of dazzling. "I can hardly tell you how appealing that thought is."

"Do you live close?"

"About three and a half hours by bus," she said, shrugging her shoulders. "That's door to door."

"Bus? You took a three and a half hour bus trip to do this?"

"I did. There's a train, but the bus can be as much as fifteen pounds less."

"That's a hell of a time investment!"

"It is," she said soberly. "But I enjoy it, and if I have three people scheduled, I earn enough to make it well worth my while."

Gillian looked at the empty chairs next to them. "You don't have three."

"Oh, but I do. They, like you, paid in advance. Even if Deep Dive gives them a refund, which they rarely do, I'll get my standard rate. I couldn't think of doing this otherwise."

"They're not going to show at this point. Why don't you go on home? I hate to think of you spending the whole night on a bus."

"I'll wait until after six, when the fare drops significantly." A sly smile made her eyes twinkle. "No one's expecting me home until nine or ten, so I'll enjoy my free time. Goodness knows I have plenty to do." She sat up straight and tried to look businesslike again. "But you've paid for this time if you'd like to use it. I could talk about the Royal Mile even if we're not walking it…"

Taking another look at the weather, Gillian said, "Even though I'm dying for a nap, I'm not in a hurry to get any wetter. Maybe the rain will stop soon."

"Many say it helps to stay up when you're traveling east. It also helps to get some exercise. Preferably in the bright sun." That impish smile flashed again. "You should have vacationed in Spain."

"My relatives aren't from Spain, as far as I know, that is. I bet this is something every American says, but I'm here partly to do a little research on my ancestors."

A sweet smile curled the edges of Torie's mouth. "I hear that often. Actually, the Lindsay clan hails from my area. Not far from Aberdeen."

When she said her town, her accent really kicked in, rolling the "r" so hard Gillian was afraid she'd sprain her tongue.

"Aberdeen, huh? Maybe I should go down there to start. There's no reason for me to be in Ed-in-burra," she said, feeling a little tentative about pushing her agenda.

"Up," Torie said, pointing at the ceiling. "Aberdeen's north of Edinburgh."

"Hmm. As you can tell, I know nothing about Scotland."

"Nothing? Truly?"

"Nothing. I recently found out I have a nineteenth-century Scottish ancestor, and I was desperate to get away for a while, so..." She shrugged. "Flights weren't too expensive, and hotels were kind of a bargain." Pointedly looking outside, she added, "I wonder why?"

"Oh, it rains year 'round, I'm afraid. Scotland as a whole has some of the worst weather on the planet. Truly," she added when Gillian looked skeptical. "Ireland, Scotland and Wales all vie for the title of dreariest place on earth. I think we might win this year." She stuck her arms into the air like she was celebrating a touchdown. "But Edinburgh doesn't get this kind of downpour nearly as often as we do up north. They usually have more of a mist." Her face lit up when she smiled again. "Just enough rain to keep your windscreen streaky."

"So, this is your career? Taking seven-hour round-trip bus rides to slosh through the worst weather on the planet?"

She nodded. "This is just one of my jobs, but it's my favorite. Well, I'm doing another nice one tomorrow. I'll be climbing around a hundred and sixty steps to have a view of the easternmost point on the mainland."

She looked pleased with herself, but also a little sly, like she really wanted Gillian to ask what in the hell she was talking about.

"If I'm supposed to know what you're referring to..."

"No, you're not," she said, her soft laugh making her eyes crinkle up. "I'm a lighthouse attendant."

"Get out!" Gillian looked down to see her hand on Torie's shoulder, then realized she'd pushed her hard enough to make her head rap against the window with surprising force.

"I'll say I'm lying if that will stop you from hitting me again," she said, reaching up to tentatively probe the spot that had made contact with the glass.

"I can't believe I did that!" Gillian closed her eyes, then made her hands into fists and held them close to her face. "I'm not usually so excitable, but I've never been to a lighthouse, even though they fascinate me."

Torie's hand hovered above her head for a second, then dropped to rest on the table. Her expression was just short of incredulous. "You've never been to a lighthouse? *Never?*"

"Ohio's in the middle of the country. You don't need lighthouses on the Scioto River."

"But they have them all over the coastline, don't they?"

"They do…I think. I go to New York all the time for business, and they must have one or two hidden somewhere around there, but I've never searched for one. Too busy."

"So, you're fascinated by something you've never seen." She laughed. "Like Bonnie Prince Charlie in exile in Italy, dreaming of Scotland."

"Sure," Gillian said, having no idea what she was talking about. "Why not? I don't know why I like them so much, but I've been interested in them since I was a kid." She reached into her bag and tugged her keys out, displaying a red and white striped lighthouse key ring. "See?"

"Would you like a tour…?" Torie started to say. Then she stopped abruptly as her eyes got big. "I'm sorry for being so forward. That's not like me—"

"Yes!" Gillian knew she should let her bow out gracefully, but she really, *really* wanted to see a lighthouse.

"I would love to take you, Gillian. But it's a long drive. And you'd have to come up to Aberdeen first."

"I don't mind a bit. I'll see someplace new."

"All right," she said, still tentative. "Deep Dive doesn't cover Aberdeen, so I'm free to make my own arrangements. I could do a tour for the same amount you paid for today."

"Done," she said decisively.

"Are you sure? I feel like I've pushed myself a bit."

"I'm sure. Completely sure."

"All right, then," she said, chuckling softly. "I like it when someone knows her own mind."

"Why don't we do this up right? Could I hire you for the whole day? I'd love to see where the Lindsays come from. Do you have time?"

15

"Hmm," she said as she took her phone from her pocket and checked it. "I don't see how that can work. By the time you get to Aberdeen, the day will be half gone."

"Monday?"

Torie took another look at her phone, sneaking a puzzled glance at Gillian while she waited for her calendar to appear. "I start on Monday morning at six, but I'm finished by ten. That evening I'll work from five until eleven. But that leaves me a block of time in the afternoon, if that would work for you."

"It does. We can do the lighthouse tomorrow, and tour around looking for Lindsays on Monday afternoon."

"We could do that…" She trailed off, seeming very tentative. "But that would leave you with so much idle time."

"Don't worry about that. I'll take the train to Aberdeen in the morning, we'll go to the lighthouse, then I'll get a hotel in town. On Monday, when you're finished with your early morning job, we can get together for a few hours—until you collapse from exhaustion."

The smile Torie gave showed no hint of fatigue. "It might sound like I work a lot, but compared to a few years ago, I barely do a thing."

⚜ ⚜ ⚜

They'd finished their drinks long ago, and had completely wasted the hour-long respite from the storm, which had now begun again in earnest.

"Now what?" Gillian asked, staring glumly out the window. "Why'd you have to be so interesting? I could have been dry and asleep by now."

"I'm not interesting on purpose," Torie said, pleased to hear that Gillian found her so. "I'm simply a student of Scotland and her people, and I've been blessed with a good memory. Thankfully."

"Well, we've hogged this table forever, and have only succeeded in timing it so that it's raining harder than ever—if that's even possible."

"Oh, it's possible. The evidence is right there." She pointed at a man in a business suit running down the sidewalk with water flowing down his face like he was in the shower.

"I guess it hardly matters. I've ruined my shoes, my raincoat's a piece of crap, and my sweater hasn't dried out much at all."

Torie hadn't been bold enough to ask why Gillian was so ill-prepared, but she hinted at it now. "Are your boots in your suitcase?"

"Boots?"

The curious way she cocked her head showed she was bootless.

"If you're going to be here for over two weeks, you might consider buying some." Torie let out a quick laugh, hoping she hadn't shamed Gillian. "They're not mandatory, of course, but if you don't want to have to stay on pavement, you might want to pick up a second pair."

"Second pair? I don't own rain boots. If it's raining, I wait until it stops." She shrugged, seemingly telling the truth.

"Don't you have a job?"

"Sure. But I park in a garage that connects to my building. I only have to run from my house to my car, which is just a few yards. I have *winter* boots," she said, her eyes brightening. "But they're for work. They're too dressy and uncomfortable to wear when I'm going to be walking a lot."

"Um, do you have a waterproof jacket? Even though I promised it wouldn't rain again, I might have been lying."

"Yeah, you might have been," Gillian smirked. "I checked my weather app when you went to the bathroom. Tomorrow's supposed to be nice, then it's right back to rain."

When she turned to observe the storm, Torie took another look at Gillian, trying to guess how well-fixed she was. *Very* was the obvious answer. From her perfectly cut shoulder length brown hair to the camel-colored cashmere sweater she wore, everything looked first-class. The gold and silver watch that hung rather limply on her wrist was another clue, especially with the tiny diamonds that stood in for the numbers on the face. "If you don't mind spending a little money, I'd advise proper rain gear and a pair of boots."

Without a pause, Gillian nodded, making it clear money wasn't a pressing issue. "Where should I go? I want everything you have." She let out a little laugh. "I'd say I'm not usually so ill-prepared for a trip, but that's a bold-faced lie. I'm perfectly organized for business trips, but on vacation my usual tactic is to search for cheap flights and a good hotel, and take off without another thought."

"You're serious?" Were there really people who spent thousands of dollars on a trip they'd given no thought to?

"I am. I'm still amazed at myself for booking this tour—which I haven't taken," she added, chuckling.

Admiring her candor, if not her planning, Torie said, "You're the first American I've met who doesn't have a tour book in your hand or on your phone. I usually have people following along as we go, ready to point out anything I say that differs from their little bibles."

"I don't even know the names of the big cities. I just know my great-great-great-great grandfather left here in 1820, and that no one from his direct line has ever been back." She let out a sheepish laugh. "I only know that because I went to a family reunion this summer and spoke with a cousin who's gotten into genealogy. I didn't even know we were Scottish before July."

Torie stood and extended a hand to pull Gillian from the bench. "If you've got a good guide, that's all you need." She gave her a confident smile. "And you've got an ace. Let's get you kitted out."

⚜ ⚜ ⚜

Torie knew where people with money shopped. She herself wouldn't have dreamed of searching out brand names and the latest styles, but she tried not to judge those who did. There were a couple of popular outdoor gear shops nearby, with one of them in the general direction she had to walk to catch her bus, so that was her choice.

Gillian had clearly given up even trying to stay dry. She had the hood of her coat up, which had oddly kept her hair pristine, but she'd given up on the shoes, for she plowed right through deep puddles without pause. The rain didn't inhibit her ability to talk, either, since she never stopped as they leaned into the driving wind.

"I forgot to bring an umbrella. Clearly, I need one," she said as her shoes splashed through at least three inches of standing water.

"Unless you want to bother with buying a very sturdy, substantial one, I wouldn't. This wind will whip it inside out by the time you've walked ten steps. I'd stick with a hood."

"I've got a sturdy, substantial golf umbrella—at home," Gillian grumbled. "My dad's old one. I'm sure it's keeping my closet perfectly dry at this very moment."

"Oh, closets get grumpy when they're wet. Wise choice." Torie lifted her hand to point. "If we can cross this street without drowning, we'll be home free."

"I've never been so wet!" Gillian yelped, once again stepping into what had to be ice cold water to venture into the street. That first step might have been her last if Torie hadn't grabbed her forcefully and pulled her back.

"You have to look to the right!" she gasped, heart racing.

She blinked the rain from her eyes, then nodded. "I haven't had to cross a regular street since I got here. I was just wandering up and down the Royal Mile…"

"It's *vital* to remind yourself to look to the right," Torie said, hoping Gillian's somewhat vacant gaze didn't mean the instruction had gone over her head.

"Right," she said, with her pale eyes locking onto Torie's. "I've been to London before, so I know the drill. My brain's just not working at the right speed."

Torie kept a hand on her arm just to be safe, and they finally made it to the vestibule of the building, with Gillian roughly peeling her limp coat from her body. "I would burn this, but it's too wet to catch fire," she said, glaring at it as it dripped onto the floor. "These shoes too."

Torie couldn't stop herself from laughing at Gillian's bare feet as she pried off the sodden shoes, toes so cold they were a faint blue, with bright pink toenails giving them a second spot of color.

"Let's start with boots. I don't want you to get frostbite."

"I think I've got to find some pants first."

Torie blinked at her for a second. "I take it you mean trousers. Pants are an entirely different thing."

"They are?"

"Pants are worn…under trousers."

"If they sell underwear here," Gillian said, clearly not embarrassed, "I'm buying some. I could wring mine out."

"I suppose we'll have a look. I hadn't planned on outfitting you from head to toe, but I think we'd better."

❦ ❦ ❦

Gillian swallowed hard when all of her purchases were totaled. She hadn't expected to spend nearly more than her air fare on clothing, but she'd be able to wear all of it when she got home. As she tucked her credit card case away, she caught sight of Torie watching her intently.

"That jacket looks very nice on you," she said, starting to blush. "The unlined black one would have been warm enough, but that one makes you look…" She trailed off, then spoke again, with the color in her cheeks growing. "It's very attractive."

"I like it," Gillian said, taking a look at the color one more time. It was close to tangerine, but the bright color would be a plus when she wore it for early morning bike rides. "I'm ready for anything Scotland can throw at me now." After she signed the receipt, she met the clerk's eyes and said, "If I leave my coat and shoes here, will you throw them away for me?"

"No!" Torie said, then stopped and lowered her voice. "I mean, are you certain you want to do that? Your coat looks nearly new."

"It is, but what good does a raincoat do if it doesn't keep me dry? I'll buy one that works when I get home."

"There's a resale shop I pass every day. I'll take it there and see if they're interested. It's too nice to chuck."

Gillian gave her an indulgent smile. "If you want to carry a heavy, wet raincoat all the way to Aberdeen on a bus…be my guest."

"The shop won't pay straight away. But if they sell it, you'll get half of the purchase price. I'll send you the money."

"No need. You can consider that your fee for your troubles."

The clerk folded the coat and put it in a plastic bag. As Torie reached for it, she said, "Could you add the shoes too? If I dry them properly, they'll fetch a good price."

Gillian watched her smile grow as she folded the bag and put it under her arm. Torie looked as pleased as a kid on Christmas, but that only made sense. Any woman who had to make a seven-hour round-trip bus ride just to earn a few bucks was not the kind of person to throw perfectly good, although sopping wet, clothing away.

🌿 🌿 🌿

It was out of her way, but Torie walked Gillian to her hotel. She was now dressed properly, with her brightly colored jacket, a white turtleneck "base layer" made from a fabric that promised to dry quickly, navy-blue rain trousers, matching Wellies, and a pair of wind and waterproof gloves. Beneath the trousers, the same base layer would protect her legs even if the temperature plummeted. Torie had been unable to stop herself from urging Gillian to be more careful with her money, but Gillian had quickly rejected her idea to save twenty pounds by purchasing ankle-length Wellies. Clearly, she didn't believe she wouldn't be knee-deep in water for every one of her sixteen days in Scotland.

The healthy glow her cheeks had born earlier was beginning to fade, and her bright blue eyes had lost their luster. She probably could have found her way to her hotel on her own, of course, but Torie wanted to make sure she was delivered safely. When you had a client willing to pay for a tour of a place you were going anyway, you had to protect your asset.

They reached the entry of a very nice hotel, one where Torie had frequently picked up clients. The doorman, a man she'd seen many times, held the door wide, greeting only Gillian with a very proper, "Good evening, ma'am," then sparing a quick wink for Torie. She wasn't sure what he meant by that, but it was an uncomfortably familiar gesture.

The economic divide between guide and client got wider when Gillian took out her wallet and extracted a couple of notes, then pressed them into Torie's hand. "I truly appreciate how much time you spent with me today. Thank you," she said, her voice taking on an earnest quality.

"This isn't necessary," Torie complained, trying to hand the money back. "You paid for a tour, not shopping. I had *fun* this afternoon, Gillian. It wasn't work."

"Don't you normally accept tips?" she asked, her gaze boring into Torie.

"Well, yes, but—"

"I'd tip anyone who spent her whole afternoon with me." She shut her mouth as her eyes got slightly larger. "I'm not insulting you, am I? I don't know tipping customs in Scotland…"

"Of course you're not insulting me. But shopping isn't what you paid for."

"But it's what I wanted," Gillian insisted. "Now, how are we going to set tomorrow up?"

Torie quashed her discomfort to concentrate on planning. Timing was critical. "You'll need to take an early train to Aberdeen. I believe there's one around eight, if the prospect of that isn't too horrifying. I'll check the schedule and text you."

"Early is fine. You've got my number."

"I do indeed. I'll fetch you from the station in Aberdeen, and we'll head out. Would you like me to make a reservation for you at a local hotel?"

"Sure, if you don't mind."

"What do you like? Historic, modern, one with a spa…?"

"Spa?"

"Exercise facilities, massage services, facials…"

"I wouldn't mind that, but I'm not too particular. I just hate old places filled with knickknacks. I like clean and uncluttered. Quiet is a big plus."

"I can do that. I'll make it for one night?"

Her smile dimmed as a disappointed look covered her face. "We're not going to spend time together on Monday? I thought…"

"Oh! I wasn't sure if you were serious about that. I can spare the time, Gillian. I just didn't want to pressure you."

The smile grew past its previous brightness. "I'm not very easy to pressure. I don't have a thing on my agenda, other than where you lead me. So if you think you can keep me busy in Aberdeen, I'm happy to stay there for a few days."

"Well, Aberdeen is a fine city to live in, but there aren't many 'must see' attractions for tourists. It's more of a business hub for the oil industry."

"I'd like to relax more than anything. When I'm alone, I'll sleep late, and have breakfast in bed. Then we can look around in the afternoons. How does that sound?"

"Like a dream," she said, sighing. "I'll make your reservation through Tuesday. Then we can reassess."

"Awesome."

Standing there with her big smile, uttering that ubiquitous adjective, Gillian seemed one hundred percent American. Very becomingly so. She extended her hand, and shook Torie's in a firm, businesslike fashion.

"If I were you, I'd have a light dinner, then head straight to bed," Torie said.

"I'm going to do just that, but I'm going to skip dinner. I'm too tired to chew."

"That's even better. In the morning, get up and have breakfast at your normal time. That will help reset your body clock."

"I'll do that. I guess I'll see you tomorrow then."

"You have my email and my mobile number. Just text me to let me know you've made the train. I promise I'll be there to pick you up."

Despite her fatigue, Gillian's smile still packed a lot of energy. "I don't have a doubt about that. You give off the air of someone I can count on."

"I'm glad the air is telling the truth." She started to walk backwards, waving as Gillian turned and headed for the front desk. When Torie exited, she glanced at the doorman, who once again gave her a knowing wink that had an air of lasciviousness to it. He'd undoubtedly seen Gillian pressing cash on her. Did he think she was a sex worker? She laughed to herself, thinking that if she had been, she would have been able to work not just fewer jobs, but fewer hours as well.

Chapter Three

When Gillian stepped out of the Aberdeen train station on Sunday morning, she held her hand over her brow to shield her eyes from the bright sun. They'd agreed to meet outdoors so Torie could soak up some Vitamin D while she waited, but Gillian wasn't exactly sure where— Then she heard a cheery voice say, "You never thought you'd see that golden orb in the sky again, did you."

"Good morning," Gillian said, turning to find Torie dressed for a sunny, cool day. Another wool jacket, this one forest green, topped a navy fleece worn over a pale blue blouse. A darker green scarf was wound around her neck, a slight nod to the cool weather. The sun made her hair glow like a halo, red and blonde strands standing up to catch and reflect the light.

"You look awfully nice," Gillian said. She gazed at the fleece for a moment. "Is that a vest? If so, I see a trend."

"A…vest?" Looking down, she grasped and tugged the bottom of the garment. "Do you mean my gilet?"

"If gilet means vest, then yes," she said, chuckling.

"You wear a vest *under* your blouse. I actually have one on, but you shouldn't be able to see it," she added, laughing along with Gillian. "I'm always cold."

"That means you're wearing…" She narrowed her eyes and thought. "A vest, a blouse, a gilet, and a jacket?"

"I'd call this a blazer, but I suppose it's also a jacket. Along with leggings and jeans. It's a rare day I don't have to wear a vest and leggings."

"I have the long underwear I bought yesterday in my bag." She looked up at the sun and gave it a scowl. "I don't trust it to stay nice out, so I came prepared."

"But you're not wearing your rain boots, so you're also an optimist."

"I thought I could trust the sun to stay out for a few hours. But my boots are in my bag if I need them. I just prefer running shoes."

"Trainers," Torie said as she grasped the handle of Gillian's bag and started to wheel it toward the parking lot next to what looked like an upscale shopping mall.

"I knew I'd have to adjust to Scotland, but I didn't think I'd have to learn new words for everything!"

"We have an advantage. We watch American TV, so we hear most of your expressions. But I doubt you watch many programs that are produced in Scotland."

"I've seen a few Ewan MacGregor movies. Does that count?"

"It does," she said, revealing an indulgent smile. "Extra points for James McAvoy, Kelly MacDonald, or Rose Leslie, noted Aberdonian."

They walked to a small white car, where Torie used her key to open the trunk. "Och, the boot's nearly full. Do you mind if we put your things on the back seat?"

"Boot? Is that the trunk?"

"No," she said, grinning slyly. "It's the boot. You can incorrectly call it whatever you want, of course."

Gillian took a look at the junk piled up in the trunk. A kid's biking or skateboard helmet, splattered with decals, a backpack, partially open and stuffed with plastic parts to some building project, and a couple of plastic cases like the kind that held power tools. "Your boot looks well-used."

"Always," she sighed, then shut the lid. It took a little work, but she wedged Gillian's wheeled bag as well as her carry-on onto the tiny back seat, then let out a breath, looking proud of herself.

Since Gillian hadn't been helping, her attention had drifted to a pair of huge ships docked just across the road. "Is that a…port?"

"Indeed, it is. The port of Aberdeen has brought us trade, commercial fishing, ship building, and now a mix of container ships and ferries, along with serving the needs of the oil industry. We're the energy capital of Europe, you know."

"I did not know," Gillian said. "Is that a…river?"

Torie pointed to the gray water in the distance. "That's the North Sea, provider of our lovely, temperate weather. Right in front of us is the River Dee. I live just on the other side of it."

Gillian didn't comment, privately wondering how close Torie lived to this very industrial area. She hoped there was a pretty, tree-filled neighborhood hidden behind all of those oil storage tanks.

As they got into the car, Torie said, "We've got an hour's drive. Barely enough time for me to astound you with my knowledge of lighthouses." She let out a laugh. "I really do know a lot about them, truth be told."

"Mmm hmm. I see how this goes. While I was idly wishing I lived near a lighthouse, you did the mature thing and read up on them."

Torie was fussing with her seatbelt, which hadn't seemed to have retracted properly. "Well, I have read a bit, but my knowledge comes from experience. I lived in or near a lighthouse for most of my youth."

Gillian found her hand involuntarily wandering off her leg to slap Torie once again, but she managed to restrain it at the last second. "Get out! I've never even seen one from a distance, and you've lived in them?"

"I have," she said, smiling proudly. Her phone rang and she tugged it from her pocket to gaze at it for a moment. "Do you mind?"

"No, go ahead."

Gillian was surprised to have her get out of the car and move a few feet away. The windows were up, so she couldn't hear much, but in just a minute Torie was gesturing with her hand, making a fist, then slapping herself on the thigh. Her cheeks were getting redder by the moment, and when she shut off the phone and stuck it back into her pocket, Gillian could see her take in a deep breath and try to compose herself.

When she opened the door again and slipped into the driver's seat, she asked in a conversational tone, "Do you have children?"

"Not a one. I had an aquarium, but I got tired of paying people to take care of it when I was away. How about you?"

"I'm responsible for one wee bairn. And if I could get my hands on him, you'd be able to watch an old-fashioned skelping."

"Skelping is…?"

"A beating. Which he richly deserves." She let out a tired-sounding sigh. "But I'd never lay a hand on him, which he takes advantage of." She shook her head briskly. "Back to happier topics. We're going to follow the A90 the whole way, so I can talk without having to look at my GPS."

Given the anxiety she could nearly see emanating from her body, Gillian had to fight with herself to not ask what was going on with this kid. But she didn't want to pry into Torie's private business. And this was clearly private, or she wouldn't have gotten out of the car to take the call. "That sounds good," she said. "Um, are you sure this is a good day to do this? I could…do something else if you have something you have to take care of."

"No. Thanks, but no," she said, with a thin smile covering her face. "I've built my schedule around doing this today. I'm quite glad to have someone to share the drive with. Especially when the sun's shining like it is. The weather's too glorious not to share it."

"It is that," Gillian agreed. "Oh, I meant to thank you for all of the info you sent me. Were you up all night compiling it?"

"No, no, not at all. I wrote most of it on the bus. I carry a tablet computer with me at all times, just in case. What did you think of my fee? Is it all right?"

"No," she said, giving her a frown. "It's way too low. For four hours of your time yesterday, I paid a hundred and fifty dollars. That's thirty-seven fifty an hour, which seems like a fair rate."

"No! I only get half of the fee Deep Dive charges. Fifteen per hour is a very good rate for me, Gillian. Really. It's more than I make at my other jobs, and I enjoy this more."

"I won't pay less than twenty. Final offer."

A genuine smile lit Torie's face, making her look about twenty years old. "Well, you're in my car, and it would be rude to toss you onto the motorway, so I'll accept your final offer. But I'll only charge you for the time we're actually touring. When I'm at the lighthouse, I'll have to switch hats and be an attendant. Fair enough?"

"Fair enough."

Torie pulled her tiny car onto the road, with Gillian barely stopping herself from screaming and wrenching the wheel to the right. *They drive on the left,* she reminded herself sternly. *Look right, drive left.*

Fighting the instinct to grab the wheel, Gillian looked out at the stately gray buildings, with the sun glinting off flecks of something in the stone. The city fathers must have gotten a very good deal on an entire quarry, since nearly every building was covered with it. "Do you have a big quarry nearby?"

"It's called Granite City for a reason," Torie said, smirking. "The suburbs aren't quite as granite-clad, but most of the city is. Some of us love it," she said, her contented smile showing she was one of them.

"It's nice," Gillian decided. "Shimmery."

"Aye," Torie said sagely, "when the sun's shining at the proper angle." A cute smile settled onto her face. "Which it's going to do for fifteen consecutive days."

"That's the request I've put in." Gillian turned to watch Torie, *from the passenger's seat,* maneuver the car onto a bigger road. Years of driving from the left-hand seat had thoroughly indoctrinated her. Torie simply should *not* have had a steering wheel in front of her. Taking a deep breath to calm her nerves, she said, "Why don't you tell me how a woman became a lighthouse keeper. I've always assumed men were up in those little crow's nests."

"I think crow's nests are on ships. And you're right, most keepers were men. But it wasn't odd for a woman to be a keeper. That term's no longer valid, by the way. We're merely attendants now."

"The difference is…?"

"When I was a girl…" She stopped and laughed. "I sound older than I am, which is quite old enough. But when I was a girl, many of the houses were still manned by keepers. My father was one from the time he was a young man until mechanization rendered all of the keepers redundant."

"I guess I'm surprised they weren't always mechanized. Did your dad have to turn the light around by hand?"

Torie gave her a puzzled glance, making Gillian guess she'd asked a stupid question. "The houses I'm familiar with had lights that flashed at specific frequencies. They'd been on timers for many, many years."

"That sounds more reasonable," Gillian said, laughing at her own ignorance. "The keepers would have gotten really tired if they'd had to turn a crank all night long."

"Aye, they would have," Torie said, chuckling. "Keepers were busy enough, monitoring the light and making repairs. They were also charged with keeping an eye out for disabled ships, and all sorts of other issues too numerous to mention."

"You're saying that at some point they mechanized the whole thing, right?"

"Correct. At that point, my granny was getting on in years, so we moved into her flat in Aberdeen. We're still there," she said, letting out a sigh that sounded wistful.

"That meant your dad had to find a new line of work?"

"He did, but he's never been as happy as he was when he was a keeper. In Salutem Omnium." She snuck a quick look at Gillian. "For the safety of all. That's the keeper's motto." She made a face, then shook her head. "Leaving was difficult for him, since I believe it was his calling. He's not had that since." Her lips pursed briefly, then she let out a breath and adopted a happier expression. "My mum went to work for the first time when we moved to Aberdeen. She'd always wanted to, but I think she imagined that working would be more glamorous than it's turned out to be."

"Does she have a good job?"

"Good?" Torie gave her a quick glance. "She cares for an elderly woman who's unable to care for herself. The pay isn't much, but the schedule fits very well." Her smile reflected what must have been very fond feelings for her mom. "She loves to care for people, and the woman she works with is a lovely person. My mum would help her for free if we didn't need the income."

Gillian knew she was probing, but she couldn't help it. She loved drilling down deep when she was learning about something she was interested in, and the ways of the average Scot was on her list. "How did you pick up this attendant's job?"

"Oh, it's not really my job. For largely sentimental reasons, my dad agreed to stay on as an attendant. The job requires only a monthly visit, and a report to the Northern Lighthouse Board if anything's amiss."

"One day a month?"

"Well, four days in total, since he's responsible for all four houses in Aberdeenshire. He had five, but they closed the one in Kincardineshire a few years ago."

"Um," Gillian said, "so he kind of does his old job, but doesn't get his old salary?"

"Oh, the money's a pittance, but it means something to him to be on the job for forty years. Next year's his anniversary, and then we can stop this cat and mouse game. I might try to get the job on my own, but that's still up in the air."

"Wait. You do the job *for* him?"

"Oh." She laughed. "I'm expecting you to figure a lot of things out on your own, aren't I? My father's knees should both be replaced, but he's mastered the art of dismissing the pain every time he gets near the top of the NHS waiting list. They hurt horribly, are very unstable, and we're all afraid he'll fall and kill himself just walking about. Climbing the lighthouses is physically impossible, and has been for years."

"Years? You've been covering for him for years?" She tried to keep the amazement from her voice, but realized she'd not done well.

Torie smiled and shrugged. "Every year he says he'll have the surgery. He's afraid," she added quietly.

"What will happen when he's reached his fortieth anniversary? Will he get a gold watch?"

"A gold watch!" She laughed, shaking her head. "I don't expect anyone will notice, save for my father. But it's no bother to do the job. You'll see."

Torie doubted anyone would ever attempt to write her biography, but if anyone did, they should start with the reams of notes Gillian must have secretly been taking. In all of her years, no one, save for Aiden, when he was about seven, had ever seemed so interested in her. It certainly didn't seem sexual, although Torie was so out of practice she might have missed an obvious pass. But Gillian didn't look or act very gay, again, if Torie recalled how lesbians acted. No, it simply seemed that Gillian was insatiably curious—about nearly everything, and Torie was the only thing available at the moment to fix her agile mind upon.

"You were saying you started secondary school when you moved to Aberdeen, right?"

"That's correct. It seemed like a very big city to me, the largest town I'd ever lived in, but I got used to it eventually."

"Where did you say your last lighthouse was?"

"Fair Isle. An island in Shetland so tiny I literally knew the name of every single person who lived there. I think that was around sixty people."

"Get out!" Gillian yelped, with her hand lifting to potentially get in another punch. She grabbed the right with her left and wrestled it back onto her lap.

Did she have some sort of neurological disorder?

"I'm being perfectly honest," Torie said. "You can see why I'd have culture shock in Aberdeen after our posting in Fair Isle, plus my summers in Orkney."

"That's where your mom's family was from?"

"Correct. I spent every summer helping out on the family croft." She paused, and clarified, "A croft is a small farm, by the way. The Sinclairs are mostly gone now, but they were Orcadian crofters for generations."

"Sinclair?"

"Uh-huh."

"That's a Scottish name?"

"I do believe it is," Torie said. "It's very common around there. Why?"

"My mom was a Sinclair." She blinked a few times, looking very puzzled. "I don't think she was Scottish, though. At least she never said she was."

"Has your mom ever talked about her family origins? I suppose Sinclair is common in England, too."

"Not that I remember," Gillian said, her head barely shaking. "I'm sure I asked, but she wasn't much for talking about the past."

"Your mom's gone?"

"Uh-huh," she said, turning to idly glance at the pasture dotted with white sheep.

"I'm certain you would have asked," Torie said, chuckling softly. "You're a very curious person."

"Oh, damn, I'm grilling you like you're a suspect," she said, slapping her hand over her eyes. "I'll shut up and just enjoy the drive."

"No, no, I love having someone to talk to. But I should be talking about Scotland, not myself. That's what you're paying for, Gillian."

"You're right," she said, continuing to gaze out the window. But the more Torie talked about Scotland, the fewer questions Gillian asked. She was clearly someone who liked to hear about people, rather than facts and figures. As any good guide should, Torie tightened up her spiel, dropping in some tales about the people who'd worked the lighthouses, and the privations they'd suffered. That brought Gillian back around, and she started to ask for more detail, assuring Torie that she'd nabbed her interest once again.

It didn't take long for the city and the suburbs to disappear, leaving them in less populated, more rural areas. Then the small towns vanished, and cows began to appear, contentedly munching on long, very green grass. Gillian had seen a lot of cows in Ohio, but they weren't eating verdant grass in November. It certainly didn't seem warmer in Scotland, but the grass hadn't gotten the memo.

Whenever the land started to look a little bare or patchy, the cows would give way to sheep, who could clearly survive on less fertile land.

Torie was talking away, providing a wealth of details about lighthouses, their role in keeping ships and sailors safe, along with little snippets of info on their design. That was all interesting enough, but facts and figures only lodged firmly in Gillian's brain if they had to do with her job. She couldn't name all fifty states to save her life, and tended to blow off any details that weren't connected to people she knew.

She understood that Torie had to give her some background on the actual structure of lighthouses, but Gillian wanted to see them, to climb the stairs, to gaze out at the sea. It really didn't matter how many there had been, or who built them, or how sturdy they were. She wanted the real experience.

They were about fifteen miles from Aberdeen when she saw her first unbroken view of the sea, off to her right, sparkling in the sun. "The water's right there!" she gushed, drawing a puzzled look from Torie.

"You seem very impressed by large bodies of water. Didn't your flight cross the Atlantic?"

"Of course it did. But I've never seen the ocean from a car."

Torie gave her another suspicious look. "Your family didn't take you to Florida in the winter? I thought that's what everyone did." She laughed a little. "It seems like every Scot makes a pilgrimage to Florida at least once in their lives."

"Not us. We actually didn't take many vacations. Both of my parents liked work better than family life." She shrugged, knowing that was an awful thing to say, but having gotten very accepting, nonjudgmental vibes from Torie.

As she'd hoped, Torie simply nodded, then went back to talking about the Northern Lighthouse Board.

After another fifteen minutes, Torie hit her blinker and they exited onto a smaller road. The ocean was close now, with Gillian easily able to smell its salty tang. Torie slowed down as they entered a more built-up area, and they passed some awesome rocky cliffs that plummeted down to the sea. "How high were those?" Gillian demanded.

Torie gave her a quick smile. "I'm not sure, but I wouldn't want to have to jump. We're almost there," she said. "If you keep looking to the northwest, you'll see her soon."

Gillian leaned forward, like that few inches would make a difference, then she squealed with delight at her first glimpse. In the distance, with rocky cliffs in the foreground, the lighthouse stood proud on a spit of land, with the glimmering sea shining so brightly it hurt her eyes. She wanted to speak, but only a satisfied purr came out.

Finally, they were close enough for her to make out details on the structure, to see a crisply painted wide red stripe upon the blinding white background, and a smaller red ring near the black lantern, pleased with herself for having recalled its technical name. "It's so beautiful," she said, realizing she was whispering.

"It is that," Torie agreed. "I've not seen them all, but I've seen many, and this one stands proud."

They parked on a tiny bit of land near the jagged, rocky shore, got out and walked across a short land bridge to the small parcel of land the lighthouse sat upon. "1827," Torie said, leaning her head way back as she looked up. "Designed by Robert Stevenson, but built by an Aberdonian."

"You said he was Robert Louis Stevenson's grandfather?"

"He was indeed. Scotland's pre-eminent lighthouse builder as well. The tower's thirty-five metres tall." She paused, adding, "About a hundred and fifteen feet."

"Thank you," Gillian said, bowing.

Torie just smiled, continuing to state her facts. "The light flashes white every five seconds, visible for twenty-eight nautical miles."

"On a clear day."

"On a clear day," Torie agreed, her charming grin sending a little zing down Gillian's spine. Or maybe it was the lighthouse that gave her the chills. She stood in front of a massive reddish-orange steel gate with golden letters affixed to it that spelled out "Buchan Ness Lighthouse." That spiffy sign certainly didn't look like it had been there in the nineteenth century.

"Are we going up? I'm ready to run ahead and start without you."

"Have a little patience. Remember, I'm working now, so I'm setting the pace." She carried a tote bag with all sorts of things jammed into it, and she removed a big ring of keys that lay on the top. Keys of every size and shape jangled when she shook it, then brought it close to her face for inspection. "This one's next to the blue ball, I think." She, or her father, had put beads on the big ring to separate the keys for the different houses, and she quickly plucked the proper one from next to the blue ball. After opening the gate, they walked up to the door of the lighthouse, and Torie slid the key into the lock and turned it. A sharp "clack" showed it had worked, then she used the next key to open a more modern lock that sat higher up on the door. That one opened as well, then Torie pushed the door open.

Gillian peered inside, then gasped. "The staircase is awesome!"

She stood right in the doorway, staring. The stairs had obviously been crafted back when builders as well as the government wanted a beauty return on their investment, and they had definitely gotten their money's worth.

The stairs themselves were probably made of concrete, but they were painted white, with the middle of each a deep red, looking like a carpet runner.

It took her a minute to figure out how they held together as they spiraled up the tower, but she finally had it. A wooden bannister curled up from the first stair, with a white painted wrought iron spindle encased in each step.

Gillian wasn't at all sure how the stairs were attached to the tower wall, but they definitely were. But with no hardware or brackets, it looked like they were held in place only by the fairly delicate spindles and the handrail, which actually looked seamless, although that was a total impossibility.

The staircase took up the majority of the tower, with a little space on the first floor for access to a very large metal-covered panel, probably the mechanicals Torie had spoken of. Other than that, it was just a tower with a magnificent staircase.

Gillian was so transfixed that she started when Torie spoke softly behind her. "The light itself is still owned by the lighthouse board, but the tower and the keeper's cottages are privately owned now. They renovated the whole property over a period of years, and it's looking awfully nice. It's in the best shape of any I've seen."

"Someone lives here?"

"The owners rent the cottages out, but they could live in one if they wanted to." She laughed. "Given they could afford to buy this property and bring it up to this standard, I'm betting they have a magnificent home somewhere else."

"But why would you ever leave?" Gillian asked, still staring at the stairs.

"Because you were freezing cold, bored to death, lonely for companionship, sick of the same view... I could go on."

"Those are not the words of a romantic," Gillian said, a little disappointed that Torie seemed so blasé. "I haven't even been up there, and I'm already sure you're going to have to pry me away."

"There's no bathroom," Torie said, batting her eyes. "You'll come down soon enough."

"Can I go?" She was already inching toward the stairs.

"Of course. I'll check things out down here and come up in a minute."

"Do you need help?" she asked, hoping her offer was rebuffed.

"I do not. I just have to check the batteries, take a look at some wiring we had replaced last month, then peek around for water leaks or anything that's out of place."

"I'll be upstairs." As she started to climb, the white painted stuccoed walls closed in on her a little bit. She wasn't claustrophobic, at least not that she knew of, but she guessed the sensation would bother those who were. She started up way too fast, and even though she was in good shape, Gillian was panting by the time she was halfway up. Her heart was racing, too, really thrumming in her chest.

"I thought I was fit," she called down.

"There's nowhere to rest. Usually, when you climb flights of stairs you get a little break with each landing. Not here."

"These little windows are cute!" She put her hand into the deep recess that had been cut into the wall to allow for a bit of natural light.

"Indeed. They're not very wide, but they're worth a peek."

"No way. I'm not going to spoil my view. It's all or nothing."

Gillian slowed her pace, keeping her eyes on the sunlight streaming across the space directly above her. That probably wasn't smart, since it let her see how slowly she was closing the distance. But she kept making progress, now using the handrail to steady herself as she finally reached the top, breathless and sweating. Her jacket was off, and she was tempted to whip her sweater off as well, but then she steadied herself and looked out, immediately forgetting her shaking legs and the sweat trickling down her back. In front of her, in three directions, all she saw was the deepest blue water on earth. She made some kind of pleasured sound, then leaned on an iron railing to stare, transfixed.

The day was remarkably calm, with not a single whitecap on the glassy surface. This was just what she'd imagined it would be like up in a tower. Nothing but nature's magnificence. No people. No noise. Just beauty. Her eyes began to adjust and let her take in different kinds of birds, white, and black, and gray, some with bright yellow bills or feet. Then a flock of odd birds flashed right by her, beaks and feet a dull orange. They beat their wings so fast they were a blur, then they dove for the ocean, with most of them hitting the water like dive-bombers. Squealing with delight, Gillian grabbed a pair of binoculars and tried to follow them, but they were so fast she couldn't begin to keep up.

"Having fun?" Torie asked, nearly making her drop the binoculars.

"What are those birds?"

"Puffins," she said, then took the binoculars from Gillian's hands. She studied them for a minute, then said, "They shouldn't be here at this time of year, though. They're pelagic—"

"Pelagic?"

"Birds that spend almost all of their time on the open water. See how dull their beaks are? In the spring, when they come back to mate, they'll be bright orange. Their feet too."

"I'll come back," Gillian said without a pause. "I want to see them again."

Torie grinned widely. "I come out the last Sunday of every month, unless I've a tour scheduled. Come back in April or May. They'll be going crazy then, feeding their chicks."

Gillian found herself slapping Torie's shoulder again, unable to keep from battering her. "You have a key to this place and you only come once a month?"

"Just once," she said soberly. "I have to visit the other three stations too, and I never know how long I'll have to spend. I usually don't schedule any of my other jobs on lighthouse days, so four trips is about all I can manage financially."

"Why do I keep hitting you?" Gillian asked, covering her eyes with a hand. "I'm not usually a violent person."

"You're excited."

"I really am," she agreed, a little embarrassed to be carrying on like a child. But she was in a foreign country, she was with someone she'd never see again, and for a change she didn't have to act like a cool, calm and collected adult. She was on vacation from *everything*, including her composure.

"I don't blame you for thinking this is a taste of heaven," Torie said, sounding a little wistful again. "You look out there on a day like today and you just see the beauty. But when you're up in one of these houses and the waves are crashing against the base so hard your teeth chatter, you look at it with a different perspective."

"You don't love it?" She knew she sounded like a kid asking if another kid believed in Santa Claus, but she couldn't imagine not loving every single thing about this experience.

"I *do* love it," she admitted. "It's part of me. I just see…more than the beauty."

Gillian grasped a wooden stool and sat down, still staring out at the endless ocean, so blue and clear it was almost painful. "How much time did you spend up in the tower when you were a kid?"

Torie leaned against the metal railing that encircled the space, and gazed out for a minute. She had such a thoughtful expression on her face, sober and reflective, with her intelligence radiating out through her chocolate-colored eyes. "It depended on the station. I can remember being young, maybe five or six, and just having learned to read. I'd lie on the floor and rip through my little books for hours at a time while my dad made his rounds. Those are such good memories," she said, her voice catching a little.

"Some of your lighthouse memories weren't so good?"

"Oh, they were all fine," she said, dismissively. "But some of the stations were very isolated. It was hard being ten years old, with a new baby in the house, and no friends who could come over and play. I was lonely then."

"Your mom had a baby when you were ten? That's a big gap."

"They say she was their happy accident, but…" She shrugged. "When my dad was made redundant, my mum found a job right off, leaving me to help my granny watch my sister. No kid wants to do that."

Gillian nodded. "I'm the eldest, too. But my sister's only four years younger."

"Do you get along with her now?"

Gillian gave that a moment's thought. "Ideally? I'd be an only child." She laughed, thinking that her parents would probably have surrendered *her* if they'd had to reduce their flock. "How about you?"

"The same," Torie said, avoiding Gillian's gaze as she turned slightly to stare out at the tranquil, endless sea.

A loud "bang" and a mild curse, spit out with a surprisingly rough Scottish accent had Gillian leaning over the railing to look down upon Torie, who was oblivious to being observed. She looked so darned cute it was a crime, and Gillian let herself indulge in some girl-watching.

She wasn't usually attracted to long, lean women. Especially ones with short hair and very modest breasts. But when Gillian watched Torie lying on the floor, squirming around like a snake as she put all of her effort into loosening some sort of mechanism with a big wrench, she gave off some very compelling vibes. There was something very feminine about her face, with a pleasant broadness across her cheekbones, allowing plenty of room for her big, brown eyes. Then her face narrowed to a delicate chin, so fine it could have been modeled after a porcelain doll's.

The sun shone down through the tower to land on her face, with her hair shining like spun gold, strands of deep red making it even fiercer. Gillian wanted to set her chin in her hand and rest her elbow on the railing to watch, but she had a firm policy against wasting her time on straight women—especially married ones. Still…if Torie squirmed around a little more, her shirt might ride up. For some silly reason, Gillian loved to look at a woman's unexpectedly uncovered skin, and she bet Torie's belly was as pale and soft as a baby's. Despite her reddish hair, she didn't have freckles…maybe because the sun shone so infrequently.

Gillian shook off the longing, then turned back to stare out of the windows. Maybe she'd check out a dating app for her evening's entertainment. Anyone she hooked up with would be in the market for a stranger to ogle her, unlike Torie, who was simply trying to earn what sounded like a very meager living.

Two hours later, Gillian realized she'd sat on the hard stool for so long her legs had gone numb. Standing, she waited for the pins and needles to die down, then leaned on the little shelf that ringed the small, circular room, providing a handy place for papers, binoculars, and a book on identifying bird species, along with a cheap crossword puzzle magazine. She could hear Torie tinkering, but hadn't yet asked what she was up to.

"How's it going down there?" she called down.

"Good. I'm replacing the grout in the windows. The sun dries it out."

"The what? I thought this was the gloomiest place on earth."

"The little we get," Torie called up, chuckling, "really bakes this grout. I'm nearly done. Want to stay longer? I can climb up again."

"I want to do more than stay longer. I want to move here—today. But I guess I'm ready to take off. My eyes are burning from staring at the water for so long."

"I should have told you to bring polarized sunglasses, but it never occurred to me."

"I didn't pack sunglasses, and I think I've boosted the Scottish economy enough without buying another pair. Be right down."

Going down made her thighs quiver, giving Gillian extra resolve to hit the weight room at the gym now that biking season was nearing its end. When she reached the bottom, the front door was open and Torie was standing a few feet away, talking on the phone. The signal must have been bad, for she was nearly shouting.

"I'm not *asking* you to cook a meal. All you have to do is turn on the oven. Turn it *on*," she repeated slowly. "Gas mark six. *Six*."

Gillian stopped and walked away from the door, trying to avoid eavesdropping, but it didn't work. She heard every word.

"He's hungry when he gets home from football, and if he doesn't eat something healthy he'll wind up stuffing himself with crisps." A long pause. "I'm not telling *you* not to eat crisps. You're an adult. I simply want Aiden to have more fruit and veg."

She was quiet for a minute, then said, "I'd love it if you'd just heat up the dish that's lying right on the shelf in the fridge." She let out a sigh that sounded like a woman who was ready to throw in the towel. "I know you're trying, and I didn't mean to speak so harshly. Just try to get him to eat what I prepared, all right? I know. I really do know. But he'll be more alert to finish his schoolwork if he eats something healthy." Her voice lowered and sounded much sweeter. "I love you, too. See you when I get home."

Her attention was glued to the phone, and when she walked back into the room she looked up sharply when Gillian purposefully made a noise to let her know she was there.

"I thought I'd have to drag you down by the heels," Torie said, showing a tight smile.

"I managed to tear myself away. But it wasn't easy. Ready to go?"

"I think I am. Just let me check the box again." She opened the metal door to what was, as Gillian had suspected, a massive electrical panel. Inside were brightly colored wires, neatly laid out, along with some levers.

"Is all of that just for the light?"

"It is." She shined her bright flashlight into every nook and cranny. "Looks good." As she shut the door, she patted it. "Panels like this replaced anywhere from six to eight people per house. It makes perfect sense that the board chose to automate, but those were good jobs for a lot of people."

"That's the way of the world," Gillian said. "You can't fight progress."

"Oh, you can, but it's usually futile." They walked outside, with the sun still bright and warm, but already sinking in the sky. "A lot of people rioted against the industrial revolution. Some thought they were mad to risk their lives to protest a mechanical loom, but those people knew their way of life was changing forever, and couldn't be easily replaced." She started to lock the door, her keys tapping against one another the same way they'd undoubtedly done for a very long time. Long before someone had the ability to automate the entire system. "Lighthouse keepers were integral members of the community, with steady incomes, and a modest, but livable retirement benefit. But even though they were skilled workers, those skills didn't translate well to other jobs. My father doesn't know a single keeper who did as well after being made redundant. They lost not only a unique way of life, they lost their futures."

"I wish they would have phased them out more slowly," Gillian said. "Or at least have given them some warning."

Torie smiled wryly. "My father was one of the last keepers in all of Scotland. They automated the first house before he was even born." She shrugged. "The life appealed to him, even though he had to have known it was time-limited."

"Mmm." Gillian had nothing to say to that. Wishing for progress to stop was a luxury a man with a family shouldn't have opted for, but she wasn't going to voice that opinion.

Once back in the car, Torie buckled up and started to drive. "How are you feeling? I was afraid you'd have jet lag, but you seem perfectly fine."

"Oh, right," Gillian said slowly, recognition dawning. "That's why my legs got tired so quickly. Or at least I can make myself believe that."

"You're feeling good?"

"I'm very good. I should get to bed early though. And I'm sure you want to get home."

Looking contemplative, Torie said, "I was going to suggest we have our evening meal together. I did a little work on the Lindsay clan last night, and I could tell you what I've learned."

"You *were* up half the night looking things up for me!"

"No, no, I've got good resources. It took no time at all."

"Well, I have to eat, but I can just order room service if you want to get home."

Torie's phone buzzed, and she rolled her eyes as she moved the car to the shoulder to take a look at it. "One moment," she said, then started to text, furiously typing so quickly her thumbs were going to callus. When she finished, she let the phone rest on her thigh. She spoke again, her voice calm, but weary. "I have no reason to rush home if you'd like to eat together. What do you call your evening meal?"

"My family called it dinner, but supper isn't an uncommon term in America." She tried to figure out if the offer was genuine just from reading Torie's expression. "If you'd like to eat together, I'd love to. But I could also put my sweats on, lie on my bed and watch TV while I eat whatever the hotel kitchen can produce."

"How do you feel about a good, but very casual chippy?"

"I love good and casual, but I have no idea what a chippy is."

Smiling, Torie said, "I thought you might not. Do you like fish and chips?"

"I've had fish and I've had chips, but not together. I'm willing to expand my horizons."

They hit town early, with the setting sun warming the car until it was just short of uncomfortable. Torie rolled down her window a little and said, "They have a few chairs at the chippy, but it's usually crowded." She turned briefly to catch a glimpse of Gillian, avidly staring out the window, seemingly fascinated by Aberdeen. "Fair warning. The whole place smells of hot oil."

"Do you write restaurant reviews in your spare time?" Gillian asked, chuckling. "You're going to have people knocking each other over to get in there."

"No, no," she said, laughing. "I thought you might like to check into the hotel while I go for takeaway. If you don't mind eating in your room, that is. If you're like me, eating good chips in your pajamas is heaven."

"Sold. But you've got to let me pay for dinner. In my mind, you're still on the clock."

Torie nodded. "Agreed. But if you pay for dinner, I'm off the clock."

"You're a wily one, Torie. Always thinking of ways to earn less money."

"That's the story of my life," she said, not kidding in the least.

They drove through a good portion of Aberdeen, with Gillian marveling at the uniformity of the housing stock. Nearly every building, from a tiny shop to a soaring church was faced with granite. Now that the sun was setting, the buildings favored by it glowed a warm golden color. "Was everything built at once?" Gillian found herself asking.

"No," Torie said, letting out a laugh. "Even though we were significantly damaged during the second world war, the worst of that was around the docks. Knocking out our shipbuilding capabilities was a priority, as you'd guess." She took a glance at the buildings they were passing. "These homes aren't very old. They were probably built in the 1950s or 60s, but the older parts of the city are mostly nineteenth century. We had a lot of locally quarried granite, so it was cheap. You go with what you've got."

"I love it," Gillian said, not adding that the ubiquitous nature of it might get old quickly. "Where are we heading, anyway? It seems like we've already passed the bigger hotels."

"We're going a little farther out." She fixed Gillian with a warm smile. "I get a discount at the place I work, so…"

"You work at the hotel I'm staying at?"

"I thought it best. I know it's good quality, and very quiet. With my discount, it's well worth the price." The look she revealed the next time she turned was a little less confident. "That's all right, yes?"

"Oh, sure. That's perfect. Really." They were on a curving road in a fairly bucolic area that could have been in one of the more exclusive suburbs in Columbus, then Torie hit her blinker and pulled up to a very attractive boutique hotel. You could tell from the parking area that it was going to be casual, but classy.

"Here we are," Torie said. She stopped the car near the entrance, hopped out, then started to wrestle the bags from the backseat.

"No valet?" Gillian asked.

"Oh, someone will be out, but I'll have you sorted by the time he arrives." She put the bags in the vestibule, then got back into the car. "The reservation's under your name. Just text me with your room number, and I'll come right up with our food."

Gillian nodded to the guy who raced up to her, too late to do anything except hover, then leaned close to Torie's open window. "I'll have a cold drink ready for you. Beer? Wine?"

"A beer would be lovely. Anything at all. I'm not particular." Then she was gone, racing away to continue to serve, a state Gillian guessed was her usual.

Thankfully, the chippy had been in fine fettle, with Gillian raving over the food, even when she learned chips were, in her mind, crisps. The thought of fish and crisps simply seemed wrong on every level to Torie, but you could never guess what Americans would consider good pairings.

Gillian had ordered a couple of bottles of brown ale, and Torie finished hers and set the bottle down with a thump. "Very good choice on the ale. I'm going to have to remember that name. We don't serve it at my pub."

"You don't work at a brewpub that has every beer known to man? We're drowning in beer in America. We went from everyone drinking four or five national brands to microbreweries so small they're run out of people's garages."

"Oh, we stock beer. Plenty of it. Cask ales, mostly. But we specialize in whisky. We claim to carry over five hundred different ones, but I'm certain no one's ever counted."

"What?" Gillian yelped, her eyes popping wide open. "How can you keep track?"

"Oh, we don't. Most of it's hidden away in a storage room, never touched. Someone tried to alphabetize it, but that was years ago. I don't think the owners made a plan to have so many brands. It's more a failure to keep the place tidy and organized. That's what you get when your pub is over a hundred and fifty years old."

"Ahh. I didn't realize you worked in a historic place."

Torie laughed. "It's old and untidy, not historic."

"Mmm. You work tomorrow night?"

"I do."

"Maybe I'll wander over and have you pour me a shot of your favorite whisky. Can I walk from here?"

"I suppose you could, but it would take you an hour or two." Her phone buzzed and she pulled it from her pocket and narrowed her eyes as she read. "Do you mind?"

Gillian started to shake her head, but Torie was already in the bathroom, trying to speak quietly. "Hi, Mum. What do you need?"

"I don't *need* anything, but there's no food in the house, sweetheart. I thought you could pick up some takeaway if you're coming home soon."

Torie counted to ten, certain she'd made enough to serve four. "Did Dad and Aiden eat what I made for his tea?"

"I don't know about that. Your father's napping in his chair, and Aiden's gone. But I'm certain there's nothing in the fridge."

"What can I get for you?" Torie asked, not willing to make a point of the missing food. It was gone, no matter if it had been eaten or thrown out. "I had fish and chips. Would you like that?"

"From the chippy I like?"

"The very one."

"Could I have the chicken dish? The one with the bacon?"

Sighing, Torie said, "Do you want the white pudding or the haggis?"

"You know me. I prefer pudding over haggis any day."

Her mother was borderline diabetic, and more than three and a half stone overweight. Yet she wanted a chicken breast and white pudding wrapped in bacon, dipped in batter and deep fried. But her mum was almost sixty, and was clearly competent to make her own choices—even when they weren't healthy ones. Of course, Torie's fish and chips weren't on any doctor-recommended list either, so she had little room to talk.

"You can have whatever you like, Mum. I'll be home straightaway."

"Don't rush. I know you're working."

"It's fine. See you soon."

When she emerged from the bathroom, Torie gathered up the bags the food had been in. "I've got to run. My mum's just home and can't find a thing for supper."

"You live with your mom?"

She started, realizing she'd been too forthcoming. Spending casual time with Gillian was making her lower her guard. "With both of my parents. I never have to worry about being lonely." Once she had everything compressed into a small pile, she picked it up and said, "I'll dispose of this once I get home. You don't want your room to smell like a chippy."

"You don't have to do that!"

"No bother. About tomorrow. Will you have finished lying in bed, munching on scones dripping with jam by ten? That's when my shift is over."

"I think so," she said, smiling. "Will you just come up?"

"I'll text you," she said, knowing she'd draw too much attention climbing the stairs to a guest's room in her server's uniform.

"Great. Have a good night," Gillian said, walking her to the door.

They stood there for a moment, with a slight feeling of discomfort coming over Torie. They didn't know each other well, but they were already too well acquainted for a handshake, yet not nearly enough for a hug. So she simply smiled. "Get some rest. You don't want any jet lag to sneak up on you when you're not looking."

"I'll do that. But first I'm going to watch some TV. I want to learn some Scottish expressions so I can decide if you're screwing with me."

"That's wise," Torie agreed. "I'm but one of a nation of tricksters."

CHAPTER FOUR

THE NEXT MORNING, GILLIAN NEARLY skipped down the stairs of the hotel after Torie's text came in, alerting her that she was waiting in the parking lot. The little white car pulled up near the entrance, and the doorman raced over to open and hold the door when he saw Gillian headed for it.

"Have a lovely day," he said, giving her a bright smile.

"Thanks. I'm planning on it." She got in and waited for him to shut the door, then she started to secure her seatbelt. "Sorry I didn't get downstairs to eat in the dining room. I just couldn't get it together." She turned to face Torie, nearly letting out a gasp when she was met by a very pale face and bleary eyes. "What... Are you all right?"

"Of course," she said, with very little enthusiasm. "Don't I look all right?"

That was a tough one. They didn't know each other well enough for Gillian to be frank, but she'd already stuck her foot in it.

"You look great." If Torie was going to lie, she was going to join right in. "I like that vest...I mean...giblet?"

"Gilet," Torie said, managing a weak laugh. "I'd call this a waistcoat, and it's one of my favorites as well."

"It's fancy. Is that silk?" It really was a pretty vest. Like something a very fancy guy would wear to a formal event—a background of midnight blue with pink lines turning into a kind of windowpane plaid.

"I think so. I have people at all of the second-hand shops here and in Edinburgh on the lookout for gilets and waistcoats that I can alter to fit. I have more than I should admit, but I wear one nearly every day."

"I should find something that gives me a signature look. I look like every other woman in the corporate world."

"That's not such a bad way to look," Torie said, giving her a smile that had a little more punch to it. "I wouldn't mind looking prosperous and professional."

"I hear a compliment in there, and I'll take it, even though I think I look pretty boring."

"That was definitely a compliment. So? Are you ready to start digging into the secrets of the Lindsay clan?"

"I really am. All I know, and I stress the 'all,' is that Hamish Lindsay left Scotland from Leith in 1820. He was just twenty years old, listed as a laborer, and was traveling alone. In the 1830 census, he was married, with kids, and living in Ohio. That's where we got our start in the new world."

"And you don't know a thing about the old."

"Correct. But I have a feeling that's about to change. I can tell you're not going to let me go home without a little more knowledge under my belt."

A very attractive smile greeted that comment. "You know me well enough, then. I promise we'll find some things out. If nothing else, you'll see where your clan leader lived for hundreds of years." She checked her watch. "Actually, you'll see that in less than an hour."

"Really? How can you know that?"

"Because I know where Edzell Castle is. And soon, you will too."

"Edzell? Doesn't sound Scottish."

"But it is, lassie. Dinna worry yer heid."

They wove through a relatively congested part of town, edging their way south. Torie concentrated on her driving, speaking less than normal. But that might have also been because she hadn't slept, or had been in a fight with her husband, or had a devastating headache. All Gillian knew was that something significant was either troubling her or she was ill. You just didn't look like she did without cause. But Torie was clearly keeping the wall between client and friend up, and Gillian didn't want to push if she didn't want it to be breached.

By the time they'd left the busy streets of Aberdeen, Torie seemed able to be more conversant. "Did you sleep well?"

"Very well, actually. My room was quiet, and the bed was nice and soft. Just how I like it. The price was right, too. I'm used to New York rates, so this was a welcome surprise."

"I could have found you a more expensive, more luxurious spot. But I wanted you to have good value for money."

"No complaints. So? How many hours do I have you for today?"

"I clock in at five. That means we'll have to leave the Lindsay fiefdom by half three. But that should be plenty of time. It's not an extensive place."

They drove for a while longer, with Torie's phone buzzing softly time and again. She didn't answer the calls, giving the device a quick glance to dismiss every one. Given her many jobs, she probably had a lot of inquiries to keep up with.

"You don't really think I'm related to the people who owned this castle we're going to, do you?" Gillian asked.

"If you're talking about being a direct descendant of the earl, that's very unlikely. But you could well be a descendant of one of the movers and shakers back when the Lindsays were a very big force in this area. It's easier to fall away from titles and lands than it is to keep them."

"Given my ancestor was a laborer in 1820, his branch had fallen quite a bit."

"Mmm," she mused quietly. "That was a tough time in Scotland. We…" She gave Gillian a quick glance. "I mean Britain, had been at war with France since…" One eye closed as she thought. "From 1793 until 1815. There was a slight tax to pay for the war, but mostly they financed it with debt. That obviously had to be paid off."

"Ouch!"

"It was a big ouch. I know there's grumbling in the US over the amount of money you've spent in Iraq and Afghanistan, but your bill for those wars was nothing compared to the tab England racked up over the years they fought France."

"I'm good with profit and loss," Gillian said. "What was the bite?"

"Two hundred percent of the GDP."

"Two hundred?" Gillian stared at the side of her face. "That's not sustainable —at all."

"It wasn't," Torie agreed. "Unemployment was high due to all of the soldiers who were now trying to find jobs, and inflation was through the roof. It was a tough time all around."

"But Britain won, right?"

"You've not heard of Waterloo?"

"Oh, sure." She hesitated, then told the truth. "I know Napoleon lost the battle, but I didn't really know who'd won. I'm pretty hazy on European history."

Torie shrugged amiably. "You can afford to be. Being geographically isolated must be nice, especially given that Canada and Mexico haven't spent hundreds of years trying to run you over."

"I never thought about that, to be honest. But I guess it has been nice not to have our neighbors trying to take our land. Recently, at least. We had some skirmishes back in the day." She laughed a little. "Don't ask me for details, but I'm supposed to remember the Alamo for some reason."

Torie nodded. "It's obvious that unemployment, dropping wages, and rising prices didn't make for a happy populace. Plus, this was just a few years after the French Revolution. That let people in Britain see you could overthrow the monarchy and live to tell the tale."

"Oh, right," Gillian said. "Wow. That must have been a wild time to be alive."

"I'd say so. Given that your ancestor, and many others like him left his home, he must have decided things were a bit *too* wild for him. Or he had no choice."

"You mean…he could have been *sent* to America?"

"That wouldn't have been likely. Britain sent undesirables to Australia for the most part. But his circumstances could have been so poor that he had little to risk. He was a laborer, you say?"

"Uh-huh."

"That likely meant he didn't have a skilled trade, and he obviously wasn't a landowner." She smiled. "Hamish wasn't a castle dweller, but as I said earlier, you only needed a few older brothers to find yourself out of luck when it came to land and titles."

"I think democracy and capitalism is a better bet than a monarchy and landed gentry."

"I do, too. But oligarchy always seems closer than we'd wish, doesn't it?"

"That's when…" She was *sure* she knew this. "Just a few families control the wealth, right?"

"Right. It's tough to break into that one percent, as you Americans call it."

"I'm not part of that crowd," Gillian assured her. She didn't add that she wasn't too far down from it. Being in the top ten percent wasn't anything to be *ashamed* of, but it was rude to boast about it.

☙ ☙ ☙

It was time for lunch when they arrived at the castle, but unless Torie had packed a picnic, they weren't going to eat. Gillian had been keeping an eye out for the last fifteen minutes of the drive, prepared to suggest they stop for a bite, but she'd seen nothing but sheep and deep green rolling hills. If there had been a village, it had been well hidden.

The castle itself was a relatively modest structure that had been knocked around by time and weather. The roof had been lost many years earlier, along with all of the windows and doors. But the stone frame was nearly fully intact, making it clear exactly how it had once been set up.

"Impressive," Gillian said, smiling at Torie when their eyes met.

"We're the only car in the park," Torie said, making a face. "I didn't call to check their hours. Many places are only open on weekends in the winter."

"Well," Gillian said, as they continued to walk toward the building, "it's not like you could see much if you were inside. I mean, it's not furnished or anything."

"No, that would be difficult. I've never encountered furnishings that can stand up to the elements. Still…" She looked so downcast that Gillian was tempted to hug her. "I should have checked. You're paying good money to see this area."

"Don't worry about it. You've been telling me about the Lindsays for the last hour. I have a good sense of who they were." She paused a second. "A bunch of hotheads who fought with all of the neighbors."

"That's what everyone did," Torie said, chuckling along with her. "That's how you survived. Skirmishes, outright wars, beneficial marriages… Whatever worked to keep the land you had and increase it every time you had the chance."

"Sounds like people had a lot more energy before they got TV," Gillian said, trying to make Torie laugh again. She had the prettiest smile when she leaned her head to the side and let a good one out.

"I can't imagine what they'd think if they saw how easy our lives are. Their entertainment options were staggeringly limited. Most people couldn't read, but that was just as well since books were so rare. And don't think they were eating interesting food. You had to go well out of your way to find spices in the fourteenth century in Aberdeenshire."

There was an attractive fence around the whole site, and they leaned on it as they regarded the building. "I bet you can see what this place looked like, can't you? I mean, back then."

A slight blush colored her cheeks when Torie nodded. "I have a good imagination, and I use it to bring places like this to life."

"That's underselling yourself. It's your knowledge, not your imagination that helps. You know what they wore, how they cut their hair, what they ate, the games they played." She gave her a poke on the shoulder. "Admit it."

"All right. I'll admit that." She blushed a little deeper. "When I was at university, I spent a summer working as a researcher for a BBC series about medieval Scotland. I had the time of my life," she added, sighing. "Seeing the ideas we put forward brought to life was unspeakably exciting."

"That's so cool! Couldn't you make a living doing things like that?"

She shook her head. "The market for historians consulting for TV isn't as robust as you'd hope. But I'd love to do another."

"Is that what your degree is in? History?"

"Yes. Scottish history. I was well on my way to earning my PhD, but…my plans changed. I could have shifted course and gone for my masters, but I still would have had to write a thesis." She shrugged. "If I'd had time for that, I could have powered through for my PhD, but I didn't have the time, so I let it go."

"I have a bachelor's degree in marketing," Gillian said, "and I couldn't tell you the first thing about the history of marketing." She thought for a moment, with Torie gazing at her curiously. "Actually, you remind me of a math teacher I had in college. I wasn't looking forward to taking the class, but she was so into it that I wound up taking more math than I had to, just to spend another semester with her."

"Thank you," Torie said, shifting her gaze to let it drop to the ground, clearly shy about being complimented. "I wish I could have finished my degree, but being out here in a lovely spot with an interested visitor isn't a bad way to spend the day. And I never have to mark an uninspired essay."

"I'm as interested a tourist as you're going to get. Will you take me around and tell me how my relatives lived? I'd love to hear about how they got their food, how they cooked it, what they did for fun."

"Are you sure? Most people just want to know the big picture."

"I'm sure. I'm a little picture person. I like to think about individuals."

"All right then," she said, her smile growing until she looked happy, and healthy, and stress-free. "Let's start in the fifteenth century. That's when the Earls of Crawford, which was the title the Lindsay clan had been granted, built this castle over the ruins of a previous one. Try to imagine what it was like to have no modern conveniences at all. No electricity. No proper machines. No complex tools. Just a large number of people; clan members, servants, even serfs in the early days. They tamed the land and built their homes by hand with simple tools. Let's talk about how you did something as routine as prepare a meal without gas or electricity or a true oven or refrigeration…"

Somehow, they'd managed to spend the entire afternoon walking around the property at a snail's pace, with Torie extemporaneously conducting a graduate level course in the history of the Lindsay clan at Edzell Castle. Gillian was pretty sure she hadn't previously known much of the information she so effortlessly revealed. But Torie was clearly the kind of woman who worked hard to do a good, thorough job. Of course, she could have been making all of it up, but Gillian was certain she hadn't done that. She was a scholar, who generally didn't get to use her years of study for anything more taxing than serving breakfast and drinks, and that was a damn shame. Torie clearly would have been an excellent teacher. So, what was she doing dragging her butt all over Scotland, giving tours to tourists when she wasn't carrying trays of breakfast or beer? There had to be teaching jobs for people who didn't have PhDs.

The wind picked up, and Torie took the knit scarf she wore and tightened it around her neck. "It's gotten colder," she said, then let out a gasp when she checked her phone. "We've done nearly nothing and have to leave." Her eyes widened further. "Good God! I've not given you a thing to eat!"

"It's fine," Gillian said. "I've barely thought about lunch, and I'm definitely not ready to leave. Actually, I want to run right over to the Cairngorms, since we're so close."

Torie's smile was indulgent, like you'd give to a kid who wanted something truly silly. "We're close to the far eastern edge of the park. To really see the beauty, you'd go to the Highlands. That's where it's stunning."

"When can we go?"

"*We?* You want me to take you? Wouldn't you be better off with someone more outdoorsy? There are some remarkable trails for hill walking..."

"If you'd rather not..." Gillian said, her disappointment growing by the second.

"No," Torie said, grasping her arm and giving it a squeeze. "I'd love to go. I'm just not sure that hiring me is the best use of your money."

Gillian started to head back toward the car. "If that's your only concern, you can skip right over it. I like hearing about people. I can find someone to take me hiking or whatever back home. But no one in Columbus knows a thing about Scottish history."

"I'm sure that's not true," Torie said, chuckling. "But there might not be *many* Scottish historians at your local university. You might have to search a bit."

"Well, I've got you here now, and I'd like to keep you. When can you go?"

"Mmm." She paged through her calendar. "As I think I've said, I've got to work every day this week. I'm off Sunday evening, then it's back to more of the same next week." Her brow furrowed. "No tours so far, though. Just my two standard jobs."

Years of having to be pushy for her profession had spilled over into her personal life, meaning Gillian rarely let a wish go without putting on a full-court press to have it realized. "I'm paying you more than you make as a waitress, right?"

"Right," she said, nodding.

"Then why not have someone sub for you? Or do you have to get home for...family things."

"Normally, I would," she said, some of the sadness that had infused her face earlier in the day coming back. "But Aiden's going to be away for a few days—at least. I suppose I could manage to slip away. I'll just have to find someone to cover my shifts…"

"Let's go back now. You can work tonight, then find someone to cover you until…" She thought for a minute. "Can you be gone for a whole week?"

"A week?" she said, her dark red brows rising to their full extension. "Have you gone mad?"

"I don't think so." She made her plea even more earnest than she probably had to, really selling it. "I doubt I'll ever come back to Scotland. Having you along will let me see things I'd never see, and help me understand them. I'd love to go all the way across the Cairngorms, then head up through the Highlands. You do know a lot about the Highlands, don't you?"

"I do," she said, clearly proud of her knowledge base. "And what I don't know, I can research to death."

"Then let's do it!" She grasped her by the shoulders and gave her a brief shake. "It'll be like a vacation for you, but you'll get paid."

Her smile disappeared in a second. "I don't think I can afford to stay in the kinds of places you'd like, Gillian. Nor eat all of my meals in a touristy area."

"Accommodations and meals on me. And I'll pay you from the time we leave in the morning until we stop for dinner."

"No, no, that's too much," she said, shaking her head so hard her spiky hair quivered. "I normally work ten hours a day. I'd be very happy with a hundred and fifty." She fixed Gillian with the most earnest look she thought she'd ever seen. "I don't eat much, and I can easily sleep on a sofa." She brightened a bit. "I'll bring a sleeping bag."

"You will not," Gillian said. "I'll gladly pay for two bedrooms, but if you'd rather I scrimp, I'll happily share a room. But you'll have your own bed. With a mattress," she added, chuckling. "The days of the Lindsays living like kings while their staff slept near the stone hearth are over." They started to shake on it, and she added, "And I'll pay you two hundred a day. I'll ask so many questions you'll feel like I've robbed you."

❦ ❦ ❦

At one thirty that night, Torie opened the door to the family home, surprised to see her mother still awake. The telly was on, but the volume was very low, so low Torie couldn't tell what kind of program was playing.

"You're up late," she said when her mum looked up.

"I suppose I am." She yawned, sticking her arms up in the air and stretching. "I lost track of time." Starting to get up, she let out a pain-filled grunt, then steadied herself. "If you can manage," she said, "avoid getting old."

"I'll take old over dead," Torie said, smiling when her mum gave her a fond look.

Then strong arms enfolded her, and Torie sank into the hug.

"Get to sleep," her mum said. "You have to be up awfully early."

As she pulled away, Torie said, "Not tomorrow. I'm going to stay in my snug little bed until half eight."

"How...?"

"I'm taking a client on a tour across the country, and she doesn't want to start until nine." Her smile grew. "I could hardly be more excited."

Clearly puzzled, her mum said, "How can you cross the country and be back for work?"

"We're staying for a week. After Kirsty snatched Aiden away, there was no reason to refuse the job."

They were standing close to each other, and Torie could see her mother try to put on a bright face. "He'll be back," she soothed. "He's only trying to feel independent."

"You know I'd be thrilled to have him reunited with Kirsty, Mum. But it's too soon."

"But he's gone," she said, pragmatic as usual. "The bigger question is how you can manage every meal in a restaurant, lodging—"

"My client's paying for lodging and meals. Plus, I'll get a flat fee for each day we travel."

That obviously didn't allay her concerns in the least. Her brow furrowed even deeper. "You're taking up with a stranger for a full week? You can't know what kind of person this is. What if he..." Her lips pursed and she made a face that would have been funny if she hadn't looked so concerned. "How do you know he's not..." She started again. "What if he's more interested in you than the landscape?"

"My client's a woman, Mum, and I'm sure she's interested in the landscape."

In a flash, her mum's cheeks gained a little flush. "I didn't mean to imply—"

"It's fine. Really." Torie put her arm around her and guided her toward her bedroom, a very short trip. "I'll be paid well, and I'll be able to catch up on some sleep. I'm really looking forward to this."

"If you're sure," she said, clearly not convinced. "You know how I worry."

"I do. But this will be good for me, and I'll clear fourteen hundred pounds." She stopped. "Or maybe she's thinking in dollars. We'll have to clear that up."

"Take care of yourself." She hugged Torie one more time, then placed a soft kiss onto her cheek. Even after work her body still bore a faint trace of the lavender-scented powder she'd worn for Torie's entire life. "And keep an eye out for deer crossing the road. They can dart out in front of you before you have a moment to react."

"I'll be careful. I told Aiden to call or text you every day, so if you don't hear from him, give him a wee bell, all right?"

"I'll keep track of the lad, Torie. You don't have to worry about him."

They kissed one more time, then Torie turned off the telly and headed straight for Aiden's bedroom, where a bed larger than her own awaited her. The bed was a wreck, but she merely pushed aside all of the junk and dirty clothes to fall onto it, letting out a hearty sigh. It smelled of boy and grass and earth and some kind of sweet, possibly something stuck to the pillow, but she was too tired to do anything more than kick off her clogs and try to shut off her mind.

CHAPTER FIVE

THE WEATHER DIDN'T LOOK PROMISING when Gillian stepped outside on Tuesday morning, with the sky a dull, flat gray, and even darker clouds off to the east. At least she thought it was the east. It was hard to tell when you couldn't be sure where the sun should be. She was still studying the skies when a car horn sounded. Looking up, she spotted Torie's little vehicle. The bellman was missing again, but he wasn't needed. Torie put the car in park and ran around to the rear to open the trunk.

"Look at all of the room!" she said, clearly pleased with herself. "All of the things I had in the boot are now stuffed into a wardrobe, but I'll worry about all of that when I return."

"Thanks for agreeing to come with me," Gillian said, turning to take a look at Torie's vest—this one bright red wool with small gold buttons. Seeing the red color so close to her hair made it even more clear that gold was the predominant shade. At least on a dreary day.

"You don't need to thank me. Getting away for a few days is a dream come true." Her smile was a little tight. "I'm very happy to be doing this."

"You don't get away much?"

"Not much at all. Rarely, in fact. This is honestly a treat for me."

"That's very good to hear. So? Where do we start?"

"We have many options. Perhaps too many. Maybe we should stop for a hot chocolate and make some plans."

"I overslept," Gillian admitted. "They brought my breakfast up at 8:30, but I was sound asleep. I jumped in the shower, and when I finally sat down to eat, my eggs were cold. I could definitely use a muffin or something."

Torie smiled at her. "You should have called. There's no hurry."

"I didn't want to inconvenience you. I like to follow through on my promises."

"Let's stop for a tick. We can get organized and get a few bites of food into you."

"Did you eat?"

"I did. But I can always use another cup of coffee."

They drove back to the center of town, then spent a few minutes finding a place to park. They eventually wound up at the ubiquitous American coffee chain on what Torie referred to as the High Street. It was a nice branch, more spacious than Gillian was used to, with lots of comfortable leather chairs.

Hot chocolate tasted better when served in heavy, ceramic mugs, and Gillian relaxed in her chair, smiling at Torie's hastily arranged prop. On a table, she'd unfurled a detailed map of Scotland, with small orange stickers placed at various spots. "We're right here," she said, pointing to the northeast coast. "All of this is the Cairngorms." She let her hand hover over the middle of the map, a very large spot of green.

"And the Highlands are…"

"All of this," Torie indicated most of the west coast. "The Highlands and the Islands."

"Ooo. Where's the Sinclair island?"

"My Sinclairs are way up here," she said, smirking. "And no, I hadn't planned on going to a Sinclair castle, even though there are many of them." She laughed a little. "One of them holds Rosslyn Chapel, which is probably worth a trip, but it's in Midlothian. That's nowhere near the Cairngorms."

"I'm interested in the park, but…" Gillian let her gaze settle on those tantalizing islands floating up in the corner of the vast field of blue. "The islands are pretty compelling. Looks like there's a lot of them."

"Around seventy, I believe. But only twenty have permanent settlements." She had a capped pen in her hand, and she circled the area several times. "Do you honestly think you want to go to Orkney? Really?"

"Is it hard? Would we be able to find a place to stay?"

"In November?" She laughed. "We'll have little competition for rooms, but many smaller places close for the season. Hmm…" She looked contemplative for a moment. "There are a few good-sized hotels that stay open all year. I could make a few calls."

"Will you? Just so we know what our options are."

Smirking, she picked up her phone and paged through her contacts. "You don't mind boats, do you? The ferry takes five or six hours to get to Mainland."

"*Hours?*"

Torie put her pen on Aberdeen, then slowly traced a dotted line that eventually led to the island. "It's not close."

"Check on hotels. If everything works out, I'd love to go. If not, we can stick with our original plan."

"Which was what? I don't believe we had one other than 'I want to see all of Scotland in a week.'"

"That's exactly my plan, and if I'm not wrong, the Orkney Islands are in Scotland." She put her finger on the grouping and moved it slowly to the east. "But I think they might be closer to Scandinavia."

"It might not seem like it, but they're much closer to the Scottish mainland. You have to get up to Shetland to be close to Norway, and it wouldn't surprise me a bit if we wound up there." She tapped Gillian on the head with her fingers. "You are not afraid to explore the unknown. Actually, I'd call you impetuous."

Gillian nodded her agreement to that. She didn't have many fears, but being trapped in a rut was definitely one of them.

Gillian didn't seem like most of the business people Torie came in contact with. All too many of the hard-driving know-it-alls she'd met tried to *give* a tour rather than take one. But Gillian patiently sipped at her hot chocolate, perfectly content to let Torie make all of their arrangements. Besides being oddly passive about the details, Gillian didn't care how much or how little they spent, nor how long they stayed in any particular place. It was strange, but so much nicer than being second-guessed over every detail. Of course, Torie had never actually taken anyone on an impromptu week-long tour of Scotland. She still wasn't quite sure how this had all fallen into place, but here she was, making reservations on the five o'clock ferry.

When she'd finished, she put her phone on the table and said, "We're set. I have a friend who has a friend who rents out her home. It's not far from Kirkwall, where the ferry lands, and it's on the water. The very good news is that we'll have access to a long beach, and I doubt we'll see another person out there." As Gillian's eyes lit up, Torie felt a burst of pride at having easily arranged things she knew would make her happy. Yes, part of that was being a good guide. But another part was that Gillian seemed delighted by just about anything you did for her.

"I've always wanted my own beach," she said, grinning like a child with a treasured toy. "Which is an odd wish for someone who's never been to the ocean. Is the ferry soon?"

"I'm afraid not. We've got over five hours to kill. What's your pleasure?"

"Got any more lighthouses?" she asked, blue eyes twinkling.

"Mmm. If we rush, we could get up to Fraserburgh and see a good one. The lighthouse museum is there too, which is worth a trip."

"I'm willing to rush. Let's go."

Torie gripped the hem of her jacket and tugged her back down. "I don't think they do tours during the week in the winter. It's a long drive if you're not able to climb the tower."

Gillian plopped down and set her chin in her hand. "I don't think I'd like having a tower right there and not be able to climb it."

"We do have a proper lighthouse in Aberdeen, you know. It's one of mine, as a matter of fact."

"You have keys?"

"I do," Torie said, chuckling at the excited expression on Gillian's face. "It's not as grand or as tall as Buchan Ness, but it's close."

"Sounds like it won't take long to check it out. Is it by where we catch the ferry?"

"Just a few minutes from there."

"Then why don't we stay right here for a while and continue to plan our trip? I'm getting the impression that you're not as extemporaneous as I am."

"You're not extemporaneous," Torie scoffed. "You're haphazard. And I *would* feel better if I had places lined up for the rest of the week. I want you to be satisfied with our accommodations, Gillian. Your only trip to your possibly ancestral home should be one you'll always remember." She laughed at the absurdity of their plans. "You will acknowledge that we're not at all sure your mother's people were from Scotland, right."

"But you said the Orkneys were full of Sinclairs."

"First, it's Orkney, not the Orkneys. Second, I looked up the surname this morning when I was unsuccessful at staying in bed. Sinclair was first recorded in the Domesday Book, which means it's also an ancient English name." Gillian's eyes took on a sparkle, and Torie jumped in again. "We are *not* going to England, so dispose of that thought right this minute."

She settled back in her chair and waved a hand in the air. "I have no evidence I'm not Scottish on my mother's side, so I'm claiming the...I'm claiming Orkney." A half smile made her look particularly cute. "My vacations have been few, badly planned, and entirely forgettable. Because I'm with you, I'm certain this one's going to be different."

⚜ ⚜ ⚜

They'd spent so much time planning that Torie was ready for a meal when they'd finished. "It's time for lunch, but I have a craving for a rowie," she said, slapping herself decisively on the thighs. "I'm not sure why all of our iconic Scottish dishes are so bad for you, but I'm craving either a rowie or a bacon butty, neither of which will increase my longevity."

"I don't know what either of those are, so I can't help you decide."

"You poor thing," she sighed. "All these years on earth, with a delicious rowie never having passed your lips." She stood and packed all of her materials into her nylon carryall. "Let's fix that omission right now."

"It's starting to rain," Gillian said as she gazed out the window.

"So it is." Torie reached down and pulled on one of the strings of Gillian's hood. "You're prepared."

It was barely drizzling when they stood in front of the coffee shop, with Torie doing some calculations. "The best rowie I've had is in Peterhead, which is too far to even consider. There's a pretty good one about a mile from here, though. Walk or drive?"

"I can walk, but it looks like it's going to start to rain harder…"

Torie laughed at that. "You're still scarred from your first day, aren't you."

"Little bit," Gillian admitted, showing a reluctant smile.

"We can drive. I generally hate to use my car for short trips, but I'll make an exception for you."

As they started to walk back to the car, Gillian said, "I can't imagine what rowie means. It certainly doesn't sound like something you'd eat for breakfast."

"Oh, it's got more titles than the queen. Aberdeen roll, rollie, rowie, buttery. They all equal artery-clogging goodness."

"And a bacon buttery is different?"

"Bacon *butty*," she corrected. "Completely different. They're both savory, but the rowie generally has no meat. Just lard," she added, smiling. "It's not for vegetarians." Gillian was giving her a curious look, and she added, "A butty is very common all across Britain. It's either bread or toast or a bap, buttered, with bacon and either brown sauce or tomato ketchup. I like mine the traditional way. Untoasted buttered white bread, bacon and brown sauce." She kissed her fingertips. "Delicious."

"I like bacon," Gillian said, "but I can't imagine wanting any kind of brown sauce on it. Should I stick with a…rowie? It sounds safer."

"You might also be tempted by a savory pie. They make a bridie that my father loves."

Gillian shook her head. "Three days and I still only understand about half of what you say."

"That's not a bad score. By the end of your trip, I bet you're all the way up to sixty percent."

They were still a couple of blocks from the car, and Gillian said, "You called this High Street, didn't you? But the signs say Union."

"Ahh. Yes. High Street's a generic term to indicate the main shopping area of a town." Letting her gaze travel down the road, she shrugged. "Perhaps we should rename it. It doesn't represent our best or most popular any longer. Now it's mostly charity shops and Döner kebab spots."

"I can't figure Aberdeen out," Gillian said. "Most places look prosperous, but…" As they passed the churchyard of St. Nicholas, a few people living rough were having a loud, drunken argument. "I've also seen a lot of people who look pretty down on their luck."

"A lot?" Torie asked.

"Well, three or four. That would be a lot for a nice part of Columbus."

"Mmm. I suppose I don't notice." She took a look at the people shouting from the churchyard, two men and a woman squaring off like they were actually going to start throwing punches. "Many of our best shops moved to the indoor mall. The one by the train station."

"Oh, right. That looked nice."

"It is. But when that opened, the High Street took a hit. It doesn't take long for the whole tone of a neighborhood to change. You won't see the cream of society shopping for their ball gowns and tiaras around here any longer." She took one last look at the churchyard, hoping the young woman who was yelling the loudest could handle herself against the much larger men. With a slight flutter of pride, she praised herself for not attempting to intervene. Trying to break up a rammy between alcoholics and drug addicts was not only rarely successful, another one would start before the dust had settled on the first.

Gillian rarely indulged in high-fat or high-cholesterol foods. Luckily, she simply wasn't drawn to them. Her thing was sugar, a craving she had little control over. But she could appreciate the prodigious use of butter in a pastry, and she was pretty sure she could become a fan of rowies without too much trouble. She'd just had a bite of Torie's, slathered with butter, then decided to get one of her own. It tasted more like a flattened croissant than anything else, but decidedly saltier. She couldn't imagine smearing it with jam, as Torie said many people did, but that was probably also a taste she could acquire. What she wouldn't consider was a bridie, which looked like a small calzone. Minced steak, beef suet and onions were never going to be on the menu for a breakfast treat while she was in charge.

"Should we get a couple of steak pies for our trip?" Torie asked, eying a flaky-looking pastry. "They make good ones here."

"Mmm, I could eat a steak pie, but I think it would have to be hot. But don't let me stop you."

"Well, maybe just one," she said, smiling like she was doing something slightly wrong. "They're better hot, of course, but they're not bad cold. I always get hungry when I travel."

"Couldn't prove that by me," Gillian said, now assured that Torie didn't mind being teased.

The paper bag Torie was handed had grease stains on it within five seconds, but she found a plastic bag in her purse and wrapped it up neatly, looking as happy as a clam. Given she was so thin, she must not have indulged in lard-infused pastry very often—unless she normally left her car at home and ran everywhere.

"All right then. We've been fed, we know our plans for the week, and we've got a few hours to kill. We can go take a look at the lighthouse…in the rain…or —"

"Lighthouse in the rain," Gillian said, not missing a beat. "I'm dressed for the weather. Scotland can't sneak up on me now."

They blew the rest of the afternoon checking out the local lighthouse, but it had been entirely enshrouded in fog. But Gillian didn't mind too much. She had another lighthouse under her belt, even if all she'd actually seen was a gray cloud.

There wasn't much more to do with the limited time they had left, so they headed over to the ferry as soon as possible. Gillian had no idea how large the boat would be, and was kind of stunned to see that it was truly massive. After driving the car right onto the thing, they climbed the stairs to enter a very… swanky was the word that came to mind, lobby. It looked like the front desk of a modest hotel with grand aspirations, with thick carpeting, a wide staircase going to an upper floor, and uniformed men sitting behind a wide counter. Torie led the way, sailing past the crew to grab two cushy reclining chairs at the very back of a section that held about thirty of them. On the front wall that separated this section from the next, a big television was playing one of those dancing competitions that seemed unreasonably popular to Gillian.

"If we stay back here, we won't be bothered by the telly," Torie said. "Up front, there's a quiet area, and behind us is a bar, a cafeteria and a slightly more formal restaurant. Of course, there are nice cabins on the upper floor, but I assumed you could remain upright for the journey. Was I right?"

"I'm amazed! I was expecting the Staten Island Ferry. I thought there would be benches around the perimeter, and maybe a place to buy chips and candy."

"This is Scotland," Torie said, turning up the accent. "If we're going to be trapped somewhere for five hours, there will be several bars."

Gillian almost wet herself when a massive horn sounded. "We're leaving soon," Torie said. "Want to go outside and see the harbor slip by?"

"Definitely."

"We can leave our things here," she said, seemingly seriously.

"Here? Right here?"

"Come on," Torie said, tugging on the sleeve of her jacket. "Let's go see our local lighthouse from where it's supposed to be viewed—from the sea."

❧ ❧ ❧

The ride was remarkably smooth, given the size of the waves earlier in the day. But it was still a little bouncy, too rough for Gillian to risk upsetting her stomach. Her fellow passengers weren't as delicate as she, since a few guys parked themselves at tables near the bar and pounded beer like they hadn't had a drop of liquid in days. Torie didn't have a drink, but she dug into that cold steak pie like a trouper, a satisfied grin never leaving her face.

"Sure you don't want a bite? Last one," she said, piercing the final bit with her fork.

"I'm going to stick with a bag of chips."

Torie shook her head gravely. "Crisps. You'll confuse the whole island if you insist on calling them chips, and we're confused enough."

❧ ❧ ❧

They arrived just after eleven, and as they followed the other cars off the ship, Gillian got a lesson in what real darkness looked like. As soon as they were past the lit parking area, the road turned pitch black. She wasn't even sure how Torie could stay on the macadam, but she drove at a quick clip, chattering away while Gillian held onto the door and the dashboard, just in case.

"Do you know where you're going?" Gillian asked.

Torie turned, with her mouth dropping open. "You don't?"

"No!"

"Teasing," Torie said. "I've got it under control. You can let go of the car, by the way. Gravity will keep it on the road."

Swallowing her embarrassment, Gillian said, "I've never been anywhere so dark. How can you even tell where you're going?"

"Mmm…I have headlamps," she said, smiling again, clearly enjoying this.

"I realize that, but…" She peered out the windshield. "It's so dark."

"Then it's good I'm driving, because it seems appropriately dark to me."

They turned right when the car in front of them turned left, then they were the

60

only people…anywhere. Torie slowed down just a tiny bit, then she pointed to her right. "The sea's right there."

"Where?"

"The dark part."

"It's all dark!"

"No, no, the water's much darker. Look up ahead. There's a croft. They've got a light on."

It looked like they had a light the size of Cincinnati, but it got smaller and smaller as they drew near, eventually turning into a single porch light, probably guiding some poor farmer home.

After about fifteen minutes, Torie slowed down a little more, then turned onto an even smaller road. "Almost there."

Gillian was sure they were going to drive right into the ocean, but Torie put on her blinker for no reason at all, then turned left onto a gravel drive.

"Is there a house here?"

"You might want to visit your eye doctor. The house is five metres away."

"I have no idea how far that is, so I'm going to assume it's like a mile."

Chuckling, Torie said, "Don't run into a wall when you start off on your trek. We're so close I could pick you up and toss you to the front door."

Gillian stayed behind Torie, letting her run into any walls that needed running into. She used a code to open the door, shrill beeps seeming very loud in the unearthly silence, then flipped on a light and suddenly they were in a house. A simple, modest one, but a home nonetheless.

"Not bad for forty pounds a night," Torie said, nodding her satisfaction. She flipped on all of the other lights, making the place warm and cheery. It looked like it had been decorated by Ikea some years earlier. But hosting frequent guests would ruin the furniture, so buying inexpensive things only made sense.

"Bigger bedroom is yours," Torie said. "Smaller is mine. Your bags will arrive in a moment."

Gillian looked around, satisfied with their choice. If she'd been alone, she would have stayed at the nice-looking hotel near the harbor, the one that she'd seen ads for on the ferry. But she knew Torie would prefer saving a little money.

Her suitcases were rolled down the hall, then Torie said, "You may use the bath first. I'll get the furnace started."

Just then, Gillian registered how friggin' cold it was! Clearly, she'd forgotten to pack a few things that were mandatory for Scotland. Thermal pajamas…along with booties, gloves, and a stocking cap.

CHAPTER SIX

THE INSISTENT PATTER OF RAIN on the roof slowly woke Gillian from a sound sleep. A sound, restful sleep. For the first time since she'd arrived, she felt close to normal. Her synapses were firing at their usual rate, and all of the fog in her brain seemed to have cleared. Her body had recovered too, with her usual drive to get up and make her muscles work thrumming away. But she wasn't sure what she should do to get her heart-rate up. Running in a cold rain didn't sound like much fun.

She lay there for a minute, trying to determine if Torie was up yet. The house was ghostly silent, with not even a ticking clock to disturb the peace. She'd left the curtains open, hoping to have the sun wake her, but dawn hadn't broken yet. Lazily, she rolled over and took a look at her watch. *Eight thirty.* Dawn had come and gone, leaving little evidence of having visited at all.

There was only one bathroom; a very simple toilet with an odd flushing mechanism, a small shower enclosure, and a tiny sink. No elaborate towel warmer like she'd had at Torie's hotel, nor was the floor heated. That was going to be a problem. She hadn't brought pajamas, since she slept naked or in a T-shirt at home, nor had she thought to bring slippers. Clomping to the bathroom in her rubber boots was an option, but was it worth having Torie laugh at her? Yes. It truly was.

She'd slipped into her new thermal underwear to sleep, so tossing the covers off wasn't a huge shock to her system. But she couldn't convince herself to wear the damn boots. She really didn't like to look silly, even though she knew that was just her vanity rearing its ugly head.

After adding a pair of socks to the ones she had on, she grabbed her toiletries kit and her clothing for the day and dashed down the hallway to the bath. It was cold…no other word would do. But when she turned the water to scalding hot, it got up to an acceptable temperature pretty quickly.

That's exactly how she washed herself—quickly. Then she dried off with the thin towel and slid into her clothing so fast she must have set some kind of record. After doing all of the other small tasks she normally performed, her teeth were clean and shiny, and her hair looked good for not having been washed. As she exited the room, she nearly ran into Torie, who was coming in the front door with a couple of net bags full of groceries.

"You wore your Wellies to the bathroom?"

Grimacing, Gillian said, "Of course not. I'm dressed for the day, which will require boots—as always. How'd you sneak out without my hearing you?"

Smiling, she said, "Moving about stealthily is one of the many skills you develop when you have a colicky baby in the house. I can pass through a room without even disturbing the air. Breakfast?"

"Yes, please." She walked over to the counter and started to unpack while Torie shrugged out of her dripping jacket. "How long are we staying? A month? Not that I mind…"

"Two nights. That means two breakfasts, two lunches and one dinner. I think I've got everything we need."

"Did you have to go far?"

"Not very. Just a bit past where the ferry came in. There's a Tesco," she said, making her eyebrows pop. "We didn't have that when I was a bairn." She laughed. "I guess that's why we had lamb or mutton so often. We ate what we had."

"Is your grandparents' croft nearby? I'd like to see it if it is."

"I'd be happy to run you by, but it's not much to look at." She looked up and assessed the house for a moment. "Their home wasn't very different from this one, honestly. The outside is almost identical, but we had a nicer fence."

"I haven't looked," Gillian said. "Of course, it was as dark as a cave when we arrived…"

"Is Columbus, O-hi-o lit up like Times Square? Do you have neon lights on all of the major streets?"

"No, but we have lots of houses and stores. That brightens things up." She went to her room and got her coat, then pulled up the hood and slipped her gloves on. "I'm going to ignore the rain to take a look outside. Do you mind?"

"Not a bit. I'll start breakfast. Do you like eggs?"

"I do. I'll eat just about anything."

"Bacon?"

"Sure."

"Tea? I didn't buy coffee since I didn't want to waste money buying filters for that ancient machine."

"I'm fine with tea," Gillian said, even though she would rather have had bad coffee than good tea.

"Then go explore. I'll have breakfast ready in fewer than ten minutes."

Gillian started to go, then paused at the door. "Do you mind cooking? If you'd rather not, we can go out for our meals."

"You're not going to fight me to take over in the kitchen?"

"Never. I can cook, but I generally stick to sandwiches and salads. I'm always rushed for time at night."

"Then I'll be in charge of meals." She gave Gillian a very contented look. "I love to cook, but I rarely encounter many adventurous taste buds. I'm looking forward to this."

"If you are, I am. Just don't try to make me skip meals like we did yesterday *and* the day before. I like three squares a day."

"Squares of what?" she asked, turning briefly to incline her head.

"Ha! Two can play this game. I'm going to use my most uncommon American expressions and stump you. I owe you many!"

Torie let out a devilish laugh. "We use the same expression, Gillian. I'm having you on, which I'm finding is very easy to do."

🌿 🌿 🌿

After breakfast, Torie peered out the kitchen window, and when she turned again a broad smile lit her face. "Guess what's going to happen soon."

Gillian cocked her head, listening intently. "I don't hear rain at the moment, but I'm sure it'll be back soon."

"You're so cynical! While it might rain a drop or two, I'm nearly certain the sun will come out. Maybe soon."

"How can you tell?" Gillian went to the window to see layers of gray, none of which looked like they were going to scatter to reveal a glorious sun.

Torie shrugged her shoulders. "It looks obvious to me, but I can't really say why." She stuck her foot out to tap Gillian's boots. "I'd leave those on, though. You'll need them at some point."

"Do you have rain boots for babies? I have an image of tiny Wellies in place of the knit booties we dress them in."

"Uh-huh," Torie said, always willing to humor her. "Why don't we go for a walk and talk about what we'd like to see while we're here? I have a lot of options for you to choose from."

"I'm ready. Just let me get my jacket."

She was back in a flash, and they walked out together. "Key?" Gillian asked.

"There's no need. I'd be surprised if anyone went down this road in the next hour, much less someone going door-to-door, looking for treasure."

"You sure?"

"Me sure," Torie said, always ready to take Gillian's expressions and turn them around a little.

They just had to cross the narrow road, then traverse some soggy soil to get to the sea. It actually looked more like a lake to Gillian, calm and inviting. The grains of sand were pretty big, nothing like the powdery white fluff tropical beaches allegedly bore, but it was still nice. Not to mention tranquil.

"So far, I'm loving Orkney," she said. "Not many people, no horizontal rain. See how easy I am to please?"

"I'm starting to," Torie said, giving her a longer look than was necessary to make conversation. "As a matter of fact, I think you'd be awfully easy to live with."

"Mmm," she said, nodding. "No one has tested that ability for a very long time. Not since college."

"Really? You've never lived with anyone?"

"I haven't." A slew of thoughts started to race through Gillian's head. How much should she reveal? How would Torie react to knowing she was gay? Were her questions just polite filler tour guides used to make time pass more quickly? Picking the easy way out, she turned the question around. "How about you? Have you always lived at home?"

For a second, a frown formed on Torie's otherwise unlined face. She shook her head briefly, then said, "I lived with a partner for a few years when we were both students in Glasgow." Her normally carefree smile returned. "That's been a while, hasn't it?"

"It has." Gillian wasn't sure where to go with that, so she pivoted. "So? What's on the list for today?"

Now Torie looked completely normal. Confident and excited about her topic. "That depends on your mood. There are some fantastic Neolithic sites nearby, but if you're not a fan of ancient history, I've always got a lighthouse in my back pocket. Actually, if that's your choice, we can start making our way to one in just a half hour."

"Why the time limit?"

"It can only be reached at low tide—with boots." She checked her watch. "That's at ten, but we can go now if you don't mind the rocks being a little slippy."

"Slippy?" Gillian asked, grinning. "I like slippy."

"And I know you like lighthouses, even though this one is a bit underwhelming."

"I'll take any kind. And I could be persuaded to peek at a Neolithic thing if you really think it's worth it."

"Do *I* think it's worth it?" Her chin lifted when a hearty laugh bubbled up. "If I could transport myself in time, I'd do it in a second. Being among the early human settlers of Scotland would thrill me to the marrow. Whether you share my sensibilities is another issue."

"Then we'll just have to run a controlled experiment and find out."

Torie was really in her element. Gillian thought she might have been imagining it, but it seemed like Torie's accent got stronger as they ventured further into the rugged, spare beauty of Orkney.

Torie insisted the land was fertile, and the climate mild, but Gillian had to guess they were using different scales. To her, the flat landscape was a nice shade of green, but the grass or ground cover was short and uninspired. Clearly, November wasn't when you'd expect crops swaying in the sun, but the land didn't look like it had ever been cultivated. She didn't see a single silo or barn, and the fallow acres of dirt she was used to at this time of year in Ohio were nowhere to be seen. In her unschooled opinion, the land looked like it would make decent, but not lush pastureland.

Torie must have been an amateur meteorologist, since her prediction was coming true. As they drove, the clouds that had seemed like a heavy blanket began to part, with streaks of golden light peering out, then disappearing in a matter of seconds. Maybe that was all the sun they'd get, but Gillian found herself scanning the sky constantly, trying to guess where the next rays would appear.

While she was obsessing about the skies, Torie was rattling off tidbits about Orkney. Given they hadn't planned on visiting, she couldn't have just brushed up on her knowledge. It had to have been cemented in her mind, which was pretty cool. She knew the land down to the bedrock, properly identified, of course. Torie knew this place deeply, and just as clearly loved it in ways that Gillian was a little jealous of. While she was happy enough with Ohio, she'd never taken the time, nor had the interest, to know it deeply. But she and Torie obviously didn't share the same outlook. Gillian was pretty sure North Dakota, South Carolina, or West Virginia would please her just as much as Ohio did. To her, it was only a place to live.

They'd been close to the sea on their drive, but had passed nothing even resembling a town. "You haven't told me much about Kirkwall," she said. "Are we in…the suburbs?"

Torie shot her a glance. "Why, yes," she said slowly. "We're on the ring road so we can avoid the awful traffic. Most people take one of the many commuter trains to…" She paused, then started to laugh. "I'm sorry, but some of your questions make me—"

"Screw with me?" Gillian asked. "Not that I mind. You don't make me feel as dumb as I probably am."

Torie gave her a quick smile. "No one has ever accurately called you dumb, Gillian, so don't even pretend they have. You're just…surprisingly naïve about small towns." She sat up a little straighter, and Gillian could see that she was trying to get back into tour guide mode. "I haven't made things clear. We're in Mainland, which is the biggest of the Orkney Islands. The vast majority of the population lives here, with Kirkwall, where our ferry came in, the largest town. There's one other real town, and that's about it."

"So we're not on the ring road?" she asked, laughing a little.

"We're on the main road. That's why we see an occasional car."

"How many people live here?"

"In Mainland? I'd guess seventeen or eighteen thousand, with at least ten thousand of those in Kirkwall. That's where the action is."

"Maybe *they* have a ring road."

"Maybe," Torie allowed. "I haven't been here for a few years. You never know what they'll get up to."

They arrived at a parking area, an elevated spot above a bay that was, at the moment, gone. "Is there much water here normally?" Gillian asked as she got out of the car and stared out at rocks of all sizes.

"Quite a bit. A couple of metres, depending on the season."

"Okay," Gillian said, closing her eyes. "Give it to me one more time. How far is that?"

"About three and a quarter feet. Think of it as slightly longer than a yard."

Narrowing her eyes, Gillian said, "Why's it so easy for you?"

"We didn't start using the metric system until quite recently, you know, historically speaking. Many of the older people in my life never adopted it, so I was exposed to the imperial system quite a bit. But your temperatures give me a lot of trouble. I can't do the Fahrenheit conversion well at all."

"That's something," Gillian allowed. "I don't have to feel too dumb."

"You're not dumb in the least, but your leaders were dumb in refusing to go metric. It must cost the world a huge amount to have to adapt to US standards."

"We used to be able to get away with that kind of thing. But we're not going to be the big dog wagging its tail for long. China or India's going to be calling the shots in the near future."

"As a reluctant member of the formerly indomitable British Empire, I feel your pain," Torie said, with a cute smirk lifting the corner of her mouth.

They started to cross the Sound of Birsay, now just deep enough to get your ankles wet, and that was only if you made a misstep and didn't get firm footing on one of the nearly flat boulders.

Gillian had superb balance, stretching out her long legs to lightly hop from rock to rock, making Torie have to redouble her efforts to keep up.

"This is so much fun!" Gillian called out, turning her head. "I feel like a kid."

That's just how she looked. Like a child delighting herself with a small act of bravery. Actually, given that the rocks could be very slick, Gillian was being slightly foolhardy. But she was enjoying herself so much Torie couldn't make herself be the scolding adult—for a change.

The Sound was fairly wide, taking them about ten minutes to cross, but they made it without incident. Gillian jumped onto the incline that led up to the settlement, her boots slapping noisily onto the stone. "Made it," she said, looking proud of herself. She stood very still for a minute, then tilted her head toward the sky.

"This might sound silly," she said quietly, "but when you have a clear, sunny day you don't think about it much. But when the sun's playing tag with you, you really look up and take notice every time it comes out."

"That doesn't sound silly at all," Torie said. "I know exactly what you mean." She stood next to her as they faced the Sound, where the sun now glittered off the large, flat rocks worn smooth over the millennia.

"Those stones are so pretty." She pointed to the water pooling around a few of the small ones. "Check that out," she said, her voice filled with awe. "It looks like tiny little rainbows in there."

"It is nearly magical," Torie agreed.

"And some of the big stones we jumped across are so flat they look like a stone mason worked on them."

"Just water and time," Torie said. "Sometimes I put myself in my place by looking at stones like this." She saw Gillian face her and cock her head. "When I think of how many thousands of years it took to wear a rough stone down it reminds me that my time on earth is not even a tick of the clock. Sobering, but accurate."

"Yeah," Gillian sighed. "Makes you want to tell your boss to kiss your butt when he loses his mind over a report that's an hour late. Get some perspective!"

"Right," Torie said, patting her back. "Next time you get called out, remind your boss that no report will matter in a hundred years time."

"A hundred years?" Gillian laughed. "How about a week? All we do is chase our tails." She let her head lean all the way back, with the sun illuminating her face. "But I get paid, so I guess I should shut up." When she stood up straight again, she turned to continue to climb up the long slope, with Torie walking alongside her. "We've got a historic thing and a lighthouse here?"

"Beautifully put," Torie said. "Lighthouse first?"

"Always."

They skirted the gift shop, where Torie noticed the site was closed for the winter. But there was no way to seal it off, so it hardly mattered.

After going through a gate that allowed access to the lighthouse, they started to walk up a fairly steep pasture, still green and vibrant.

Gillian stopped to point at the flock of sheep just over the crest of a hill. "Will they mind us walking by?"

"They'll scamper away as soon as we get close. Just watch where you're walking. It's hard to find a spot where they haven't made a deposit."

"Eww!" she said, looking down. "It's everywhere!"

"It is indeed. Fertilizer. All organic."

"Well, it doesn't smell as bad as cow manure, so there's that."

They made it up the next gentle slope, then stood by the lighthouse, a pretty underwhelming one. Since it was atop a tall hill, there was no need for a tower. The light perched on a single story house, painted white with the usual pale gold with just a crenelated top to give it a little spark.

But Gillian still had a delighted look on her face as she walked around it, then took her camera out and snapped a few photos. "Good, but not great," she decided. "I've become a connoisseur in less than a week."

"You're a quick study."

"The view's great, isn't it? When the sky's filled with those big, white clouds, and the sea's such a beautiful color, it can take my breath away."

"Mine too," Torie said softly. "It's so nice to have a client appreciate the little things."

"Little? Look down at those cliffs! I've never seen anything cooler."

Trying to see through Gillian's perspective, Torie had to admit the cliffs were gorgeous. They were simple sandstone, one thin layer lying upon the next, but they were a beautiful dark orange, very jagged and irregular where the battering sea had washed chunks away. Grass covered the cliffs right to the drop-off, and it was still bright green and long, looking like a welcoming carpet. "It is lovely," Torie said. "Tranquilizing."

"That's exactly it. If I plop down right here to stare at the sea, will you tell me about that Neolithic site next door?"

Torie did a quick visual inspection to make sure the sheep hadn't made any deposits, then slipped to the ground. "There are Neolithic sites nearby, but this one was built by the Pictish people, with lots of Norse influence."

"Pictish?" She paused for a second. "Norse?"

Torie smiled up at her, so pleased that Gillian didn't let her pride get in the way of asking any question that occurred to her. "The Picts lived in this area for quite a while, until the Norsemen, or Vikings as they're also known, came."

"I thought Vikings were Swedish. No?"

"They were a Germanic people who lived all over Scandinavia. It looks like they and the Picts lived together, maybe even peacefully, for a few hundred years, but then the Pictish language died out completely. It's not clear why that happened, but all they left are the symbols they carved, a little jewelry, and parts of settlements. This is a very good one," Torie added. "But all of Orkney is excellent for exploring early sites. They say you can't dig down two feet and not hit something very old here."

Gillian sat down next to her and leaned back on her hands, sunning herself like a cat. "You can keep talking," she said, with her voice having grown soft and reflective. "I'm interested."

"Remember how I said we wouldn't be very close to Scandinavia in Orkney?"

"Uh-huh."

Torie pointed off to the northwest of Birsay. "That's the Norwegian Sea in the distance, so we're also not very far away."

"I knew it," Gillian said, chuckling. "Actually, I knew no such thing."

"Well, we're close enough that Orkney's been visited by northern peoples many, many times through the centuries. Sometimes we got along, sometimes we didn't. But it's not rare for people here to think of themselves as different from the rest of Scotland. Many people feel at least as much Viking as they do anything else."

"Didn't you say you think you've got Viking blood?"

"Oh, yes, I'd have to. But I identify more with the Picts." She laughed a little. "Probably because less is known about them. They're mysterious, and that caught my interest when I was a student."

"This is so nice," Gillian said. She lay flat on the ground, obviously relishing the warmth of the sun now that it was shining brightly. "I could stay here all day. Just keep talking," she sighed. "Between your voice, the sound of the waves hitting the cliffs below us, and the birds I keep hearing, I could be lulled to sleep."

"I'm happy to talk. And if you fall asleep, I promise I'll wake you before the tide comes back in. Even though it feels warm now, it wouldn't be if we had to wade back to the car."

They got back to the car while the Sound was still mostly dry. Gillian hadn't been kidding when she'd said she would have stayed all day, but when your access depended on the tide, you didn't get to decide your own schedule.

Torie had continued to march through history, and she was now talking about the Neolithic people again. Gillian's mind was wandering, but she stopped her at one point. "Wait… What? Did you say fifty centuries?"

"I believe I did. If you can hold on for about ten minutes, I'll show you something very impressive that people who lived right here around fifty centuries ago erected."

"If something's still standing after five thousand years, it's worth a peek," Gillian said.

The sun had been about to set, and the wind had picked up by the time Torie parked her car next to some tall stones standing in a field, arranged in a semi-circle. Gillian was certain Torie had her dates right, but she was having a hard time believing her.

"How deep are they?" she asked, looking them over. "I mean, if they went down twenty feet, I could see how they're still upright, but…"

"They're not that deep," Torie said, chuckling. "But they're in the ground pretty securely. We've had many instances where farmers tried to knock down standing stones to have a little more pasture, but most of them gave up when the task proved more difficult than they'd assumed. Not everyone appreciates antiquity," she said.

"And you're telling me these are older than Stonehenge?"

"Stonehenge? Ha! Our stones were fifteen hundred years old when the first of their stones was planted into the ground. It's entirely possible they got the idea right from here."

"You're saying Stonehenge just had better PR?"

"I've never thought of it that way, but that's exactly what I'm saying. We needed a catchier ad campaign."

"It might be a little late for that," Gillian said. She took a look at her watch. "Hard to believe it's only four-thirty, but the sun has gone to bed."

"How about an early dinner?"

"Um, I think the proper term is late lunch, but I'll take whatever you're offering."

Torie winced audibly. "Why did you let me skip lunch again? You've got to speak up!"

"Not to put too fine a point on it, but we haven't passed anyplace to eat. I'm used to seeing food dangling in front of me every five feet. I keep thinking we'll see something around every corner, but it's just more standing stones." She reached over and gave Torie a playful slug on the arm. "I'm fine. We'll have dinner early, then, since I'm exhausted by nine, I can indulge myself and go to bed when I really want to."

"Nine," Torie repeated, sighing. "The thought of going to bed at nine makes my mouth water."

"We're old!" Gillian whined. "How in the hell did that happen? It seems like yesterday that I could stay out all night, then jump up and get to work on time. Where did that go?"

"Mmm. That was another lifetime for me. I've been struggling with sleep deprivation for twelve years."

Gillian was going to probe a little. To ask for some details about this kid—like who was watching him. If he had a father in the picture, shouldn't the guy be working so they could afford their own apartment? But there was no way to do that tactfully. She'd just have to wait and see if it came up. If not—she wasn't above being less than tactful.

❧ ❧ ❧

When Torie had made her early morning trip to the market, she'd bought only enough food for meals. Now, snacks were needed to tide Gillian over until dinner. She actually ate like Aiden, which was odd for an adult woman, but she was lean and muscular, so she must have needed the calories.

Torie carried a basket that was getting heavier with every item that Gillian tossed into it—cheese, crackers, biscuits, and more sweets than she could have possibly consumed in a few days.

"I think I'd better get busy and start baking," Torie said. "Or we could save time by your sticking a spoon in a bag of sugar and shoveling it in."

"I like sweet things," Gillian said, shrugging.

"Put those biscuits and sweets away and I'll make something good. As a matter of fact, if you don't mind having a kick to your sugar, I could make whisky tablet."

Gillian cocked her head. "That's…what?"

"Sugar, butter, condensed milk—"

"Perfect," she said, grinning. "Make a lot."

"We'll need some whisky. Just a small amount…"

"Not too small. I want to learn to like it. I've been drinking vodka my whole adult life, but it's time to embrace the dark spirits of my newly discovered heritage."

"You've never had whisky?"

"Not that I can recall. Of course, some of the parties I went to in college are a total blur."

"Mmm. Then we should probably get a blend to start. Something that isn't too bold in any of its elements."

"Done. Tell me what to get."

After they'd checked out, Gillian stopped at the bank to withdraw some cash. Torie looked up to see her examining the notes with great concentration. The door opened and she slid in, then extended her hand to show a fifty-pound note to Torie. "What's this?"

"Besides fifty pounds?"

Reaching over with her other hand, she pointed at the words across the top. "Who's the Bank of Clydesdale, and why are they issuing bank notes?"

"Oh. Three of our banks are allowed to do that. They keep the colors the same as the ones issued by the government, but…" She shrugged. "It's just what we do."

Another bill appeared before Torie's face. "This one's plastic!"

"It is. We're slowly switching to polymer. It feels odd, doesn't it?"

"It's all odd," she said, fanning the notes out. "These are from two different banks, and I have no idea who these people are. It's like Monopoly money."

"It still spends," Torie assured her. "Although I've had trouble with it in England once or twice, I guarantee you can buy whatever you want here with those notes, even though you don't know who the portraits represent."

"I feel very far from home today," Gillian said. "But I like that." She buckled her seat belt and placed her hands on her thighs. "Now it's time for you to feed me. Let's make it snappy."

Gillian forced the last bite of a delicious cheese-crusted beef stew into her mouth and flopped back against her chair. She chewed for a few moments, then patted her belly with both hands. "I feel so Scottish. Now that I've had neeps and tatties, I can probably petition for citizenship."

"I think you've had tatties before. Or do they not have potatoes in America?"

"Rumor has it. I liked the combo, though. What did you call it?"

"Clapshot, when you add butter and chives. That's an Orkney variation."

"Well, it was the best meal I've had all week. No, scratch that," she amended. "Best I've had this year. If you get tired of giving tours, you could make a good living as a chef."

"I love to cook," she said, looking down at her plate, always seeming embarrassed when she was complimented. Their eyes met, and she added, "But it makes it much more fun when I see how much it's enjoyed."

"I'm at my enjoyment limit. Thank God it's only six. I can digest my dinner for a while, then get at that fudge thing."

"Tablet," Torie corrected. "It looks like vanilla fudge, but it has a different consistency." She stood and started to gather the dishes, but Gillian jumped up and took them from her.

"You can sit on a stool and watch me clean, but you can't help."

Torie let out a happy-sounding laugh. "That's an offer I'll never refuse. It's a fight every day to get Aiden to help."

The cottage, while certainly not fancy, was relatively modern, having clearly been updated in the last twenty years. The kitchen was modest, but had every convenience, including a dishwasher. But Torie had used every pot and pan she could find, and some of them would have to be hand-washed. Gillian squatted in front of the sink and poked through the cleaning products nestled in the small space. Finally, she took everything out and inspected each container. "I'm not familiar with any of these things," she said, feeling unreasonably miffed. "I'd think they'd have *something* from Channing Brothers."

"Why's that?" Torie pulled out a stool from under the counter that bisected the living area from the kitchen, and now sat with her elbows resting on it.

"Inherent bias. I've clearly bought the company line that our products truly are the best, even though I haven't tried all of them."

"'Our?' Do you work for them?"

"I do." Gillian got up and put everything but the dish soap back where she'd found it. "I haven't mentioned that?"

"You haven't said a word about what you do. I've been trying to guess, but I don't know enough about corporate America to get very far." She let her dark eyes roam over Gillian for a minute, her gaze so interested, so intent, that Gillian could feel her cheeks start to color. "I can see you in a well-cut business suit, holding a meeting. A few clients are leaning forward, hanging onto every word, ready to snap up the hook you're dangling in front of them."

Laughing at the image, Gillian said, "That's how I'd like it to go, but that's not often my reality." Slightly embarrassed, she got back to the products. "The label's washed off this, so it might be ours." She squirted some soap into the sink as she ran the water to heat it. Leaning over, she sniffed the air as the warm water released the chemicals. "Oh, this is ours," she said, feeling a little silly to be so excited. "I'd recognize that scent anywhere."

"That's Pixie, which I thought was a British soap. My mother grew up using it, so I make a habit to buy it at home, even though it's often more expensive."

"Thank your mother for me. Brand loyalty is what keeps us going. Pixie's made by Bristol Soap, which we own. This little dishwashing liquid is Bristol's sales leader."

"Interesting. I suppose you can never tell who owns whom anymore, can you."

"It's not easy, but it hardly matters which corporation's behind a product. The product has to stand on its own."

"What do you do for Channing Brothers? They're obviously a very large company, since I've heard of them."

"Marketing. I handle all fabric care products in North America."

"I'm not certain what that means. Do you *make* detergent?"

"No, no," Gillian said, laughing. "I'm much better at marketing it than I would be making it."

"Then you're in sales?"

"Not exactly. I'm in charge of advertising our products and getting them into the right stores. I suppose marketing is awfully close to sales, but I don't go door to door with a suitcase full of samples." She laughed again. "I probably wouldn't be great at that, but I'm good at figuring out how to effectively spend an awful lot of money on advertising."

"What's an awful lot? I have no idea how much it costs to convince people to buy laundry detergent."

"Well..." Gillian was going to evade the question, then she realized that was silly. Torie wasn't an industrial spy. Or if she was, she was really committed to a long con. "Last year my advertising budget was a hundred and three million dollars."

Torie's chin nearly hit the counter. Gillian hated to admit what a charge she got out of surprising people with how big Channing Brothers was, but she really did dig it.

"Are you truly serious? A hundred and three million dollars just to convince North Americans to care for their fabric?"

"I am totally serious." She dipped a pan into the sudsy water and started to scrub it with a plastic scour pad. "Our gross on Bam!, our biggest seller, is larger than some countries' GDP. We're huge."

"And you're in *charge* of marketing?"

"For fabric care only." She didn't want that to sound like an insignificant sector, so she added, "Fabric care represents forty percent of our global sales. I worked hard to move over after starting off in oral care. You can do a lot more with fabric than you can with teeth."

"I'm stunned," Torie said. "Truly stunned. You don't seem nearly old enough to have such an important job."

"If you keep feeding me, and we don't drown from the rain, I'll turn forty in March."

"I'm still impressed. I don't know a lot about business, but I've gotten the impression we move up the corporate ladder at a slow pace here."

"We can go quickly, but I'm no longer the wunderkind I was when I was getting promoted every two years. My boss is in my way now, and if he doesn't move on, I can't move up."

"Still… You've accomplished so much, Gillian. Your family must be so proud of you."

"Proud?" She turned her back to scrub at the baked-on cheese for a minute. "Well, my parents were both gone before I started to work…"

"Both?" Torie said, her voice growing soft in an instant.

"Both. My dad died when I was a freshman in college, and my mom just a week after I graduated." She shrugged. "My sister's never said she's proud of me, but…" She trailed off. "Um, to be honest, my parents wouldn't have been happy with the path I've chosen." She finished scraping the burned-on bits from the pan and set it aside. When she turned, she caught Torie gazing at her intently. She got up and moved to stand close by, then said, "Tell me why your parents wouldn't have been impressed by your achievements. I can't imagine a good reason."

Having little interest in talking about it, Gillian forced herself to get over her reticence and have a serious conversation. After rinsing the last pan and putting it on the counter, she twitched her head toward the living room and walked over to take a seat before the fire.

Torie sat across from her, their knees almost touching in the small space. Besides the intimacy of the room, there was a warmth in Torie's gaze that made Gillian swallow her discomfort and let it out.

"Um, my dad manufactured auto parts. His company wasn't huge, but he had some sizable contracts with Detroit. To keep his prices competitive, he had to do the manufacturing in Mexican border towns."

"Uh-huh," Torie said softly, her gaze never leaving Gillian's face.

"He spent most of his week shuttling between his two plants there and headquarters, which was in Columbus. Add in routine trips to Detroit, and he was hardly ever home."

"I don't think that's uncommon. Sometimes your job changes in ways you couldn't have predicted."

"True. But I knew exactly what his job entailed, and that's why I steadfastly refused to be part of it." Even now she felt the sting of his hurt. He'd never understood her refusal to work in the office, even during summer vacations.

"He was upset...?"

"Very. I think he felt I looked down on him. Like the job wasn't glamorous enough. But that wasn't it," she insisted, hearing herself trying to convince Torie of her truth. "I just didn't want to be on the road all of the time." She shrugged. "I should have said that. Instead, I told him the other reason."

"I feel like I'm dragging this out of you," Torie said, gently touching Gillian's knee. "You don't have to tell me if—"

"I was eighteen," she said. "And I thought I knew everything. I mouthed off one day and told him I couldn't exploit people like he did. He was paying his Mexican employees next to nothing, and I told him I couldn't be a part of that."

"Ooo," Torie sighed. "That must have hurt."

"I'm sure it did. We went through a few months where he barely spoke to me." She let out a shuddering breath. "Then he was killed when the private plane he'd managed to hitch a ride on went down in a storm." She met Torie's wide eyes and nodded. "We never resolved it. We never can," she whispered, feeling the familiar tears begin to sting her eyes.

"And then you lost your mother so soon afterward..." Her hand gripped tighter. "I'm so sorry."

"It was bad," Gillian admitted. "My mom took over my dad's company, even though she had no experience in running manufacturing plants. Then *she* was gone constantly. I was away at college, so I didn't have to adjust to that, but my sister sure did."

"Was your mom's death sudden?"

"Very. She had a heart attack."

"So young?"

"Uh-huh. We found out she'd been using anxiety medication along with some other stuff. I don't even recall what it all was, but she was medicating herself to be able to function on just a few hours of sleep a day. That, combined with an undiagnosed structural problem with her heart, let her go to bed in a hotel in El Paso, and never wake up."

"You poor soul," Torie soothed. "You and your sister must have been devastated."

"We were. How could you not be? But Amanda was already enrolled in a summer language institute, so she packed up and left home just a few days after the funeral. Then we both started school again in the fall. She went to Kenyon, and I went back to Chicago to get my MBA." She let out a weary breath. "Sometimes deaths in the family bring you closer, but that didn't happen with us."

"You could always try to get closer now," Torie suggested, her tone very gentle and respectful.

"I don't think so." She turned to watch the processed log burn away, the red and gold flames mesmerizing her for a minute. "Amanda met her husband at Kenyon and she just kind of slipped into Rick's family. She's one of them now."

"You don't even spend holidays together?"

"Not if I can go to my best friend's house, which I usually can. I like Rick's family, but I always feel like an add-on, you know? Ideally, I find someone to take a trip with over Christmas, but I haven't had any luck the last two years." She knew her smile was filled with sadness, but she couldn't do much about that. "I need more outcast friends."

Torie gave her a brisk pat on the leg. "I think it's time for a drink. Join me?" When she stood, her phone buzzed, and she took a look, then texted back and forth for a minute. "I can relax," she said, letting out a sigh. "Aiden's in for the night. He'll probably have pizza for dinner, but at least I know he's safely battened down."

Gillian couldn't help herself. Torie had left the door open, so she walked through it. "Your parents watch your son when you're away?"

"My son." She stared blankly for a moment. "Oh! No, no, Aiden's not my son. He's my nephew. My parents and I have had custody of him for almost his entire life, but he's my sister's boy."

"Oh, shoot," Gillian said, starting to laugh. "I had this whole scenario laid out for you, with an unhelpful husband and…" She shut her mouth quickly. "I…"

"It's all right," Torie said, gently rubbing her back as she passed by. "I have a largely unhelpful, but truly lovely father. You must have heard me on the phone with him."

"I didn't mean to eavesdrop, but I couldn't…"

"It's fine. I've nothing to hide. My dad and my mum are wonderful people, but they're not up to managing a twelve-year-old boy. Aiden's learned how to manipulate them to get exactly what he wants, then I get home and have to be the enforcer. It's not a great deal of fun," she said, clearly an understatement.

"Your sister is…?"

Torie pulled out two rocks glasses from the cabinet, then produced a small pitcher that she filled with water. She put everything on a tray and brought it over to place it on a small table. "I need a drink before I can talk about Kirsty." She stopped abruptly, looking at Gillian carefully. "If you want to hear the story, that is. I don't want to—"

"I'm interested," Gillian said. "I told you I'm going to learn to like Scotch on this trip, so what better way to start than to share a drink while you tell me about something that's clearly important."

With a warm smile, Torie said, "We call it whisky, and I'm not sure you can force yourself to like it, but I'll help in any way I can. Every new whisky drinker boosts our economy."

Torie poured a little whisky into each glass, then said, "Just let this warm in your hands for a moment. Take a sniff. You should be able to detect a lot of different aromas."

"Nice," Gillian said, doing as instructed. "I should take to this easily. My father used to drink Scotch on the rocks, so maybe I have a genetic predisposition to like it."

Torie looked up sharply. "I hope he didn't waste his money on a good malt. Ice completely obliterates the top notes, like citrus and honey. I'd only recommend ice when you're drinking a modest blend and the day is infernally hot." She smiled. "In case you hadn't guessed, that's a rare day in Scotland."

Torie concentrated on adding small amounts of whisky to each glass, then she held the pitcher over one. "I like a splash of water, but many don't."

"I'll try it your way."

"I think water opens up the flavors a little, lets them breathe." She handed the glass to Gillian, and they touched the rims. "Slàinte," Torie said quietly. "Cheers."

"I'll drink to that."

"Take wee sips and let it rest in your mouth. It should warm you from the inside out, something we need more often than not."

The first sip went down well, warming, but not burning her esophagus the way alcohol sometimes did. "It's nice," Gillian said, smacking her lips. "It reminds me of the few times I've had a good brandy."

"I just like a wee dram. Neither of my parents drink much, or often, nor do I, but my sister has made up for the three of us falling behind."

"She's an alcoholic?" Gillian asked gently.

After taking another sip and letting out a sigh, Torie said, "Unfortunately, she's both an alcoholic and a drug addict." Her expression brightened, but it still didn't look entirely happy. "But she's been clean and sober for nearly a year this time. We've been trying to give her more control, along with slowly increasing visits from Aiden, but waiting isn't something she's historically been good at. The last month has been difficult for me, but it's also putting stress on Aiden, which I hate."

"You seemed really upset the day after we met. Was that part of this?"

"It was. He was supposed to stay home that day, but he went to her flat during his homework time." Torie closed her eyes for a few seconds. "She's his mother, and I want them to spend as much time together as they both want, but I'm worried. He seems just like she did at the same age—easily influenced, little motivation, not a star at school…" She let her head lean back against her chair. "If he gets into trouble like she did, I simply don't know what I'll do."

"She's a lot younger than you are, right?"

"Ten years."

"Then how can she have a twelve-year-old?"

Torie lifted her head, then looked Gillian right in the eye. "My sister was just fifteen when she had Aiden."

"God damn," Gillian whispered. "She was a child herself."

"She was." Sitting up taller in her chair, she took a long breath and said, "As I've said, my parents are lovely people. But neither is skilled at setting limits and all of the other things parents should do. That was fine for me, since I didn't want to tear the town down. But Kirsty did, and they let her run wild. I was at uni when the worst of it started." She tossed the last of her drink back and shook her head. "I'll always blame myself for not being more involved. The spring and summer I worked with the BBC was when she took up with an older crowd and got pregnant. The baby had to go through withdrawal," she said quietly. "For all we know, that's permanently altered his brain chemistry."

"Damn," Gillian breathed, shaken by the story. "That must've been so hard —for all of you."

"It was. At the end of my term, I got permission to take a leave of absence and came home to take care of the baby. Then my granny broke her hip and needed as much tending as Aiden did..." Shrugging, she said, "Twelve years later, I'm still hoping to one day leave home."

After letting that statement hang in the air for a minute, Gillian quietly said, "I can't imagine how unhappy I'd be if I'd had to stay at home when I didn't want to."

"It's not ideal," she admitted, "but we make do. Sometimes you have to work with what you have rather than long for what you don't." A little smile crept across her lips. "No matter how things have gone, I'm still in a much better position than nearly all of the people ever born. That's rather soothing, isn't it?"

Gillian nodded, but her heart wasn't in it. Torie was comparing herself to millions of people, most fighting their way through the chaos of an utterly unpredictable life. But she'd been born into an industrialized, democratic nation, and she had every right to mourn the loss of her autonomy, her career, and most importantly, her dreams.

⚜ ⚜ ⚜

After getting used to the taste of whisky, having it added to sugar, butter and condensed milk seemed like a perfectly reasonable choice. Now Gillian was starting to feel a little sick, just at the point where another bite of the sugar-laden treat might send her over the edge. But the damned tablet was so good she had to risk it. After she'd popped another square into her mouth, Torie confiscated the pan and the knife and carried them both into her room. When she returned, she said, "I'm hiding the rest. You have the appetite of a toddler!"

"Always have. I keep waiting for it to catch up with me, but I'm the same size I was when I graduated from college." She crossed both sets of fingers. "If my metabolism changes, I'm not going to be able to resist, so I'm really hoping middle-age doesn't mess me up."

"You've not mentioned anyone special in your life. Has there been...?"

"Sure." She looked down at her unadorned hand, wondering if it would ever be decorated by a gold band. "I've never been married, but I've had some relationships that were pretty significant." Her usual tactic was to brush past her sexual orientation, but Torie seemed like she'd be open-minded and interested in her reality. "Um, I was dating someone last year, and we were starting to... Well, I'm not sure we were going to make it to the next level, but I was willing to try." She took in a breath and finished. "She taught at a Catholic high school, and was *very* paranoid about anyone finding out about us. Having to watch every step got old pretty fast, so I called it quits."

Torie's eyes nearly flew from her skull. Her mouth opened, then closed for a few seconds. "You're a lesbian?" she finally asked.

"I am. No one at work knows, so I guess I'm a stealth lesbian. Is that...?" She gazed at her, almost certain Torie had turned a little pale. "Are you okay with that?" *What a dumb question!* Was she going to turn straight if Torie didn't like it?

"Sure. Of course." She kept nodding, vacantly.

In Gillian's experience, the more someone insisted they were fine with lesbianism, the faster they made an excuse to head for the hills. But Torie didn't do that. Instead, she cleared her throat and quietly said, "So am I."

"You are?" Gillian was sure her cheeks were turning pink. *This was such an awkward conversation!*

"I am." Looking away, she gazed into the fire, not blinking. "It's been so long since I've been with a woman that I might not be able to honestly call myself that. But I am," she said, her voice gaining a little force. "I *am*."

🌿 🌿 🌿

At eight o'clock, Gillian quietly put their glasses away, then turned off the light in the kitchen. Torie was sound asleep in her chair by the fire, and Gillian was tempted to put a blanket over her and let her wake on her own. She stood next to her for a moment, observing her as she slept. She was *such* a pretty woman, with a delicate, almost fragile bone structure that gave the planes of her face very well-defined angles. That's why she looked younger than she was. Good bone structure helped a lot. But she was much more than a pretty face. Torie was a good person. A loyal, dutiful daughter, who'd sacrificed an enormous amount of autonomy for her family's sake. And if she ever bitterly complained about her situation, she certainly hadn't done so in front of Gillian.

She started to bend over to put a hand on her shoulder to wake her, then abruptly pulled her hand back as she realized her rule against chasing after married straight women no longer applied. But a woman who was raising a difficult child, while saddled with a drug-addict sister, along with a pair of ineffective parents was more toxic than heterosexuality—by a long shot!

Gillian had always been careful when it came to attraction. In Torie's case, she needed to be more than that. No matter how nice a person she was, she was knee-deep in family junk, and that canceled out both her kind heart and pretty face.

Waking in the pitch blackness, Gillian pummeled her pillow, trying to relax enough to fall asleep again. After fifteen minutes of tossing and turning, she sat up and tried to get her thoughts in order. Her phone was lying next to her, and she checked the time. On the off chance she was home, she dialed her closest friend Kara. The phone rang four times, then a slightly agitated voice said, "Are you all right?"

"Of course. Are you busy?"

"Not too. I was just checking on the baby. He's got a little cold, and he was making some funny noises. But he's sleeping, so all is well."

"Is Ben around?"

"Uh-huh." Kara paused a second, then said, "Gillian, what's going on? It's the middle of the night in Scotland."

"I know. I just didn't want to get into something if you're going to have to hang up right away."

"I'm all yours. The kids are asleep, and Ben's watching a football game where it's still sunny."

"Los Angeles," Gillian heard him call out.

It took a second for her to get all of the time zones right, then she said, "When was the last time I had a crush on an unavailable woman?"

She could hear Kara's heels clicking, figuring she was crossing the family room to go into the kitchen. Ben usually didn't pay any attention to her phone conversations, but every once in a while he couldn't get enough gossip. Given that Kara spent her days keeping attorney-client conversations private, she generally continued that practice at home. The room changed the tenor of Kara's voice, making her sound like she was much closer.

"Repeat that question, please?"

"I think you heard me. When was I last interested in someone I couldn't, or shouldn't, have lusted after?"

"College, I guess. No, when you were getting your MBA. You had a crush on that—"

"Professor," she interrupted, sighing. "Lucia Santos Muñoz, the prettiest woman Spain's ever produced."

"Uh-huh. I just remember you threatening to ask her out—while class was still in session. You couldn't even wait to see what grade she gave you!"

"I did great in that class, mostly since I lingered on every word that came out of her gorgeous mouth. But you were right. No smart professor would have gone out with a student while she was still in school. Maybe I should look her up. I need to take my mind off my current crush."

"Any facts at all would help," Kara said. "Pick one."

"Okay." She took in a breath. "I met a really cute woman the day I arrived. She's a tour guide, and I proposed she take me on a private trip across Scotland. Now we're in a cottage that's nearly in Norway, and I just found out she isn't married. Even better, her kid is really her nephew, not her son. But best of all, she's a hundred percent gay."

"Have you been drinking?"

"I had a drink, but I'm sober."

"Doesn't sound like it. Who *is* this woman?"

"Her name's Torie, and she's soooo pretty," she said, knowing she sounded like she was twelve. "Super smart, too. Good sense of humor. Doesn't take herself too seriously."

"Let me guess," Kara said, sighing. "A Latina, medium height, dark hair, dark eyes, curvy, big ti—"

"Tall, thin, pale, nearly flat-chested and...she's a ginger," Gillian interrupted. "She *does* have brown eyes though. Big, dark, soulful ones."

"Well, you're certainly going outside your comfort zone. So, what's her problem? Why's she unattainable? Except for the fact that she lives thousands of miles away."

"Eh," she said, dismissing that detail without a second thought. "Distance isn't a problem these days. It's her family situation."

"God, I can't even imagine what would—"

"Stop guessing and let me tell you. She lives with her parents, and all three of them help raise her sister's kid. He's twelve, and is giving her fits."

"Not good," Kara said, soberly. "I bet she's doing all the work."

"Oh, she definitely is. Her parents sound like nice people, but they're ineffective. Torie dropped out of a PhD program to take over, effectively giving up her future. Now, instead of being a professor, she runs around Aberdeen tending lighthouses for her dad, along with three other jobs."

"*How* many drinks have you had? I thought I just heard you say she tends lighthouses."

"I did," Gillian sighed. "But I think she actually does that just to get away and have a few hours to herself. She can't be paid much to make sure a light's on."

"She's a full-time tour guide?"

"And a waitress, and a bartender. For all I know, she has a paper route, too. God knows she's willing to do just about anything for a few bucks."

"Well, if you don't think distance is a stumbling block, why not give it a try? You could help her out a little so she didn't have to work so hard. Are you getting your full bonus this year?"

"Sure am. Every soapy little dime."

"Give her half of it and she could just do the tour guide thing. The kind of money you make is *life* changing, G."

"How much would I have to give her to lose the kid?" she said, her voice growing dark. "Her sister's an alcoholic and a drug-addict, Kara. Torie's going to be wrapped up in some kind of drama for the rest of her friggin' life."

"God, that sounds awful. Is she as bitter as I'd be in her shoes?"

Gillian let out a laugh. "Nowhere near how either of us would be. She seems disappointed, but resigned."

"Freaky."

"I know. I'd give the kid back to my sister and hire one of those sobriety monitors famous people use. Then I'd move as far away as possible."

"You really would," Kara said. "You're the least maternal woman I've ever met."

Stunned, Gillian spluttered, "Wha... What?"

"I didn't mean that as an insult, G. You just don't care for kids. You're *nice* to them, but you'd hate having one of your own."

"I can't argue with that, but it still sounds like an insult. Women are supposed to want kids. It's our biology."

"You like being in charge, and God knows you never are when you have kids. But just because you want a more predictable life doesn't mean you're not womanly. You're just not motherly."

"Well, I'm going to do my best to ignore the big, sexy, dark eyes that keep distracting me. Having a kid is bad enough. Having a troubled sister who really owns him is a red flag I can't possibly ignore."

"Mmm, *own* is kind of a harsh term when it comes to a child... Just saying," she added, laughing.

"Noted. I'm going to try to sleep now. Thanks for talking me down."

"Are you having fun even when you're not looking at a pretty girl?"

"I am so glad my cousin Joni told me I was part Scottish. I *love* it here," she said, her enthusiasm making her sound like a kid. "I'm not even sure why I like it so much, but it's super cool. If the weather was better, they'd have so many tourists the island would sink into the sea."

CHAPTER SEVEN

SLEEPING FOR NEARLY TWELVE HOURS hadn't made as big a dent in Torie's sleep deprivation as she'd hoped. But her body wasn't nearly as fatigued as it usually was, which was a very pleasant sensation. She could deal with a slow-firing brain with no problem at all.

After stretching to get a few kinks out, she stood, then grabbed the blanket and tossed it over her shoulders. They should have turned the thermostat to at least sixteen, but she'd been so groggy when Gillian had woken her the night before, it had been all she could do to kick off her shoes and climb into bed.

Quietly, she tip-toed down the hall, then realized she didn't have to be so quiet. Gillian was clearly a sound sleeper, her heavy breathing sounding through the open door.

Torie found the thermostat and set it for a reasonable temperature, warm enough to keep their blood from turning to sludge, but cool enough to not be wasteful.

While waiting for the kettle to boil, she grabbed a stool and sat, leaning against the counter much the same way she'd done the night before.

How had she missed the signs that Gillian was gay? Maybe she'd simply stopped looking for them. Knowing you couldn't have something sometimes made you stop thirsting for it. But if she were to thirst, Gillian would be exactly the kind of woman who could quench her desire.

Smart, clever, pretty, and, most of all, kind. Only a kind woman would listen to your tale of woe for the better part of the night and offer only encouragement. Not once did she throw out any of the platitudes so many people were all too quick to regurgitate. God *did* give you more than you could handle. Everything *wouldn't* necessarily turn out for the best. Fate had *nothing* to do with her little sister developing a drug habit. It had been a series of bad circumstances, ineffective parenting, and probably a genetic predisposition for stimulus that had led Kirsty down a dark path. But Gillian blessedly hadn't tried to wish the truth away in a few words. She'd just listened. Those pretty blue eyes had locked on Torie as she listened attentively. And that was a very welcome gift.

Yes, Gillian was exactly the kind of woman any lesbian Torie knew would pull out her eye-teeth to nab. But Torie didn't have the skill, much less the style, or the money, or the cachet that it would take to lure a woman like Gillian into her bed. And even if all of that hadn't been true, having a mother, a father, and a quarrelsome nephew sleeping a few feet from her would have scared away the most avid pursuer.

❦ ❦ ❦

Torie looked up from her porridge to see Gillian cutting another bite of tablet. "Eat your porridge," she growled playfully. "This is like traveling with Aiden. Both of you would die of malnutrition if someone wasn't watching over you."

Gillian held up the tiny bite remaining. "This is superior to hot cereal." She took a tentative bite of the porridge, then wrinkled up her nose. "My mother used to try to get us to eat oatmeal, but we fought her."

"You must exercise a lot to be able to eat like a child."

"I do," she admitted. "I ride a bike…a lot."

"Daily?"

"No, not daily," she said thoughtfully. "Usually just on the weekends, except in summer when it stays light later. But I routinely clock a hundred miles on a good day. Pretty intense."

"I would say so!"

"Aaand…I go to the gym to work on my core and stay flexible. I burn a lot of calories."

"Mmm, I'd love to have the time for bike rides. I used to ride everywhere in Glasgow."

"Um…" Gillian seemed to hesitate, then she spit out her question. "I can see how you wouldn't have time to finish your PhD, but why did you never get a teaching job? Couldn't you teach at the high school level?"

"I could have, I suppose. I'm sure I would have had to take some classes to qualify, but I was never motivated to do that. It's only in the last couple of years that my life has been predictable enough for me to even consider having a single, full-time job."

"Okay," she said, her head bobbing slightly, encouraging Torie to respond. "Why not think about it now?"

"I'm sure I make as much doing what I do now, and with much more flexibility, than a beginning teacher would earn."

"Mmm." She took another tiny bite of tablet and chewed thoughtfully. "But wouldn't you get other things…" She frowned slightly. "Like professional satisfaction from teaching a subject you loved?"

"Teaching wasn't my primary goal. My long-term plan was to finish my degree, then try to work for an NGO."

"A non-governmental organization?" Gillian asked, her puzzlement clearly growing. "How would that work?"

"Many NGOs hire people like me to implement programs targeting diverse cultures." She smiled. "Historians are quite good at things like that."

"But you think you'd need your PhD to have a chance at that, right?"

"Well, yes, I think so." She took a breath, feeling her heart skip a beat at the mere possibility. "I'd give anything to finish. But what I have to give isn't going to get the job done."

They were scheduled on the late afternoon ferry to Inverness, giving them time to squeeze a little more out of Orkney.

They headed for a Neolithic structure Torie claimed would thrill Gillian to the bone, but she honestly didn't much care where they went. She liked *Scotland,* the land, the sea, the hills, the rough, wild beauty of the place. What had been there many thousands of years ago was all well and good, but she loved it right now, weather be damned. Actually, if she was honest, part of what she loved about the country was the wild, extreme weather. Anyone could love Hawaii or Bermuda. You'd have to be very hard to please to not like lush, tropical greenery and beautiful beaches, with the temperature not changing much throughout the year. But Scotland dared you to love it. It showed you its worst and left you to take it or leave it—and Gillian definitely wanted to take it.

As Torie started her little car, Gillian turned to catch a look at her. As usual, she looked so cute Gillian wanted to pinch her cheek. Today she wore a yellow pullover sweater, with a pale green waistcoat that had a yellow stripe running through it. Perfectly matched, as always. Gillian assumed she found the gilets and waistcoats, then searched for a blouse or a sweater to match. However she did it, she always looked polished and well put together.

There wasn't even a hint of tension between them, which was more relieving than she cared to admit. She liked Torie so much she didn't want to do anything to upset the rapidly growing friendship they had going. She took another quick look, admiring the intelligence radiating from her perceptive gaze. Smart women were sooo sexy.

Her mind started to wander, creating flights of fancy that started to get away from her. Aiden was almost thirteen. In only five years he'd be going to college. Five years wasn't too long to wait to see if you had any chemistry, right? She almost slapped herself on the head, but Torie would think she was nuts.

Which she was. What kind of stupid plan was that? Be pen pals until Aiden disappeared, and then switch over to being girlfriends. Very sound plan. For an idiot.

❧ ❧ ❧

It seemed that the more popular chambered burial cairn was at Maeshowe. But Gillian didn't want to go on a guided tour, which was required there. So they were heading to Sanday, an island they could reach by a causeway, to see a small, less well-preserved site.

It wasn't raining. Not even a drop. But the skies were the flat, leaden gray that Gillian now took as a good sign. When there were many shades of gray, some of that gray was filled with rain. A nice, uniform gray was almost the equivalent of a clear blue sky.

Gillian had been staring out at the landscape for a while, finally saying, "I believe you when you tell me the land here is fertile, but why are there no trees?"

Torie gave her a cute smile. "Global cooling."

"Cooling?"

"Not now," Torie said. "A few thousand years ago. When humans first arrived the land was lightly forested. But they needed wood for fire and housing, and they might not have been careful about how they harvested the trees. The science of timber management wasn't very well developed," she added, letting out a short laugh.

"You're saying they cut everything down? They didn't even leave saplings?"

Torie smiled at her. "I'm not saying that. All we know is that there had been forests, then they were gone. It was probably a combination of cutting trees for their immediate needs and a distinct cooling trend that made the entire area pretty inhospitable for quite a while. The land changed dramatically partially because people focused on the present, with little planning for the future."

"Huh. Good thing we're so smart now," Gillian said wryly. "Many thousands of years have taught us basically nothing. Why do people care so little about—" She shut her mouth abruptly. "I'm not going to get into it. I'm on vacation, and I'm going to stop banging my drum about all of the stupid things we're doing."

"That's not a bad plan," Torie said. "There will be plenty of stupid things to rail about when you return."

"Never-ending," Gillian grumbled, turning her head to stare out at the flat, treeless land.

❧ ❧ ❧

They were the only car parked near the structure, which perked Gillian up even more. She loved being alone and making her own observations, rather than

92

having someone tell her what was important. Well, Torie could, but she was the only tour guide Gillian wanted to listen to. It had taken her a long time, but she now realized she didn't want to listen to a guide. She wanted to have a conversation, and that was only possible on a private tour. Her realization would cost her a fair amount going forward, but she thought it was worth it. It was so much better learning about what interested you, rather than hearing a spiel meant to appeal to everyone.

When they got out of the car, Torie looked up and acknowledged what Gillian had already determined. "I'm so glad we've got a nice, dry day."

"Me too. It must be close to fifty degrees. No wind."

"I'd say it's close to ten, but I'll accept your fifty, even though that sounds like a sauna." They started to walk, passing cropped grass probably tended by the sheep in the distance. "Do you know much about the Neolithic era?"

"Just what I learned yesterday."

"Well," she said, the essence of patience, "this structure is called a cairn. Cairns come in many forms, but essentially they're stacked stones. This one is a chambered burial cairn, built around five thousand years ago. When it was discovered, in the 1800s, they weren't at all careful in their excavation. Anything fragile or small was lost, but they did discover human bones, clearly laid out in a respectful fashion. Think about it," she said, with her voice taking on the slow, dreamy quality it did when she considered the distant past. "You had nothing but very rough tools. You could make fire, of course, and create shelter, but that was it. And still…" She took in a breath, turning her face to let the wind tousle her hair. "You spent the time and the effort to construct this tomb. Think of how important that must have been to you."

Gillian nodded, trying to see this from Torie's perspective. It wasn't easy, but when she tried to think of the builders as earlier versions of herself, it got in. "I think I get it," she said. "You actually needed every waking hour to find food, stay warm and protect your family from threat. But you worked on this tomb instead. This was your priority."

"Right," Torie said, nodding. "And not only that, you spent years designing and building it so that the sun split the opening at sunset on the winter solstice." She let out a soft laugh. "They didn't have a chart to tell them when that was going to be, mind you. They had to figure it out through years of painstaking observation."

"And given how rarely you see the sun on any given day in December…"

"Too true," she agreed, laughing along. "It might have taken them twenty years to be certain it worked, even after they were sure of the date. What are the odds of the sun shining on a specific day at a specific time?"

"Slim," Gillian said, certain it might have taken longer than twenty years.

The cairn was tallish, and created of dry stacked stones, forming a mound now covered with turf. It was an incredibly tidy structure, with the stones so well fitted that it was hard to believe it hadn't been built recently. As they walked down a short entry path, Torie said, "This part used to have a roof. Most of it was destroyed, but..." She dropped to her hands and knees. "This part's still here. Not claustrophobic, are you?"

"Not that I know of. But if I get scared, I'm backing out."

"Once we go about three metres, we can stand up. It's very roomy inside."

"I've already forgotten what that is," Gillian grumbled, "but I'm glad I have my rain pants on."

"Rain *pants*," Torie said, laughing to herself. "The image I see is rubber knickers."

"Those could be sexy," Gillian said. She took a look at Torie. "Like if you were into rubber."

Torie stopped and they gazed at each other for a moment, before they both started to laugh. "That doesn't work for me."

"Nor me. I try to sound sophisticated, but I'm a simple mid-westerner at heart."

"Bring your mid-western self along now. We've got some distance to cover." They moved forward on their hands and knees, with Gillian experiencing a slight wave of anxiety when it got a little too dark. Then Torie was standing up and she switched on a small flashlight she carried, rescuing Gillian from having to crawl out backwards like a sniffling child.

"Made it," she said as she stood and brushed off her knees. "I bet these folks didn't have water-resistant clothing."

"Just animal hide. I bet they would have sold their firstborn for some impermeable fabric filled with down. Can you imagine how much better their lives would have been?"

"I bet you can," Gillian said, hearing the fondness she'd begun to feel for Torie slide right out of her mouth.

"I can," she agreed. She held the light up to the wall, saying, "Norse invaders arrived a few hundred years after this was built. You can see some graffiti here and there. People have always wanted to show they've been somewhere. Like carving your initials into a tree."

"I like it here. I'd like to be here at the solstice."

"You're already coming back in the spring to see how orange the puffins are. Now you want to come back in just over a month? You're going to need some extra vacation time."

"I don't usually take what I'm owed, so I'll be making up for lost time. Literally."

"We'll be here, waiting for you," Torie said. "This cairn isn't going anywhere."

"I'd better see about transferring to our London office. I could get here in a few hours from London, right?"

"A few hours?" She smiled at that. "That's a little optimistic, but I'm discovering you're a very optimistic person."

That wasn't really how Gillian would have described herself, but if Torie thought she was, maybe that was the truth.

Back at the house, they had plenty of stew for a good lunch, and now that Torie had built another fire the cottage was toasty warm and cosy. Sitting at the dining table, Torie watched Gillian eat, reassured that her normal appetite wasn't nearly as wild as it had been the day before. If that had been her usual, it would easily have taken four meals a day to satisfy her.

"So, tell me about Columbus, O-hi-o," Torie said. "You must love it, since you returned after you got your MBA."

Gillian shrugged. "Columbus is all right. It's big enough for good entertainment options, but small enough to not spend hours commuting."

"Hmm. Not a ringing endorsement."

"No…" She took another bite, chewing thoughtfully. "I always assumed I'd live in a big city. Actually, I thought I'd stay in Chicago after I finished school. But I got the offer from Channing Brothers, and it was too good to pass up." She let out a sigh. "I guess I felt a little guilty about being so far away from my sister." When she looked up, Torie could see a bit of longing in her eyes. "But she was all wrapped up in her future husband's family by then. She didn't need me."

"Oh, I bet she was thrilled you were returning home."

Gillian shrugged. "She said she was, but we'd sold our family home after our mom died. Instead of returning to Columbus, Amanda spent her vacations in Cleveland with her boyfriend—her new family."

"But you had other reasons for staying, right? I mean, you've been there your whole life, Gillian."

She dropped her fork and moved her chair back, gazing at the wall behind Torie's head for a minute. "I definitely liked growing up there, but I've been thinking it might be time for a change."

"A big change?"

"Maybe," she said. "It's probably a silly instinct, but I've been thinking about starting over someplace."

"Why is that silly?"

"Mmm. Because my biggest complaint is my boss. I feel trapped in my job, and I haven't been able to figure out how to switch to another product line. Ron's not going anywhere, but until he does, I'm not either." She shrugged, looking quite miserable. "I like working for a major corporation, and Channing Brothers is the biggest game in town. I'd need to move to Chicago or New York to find a comparable job."

"Is your boss difficult to work for?"

"No, not usually. But he steals from me. *All* the time," she stressed.

"He steals from you? How do you mean that?"

"My ideas," Gillian said. "I work my butt off to come up with plans, and he presents them as his own. That makes him look good, but it's not doing a thing for me. I'm pretty certain he doesn't talk me up to his boss, so I might not even be considered for Ron's job if he ever leaves. It sucks," she said, pouting.

"Can't you complain to someone?"

"Sure. I could march right into the Global President's office and unload on Ron. And I might as well take a knife and plunge it into my own chest. At my level, you don't go crying to higher ups."

"Why? Isn't he there to support the employees…"

"No," she said firmly. "But even if he were, I'm not an employee. I'm a vice president. When I have problems, I'm supposed to be able to solve them myself." She paused for a second. "That's not the policy, of course, but it's the reality."

"Does Ron dislike you because you're a woman or a lesbian?"

"Dislike me? Ron's crazy about me. For some reason, he views me more as a peer than an employee." She let out a quiet laugh. "Actually, sometimes he seems to view me as his superior. And he doesn't know who I date. No one at work does." The expression she wore was the first time Torie had seen her look truly downhearted. "For all my co-workers know, I go to work, then go straight home and watch TV, alone, until it's time to punch in again. That's what they prefer."

"Do you have friends who…" She tried to think of what would make her feel better in Gillian's situation. "Friends you're close to?"

"My current stock of close friends is a little sparse right now, but I have Kara, my best buddy."

"That must help. Having someone you can vent to…"

"Kara has young kids, and you know how little time you have to spare when you're working full time and raising a family. We don't talk enough to really let me complain to my heart's content."

"How about your sister?"

"No way," she said, looking more glum by the minute. "We've never had that kind of relationship. We're very topical." Gillian leaned over and set an elbow onto the table. Resting her chin in her hand, she said, "I'm being childish. I just have this desire—a really strong desire—to go somewhere else. Almost anywhere, honestly."

"Let's trade jobs," Torie said, really trying to sell it. "It will take a while for your employers to figure out I know nothing about marketing soap, and you might have to make up a lot of facts and figures about Scotland, but you seem very creative. Aiden would love the change, and you'd have a clean slate with my sister." She stuck her hand out. "I know nothing about O-hi-o, but I'm willing to jump in. Deal?"

A cute grin made Gillian's face light up. She started to extend her hand, then pulled it back. "Do I have to wait tables?"

"You may take any scut job you like, so long as you have Aiden's tea ready when he gets home from school."

"Ohio's not all bad," she said, continuing to grin. "Maybe I'd better spend a little time counting my blessings."

CHAPTER EIGHT

ON THE WAY TO THE FERRY, Torie stopped to point out the family croft, now owned by the descendants of one of her grandparents' longtime neighbors. As she stopped the car, she pointed to a small house, noting that it wasn't in fine repair. "Sinclairs inhabited that house for a hundred and fifty years. My mother's grandfather built it at the edge of his pasture, which had been in the family for unknown generations before that."

Gillian gazed out, not commenting for a minute. "And your family wasn't able to keep even an acre?" There was so much sympathy in her voice that Torie almost cried.

"It never occurred to us," she said, sighing. "But I doubt we would have been able to. My mum has two brothers and a sister, and they all needed the money from the sale." She stared out at the land, watching the sheep, who appeared completely still. "They didn't wind up with much, but we were able to get Kirsty into a private treatment facility with the funds." She met Gillian's eyes. "My mum did the right thing in sending her, but Kirsty was using within a month of graduation. A total waste of hundreds of years of Sinclair labor."

"But you have to do whatever you can to save your kid's life," Gillian said quietly.

"You certainly do. I guarantee my mum has no regrets." She gave Gillian a quick smile, started the engine, and drove on, glad Gillian hadn't asked for her personal opinion on the investment.

❦ ❦ ❦

They'd decided to depart from a different port they'd arrived at. Stromness looked like it *might* have had something going on during the summer, when lots of tourists took the relatively short ferry ride from the mainland. But on a gray, chilly November afternoon at dusk, all Gillian noticed were the shuttered shops inhabiting the dull gray buildings. The only sounds of human habitation came from the two pubs, both of which were doing decent business for late afternoon. They chose the livelier one for a drink before they sailed, mostly to have a place to sit.

When they entered the dark space, Gillian looked around, noting that a few of the patrons were backpackers, and a few more must have parked their touring bikes outside. Some people carried suitcases, but some seemed like regulars, including a totally trashed guy at the bar who leered at her with what she was certain he thought was a charming smile.

"Would you like to go up to the bar?" Torie said, with a twinkle in her eye. "I think you have an admirer."

"Oh, no, I'm pretty sure he's looking at you." Chuckling, she added, "His eyes are almost crossed, so it's kind of hard to track them."

"I'll go," Torie sighed, sounding playfully aggrieved. "But you're paying. I was going to have a pint of the local dark beer. Join me?"

"Sure. Just don't come back with company. This isn't my day to fall for the charms of men."

Torie returned quickly, having successfully ignored the histrionic mugging the poor drunk at the bar was attempting. "Good lord," she said, setting the beers down. "Some people are truly shameless."

"He's obviously a believer in the 'try 'em all' school. If you hit on a thousand women, you might find one taker." She took a sip of her beer, dark and syrupy-looking. "My!" she said, eyes wide. "That packs a punch."

"Actually, the alcohol content isn't very high, but the malt and the chocolate notes really hit you, don't they? This is one of my favorite beers, and I assumed you'd like it because it's sweet."

"I don't normally indulge my sweet-tooth as much as I have recently. I'm definitely in vacation mode. When I get home, I'll go back to watching what I eat."

"Then I won't share the recipe for whisky tablet," Torie teased.

"Please don't." Gillian laughed softly. "Although that might spur me on to find a girlfriend who can cook. It's been a while since I've had one of those."

"We've got some time, so why don't we share coming out stories? That's one thing that binds lesbians together all around the world, right?"

"Sure." She smiled, knowing this was going to be short. "I didn't have a clue that I might be gay until I was in college. A girl I liked waaaaay more than I would have if I were straight came home with me for Thanksgiving. That first night, we snuck out of the house after everyone was in bed and stood in the back yard, freezing our butts off, while we smoked some weed."

"This isn't the usual lead-up to a coming out story," Torie said, grinning.

Gillian held her hand up. "I'm getting there. We got *totally* wasted, then went back to my room. We were giggling like maniacs while we tried to change into our pajamas. Then Catrina put her hand over my mouth to stop me from laughing so loud. I still can't understand what made me do this, but I licked her hand. We stared at each other for a couple of seconds, then stripped out of our clothes like they were burning us. A second after that, we were lying on my bed, rolling around like we were on fire." She waggled her eyebrows, trying to look silly.

"In your parents' house?"

"Uh-huh. I was stunned, but once we started, you couldn't have paid me enough to stop."

"Very bold of you," Torie said. "You weren't freaked out?"

"Freaked out?" She gave the question just a moment's consideration. "I guess I should have been, but I was too obsessed with getting my mouth on every part of her I could reach."

"She'd done this before?"

"No idea. We weren't really conversing at the time."

"Well, maybe not at that moment, but weren't you curious?"

"I was curious about a lot of things, but we never had another conversation…about sex or anything else. I'm not sure how much time had passed, but I blinked my little eyes open to find my mother in the doorway."

"Ahhhh!" Torie covered her face with her hands. "That's so wrong!"

"It was as wrong as wrong gets. Want the full text of her comments?" She tried to make herself look stern and powerful. "Be ready in ten minutes, Catrina. You're going to the airport."

"Oh, my God! What did you do?"

"I just sat there, too stunned to move. Catrina put her clothes on and took off with my dad, who was half-asleep and clearly confused."

Torie grabbed her sleeve and gave it a rough yank. "Tell me more! Don't leave me hanging!"

"There isn't much to tell. Catrina was crying. I was crying. It seemed like just seconds before she was gone."

"Did your dad just slow down and kick her out of the car? Give me some details, woman!"

"I have no idea," Gillian said, holding up her hands. "She and I never spoke again. In fact, she'd turn and run if she saw me on campus."

"You're serious," Torie said, obviously stunned.

"Completely. It took me another term to get up the nerve to approach another woman, but I finally did." She let a smile show. "To this day, I haven't had sex when a woman's parents are on the premises."

"I want to know what happened that *night*," Torie insisted. "Did your mom knock you around?"

"God, no. Nothing happened. After my mom left my room, she didn't return. She was cold and withdrawn for the rest of my visit, but that wasn't all that odd." She shrugged. "We never spoke of it again."

Torie picked up her glass and drained a third of it, then wiped her mouth with the back of her hand and slammed it onto the heavy wooden table. "You've got to be lying."

"All true," Gillian said, raising her hand like she was taking an oath. "My sister's continuing my mom's tradition of showing no interest in my private life, since she's never, ever asked who I'm dating, or even *if* I date. She and her husband are the most incurious pair in the world."

"How…" She blinked a few times, then turned quiet. Like she was afraid to ask another question.

"I know it's weird. But it's not weird for my family. We don't talk about anything that might be uncomfortable. I can only assume Amanda knows I'm gay, but she doesn't want to have it confirmed. So we all act like I have no private life."

Torie's dark eyes squinted until they were almost closed. "But doesn't that keep you at a certain distance?"

"Uh-huh. It sure as hell does." Then she picked up her beer and chugged it, letting the chocolatey ale warm her chilled insides.

☙ ☙ ☙

After a few minutes of vaguely uncomfortable silence, Gillian watched the backpackers pick up their gear and noisily make for the door.

"We don't have to leave now," Torie said, "but it wouldn't hurt to get in line. Are you ready?"

"Sure. Let me say goodbye to that handsome fellow at the bar… Oops. He's down for the count."

Torie watched him for a moment, coolly assessing his state. "I've had to muscle fellas like him out of my bar at the end of the night. If there aren't strong, helpful men around, it's a challenge."

Gillian was tempted to once again suggest that teaching high school might be a good option, but Torie didn't seem to like having her job choices questioned. If she didn't mind having to strong-arm guys from her bar, it was truly none of Gillian's business.

They boarded the ferry at four thirty, and by the time they were standing outside on the deck with the smokers, the sun appeared for the first time that day, only to bid them goodbye as it sank below the horizon.

"That was just rude!" Gillian said, trying for outrage. "The sun just wanted to show us it could have been shining all day long, but chose not to."

"It can be cruel," Torie agreed. She went to the rail and leaned over, staring down at the water. When she lifted her head, she said, "On the port side, we'll pass Hoy in a few minutes. There's a geological feature at the tip of the island called the Old Man of Hoy. It's fairly impressive."

"Then let's stay on the port side. I've got my gloves," Gillian said, pulling them from her pocket. She zipped her jacket up tightly, then patted a sleeve. "Best jacket I've ever owned. Rain proof, lined, but with vents in the pits to keep you cool."

"It's a nice one," Torie agreed. "I'll keep an eye out for one like it. Mine isn't nearly warm enough."

"Want to go inside? I can see the Old Man of Hoy through the window."

"No, no, I like being out. I've got on four layers. That should be enough."

They stood there in the gathering gloom, watching the water churn as the engines kicked in, the gentle shaking of the boat calming Gillian's unease.

Every single time she spoke about her family's reaction to her orientation, she felt a real sickness in the pit of her stomach. But she didn't want to continue to ignore the feeling. It was too important to brush aside forever. It was time to get over the hurt. Actually, maybe it was time to stop the charade and move on without going through the motions of having a "family." She'd had offers through the years, but had always chosen to stick with Channing Brothers. It was time for a fresh start. She'd never been to the west coast, but she bet she'd like it. And New York wasn't bad, even though it was awfully noisy…

Torie's soft voice cut through the wind that rushed past Gillian's ears. "I don't know why your story got under my skin so thoroughly. Mine's not too far from it."

"Tell me," Gillian said. "I'm always interested in any story where my family doesn't seem cold and unfeeling." She tried to laugh, but it didn't come out with much joy.

"Well, my parents aren't cold, but they *are* reticent to speak of things they don't know much about. I came out to them when I was in college, too. They took the news with a certain caution," she said, drawing out the word. "I had a girlfriend, and they were perfectly nice to her. But when I had to return home to tend to Aiden, Sheila and I broke up. Since then, my parents have never asked a question about my personal life." Shrugging, she added, "Maybe they think I won't miss having one if we don't talk about it."

"Like that could happen." Gillian shook her head. "Why'd you break up?"

Another shrug. "It was clear I wasn't going to be able to return to Glasgow for many years. Sheila was also getting her PhD, and was very, very busy. I didn't have time to visit her, and my home was too small for guests, even if Sheila had the time to come. It just became clear that our timing was off." She stared into the water, watching it flow for a full minute. "She teaches at a university in Wales now. Married. Two kids." Her voice caught when she finished her tale, and Gillian's heart broke for her. "Sheila got the life I wanted. The life we were going to build together."

Once they were back inside, Torie found seats while Gillian went for another beer. While she was alone, Torie gave herself a pep talk. She was being paid to give Gillian a good time, not a stomach ache. This trip wasn't supposed to revolve around her crying on a client's shoulder about her life. That nonsense had to stop.

"So," she said, boosting her smile when Gillian returned with another pint of dark ale. "We're scheduled for two nights in Inverness, then two on Skye, but that leaves us one more day to play with. I was thinking we could keep heading south, and maybe stop at Oban. Besides being the home of one of my favorite distilleries, I've read about a fantastic bike ride we could take to Taynuilt."

"Bike ride?" Gillian asked, eyes glittering.

"Uh-huh. It's a tough grade up from the glen, but it's only about twelve miles. That's nothing for you, but I think I could make it—eventually."

"Sold! I was hoping I'd have at least one opportunity to ride while I was here. Can we rent bikes in Oban?"

"We can. I'm not sure the bike hire place is technically open at this time of year, but I know the owner a bit. If he's around, he'll get us sorted."

"Bike riding after a visit to a distillery. Now that's the Scottish trip I was looking forward to," Gillian said, looking pleased as she took another long drink of her beer.

They'd been on the road for about an hour, with a couple more hours to go. Gillian kept looking out her window, amazed at how utterly dark it was. "It's almost eight, so it *should* be dark, but do you normally get enough sun to… whatever sun does for you?" She chuckled softly. "I know it's important, but I forget why."

"Of course. We get about eight hours of sunlight at this time of year."

Gillian gave her a wry look. "You get an hour—on a good day." Her look turned into a warm smile. "And this was a very good day. I loved being on the water. Maybe I should have been a ferry boat captain. I bet I'd like that."

"I'm so glad you had a good day. Most people think that ferry's an utter waste of time."

"You like being on boats, don't you?"

"Oh, I do. But my mind always wanders to what it would have been like to have to cross that straight a thousand years ago." She turned to meet Gillian's gaze. "We'd have had to start before dawn, then paddle our arses off, rushing to make land, find shelter, and light a fire. The cold sneaks up on you in November, no matter how warm the day has been. When you're wet and cold and hungry…"

A curious smile turned the corner of Gillian's mouth up. "You do this all the time, don't you. Think about the past."

"All the time," she admitted. "It's nice to know facts and figures and dates, but history has always appealed to me for the stories."

"You were interested even as a kid?"

"Definitely. My mum didn't have a lot of education, but she always encouraged my curiosity. Twice a week, every week, we'd go to the library and pick up any book we could find that told good stories of earlier eras. I'm sure I've read every social science book written for children if it was published during my youth."

"You switched to adult ones at some point, didn't you? I don't mean to disparage your degree…" Gillian laughed at her own joke. "I'm a little jealous that you found something that appealed to you when you were so young, and managed to stick with it."

"That's not true for you?"

"No. I majored in a business discipline because my father pressed me, but I never found it very interesting. I did well, but only because I'm a hard worker."

Torie reached over and slapped her leg. "Don't be jealous. Which one of us is making a living from our education?"

"That doesn't seem as important to me as it once did. I guess being on the edge of forty has made me reassess—at least a little."

"Reassess your job?"

"Not the entire job, no. I like what I do," she said, feeling more confident with that statement. "And I'm very good at it." Pausing for a moment, she continued. "I've worked hard. Really hard. I've jumped through every possible hoop. And we don't take vacations like you guys do. I've lost at least twenty weeks over the years, just to make sure I didn't miss anything important. Eventually, I got the job I wanted. But now what?"

"Um, continue to work like you have for a more important job? I think that's the goal, isn't it?"

"That's what I thought I'd do," she admitted. "But I'm changing my mind. How will my life be better if I get Ron's job?"

"I can't guess. But you must have some idea."

She shrugged. "Oh, I'd earn more money, and I'd have more control. But I'd have to work more hours doing non-business stuff. Like I'd have to pick a charity and get on the board of directors. Stuff like that. I'd have to entertain clients more often, too. They'd want me to take a golf membership at the best club in town so I could take clients out for a round. But…that's it. How would my *life* improve?" She stared out at the dark landscape, feeling glum. "How would that give me more?"

"More what?" Torie asked gently.

"Connection. Love. And if not love, at least companionship." She turned and faced her, letting her sadness show itself through her eyes. "I want to love someone, and be loved in return. I've made Channing Brothers my whole world, but they don't love me. The brothers have been dead for a hundred years," she added, trying to make light of her dilemma. "They're awful boyfriends."

"Aren't most people at your level married? Is there some reason it's harder for you…" She trailed off, realizing she was probably probing too deeply.

"Yeah," Gillian said. "It's harder for a woman. Especially a lesbian. At least it has been for me."

"Tell me about that. I'm interested, Gillian. Really."

"Well, I've told you I'm not out at work. If I found someone to love, I probably couldn't keep that up."

"And that worries you?" Torie asked gently.

"Not…" She thought for a minute. "I'm not worried they'd fire me or anything, but… Work has always been my priority. It would take me a while to adjust to having my personal life be part of the conversation."

"It never has been?"

"Never."

"But you know about your co-worker's lives, right?"

"A little. Men don't spend a ton of time talking about their lives, but I know who's married and how many kids they have. You can tell who's happy and who isn't. But they don't know *me*," she said. "Not at all."

"But you don't want them to…"

"No, that's not exactly true. I don't want to have my private life affect my career. That's all. If I could be open about everything and not have it hurt me, I would. I just don't trust that's true."

"Because you're a woman?"

"Partly." She thought for just a second, then decided to reveal something she rarely talked about. "Here's an example. I…um…I broke up with someone I was in love with because she wanted to have a baby. I just…" She closed her eyes and took in a deep breath. "I couldn't see how I could shoulder half of the responsibility while I was traveling so often and working so many hours. So I said no, and I wouldn't change my mind, even when Grace told me it was a deal-killer for her."

"Oh…" The silence stretched out until Torie must have felt compelled to say more. "It's not a good idea to have a baby unless you're *really* committed to the idea. Trust me on that."

"I know that's true. But what do you do when someone you love wants something you don't? If I'd been a guy, Grace wouldn't have expected me to do half of the work. She would have done like my straight girl friends have and just accepted that the childcare would mostly be on her."

"That's not fair," Torie said. "Especially if Grace had a job. Did she?"

"Uh-huh. A great one. Better than mine, really. But she would have gotten to take twelve weeks of maternity leave. Believe me," she said, letting out a soft laugh, "I remember all of the details, even though it's been nearly ten years."

"I'm sorry it didn't work out," Torie said. "You must have been crushed."

"We both were," she said, feeling like she might cry. "When I wouldn't change my mind, she technically broke up with me, but all of our friends blamed me for being so inflexible."

"That's not being inflexible," Torie said, her gaze full of empathy. "Having a child just to please your partner is a very bad idea."

"I thought so. But Grace was sure I'd change my mind if it was my child." She shrugged. "I really could have used some advice from the people I worked with. You know… Someone who had the same kind of job, with the same kind of stress. But I couldn't talk about it with anyone without coming out, something I just wasn't willing to do."

"But not coming out means you're unable to talk about all sorts of things, Gillian."

"I know. Believe me, I know. But I don't trust my boss or many of my peers. I think they'd use it against me if they had the chance. And I've worked too hard to get to where I am to throw it away for a little more camaraderie."

"I'm sorry," Torie said. "That must make your job a lonely place."

Gillian thought for a second, then shook her head. "I'd rather be lonely than have to look over my shoulder every minute. I've just got to work harder to find friends outside of work. I've let that slip," she admitted, not at all sure how to rectify the problem.

CHAPTER NINE

WHEN GILLIAN WOKE, SHE STOPPED in the bathroom for a quick visit, then pulled her blanket from her bed and covered her shoulders. Going to the window to look out, she was a little disappointed. She'd been sure the darkness of the previous night had been hiding glorious peaks and valleys, since her ears had been popping constantly. But all she saw now was an attractive town, with a pretty river that seemed to bisect it.

"The sun's about to blind me," Torie said. Gillian turned to look at her, seeing that her eyes were still closed.

"How can you tell?"

"I can feel it on my legs. Nice," she said, looking very happy. "Is there anything better than having the sun warm you while you're still in bed?"

"Yes," Gillian said, chuckling. "I could spend all day thinking of things I like better. But I'm glad a little sun does it for you." She grasped the sheer curtain and pulled it aside. "I thought I'd wake to mountains, but I got a little river instead."

Torie opened her eyes and got out of bed, stretching a little before she walked over to Gillian. She stood in front of the window for a moment, looking pretty happy as the sun hit her face. "There are mountains everywhere," she said. Turning to reveal her smile, she added, "Just not right there. But you'll see some as soon as we start to drive. Promise."

❧ ❧ ❧

They'd decided to stop for a brief visit to the battlefield at Culloden, then hightail it down to Skye for what Torie was sure would be a great fireworks display.

During their walk around the battlefield, Gillian had been so attentive, so respectful that Torie got a feeling for how it would be to teach a class of very earnest undergrads. In fact, she'd met very few undergrads who were as attentive as Gillian, but there had to be *some*.

It was odd, but Gillian knew almost nothing about Scotland, and just a tiny bit more than nothing about the UK. Didn't schools in the US teach European history at all?

But her lack of knowledge didn't seem to hamper her interest in the battlefield. She still probably couldn't explain exactly who the Stewarts were, much less the Hanoverians, but she understood that a lot of people died in a very short time on this ground, and that they'd given their lives defending what they thought was a massively important principle.

"So? Whose side are we on? The Stewarts, right? We're Bonnie Prince Charlie fans?"

"I'd say that most Scots today would be on his side," Torie allowed. "But it's hard to look back on that time with any kind of current equivalent. It's certainly not that Charles or his father were going to install a democracy if they'd overturned the Act of Union. It was just a matter of having more local control." She shrugged. "*Some* local control, that would, as usual, be in the hands of the most powerful. No one was going to ask a crofter who owned five acres of land what he thought."

"No one ever has," Gillian agreed.

They set off at noon, and by 12:01 Gillian was asking questions. "I'm trying to get myself oriented. I know we're going to the Highlands, but I'm not really sure what that means."

"We're going *through* the Highlands to reach Skye, which is actually an island. It's part of the Inner Hebrides."

"Mmm," she said quietly. Torie could guess what the next question would be, and she smiled when it came.

"That must mean there's an Outer Hebrides?"

"There certainly is. Many, many islands, most of them uninhabited. You might have heard of Lewis or Harris?"

"I've seen ads for Harris tweed. Is that what you mean?"

"Precisely. Lewis and Harris share an island, and that's where the majority of people in the Western Isles live."

"Okay." She nodded soberly, clearly trying to get the geography to make sense. "But we're not going there, right?"

"I wasn't planning on it, but it's possible to jump from island to island via ferry. A lot of people do that."

"I love ferries," she said, with her voice taking on the excited tone Torie had learned she had to quell quickly.

"I do too, but we need some firm plans, Gillian. It's all too easy to get sidetracked. I'm sure you'll enjoy Skye, so let's focus on that."

"All right," she said, sounding a little disappointed. "But I thought we were going to really see the Highlands."

"We're going to be driving through them for over three hours today, and I'll return home via a different route. So we'll have about seven hours of Highland scenery to enjoy. If you're interested, I can rattle on about them for seven hours without a problem."

"I'm all for hearing about them. But don't pass up anything that's particularly pretty, okay?"

"Consider it done," Torie said, smiling to herself when she thought of how enjoyable it was to tour with someone who had a nearly insatiable appetite for information. "How do you feel about waterfalls?"

"The ones I've seen pictures of have been pretty great. Why? Is there one around here?"

"There is. It's not a tall one, but it's quite pretty. Interested?"

"One hundred percent," she said, her voice nearly a purr.

Torie hadn't been to Rogie Falls for a few years, but she'd always found it a peaceful respite. They parked in a paved lot and got out, with Gillian immediately cupping her ear and leaning her head toward the trees.

"I don't hear a waterfall."

Chuckling, Torie said, "It's pretty, but it's not going to fill you with awe. Lower your expectations."

They started to walk along a wide path, surrounded by silver birch, some rowan, and a few larch. The trees were tall, but thin, pretty normal for this part of the Highlands. But the birch had already turned, now showing a profusion of gold and yellow leaves atop their crowns.

"I like this already," Gillian said, taking in a deep breath. "The air feels clean, and it even smells good. Is that from the trees?"

"Maybe. I love the smell of a forest, even though this is a meager one."

"It's pretty nice," Gillian said. "Tranquil, for sure. Are the white trunks birch?"

"They are. I assume you have birch in Ohio?"

"Uh-huh," she said, so busy looking around she sounded a little distracted. "We had a couple in our front yard when I was growing up. They weren't old, though. My dad had them planted." Her smile grew wider. "These remind me of that, but these are a heck of a lot taller." She stopped and cupped both ears. "I hear water!"

"I do too. We're close."

Torie picked up the pace, having seen how excited Gillian was by the prospect of falling water.

"Nice!" she crowed the minute the thundering water was within sight.

"It is nice," Torie agreed. "And there's a bridge we can walk across."

Gillian's slightly longer legs let her race ahead, reminding Torie of a happy dog who kept turning back to make sure her owner was following along.

"Epic!" she said, standing upon some big stones to get a better perspective on the falls.

Torie stood alongside her and took in the vista. It really was well worth a stop. While the falls weren't terrifically tall, the water cascaded down a long series of boulders, creating quite a noise.

"Bridge!" Gillian said, taking off to walk across it, holding onto the railings as the bridge swayed under her weight. When Torie joined her on the other side, she was laughing. "I had no idea it was going to move!"

"I wouldn't want to be on it during a serious gale," Torie agreed, "but I love it. It sways just enough to get your heart pumping a little harder."

"A lot harder when you've never been across a bridge that moves. But it was cool. I'm going back," she said, taking off before Torie could say a word.

Torie had been right about the mountains being all around them. At least Gillian's ears were sure she'd been right. But it was surprisingly hard to know you were actually *in* mountains, even though she wasn't going to admit that. They went up a little, then down a little, never doing the thing Gillian assumed they'd have to do—climb straight up some massive peak, able to look down at a valley floor hundreds of feet below. The cartoons she'd watched as a child obviously hadn't portrayed the mountain driving experience accurately.

She felt a little dumb having to admit what scant attention she normally paid to the natural world. It was only having Torie's perspective, listening to her interweave the story of the Scottish people with their unique and beautiful land that caught her interest. But now that she was actively trying to appreciate the landscape, she had to admit it was glorious.

Many of the trees had lost their leaves, but every once in a while they rounded a bend that revealed an autumnal display that made her breath catch. She was still tingling from the afternoon sun hitting a small loch, with layers of red, orange and yellow trees looking like they'd been neatly stacked to climb the side of a steep hill. The reflection of the trees in the water, creating a mirror image, was going to stick with her for a long time. She'd begged so earnestly that Torie had actually turned around to find the best spot to take pictures. Now

Gillian was planning on where she'd place the photo she was going to frame. People might wonder who the beautiful red-headed woman was, but once Gillian had seen her standing by the shores, she couldn't resist capturing her as well. Torie Gunn and the beauty of Scotland were simply too intertwined to fail to include her.

🌿 🌿 🌿

Even though they hadn't taken a very long break at Rogie Falls, it was almost completely dark when they finally reached the Skye Bridge.

"Is this the...sea?" Gillian asked, staring out at the water.

"This is Loch Alsh. It separates the mainland from Skye."

"Cool. I love being on an island, even though I never feel like I'm on one when I'm on one."

Torie shot her a look, and Gillian flinched. "I kind of thought you'd feel like you were on an island, but you just feel like you're on land."

"Well, you are," Torie said, clearly unable to keep herself from laughing. "But you're close to water on all sides. That's the key, you know."

"Mmm. I've never really been on an island before this last week."

"I think New York City is an island." Torie gave her a quick look, raising an eyebrow.

"Now you're just screwing with me! I bet you think I'm some country bumpkin who's never seen anything more exciting than the state fair."

"Don't be silly. You've just not been a traveler, which surprises me, since you seem so interested in everything."

"I am," she said. "But I've never prioritized travel. But that's going to change. No more letting my vacation lapse." She laughed. "Next time I'm in New York, I might take one of those tour boats that goes all around it. Then I can check its island status."

Torie gave her a quick pat on the leg. "I'm certain you'll do just that. Now we don't have reservations for tonight. I couldn't find anything that looked quite right, so I thought we'd take our chances, hoping the place I reserved for tomorrow had a cancellation. Want me to pull over and make some calls?"

Gillian took her phone out and saw that her cell signal was decent. "I can do it. Do you use any particular site?"

"Not for Skye. I made reservations for a place named The White Stag. I've got their number on my phone."

"I can find them." She got the number, then dialed. "Good afternoon," she said. "I've got a reservation for tomorrow. Lindsay?"

"Yes, ma'am," the woman said, her accent so strong Gillian had to let her mind process her words for a second.

"I was wondering if you had a room for tonight, too."

"Och," she sighed. "We're quite busy because of the festivities." She was quiet for a minute, then said, "We have the Laird's Suite available, but I'm afraid that's all."

"Is that a room?"

"Oh, yes, ma'am. It's a two-bedroom suite. Quite lovely. It's..." She trailed off. "You've reserved a double room on the top floor. I'm afraid the Laird's Suite is quite a bit more expensive than the room you've booked."

"How much?"

"Twice as much, I'm afraid," she said, or at least that's what Gillian guessed she said.

"Is it available for three nights?"

"It is. Yes, it is."

"We'll take it," she said, hoping Torie didn't feel *too* bad about her throwing her money away. "We'll be there pretty soon. We just crossed the bridge."

"Will you be joining us for dinner, Ms. Lindsay? We're having a chef's tasting menu tonight. It's sixty-five pounds per person, and includes five courses."

"We want to go to the fireworks... Can we get an early reservation?"

"Six o'clock?"

"Perfect. For two," she said, knowing Torie was going to flip her lid. But Gillian was ready to sit down and let someone else cook for them. She hadn't been crazy about the Indian food they'd had in Inverness, and, as usual, they'd missed lunch. She knew she was a spoiled American princess, but sometimes you just had to admit who you were and damn the consequences.

❦ ❦ ❦

"I'm not even going to ask," Torie said after they'd been shown to their suite, which was actually a small, freestanding building near the back of the property. It was nice, definitely nice, but not very luxurious, at least in Gillian's opinion.

Through the years, she'd stayed in some remarkable hotels, and had climbed the status ladder to a rank that now allowed her consistent upgrades. Gone were the days when she had to be happy with a small room with a view of a parking lot. But she wasn't going to diminish Torie's glee at having a whole room filled with just a big soaking tub. If Gillian had designed the room, she would have enclosed both bedrooms instead of leaving the king-sized bed right in the middle of the main room. Not doing that, while dedicating a room for a tub was just silly. A builder, rather than a designer, had probably done the work, repurposing an out-building on the property. But she wasn't going to utter a single criticism. No one appreciated a spoiled person complaining that she wasn't being spoiled quite enough.

A little before eight, Torie drove along in a long line of cars waiting to enter the grounds of Dunvegan Castle. From the road, the architectural elements of the castle had been accented with perfectly placed lights, making it look both dramatic and welcoming.

"My first castle," Gillian said, sighing.

"I wish we could go inside. But they closed for the season a couple of weeks ago. No more tours until Easter."

"Easter! They're closed half the year."

"Or more, depending on when Easter is. It's too expensive to keep a place like this open if it's not filled with tourists. Heating every wing alone would slay them."

"When I come back to see the puffins…"

"You're certainly coming up with a very comprehensive list for your second visit," Torie teased. "You won't have time to take in anything new, since you'll be backtracking on what you've already seen on your first trip."

"Maybe this is the first of many trips. I have a friend who goes to Bermuda every single year. And God knows Scotland's got more things to see than Bermuda."

"I haven't been," Torie said, "but I can tell you where I'd rather spend a week in February, and it's not Scotland. The thought of sand between my toes while I powered through an extra-large tube of sunblock fills me with delight."

Gillian had no idea how big the Isle of Skye was, so she couldn't guess how many people lived there. But she would have been surprised if nearly everyone from the island wasn't at the castle tonight. There wasn't an American accent within earshot, so it didn't seem like a particularly touristy event. Rather, people were calling out to each other, offering greetings and hugs, with a zillion little kids running around like flocks of sheep—no real idea of where they were going, following a leader who was equally perplexed. "How are these kids going to find their parents?" she said, amazed at how young some of the free-range kids were.

"Oh, they'll be scooped up eventually," Torie said. "It might take a while to sort them out, but no one's in a hurry."

"Aren't they…?" She started to ask if it was dangerous to let kids run around in a crowd, then realized how silly that was.

"Aren't they what?"

"Nothing. I was thinking like an American. We believe the world is a very dangerous place."

"It can be," Torie said, smiling up at her. "But it's generally not. Bad things can happen no matter how careful you are."

"I suppose that's— Yeow!" The first blast nearly made her wet herself.

"Big one," Torie said, her eyes bright from the blue and white streaks the explosion had trailed across the sky. "This is going to be good."

It *was* good, one of the best displays Gillian had ever seen. Having the colors reflecting off the dark skin of the castle definitely made it more special, but whoever set this up did a great job of timing, letting the smoke clear before they lit the next rocket. It was a little slower pace than she was used to, but she found she liked it better.

The crowd made very appreciative noises, "ohhing" and "ahhing" with every major blast, with kids still running around, some of them holding their hands over their ears. The whole thing was so darned wholesome it actually made Gillian tear up.

Taking a look at Torie as a bright blast lit her features, she had an irrational desire to take her hand and hold it. Actually, she wanted to grasp it in her own and clasp it to her chest, letting Torie feel her heart race.

That was crazy!

Tearing her eyes from Torie's classically beautiful features, she tried to get hold of herself. Yes, Torie was the epitome of what she wanted in a woman, but she had baggage. *Major* baggage. To snap herself out of it, she thought of a grumpy twelve-year-old, sitting on the pristine, buff-colored sofa she kept in the den, glaring at her as he took a can of soda, shook it roughly, then popped the top, letting the spray hit the ceiling, with a fine mist staining every piece of her carefully chosen, quite expensive, furniture.

Giving Torie another quick look, she sighed in defeat. She still wanted to hold her hand.

⚜ ⚜ ⚜

The last major boom was still echoing in her ears when Torie turned to Gillian and said, "Now comes the unique part."

"That wasn't…? That wasn't it?"

"There's more," she said, grinning. The groundskeepers were maneuvering something big into place, then they removed a tarp, exposing a full-sized replica of a Viking longship.

"Boy, that's cool," Gillian said. "I don't think I've ever seen one of those. Can we get close to… Ahh! They set it on fire!"

"Sure did," Torie said, laughing at the expression on her face.

"Why'd they do that?" Gillian said, speaking loudly so her voice would carry over the cheering crowd.

"For the spectacle. You know we were invaded by the Vikings for hundreds of years. Sometimes we celebrate them, sometimes we set their ship on fire. It all depends on our mood," she said, chuckling.

"That's kind of awesome," Gillian said, staring avidly as the flames climbed up the sides of the boat.

"You're saying they don't burn ships at the fireworks displays in O-hi-o?"

"They do *not*," Gillian agreed, staring at the inferno with just as much interest as the kids who'd come to a stop in front of them, all equally transfixed.

🌱🌱🌱

They took the long way back to the car park, going as close to the burnt shell of the ship as they could, trying to see a bit more of the castle. By the time they'd reached the car, many of the nearby vehicles were gone, but when Gillian opened her door, she didn't move to sit. She leaned on the top of the door, quietly saying, "I don't want the night to be over."

"Ooo. Did you have fun?"

"I had a fantastic time," she said, showing her teeth when she smiled. "I know this is partly because I'm on vacation, but I feel younger than I have in years. Childlike, actually. It's a wonderful feeling."

Torie walked over to her, fighting the instinct to give her a hug. But Gillian was practically begging for one. She looked like she truly craved some physical contact, but maybe that was just Torie shifting her own desires. She couldn't even *think* of hugging a client. Any client. Maybe at the end of the trip… She shook her head roughly, refusing to even let herself dream of having an intimate moment with Gillian.

Clearing her throat, Torie said, "I'm very, very glad you had such a good time tonight. This was more fun than eating Indian food in a small double room in Inverness, wasn't it?"

That earned her a wry grin. "I could get used to that. I just didn't grow up eating anything very…unique. When I come back to see the puffins, and the winter solstice in that claustrophobic thing in Orkney, and this castle, I'll spend some time getting acquainted with Indian food." She laughed. "Something I really didn't think I'd encounter in Scotland."

"We'll add haggis to your list of things you have to try. Now *that's* Scottish."

"Haggis is…?"

Torie patted her arm and walked back to the right side of the car. "Something you might enjoy if you didn't know exactly what it was, or how it was made. Trust me. We have a few things that fall into that category."

❦ ❦ ❦

By the next morning, the weather had turned cold, and while it wasn't exactly raining, the air was so heavy and thick it felt like you were inhaling a mist. Gillian wasn't able to see farther than fifty yards, but Torie assured her that climbing a steep peak in heavy fog wasn't dangerous. Of course, people who set a big boat on fire when kids were running around unsupervised probably weren't the best judges of safety.

She bent over and tightened the laces of the shoes she'd bought that morning. They were the perfect shoes for Scotland. A cross between running shoes and hiking boots, and entirely waterproof. The thick black tights she wore were another splurge. She could have gotten by with her jeans, but she didn't want to run the risk of them getting wet. Nothing annoyed her more than soggy jeans. Of course, she owned black Lycra tights. Cold morning bike rides in November required them. But she hadn't packed very carefully. That omission was good for the Scottish economy, but not-so-good for her credit card, which was going to melt if she didn't stop whipping it out every other minute.

Torie, in Gillian's opinion, wasn't dressed properly for a hike in the fog. But she probably had five or six layers hidden under her rain jacket, and another one or two beneath her jeans. And if she was certain her regular running shoes were up to the task, Gillian really couldn't argue with her. Well, she could, but she'd learned that Torie nodded politely when presented with a suggestion, then did exactly as she wanted. Torie Gunn was no pushover, which just made her all the more attractive.

Torie had insisted that this hike up the Quiraing was one of the most popular in all of Scotland, but there had only been about fifteen cars nestled along the road when they'd arrived. Maybe the locals were sitting around a roaring fire, thinking about taking on the Quiraing on a more hospitable day.

Looking up as they stood at the foot of the trail, Gillian couldn't really pick much out, but there was a looming, dark presence above her. It was really pretty Gothic, and if she'd let herself, she could have let her imagination run away with her. Then Torie stood beside her and said, "Want to race?"

"I'll take you on for some sprints, like…fifty yards at a time. But I'm not running where I can't see."

"Such a careful girl you are," Torie said. "Come on, then. If you won't race, you might as well walk."

They started off on a narrow path that had probably been created by sheep, but Gillian's new shoes easily shrugged off the uneven terrain, and in just a few dozen yards she was able to stretch her legs out and get into the climb.

Even though she'd ridden up every significant hill in central and southern Ohio, Gillian had done almost no hiking in her life. It always seemed more fun to ride. But walking definitely had its charms, allowing her to focus on the path and her breathing and her balance. It was fun, really, reminding her once again of being young, of taking on challenges that seemed a little daunting, but powering through anyway, oblivious to the danger, sure of her invulnerability.

As she climbed, she spied some massive…spires in the near distance. They were quite tall, and very irregular. But it looked like she might be able to scramble up them… Without checking with Torie, she started to crab-walk up one of the spiky peaks, turning to see that Torie was right behind her, head down, clearly exerting herself. *God, this was fun!* No map, no path, no signposts. Just a craggy hill that needed climbing for no reason at all. They might have to slide down on their butts, but she'd figure that out later. For now, all she wanted to do was keep climbing, making her body react to the stress just like she'd trained it to do. Whether on foot or on a bike, the key was to keep going, eating up the terrain one inch at a time.

Torie's thigh muscles twitched sporadically, strained and weary. She snuck a quick glance at Gillian, who was obviously at least twenty-five percent mountain goat.

Gillian was gazing out of her window, giving Torie another moment to take another peek at her legs. They'd been together for over a week, but today had been the first time Gillian had worn anything form-fitting, even though her legs should have been showcased in every way possible.

Torie hadn't even been aware she was so attracted to legs, but she most definitely was—at least when Gillian's were the ones in question.

Her years of riding bikes, combined with her height gave her long, supple muscles that her black tights lovingly caressed.

Their walk had been around six kilometres, definitely enough to stress Torie, who, though she was on her feet constantly, rarely had the opportunity to stretch her legs for much of a climb. Gillian, of course, had acted like they were window-shopping, barely breathing heavily as they scrambled around, investigating every part of the walk.

She'd been fresh and ready to go when Torie suggested a favorite restaurant for an early dinner, even though it entailed a long, winding drive.

"I really enjoyed dinner," Gillian said, turning her head unexpectedly to meet Torie's eyes.

"Right!" she said, feeling silly at having such a meager response. "Um, that was my kind of meal," she added, trying to get her brain to work properly. "A spicy vegetable curry over rice hits my sweet spot."

"Mine got hit, too, even though we didn't eat the same thing. My salmon tasted like it had been caught five minutes before it was served."

"Might have been," Torie said, "but I don't think the chef has time to go fishing. He runs that place with only one person in the kitchen with him, and one server."

"It was a good meal, topping a good day. A very good day." She eased her seat back a little and let out a breath. "The wine was good, too. Wish you could have had some."

"Mmm. That's a little too much alcohol for me when I'm driving. I'll have a beer if I've got a couple of hours before I have to get in the car, but wine hits me harder."

"Me too," Gillian said, laughing a little. "I don't think I'm going to need my wee dram of whisky before bed."

They'd driven most of the way across Skye to reach the restaurant, and now they were the only car on the pitch-black road, climbing a hill that would have given them a great dramatic view of a glen if they'd been there a few hours earlier. Torie sighed a little, disappointed they hadn't gone this way before now. But even with three days you couldn't begin to see all of the striking landscapes hidden within Skye.

When she reached the peak, a chill hit the back of her neck. There was just a hint of green in the sky. Maybe… Were they lucky enough? *Yes!* "Look," she said, immediately pulling over to the side of the road and turning off the car.

"What in the heck?"

Torie was certain Gillian had never seen them before, given she herself had only seen them about ten times in her whole life, and they were relatively common in Scotland. "The aurora borealis," she said, her voice taking on a reverent tone. She opened her door and walked toward the hood of the car, leaning against it to soak up some of the warmth from the engine. Gillian was next to her in moments.

"This is normal?" she asked, with a hint of concern in her voice. "A spaceship's not going to land, is it?"

"Normal. Not common, but entirely normal."

"Is this the Northern Lights?"

"It is." They were both silent as the air seemed to throb with color, shades of vivid green giving way to a deep purple near the horizon. "Ooo," Torie purred. "I hardly ever see purple." She took in a breath. "This is special, Gillian."

She didn't respond, but Torie tore her gaze away momentarily to catch her looking absolutely stunned, mouth slightly open, eyes as wide as they got.

"Can I take a picture?" she asked, sounding a little tentative.

"Of course you can. It's real," Torie said, chuckling. "This isn't a hallucination."

She pulled her phone from her pocket and took picture after picture, then put it away and continued to just stare, with the wind whipping her hair around her head.

"I'm getting cold, but I don't think I care," Gillian said. "Can we stay here all night?"

"We could, and I'm willing to stay as long as they last, but they could disappear at any moment."

"No!" she moaned. "I want more."

"Let's sit in the car for a minute. My hands are getting numb."

Torie thought Gillian might just ignore the cold, but she complied. The car wasn't a whole lot warmer, but it cut the wind, which was the problem.

"How cold is it?" Gillian asked. "Below freezing?"

"Oh, gosh, no. It's probably six or seven degrees. At this altitude it doesn't often freeze at this time of year."

"Wish I knew what six or seven meant. I'm going to assume it's ten below zero." She let out another heavy sigh. "If I knew this was a possibility, we would have been outside all night—every night."

Torie laughed. "Then I'm glad you were clueless. The islands are good places to see them, but they're never guaranteed. I've been checking an app I have, but it said there was a zero percent possibility for tonight."

"So, you've been looking for them?"

"Of course. I knew you'd love to see them. But, like I said, I didn't expect them tonight."

"What are they?" she asked, leaning close to the windscreen as she stared.

"Mmm. Sun flares? I think some solar particles get through the earth's magnetic shield and mix with oxygen and nitrogen to cause the color. I forget whether oxygen or nitrogen causes the green and yellows, which are most common, but the other gives you the pink and purple."

"Pink?"

"No pink tonight. Just the thin line of purple there that's…gone," she said. "Bye-bye, pretty purple."

Gillian let out a disappointed grumble. "The green's still awesome. Doesn't it look like the air's dancing?"

"It's doing something," Torie agreed. "It's more of a shimmer to me, but I see your point."

"I really hope you're not too cold, because I have to stay here until this is over. You can leave me by the side of the road if you need to, but I've got to stay." She still hadn't taken her eyes off the sky, staring so hard she was going to get a headache.

"I'm with you until the bitter end," Torie said. "I didn't see them at all last year, or the year before, for that matter. I'm all in."

Nodding, Gillian relaxed a little, but she stopped speaking. She stared with such interest that it seemed she was having some sort of religious experience, and Torie wasn't about to interrupt her.

After a long while, Torie turned when she heard a faint sniffling sound. Gillian was wiping at her eyes, and she turned to quietly say, "I don't think I've ever seen anything so beautiful. God," she whispered, "the world is so awesome, and we see so little of it. As least I've only seen a tiny bit."

"Me too. Except for a hen-do in Dublin, I've never left Britain."

"I've spent most of my spare money on things," Gillian said, her voice going a little flat. "That's dumb. I've got to seek out more experiences. I've got to *see* more."

"That's a good wish," Torie agreed. "When Aiden's grown…" She trailed off, feeling a little silly to even have the dream.

"I'll be your tour guide if you ever want to come to America," Gillian said, taking her eyes off the sky for a split second. "I can show you much of Ohio, a little bit of New York City, and about a square mile of Chicago. Not much, but that's all I know."

"For now," Torie said, reaching over to give that Lycra-clad leg a pat. "Maybe you'll be traversing the country in no time at all."

"I guess it's possible," Gillian said quietly, falling into another long silence. "I don't even know why I've traveled so little," she said, startling Torie after minutes had passed without a sound. "It's like I have to be shaken out of my routine to do anything different. My friend Kara's still teasing me about taking this trip. She keeps calling it my expedition, like I'm traversing the globe."

Torie wasn't sure how many minutes passed before Gillian once again broke the silence. "What were you doing with hens in Dublin?"

CHAPTER TEN

IT HAD TAKEN OVER A FULL week in Scotland to enjoy what Gillian considered a world class meal, but she was having one today. This was the only Michelin-starred restaurant they were likely to encounter, and having a blow-out lunch was much more reasonable than a blow-out dinner, which she knew Torie wouldn't be able to relax and enjoy.

Since it was only lunch, Torie hadn't put up much of a fight, but she'd ordered the less expensive of the two fixed price menus, refusing the seafood sampler which Gillian was sure she'd like. The fifteen-pound supplement undoubtedly would have ruined her enjoyment.

"I can't imagine the guts these people had to open a top-notch restaurant way out here," Gillian said. They'd driven over a half hour from the closest town on mostly single-track roads to reach the spot.

"I think being inaccessible might add to the cachet," Torie said. "But they've earned that star. This was the most lovingly prepared food I've ever had."

"And I got to try black pudding. I'm feeling very Scottish now."

Torie nodded, a small smile on her face. "Don't order it at a manky chippy. What you had was definitely an elevated form. But I'm proud of you for giving it a try."

"I'm probably going to regret this, but I'm going to eat every bite of my Drambuie custard bread pudding, even though I'm stuffed. We're going to have to walk some of this off."

A flash of concern crossed Torie's face. "Are you sure you still want to go? We've got a long drive to reach Oban tonight, and it looks like it's going to rain…"

"It does," Gillian admitted. "But I can't ignore a noted lighthouse."

"It's waaay out," Torie insisted. "Another half hour from here. And it will be *very* windy."

"Wind never killed anyone. I've got my weather clothes. I'm impermeable."

"Your jacket and trousers might be," Torie agreed, "but I don't think that extends to the wearer."

"Close enough," Gillian said, with her eyes locking onto the bread pudding being set down in front of her. She was going to need a *very* vigorous hike to work it off, but it sure looked like it would be worth it.

༓ ༓ ༓

The day had been unrelentingly dreary, not the kind of day Torie would have ordered up for their last hours on Skye. But getting three days without any significant rain had been expecting a lot. She kept checking out the sky, sure it was going to pour.

The clouds were heavy, very low, and ranged from a wispy pale gray to a deep, dark smoke. The dark ones were the ones she feared. But Gillian truly believed having a waterproof jacket and trousers meant weather didn't concern her. She'd learn. Maybe not on this trip, but if she visited Scotland more than once, she'd learn.

"The land looks really different out here," Gillian said. "No real grass, and it's as flat as a pancake."

"Yes, this part of the island isn't overly scenic. But this boggy, scraggly land is an important part of the ecosystem. It all works together." Torie pulled over onto the shoulder to let a truck pass.

"These single-track roads sure do take a while to travel," Gillian said. "Is there a rule for who goes first?"

"Not a hard and fast one," Torie said, giving the truck driver a return wave as he passed. "I let anyone who looks like they're working go first. But on a road like this, where you can see who's coming, I try to time it so we both reach the passing place at the same time. Then neither of us has to stop." She turned and gave Gillian a smile. "That doesn't work with tourists if they haven't adapted. I can usually tell who the tourists are, though. They rent the bigger cars."

"A week ago, I would have done exactly that, but I've learned my lesson. Go tiny."

They continued on, with Gillian observing the landscape carefully. "It's kinda lunar," she finally said.

"I can see that. But I don't think they have peat on the moon."

Things started to turn green as they got close to the point, and when Torie pulled into a small car park, there were acres of verdant grass surrounding them once again.

The wind was shaking the car, making it shudder enough to finally make Gillian look concerned. "This won't blow the car over, will it? I don't think I'm strong enough to turn this little bug over if it's wheels up when we get back."

"It's never flipped over," Torie assured her, "but it's much windier than it was when we left the restaurant."

"It was around forty miles an hour when we reached the car," Gillian said. "But I lost cell service by the time we'd gone a mile. I guess we'll see, huh?"

As Gillian threw the door open, the wind caught it and threw it right back at her. She barely got a hand out to stop it from snapping her leg off at the shin.

"Good God!" she said, eyes wide. "I don't think that's ever happened to me before!"

"This isn't good," she said, "And… Here comes the rain." In seconds, the windscreen was covered with drops, then it started to drum on the roof. "It's time to turn back, Gillian. I—"

"No way! This is why I bought the gear, right? Jacket, hood, gloves, *trousers*, boots. Only my face is exposed, and it won't hurt me to have a wet face. This is our last chance. Let's do it."

"Last chance on *this* trip. You could always come back on your puffin excursion." Torie was teasing, and knew her voice reflected that.

"You think I'm kidding, but I'm going to be watching those little orange-footed birds before you know it. Come on. I want to scratch this off my list." She peered into the rain. "Where is it, anyway?"

"A long way from here. We've got to go down a steep set of stairs, then across an open pasture, then climb a little more. But there's a railing on the steps, so we shouldn't be dashed to the rocks. I *hope*."

"Nothing ventured," Gillian said, opening the door again, this time using both hands and waiting to stick her foot out until it was secure.

They made it down the stairs, but Torie would never have even attempted it if Gillian hadn't been paying for her time. While the walk probably wasn't truly dangerous, it was foolhardy. She'd been to this lighthouse many times, and knew it wouldn't show well in the rain. But while trying to put herself in Gillian's place, she had to admit she'd want to see Times Square, even during a power outage. You had different priorities when you assumed you had one chance to see something.

Once they'd climbed down the crumbling, wind-swept stairs, clearly built many, many years ago, they reached the pasture, a very wide, very green space that culminated in a dramatic ocean vista. Gillian held her arms straight out and let the wind yank, tug, and pull on her jacket and trousers. She looked like she might take flight, but she was a little too sturdy for the wind to carry her away.

"It's cool!" she said, taking off after a flock of sheep, making them complain loudly as they scampered away.

"Stay away from the cliffs!" Torie yelled.

Gillian pointed at the near distance. "That's a cliff?"

"Isn't that the sea?"

"Couldn't prove it by me. We didn't see it on the way in, so I didn't know to look for it." She tilted her head back, letting the rain slap her right in the face. "Ahh. I can smell the ocean now. It's out there, hiding."

She started for the cliffs, but Torie ran over and grasped her by the sleeve to hold her in place. "Let's stay on the path. Nice and safe."

"Where's your spirit of adventure?" she demanded, turning to face Torie. Rain was sheeting down her face, with the edges of her hood fluttering wildly as she tottered in the relentless gusts of wind.

"This is plenty adventurous for any woman." They struggled against the wind to climb a short rise, then she stood next to Gillian and pointed to their right. "There she is."

"Oh," Gillian said, clearly not impressed by the lighthouse. "Another little one."

"All of the ones on cliffs are wee," Torie said. "But this one had a cool feature. See that cable coming up from the sea?"

"Uh-huh."

"They used to bring supplies in by boat, then load them up in a little cart. The keeper would crank them up the hill so no one had to scramble down to the water. Nice feature."

"God, if they paid lighthouse keepers based on what a pain in the butt their jobs were, they would have been paid like Wall Street hedge fund managers."

"At least," Torie agreed.

They kept walking, with Gillian linking her arm through Torie's. "You're light enough to blow away," she said, blinking hard when the wind lashed across her face. "Since I could never find my way out of here, I've got to keep you tethered."

"If we get over there by the old cottages, we'll have a little protection."

"Cottages? Those awful things are where the keepers lived?"

"Those are they. Obviously, no one's bought them and spent a lorry full of money to trick them out. They're truly dismal."

As soon as they got behind the building, the wind was brought down to a manageable level.

"Whew!" Gillian said. "I'm so glad I'm not a lighthouse keeper in nineteen hundred!"

"It wouldn't be for me, either. Had enough?"

"I've got to go over there," she insisted, pointing at a spot too close to the cliff for Torie's comfort. "There's a sign."

"It's nothing. Trust me."

"But I can get a good picture over there. Be right back."

Before Torie could reach out to stop her, Gillian was racing away. She'd only gone about twenty feet, farther than Torie would have allowed, but she really was sure-footed. She extended her phone and took a few pictures, taking the time to do some panoramas, which couldn't possibly have turned out in the driving wind. Her arms were up, and the big target she presented must have made her into a sail. A gust hit her in the back and she dropped to her knees for a split second, then tumbled forward, landing on her side, still holding onto the damn phone.

Torie was next to her in a flash, heart racing when she heard Gillian crying out in pain.

"I broke something," she moaned. "God damn it. I broke my arm!"

"No, no," Torie insisted. "Give me your hand. I'll help you up."

She'd rolled into a ball, holding her right arm to her body. "I can't. I can't."

"Gillian, you've got to get up. We don't have any options."

"Call an ambulance," she whimpered.

"Ambulance? There's no cell coverage here. And it would take an hour to get here, even if I could summon help. Come on, now. You can get up."

Carefully, she rolled onto her back, eyes closed tightly, mouth contorted into a grimace. "My arm's broken, and I think my ribs are too."

Torie shielded her eyes, seeing that Gillian had fallen onto a rock that protruded from the otherwise flat ground. It was a big one, and she must have hit it at just the perfect spot. But there was no way she'd broken anything. Bruised? Certainly. But she was too fit and hardy to have a bone snap from a simple fall.

"I'm sure it hurts," she said firmly, "but we can only get you to Emergency if you can get up. I can't give you a collie-back, so you're going to have to do it on your own."

"Speak English," she growled, grimacing in pain.

Torie thought back to her previous sentence, then decided to ignore it. She simply didn't have time to translate her words into American at the moment.

Screwing her eyes closed even tighter, Gillian extended her left hand, crying out in pain when Torie tried to haul her to her feet. She was just too heavy, and Torie couldn't keep hold of her. As she thumped back onto the ground, she yelled so loudly she could have been heard in Oban, with guilt piercing Torie's heart for screwing up so badly.

"I'm so sorry," she said, dropping to her knees. She leaned over Gillian, keeping the rain from her face. "I'll help you sit up. Then you can get to your feet. I know it will hurt, but you've got to do it."

With great care, Gillian sat up, biting her lips from the pain. Then she used her left arm to slowly get to her knees, with Torie bracing her against the wind. Finally, with a great cry, she stood. "I really screwed up," she moaned. "I've got to get to the hospital."

Torie nodded, knowing that was much easier said than done.

The screen on Gillian's phone was smashed, but she hadn't even glanced at it. All she'd managed to do was slump in her seat, eyes closed, whimpering every time Torie was forced to hit a dip or bump in the road.

She held her arm tightly to her body, cradling it like a baby. Other than the occasional cry, she hadn't said a word, letting Torie worry without interruption. She had no idea where the Emergency was, assuming it would be in Portree. But she hated to go there without confirmation. Cell service was still just a wish, so she stopped at a tiny coffee house in a tiny town about a half hour from Neist Point. Gillian gave her a pleading look, but Torie patted her and said, "I've got to find out where to go. Can I get you anything?"

"A hospital," she muttered. "All I need is a hospital."

It took almost another hour to reach Broadford, and it was deep dusk when Torie tentatively pulled into what she'd been led to believe was the Emergency room.

Gillian looked up to stare out the windscreen before uttering a dismissive, "No way."

"I think this is it," Torie said, but she did have to admit it looked like a nice outbuilding for a croft. She entered the narrow drive, and saw just three other cars parked haphazardly, as if their drivers had stomped on the brakes and had gotten out with no thought at all. "I'll go check," she said. It had stopped raining, but the car park was a manky mess. Her boots were sucked into the muck as she walked, but halfway to the building she could see that it looked like a proper medical facility. Heading back to the car, she opened the door and put her hand on Gillian's shoulder. "This is it. Give me your hand and I'll help you out."

"Can't someone come get me? I need them to use the jaws of life to cut the car open. I don't think I can turn my body to get out."

"Oh, Gillian, I don't think anyone can get you out of there. You've got to take a deep breath and make yourself move."

She closed her eyes again as she took in a sharp breath and gave it a try. But she didn't get far. Torie reached in and grabbed a leg, pulling it firmly to place her foot on the ground, ignoring her cry of pain. They didn't have the luxury of giving into that now. Getting Gillian's right leg onto terra firma was more daunting, but Torie did it, with her ear still ringing from Gillian shouting a few choice curse words into it. Then Torie grit her teeth, grasped Gillian's left arm and draped it over her shoulders, getting an arm around her back to pull her to her feet. She'd surprised herself at being able to pull a larger woman from a car, but her adrenaline was clearly pumping. Gillian swayed a little, bent over from the pain, once again cradling her arm.

Torie got her in the automatic door, then set her down on a plastic chair, knowing it wouldn't be easy to get her up again. There was a little glass window at the reception area, but no one was behind it. Torie rang a bell and a gray-haired woman eventually greeted her. "Can I help you?" She looked out into the waiting room, seeing Gillian. "Oh, my, what's happened?"

"She fell out at Neist Point and landed on a big rock. She thinks her arm's broken."

"Ribs too," Gillian said, growling unhappily.

"We've had two people who fell at the Fairy Ponds, but you're our first from Neist Point. Today," she added. "I'll send someone to get her. I'll just need her name and phone number."

"Gillian Lindsay," Torie said.

Gillian piped up with her phone number, then the woman disappeared again. Torie went to sit down, gently patting Gillian's leg, trying to soothe her.

Another woman appeared, about their age, with dark hair pulled back into a twist at the back of her head. Her expression was filled with empathy, as though she were the one in pain. "What's happened?" she asked, squatting down right in front of Gillian.

"The wind knocked me over," she said. "Neist Point. Hit my arm and my ribs on a rock that was sticking out of the ground. They're broken."

"We'll have a look. Can you walk, or would you like a wheel chair?"

"Wheel chair," Gillian said without hesitation.

"Be right back." She was true to her word, returning in a flash with a wheel chair. She set the brakes and helped Gillian to her feet, with Torie noticing that Gillian was really toughening up. Nary a whimper this time.

The woman started to push Gillian toward a door to the left, saying, "I'm Annette MacLeod. You're…?"

"Gillian."

"It's nice to meet you, but I wish it were under different circumstances." She got her into a big room with an x-ray machine, then spoke to a young woman who must have been the radiographer. Returning, she spoke soothingly to Gillian again. "We'll take a picture of your arm—"

"And my ribs," Gillian said.

"We don't x-ray the ribs. The dose of radiation outweighs the benefit in most cases. We'll treat your pain, and the ribs will heal on their own."

"You're not going to fix them?" Gillian asked, looking like she'd cry.

"We'll treat your pain, Gillian. Trust me on that." Annette grasped her hand gently. "Can you stand?" She helped again, then unzipped Gillian's jacket and did a cursory exam, listening to her breathing, then lightly touching her chest. "Right here?"

"Yes," she said, her voice an octave higher than normal.

"I'll need your jacket off," Annette said, doing it quickly. Carefully, she touched various parts of her arm. "There's no obvious break, but we'll take a look, all right? We'll need to leave," she said to Torie. "This will just take a minute."

Torie really didn't want to leave her, looking so lost and vulnerable in the big room. But she was certain they wouldn't take an x-ray with her clinging to Gillian's leg. "I'll be right outside. Let's hope for a bad bruise, okay?"

"Broken," Gillian said, never wavering in her conviction.

Annette showed Torie to a small exam room. "You can wait right here," she said. "Are you Gillian's…"

"Friend," Torie said, ignoring their professional relationship. At this point, they were friends, and she was going to be right by her side until she had her back home, hopefully merely bruised.

After a wait that seemed long, but was actually only fifteen minutes, the radiographer wheeled Gillian into the exam room. She was a ghostly pale color, actually looking like she might vomit. Torie was about to ask how it had gone, but Gillian was giving off every indication she didn't want to speak. Torie sat beside her, and she put a hand on her left shoulder. Gillian nodded slightly, then leaned her head down to trap Torie's hand between her chin and her shoulder. So she wanted some comfort, but she didn't want to talk. No problem. Aiden was exactly the same way.

After about a half hour, Annette returned. She met Gillian's gaze and said, "I'm afraid you were right." She placed a laptop on the small table and pointed with her pen. "You broke the ulna, right here," she said, hovering over the ghostly image. "We've spoken to the orthopedist, and it's a very simple break. The angulation's only five percent, with a one-millimetre displacement. You won't need surgery."

"Surgery!" Gillian yelped, clutching it tightly to her chest.

"Many lower arm fractures have to be stabilized." Annette moved her own hand as if she was turning a door knob. "The bones twist around each other when you make this movement, so you're asking a lot of them. You want to make sure they stay properly aligned."

"Then maybe I *should* have surgery," Gillian said, her whole affect sharpening. "Can I speak with the orthopedist?"

"We spoke to him by phone. He's in Inverness."

"Inverness? There's no one here?"

"We have a doctor here, but not an orthopedist," Annette said. "If you have a specific question, I'll have the doctor call again…"

"You're not a doctor?"

"I'm a nurse practitioner, but the doctor will be in to see you in a minute."

"Can you send the x-ray to my doctor in the US?" Gillian said, showing more force and determination than she'd shown all day.

"We don't send x-rays by e-mail because of patient confidentiality. But we can post a CD first thing. Will that be all right?"

"I'll do it," she said, giving Torie a quick glance. "I'd like to overnight it."

"Not a problem." She looked down at Gillian's arm with a great deal of empathy. "I do hope you're left handed."

"Right," Gillian sighed. "I'm going to have to dictate for a while."

Gillian wasn't acting like a true diva, but it was clear to Torie that she didn't think this tiny emergency room in a rather remote part of Scotland was up to handling her injury. But having a task—getting hold of her doctor in America, kept her occupied. When she was busy, she didn't seem to notice the pain as much.

Torie was actually impressed at how determined Gillian was, simply not taking no for an answer until she had her doctor on the line. Thankfully, he was able to reassure her that a simple fracture would heal on its own. He even boosted her mood slightly when he guessed that she'd be able to switch to a brace by the time she returned home. That would make things easier in every way, even though Torie was certain Gillian's mind was too muddled to consider how difficult the next few days would be.

Annette returned, bearing a canister of Entonox. "Would you like a little something for the pain? It will be another few minutes until we're able to cast your arm."

"What is that?" Gillian asked, clearly suspicious.

"It's a combination of oxygen and nitrous oxide. Very quick acting."

"Laughing gas?"

"It is. Would you like some?"

Gillian met Torie's encouraging gaze.

"I guess."

She held the mask over her face and breathed in the way Annette described. After a minute or two, her whole affect changed. Her body grew less rigid, and she relaxed in her wheelchair, with a smile starting to bloom.

"This helps," she said, her voice turning a little slow and soft. "A lot."

Torie gripped her uninjured shoulder. "I'm so glad."

Annette used her stethoscope to listen to Gillian's breathing again. The exam seemed much easier for Gillian to tolerate, with her barely whimpering when she was forced to breathe in and out deeply. "What's the verdict?" Gillian asked.

Annette smiled at her. "I'm certain they'll feel much better in a few weeks."

"Weeks," Gillian said slowly. "Isn't that a long time?"

⚜ ⚜ ⚜

It was after nine when they finally made their way to the car, with Annette walking alongside to help Gillian in. Neither her tailored blouse, nor her sweater, nor her jacket fit over the cast, so she wore a hospital gown over her waterproof trousers, with her jacket draped around her shoulders. "You have your medications, right?" Annette asked.

"Don't know," Gillian said, blinking slowly. Clearly, codeine affected her quickly and dramatically.

"I have them," Torie said. "You gave her enough for a week?"

"I did. But she probably won't need them for that long. After a day or two, she'll be able to switch to straight paracetamol. Just make sure she has enough pain control to allow her to breathe deeply. You have to be on the lookout for pneumonia with rib injuries."

Gillian slid into the car like she didn't have full control of her muscles, then smiled up at Annette. "You're really nice," she said. "This is the nicest place I've ever been."

Annette patted her gently and started to close the door, saying, "I hope you feel much better very soon."

Before the door closed, Gillian called out, "Wait!"

"Yes?"

"We didn't pay."

"Pay? For...?" Annette asked.

"For everything you did. They can't bill me since they didn't even ask for my address."

"There's no charge," Annette said. "You've had an accident, Gillian, not some elective procedure."

"Free? This was all free?" Her gaze slowly traveled from Annette to Torie. "Scotland's a wonderful, wonderful place," she sighed, letting her head drop back. "You're all so nice."

"This won't be so bad," Gillian mused as they pulled out of the car park. "I'll be fine in a few weeks." Turning her head, she said, "Are we going to Oban now?"

"We are not," Torie said firmly. "We're going right back to the hotel. They hadn't let the room, so we lucked out."

"Oh. Right." Gillian tried to stop herself from whining. "Doesn't make sense to go to Oban to ride bikes at this point." She turned, seeing Torie's concerned expression. "When I come to see the puffins, I'll go on a long ride."

"I think we'll stay right here until you feel better," Torie said. "I hate to have you paying so much for a room when you're not enjoying Skye, but... I could take you to Aberdeen. You could have my room. If Aiden's back, I'll sleep on the sofa."

"Torie," Gillian soothed. "I'm going to be fine. It feels so much better already. I might be ready to start exploring tomorrow. You'll see."

Another worried look headed Gillian's way. Torie didn't seem like a pessimist, but she clearly wasn't buying that prediction. She just wasn't aware of Gillian's awesome recuperative powers.

The pain meds were still working well. So well that Gillian tried to help with the luggage. Torie was really going to have to keep an eye on her, because she would be very unhappy if she tried to yank on a suitcase with her sore ribs.

Once they were in the room, Torie said, "Do you want to put your long underwear on? I'll have to cut off a sleeve..."

"How am I going to..." She stared, open-mouthed. "I can't get anything over my arm!"

Torie gave her a long look. Her cast kept her arm at a ninety-degree angle, wrapping around her thumb to travel all the way up to her biceps. Literally nothing she owned would fit over it.

"We're going to have to buy you a few inexpensive things that you won't mind ruining."

"Oh, great. Everybody looks good in disposable clothes."

"I'll go get you something in the morning." She tossed one of Gillian's suitcases to the bed and opened it to find her long underwear. "I hate to ruin these. Do you have a T-shirt?"

"I do, but I like it," she said. "It's the only thing I still have from college."

"Hmm…" She stood with her hands on her hips, then made a decision. "I'm due for a new thermal top. Giving mine to you will spur me on to purchase a replacement."

"No, no, cut mine up. I don't care."

"I do," she said, ignoring Gillian's complaints. In a few seconds, Torie had her white top out, flinching a bit when she sliced the sleeve off with the knife she always carried when traveling. Holding up the shirt, she said, "Ready to put it on?"

"Yeah. Just let me…" She tried to shrug out of the hospital gown with one shoulder, which wasn't humanly possible.

"Let me help you." Torie untied the gown, then started to slip it from Gillian's shoulders. She caught it and held it against her breasts, letting Torie wrestle her into the snug thermal top.

"Can I have my thermal pants? *Trousers,*" she corrected, making Torie laugh for the first time in a few hours.

"I don't think you'll be able to get them on, but feel free to try."

"I've got one good arm," she said, holding onto the bottoms as she went into the bathroom.

She was gone long enough for Torie to place Gillian's suitcases on the floor, then find her phone charger. Despite the cracked screen, the phone seemed functional.

The door opened, and a flushed Gillian stood in the doorway, jeans open and pulled down only a few inches on one side. "This is ridiculous!"

"It takes more work than you'd think to get undressed," Torie said. "When my granny broke her hip, she was utterly helpless for quite a while. I got good at dressing adults," she said, trying to make light of what she assumed would be embarrassing for Gillian.

"The rain pants were easy, but these jeans will not come off. They're kinda snug," she admitted. "I shouldn't have worn the skinny ones today." She grasped at the fabric that had flapped open. "Normally I just shimmy out of them, but it hurts to shimmy."

"This will just take a second." Torie walked over to her and whisked them down in a flash, refusing to allow herself to take a close-up view of Gillian's gorgeous legs. "Pants?"

"Trousers," she grumbled.

"I meant, do you want your pants off?"

"I can do that," she insisted, grasping her thermal bottoms again. "I'm not paying you enough to strip me naked."

Torie didn't comment, knowing they were going to have a bigger issue when Gillian wanted to wash. There was no earthly way to shower and keep a cast dry, and her ribs were going to hurt too much to get into the tub without a great deal of help—preferably a fork lift.

After taking another dose of codeine, Gillian tentatively got into bed, with Torie propping up her arm with the pillows from the sofa. "Can you lie on your back to sleep?"

"I lie on my right side," she said, clearly annoyed. "Exclusively."

"Well, the good news is that Annette said your ribs would feel better if you slept on the bruised side. But you don't want to do that right away. Lying on that cast would not be fun."

"I should be all right." She blinked slowly, looking so young and innocent she almost brought Torie to tears. "I still have a lot of pain, but the drugs make me not really care."

"Want me to put some pillows under your knees? If you're not used to sleeping on your back it might get stiff."

"You're off the clock," Gillian said, her voice full of fondness. "Go read something or watch TV. Enjoy a moment's peace."

"No TV for me. I'm going to sleep. Today was…" She was going to reveal that the day had taken a lot out of her, but that was silly. She hadn't fallen and broken an arm. "I'll be glad to greet the morning," she said, leaving it at that. "Are you sure you're all right?"

"I'm fine." With their eyes meeting one more time, she said, "Thanks for everything today. Without you, I'd still be lying on the ground, waiting for that ambulance to come."

"Without me, you wouldn't have known about the lighthouse at Neist Point, so don't give me too much credit." The instinct to bend over and kiss the top of Gillian's head was almost overwhelming, but she fought it. Blurring those lines could only lead to trouble. "Call me if you need anything. *Anything*. All right?"

"Okay. You can leave the light on. I'm going to check the news."

"I'll bring your computer. Hold on."

As Torie turned to fetch it, Gillian said, "I can just use my... What happened to my phone?"

"Neist Point happened. That was one malevolent rock."

CHAPTER ELEVEN

WATCHING THE LED NUMBERS ON the clock change was about all Gillian could manage. Seeing five o'clock appear cheered her up a bit, knowing the night was almost over. When she heard Torie get up, she called out, "Can you bring me some pain pills when you have a minute?"

"Be right there," she said, with her voice sounding a little rough from sleep.

Moments later, Gillian watched Torie make a cup of tea over by the mini-fridge. She was so efficient, so competent, insisting the drugs would go down better with something warm, then starting to make herbal tea before Gillian could lodge a protest.

"Here we go," she said, sitting on the edge of the bed to hand the mug over. "I'd take two tablets. They'll help you get back to sleep."

"I haven't done much of that," she admitted. "I cannot get comfortable lying on my back."

"Try to think of something soothing," Torie said. "Even if you don't sleep, you'll be resting."

"Mmm. I'm not all that fond of resting." She swallowed the pills and handed the mug back. "I'm learning all sorts of new things about myself, none of which I wanted to know."

❦ ❦ ❦

Two hours later, when Torie tip-toed into the main room, dawn was breaking over the mountains, promising a clear morning. She'd been up for a while, but had stayed in her room to avoid waking Gillian. But now she was hungry, and thought she might be able to sneak out to walk over to the lodge. But the second her foot hit a creaky floorboard, Gillian gasped and started to groggily sit up. "Damn it," she growled, clutching her arm. "I was hoping this was a bad dream."

Torie walked over to her and sat on the edge of the bed. "You can't get comfortable, can you."

"Not at all." Her hair was a mess, her eyes were swollen and puffy, and her skin was a little blotchy, making her look like she hadn't gotten a moment's sleep.

Torie gently traced the part of her hand that extended from the cast. "You've got some swelling there, but it doesn't look too bad. How are you feeling? Is your pain under control?"

"Not very." She ran her hand along her rib cage, then pulled her top up, exposing her belly. It took until that minute for Torie to notice how snug the top was. Gillian's remarkably perfect breasts were highlighted like spotlights were aimed at them, revealing pert nipples, hardening from the chilly air. "Am I bruised?"

Torie blinked, unable to get her mouth to work. Finally, she murmured, "Mmm-hmm," and tried to concentrate. With the gentlest touch, she barely moved the skin, tracing red and purple bruising along Gillian's side. "It doesn't look too bad, but I'm sure it hurts."

"I'd like something to settle my stomach. Then I can take some more pain pills. I feel like I need them so I can breathe." Tentatively, she tried to take a deep breath, just the way Annette had instructed her. But she gasped in pain and stopped mid-attempt. "Can you help me get up?"

"I'll try. Just give me a minute. I want to figure out how to do it without putting stress on your ribs."

"That won't be easy. I'm finding that you use them for *everything*."

"I'll get behind you and push your trunk. Pulling on you doesn't seem like a good idea."

"Mmm. I'm not sure how that will work, but I'm willing to try. Tonight, I think I should prop myself up higher. That will encourage me not to try to roll over, which I did about twenty times, waking up in pain every single time."

Torie got up and slid onto the bed behind Gillian, then slipped her hands under her back, feeling the warmth of her body as it settled against her. "I'll go slow," she said, mouth bone-dry. "Just relax and let me do the work."

"Are you sure you can lift me?"

"I am. I'm stronger than I look."

"That's good," Gillian said, joking for the first time. "Because you don't look strong at all."

"Here we go," Torie said. "Just stay loose and let me do this."

Gillian's body was rigid with tension, but Torie could tell she was trying not to use her muscles to help. It took some effort, but Torie got her hands well down her back and used her whole body to push, managing to get her into a sitting position with a minimum of whimpering.

"So much better," Gillian sighed. "But who's going to do that for me when I'm back home?"

"You'll feel better by then. I can be your ribs until Sunday, and I think that will get you through the worst of it."

Gillian put her feet onto the floor and stood, wobbling for a second as she reached out to grasp Torie's shoulder. "Kinda woozy. Too much codeine."

"Need help in the bath?"

With a smirk, Gillian said, "I *definitely* don't pay you enough for that. But I've been thinking all night about how I'm going to wash."

"We'll do that after breakfast. Oh," she said. "You don't have clothes to wear to the lodge. I'll go fetch something for you to eat. Anything in mind?"

"I want whatever's full of sugar. Pancakes, waffles, sweet rolls. Just don't bring me anything even vaguely healthy."

"I can handle that," Torie smirked. "Want me to stay while you use the bathroom? I want to make sure you can get up."

"I can," she said, using one hand to turn her toward the door.

"I've got to get my jacket," Torie said, making for her room.

"Wear mine. It's right by the door. It looks cold out. You'll like the added insulation it has."

Torie picked it up and shrugged into it. "It's probably one size bigger than I'd normally pick, but now I'm even more jealous." She wrapped it around her body and hugged herself. "It's so *warm.*"

Gillian gave her a pat and urged her to go. "I don't want you listening to me if I start crying when I sit down to pee. Go. Go," she said, giving her a slight push.

"I'll be back in a few minutes. *Please* be careful. I don't want you getting dizzy and falling."

"Don't even say that word," Gillian said, scowling. "That's my least favorite word of the day."

🌿🌿🌿

Gillian might have thought she wanted sweet, nutrient-free food, but her heart clearly wasn't in it. She was upright, sitting on the sofa, with her hair combed, and her face washed. But she didn't look well at all. Every time Torie took a look at her she felt a burst of regret for her situation. Essentially losing five days of her vacation, a vacation she'd been enjoying so much, had to be hitting her hard. But the feeling Torie couldn't shake was her complicity in Gillian's winding up at Neist Point at all.

Gillian couldn't really be blamed for ignoring the inherent danger imposed by a very windy, very wet point out at the tip of the island. Torie, on the other hand, knew it had been a risky decision, but she'd put up very little resistance, thinking that pleasing a client was her top priority. That had been wrongheaded. Pleasing a client while keeping her *safe* should have been her goal. But she'd let the safety aspects glide by, and now Gillian was suffering.

"You don't seem like your breakfast is going down well," Torie said. "Can I get you something else? Maybe some toast or something bland?"

"No, thanks," she said, offering up a wan smile. "I'm just feeling weird. Slow," she added. "Really hazy up here." She pointed at her head with her index finger.

"Maybe the codeine's not agreeing with you. What do you normally take for pain?"

"Not much. Ibuprofen when I get my period." She shrugged, then winced when the gesture must have tugged on her ribs. "I guess I'll lie down again. Maybe I'll feel better if I get more rest." She started to get up, then sank back onto the sofa to gaze at Torie with a puzzled expression. "Don't you have to get home? We were going to head back to Aberdeen tonight, right?"

"Don't worry about it. Everything's fine at home. I can get someone to cover for me."

"But it's been a week. I don't want you to…"

"It's fine, Gillian. Come on. I'll help you to bed, then I'll go buy some things that will fit over your cast."

She gave it a baleful look. "Whatever I get, I'll have to cut the sleeve off."

Torie took another look, reluctantly agreeing. "That's probably true. I'll get something inexpensive."

"I don't care," Gillian said, biting at her lip as she forced herself to her feet. "Take my ATM card and get some cash to pay for stuff. My PIN number's 3198."

"I can charge things…"

"I don't mind." She sat on the bed, looking like she was afraid of lying down again. Torie walked over to her and once again scrambled around until she was braced against the headboard. "Just relax and let me guide you down," she said, pleased when Gillian did exactly that.

It took some work to climb out of the spot she'd left herself in, but Torie finally stood next to the bed and arranged pillows under the cast, adding another to Gillian's side to support her ribs. "I won't be gone too long. I'll bring lunch, all right?"

"Sure. Whatever."

Torie stood there for a second, waiting for a little joke or something. She'd gotten so used to Gillian's teasing that its absence was slightly jarring. Their eyes met, and she reached down to pat her leg. "You'll feel better when you've gotten some more sleep," she promised, not at all sure she was being honest.

It took quite a while to find inexpensive clothing on the island, but Torie had a lot of experience in ferreting out deals. When she walked in the room, carrying big bags full of clothing, she thought she heard Gillian making some kind of sound, but her eyes were closed and she didn't move.

Quietly, Torie put everything down, then tip-toed over to her. "Gillian?" she said, as she sat on the edge of the bed and touched her damp cheek. "Are you all right?"

Her eyes didn't open as she shook her head. "I'm…" Fresh tears spilled from the corners of her eyes. "I feel awful." Wiping at her eyes with the back of her left hand, she mumbled, "I'm sorry for acting like a baby. I just can't…"

"You're sad. Justifiably," Torie added. "I don't know exactly how you feel, but I have a rough idea, and it's awful."

She finally opened her eyes, red-rimmed and swollen. "I never do this. I'm not a crier."

"You need to," Torie soothed, stroking her hair. "You're sad and you're upset and you're hurt."

"I've never been hurt before," she said quietly. "It's kind of awful." She gazed at her cast. "I feel like my body's betrayed me." With a dramatic sigh, she added, "I haven't been bothered at all by the thought of turning forty, but I guess I'd better get used to things like this happening. I'm on the downhill side now."

Torie hated to laugh, but she couldn't hold it in. "Now you're being silly. You bashed your arm on a big rock. That has nothing to do with your age. Come on now." She gave that powerful leg a playful slap. "You have the body of a thirty-year-old. A really fit thirty-year-old. You'll be in pain for a bit, then you'll bounce right back."

"You think so?" she asked, her voice shaking a little.

"I know so. You'll feel a little better every day, and when you get home you can get this cast taken off. When you're not carrying this massive thing around I guarantee you'll feel close to normal."

"Thanks," she whispered, closing her eyes again. "I'm embarrassed I'm being such a baby. Thanks for not making me feel stupid."

"I want you to feel safe," Torie said softly, leaning over a little as she started to instinctively press a kiss to her head. But she pulled up just as she was about to deliver it, meeting Gillian's eyes, which batted open as she got close. Embarrassed, she put her hand to her head and ruffled her hair. But Gillian didn't brush off the gesture. Instead, she looked directly at her and said, "I feel safe with you." Her eyes darted to the side, breaking the intimacy of the moment. "You're very maternal." A tiny frown formed, then she added, "I mean that in the most complimentary way. I mean…" Now even quieter, she said, "I don't ever remember my mom making things safe for me." When their eyes met again, she added, "Being cared for is a very nice feeling."

"I do care. We're becoming friends, and I'm very happy for that," she said, feeling a swelling in her heart at the open, trusting look Gillian was giving her.

"We are," she agreed, holding the gaze for a few moments. "Is there any way you can make me well enough to go on that bike ride? I can't tell you how much I was looking forward to that."

"I wish I could," Torie said, sitting up tall. "You're going to have to put that on your list for your next trip. Maybe you can bring your bike. A lot of people do."

"I've done that," Gillian admitted. "Almost all of my vacations have revolved around bike tours or races."

"Then I'll make it a point to research the best routes. I'll have a trip all lined up for you when you come for your puffin run."

"Will you ride with me?" she asked soberly.

"Um…" There was no way she could keep up with Gillian. Even for a short trip. But she needed some comforting today, and if that included lying to her, who'd be hurt?

"How could I resist? I'd better start training in the next five minutes if I don't want to slow you to a crawl, but I'll do my best." She patted her shoulder. "Want to rest a little more?"

"I should get up…" At that moment, she looked like a little girl. A confused, sleepy little bairn who knew she needed a nap, but was afraid of missing something important.

"Come on." Torie patted her shoulder, then tucked the comforter around her. "I want you to think of the calmest, most tranquilizing place you've ever been. Clear your mind of everything else."

"Orkney," she said as her eyes fluttered closed.

"Which part?"

"When we were by those awesome cliffs, and you could hear the waves crashing against the rocks."

"Then think about the waves as they thrummed against the stone, how moist and clean the air was. Let the feeling you had then envelop you, Gillian. Let it soothe you."

She simply nodded, her eyes closed tightly, the beginnings of a smile starting to form.

Torie sat there for another few minutes, letting her body press against Gillian's, hoping to reassure her. Pondering the comments Gillian had just made, she turned them over and over in her head. Did things just not generally upset her? Or did she try to keep a tight lid on her emotions? Gillian honestly seemed very carefree and content, which was a bit odd, given the losses she'd suffered. But when she thought of it carefully, Gillian was probably the happiest person she knew.

All they accomplished that day was resting and watching TV, but Torie didn't have a single complaint. Given she was always sleep-deprived, she napped nearly as much as Gillian did, and by the time she woke on Thursday, she felt better than she had in a couple of years.

But reality was calling, and she had to get back home. Getting Gillian in shape to travel wasn't going to be easy, but they started tackling it just after breakfast, when she'd finally gotten three pieces of toast and jam into Gillian's empty stomach.

They stood in the bathroom together, with Gillian holding the thermal top to her breasts. "I think I just need you to wash my left armpit," she decided.

"And you think you can do the rest? I truly don't mind helping, Gillian. I can be very clinical when I need to be."

"I think I've got it. Sure you don't mind?"

Torie lathered up a cloth and rolled her eyes. "This is not a difficult job."

Gillian raised her arm as well as she could, shivering in the chilly room. "No one has washed me since I was a baby. I swear I'm regressing."

"No long showers with a girlfriend?"

"Don't think so. Never living with a woman gives you fewer opportunities for playing around like that. Maybe that's what I should get myself for my birthday. A woman I can shower with." When she smiled, Torie felt her heart start to beat a little harder. Gillian could have had that wish without even trying. Why didn't she know that?

The prospect of putting on a butt-ugly black sweatshirt with a sleeve cut off was bad enough. But getting a bra on was just not going to happen. Even with help, which she was *not* going to ask for, the thought of that band of elastic pressing against her ribs made her sick to her stomach. "Okay," she said, dropping her towel as she turned her back to Torie. "I'm going to need two things. First, help getting the shirt over my head, and second, you're going to have to judge a bounce test."

"Bounce test?"

"Yeah. You're going to have to check me out to make sure my boobs don't bounce too much without a bra."

Torie didn't comment right away, busily trying to wrestle the sweatshirt around Gillian from the back. But once it was in place she stood in front of her and gave her chest a quick look. "The fabric's really thick. You look fine."

Gillian put her left hand to her breast and rubbed it briskly. "Can't see my nipple?"

Another brief glance. "Not unless I stare, and if anyone's staring at your breasts..." She shrugged. "Bap 'em wi' yer cast."

"Are you sure I look okay?" She was sick of herself, having been reduced to a crying, whining, needy mess. But she knew people would be staring at her because of the cast, and wanted to at least look presentable.

"You look just fine. I know you'd prefer to wear a nice blouse and a soft sweater, but I couldn't participate in ruining any of your expensive things."

"I appreciate that you went out of your way to buy this stuff," Gillian said, dreading having to put on the windbreaker that had to be a men's extra-large.

"I know this isn't anything you'd choose," Torie said as she picked up the jacket. "But it will keep the rain off you. You can burn it when you leave on Sunday."

"Melt," Gillian said, fingering the material. "I don't think this would burn."

"Come on," Torie said, holding the jacket and shaking it. "I spent a half hour measuring sleeves to make sure this would go over your cast."

"I really do appreciate that," Gillian said, feeling herself start to tear up again. *What was happening to her?*

Torie got the jacket over the cast, tried to settle the elastic around her wrist, then rolled up the sleeves, which were at least six inches too long. She'd done a good job of finding a jacket that fit over the cast, but the body of the coat hit her in the middle of her thighs, making her look like she'd mistakenly picked up a jacket that belonged to a lineman for Ohio State. But it would keep the rain off, a meager, but attainable goal.

"You look perfectly acceptable for traveling," Torie said, her smile a little overly-enthusiastic.

"Let's do it." Gillian forced herself to at least try to act perky. "I mean, you do everything and I'll supervise."

"Go with your strengths," Torie said, hefting Gillian's suitcases as she made for the door.

🌿 🌿 🌿

They took the most scenic route to the bridge, even though it wasted a little time. But Torie wanted Gillian to at least have a pretty drive back to Aberdeen. Just before they left the island, Torie slowed down when she spotted a guy standing near the Straight, playing his pipes. She pulled over when Gillian met her eyes, clearly surprised.

"He's out here alone? Why?"

"He's busking," Torie said. "It's not unusual to have someone out here playing. Nice backdrop. Good photo op."

"If I can haul my butt out of here, will you take my picture with him? I want to send it to my buddy to show her why I haven't thrown myself off a cliff yet."

"Not sure I get the reference," Torie said, helping Gillian out of the car.

"I'm really not used to being unable to take care of myself." She stood and looked out at the water, with the peaks of the Highlands looming up behind it. "If I was at home, I'd have to have someone come hide the knives. But here…" She reached up and wiped at her eye, clearly unable to stop her emotions from spilling out without warning. "I'm so crazy about Scotland, I'm able to ignore the pain and try to enjoy myself." She patted her back pocket. "Do you know where my wallet is? I've got to give this guy some money."

"I've got a fiver on me," Torie said. "Is that too much?"

"Add it to my bill," Gillian said, taking it and walking over to the piper. Then she signaled Torie as she lifted her left hand with a thumb's up sign, leaning her head toward the piper playing away.

"I got a good one," Torie said. "At least I think I did. It's a little hard to tell with the screen this badly cracked."

"That phone's a month old," Gillian grumbled as they got back into the car. "But I'm not even going to complain. Small price to pay for finding my true love."

"What?" Torie said, whipping her head around so quickly she might have strained her neck.

"Scotland. I'm going to love it here."

"What exactly do you mean?"

"I'm thinking of ways I can stay. In Scotland. Not right here." Her gaze traveled around the Straight. "Although staying right here is tempting."

"Do you have some *recent* Scottish ancestor you haven't told me about? Or are you going to enter into a sham marriage?" She lifted her shoulders. "Otherwise, it's not easy to get citizenship."

"I don't need citizenship. I just have to get residency."

"Also not easy."

"No, but I bet I could figure it out. Some Scottish company must need an ace marketing wizard."

"You're serious," Torie said, gazing at her intently. "I think you really are."

Gillian smiled, looking like a contented cat. "I really am. I love it here," she said quietly. "I love the geography, I love the water, I love the people. I love the fact that you might declare your independence, and I want to be here to watch an autonomous Scotland come into being."

"Gillian," she said, soothingly, "it's fun to fantasize about moving to a new place when you travel, but another to actually do it."

"I know." She looked at her for a few seconds. "I'm sure there are plenty of bad things about living here. But its taken my being away from home to acknowledge how unhappy I've been. I keep thinking it's my job that's making me so unhappy, but it's more than that." She swallowed as a sober look crossed her face. "It's much more than that."

"Tell me. What's making you unhappy?"

After blowing out a breath, she said, "I've known you for a little more than a week, and I've told you more about my life than I have most of my friends. I don't have many deep connections, Torie, and even though I know that's my fault, I don't have them because I don't know many people I want to go deep with. I want a new start." She shrugged. "It's as simple as that. I want to start over and get to know people who truly want to know the real me."

Torie bit her tongue for a moment, then decided to spit it out. "Um, do you think being in the closet's part of the problem?"

She shrugged one shoulder, a trick she'd managed to teach herself pretty quickly. "I don't think so, but people blame every problem you have on your being private about your life. I guess they could be partly right. I'm not sure."

"Well, it's hard for people to know the real you if you don't tell them about something pretty important…"

"I'll be more open when I move. I will," she said, nodding.

"What about your sister? Wouldn't it be hard to leave…"

She made a dismissive gesture with her hand. "She wouldn't miss me if she never saw me again."

"That can't be true," Torie insisted. "It can't be."

"I'm not saying she hates me or anything, but I only see her once in a while. I think I'm an obligation for her. She puts as much effort into seeing my father's aunt who's in an assisted care facility as she does me. You know… She dutifully takes her a fruitcake and a lap blanket at Christmas."

"Oh, Gillian, I wish you had more. I don't think I'd choose my parents as friends, but I love them with all my heart. I truly like them, too, even though they both frustrate me to the core." She reached over and touched Gillian's leg, trying to connect with her. "We've been through so much together, and I have so many fond memories from my childhood. You honestly don't have that?"

Gillian shook her head. "I recall the few vacations we took together, but it's the places I think of, not my family."

"No fond memories of playing with your sister when you were small?"

"None I can think of," she said, clearly wracking her brain. "Four years is kind of a big gap when one of you is seven and the other three."

"And you have little in common now, right?"

"Well, given she's an avid Republican, and I think they're slashing away at the foundations of our democracy…"

"Is she afraid of immigrants and Muslims and your formerly close international allies?"

"If she is, she's never said so in front of me. We've had a grand total of one talk about all of this." She sat quietly for a few seconds, then said, "I made a plea to get her to see that electing the Manchurian Cheeto was a horrible idea, but she seemed to believe that traditional Republicans would take over. Since then, we've both avoided bringing the topic up."

"That's probably not a bad idea. I've done the same since our Brexit vote. It's too late to change the outcome, and arguing isn't productive."

"No, it's not. Up until a few years ago, my interest in politics had been largely nonexistent. I'd probably be happier if I went back to being uninformed." She graced Torie with a wide smile. "But I should know who the president of my new home is."

"Um, we don't have presidents. Nicola Sturgeon is the first minister of Scotland. How's that? Or do you want me to get into how we share power with Whitehall?"

"I'm happy with my Sturgeon," she said, chuckling to herself. "Love the name."

Gillian leaned against the window, eyes turned to the rugged, achingly beautiful landscape they'd just left. She felt a visceral need to stay, to explore and soak it all in. If she'd been healthy, she just might have done that, surprising the heck out of Torie.

Before this week, she never would have thought she'd be bowled over by massive geological formations with a grassy covering. She'd always been a tree girl.

Since she was small, she'd loved the big specimen trees that turned lovely shades of green, yellow and red depending on the season. They graced the curving lanes of her suburban childhood town, stood proud in front of her church, and blocked the wind around farmhouses all over Ohio. But most of what she'd seen so far in Scotland was, to be kind, a little deficient in the tree department. Scotland made up for it in drama, though, with the cliffs and crags the earthquakes and volcanos had visited upon the land making her gasp in surprise every hour or so.

Once the road turned to prevent her from seeing the island she already missed, Torie said, "About five thousand years ago, the Highlands were a nearly perfect ecosystem. Brown bears, wolves, moose, elk, boar, aurochs, lynx, beaver... All working in harmony to support a wide range of forest, savannah, scrub, peatland, bogs." She let out a sigh. "All of the predators are gone now, and if we don't work harder, the deforestation will reach a point where we can't bring it back, no matter how hard we try."

"Global warming?" Gillian asked. They were gaining a little altitude, and were very quickly surrounded by what looked like a very healthy forest to her.

"That doesn't help, but as I told you on Orkney, we'd started to destroy the forest in Neolithic times. When you start cutting down trees for homes and warmth, things get out of balance. But it was the introduction of sheep and cattle that accelerated that. Farmers and shepherds aren't fond of trees," she said, letting out another short, sad, sigh. "Then the predators were hunted to extinction, leaving far too many red deer."

"The deer are cute," Gillian said. "Actually, they're pretty. They remind me of you."

"I look like a deer?" Torie tore her attention from the narrow, twisty road to give her a startled look.

"Not you, per se. But when the sun hits them, their fur... Is it fur or hair?"

"Hide, I'd think, which I suppose is hair. Go on," Torie urged. "I want to hear how this ends."

"They look red, but also a little gold." She was at the limit of her ability to describe the animals, stopping to add, "That's how your hair looks when the sun hits it. Red and gold at the same time."

"Hmm." Torie turned quickly to reveal what Gillian hoped was a pleased smile. "I suppose there are worse things to resemble. I have a photo of myself standing next to a Highland cow, and I have to admit we could have been sisters."

"You look like you belong here," Gillian said, a little jealous that her small amount of Scottish blood made her look just like most white people on earth—brown hair and skin that tanned rather easily.

"If I could go back, I'd live here five thousand years ago. I'd love to have been here when this was a proper forest."

"You might have been eaten by a bear," Gillian teased. "Or frozen to death. You're cold all the time now, and you've got warm clothes and artificial heat."

"I'd risk it," Torie said, her mouth quirking up in a big grin. "The last five thousand years of coddling have weakened my constitution. I would have been tougher then."

"You would have been cutting down trees as fast as you could manage, just to keep a fire going. Admit it."

"I'd only take what I had to. I'd have been the first conservationist." She laughed a little. "I'd probably have been very unpopular, but I'd try to convince people to huddle together for warmth. Fire's overrated."

"If anyone could convince a bunch of freezing, soggy people to huddle, it would have been you," Gillian said, easing her seat back an inch to take some of the stress off her ribs. She let her eyes close halfway, taking in the undulating terrain, the sharp curves, and what she still considered pristine forest in what was now her new favorite place in Scotland.

Gillian was sound asleep, snoring softly. Hard to believe the car was more comfortable than her bed had been, but sitting up might have helped her ribs. Whatever the reason, Torie was very glad she was finally getting some rest.

They were heading back to the hotel in Aberdeen, but Torie couldn't figure out why. Gillian hadn't even gotten a taste for Edinburgh, nor set foot in Glasgow, yet she wanted to return to Aberdeen, a place that held few highlights. That might have made sense if Torie had the rest of the week free. It was undeniable they were attracted to each other. Anyone with the slightest bit of sensitivity would have seen that, but neither of them had made an overt move, and Torie had already convinced herself not to even consider doing so.

But Gillian was clearly planning on spending time together, even though Torie had made it clear she couldn't think of taking any more time off work.

When they drew near the city, with the traffic causing her to slow and merge more frequently, Gillian woke slowly, letting out a few pain-filled whimpers.

"I'm sorry I woke you," Torie said quietly.

"It's okay." She rubbed her eyes and sat up, wincing audibly. "I'll need some more pain meds. Are we just about there?"

"We are. Um, what are you planning on doing for your last few days?"

"No plans. I thought we could…" Torie could see her swallow nervously. "You're free in the middle of the day tomorrow, aren't you?"

"I think I can manage two hours, but I'm afraid that's all."

"Two hours?" she asked, her pale eyes opening wide.

"I think so. Aiden's back home, so I need to spend a little time with him. I want to have his tea made when he gets home from school so we can go over his homework before I go to work. I'll come by your room as soon as my morning shift's over, but I truly have to leave by noon…"

"Am I going to annoy you if I'm here? Be honest," she said, showing the forthright personality she'd evinced only sporadically in the last two days. "You won't hurt my feelings."

Torie knew that was a lie, but she could tell the truth without a second thought. "I love spending time with you. There's just not a lot to do here. Are you sure you don't want me to make up a list of things for you to see in Edinburgh?"

"Not unless you want me to leave." She shrugged. "I'd go home early, but I checked with the airline and there's no availability for reward seats. I thought I'd just lie around and rest. That's what I'd do at home, since I can't manage much else. At least at a hotel I can order room service."

Torie pulled up in front of the hotel, but before she could utter a word the youngest, least confident bellman had Gillian's door open, greeting her. "Welcome back, ma'am," he said tentatively. "Checking in again?"

"I am, but I need a minute."

"Oh. Sorry," he said, quietly shutting her door like she'd snapped at him.

"You're going to work now?" Gillian asked.

"I am. I'll just make it."

"Okay. Okay." She shook her head and opened the door. "Come by when you're free in the morning. I'll be here."

"See you," Torie said, afraid she'd cry. That had never happened with a client!

"See you." She reached for the door rather awkwardly, but got it open just as Torie was unfastening her seatbelt to race over and help. Then she was out of the car, guiding the bellman to her bags after Torie popped the boot open.

A horn honked sharply, and Torie put her car into gear and took off. Even if she heeded the warning bells that were going off in her head, they'd have to meet up again. She hadn't been paid!

CHAPTER TWELVE

THE DINING ROOM OF THE hotel was empty for a Friday, with Torie serving a total of five people, all of whom seemed to have colds.

For her entire shift, thoughts of Gillian filled every corner of her mind, nudging and annoying her. Knowing she was right upstairs made it worse. So much worse. A powerful yearning made her want to whip off her apron and run right up the stairs. But she couldn't. Not when she was the only server on duty.

The facts she'd been fighting were not up for debate. Gillian was the first woman she'd been interested in for twelve years. Seriously interested in. Sexually interested in. There was no doubt that Gillian possessed all of the physical qualities that appealed to Torie. Actually, she had more of them than either of her previous girlfriends. But the one thing she couldn't ignore, the one thing that scared her to her depths, was having just a taste of the connection she'd missed so badly for the last twelve years—only to have it taken from her.

She'd never had a fling, and was terrified to have her first with Gillian. A local woman who didn't appeal to her strongly might have been safe to experiment with. But Gillian appealed to her in every way possible, and Torie knew that sliding into a physical relationship with her would gut her when they had to part—in just two days. But the pull was overwhelming. Every lusty part of her wanted to march up to Gillian's room and take her in her arms. They'd figure out a way to work around the bruised ribs and the broken arm.

She closed her eyes for a few seconds, imagining how it would feel. With a sigh, she forced herself to admit she'd be perfectly happy just to kiss her. Any kind of physical connection would soothe her soul and help her feel like a sexual being once again. But was that an instinct she *should* give into? How did you know which desires were better kept in your head, and which should be jumped on with alacrity?

Gillian paced across the plaid carpet, waiting for Torie to arrive. She'd never been so nervous about meeting a woman, but her mind was a whirling mess of conflicting thoughts.

It would be a ridiculously stupid idea to get involved with Torie. The fact that she lived several thousand miles away was the *least* of the problems they'd have to overcome, and that was saying something. But a woman who'd given up her personal life entirely to raise her nephew…revealed something. Something important. Yes, it was a noble gesture. You couldn't argue that it wasn't. But every minute of Torie's day wasn't taken up with parenting the kid. If she'd made herself a priority, she could have switched her schedule around to have some free time. But even if she couldn't have done that, there must have been a lesbian in Aberdeenshire who had a few hours available in the middle of the day, right? If she was really a sexual being, wouldn't she have figured out a way?

There was a soft knock at the door and Gillian's heart thrummed in her chest. When she opened the door, her eyes met Torie's and every qualm evaporated, replaced with a burning desire to impress her, to charm her, to make Torie want her as much as she wanted Torie.

"Hi," Gillian said, trying not to look nervous. She'd made multi-million-dollar presentations and been calmer than she was today.

"Hi," Torie said, touching her lightly on the arm. "Nice sweatshirt you have there."

"Oh, yeah. My shirt." Gillian had managed to iron her khakis and polish her shoes, all with one hand. It had taken an hour, but she'd gotten it done. Using her left hand to blow her hair dry had also taken a ridiculous amount of time, but it looked damn nice, if she did have to say so herself. But all Torie noticed was her raggedy shirt, the only one she could get on.

Forcing herself to ignore the slight, she focused on Torie. Reaching out, she rubbed the black and white fabric of her waistcoat between her fingers. "Wool?"

"Uh-huh. I'd call this a Donegal tweed. See the slubs woven into it?"

"Slubs?" Her thumb was still running across the fabric. She'd chosen to test the material at the arm hole, and now her fingers were close to Torie's body. So close she could feel her warmth.

"That's what they're called," she said, looking down at Gillian's hand, which had lingered far too long.

"Pretty."

"I added these silver toggle-like closures. It had ugly buttons." She let out a laugh. "I shouldn't admit how much time I spend making my gilets and waistcoats absolutely perfect. I could have invented something important if I hadn't been goofing around making sure my buttons were proper."

"It's important to look nice, too," Gillian said, settling down onto the bed. "Did you have a good shift?"

"Not really. But I'm not tired, which is nice. Having no customers was quite refreshing."

"Should I have come down…?"

"Of course not. Did you have any breakfast?"

"I finally made myself eat porridge," she said, smiling. "I skipped dinner last night, so I needed something to fill me up. It was actually pretty good. I liked the berries they put on it."

"Mmm," Torie said, her gaze sliding over to the desk where the remnants of Gillian's porridge lay. "I could use another breakfast. I didn't have time for much this morning."

"Let's go have some," Gillian said. "I could use another cup of coffee." She stopped abruptly. "You have time, right?"

"I'd like to be home by noon," Torie said, sticking to the schedule she'd mentioned the previous afternoon. "I don't know this area well, but I can ask for a recommendation at the front desk. The staff's very knowledgeable."

"Let me get my coat so I can dazzle people with my look," Gillian said. "I assume everyone will soon be wearing a dark blue plastic jacket four sizes too big. I like to set trends."

Torie helped her on with it, and they walked toward the door. Right before they got there, she turned and regarded Gillian with a warm smile. "Even in a cheap, ill-fitting jacket, you can't dim your charm. It's too elemental a part of you."

No one at the hotel could name a good local place for breakfast, so they had to return to the city centre. But that only took her about a mile out of her way. A distance Torie was more than willing to travel to spend more time with Gillian. The tearoom was a little anachronistic, almost from another era. But Torie wasn't paying much attention to her surroundings. Gillian's work personality was fully engaged, and she'd begun a long, thoughtful bit of rumination on what she assumed was the difficulty of segmenting the market for various types of condiments. She had a bottle of HP sauce in her hand, which she used as a prop.

She'd been talking for several minutes, with Torie offering only encouraging nods and an occasional "I see," to keep her going. She did, in fact, want her to keep going. When Gillian was locked onto a topic she understood, she was sexy as hell. Torie had always been enamored of brainy women, and Gillian's effortless use of terms of art Torie had never heard before made her seem even brighter than she was—which was considerable.

Even though she clearly didn't like her boss, anyone could see that Gillian truly loved marketing. She rattled off numbers and percentages like she had a calculator in her head, a talent Torie was sorely lacking. Surprisingly, Aiden was the member of the family who had any capacity for maths. His father, whomever that had been, might have inadvertently given him that gift.

Thinking of Aiden broke her concentration, and she discretely checked the clock over the doorway. But Gillian had an eagle-eye for watching her subject, and she immediately said, "Running out of time?"

"I should go soon. I've got to go to the market, then start cooking. I try to tempt Aiden with something healthy, which only works if I can hide all of the things my father likes to snack on."

Looking like she was closer to Aiden's age than her own, Gillian fussed with the bottles on the table for a few seconds. "I'd like to meet your family. Would that be..." Her gaze slid from the condiments to settle on Torie's face. "Weird?"

"Weird?" The offer was so unexpected she was caught off guard. Thinking, she finally shook her head. "Not weird, no. Normally, I'd love it, but I don't think this is the perfect day. After being gone for a week, I need time alone with Aiden."

Gillian held a hand up. "You don't have to explain. He'd probably think it was weird."

"Gillian, you're not a client any more. We're friends." Embarrassment crept onto her cheeks as she felt them color. "That's why it's hard for me to bring up the fact that you haven't paid me..."

"Oh, my God!" She looked like she might faint, with all of the color draining from her face. "I swear I wasn't trying to stiff you!"

"That never crossed my mind. You're not—"

"Did you keep track?" she asked, possibly hyperventilating.

"Yes, of course." She pulled out her phone and turned it around so Gillian could see the note she'd made. "I stopped logging the hours on Tuesday afternoon. We weren't touring together after your accident. Things had changed."

Shaking her head, Gillian said, "No, we weren't touring. You were acting as my nurse. I'm paying you double for Wednesday and Thursday."

"No!"

"Yes," Gillian said. She took her checkbook from her bag, then stared at it for a moment. "I don't know if a check will go through if I have to write with my left hand. Will you fill it out for me?"

"You want me to forge your signature?"

"Sure. Unless you want cash. I don't know how much I can take out of an ATM per day..."

Torie took the checkbook and the pen and filled out the amount, tempted to lower it. But Gillian was watching so carefully she would have noticed.

Luckily, she didn't realize she was paying in dollars, rather than the pounds she'd agreed to. Still, it was awfully thoughtful of her to be so remarkably generous. But when Torie thought about it, she would have been surprised if she'd been any other way. Beautiful, sexy, smart, thoughtful, emotionally connected, and generous to a fault. Either the women of Columbus, O-hi-o were remarkably picky, or Gillian was expertly hiding some very serious flaws.

If anyone had told Gillian that she'd spend the next to last evening of her vacation in what could only charitably be called a dive bar, she would have never believed them. But here she was, waiting for Torie to pull a pint for a customer, a youngish guy who looked like he'd just finished some form of construction work. The stool next to him held his hardhat, and even in the dim light she could see how pale his forehead was compared to his ruddy cheeks. Wearing a hat all day when you worked outside wasn't the way to have an even tan—even in rainy Scotland.

If Gillian had her way, she'd take Torie by the hand and lead her out of this place—never to return. Maybe the dim light that barely illuminated the old sign out front had made it look particularly glum, a granite-faced single-story building in a short line of them, but once inside it hadn't gotten any better.

The place was old, dark and mostly covered with wooden paneling. For most of its life, every patron must have been a chain smoker, with the smell thoroughly permeating the wood, making the whole place smell like a giant ashtray. But it was the clientele, not the smell that was the problem.

Essentially, Torie was naturally friendly, outgoing, conversational. She should have been working somewhere that would showcase those skills. Somewhere she was *rewarded* for those skills, which few people had in abundance. But she was a different person here. Her personality was muted. Now she was polite, businesslike, efficient, and mostly silent, without a drop of warmth in her posture or her language. Gillian didn't blame her for being so reserved, since she would have acted the same. The few patrons at the bar seemed like they lived to drink. Each man was alone, spaced out so they didn't have to interact with one another. Heads down, lost in their private pain. Thankfully, none of them pestered Torie, probably because she was behaving like she had no personality at all. She'd undoubtedly learned that it was a bad idea to be too friendly. Gillian just hoped she hadn't learned that the hard way.

Now, she sauntered down the space behind the long, dark, wooden bar, with a charming smile on her face, reserved, on this night, only for Gillian. "Hey there, lassie. A wee dram?" She'd amped up her Scottish accent, the one that made Gillian laugh each time she pulled it out.

"Is that a particular accent? Or do you just make yours bigger?"

"It's particular," she said, sticking with it. "But I'm nae gonnae gie ya aw ma secrets. Ye ha tae earn ya knowledge."

"I guess I'll take a drink, since I think I'll strike out in the accent-naming game. All I could do is call out the towns we've been to, and that seems like cheating."

"It also won't work," Torie said, picking up Gillian's water glass to refill it. She walked away to gaze at the bottles displayed before a mirror, then returned with a splash of amber liquid. "My treat."

"You mean the bar's treat."

"No, mine. I'm allowed one drink a night, and I'm giving it to you. Your expression shows you're in some pain. Am I right?"

Ignoring the question, Gillian said, "You're allowed to drink? At work?"

"This is Scotland," she said, turning up the burr on the accent to full-throttle. "One wee drink's barely enough to wet a lassie's whistle."

"If your whistle needs wetting, I can pay for my own," Gillian said. "I don't need to swipe yours."

"No, I never have the one I'm allowed. On the nights I have a backup, I pour one for him when he comes in at nine."

"Ooo, I'd love to have someone pour me a drink at work. Maybe I'll put that in the suggestion box." The door opened and a pair of guys walked in, engaged in a spirited discussion about something Gillian couldn't make out. "Looks like you're starting to get busy.

"Don't think so. Thursdays are always dead." She started to walk toward her new customers when the door opened again and two couples walked in, talking loudly. "You might be right about my getting busy." She lifted her hand and waved, just twitching the tips of her fingers slightly.

Gillian watched her walk, hoping the men at the bar weren't observing her. A guy could always tell when someone was checking out a woman's ass—which she most certainly was. Damn it to hell, she most certainly was.

Gillian's silly plan had been to linger at the bar for Torie's entire shift. She'd argued against that, of course, knowing it would bore her to death, but Gillian had been resolute. Now it was barely half nine and Torie noticed her chin repeatedly hit her chest. Giving her a nip of whisky might have been a bad idea.

Approaching her when she had a spare second, Torie grasped her arm and gave it a shake, waking her. "I'm calling you a cab."

"I'm fine," she said, trying to look alive.

"No, you're not. You're still taking drugs, you're still stiff and sore, and you're badly in need of rest." Seeing the disappointment in her expression, she added, "You need to get to bed early since I'm going to pick you up at seven."

"You are?" she asked, brightening. "Don't you have to work?"

"I found someone to cover for me for breakfast. I'll have to work in the evening, but I'm taking you to a pretty unique lighthouse tomorrow. Just make sure you wear your boots, no matter the forecast."

She held up her right arm. "I can go up the tower like this?"

"You can. It might be a little dicey, but I know you'll enjoy it."

"Can't wait," Gillian said, looking like she'd be happy to sit right where she was, waiting until it was time to leave.

CHAPTER THIRTEEN

GILLIAN WAS PACING IN FRONT of the hotel when Torie pulled up a few minutes before seven. When she got in, careful to keep her wincing at a minimum, she pointed down at her feet. "I've got my boots on, but it doesn't look like I'll need them." Turning as she fumbled to buckle her seatbelt, she smiled and said, "They're predicting crystal blue skies. The people at the BBC wouldn't lie, would they?"

"Not intentionally. But given that the sun hasn't come up yet, we don't have much to go on."

"You know," Gillian said, leaning back in her seat to gaze pensively at Torie. "I haven't seen a repeat of a gilet or a waistcoat, and each one's nicer than the next. Do you have a separate room for all of them?"

"I do not. I'm just good at organizing my things and stowing them in every conceivable bit of space." She glanced down. "I got this one when I was at university. There was a very good second-hand clothing store in Glasgow, and whenever a gilet or a waistcoat came in, the owner would save it for me. I love paisley, don't you?"

"I do. The bits of gold and red in that dark blue background really set it off."

"We could have gone to Paisley if we'd started in the Cairngorms like we'd planned," Torie chided. "It's just a few miles away from Glasgow."

Gillian had been looking out her window, still amazed at how similar the buildings were in their matching granite facades. She must have misheard, and idly asked, "How do you go to a pattern?"

"Paisley's a town," Torie said, chuckling.

"It is?"

"Sure. They sold so much of a certain Persian pattern that people started calling it a Paisley design."

"How about plaid? Is that a town?"

"Um…" Torie gave her a quick look. "You're kidding?"

"Absolutely. If that sounded dumb, I was definitely kidding."

"Then we'll assume you were, since that was…" She smiled. "Not dumb, but…"

"Dumb," Gillian said. "I think my brains got a little scrambled when I fell."

They got out of Aberdeen quickly, since it was a bit early even for day trippers. Then they headed north, skirting the coast. "It will only take about twenty minutes from here," Torie said. "I normally wouldn't have yanked you out of bed so early, but this job requires careful timing. I think we'll be able to stay for about an hour—if we're lucky."

"Oh." Gillian tried to swallow her disappointment. "Do you have to go to work when we're finished?"

"Not until five, but timing's critical for the lighthouse."

The grin that covered her face was a little sly, which piqued Gillian's interest all the more. "Can't wait."

They were cruising down a wide, beautifully maintained stretch of road when Torie said, "Cover your eyes for a minute."

"Cover my..."

Torie's hand clapped over Gillian's face, but she failed to get the left eye completely covered.

"Oh, God, I'm gonna be sick!" Gillian wailed.

"I warned you. I did everything I could to spare you."

"Our so-called president wasn't satisfied with ruining America? He had to come over here and plunk a golf course down?"

"Don't mention his name around here. The promises he made and swiftly broke would fill Loch Lomond."

"My pleasure. Damn," she said, shivering. "This lighthouse is going to have to be nice to get that taste out of my mouth."

After leaving the main road, they hugged a beautiful sandy beach that was completely empty. "Shouldn't someone be out here walking a dog or something?" Gillian said. "It's beautiful!"

"It is, isn't it? This is my favorite of all the lighthouses in Aberdeenshire. I like nearly everything about it."

Torie turned again and parked the car on a slight bluff right as the sun rose majestically, breaking through the low clouds on the horizon to cast warm, nearly orange light onto their faces.

"God, isn't the sun wonderful," Gillian sighed. "I promise I'll give thanks for it when I'm back home. Having it be an infrequent visitor for two weeks has shown me how good our weather really is."

"Well, you might have more sun, but you don't have a lighthouse in Columbus, O-hi-o," Torie teased, enunciating each syllable the way she did every time she mentioned the state.

As soon as they got out of the car, Gillian assessed the huge sand dunes that blocked the view of the sea. "Do we have to climb over these?"

"We do not." Torie led the way, carrying her tool bag. She walked around the first dune, revealing a wide space where the sand was perfectly flat.

"Awesome!" Gillian cried when she caught sight of the lighthouse, illuminated by the brilliant sun just beginning to creep up behind it.

"That's such an Americanism," Torie teased. "A nice one," she added when Gillian looked at her.

"Well, what other word should I use? You take me out here right when the sun's rising behind a gorgeous lighthouse. There are all sorts of cool rocks and boulders everywhere. And…" She whipped her head around to stare. "How do we get there? It's in the water!"

Torie pointed at her boots. "The hard way. But we'll be fine. Low tide is in…" She checked her phone. "Thirty-two minutes."

"Let's go!" They walked across the hard-packed broad beach, with Gillian leading the way. She actually wanted to run, but knew she'd just look silly slapping along the sand in her boots. Wincing when her ribs began to ache wouldn't add to her image, either. "We just walk across these boulders?" she asked when they reached a little grouping of them with a couple of inches of water at their bases.

"Or go around." Torie did a neat little turn, then waved from the other side of the boulder.

"Oh, sure, *anyone* could go around. I was going to show how stunningly agile I am. Or used to be."

"You'll be jumping over rocks again in just a few weeks. I think we'll have a clear path, but we had a big storm two weeks ago, and that can change the contour of the beach pretty dramatically." Torie got in front of her to be able to look right into her eyes. "The rocks can be slippery, so I want you to hold my hand. Be very careful, but try not to be tentative. Can you manage?"

"I can," she said, appreciating that Torie realized it could be just as dangerous to be hesitant.

Gillian let Torie pick the best path, holding onto her hand loosely. Every few seconds she demanded they stop for a photo, with Torie indulging each request. "You couldn't have made me happier," Gillian said when they were just a few yards away from the structure. "Waaaait a minute! I have to climb up that ladder?"

"Not if you don't think you can do it." She gazed into Gillian's eyes for a moment. "I spent a lot of time thinking about this, and I can *see* how to do it.

Given how strong and agile you are, I don't think it'll be a problem. But if you're not up to it, I don't want you to try. We'll put it on the puffin to-do list, okay?"

Gillian gazed up. She'd break her neck if she fell. No question. "I'm game," she said without another thought.

Smiling, Torie said, "I'll go first, then you follow after I get up to the quarter-deck. I'm sure the ladder's sturdy, but there's no sense in testing its capacity."

The ladder folded down, probably to keep the seawater off it during high tide. Torie seemed to know exactly how to get it set right, and when she had it ready she started to climb. For the first five steps, she used just her left hand, pulling herself up, then loosening her grip to clamp onto a higher spot.

"Got it," Gillian called up, adding a thumb's up sign. Torie got serious then, climbing like someone who'd been scaling buildings her whole life. Never a pause in her determined, sure movements as her right, then her left hand reached up and pulled her body along. Once she'd climbed over the ladder to stand on a solid surface, she leaned over and shouted, "It feels fine. Come on up, but *please* take your time."

Gillian stashed her phone, then followed, finding it a heck of a lot harder to climb a ladder with one hand than she would have guessed. She was tentative at first, but when the movement didn't hurt her ribs too badly, she gained a little confidence. The best part of the experience was that Torie wasn't babying her. She *hated* that. When she reached the deck that surrounded the tower, she leaned her head back, with the warm sun hitting her right in the face. "I'm happy," she said simply. "Really happy."

"Let's get in there. Only sixty-four steps to the top, with a railing on both sides."

"Sixty-four? Child's play."

Torie used her enormous set of keys to get the door open, then they stepped inside. It wasn't a showplace. Far from it, as a matter of fact. The interior was covered with white subway tile, a type Gillian had seen frequently in Scotland. That was uninspiring, but the real eye-sores were the electrical panels and what must have been the mechanism for the fog horn. They had to have been thirty or forty years old, and had been treated roughly. There was also a large, ancient water tank, along with lanterns and buckets and other junk that had accumulated over the years.

"Not very pretty down here, but the keeper's room is perfectly nice. Go on up," Torie said. "I'll run through my checklist, then come up and join you."

Gillian didn't need convincing. She scampered up the stairs so fast she got a little dizzy. But then she reached the top and saw the bright sun warming the space. The view was spectacular. Miles of pristine beach, with moss-covered boulders plunked down onto the sand in a completely random pattern. As she took in all in, a flock of birds raced across the expanse, their skinny legs glowing yellow in the bright light.

She'd been disappointed they wouldn't be allowed to stay long, but just the few minutes they'd have would stick with her for a long, long time. She was perched on a stool, chin in her hand, staring hard when Torie came up behind her. "Penny for your thoughts," she said softly. "But I bet I know what they are. You're trying to figure out if you can get the keys away from me and live here."

"No," Gillian said, standing to turn and face her. The sun was in Torie's face, making her captivating hair glow like it was aflame. Gillian couldn't explain why she'd never been attracted to a red-haired woman, since they were gifted with the coolest color imaginable. Today, the different shades of red and gold shimmered in the sun, and Gillian found herself boldly staring right into Torie's face. She knew it was her turn to talk, but she had a tough time making the words come. Finally, she got a few out. "I'm thinking of having to leave tomorrow."

"Aww." Torie moved to the side, getting out of the direct sun. "I'm so happy you've had a good vacation. When someone doesn't want to leave, I know Scotland's hooked them."

"It's not Scotland," Gillian said, her tone sober and slow. "It's you." She was sure Torie wasn't surprised, but her mouth opened slightly as she blinked. Gillian was in deep now, so she kept going. "I don't want to leave *you*. There's something between us, Torie. Something great. I *know* it."

Still not responding verbally, Torie leaned against the small ledge that circled the light keeper's room, her dark eyes staring at Gillian.

She hadn't said "no," so Gillian kept pushing. She took a step, getting very close to Torie, who hadn't backed away. Gillian put her hand onto Torie's cheek, massively cheered when she leaned into it.

It might have been polite to ask for permission, but she wasn't that kind of woman. When she had a goal, she went for it. And right now, the only thing she could focus on, the only thing she wanted, was to wrap her arms...arm around Torie and kiss her. Tentatively, patiently, she moved closer, watching Torie for even a hint of rejection. But she just kept staring at Gillian, her posture open, lips slightly parted.

Her desire to grab Torie in a crushing hug was strong enough to make her light-headed, but Gillian didn't give in to that need. Instead, she surprised herself by getting so close she could see flecks of gold in her eyes, then quietly said, "I want to kiss you."

Torie didn't reply. Her head tilted slightly, offering up her lips for Gillian to close the scant distance. But she didn't. Reaching up, she used her left hand to tenderly brush along Torie's hairline, reverently touching the soft strands of red and gold.

Torie's eyes closed as Gillian continued to touch her, now moving down to trace her features, nearly dancing across those delicate planes.

Finally, she let her fingers rest on her sculpted chin, holding it gently as she took her in, trying to memorize each beautiful curve and angle. Torie's eyes had closed, and she tilted her chin forward a little more, clearly signaling permission. But Gillian held back, waiting, unwilling to hurry this along. This was important. Maybe the most important moment of her life, and she not only didn't want it to end, she didn't want to begin.

Torie's eyes fluttered open, bearing a question. When their eyes met for a heated second, she took the lead, letting out a soft whimper as she placed her hand on the back of Gillian's head and pulled her forward.

With the most tender touch imaginable, their lips gently brushed together. Then Torie's breath caught, the sharp intake of air reaching Gillian's ears. Thankfully, Torie didn't show the slightest sign of regret about taking the lead. Instead, her hands settled onto Gillian's hips, then gripped gently.

That was all it took for Gillian to press forward without a single qualm. Now her arm wrapped around Torie's waist, pulling her against her body firmly. As Torie's head tilted, Gillian followed her, kissing her with all of the intensity that burned in her soul. Her beguiling scent, the softness of her pink lips, the feel of her body, so thin and reedy it was almost delicate, made Gillian reassess for a second. Maybe she was pushing too hard. Maybe Torie wasn't *able* to distance herself in the small space. But Gillian had seen her zoom up that ladder, had watched her wield a heavy wrench, had witnessed her grasp overpacked suitcases to toss around like feathers. She was slight, but strong. Physically and emotionally.

Finally, Torie's hands slid around to Gillian's back, where they crept up, carefully touching her, exploring her body, testing the muscles like she was trying to learn her anatomy in mere moments.

Gillian's hand rose to settle on the back of Torie's neck, pressing slightly, making their lips merge again. That brought out a sexy sigh, with Torie's warm breath caressing Gillian's cheek. A quiet moan broke the kiss, then Torie buried her face into Gillian's neck. "What are we going to do?" she whispered.

"More of this," Gillian said, certain despite her nerves. "Don't you like this?" she asked, whispering into her ear as her hand slid under the vest to settle just inside her waistband and pull her close. Their lips met again, hungrier, needier this time.

Torie's hands slid past her ears and held her head still as she kissed Gillian with a burst of intensity that nearly sent her to the floor. Then she pulled away decisively and stared into Gillian's eyes.

"I nearly raced up the stairs yesterday morning to bang on your door," she said, her eyes closing briefly. "I had every intention of wrapping my arms around you and having my fill. But I…" She took in a deep, shaky breath. "I couldn't. I don't *do* this, Gillian. I never have."

"Do what?" she asked gently, giving into her need to stay connected by running her hand up and down her arm. "What do you think I'm asking?"

"To have sex. And I want that, too. More than you'll ever know." She wrapped her arms around Gillian once again, then let out a weary-sounding sigh and rested her chin on her left shoulder. "I'd forgotten how fantastic it was to have someone want you as much as you want her."

"Oh, I *do* want you," Gillian said, her chest pulsing with excitement now that she knew her feelings were returned. "But if that's all I wanted, I would have tried to start something a week ago." She pulled away to be able to gaze into Torie's troubled eyes. "I don't want a one and done. Really," she stressed when she saw nothing but doubt reflected back.

"How can we have anything but?" She removed her hands from Gillian's body and purposefully sidestepped her to walk to the opposite side of the room. That felt like a kick to the shins, but Gillian tried not to take offense. This was clearly hard for Torie to get her head around.

"Um…" Gillian stuck her hand into her armpit, giving herself half of a hug to make up for Torie walking away. "How does any couple start? They just… start."

"When they live three thousand six hundred and thirty-four miles from each other?" she demanded, her gaze hot. "What do they start? A string of e-mails?" Her expression shut like a vault. "Until one of them realizes it was a silly dream and just fades away?"

"What?" Gillian stormed over to her, her boots making the old floorboards creak noisily. She stood right in front of Torie, glaring at her. "Are you seriously questioning my motives? Or are you just saying I don't know what I want? Either way, that was a very insensitive thing to say!"

"Listen to yourself," she said, not backing down. "You come to Scotland for the first time, and in a matter of days you're talking about moving here! You don't know the first thing about the country, the people, the climate, the job opportunities. But you claim you're dead serious about it. That's not normal!" she shouted, spitting each word out precisely, eyes blazing. "How can I trust what you're saying about us?" She turned to move away again, obviously wanting to keep a physical distance between them. When she spoke, she sounded tired, or maybe just worn-out. "I've had a lifetime of promises, Gillian. All of them unfulfilled. At home, at work, from relatives, girlfriends, clients." She looked up, with the scars of those broken promises etching her face. "Do you know how many people promise to write a glowing review of my tours? Hundreds. Do you know how many have done it?" She held up four fingers. "Four people have followed through."

Gillian's heart was beating so fast she thought it might explode. "You're comparing me to some chump you walked around a castle for an afternoon? We've been together every day for nearly two weeks! We've shared so much!" Her mouth snapped shut. "At least I have. Maybe you tell every tourist your story, but I don't! I opened up to you. I showed you what's in my heart!" For the third time in recent memory, she started to cry, wounded to the core that Torie could lump her in with a bunch of anonymous strangers.

"No, no, that's not it," Torie said, closing the distance between them in two big steps. She tentatively put her arms around Gillian, then tightened her hold when she reluctantly settled against her body. "I'm sorry I said that. It's not what I meant."

"What did you mean?" she asked, her voice muffled.

"Just that I..." she trailed off. "I can't..." Sucking in a shaky breath, she said, "I can't afford to believe you. I have so little faith left." Then she began to cry as well, fat tears trailing down her soft cheeks. Gillian lifted her hand and flicked them away with her thumb, gazing into Torie's troubled eyes.

"Shh," she soothed, desperate, but unable to get both arms around her. "This can work. It can." Her hand slid up and landed on Torie's shoulder, and she held her at arm's length as she tried to get control again. "You don't have to believe me now. You just have to give me a chance."

"I want to," she said, her shoulders starting to shake as the tears fell again. "I want to so badly."

Gillian grabbed her and pulled her to her chest with a "thump". The hug she gave her was forceful, and as emotion-filled as she could ever recall giving a woman. "I won't disappoint you. I swear I won't."

"I have all the promises I can handle," she murmured softly. "I can only trust behavior. You're going to have to *show* me that you care." Their eyes met again, so close Gillian could focus on how pale her normally dark eyes were in the harsh morning light.

"I'll show you," she promised. "You won't ever doubt how serious I am about this."

"This? Define this. What exactly are you promising?"

That caught Gillian by surprise and she had to spend a moment thinking. When she was sure, she spoke again. "I promise this isn't just a vacation fantasy. I promise I want to try to have a relationship with you. And I promise to be honest with you and let you know my feelings." She shrugged. "That's all I can promise now, but I think that's a lot." She swallowed, with her feelings just about ready to overflow again. "That's a lot for me."

A gentle smile tried to form on Torie's trembling lips. "That *is* a lot."

"How about you? What can you promise?"

Her eyes closed for a few seconds, then blinked open. "I promise I'll try to trust you. I promise I'll try to be open to having a real relationship." Her tentative smile faded. "But I'm obviously more of a pessimist, or maybe more of a realist than you are. It'll be hard, Gillian. Very hard."

Gillian tenderly caressed her cheek, loving the feel of her skin against her fingers. "Did you make up that number? What was it? Three thousand—"

"Three thousand, six hundred and thirty-four miles," she said, with a slight flush rising on her cheeks. "I looked it up when I was trying to stop myself from thinking about you the other night." She shrugged. "It didn't help."

"Ooo," she said, reaching out to tickle under her chin. "You were thinking about me?"

Torie playfully slapped her hand away. "I think about you the whole day! And worse, I think you know that. For someone like you, landing me's as easy as shooting a fish in a barrel."

"Someone like me? What's that supposed to mean?"

"Oh, for goodness sake! Look at yourself! You're beautiful, even in a ripped-up sweatshirt. You're classy, and bright, and filled with potential. You're as kind as nearly anyone I know, intensely interested in me, polite, refined, passionate..."

"What do you mean that I'm as kind as *nearly* anyone you know," Gillian said, hoping it was clear she was teasing. "Who's got me beat?"

"Just about everyone who works with addicts," she said, knocking the smile from Gillian's face. "Those people deal with lies and broken promises and mangled lives every single day, but they stay positive, for the most part. The best ones are like saints to me."

Gillian once again wrapped her in a hug. This one gentle and as comforting as she could make it. "I'm so sorry you have to know those people, even though you clearly care for them. I'm sorry your family's gone through so much." Pulling away so Torie could clearly see her face, she added, "Wouldn't you like to have someone on your side? Someone who's always got your back? Someone you can always talk to?"

Torie's head nodded slowly as the tears returned. "I'd love that more than you'll ever know." She rested her head on Gillian's shoulder again, murmuring, "I have to be strong for my family. I have to be a parent to Aiden. I have to be on guard with my sister, so she doesn't take advantage of me again. I have to be upbeat and friendly for my jobs. I don't have anyone I can just be myself with. I truly don't."

"You do now," Gillian said softly. "You do now."

Torie nodded, gave Gillian a slight smile, and stood tall. Taking her hand, she turned it so she could see the face of her watch. "It's half eight. We've got to go or we'll have to swim back."

"Are you still planning on working tonight?"

"I am." She smiled, this time a wide, full one. "But I was hoping to spend the day with you. I don't think… With your flight tomorrow, I don't think we'll be able to see each other."

"As long as I can get down that ladder, I'm ready for anything."

"Down should be easier," Torie said, clearly just guessing.

Going down the tower staircase was easy, given the sturdy handrail. But when they got to the quarterdeck, Gillian started to feel some anxiety building. It was easier to look up at a thirty-foot climb than to look down at a killing fall. Her trepidation must have shown on her face, since Torie said, "I've got a plan."

"Build a ramp? Shouldn't take long…"

"That would work, but I've got a different one." She put her tool bag down and swung a leg over the parapet, planting her foot onto one of the rungs of the ladder. "I'm going to stick right behind you. If you lose your grip, I'll catch you."

"Catch me!" Gillian had shouted her response, surprising herself. "You can't catch me," she said, a little quieter now.

"Yes, I can. Come on. I'll move down a little to give you room to get on. If we work together and take careful steps, we'll figure this out."

Gillian wanted to protest, but the thought of having any assistance helped a lot. Her brain was able to switch from terrified to calculating how to avoid kicking Torie in the head.

"Here goes," she said, swinging a leg over to secure it against a rung.

Torie climbed back up, getting so close her head was right in the center of Gillian's back. "I'm right here," she said. "I've got you."

"Thank you," Gillian sighed, fairly certain she would have had a heck of a time doing this on her own. "Ready?"

"I'll give the orders. When I say 'step', move your right foot to the next rung, then we'll follow with our left. Got it?"

"I do. Let's do it."

"Step," Torie said clearly.

Careful to keep her foot close to the rungs, Gillian moved down one, feeling almost enveloped by Torie's protection. "Good?"

"Perfect. One step at a time. We've got this."

"I think we do," Gillian said, confident this task was just the first of many they'd tackle together.

⚜ ⚜ ⚜

After Torie made the climb and the descent again to pick up her tools, they walked back to the beach, with the tide already starting to rise. If they hadn't had boots on, they would have been wet to their shins.

Torie put her tool bag in the trunk, then dug around in the space to pull out an old woolen blanket. "Why don't we sit on the beach for a little while and enjoy this magnificent day."

"It's not even fifty degrees, but I'm game if you are."

Torie took the blanket to a spot protected on three sides by sand dunes, laying it out carefully. She helped Gillian get to her knees, then plunk down, with the move not hurting her ribs nearly as much as it would have just two days ago. "This is pretty nice," Gillian said as she put her left arm around Torie's waist and leaned against her.

"I sat on the proper side," Torie said, grinning. "I haven't asked for a health update today, but from the looks of it, you're feeling better."

"At least twenty percent better," Gillian admitted. "My arm doesn't hurt much at all." She flexed her fingers. "Actually, my hand hurts worse than the arm. It feels like I'm wearing a really tight glove."

"The swelling's not too bad," Torie decided, looking at it carefully. "Ribs?"

"Still a problem. But I think I can figure out a way to lie next to you and still be able to move around." She let her most charming grin emerge. "We're going to my room, right?"

"Your room?" Torie's eyebrows rose as Gillian's hopes fell just as dramatically.

"Don't people starting a relationship want to celebrate?"

Torie lifted her knees, then wrapped her arms around her shins. The sun was shining onto her face, strands of her hair gently blowing in the surprisingly light wind. She looked as beautiful as Gillian had ever seen her, but the expression on her face was not the one Gillian had dreamed of when she'd let herself idly wonder about their first time together. "It didn't dawn on me that you'd want to…"

"It didn't dawn on you?" Gillian asked, gently scratching across the dark blue fabric of Torie's woolen jacket. "Is that something you want to talk about? I mean… I think most people want to get to know each other before they commit, right?"

"So… This would be a test?" she asked, turning to arch an eyebrow.

"Of course not. Jesus!" She started to lean forward to mirror Torie's pose, but the pain in her side stopped her dead. "If you've got some sexual hang-ups, we can work through them. But if you don't generally like having sex…" She swallowed nervously. "That's a bigger problem."

The look Torie gave her was a long way from friendly. "What happened to having someone who's always on my side? Someone to support me no matter what?"

Gillian closed her eyes for a second, partly to avoid Torie's heated glare. "I'm crazy about you," she said quietly. "And I want to have a decidedly sexual relationship with you. But if that's not what you want, I'll simply be your friend." She reached out and rubbed across her back again. "I'll be there for you no matter what, Torie. I promised you that, and I keep my promises. But I'm looking for a lover."

She nodded a couple of times, then made sure the blanket was under her head before she lay down, staring up at the blue sky. "I want a sexual relationship too," she said quietly. "But I think I process things slower than you do. You're ready to go from client to lover in an afternoon, and I'm simply not."

It hurt to turn her body, so Gillian stayed where she was, facing the surprisingly docile sea, the waves lapping the shore so gently it looked more like a lake than the imposing body of water she'd seen for the last two weeks. "How long do you think it will take you? Days? Weeks? Months?"

"If you lived in Scotland? Probably weeks. But you don't," she said flatly. "Remember when I said I judged people by their behavior? I need to see some of that before I'm ready to be that vulnerable with you. I'm sorry that's not how you feel, but I can't rush this."

"Because you don't trust me yet."

Torie put her hand on Gillian's hip and stroked it gently. "That's not exactly true. I do trust you in many ways. But I don't yet know how committed you are to following through."

"On moving?"

"That's a big one," she said. "I still think it's near madness to decide to move to Scotland so quickly, but at this point I'm taking you at your word. But I'll need to see some progress before I trust you'll follow through."

"So…? If I can't find a way to move, you're not interested?"

"Am I interested in being committed to you if you choose to stay in America? I'd still care for you, but I think I'd keep looking for a woman I could actually touch."

"Understood," Gillian said, nodding decisively. "You'll be surprised, but pleased when I show up at your door."

"It's going to be harder than you think to get residency," Torie said. "But there are ways to get you in if we make a go of it. They'll take time, but you're worth the investment. You really are."

Gillian let that thought percolate for a few seconds, then said, "But you just said you'd want to wait weeks to have sex even if I lived here. So, it's clearly not just a worry about my commitment to move."

"No," she admitted, her voice very soft. "It's not only that." Torie sat up and moved around so they were facing each other. "I haven't had a lot of experience. I've only been with two women, and the last time I was even kissed with any heat was nearly thirteen years ago. I'm very nervous about having sex, with you or anyone else."

Gillian put her hand on her knee, able to feel it shake under her fingertips. "Then why don't we go to my room and just fool around a little? We don't even have to get naked. It can just be a first step to help make you more comfortable."

"I don't think so," Torie said, hesitating a little. "Once I'm sure you're serious about this, I don't think I'll have trouble getting over my nerves. But I'm just not used to the whole idea yet. Do you understand that at all?"

"Mmm." Gillian tried to see this from Torie's perspective, but it was so different from her own that she wasn't doing a very good job of it. "I hear you, and I accept that's how you feel, but I'm just the opposite. Touching you would make me feel closer to you. And if things *didn't* work—we'd at least have today."

"Oh, that's not how I am at *all*," Torie said. "If I made myself vulnerable enough to have sex with you, and then you disappeared? It would take me years to get over that. *Years*," she insisted.

"Why am I the one who's going to bail? You could decide you don't want to continue. Don't paint me as the flake, Torie. That's not me."

Torie composed her expression, then sat quietly for a few minutes, clearly thinking. "I feel like I know you pretty well. But two weeks isn't all that long, no matter how you view the timeline. I'll admit I'm worried that this is more about sex for you than commitment, but that's just how I defend myself. I protect myself whenever possible, Gillian. That's the only way I've been able to stay as happy as I am. I'm careful."

"Have you ever been unsure about something, yet done it anyway? Have you ever ignored the little voice in your head warning you that something's dangerous?"

"I might have when I was younger," she said, "but generally not."

Gillian grasped her hand and brought it to her heart. "Isn't it time to take a risk? Sex definitely isn't the only thing on my mind, but having to wait until the puffins' feet turn orange seems kind of crazy to me."

With a sly smile, Torie said, "Have you ever paid attention to the little voice in your head that warns you something's dangerous?"

"Um…" She thought hard for a moment. "Not about anything that might give me pleasure." Letting out a laugh, she said, "Well played."

"I honestly think it might be good for you to get used to deprivation, since you're going to face a lot of it." Her gaze grew significantly more intense. "You *do* plan on being committed to me, don't you? I don't want to simply be your European girlfriend."

Gillian put her hand up, like she was taking an oath. "Exclusive. Promise." Shaking her head, she said, "I can't believe I'm promising to be exclusive with a woman who won't sleep with me for months, but it appears that I am."

Torie got onto her hands and knees and leaned forward. "I won't sleep with you, but I will rain kisses upon your lips." As their mouths met again, Gillian felt that chill go down her spine, like thousands of tiny hands were massaging her central nervous system.

"You're going to have to keep that up for the rest of the day to satisfy me."

Torie grinned at her. "If we keep kissing like I want to kiss you, I guarantee you won't be satisfied." She leaned in again and delivered a scorcher, leaving

Gillian panting with need. "Be careful what you wish for," she said, patting Gillian's cheek as she sat back down and gave her a well-deserved smirk.

CHAPTER FOURTEEN

A DAY LIKE THIS HAD BEEN worth waiting nearly thirteen years for, Torie decided. After working together to make her comfortable, Gillian now lay on the blanket, peacefully resting as the sun warmed her face. Every few minutes she'd bat her eyes open and ask for a kiss, which Torie speedily delivered. They'd been chatting, but their conversation came in fits and starts, with both of them seemingly happy to speak only when she had something worthwhile to say.

After bending over to place a gentle kiss to Gillian's lips, Torie let her mouth travel to her ear, where she whispered, "Guess how much rain Aberdeen gets."

"How much rain is there?" Gillian lazily asked. "That much."

"No, no, no," Torie teased. "Annually, we get seven inches less than rainy Columbus, O-hi-o."

"No way!" Gillian's pale blue eyes were wide open now.

"It's true. We get rain more often, but the amount is less."

"You definitely get rain more often," Gillian agreed. "More often than anywhere I've ever been."

"We have dryer months. November isn't the best time to visit—for weather. But it's a fine time to meet a girl who's crazy about you."

"I'm crazy about you too," Gillian said, her smile making her look so happy it made Torie's heart beat quicker. "What other facts do you have? You've clearly been studying."

Chuckling, Torie said, "I was trying to convince myself it was mad to even consider your wanting to come here. Most of the numbers aren't in our favor. Like the fact that we get two hours less sun per day in the winter."

"That's not good, but I'm usually at work. I can get one of those light boxes to relieve my seasonal affective disorder."

"But we get two extra hours of sun in the summer."

"A day?" Gillian's eyes went round. "Two hours a day?"

"Indeed. When I was a child, spending my summers in Orkney, it was nearly impossible for my granny to get me to bed. I couldn't wrap my mind around going to sleep when it was nearly fully light out."

"We'll play golf after I get off work," Gillian decided. "I love to practice my putting when the temperature has cooled off."

Torie wagged her finger at her. "There's not much to cool. Our temperature doesn't vary a lot. You might miss those warm, Ohio summers."

"No sweet corn and tomatoes sold at local farm stands?"

"It's possible to grow them," Torie said, "but it takes planning. This is not their natural environment. You have to trick the seeds into thinking they're in Spain."

"Then we'll go to Spain. My counterparts in London are always running off to Europe for a long weekend. We'll go eat tomatoes and melons until they're coming out of our ears."

Torie nodded, willing to let Gillian come up with any sort of fantasy that appealed to her. It was too early in the game to douse all of her hopes so cruelly. "We grow lovely strawberries and raspberries and blueberries. That makes up for a lot, doesn't it?"

"I think it does. I love a good berry."

Lying next to Gillian, Torie took her hand and clasped it to her chest. "I love dreaming about the future. I haven't done this hardly at all for the last few years, not even realizing how much I've missed it."

Turning her head, Gillian said, "How will we keep in touch? Can I call you every day?"

"*Every* day?"

"Uh-huh. I was thinking I could call when I wake up. That's like eleven o'clock here. You're free then, right?"

"Usually," she admitted.

"I thought that would be a great way to wake up. I wouldn't ever hit the snooze button if I knew I was going to get to talk to you."

Rolling onto her side, Torie tucked her arm around Gillian's waist and cuddled up to her. "This has been the best day of my life," she murmured. "All I was hoping for was a chance to show you my favorite lighthouse. But I've somehow managed to find myself in possession of a girlfriend. A wonderful one," she added, feeling a tingle start at her neck and work its way all the way down.

They spent the early afternoon wandering around the city center, shopping for keepsakes. Gillian bought several pair of whisky tasting glasses, two wooden swords as well as several books for her nephews, and Lindsay tartan scarves for herself and her sister. Torie was surprised to see her buy a very expensive hand-knit sweater for her friend Kara, but she was learning that Gillian didn't consider price when she was shopping. As they were getting ready to leave, Gillian stopped to grasp a wee stuffed bear. "Does this come with different clan names?"

"It does," the clerk said. "It takes a few weeks to make them up, but we can use any of the popular names."

She held the bear in her hands, lightly touching its tam. "So, it gets a new hat, a sash and a kilt?"

"It does. Along with the medallion that shows the name."

"Is Gunn a popular name?"

"It is," he agreed. "Would you like one?"

"I would," Gillian said.

Torie found herself saying, "Make it two. One for Lindsay." The words were out of her mouth before she'd even checked the price! She actually wasn't sure if she was supposed to keep the Lindsay or the Gunn, but she didn't truly care. Gillian had turned her world upside down, and all she could do was hang on and see where she landed.

❧ ❧ ❧

It was just three when they reached the hotel. Gillian knew Torie didn't have to be at work until five, which meant she had a full hour to spare—if she wanted to. Given how clear she'd been that she wouldn't even allow the possibility of having sex, she might have considered just slowing down to toss Gillian out of the moving car.

But she pulled into a parking space quite a distance from the front door, giving them some privacy. As she turned to Gillian, a disappointed look crossed her face. "You're not going to be comfortable sitting here for long. I can tell it hurts you to turn to the right." She gently touched her side. "Are you due for some pain pills?"

"I stopped taking them yesterday morning. Of course, now I'm regretting that..."

"Why did you stop? Were you feeling that much better?"

"Not really. But I knew I wanted to tell you how I felt about you, and I didn't want to be loopy when I did that."

"Och... That's so thoughtful." Torie reached across and covered her casted hand. "Let's go up to your room. The whole dining room will be talking about me by morning, but I don't care."

"Tell people I'm your cousin," Gillian said, struggling to get her seat belt off.

"Hold on." Torie got out and raced around the car, then squatted down and freed her, but not before leaning in to give her a surprisingly tender kiss. "Anyone who saw us together would realize I was wild for you."

181

"Then let's go ruin your reputation." Gillian got out with a small assist, then took a breath. After sitting for a long time, she was always stiff and sore, but today was worse. Not taking the pills had been good for her thought processes, but not as good for her pain receptors.

Torie went to her left side and clutched her arm. "Need some support?"

"I don't need it, but I'd like it."

"Then you'll have it." They walked to the front door, and crossed into the lobby. Torie waved to the clerk on duty, then they walked up the stairs to Gillian's room.

"Was that all right?" Gillian asked. "I honestly don't want you to be uncomfortable at work. If you'd rather leave right now…"

Torie pulled her arm close to hug it. "I care much more about how you feel. If you want me to stay for a bit, I will."

"Then you will," Gillian said, placing her key on the sensor.

They went inside, with Torie gazing around the room for a moment, like she'd not seen it before. "How many times did you call to ask for extra pillows?" she asked, taking in the mountain of down and fiberfill the housekeeping staff had tried to make look normal.

"Just twice. I asked for a lot, but they thought that meant two. They eventually got the message though. I put three under my head, two under my arm, and another two under my knees."

"Are you sleeping well?"

"Not very. Actually, not well at all last night. My body prefers to be heavily medicated. It's just my brain that doesn't like to be jumbled."

"Poor brain," Torie said, brushing across Gillian's head with her fingers. "I bet you'll sleep better when you're home."

"No, I'll sleep better when I get this cast off. I'm going to see a doctor on Monday, even if I have to call every orthopedist in Ohio."

"They said you'll still need a brace," Torie reminded her. "Are you sure that will be substantially better than a cast?"

Gillian let out a laugh. "I have no idea, but I've convinced myself it will be. Don't ruin my fantasy," she insisted, giving Torie's shoulder a poke.

Grasping Gillian's left hand, Torie put it on her waist, then stepped close, close enough that they were nearly nose-to-nose. "We've got about forty-five minutes before I have to leave. I'd love to spend that time being close with you." She slid the arm further around her waist, pressing against Gillian until their breasts compressed. "Would you like that, too?"

Gillian felt her eyes close briefly, without her commanding them to. "I would."

"Want to lie down? I know it can be uncomfortable…"

"I'm willing to risk it," she said, unable to think of a level of discomfort that would make her refuse.

"What works?" Torie led her to the pillow-strewn bed.

"I need to be kind up upright, so…"

Torie assembled the pillows so they each had three. She helped Gillian lie on her left side, then climbed onto the bed, facing her. "This is nice already. I really look forward to the day we do this like it's the most natural thing in the world." She kissed her fingers and placed them in the middle of the cast. "And to when you can jump into bed without those lines on your forehead." She eased the tension with her fingers. "Does this hurt too much?"

"Not really. It just takes a few minutes for everything to adjust." She moved an inch or two to her left, then came back to the right, trying to find the sweet spot. "I think I'm good." As the pain began to settle, she said, "I usually move around a lot in bed, but I'm afraid you're going to have to take the lead today. I'm kind of stuck here."

Torie let out a sly laugh. "I wouldn't have suggested this if you were at your normal capacities." She put her hand on Gillian's chest and leaned into her, sighing as their lips merged sweetly. "I hope this is just the first of many times we lie in bed together."

Gillian lifted her hand to stroke across Torie's velvety soft skin. Feeling the delicate bone structure under her fingers nearly made her cry. She wanted nothing more than to touch her—just this way—for days on end. "I…hope this doesn't come out wrong, but I'm… I don't feel the need to pounce on you like I normally do."

"Pounce?" Torie asked, her eyes widening.

"Mmm, I had a feeling I wasn't putting that right." She closed her eyes for a second so she could think without distraction. "I want to have sex with you. That isn't in doubt. But I want a lot more, and that's not common for me." She could feel a grin start to form. "I like this feeling. A lot."

"You're saying you're happy you don't feel a huge amount of sexual drive for me?" A questioning eyebrow rose.

"Oh, but I do," Gillian said. "If you hadn't made it clear we weren't going to do that today, we'd have been doing it for a long time already. No one in my life *needs* a present from Scotland," she said, chuckling. "We'd be resting up for another round right now." She leaned close and gave Torie a lingering, gentle kiss, feeling a chill run through her when fingers slid along her scalp. "Yeah," she murmured, "maybe we'd be on round three. I think it'll be hard to go slow with you."

"You say the silliest things," Torie said, tracing Gillian's lips with her fingertip. "All kinds of fantasies come tumbling out of here."

Gillian grasped her hand and held it tightly. "That's not a fantasy. That's what will happen when we're together." With another soft kiss, she said, "But I'm willing to wait. I'm kind of looking forward to exploring what it's like to be with someone you want more from. And God knows I want more from you."

"How do you *know* that? After just two weeks, how on earth do you know that, Gillian?"

"I can't say," she admitted, "but I've never felt quite like this. Normally, I'm attracted to a woman, then I start to want her, then I have her. After that, I decide if I want to know her better." Once again, she stroked Torie's cheek. "It isn't like that with you. My desire for you grew along with my need to know you better." Her smile was so wide it made her cheeks hurt. "I think that's a more mature way of starting out. Maybe I'm finally growing up."

"Don't grow up too much," Torie warned. "I like that you're impetuous."

"Oh, I don't think I can change much," Gillian admitted. She had to use her casted arm, but she got it placed across Torie's hip. "This was such a good idea," she sighed. "Letting our bodies get to know each other better is a perfect way to end this vacation. Kind of like a play date."

"I wish we could play together for a long, long time," Torie whispered. "There's so much I want to know about you. I'm interested in everything…what your life was like when you were growing up, how you feel about so many things, what your goals are, what's most important to you…"

"We'll get there," Gillian assured her. "We'll build that knowledge base piece by piece until we know everything there is to know."

"I know I want to kiss you some more," Torie murmured. "I don't think I could possibly do that often enough."

"There's something we have in common. A shared goal."

Torie's arm encircled her tenderly, then pulled her close. It hurt enough to make Gillian suck in a sharp breath, but she would have gladly suffered far more for another spate of Torie's gentle kisses. Memories of them were going to get her through the next few months. She wasn't sure how she knew that was true, but she would have bet just about anything on it.

Being in control made the experience *so* much nicer. Gillian wasn't generally overpowering, or demanding, but she clearly had an agenda. And when she had one, she tried to nudge people along so they got on board. She was a little like a sheepdog in that way. She didn't need to growl and threaten. A slight bump with her head or a gaily wagging tail made it clear which way you should turn.

But now, with Gillian lying mostly on her back, graciously allowing Torie to set the pace, all was right in the world.

It had been forever since she'd been in bed with a woman, and even then she wasn't often in charge. Sheila had been a faithful, gentle, loving partner, but to say she was careful and restricted in what she liked in bed was an understatement. But today, in the amazingly short time they'd been playing with each other, Torie was certain Gillian and Sheila were going to be nothing alike.

As soon as Torie ramped up the heat of her kisses, Gillian responded, staying right with her. She didn't push—at all, which was fantastic, but she made it clear she liked every single thing Torie did, and was up for more of it. Such a relief!

Torie truly didn't want to lose control this afternoon, but she had so much desire pulsing through her body that she wasn't at all sure she could hold back. Gillian's body was such a turn-on it seemed like it had been created with Torie's libido in mind. She'd *never* been with a tall, trim, athletic woman, but ever since she'd been a bairn she'd settled herself in front of the telly to watch every moment of the Olympics, almost exclusively interested in women's sports. Gillian wasn't quite as tall as some of the volleyball players she'd lusted over, but she had that kind of body—lean, muscular, and powerful. *God*, what she'd give to see her in a pair of skin-tight shorts.

Her tongue slid into Gillian's mouth as her hand roamed up and down her thigh, exploring the long muscles that made her heart race. A groan escaped from her throat, and when Gillian let out a soft laugh she could feel her cheeks flush. But she purposefully refused to let herself be embarrassed about showing her appreciation for Gillian's body. They were mature women who had both been through a lot. They'd earned the right to claim their bodies and all of the pleasures they would yield. Those years of being shamed for having too much desire were in the past. With Gillian, she would own her wants and her needs. They were starting from scratch, and she could hardly wait to begin.

They stood in front of the door, holding each other as well as they could. Gillian was clearly hurting, with Torie feeling a lingering bit of guilt for getting too enthusiastic when they were lying together. But she was certain Gillian hadn't wanted gentler treatment. She'd taken some pain pills, and now had the silly look she got when taking her medication. Kind of like she was drunk, but without the sloppiness alcohol caused. In fact, she seemed close to normal, but with everything at half speed; smile, speech, and reaction time.

"I wish I could go to work with you and just stare at you as you prowl up and down behind the bar. You have a very sexy strut, you know."

"Not normally," Torie said, chuckling. "When you were at the pub, any strutting was purely for your benefit, and even that was pretty inadvertent."

"Pretty?" Gillian tickled under her chin. "Was it a little intentional?"

"I don't think so, but I can't be responsible for my subconscious mind. It clearly knew I was tremendously attracted to you."

"If I wasn't going to be sitting on a plane for hours tomorrow, I'd go with you anyway. But I'd probably fall off my stool. You're a baaad girl for talking me into taking two pills."

"You needed them. Now I want you to order some dinner, watch a little telly, and go straight to sleep. Lights out by nine, all right?"

"I think they might be out by six."

"I've got to work until ten tomorrow, and your train's at half nine, so we likely won't see each other. Is that…all right?"

"It's fine. Today's all I need." She leaned forward, with much of her weight resting on Torie. "I had the nicest day I can ever recall having."

"Me, too." Torie staggered a little, then set Gillian back on her own feet. "I hate to go, but I must. One last kiss?"

Gillian settled herself, then gave it her all, pressing Torie into the door as the heat of their shared passion pulsed through their bodies.

Torie finally broke away, caressing Gillian's flushed cheeks. "That was a proper knee-trembler," she said, lightly kissing her forehead as she let out a shaky breath. "Enough to hold me until the puffins' beaks are glowing orange."

"Until then," Gillian said, leaning against the wall, her own knees obviously trembling as well.

"Bye," Torie said, implanting that final image of Gillian in her mind. A sweet-faced, incredibly sexy woman, with a lazy smile and eyelids too heavy to keep open.

🌵 🌵 🌵

It took some real salesmanship, along with twenty pounds, but Torie finally found a fellow server to come in early and cover her last hour. The drive to the train station wasn't long, but there was more traffic than usual for nine o'clock in the morning—or at least it seemed like it was worse. Maybe Torie was just so anxious about getting there in time that her internal clock was off.

She found a spot in the car park since the stores weren't open yet, then ran around the complex to enter the train station. Not having taken the time to spruce up, she still wore her uniform; the plain, short-sleeved, white polyester blouse and black knit slacks that probably reeked of eggs and sausages. But they'd have a few minutes together before Gillian's nine thirty train, and that was her only goal.

The station was busier than she'd expected, with people loitering around waiting for the Edinburgh train announcement. But she knew just where to go, having made this particular journey many times. For the first time since five thirty that morning, Torie stopped to take a look at herself when she skidded around a corner and caught a look in a mirrored sign hanging in an empty pub. It wasn't a pleasant surprise. She hadn't had time to apply enough hair gel to make tufts of her hair lie in what she considered attractive disorder. Now it was simply run-of-the-mill disorder, not at all what she was going for. Her blouse didn't have any obvious stains on it, but white wasn't her color. It always made her look even paler than she was, or maybe she looked pallid. Whatever you called it, it wasn't ideal. At least she hadn't had to wear her raincoat today. The loden green wool jacket she wore gave a little life to her skin. For a second, she tried to make her hair comply, but it was a wasted effort.

She took off again, nearly running. When it was clear a businesswoman's determined path was going to intersect hers, she slowed, then tried to time it so she could sweep around her. But the privileged jerk slowed down too, clearly not as determined as she looked.

The station was often populated by this sort in the morning—local people going to Edinburgh for a meeting or some cultural event. They never knew where they were going, but that didn't stop them from clogging up the main paths while they checked the announcement board.

After rushing around the woman, some internal monitor made her slow, then stop. "Gillian!" she called, unable to get her feet moving again. The tall, trim, impeccably attired woman didn't hear her, and Torie spent a few seconds trying to reconcile this woman with the silly creature who'd stomped around Scotland in a tangerine slicker and rain boots for the past two weeks.

This was a *business*woman. A successful one. She had the direct, level gaze that women of her rank effortlessly pulled off. The kind of look that gave you the clear message it wouldn't be in your best interests to mess with her, even though there was nothing rough or threatening about her look. It was more that she was so sure of her place in the world that she didn't need to posture. Kind of like a fast, dangerous animal lying in the sun. A puma or a cheetah or a lion. It looked so docile—but only because it had the ability to decimate slower-moving prey at will.

Standing there in her cheap blouse and slacks, Torie knew she looked like she should be cleaning the place, but she couldn't resist her. Not for another moment. Once again, she called out, "Gillian," then finally got her clunky black clogs to propel her across the marble floor.

Gillian turned, and her face lit up in a glorious grin. Like she hadn't even noticed that Torie looked like hell. In fact, Gillian's eyes never moved south of Torie's. They were locked there as she smiled.

They fell into each other's arms, holding on tightly. "It took all of my salesmanship, but I finally convinced someone to cover for me," Torie said. "I couldn't let you leave without seeing you again."

"I've been wandering around here for a half hour, hoping you'd figure out a way to come." She kissed her cheek and stood up straight. "I knew you'd try."

"Already I have no secrets?" she asked, laughing nervously. "This is awfully soon to be so exposed. We've only had one date—a great one, by the way, but still…"

"I know you're thoughtful. To the core."

"You look so…adult," Torie said, laughing at herself. "I mean, you are an adult, but…" She patted the black jacket draped over Gillian's arm, partially hiding her cast.

"I had a big client meeting on the day I left, so I had to spruce myself up a little. Thankfully. If I hadn't had this sleeveless dress, I'd still be in that black sweatshirt."

Torie grasped the fabric of her jacket and let the curly loop of the weave snap up as her thumb slid across it. "Boucle wool. Nice."

"Uh-huh. I have three other black suits, and it's nearly impossible to tell one jacket from the other. I have to resort to looking at the labels."

Torie tugged on the collar of the jacket to expose an Italian designer's name. Gillian just shrugged, looking only slightly embarrassed. "I have to look nice. Part of the job."

"You do. You really do," she said, stepping back a little to take a good, long look at her. "No raincoat?"

"I gave it to you!"

Torie laughed. "I forgot all about that. The resale shop hasn't sold it yet, but they were certain it would go. They were impressed with the quality."

"Did you tell them it wasn't waterproof?"

"I did not," she said, chuckling. "Caveat emptor in a resale shop. Besides, the women who'd buy that coat aren't trudging across Aberdeen in a downpour. They're like you. Pampered."

"Pampered?" She lifted an eyebrow, looking even more imperious.

"Yes. Pampered. You clearly are." She took her hand and placed a quick kiss to the tip of a nail. "How long will it be before you're having a manicure?"

"I've got a two-hour layover in Chicago. I was planning on having one there."

"And a massage?"

"No," she said, chuckling. "It was bad enough having to ask the poor woman at the front desk to zip me up. I won't do that twice in one day."

"Did you ask her to perform the bounce test?"

"I've figured out how to slither into my bra. It's not easy, and it's not fun, but I can do it."

"What else is on your agenda for when you get home?"

"Mmm, I'm getting a haircut tomorrow night," Gillian said, laughing at herself. "I knew I'd look shaggy after my trip. " She started to say something else, then revealed a slight frown. "Women are judged much, much more harshly than men in corporate America. Every woman VP at my company works hard to hold it together, while the guys just have their pants let out when they gain twenty pounds." She took in a breath, then put her hand on Torie's shoulders. "Why are we talking about this? Shouldn't we be kissing?"

"Here?" Torie looked around at the scrum of passengers huddling alongside them.

"Let's find a quiet corner. I've got five minutes before I have to board."

"Then let's go," Torie said, grasping the handles of her suitcase and heading for the proper track, which had just been announced. Gillian followed along a few steps behind, owing to her black heels, which made her look seven feet tall. Seven feet of utter loveliness.

The train was five cars long, and Torie raced down the platform, going just past the last entry door. Then she stood behind a large square support beam and extended her arms. Gillian arrived a few moments later, slightly winded, but she smiled and snuggled up to Torie immediately. "This is better," she murmured.

"I'm going to miss you every moment we're apart," Torie whispered. "Every single moment."

"Me too. It's going to be hard. We can't kid ourselves about that." She lifted her head and gazed into Torie's eyes. "But it's going to be worth it. I promise that."

"Please kiss me." Torie closed her eyes and let her head lean back so Gillian, with her added height, could more easily reach her.

The noisy platform, the diesel fumes, the call of the conductor, even the rumble of an incoming train all disappeared the moment Gillian's lips pressed into hers. She was transported to a perfect place. A place where she felt safe, and wanted, and desired, and cared for. A place she wanted to live. Permanently.

Through the acrid fumes of the engine, she could still detect Gillian's scent. Clean and slightly floral. As kisses covered her mouth, then her cheeks, she concentrated on locking that lovely scent into her memory, along with the warm safety of Gillian's embrace, an embrace she needed more than she could have imagined just one day ago.

"All aboard!"

Torie grasped the handles of the bag and started for the first car, where the conductor gave her a frankly puzzled look. Gillian was probably the first passenger ever to join the train from the direction of the engine. Torie hoisted the cases into the car, then grasped Gillian for one final kiss. It was a fantastic one. One she'd hold close for as long as she possibly could. Then Gillian gracefully stepped into the car and peered over the shoulder of the conductor, who stood on the bottom step and waved to the engineer. Gillian stared at her intently, but they didn't wave to each other. Their gazes were locked together until the train whisked her away, back to her real life—the life Torie fervently hoped she wanted to flee as much as she'd claimed.

CHAPTER FIFTEEN

AT EIGHT O'CLOCK THAT EVENING, Gillian stared at her phone, trying to recall if she'd set it for local time. Her body thought it was much, much later, so the phone must have updated itself. She was afraid she'd fall asleep in the manicure place and miss her connecting flight if she didn't keep herself busy, so on the off chance she wasn't involved in some intensive mothering, she dialed Kara and waited through three rings.

"Are you home?" Kara's warm voice asked.

"Chicago. I got through immigration without a problem, which was reassuring. I assumed I'd be on an enemies list."

"Oh, what a happy sounding woman you are. Is anyone coming to pick you up?"

Gillian let a moment pass. "Who do you know who might do that?"

"I'll take that as a no, but since that's an unacceptable answer, I'll be there."

"No way! I don't land until ten fifteen. I'll just grab a cab."

"The kids will be asleep by then. I'm coming to get you, and I'm hanging up now so you can't convince me not to. Text me your flight number so I can track it. Otherwise, shut up. Byeee," she said, giggling.

Gillian looked at the phone for a moment, then dutifully texted her info. It was so nice to have a friend who bullied you into accepting a true kindness.

Kara's dark blue luxury SUV snuggled up to the curb, and Gillian waited as the trunk lid rose slowly and regally. She started to wrestle with the heavier of her bags when it was taken from her hand.

"I'm not going to have you throw your back out from using just one arm." Kara put her hand on Gillian's shoulder and pulled her close for a kiss.

"You're too nice to me."

"Why are you nearly naked? Bare arms in mid-November?"

"I threw my raincoat away. Not that I could have gotten it on…"

"Why didn't you buy another? I'd think Scotland, of all places, would have the best in the world."

"I couldn't try them on, so…" She shrugged. "I'm supposed to get the cast changed out for a brace. My clothes might fit over that. I *hope*."

The bags were loaded, but just before Kara shut the trunk she said, "Is that whiskey I smell on your alcohol-infused breath? Is that what you're taking for your owie?"

"I'm trying to stay off the codeine, so I had a little Scotch, as you Philistines call it. I know it as whisky—minus the 'E'. It's my new drink. Vodka is dead to me." She said this with what she knew was a ragged attempt at a Scottish accent, but tired as she was, it sounded pretty good to her ear.

"I'd better sell my Grey Goose stock," Kara teased. "Demand will shrink by several percentage points." She guided Gillian over to the passenger side, helped her in, then fastened her seatbelt just like she did for her children. Leaning in close to gaze into Gillian's eyes, she said, "Are you still in pain?"

"Not much. My ribs still hurt, but I'm doing much better. The awesome Lindsay recuperative powers might be kicking in."

Kara patted her, then walked around to the driver's side, got in and fastened her belt.

"So...," she said, "you've taken to drink to keep your libido in check?"

"I have not," Gillian said dramatically. "In fact, my libido's not in check. It's in charge. Or..." She tried to order her thoughts. "That's not true, either. But my heart is, and it's crazy about Torie. One day this spring I'll let my libido start running my life again."

"This time, I *know* you've been drinking," Kara said as a traffic enforcement officer signaled her to move away from the curb. "You're making no sense at all. Where did you leave things?"

"I left my heart in Aberdeen," she sighed. "Now I have to spend the next few months convincing Torie to keep it."

❧ ❧ ❧

On Monday morning, Torie exited the hotel to step out into a mild drizzle. When her phone rang, her heart started to beat faster when she saw the name in the display.

"What a nice companion for my drive home," she said, sighing with delight. "How are you?"

"Slow, grumpy. Normal for me. A more interesting question is, how are you?"

"Well, I suppose the only good news I have is that I'm not only dry, I'm warm. A very thoughtful, very generous woman left her coat for me. First time I've had a present waiting at the front desk when I arrived at work."

"Do you like it? I know it's a little big, but..."

"It fits perfectly over my wool jacket. And while I never would have picked such a bright color, maybe it's time for me to run a little wild. Thank you, Gillian. Your generous gesture wasn't necessary, but it was greatly appreciated."

"I wanted to keep you warm. Thinking of you wearing my jacket makes me feel closer. I know that's weird, but it does."

"I miss you," Torie sighed as she got into her car. "Aiden commented on my mood this morning, so it must be awful! Boys his age usually don't notice if an adult's bleeding from her eyes."

"What a nice image. Your shift was good?"

"What are you doing right now?" Torie asked, hearing Gillian banging around noisily.

"Making coffee. I've only got about five minutes before I attempt to wash myself. Takes forever."

"Is this what you want to do? Just check in? We can, of course, but most of my days are close to identical. We won't learn much about each other if all we do is exchange platitudes."

"You sound grouchy," Gillian said, immediately switching into the personae Torie had come to rely upon. The open, expressive, interested one. "Tell me about that. What's going on?"

"I'm fixated on you," she said, able to narrow it down to one word. "Well, you and me. What do we do now? Talk on the phone for a few minutes a day, hoping that lets us grow closer?"

"We'll definitely talk on the phone. I'm desperate to hear your voice. But we should do more." Torie could hear pages turning, then Gillian said, "I bought this book at the airport last night. It's called *One Hundred Important Questions*. The subtitle is *Things You Should, But Probably Don't Know About Your Closest Friends.*"

"So, you're going to ask me questions?"

"What I'd like," she said, continuing to noisily page through the book, "is to find a good question, then have each of us write an answer after we've thought about it. Doing it that way will give us time to make sure we're being candid."

"Ha! Giving me time will ensure I'm not candid," Torie teased. "The more time I have, the more I can twist things around to sound smarter or kinder."

"You won't do that. You want me to know the real you. You're not doing this to waste time."

"That's the absolute truth. I'm glad you know that, Gillian."

"So, here's today's question. What was the single happiest memory of your childhood? Got it?"

"I do. I'll think about it when I'm on the bus to Glasgow."

"Glasgow? Do you mean that if I'd been there this week, you'd take me on a tour of a real city?"

"Yes, lassie, I would have. Your timing was awful."

"My timing was impeccable," she said, clearly trying to sound romantic. "I met you, so I don't have a complaint in the world."

"I do. I wish Channing Brothers was located in Aberdeen, Scotland."

"It's not, but if we work at it, we can find a way to spend more time together. Remember, we've only had one date."

"But it was a good one," Torie said, smiling at the thought of Gillian's soft lips pressing into hers for the first, but certainly not the last time.

The next day, Torie didn't get a chance to look at her email until she'd finished her waitressing shift. But when she finally sat down, put her feet up, then opened her computer, she purred with delight when she saw the first message in the queue was from Gillian.

It read, in its entirety; "You are an unexpectedly warm, sunny day in February."

Torie gazed at the message for a few moments, imagining a lovely, warm day when you least expected it. As she ruminated about that, she thought of similar ways to describe Gillian. When one came to her, she texted it, hoping Gillian would appreciate getting a note during the day.

"You are the first sip of a carefully brewed ale." Just before she hit the "send" button, Torie gave it a little more thought. She'd considered the scent of a baby just out of the bath, a hug from your grandmother after you'd not seen her for a few months, and the aroma of a hearty stew when you were cold and hungry. None of the things she'd thought of were sexy or even romantic, but she didn't put extra time into thinking of something better. She wanted Gillian to get to know the real her, and she had to admit the smells and tastes of food and drink evoked the warmest thoughts. After sending the text, she went to warm up some food, having had next to nothing before work. She'd barely reached the kitchen when her phone rang, with the happy, upbeat ring she'd assigned to Gillian making her smile.

"I didn't expect to hear from you today, but I'm very glad I was wrong."

"I have a few minutes before I have to leave for the office. My counterpart in London pulled me into a meeting at eleven, London time, so I stayed home to take the call. I've got to get going, but I thought I deserved a little pleasure for having to get up at five to prep for the meeting."

"That's when I got up," Torie said. "Not much fun, is it."

"Not a bit. But talking to you is."

"I was hoping I'd see your response to the big question when I got home, but I'm pleased to know I'm an unexpectedly warm day."

"Very unexpected, but blissfully warm. Is there anything better than being surprised by something really nice?"

"Few things."

Some muted background noises sounded through the phone, then the quality of the call changed. "I'm walking to my car," Gillian said. "Want to ride to work with me?"

"Can you drive and talk?"

"Sure." In a few seconds, the sound changed again, now much fuller. "You're on Bluetooth."

"It sounds odd, but also intimate."

"That's me. Odd, yet intimate. Want to hear my fondest childhood memory, or should I write it down?"

"I'm on pins and needles," Torie said. "Tell me this instant."

"Well, I'm not sure what this says about me, but this is the happiest memory I can recall."

"I'm ready."

"The summer after third grade, I was on a soccer team. I hadn't wanted to play, but my parents insisted. Looking back on it, I think it must have been some kind of day care thing, since it was every morning at nine. They kept us busy learning drills and goofing around until noon, then we went home."

"Please don't let that be the whole memory," Torie said, hoping Gillian realized she was teasing.

"Tiny bit more," she said, letting out a soft chuckle. "Since my parents both worked, and Beverly, the woman who watched us, didn't have a car, I had to ride my bike. It wasn't very far, but it was farther than I'd ever been allowed to ride, and I was proud of myself for spreading my wings a little."

"Oh, I can just see you pedaling away."

"I showed up right on time for a few days, but I hated it. We didn't really do anything but stand around waiting for our turn to kick the ball once before getting back in line, a huge waste of time in my book."

"I know you still hate to waste time, so that's not surprising."

"Not at all," Gillian agreed. "I still remember what the day was like. The sky was bright blue, cloudless, there was dew on the grass, and the air felt so fresh and clean. I rode over the crest of a slight hill and saw all of the kids standing around waiting for the high school kids who ran the camp to get started."

"I can see it too," Torie said, charmed by how detailed Gillian's recollection was.

"I hit the brakes, stopped and stood there for a minute or two, trying to figure out what to do. I was *done,* but I knew they'd tell my parents if I told the leaders I quit. So I just turned around and rode away."

"You went home?"

"No way," she said, with a full-throated laugh. "I had to take advantage of my first opportunity to spend a morning exactly how I wanted."

Torie was so surprised by that comment that she didn't think of a rejoinder before Gillian started to speak again.

"That was the first day I'd ever truly concentrated on riding, listening to the wind as it whipped past my ears, sniffing the alfalfa in the fields, feeling the freedom of self-determination in a way I never had. I rode wherever I wanted, going farther and farther from home. My little legs were shaking when I finally had to admit I was lost, but I marched up to a house and asked for directions. I could tell the lady was tempted to call my mother, but I convinced her I had everything under control."

"Gillian! You just took off on your own?"

"I did," she said, clearly proud of herself. "By the time I got home, it was well past noon, but Beverly hadn't noticed the time. She asked how camp was, and I said it had been great. And it had been. Everything about that day had been great. I felt like I *owned* Columbus. I spent that entire summer exploring it. No limits."

"I'm so impressed," Torie said, her voice soft. "I wouldn't have had the nerve to do something like that until I was a teenager, and even then I would have been terrified of being caught out."

"I was *never* caught," she said emphatically. "I left the house every morning, rode around exploring, then went home for lunch. No one ever alerted my parents that I'd dropped out. Wasn't that criminal? They must not have bothered to count heads!"

"That's pretty close to criminal," Torie agreed, "but I'm glad they were negligent. Discovering you could fend for yourself at such a young age was an unexpected gift. Like a warm day in February," she added, feeling so tender toward Gillian that she ached to hold her.

"That's exactly what it was. An unexpected gift." The sounds changed again, and Gillian said, "Talking to you was an unexpected gift, but I'm at work now."

"Thanks for calling," Torie said, sighing. "I hope you have a wonderful day."

"You too. Got to go," she said, then clicked off.

Once again starting for the kitchen, Torie mused that the child had become the woman, without a great deal of change. Gillian had been, and remained, fiercely independent. Torie couldn't imagine taking off for a two-week vacation to America, all on her own. But Gillian hadn't given that a second thought. She knew she'd find people to talk to, and if she was lonely, she could hire guides to spend the day with. Was money the difference? Did she simply have more options because she could always buy what she needed? Pondering that for a while, Torie dismissed the idea. If Gillian had no money at all she'd still be independent. That was just who she was.

Taking a dish of pasta from the refrigerator, Torie continued to think as she warmed her lunch. Gillian's independence was, in many ways, an admirable trait. But did a woman who'd never lived with a partner have the capacity to be in a committed relationship? They'd never talked about that, since Torie simply took it for granted that they'd live together if Gillian moved to Scotland. But what if that's not what she wanted? The thought of continuing to live in Aberdeen with her family while Gillian was ensconced in a luxury flat in Edinburgh was not at all what Torie had in mind.

She stood in front of the hob, idly considering all of the things they had to work out. The list was monumental. But if they could continue to talk, and to write to one another, they could start chipping away at it. Slowly, but surely.

Ron was out of the office for the day, much to Gillian's pleasure, so she put her head down and continued to plow through the thousands of emails and messages that had come in during the previous two weeks.

She'd kept her direct reports on tenterhooks the day before, spending most of the day wading through email. At the close of business she'd asked them to meet with her at two, so they could get into the details of everything that had gone on during her absence. When they met, she'd spend some time calming them down or whipping them into a frenzy, whichever option was necessary.

The orthopedist she'd harassed into seeing her had an office about a half mile away. Normally, she'd take a cab, but it was a surprisingly warm, very sunny day, so she decided to walk. About halfway there, her phone rang and she took a look through her broken screen, barely able to see the photo that appeared. A stab of guilt hit her when she considered the lecture Torie had given her about family ties, so she answered and tried to sound pleased that her sister was calling.

"Hi, there," she said. "Miss me?"

"Of course. I wanted to make sure you got back all right," Amanda said.

"I did. And nothing blew up while I was gone, so Channing Brothers is well too."

"Did you have a *wonderful* time?" Amanda asked, always sounding a bit like a cheerleader or a pre-school teacher.

"I did. I feel very Scottish now."

"Where are you? I can hear traffic."

"Oh, yeah. Sorry about that. I'm walking to see an orthopedist. I broke my arm last week."

"What? Gillian!" Amanda sounded like she was going to hyperventilate. "You've *never* been seriously injured! What happened?"

"Strangely enough, the wind knocked me down. I broke one of the bones in my arm, bruised some ribs, and cracked the heck out of the screen on my phone. Bad day all around."

"That's just awful. Do you need help?"

The thought of her sister helping her get dressed was one she didn't want to linger on. Hiring a stranger would have been much more comfortable. "Oh, thanks, but I'm managing. Actually, I'm hoping this doc will give me a brace. Right now, I've got a cast from my hand to the middle of my upper arm."

"That's just horrible," Amanda said. "That must have ruined your whole trip."

"No, no, it really didn't. I had a great time," she said, unable to even attempt to hide her enthusiasm. "Best trip of my life."

"Fantastic! Did you find out more about our Scottish relative? What was his name? Hannibal?"

"Hamish," she said, chuckling. "And no, I didn't, but I'm going to look into him now that I know a little bit about the country. Did you know that Sinclair is also a Scottish name?"

"No," she said slowly. "I didn't. Are you sure?"

"It's definitely Scottish, but it could be English, too. I might look into that. All of a sudden, I'm interested in our genealogy."

"Mmm. Don't tell Rick, or he'll get interested in his. You know he's always ready to jump on any bandwagon you're on."

"He is?" Gillian had to jump back onto the curb after a taxi got close enough to brush against her skirt.

"Oh, Gillian," Amanda sighed. "You're so oblivious."

"So I've heard, but I paid no attention."

"That doesn't surprise me," Amanda said, as usual not getting the joke. Only Gillian had inherited their father's sense of humor. "Let me know if you get that cast off. If not, I can send Irene over to make dinner for you."

"I'm fine, Amanda. Really. I'll text you a photo of the before and after, okay?"

"All right. And let me know what you find out about our relatives. I wasn't interested before, but it might be nice to know a little something of where we came from."

"Will do," she said, hanging up to race across the street to the doctor's office. She couldn't wait to have the use of her hand again.

The orthopedist had clearly gone out of his way to see her, which she deeply appreciated. Gillian was rushed in, x-rayed, had the cast cut off, and a new brace fitted, all in less than a half hour. Now she stood outside in the warm sun, finally able to put her suit jacket on. The brace was pleasingly thin, with velcro straps she was supposed to adjust as the swelling went down. Now she could move her elbow, and her wrist, but both were amazingly stiff and swollen. Bruised, too, but not as bad as she thought they might be.

She'd been instructed to do some simple flexibility exercises, but they'd stressed she shouldn't move past the pain. But that meant she could flex her wrist enough to be able to type and sign her name. Given she had to personally approve every divisional expense of more than twenty-five hundred dollars, that wasn't an insignificant issue.

It was only twelve noon, and since she'd told Jennifer, her admin, that she was going to be gone for an hour or two, she slowed down as she passed the building where the city kept vital statistics. Surprising herself, she climbed the stairs and found the right room, then filled out a form in her shaky, dreadful penmanship. That was going to have to improve quickly, or the finance department would kick all of her approvals right back.

When she passed the form across the counter, the clerk said, "Are you waiting for this? There's a charge for that."

"That's fine. I'll wait."

She wasn't behaving like she normally did when she returned from vacation, but figured she was still under the spell of a certain Scottish lass. God only knew how long that would last, but she liked surprising herself.

The clerk returned pretty quickly. "No such birth in 1955."

"Are you sure?"

He looked at her with an expression full of disdain. "I'm sure."

Blinking in confusion, she said, "How about marriage records?"

"We've got 'em. Fill out the form." He indicated the one he'd passed back to her. "You've got to pay for that, too. Just because you've got the info wrong isn't my problem."

Ignoring his attitude, she filled out the request for her parents' marriage certificate. This time, Mr. Friendly found it quickly. She paid, then stood out in the hall, looking it over. By the time she reached the end of the form, she was on the verge of grabbing the first person she saw and demanding they read it too, since her eyes must have been playing tricks on her. There, on the line that said, "Place of birth," her mother had written, "Scotland." That's it. No town, no further info. Just "Scotland." What in the holy hell did *that* mean?

Torie was thrilled with the development, practically bouncing off the walls when Gillian spoke to her as she walked home from the pub that night. "Don't you see?" she said. "If your mother was Scottish, it's possible you'll qualify for citizenship!"

"It is?"

"It is," Torie insisted. "We'll have to do some research, but that shouldn't be difficult. Actually, I should do the research, given we'll have the records. Give me her birth date, and I'll get on it."

"I'll give you what she told me," Gillian said. "But given she lied about *where* she was born, she might have lied about the date, too. Nothing I know is hanging together, Torie. Nothing."

Having a small, but loyal group of Grampian police department employees be regular pub visitors had paid off a time or two, but Torie was surprised at how quickly her contact had found the information she needed. But she wasn't finished. Not by a long shot. Now that she knew where Gillian's mother had been born, she could use that information to do a proper search on the Sinclairs. By the time she was finished, she'd have them back to the stone age. She had to stop pondering her task when someone had the temerity to enter and signal for a pint. It was hard to daydream the hours away when customers insisted on wetting their beaks.

Torie felt just like she had at uni when she'd pulled some hidden bit of information out of a dusty tome. Few things gave her as big a charge as hunting down information, and no one could argue this wasn't a *big* piece of information.

She'd walked about halfway home, with the clicks of her heels the only sound on the lightly traveled street. When her phone buzzed, it startled her, even though she knew Gillian would call the moment she could.

"I've got my office door closed," she said, sounding much more relaxed than she had the previous night. "If you tell me something horrible and I scream, I don't think anyone will hear me."

"Hello, Gillian," Torie said, trying to make herself sound sexy. "I've missed you."

Gillian's tone changed in an instant, with her voice now wistful and full of longing. "Oh, me too. I can't believe it's only been three days since I've seen you. It seems *so* much longer."

"For me too. But now that I've got a project, I'm going to be very busy."

"You have a project?"

"Uh-huh. I'm going to track your family back to when our mutual ancestors were just starting to carve standing stones."

"Our…? You found my mother's birth certificate?"

"I did. Now I'm going to start researching how you'll qualify for citizenship."

"Isn't that all I need? In America, if your mom was born here, you're automatically a citizen."

"It's not that way here. I'm not sure what steps we have to take, but I'll figure it out. And then," she said dramatically, "we can explore our mutual ancestral roots."

"Tell me more!"

"Well, the thing I found most amazing is that your mother was born in Orkney."

"She was not!"

"Oh, she was. On the northernmost island. Her date of birth is as she said. She simply didn't mention her home country for reasons I can't imagine."

Gillian was quiet for a few seconds. "What sense does this make?"

"In my view? None. But I obviously didn't know your mother."

"What was her mom's name?"

"Jeannie. A lovely name."

"I meant her maiden name." Gillian let out a soft laugh. "I want to make sure it's not Gunn. I'm already worried that we're cousins."

"She didn't have a maiden name. Or, I should say she didn't have a married name. Jeannie Sinclair was a single woman. Seventeen years old at the time of your mother's birth."

"My mother was illegitimate?" Gillian cried.

Torie was standing in front of her home, but she didn't go inside just yet. First, she had to cool the flash of anger that suffused her. "That's not a word I like to hear. My nephew was also born without a named father, and there's nothing illegitimate about him."

"Oh, damn, I'm sorry," Gillian sighed. "It's just…" She trailed off, then took in an audible breath. "This is all knocking me off my stride. I don't recall my mother talking about her family much at all, but she definitely told me her father died when she was young."

"Maybe he did. Maybe he and your grandmother wanted to be together but couldn't be."

"There's no *good* reason you can't be together," Gillian said. "If a guy's not already married…" She sucked in a breath. "After hearing my mother frequently moralize about people who cheated on their spouses…" She was quiet for another few moments. "Maybe that's what happened. Maybe her father couldn't marry her mother. That might have predisposed her to have an irrational hatred of cheaters."

"I'll find out," Torie said. "I don't make these promises easily, so you can rely on this one. I'll find out what happened to your mom's family. The Sinclairs will not remain shrouded in the mists of time."

CHAPTER SIXTEEN

AT FIVE O'CLOCK THE NEXT afternoon, Gillian casually walked out of her office, after having locked her briefcase in her closet. As she passed by her admin's desk, she said, "I'll be on the third floor for a meeting, Jennifer. Feel free to take off whenever you finish up." Her keys were in one pocket, driver's license in the other, phone in hand as she mumbled something to herself as she walked toward the elevator.

She didn't do it often, but every once in a while she snuck out. Her guys would work until six or six thirty as usual, then worry about whether they should stay until she returned. When they showed up in the morning, her computer would be on, making them think she'd beaten them in as well. It was a dirty trick, but the boss had to be the last one out, and she didn't have the stamina to stick it out today. She didn't technically have jet lag, since she'd woken at four, bright-eyed and bushy-tailed. Her brain was performing properly, and she'd had plenty of energy to slog through all of the BS that had gone on in her absence. But her body believed it was eleven o'clock in the evening, and it was ready to chill. It had been pretty dumb to accept her sister's invitation to dinner, but now that she had information to share, she couldn't resist.

After slogging through downtown traffic, she headed northeast, aiming for the almost bucolic suburb of her youth. The area had been converted from farmland just a few years before her father had bought the property in the mid-80s, but it had slowly lost the more agrarian elements to now be just another leafy suburb. Rare was the property where horses were kept, something she missed. It had been nice to be a small kid and smell horses when you rode your bike down a lightly-trafficked lane.

Her sister's house was still decorated for Halloween, but that wouldn't last long. The Thanksgiving flag would probably be put out this weekend, then the turkeys, pilgrims and cornucopia window gels would show up. Their mom hadn't cared a whit about decorating or carefully observing holidays, but Amanda was fanatical about it. Every one of the multitudes of her Instagram posts chronicled her seemingly perfect life. Gillian didn't have a social media presence, but she was often tempted to start one just to post pictures of her nephews with snotty noses or grass stains on their knees. Anything to make them look like regular kids.

After a perfunctory knock, Gillian walked in and called out, "Amanda?"

"In the kitchen, Gill."

Gillian walked through the wide entryway, past the stairs to the second floor, past the half-bath, and into the kitchen. It was a nice one, she had to admit. Just redone in the last five years, with acres of granite and shiny stainless appliances.

She walked over to her sister, who was standing at the sink, and gave her a kiss on the cheek. "Good to see you."

Amanda wiped her hands, turned and gave Gillian a warm appraisal, then added a quick hug. "I was afraid you'd be dead tired, but you look fantastic." She fluffed the ends of Gillian's hair, nodding. "How'd you have time for a haircut?"

"How do you know it didn't grow slower in Scotland? If hair needs sun to grow, they wouldn't need many stylists over there."

"You poor thing," she soothed, gently touching the brace. "Does it hurt constantly?"

"Not really. I notice it when I'm trying to sleep, and if I type too much or things like that, but compared to the ribs…it's nothing."

"Ooo. I forgot about them."

"Not me. They remind me they're there every time I breathe."

"I'll warn the kids to go easy on you. They think every adult is a jungle gym."

That wasn't really true, at least in Gillian's experience. The boys always seemed shy and a little standoffish, generally ignoring her to concentrate on their parents and torture each other. "I'll speak with my abominable Scottish accent to scare them off."

Still wearing a dark gray jersey knit dress that she'd obviously worn to work, Amanda let out a gentle laugh and moved across the kitchen to tend to something on the stove. Her only nod to comfort was that she'd kicked off her shoes, and now padded around in her bare feet.

Gillian watched her glide around the kitchen, seemingly competent at cooking. She and Amanda definitely looked like sisters, with the same coloring, hair color and texture, and similar blue eyes. But Amanda had no interest in athletics or working out, being much more prone to lie on a sofa and read to relax. She was also slighter, kind of willowy. Gillian would have been surprised if she wore more than a size four, and if that Scottish wind had hit her, Amanda might have flown all the way to Ireland.

Focusing on the stove, Gillian tried to figure out why in the heck Amanda was doing anything at all to prepare dinner. She and Rick had Irene, their full-time live-out housekeeper and cook, and Gillian was fairly sure Irene normally remained until the dinner dishes were washed. Taking a closer look, she saw that Amanda was just putting a prepared dish into the oven and warming up something on the stove top. That must have been her nod to providing a home-made dinner. Actually, that was pretty thoughtful.

"Rick and the boys will be home in about a half hour. We have time for a glass of wine."

"Where are they?" Gillian asked, picking up the bottle of wine that rested in a chiller on the counter.

"Soccer practice. Indoors," she added. "They just run around the gym and trip over their own feet, but they like it."

Amanda worked in human resources for one of Columbus's largest companies, and Rick was ostensibly a stockbroker, but he seemed to be home an awful lot. Actually, they each went out of their way to be home in time to have dinner as a family whenever possible. That meant Amanda usually went in at six to be able to leave at a decent hour, but she didn't seem to mind.

Amanda took the glass Gillian offered and led the way to the living room. No one could accuse Gillian of being overly concerned with details that didn't interest her, but it took until just that minute to realize her sister's home was laid out almost exactly like their family home had been. That was kind of freaky. Choosing to live just four streets away from the home she'd grown up in, with plans to send her kids to the same school. It was like she was trying to recreate her own childhood through the boys—which seemed like an exercise doomed to failure.

"Come here and sit down," Amanda said, patting the seat next to her. "Show me your photos."

"I just have my phone, and I broke the screen when I fell…"

"Ohh," she said, clearly disappointed. "You didn't bring your tablet?"

"Forgot it. I'll bring my laptop next time." She knew they'd both forget, but that was fine. It was nice that Amanda even acted like she cared enough to look at pictures. "Actually," Gillian said, sitting next to her sister and holding her phone close to her chest, "I've got some news."

"News?" Alert as a guard-dog, Amanda stared at her like she was waiting for something cataclysmic. "Are you all right?"

"Fine. Just fine. Um, when I learned that Sinclair was a Scottish name, I decided to look into Mom's background. I'm not sure why, but I jumped right in on her family, rather than dad's. But…" She said, perversely enjoying the rapt expression on her sister's face, "here's the deal. Mom wasn't born in Columbus."

"Sure she was. She lived over by Wolfe Park. She took me to see her house, Gill."

"Nope. She was raised in Columbus, but born in…" She paused for effect. "Scotland."

"Scotland?" Amanda looked like she'd faint dead away. "How can that be?"

"I don't know. She was born on the day she claimed, but on a tiny island in a grouping called Orkney. I've got someone looking into things over there. With any luck, she'll be able to help us find out when, and why, she left."

"That can't be true, Gill. It *can't* be!"

"It is," Gillian insisted. "I found her and dad's marriage license. It clearly says she was born in Scotland."

"Why on earth would she lie to me?" Amanda said, tears starting to fill her eyes. "She *lied*, Gill. I remember her telling me she and I were born in the same hospital. That's a lie, not an omission."

"Sure is," Gillian said, tentatively settling her left arm around Amanda's shoulders, which felt *way* too intimate. But when your little sister was sitting there crying, and you were the only person around, you'd have to be a real jerk not to offer her a little comfort.

When Torie climbed the stairs after her breakfast shift on a Tuesday morning, she cocked her head at the large box that nearly covered the doorway to her flat. Peering at the label, she noticed it had been delivered by one of the overnight services, posted from London. She managed to get the door open and wrestle the box inside, amazed someone had been able to carry it all the way up.

After getting a knife to open it, she started to pull out the contents, then grinned when every possible type of laundry product was revealed, all from the giant UK corporation whom she now knew was owned by Channing Brothers. Inside was a note saying, "You'll never have to buy another bottle of detergent so long as I'm around. PS-Do you have a washing machine? I didn't think to ask. If you'll provide a list of all household cleaning needs, they will be met. GCL."

Torie picked up her phone and dashed off a quick text, knowing Gillian was just waking up. "I feel cleaner already. I have a washing machine, but no dishwasher. I'll donate the dishwasher detergent to a local women's shelter. What's the "C" for, GCL?"

Just a few minutes later, Gillian replied. "Cumberland. The only romantic thing my parents ever did was give me the middle name of the place they honeymooned, Cumberland Island, Georgia. Today's question is: Rank your desire for each of the following—money, status, power, influence, love, respect. It sounds easier than it is!"

❧ ❧ ❧

At six thirty that evening, Gillian got up and closed her office door. The floor was nearly empty, with the cleaning people already starting to do their rounds. She was bone-tired, starving, and grumpy from lack of exercise. But she dutifully called Torie, keeping her promise to accompany her home from work whenever she could.

The phone always sounded a little funny when it rang, and when Torie picked up, Gillian could feel a smile settle onto her lips. "Hi, there," she sighed. "Hearing your voice makes me feel better."

"The same is true for me. Emotionally, that is. My feet still ache like the dickens after a full shift."

"Bad night?"

"No, not really. We had a flurry of excitement when the police arrived, looking for one of our regulars. But he wasn't in, so the drama was short-lived."

Gillian bit her tongue, refusing to comment on the quality of Torie's usual customers. They hadn't been together long enough for her to start with that. "So? Did you think about today's question?"

"I did," Torie said, yawning audibly. "Sorry. I'm a little draggy today. I had a lot to say this afternoon when I was making Aiden's tea, but now I'm a little muddled. How about you?"

"Also muddled." She picked up her pen and started to twirl it around on her desk. "I didn't realize that exercise worked on my mood, but it must. I've been kind of a bear all week."

"You can't do anything energetic that appeals to you?"

"I might be able to use the treadmill, but I hate it. I'll make a note to call my orthopedist tomorrow and check on it, though, since that's my only option. I don't want to screw my healing up."

"Other than that?"

"Not much," Gillian admitted. "I'm kind of obsessed with a new marketing campaign we're about to launch. I'm going to go get some food and work on that for a few more hours."

"Mmm. You know what?"

"What?"

"This isn't working," Torie said, her breathing becoming slightly more labored as she must have started to climb the stairs to her apartment.

207

"What isn't working? Us?"

"Not us," Torie said, the warmth coming back to her voice. "Our schedule isn't working. I like the idea of talking about ideas and feelings and experiences, but we're too tired to do it at the end of the day. I'm *so* tired, Gillian, and I've got to get up in six hours."

"What can we do?"

"We're going to do what we said we'd do. We're going to write to each other every day, and speak just one or two days a week. Preferably Saturday afternoon or Sunday evening for me. Can that work for you?"

"I can make it work," Gillian said, not very happy with the idea. "We'll come up with a schedule."

"This is important. I can't get to know you with short conversations when we're both thinking of other things. We need to focus."

"Then we'll focus," Gillian agreed. "I'm going to hang up now so you can get to sleep. Deal?"

"Go have a nice dinner," Torie said. "I'll dream of you."

"Aww… I don't think you can just will that, but let me know if it works."

"I will. Goodnight, sweet Gillian."

"Wait!"

"Yes?"

"You're the first crocus poking up through the snow," she said, a little embarrassed to say, rather than write her thoughts.

"I will think about *that* to go to sleep, and I'm sure that image will bring me sweet dreams."

Gillian hung up, with the image of Torie's face filling her mind. Then she moved her repaired phone so she could stare at the best photo she had of her, standing in front of the Buchan Ness lighthouse. The first one they visited together. Torie looked *so* good. Bright-eyed and full of energy—a state Gillian was finding didn't occur often in her usual world.

CHAPTER SEVENTEEN

AFTER JUST A WEEK OF SEARCHING, Torie had a good lead. She'd found the Facebook page for people who'd traveled from North Ronaldsay, the tiny island Gillian's mother had been born on, to attend the grammar school in Kirkwall, the big town on the Mainland. They were busily planning their seventieth reunion, which amazed Torie. Being able to use not only a computer, but Facebook, showed these Orcadians were an intrepid group. After posting her query, she got a reply from a woman who was two years younger than Jeannie Sinclair, and recalled her with amazing precision.

When she returned home for her mid-day break, Torie called the number the woman had given her, anxiously waiting for her to answer. "Hello? Mrs. Tulloch?"

"Yes, this is Mrs. Tulloch."

"This is Torie Gunn, calling about Jeannie Sinclair?"

"Oh, hello dear. Let me just get the kettle, will you? It's on the boil."

"Of course." Torie smiled at hearing her accent, so like her own grandmother's. In a minute, Mrs. Tulloch returned.

"Now what was it you wanted to know, dear?"

"I'm a friend of Jeannie's granddaughter. Sadly, Jeannie died before my friend was born, but she's very interested in learning anything she can about her. Right now, we're looking for anyone who remembers anything about her at all."

"Can't your friend's mother help?"

"She's dead, Mrs. Tulloch, and she didn't speak of her own mother often when she was alive."

"Odd." She was silent for a moment, but Torie didn't rush in to try to explain. She thought she'd wait to use her powers of persuasion only if they were needed. "Well, I know a bit," she said slowly, "but I'm not sure it's right to talk about Jeannie."

"Why's that?"

"Och," the woman said, sounding a little like a bird cooing. "The girl guarded her privacy. I don't know if she'd like anyone, even her granddaughter, to know what went on."

"Oh, Mrs. Tulloch, I can't imagine that's true. My friend didn't even know her grandmother's name or that she was an Orcadian until a few weeks ago. That's not what Jeannie would have wanted, is it? To be completely unknown by her own descendants?"

The woman fell silent for a few moments, slowly saying, "Your friend didn't know Jeannie was an Orcadian? Her mother didn't tell her…"

"She didn't," Torie said. "I'm not certain why my friend's mother hid her background, but my friend just learned she was born in Scotland. My friend assumed her mother had been born in America, and learning that wasn't true has made her question so much."

"But Jeannie was the center of so much unwanted attention…" She sighed. "I'm not sure what she'd want her granddaughter to know."

"Jeannie's gone," Torie said firmly. "And if my friend learns nothing about her, I doubt anyone else will ever mention her name again. I don't know about you, but I'd want my grandchildren to remember me. That's all we have, isn't it?"

"Yes, yes, you're right," Mrs. Tulloch said, speaking with a burst of energy. "I suppose no one can be hurt now."

"That's true. You're simply helping at this point."

"All right. I'll start with what I know as fact. When she was about sixteen, Jeannie left Kirkwall Grammar School without a word, never to return…"

🌱 🌱 🌱

Torie was always bone tired after her shift at the pub, but now that she had information to share, her lethargy evaporated so easily it amazed her. She was bubbling with excitement when she texted Gillian, hoping she'd be free.

In just a few seconds, her phone rang, and Torie answered, "Orcadian info center, Torie speaking."

"Info?" Gillian said, clearly excited. "What do you know?"

"Well, now that I think about it, I shouldn't be so happy. Your grandmother had a tough time of it."

"Tell me everything!"

"Well, I found a woman who lives on the Mainland now, but grew up on North Ronaldsay. She and Jeannie went to school together, but this woman, Mrs. Tulloch, was two years behind your grandmother."

"That sounds so odd," Gillian said. "Knowing my grandmother was a real person, with her own plans and dreams. I've never thought of her as an… individual," she said quietly.

"She was, Gillian. But she took up with the wrong person, or at least a person who was too afraid to step up and do the right thing. She got pregnant the year she was due to leave school, and pretty much stayed on the family croft until she gave birth to your mum."

"Oh, wow," she said, sounding a little breathless. "I was hoping there was a really cool reason my mom hid this from us. Although what that might be is a mystery…"

"I don't know exactly what North Ronaldsay was like in the 1950s, but I can guarantee an unplanned pregnancy would have been a big story on the island."

"I bet. Any way you can find out who my grandfather is?"

"Apparently, Jeannie told no one. At least none of her peers. It sounds like it could have been anyone in Kirkwall."

"Wait. Why Kirkwall?"

"I'm skipping around too much. Let me start again. North Ronaldsay had a primary school, but the kids went to secondary school in Mainland. It was too far to take the ferry back and forth, so they boarded with local families."

"They just plunked their kids down with strangers?"

"I assume they were the parents of fellow students, or were known in some way, but, yes, the kids had to live with relative strangers."

"At like fourteen years old?"

"A little younger, I think. Secondary school started at age eleven or twelve."

"How could you do that to your kid?" Gillian said, her voice rising in indignation.

"If you wanted your child to have an education, you had to do it, Gillian. This wasn't a whim. There were no options for crofters."

"Fine, fine," she sighed. "You're saying my grandmother might have not been closely supervised, right?"

"Well, I don't know about that. Even people with very involved parents can find a way to have sex. She could have been taken with a fellow student, the ferry boat driver, a waiter in a tea room. Maybe the family your grandmother boarded with had a son…"

Sounding much calmer, Gillian laughed softly. "You're saying my poor grandmother slept with anyone who had a spare five minutes."

"Not at all," Torie said, her heart aching for the young, naive girl. "She went into hiding while she was pregnant. Mrs. Tulloch said no one saw her, which just added to the gossip. After she gave birth to your mother, she tried to stay on, but she, and her family, were *very* private people—"

"That trait didn't skip a generation," Gillian interrupted. "You had to state your reasons if you asked my mother the time."

"Right. Well, when people kept talking about her, and her baby, she decided to leave. Mrs. Tulloch didn't know the details, but she thinks a relative who lived in America helped her out. Maybe even sponsored her or something like that. They didn't leave right away, but your mother was still in her pram when they emigrated."

"That's beyond awful," Gillian sighed.

"Maybe not. Times were tough on Orkney back then. I don't think the North Isles even had electricity until the 1980s. If you're stuck out in an isolated place like that…"

"How big was it? Like Skye?"

"Oh, no. I'd guess they had somewhere around a hundred, a hundred and twenty-five…"

"People?" Gillian gasped.

"There were a lot more sheep than that," Torie joked, "but yes, definitely fewer than two hundred people. Being the focus of gossip, especially if you were ashamed of what you'd done, must have been horrible. I can easily see why your grandmother wanted to start anew."

"And Jeannie's shame filtered right down to my mom. Obviously," she added. "Otherwise, she wouldn't have been so secretive about her birth."

"That's probably true. It's crazy isn't it? All of that drama because two people had sex and created a baby."

"It's sad," Gillian said. "Shame extends over generations, doesn't it? My mom carried it to her dying day. Such a waste."

Torie simply nodded, privately wondering how much Gillian had escaped the Sinclair penchant for being secretive about sex. Was being in the closet really that different from hiding in the croft, hoping people would forget about your wee bairn's parentage?

🌱 🌱 🌱

Sunday afternoons had become Gillian's favorite time of the week. After going to the gym and running on the blasted treadmill in the afternoon, she'd stop at a gourmet grocery store not far from her house, buy some kind of composed salad, then rush home for a seriously early dinner. After changing into her pajamas and a robe, she'd race back downstairs and start a fire. That required only the flick of a switch, but it was important to have it going. Then she sat on the sofa in the living room, with the bottle of whisky she'd bought in Scotland resting on the coffee table in front of her. She wouldn't pour a dram until she'd eaten her salad and they'd talked for a while, but she didn't want any distractions.

Four weeks after she'd left Scotland, she was fully prepared for her four o'clock date with Torie, whisky and empty glass waiting, pear, spiced pecan, goat cheese and arugula salad resting on a tray on her lap, her fully-charged tablet standing like a sentry on the table.

"Call Torie," she said, and the magical little device did her bidding. After a few rings, she heard Torie's warm, beautifully accented voice caress her ears.

"Hello there, my American companion."

"Hi," Gillian said, always a little tongue tied when they first connected. "Did you have a good shift last night?"

"Good enough. I earned just under eighty-five pounds."

Their standards for what made going to work worthwhile couldn't have been more different. In Gillian's view, Torie was paid a shockingly low hourly wage, and the tips she made were a joke. But she seemed happy if she pulled in an extra five pounds for eight hours of work, so Gillian stopped herself from expressing her true opinion, limiting herself to a supportive, "Good for you."

"Have you eaten?"

"My salad's on my lap."

"Have you been to the gym?"

"I have," she said, stressing the last word. "But there's no snow or ice on the ground, so I'm *really* going running in the morning. I'm going to meet up with some of the guys from my biking group at dawn."

"Is that a good idea? Won't your brace alter your gait?"

"I think it'll be fine. If not, it's back to the gym to run on that sucky treadmill."

"Did you have time to read my response to the question of the day?"

"I did. I was surprised by it, so I'm still mulling it over."

"You were surprised?"

"Uh-huh. I assumed Sheila would have been your first love. Do you honestly think a twelve-year-old can really fall hard?"

"I do. I suppose it's a simple, uncomplicated kind of love, but there's no doubt in my mind that I loved Margaret. Nor that she loved me. If she hadn't moved to the Scottish mainland, we might still be together." She let out a gentle laugh. "Now I'm glad she moved, but I certainly wasn't then. I mourned that relationship for well over a year."

"Poor little Torie," Gillian soothed. "A wee broken heart, and no one to share it with."

"No one at all. I wasn't sure how to characterize what I felt for Margaret, but I knew not to talk about it with my mum."

"Preaching to the choir on that one," Gillian said, chuckling softly. "I learned that lesson when I was a bairn, and haven't changed my position since."

"I miss you," Torie said. "I think about you fifty times a day, always trying to figure out where you are or what you're doing."

"I do, too. When I get up, I immediately think about you, wondering how you're spending your afternoon break. Then I argue with myself over whether I should call or not. But since I'm racing around my house, trying to be the first one in, I usually lose that argument."

"I like our Sunday chats a lot. We're both finished with work for the week." Gillian could hear the sounds change, with the background becoming quieter. Then Torie's breathing changed too.

"Climbing your stairs?"

"Uh-huh. Almost home. Aiden and my father both had an irresistible craving for ice cream, and I had to rush out before the nearby shop closed."

"Do you need to go? Say no," she said, trying not to sound like she was on the verge of begging.

"Give me twenty minutes. It'll take me a few minutes to dish it out."

"All right. But tell those two they're horning in on my time." Gillian forced herself to laugh, then hung up. She'd once again had to stop herself from suggesting Torie's nephew could go get his own damn ice cream, and if Torie didn't want him out after dark, the least he could do was serve himself and his grandfather. Actually, since his grandfather could get down to the golf links to while away his days off with his friends, he could also get his lazy butt down to the store. But having that conversation was not a good idea—at all. You had to take your new girlfriend as you found her, reserving your improvement projects for when you were on more solid ground.

After telling her tablet to set an alarm for twenty minutes, she spent the time trying to eat slowly and enjoy her food. Then she poured the whisky and set the tablet onto a few books so it was level with her face. Her timer went off, and she instructed the machine. "Video chat with Torie." A few seconds later the screen brightened with Torie's face. She always held her tablet too close, which gave her a fun-house-mirror effect. But Gillian had grown to like that, finding the ever-changing contours of her face entertaining. The unpolished, haphazard way she had of doing certain things was oddly charming.

"Who's the prettiest girl in Scotland?" Gillian asked, her usual question.

"I'm not sure, but since I'm the only girl you know, I'll have to do."

Gillian loved that Torie never answered the same, coming up with a different rejoinder every single time. She was as clever as a cute little fox.

"I've seen a lot of Scotland, and I didn't run into a single woman who came close to you."

"You've seen a tiny bit of Scotland, and we saw more sheep than people. But I'm willing to encourage your delusions. Let's agree I'm the prettiest girl in Scotland, even though it's been over twenty years since anyone correctly called me a girl."

"What did you do all day?"

"My sister came for dinner, and that went well."

"She's good?"

"So it seems. She's following her routine, and I think seeing Aiden more has helped keep her from contacting members of her old crowd."

"When's her sobriety anniversary?"

"January the second will be one year. Let's hope we can celebrate with a nice, alcohol-free party."

"Wish I could be there," Gillian sighed. Then she laughed. "She'd wonder why your client from months ago was there, but we could work our way around that."

"I'm thinking about telling my family about us," Torie said. "Mainly because I don't want to spring it on them when you come back on your puffin quest. It would hurt their feelings to think I'd hidden something important from them."

"Do that. It's only been a few weeks, but I hope I've convinced you I'm not just a flaky tourist."

"You're flaky enough," she teased. "But, yes, I trust you, Gillian. When you come to visit, we're going to have a second date that will knock your socks off."

"And every other piece of clothing," she said, grinning widely. "You're probably not the kind of woman who usually has sex on the second date, but when there's four or five months between dates, I hope you'll make an exception."

"I have a feeling you're right." She brought the tablet to her mouth and completely obscured the lens when she made a loud 'smack' with her lips. "I'm very much looking forward to that date."

Gillian let out a sigh. Spring seemed so, so very far away.

CHAPTER EIGHTEEN

ON THE FIRST SUNDAY OF THE new year, Gillian got into her usual pose and commanded her phone to call Torie. But she didn't get the usual friendly welcome. This time, she got a hurried, "Call back in twenty. Raining hard. Bye!"

Unreasonably disappointed, she ate her salad and flipped on the TV, spending the next minutes watching some commentators talk about the college football playoffs like they were discussing the coming Armageddon. Some people got too worked up over things that didn't matter much at all.

When she finally told her tablet to video chat with Torie, her mood brightened in a moment. The tablet was at the proper distance, far enough away for Gillian to see Torie wearing her Christmas gift.

"Now you're really the prettiest girl in all of Scotland," she said, almost embarrassed at how pleased she was to see how cute Torie looked in the vest.

"Even though you promised you weren't going to spend money on me, I love it so much I can't be cross about it. I've never had a thermal gilet, you know."

"It's fiberfill, not down," Gillian said, "because I didn't want it to be too puffy. The color's perfect on you."

"It's a good green," she agreed. "How about you? Are your Christmas presents gone?"

"Gone?" She held up the image she'd just had framed. She'd had to pay extra for the rush job, but she honestly couldn't wait to put it on her mantle. "This will be with me until the end of my days." She angled the frame so Torie could see it. "I know I've thanked you ten times already, but I've never asked you where you got the photo. It's so beautiful it takes my breath away."

"I've never met anyone who expresses her thanks as often or as sincerely as you do," Torie said. "If I had more money to spend, I'd buy you a gift every day." She blew a kiss, then said, "I found the photo from one of those image sharing sites, then I had a friend from school add the inscription. Printing it off was no trouble at all."

"I love that the quote is from the fifth century." She made her voice sound imposing. "Beyond Britannia, where the endless ocean opens, lies Orkney."

"Leave it to me to quote a guy from the fifth century," Torie said. "I couldn't tell you the name of any current movie, but I can rattle off a large group of people who've been dead for over a thousand years."

"Speaking of things that might kill me," Gillian said, holding up the last piece of the delicious fudge-like thing Torie called tablet. "Don't make me any more of this. I'm going to have to run forty miles on the treadmill to make up for gobbling it all down, but I think it's worth it."

"Could you do that? Run forty miles, that is?"

"Doubtful." She thought for a minute. "I can...or I guess I should say I *used* to ride a hundred miles with no trouble, but running's a different thing. I'm more of a 10k person."

"I'd like to see you in your biking clothes. Or your running shorts." She let out a sly laugh. "Actually, I'd just like to see your bottom."

"You will. Everything from top to bottom will be yours to explore." She held up her arm and flexed her hand in every direction it would go. "I'm back to normal, so these little fingers are itching to explore all of your hidden parts."

"Ooo! How does it feel?"

"Good. Weaker than it was, but that makes sense. The doc said I can do most things, but he wants me to steer clear of even indoor biking for another month. I'm stuck with the treadmill now that the ground is icy, but I can swim if I want, and start to lift weights. Light ones."

"Listen to his instructions," Torie warned. "I need you in perfect shape when you visit."

"Can I buy my ticket yet? I may have to sell my soul, but I think I can manage a week in March."

"Just a week?"

"Yeah. Even that's going to be tough, but I can't wait any longer."

"Oh, Gillian, don't buy your ticket yet. I want to make sure Aiden's not on school break. Then I want to check out all of the different cities and see who's got a festival or an event that you might like. This time I want to make sure I'm prepared."

"I'm using points, so availability can be a problem. I've got to pull the trigger."

"I know, I know. But I want this to be perfect. It's not every day you travel three thousand six hundred and thirty-four miles for a second date."

"No, but I wish I'd been three times already. You just get prettier and prettier, but I can't get my hands on any of that loveliness."

"If I look better, it's only because I'm getting more sleep. Having Aiden living with Kirsty has made my life easier in every way." She snapped her mouth shut. "I hope he never knows that, but it's true. Sleeping in the tiny bit of space we partitioned off from the master bedroom nine years ago has not been ideal. My parents had to tip-toe through it to get to the toilet, and my father must have a *very* small bladder."

Gillian fought to stop herself from mentioning—again—how Torie's situation drove her crazy. But she'd gotten the clear impression Torie didn't appreciate her sympathies—or suggestions for changing things. She simply wasn't the kind of woman who wanted to dwell on her problems. "Just nine?" Gillian said, focusing on the detail rather than the concept.

"Uh-huh. We shared the bedroom until Aiden was around four. I thought he needed his own space then."

Gillian nodded, hoping the kid appreciated all his aunt had done for him. But if he was a normal kid, he expected everything he got, and still wanted more.

❦ ❦ ❦

Torie walked into her flat a week later to find a square envelope with Gillian's handwriting on it amidst the post. Quickly opening it, she found an invitation to her fortieth birthday party, with a note inside. "I know you can't come, but I'd feel like a jerk not to at least invite the person I'd most like to see. Let's make sure we're in the same city when your fortieth comes up—YEARS from now!" No one was around, so she let herself clutch the envelope to her breast, thrilled to simply have Gillian's handwriting touch her. She knew she was being ridiculously melodramatic, but she was so hungry for intimate contact that she cherished every hint of connection, even via pen.

Later that afternoon, she was at Kirsty's, watching Aiden finish gobbling down his tea. She was standing behind him, and found herself contemplating his awful haircut while reminding herself to take a photo from this angle. One day, she'd be able to produce it to embarrass him in front of his significant other.

Torie wasn't sure which football star he was mimicking, but she assumed the cut looked better in the original incarnation. Aiden's hair was stick-straight, thick, and brick red. It was honestly a lovely color, blending with his fair skin in a very attractive way. But shaving the hair from the crown down was not a good look, especially when you had a cowlick right at the top of your head. The boy looked a little like a rooster, with a hank of hair about four inches long refusing to lie down. The rest of his mop fell forward, hanging in his face, obscuring the features that were just starting to develop their adult shape. He'd turned thirteen the week before, and was still as thin as a rake, as well as a solid inch taller.

Puberty was still in the distance—a distance she wasn't in any hurry for him to cover. In her experience, boys were easier to manage than young men.

The door opened, and Kirsty entered, her nose wrinkling as she sniffed. "What did you make? Any extra?"

Trying not to show her irritation, Torie said, "I made lasagne. Aiden already ate half of that huge baking dish," she said, giving him a playful scowl. "Help yourself before he gets a second wind."

"I'm starving," she said, dropping her things and sitting on the sofa next to her son. Instead of getting a clean plate, she took his and stabbed at a square of food, prying it from the pan. "This looks great," she added, which seemed to be the most effusive "thank you" Kirsty could manage.

Even a glance would reveal they were mother and son, or perhaps older sister and younger brother. While Kirsty's hair had been bleached and dyed a few different shades of pink or blue or lilac over the last few years, when she left it alone it was just a shade or two lighter than Aiden's, and easily as thick. She kept it short, but might have been growing it out. Since she'd been in charge of her own grooming, Kirsty hadn't maintained the same color or cut for more than six months.

She was painfully thin, but Torie could see her adding some weight as she aged. She clearly had more Sinclair than Gunn genes, and they were a hefty breed. However she changed, Torie assumed she'd remain a very attractive woman. Her features were too classically beautiful to let even dull pink hair obscure them, but Torie didn't think her good looks were the lure for men. Since she'd been a very young woman, men had followed Kirsty around like mad. As hard as it had been for her to give up drugs and alcohol, Torie assumed that refraining from being tied to a man for an entire year had been just as difficult.

"Homework," Aiden said as he got up and headed for his room. When they'd decided it was time for Aiden to live with Kirsty, Torie insisted the plan would only work if he had his own space. That required her chipping in an extra hundred pounds a month to help Kirsty move house, but she was certain his privacy was worth the expense. At his door, he paused for a second and met Torie's gaze. "Will you look at it when I'm finished with the history part? You know about English kings, right?"

"A little bit," she said, not acknowledging that anyone could figure out history homework if you just scanned the appropriate chapter for names and dates. "I have to leave by half four, but if you're finished before that, I'm happy to help."

"I know history too," Kirsty called out as Aiden shut the door. "Well, I do," she said, giving Torie a scowl. "I was a keen student when I was his age."

"I was at university then, but mum used to tell me how well you were doing." Neither of them mentioned that happy period only lasted for a few more months. She took in a breath and steeled herself, then started to talk. "This past autumn," she began, "I met someone."

"You did?" Kirsty's eyes grew wide, like Torie was telling her an utterly unbelievable lie.

"I did." She knew she was blushing, but people with her coloring were always caught out when they were nervous or embarrassed. "I'm very fond of her." She let that hang out there for a minute, watching as Kirsty's brow furrowed, then the lightbulb went off in her head.

"You're queer?" she said, her mouth slightly open.

"I am."

Kirsty slapped at her leg as her head fell back against the sofa. She laughed hard for a few seconds, then said, "I used to ask Mum why you didn't have a boyfriend and she always gave me the oddest answers. I knew something was wrong!"

"I don't think it's wrong—"

She waved a hand, dismissing her comment. "Lots of girls fancy other girls now. No one cares. Does Aiden know?"

"Of course not. I'm not going to discuss my love life with a thirteen-year-old."

"Mum and Dad?"

"They know I'm gay, but they don't know about Gillian. I'm going to tell them, though. Tonight, I think."

"You're saying this is serious?" she asked, blinking her dark eyes slowly.

"It is. I'm very serious about her."

Kirsty blinked at her a few times, clearly puzzled. "Then why have you been hiding her?"

"I haven't been hiding her. She went back home. She's the woman I toured with when Aiden stayed with you."

She nodded, then said, "Oh, wait. She's the American?"

"Uh-huh. She lives in Ohio. In the center of the country," she added when Kirsty looked blank.

"Too bad. If you had to pick an American, you should have picked one from California. Or Florida. Wouldn't you love to go to Disney World?"

"I hadn't really thought of it. I'd just like Gillian to be closer."

"Well, I'd like to see Mickey Mouse. If you move there, can we come visit?"

"I'm not moving," she said, astounded that her sister had made that leap. "Gillian's talking about moving here..." She let out a sigh. "But that will require some work. Right now, I just want to see her."

"Then go visit. You don't want to let her get away, Torie. Long distance relationships are hard to hold onto."

"She's planning on coming here this spring. Do you have Aiden's school schedule? I want to make sure we don't overlap with one of his holidays."

"Mmm, I don't know where any of that rubbish is. Just call the school. They'll know."

"They probably will," Torie said, acknowledging to herself that her sister was never going to be on top of the details—no matter how important they were. But at least she hadn't given Torie any trouble about her sexual orientation. *That* was a happy development.

The following Saturday afternoon, Torie only had an hour free, but she wanted to catch Gillian when she knew she'd be able to talk. She dialed her number, then waited for the phone to ring through.

"Hi," she said, with a lot of noise in the background. "Hold on a second. I should set Bluetooth to lower the volume of the sound system when a call comes in, but I keep forgetting to read the manual."

"That's what too much money can do to you," Torie yelled. "My little car has no gadgets, so I need never read a manual unless I forget how to drive, and then I'd probably be past the point that a manual would make any sense to me."

"I like your perspective. It's nutty, but I like it. What's up?"

"You have a little time, right?"

"Uh-huh. I've got over an hour's drive to where I'm picking up a new light fixture for my front porch. I'd love to spend that time with you."

"What do you think of June for your visit? I've been trying to find the perfect time, and I think that's it."

"June?" Just one word, but she could hear the hurt in her voice. "You want to wait until June?"

"Well, yes, but only because of scheduling issues. Aiden's school break is the exact week you suggested for March."

"And he'll be with you? Not your sister?"

"He'll still be living with her," Torie said. "At least I hope he will be. But I'll need to spend my afternoon breaks with him, just like I have been. Thirteen is a difficult age, Gillian. I can't allow him to have too much time alone."

"Great," she said, clearly upset. "That's just great."

Trying to ratchet up the excitement, Torie said, "This can work better. Truly. You said you could take two weeks in the summer, while you'd be limited to one in the spring. Delaying would mean we'd have more time together. And in the summer we've got so much more to do. There's something every weekend. Something good," she stressed. "It's warmer, and the days are longer... Not nearly as crowded as July and August, either. The only problem is the midges, but they're bad all summer."

"What?"

Ooo, that was not a happy tone. "Midges. We have these little fly-like things that are unpleasant. But we have a lot more tourists then, so there are more people for them to bite. They might leave us alone," she lied. "Aiden will still be in school, and I could have enough money saved up to let me take two weeks off without worrying about losing the income."

"Torie," she said, adopting the tone she probably used with her subordinates, "I've made it clear I can help you financially. Just tell me the number, and you won't have to break your neck saving money."

"I don't want it to be like that between us. Why do something that might cause a rift?"

"Helping you out would cause a rift?"

"It might," she insisted. "Money's always a tricky thing. Let's wait until we know each other better to start with that."

"How can we know each other better if all we do is talk on the phone?"

"We do more than that," she soothed. "We write to each other every day. We're talking about important things, Gillian. Things we'd never get to if we were...distracted."

"Great. That's just great. Well, I don't want to *distract* you by my presence, so maybe we should keep this just the way it is. We'll talk on the phone and *imagine* we're in a relationship."

"That's not fair," Torie said. "Not fair at all."

"I've been trying to nail you down about dates for over a week! Are you just playing with me?"

"Never," she said, wounded. "I have never played with you. I'm simply trying to make sure we have as much time together as possible. I thought two weeks would be better than one, but if you disagree, come whenever you want." She tried to stop herself from crying, but knew she'd lose the battle. "I've got to go. Call me after you make your reservations... If you still want to come." Then she hung up, with her stomach a ball of tension. Every couple had communication problems. She knew that. But she wasn't at all happy to have Gillian sounding more like a boss than a girlfriend. That was not, in any way, a good thing.

Torie had a few hours free, so she walked over to her sister's flat to heat up something for Aiden's tea. He was lying on the sofa, watching football, and he barely picked his head up when she entered. "I have food," he said, his attention locked on the match.

"Lovely to see you, too," she said, heading into the kitchen to make sure he had a plate with some veg to go along with the chicken she knew he preferred. The child longed to eat like a caveman. She was almost finished when Kirsty walked in, and Torie let out a sigh of relief when Aiden didn't greet his mother with any more enthusiasm than he'd shown her. That was small-minded of her, but she didn't know how to stop being envious of Kirsty having spent so many years being the parent who showed up only when she chose.

Kirsty entered the kitchen and tossed her bag onto the counter. "Do you ever feel like he'd rather live alone?" She crossed her arms over her chest, looking truly put out.

"He started treating me like my existence annoyed him when he was eleven," Torie said. "I'm still not used to it."

Kirsty took a look toward the sitting room, then lowered her voice. "Can he hear us?"

"I don't think so. Besides, nothing we say interests him," she said, chuckling softly. "What's on your mind?"

"Nothing." She moved over to the bits of food left in the storage containers, picked one up and started to eat the cooked vegetables with her fingers, using them as a scoop. "When will we meet this girlfriend?"

"Oh." Torie stared at her, amazed Kirsty had any interest in her love life. "Well, we've been trying to get our schedules to work together. She'd like to come soon, but I'm trying to convince her to come in June."

Kirsty stopped as if she'd been frozen in space. "*June?* You want to wait until June? Why?"

"So we'd have more time together. She can take two weeks in the summer, but only one in the spring."

Kirsty made a funny noise, one that showed just how stupid she thought Torie's reasoning was. "If you can wait until June, you must not be very keen on her."

"I am!" she said, her voice squeaking. "I can't wait to see her, Kirsty."

"You just said you want to wait. So obviously you *can*. Having second thoughts?"

"No! Not in the least." She stared at her sister, on the verge of spitting out her thoughts. But she kept them to herself, determined to examine them in depth when she had a moment alone. Handing over a plate, she leaned in and kissed Kirsty's cheek. "Aiden's food will be ready in five minutes. I'm going to rush home to get ready for my shift." On the way out, she reached down to ruffle the boy's hair. "Eat your vegetables," she said, almost certain they'd go straight into the bin.

Once she hit the pavement, she stood still and took in some deep, calming breaths. Then she began to walk, clearing her mind of everything except Gillian. It took two blocks to force herself to admit the truth. As much as she tried to convince herself that Gillian was entirely serious about their relationship, she still didn't believe her. It just made no sense that a powerful, professional woman would give up everything—including her country—to move to Scotland to be with her. It wasn't even that Torie had a poor self-image. It all just seemed so improbable, especially for a woman who clearly liked routine and familiarity.

Gillian could proclaim her independence all day long, but she still lived in the place of her birth, she still worked for a man she detested, and she maintained a thin, but enduring bond with her sister and her family. Until Torie was one hundred percent sure of her ability to uproot herself and move to Scotland, she was unwilling to have Gillian's presence throw things into disarray, and having her visit when Aiden was on his school break was inconvenient. Obviously, inconvenience was a long way from disarray, but protecting the little things she had some control over was an instinct she had no idea how to curb.

She'd only been home for five minutes when someone buzzed the door. Her mother let the person into the building, then went to the door. Torie was buttoning up her gilet when a guy appeared at the door, holding an exuberant display of pink and white roses covered with cellophane in his hand. "Torie Gunn?"

She raced over to the door and accepted a form she had to sign. "Thanks," she said, gathering them up, then staring at the flowers as her mother stared at her.

"I know it's not your birthday," she said, laughing nervously. She'd been a little tentative about Gillian, but that's what Torie had expected. Not having a girlfriend for so long had obviously let them think she'd gotten over being gay.

"I think these are apology flowers," she said, smirking. "Gillian and I had a wee fight."

"Did she steal your last scone?" her father asked. "Those must have cost a week's wages."

"She's generous," Torie said, then pulled the card from where it had been stapled. The note was brief, but filled with information. "I'm sorry for being a spoiled baby," it read. "All of my fantasies have revolved around seeing little puffin babies and their orange feet. But I'll catch them next year. Our second date begins June 3rd and ends June 16th. Mark your calendar!"

🌿 🌿 🌿

On Friday evening, January the twentieth, Gillian sat at her kitchen table and carefully fill out form UKM, her application for British citizenship.

She had a wee dram of whisky in a glass, and she took a sip as she worked. Once she'd filed the form, she'd have to wait for confirmation of her good character, then she was in! No tests, not even a fee. Britain was an awesome country... Or was it a group of countries? She'd better figure that out before she pledged her allegiance.

Her head was swirling with thoughts, most of them of Torie. Would she be doing this if not for her? It only took a second to acknowledge she would not. Torie had done all of the research and had plowed her way through the often conflicting regulations regarding immigration, but Gillian could have easily hired someone to do the same. The fact was that she was drawn to Scotland primarily because of Torie. But she also loved the country—at least as much as you could love a place you'd spent fourteen days in. Over time, she was confident her love for the place would equal her love for Torie. But Scotland was going to have to put on quite a show to equal the charms of the prettiest girl in all of... Great Britain? Was that right? She really was going to have to check.

226

CHAPTER NINETEEN

GILLIAN STEPPED ONTO HER FRONT porch on the first Saturday in March, a bright morning chilly enough to let her see her breath. Her biking buddies had decided to drive well over an hour to some town that had both hills and what they swore was a good diner. But adding three hours to the outing just for a greasy breakfast didn't sound like a heck of a lot of fun on a day she had a big party planned—check that. On a day her *sister* had a big party planned. It was in Gillian's honor, but she had very little ownership of it, regarding it with as much anticipation as a work dinner. Nevertheless, she had to look good, so she was going to have a manicure and maybe a facial.

First though, she had to get her engine thrumming, and that meant logging some miles. She and her buddies had only been back outdoors for a week, and she was still rustier than she'd anticipated being. Running on the treadmill had been good for her legs and her lungs, but biking taxed her muscles in ways that running didn't.

Despite her joy at being on her bike, she was grumpy at the prospect of not being able to talk to Torie. She was in Edinburgh, working, and was going to be unavailable for the *entire* day. That development had knocked the smile off Gillian's face as thoroughly as a slap would have.

It was silly to be so invested in the sanctity of their weekend chats, but they truly were the highlights of her week. When you were rabidly interested in a woman who lived three thousand six hundred and thirty-four miles away, every opportunity to see her face and hear her voice was a precious one.

After just an hour of riding around town, she was bored. Maybe she was one of those people who needed to be pushed to really put in the effort. But it was almost her birthday, her girlfriend was ridiculously far away, and they weren't going to see each other for another three months. That was a set of circumstances that only a cinnamon sugar brioche could help relieve. Luckily, she could get one at an Italian Village cafe she loved, and riding there would probably burn off another ten or fifteen calories. The other several hundred she would consume would just have to hang around.

❧ ❧ ❧

Gillian couldn't pin down exactly when her party had gotten out of control, but it definitely had. Her original birthday plan had been to have Kara and her family over, have some restaurant deliver something delicious, and drink enough not to mind turning forty. But somehow she was now driving to her sister's house, where a weird mix of relatives, friends, and co-workers were going to fete her. She still wasn't sure how so many of her co-workers had gotten onto the list, but when Ron and her direct reports all mentioned seeing her at the party on Saturday, the die had been cast. Amanda was one of those people who believed co-workers should naturally be friends, so she'd probably called one of her buddies in Channing Brothers' HR department and gotten a list of names and email addresses. HR people were surprisingly cunning. She'd have to remind Torie of this element of Amanda's personality the next time she suggested Gillian confide in her about their relationship. Every HR person in Columbus would know Gillian was a lesbian by the close of business.

The party was supposed to start at six, so Gillian had decided to arrive at five, just in case Amanda needed any help. But by the time she slowly passed the house and saw that cars were jammed next to each other for a full block, she knew this was going to be a much bigger shindig than she'd wanted.

Amanda answered the door, cool, calm and composed. "It's the birthday girl!" She leaned over and kissed Gillian's cheek, adding a vaguely awkward hug. "Why so early?"

"I thought you might need help."

"Everything is under control," Amanda said, giving off her usual air of professional competence. "Come on in and have a drink. The bartender came up with a special one just for you. He's calling it The Peak. Vodka, elderflower and grapefruit juice. You'll love it."

"The Peak?" she asked, entering the house and letting her coat fall from her shoulders.

"Uh-huh. You're not over the hill, you're at the peak."

"Mmm. Yeah. That's cute." Nowhere to go but down. Really cute.

"Wow! Nice dress," Amanda said, letting her gaze trail from Gillian's shoulders to her knees.

The dress was special, if she did say so herself. A sparkling silver sheath, sleeveless, ending just above the knee. It was flashier than anything she'd ever owned, but the saleswoman had almost forced her to buy it. When a stranger who worked on commission urged you to buy a dress less expensive than the one you were leaning toward, there was no reason not to trust her.

"Did you just buy that?"

"Had to. I couldn't wear something I normally wear to work, so I splurged. Now I'm set for the next wedding I'm invited to." She wouldn't have had to buy a dress at all if Amanda hadn't decreed cocktail party attire, but it was churlish to complain about the dress code when your sister had put so much work into throwing you a party.

"I don't think I've ever seen you in something so…sexy," Amanda said, a puzzled grin on her face. "You should dress like that more often."

"Now that I'm forty, I'm going to show a whole new me. Look out," she growled, giving her sister a squeeze on the shoulder as she moved past to get her hands on that drink.

It was strange being in the odd mix, and even stranger to see people from work, especially the women, dressed for a semi-formal event. Gillian kept feeling some weird form of cognitive dissonance when she'd catch sight of a co-worker who normally wore only dark business suits slugging down a drink while revealing generous breasts that had been completely hidden at the office.

As she scooted along the edge of the crowd, Gillian reflected on the messages she'd been getting all night. People acted like she was at the top of a steep hill and was going to start rolling down at an alarming rate, picking up speed before she crashed into a wall.

Before tonight, she hadn't paid a lot of attention to her age, but maybe that had been a mistake. The guys who worked for her had seemed almost gleeful when they'd complimented her on how well she'd hidden her age, even though she'd never done that purposefully. Now that they knew she was seven years older than the eldest of them, they'd be sharpening their knives, trying to find ways to convince the higher-ups that they had the fresh, new, i.e. *young* ideas. Working for a big corporation was just like being a lion on the Serengeti. You spent every minute posturing, roaring, or looking for weaknesses in potential prey. And now the hungry young males of the pride thought she was vulnerable. *Super.*

Amanda knew none of Gillian's biking friends, not to mention anyone from her smallish lesbian roster. That meant the only true friend Gillian could pull aside and relax with was Kara. She'd left her older kids with a sitter, but the baby was such a handful she tended to bring him along whenever possible. Given Amanda's own kids had been sent to their grandparents' for the night, it was really pretty gutsy of Kara to bring the baby along without asking first. But that was her way. She did what she wanted, apologized when she needed to, and rarely suffered any consequences from her temerity. Gillian's kind of woman.

To find her, she looked for a hole in the crowd, knowing no one would want to get too close to a baby who could easily ruin your nice clothing.

"Ah-ha!" she said when she caught up to them, off in a corner, alone. Eli was sitting on the floor, patiently pulling books from Amanda's perfectly arranged floor-to-ceiling bookcases, while Kara sat on a folding chair and idly observed him, clearly bored.

Gillian squatted down, but didn't reach for the baby, assuming he was covered with something sticky. "I knew I'd find you if I searched for the marginal neighborhoods." The baby looked up at her and she reached over and tugged at his little bow tie. "Cute outfit. I've never seen him in a tie." Leaning over a little further, she cooed, "Did my sister guilt trip even you into complying with her dumb cocktail party dress requirement?"

"We borrowed the velvet vest and pants from a friend whose baby was in a wedding. I bought the white shirt and tie," Kara said. "Even your sister couldn't convince me to buy a dark suit for a baby." She flicked two fingers onto Gillian's butt. "Stand up and let me see you."

Gillian did, performing a quick pirouette. "I'm going for sexy senior citizen."

"God damn, G, are you trying to get lucky? You look *super* hot!"

"Thank you, thank you," she said, having gotten used to people staring at her like she'd revealed an entirely new side of her personality. "You're not so bad yourself." She held her hand out and guided Kara to her feet.

Kara always read as taller than she really was. Something about the way she stood made her look close to Gillian's height, even though she was only about five foot six.

Tonight, she wore very high heels, making them about level, given Gillian's sparkly ballet flats. Her fine blonde hair was done up in a chignon, exposing her pale, flawless skin, much of it exposed by the plunging neckline of her navy-blue velour dress. "I'm glad you're over here in the corner. Ben would be fighting to keep the guys off you."

She stood and stretched until she was on her tip-toes. "Delusions welcomed. Have you seen my alleged husband? We're supposed to trade-off, and he's way overdue for his shift."

"I saw him a while ago, but I couldn't get his attention. A bunch of hot women were draped all over him, so I had trouble..." She trailed off as she pointed in a vague direction.

"Funny. Hilarious, even. Why don't you watch the baby for a while? He misses you."

"Yeah, I'm really thinking about doing that," she said, backing up and waving as she went. "You have the best ideas!"

Gillian had been ignoring her boss the entire evening, but it was after nine, and she was running out of excuses. He was the center of attention in the corner by the entryway, holding court for everyone below his level, all of his minions reveling in his dominance.

She took a single step toward him, then felt a hand settle onto her waist. Her instinct was to slap it off, but, given the guest list, she had to be sensitive to slighting anyone. She'd never liked having co-workers touch her, but truly hated it when someone touched any intimate part—which in her view was anything other than a hand or an arm.

Turning to see who'd broached her personal space, her mouth dropped open when Torie appeared in front of her.

Her brain was working hard to process Torie's presence, but it simply made no sense. Then she reached out and hugged her, firmly, but briefly. "What are you doing here?" she asked, so stunned she felt a little wobbly.

"You invited me," she said, smiling. "I brought the invitation in case anyone tried to bar the door."

Gillian's hands were on her arms, and she moved back a step to take her in. She looked so pretty it was almost too much to bear. Tonight's gilet was black velvet, and probably wasn't a gilet at all, given that it covered her almost to her thighs. It had a stand-up collar, and decorative frogs holding it closed. Very fancy. Beneath it, Torie wore wide-legged black velvet slacks and simple black pumps, which combined to make her look very tall, and very slim. Some gold jewelry added a little elegance, and a small, silk Gunn clan tartan scarf tied at the neck made her look as Scottish as a bunch of heather.

"I am so happy to see you," Gillian said, her heart beating like a drum. "Can I…" She looked around and spied Kara, still in the corner with Eli. "Can I park you somewhere for a few minutes while I pay my respects to my boss? He looks like he's about to leave and I—"

Torie's radiant smile disappeared in the blink of an eye. "*Park* me somewhere?"

"I don't mean that like it sounded," she rushed to say. "I just *have* to speak with him. Just for a minute," she added, knowing this wasn't coming off well at all. "Kara's my only real friend here, and I guarantee she's the only person you'll like. Once I'm finished, I can relax and concentrate on you."

"If this is…" She took in a long breath. "If you'd rather I wasn't here…"

Now that Gillian really looked at her, Torie had the appearance of a woman who'd been up for a very, very long time. "Did you fly all night?"

"I left work at one in the morning, took the train to Edinburgh, then sat around the airport until my six a.m. flight. I've been in the air, or wandering around airports in Brussels and Washington, DC ever since. I'm *so* tired," she sighed.

"Come on." Gillian said as she put a hand on her lower back to guide her over to Kara. "I'll get you a drink and you can sit down for a little while. Then we'll get out of here." She gave her another glance. "Is that okay?"

"I see I should have told you I was coming." She bit at her lip for a second. "But I wanted to surprise you."

Leaning over so she could speak softly, Gillian whispered, "You're the best surprise I could have ever hoped for. And you'd better have an open-ended ticket, because I'm not letting you leave."

"Wednesday night," she said, offering a ghost of a smile. "From New York. That's where you'll be, right?"

"Right." She nodded. "Oh! You know I'm going to New York tomorrow! You're so smart," she added. Eli looked up from ripping the pages out of one of Amanda's home decorating magazines, then threw the wrinkled pages at Gillian, letting out a whoop of glee.

"Good boy," she said, leaning over to pet his head. "Kara, I am thrilled to introduce you to Torie Gunn. Torie, this is my oldest and dearest friend, Kara Hale."

As Kara stood to extend her hand, she gave Gillian a quick glance, clearly puzzled. "Is this a surprise?"

"A big one. A *great* one," she added. A presence at her arm made her turn. "Amanda," she said, utterly speechless for a few very long seconds. "Look who came all the way from Scotland to surprise me." Both her voice and her hands were shaking, but she kept going. "This is Torie Gunn, the woman who showed me around on my vacation."

Clearly puzzled, but too smooth to make a point of it, Amanda extended her hand and gave Torie one of her usual overly enthusiastic hand-clasps. "Showed you around?" she said, turning back to Gillian.

"I hired Torie as a guide. We spent…" Oh, boy, this was going to sound dumb. "We were together for most of my trip."

"Most of your trip?" Amanda's eyebrows nearly touched her hairline. Turning back to Torie, she blinked a few times, clearly puzzled. "And you came all this way for the party?"

"I did," Torie said. Gillian wasn't sure if she did this unconsciously, but her accent was stronger than usual. "Gillian invited me to the party, probably just to be polite, but it seemed like a fantastic opportunity to visit America. I've never been."

"Really? You've never been to America?"

"I have not," Torie said, sounding like she should have had a set of bagpipes slung over a shoulder. "Since I knew a local who was having a major event, I used that as a spur to make the trip."

"Are you staying long?"

"No, no, I'm leaving tomorrow to spend some time in New York."

"Oh," Amanda said, nodding like this was starting to make sense. "Gillian can give you some ideas of things to see. She goes there all the time."

Thank the good lord she hadn't told her sister she was going tomorrow. That would have required a whole explanation she wasn't in the mood to give.

"I'll make sure to get a list," Torie said. Then she squatted down and got on Eli's level. "Who's this little loon?"

Gillian took her sister's arm and gave it a tug. "Have you met my boss?"

"You haven't introduced me to a soul," she said, clearly hurt. "Is he the handsome guy near the front door?"

"That's him," Gillian said. "Ron Hawkins. Let's go say hello before he takes off."

"I feel awful that I haven't done the proper hostess duty to introduce everyone, but I don't know who half of these people are. I thought you'd do that…"

"Let's remedy that right now." As they moved away, Gillian gave Torie a pleading look, telepathically begging her not to be angry.

Torie looked up when a hand settled onto her shoulder. "She doesn't do well with surprises," Kara said gently. "G likes to know exactly what's coming, and when. If she doesn't…" She shrugged. "She gets thrown for a loop."

As Torie started to rise, the baby's hands shot into the air, begging to be picked up. She swept him into her arms and placed him on her hip, jiggling him until he started to laugh. "Has Gillian told you about…" She froze for a second. "That we've kept in touch?"

"I know all about you, Torie. But now I'm pissed because she obviously hasn't told you about me!" She started to laugh. "Every part of her life is segmented. Work, family, gym, biking, one or two lesbians. It's very rare to get any crossover. I think this is the third time I've seen Amanda since G and I were in college."

"She talks about you all of the time, Kara. She's just not mentioned talking about us." Her gaze traveled across the crowded room to land on Gillian, who stood with a small clique. She was clearly trying to be charming, wearing a high-wattage smile and seeming a little larger-than-life. "I suppose I've made a mess of things by coming without telling her. I simply thought..." She took in a breath, determined not to cry. Studying the baby helped take her mind off things, especially when he grabbed her scarf and gave it a stout yank.

"Stop that," Kara said, pushing his hands away. "He'll choke you if he gets a good hold." She tapped him on his cute little nose. "He's my third, and he's somehow integrated all of the tricks the first two played and amplified them. He's some kind of cyborg," she said, rolling her eyes. "But we love him, don't we?" she added in baby sing-song. Placing her hands over his ears, she whispered, "Most of the time."

"I can relate. I'm helping to raise my sister's—"

"Thirteen-year-old son, Aiden. G talks about you and everyone you're connected to so much it's kind of sickening," she said, chuckling.

"She certainly didn't look happy to see me. Well, she seemed happy for a second, then she looked like a fox caught in a snare. That wasn't what I was going for when I spent over two weeks pay to come."

"It'll be fine," Kara promised. "When you have her alone, she'll be herself. It's just all of these people that throw her off her game."

"Aren't these people her family? Her friends? Her co-workers? They're not a bunch of strangers off the street, are they?"

"For Gillian, they might as well be," Kara said, her smile fading away.

After leaping over hurdles that would have easily stopped a lesser woman, Gillian found Torie's coat, then her own, then grasped Torie's suitcase and headed for the back door. "We can sneak out and not have to spend the next half hour saying goodbye," she said quietly. "I'll apologize to my sister tomorrow."

Torie just nodded, and stayed close. Since Gillian had been early, she'd only had to park a few hundred yards away. Tempted to grasp Torie's hand, she fought the urge and walked quickly, desperate to get to her car. As they approached, soft pools of light surrounded the side mirrors and door handles.

"Your car knows you're coming?" Torie asked. She got closer and peered at the grill. "Porsche?" An eyebrow lifted in question.

"An old friend of my dad's owns a dealership. He offered me a deal too good to pass up." When Torie got in, Gillian said, "In the light, you're going to see why I got a discount. It's kinda…purple," she said, chuckling.

Torie just gazed at her, giving her the same slightly distant look she'd shown each time their eyes had met. Gillian started talking, her usual when she was stressed. "Um, I know I've been all over the place tonight, but I don't handle myself well when I'm surprised. That's no slam on you," she stressed. "I'm stupendously glad you're here. I just… I know I'm not acting like myself, but I'll be fine once we're at my house."

"It's fine, Gillian. I'm awfully tired. We'll both feel better in the morning."

"Did you sleep on the plane?" she asked as she hit a button and the car's quiet engine thrummed to life.

"Not much. I was awfully close to the bathroom."

She let out a sigh. "Why didn't you tell me you were coming? I could have gotten you upgraded at the very least, plus I wouldn't have acted so weird. I really get flustered by surprises," she stressed.

"I've clearly gotten that message," Torie said, with a definite edge creeping into her voice. "It's a bit late for that, isn't it?"

Furious with herself for bungling every part of the evening, Gillian stepped sharply on the accelerator, sending the car into its usual cat-like stride. The wheels squealed as she made two quick turns, entering a street without a single car parked on the pavement, guaranteeing no one from the party would walk by. She pulled over and put the car into park. "Could we start over? Let me show you how glad I am that you're here." She started to reach for Torie, but a hand rose, clearly signaling "stop."

"I'd rather start over when we get to your house. We're too old to sit in a car and grope each other."

"I wasn't planning on groping you," Gillian said, sighing in defeat. "I just wanted a kiss." She put the car into drive and took off again, gliding past her sister's house one more time. After punching the accelerator, they flew down the wide, winding street, not slowing until they reached an intersection with a red light.

She was about to say something when Torie spoke up. "All of these months, you've been the one asking the questions. But I think I've got one that isn't in your book."

Gillian could tell this wasn't going to be good, but she pasted on a smile and met Torie's eyes briefly. "Let me have it."

"I'd really like to know how you define yourself."

"What does that mean?"

"What's your brand integrity? You're always talking about that for your products. What's yours?"

As Gillian opened her mouth, Torie held her hand up again. "Not now. I'd really like you to think about it. Mull it over." Her voice grew soft and low. "This is important, Gillian. Honestly give it some thought."

Her house was only about six miles away, but it seemed like they'd driven around the world—twice. The silence was deafening, and all Gillian could do was repeat Torie's question in her head, again and again. When she pulled into the driveway, she could hear a quiet sound, perhaps some slight bit of approval, come from Torie.

"I wouldn't have expected this," she said quietly. "Even though I knew you lived in a house, I've only pictured you in a modern flat, high up in a tower, with an expansive view."

"That's not me," she said, not trusting herself to speak much more.

She got Torie's suitcase, then carried it up the flagstone path so they could enter via the front door. When she unlocked the door, it banged into her bike, and she held it open so Torie could enter in front of her. Then she pressed the control panel, and the rooms were slowly bathed in a warm, flattering light.

"How did that happen?" Torie asked. "One button did that?"

"Different sections are on separate dimmers. I had knob and tube wiring when I moved in, so I had to have a new panel installed. I upgraded everything as long as I had the walls torn open."

"That sounds like you," Torie said, still not revealing anything close to a smile.

Gillian parked the suitcase by the stairs, then took Torie's coat and hung it, along with her own, on the hooks by the door. When she went back into the living room, Torie was standing by the fireplace, looking at the framed photo of the Broch of Birsay that she'd sent for Christmas, along with a photo of herself. Gillian had sent it to a service to have it professionally adjusted to look like it had been taken by a pro, then had it framed to match the color of Torie's gilet that day. Standing next to her, Gillian was unsure if she should be the one to try to break the ice, or let Torie take the lead.

"Am I important to you?" Torie finally asked.

"God, yes!" She moved in front of her and grasped her arms firmly. Their eyes met and she stared into them for a few long seconds. "I've called or written to you every single day for over three months! I was so upset when you didn't want me to visit in the spring that I…" She let out a breath. "I didn't know what to do. I was so hurt."

"I merely asked you to delay, Gillian, and I had good reasons for why that made sense." She stared at her hotly. "Now imagine how you'd feel if you'd come anyway, and I parked you in the corner for twenty minutes while I laughed it up with my co-workers. Then, to add insult to injury, I didn't properly introduce you to my sister, or her husband, or my other relatives." She grasped Gillian's shoulders and gave her a shake. "Which is worse?"

"You don't understand! Those people aren't my friends. Do you honestly think I'd throw a party for fifty people and make them dress up like they were going to the opera? This wasn't for me, Torie. It just wasn't. I was playing a part and you…" She took in a breath and said exactly what she felt. "You appeared on stage, but you didn't have a scripted role. I'm sorry, but I couldn't write one for you on such short notice."

Torie closed her eyes and let out a long breath. Her voice was filled with fatigue when she said, "I don't know how long it's been since I slept, but I do know I can't think straight. Can we talk about this in the morning?"

Gillian nodded, then headed for the stairs. "I assume you want to sleep in the guest room?" she asked as she started up with Torie's suitcase in her hand. "Given we haven't even kissed…"

When they got to the top of the stairs, Torie grasped her hand and pulled her to a stop. "I got the very clear message that you didn't want to kiss me at the party. And I'm sorry, but it makes me feel cheap to grapple in a dark car." She looked down at the floor for a few seconds. "I know we've gotten off to a bad start, but I promise I'll be able to look at this with fresh eyes in the morning."

"All right. Do you have your flight information for New York? I'd like to sit together if possible."

"Of course." She took her bag from her shoulder and handed it over. "It's in here. I'm too tired to look through the papers."

"I'll have to change some things around," Gillian said, after finding the paper and scanning the details. "Is that all right?"

"Just don't make me actually have to sit *in* the toilet," she said, following along when Gillian headed for the guest room. "That's the only way my seat could have been worse."

That was kind of funny, but Gillian couldn't manage a laugh. She flicked the switch and the bedroom and bath both lit up. "There's a blanket and a down comforter on the bed. Just throw what you don't want onto the floor." She pointed to the bath. "Fresh towels are on the sink. There's also a kit with toothpaste and a new brush and floss and—"

"May I have a kiss?" Torie said after clapping a hand over Gillian's mouth. "I have about two minutes of life left in me, and I'd like to spend them getting reacquainted."

Relieved beyond measure, Gillian took her in her arms and held her tightly for long seconds, burying her face in her hair, and taking in her scent. "I've missed you so much," she whispered.

"I have too." Then she tilted her head back, and their eyes met. "I've missed you desperately, Gillian. You can't know how much."

Their lips met and molded into each other. The supple, sensuous warmth of Torie's mouth was a delightful sensation that Gillian was certain she'd never get enough of. Then Torie's gentle hand was on her cheek, patting it. "We'll talk in the morning. Wake me whenever you want. Left to my own devices, I'll sleep for thirty hours."

"I will," she said, then stepped back, forcing her hands to let go. As Gillian turned to leave, Torie put a hand on her shoulder and held her still. Then warm lips caressed her ear. "When my eyes landed on you tonight, I knew that I'd never seen a more beautiful woman. You quite literally took my breath away."

Shyly, Gillian turned and smiled. "Thanks. I…" She started to get into how she came to wear something so out of the ordinary, but Torie didn't need to know all of the silly details. Her instinct was to repay the compliment, still thoroughly charmed by how pretty Torie looked. But that would sound like she was just parroting her, and she didn't want to do that. "Thank you," she finally said, keeping it simple. Then she dimmed the lights and walked out, flinching when the door clicked closed behind her.

🌿 🌿 🌿

Gillian started when the covers were pulled from her body and a wave of cold air hit her. Then she sighed as Torie snuggled up behind her and tucked an arm around her waist. "I had to get up to use the toilet, and it seemed awfully lonely way over there," she murmured. "Back to sleep."

Dawn was just breaking, her usual time to get up, but Gillian had been awake for hours, replaying the events of the interminable night. Now, with Torie's body, if not her emotions, in sync with her own, a sense of sleepy contentment thrummed through her, relaxing her so thoroughly that she was asleep before she had a minute to start ruminating again.

CHAPTER TWENTY

WHEN GILLIAN WOKE, THE SUN was surprisingly high in the sky. Her eyes blinked open to find Torie gazing at her. Then her mouth slid into a smile.

"I've been playing with your hair, hoping to wake you, but trying not to get caught."

"I don't think I felt that," Gillian said, yawning.

"You're a very sound sleeper. Still tired?"

"Very." She stuck her arms out and shivered. "But we should get up. We've got a one o'clock flight."

"It's not quite nine."

"Nine!" Gillian flew into a sitting position. "I had to book tickets out of Cleveland to get seats together. We've got to leave in the next ten minutes!" Her feet hit the floor, then she ran to her closet. "I'm not packed."

Torie got up with a more leisurely attitude. "I haven't unpacked, so I just have to wash up. Can I help?"

"Just get ready. I can handle myself."

❧ ❧ ❧

Gillian was a woman of her word. Ten minutes later, she carried her suitcase down the stairs, looking remarkably good for a woman who couldn't possibly have bathed properly. A marine blue sweater covered a white turtleneck, and jeans so dark they looked black hugged her long, lean legs. A pair of socks that perfectly matched the blue of her sweater were covered by tasseled loafers, as shiny as they'd been the day they were purchased.

"I can't believe you made it," Torie said.

"I have to run for planes a lot. You get used to doing everything in double-time." She grabbed the lighthouse fob that held her keys, then picked up her bag as she stepped onto the wide, homely, covered porch. Torie followed, and as Gillian pulled the door closed she said, "We can stop for coffee, but we've really got to move." She handed Torie her phone. "I've got an app to make a to-go order. Can you figure it out? You can have tea if you'd rather. And the oatmeal, I mean porridge, isn't bad."

"I know that you call it oatmeal. Remember, I've spent a lot of years watching American telly."

They got into the car, and Gillian nearly flew down the drive. Torie was tempted to ask her to slow down and relax, but she'd never found it effective to request that someone be less tense. So she tried to distract herself by finding the app for the coffee giant and ordering their breakfast. If it had been her car, no one would *ever* eat in it, but it wasn't, so Torie ordered herself an oatmeal to go along with her tea. If Gillian didn't mind, there was no sense in going hungry. Or hungrier, given food had largely been missing at the party. Kara had insisted it had been excellent, but had disappeared at nine on the dot. Given the invitation stated the party was from six to ten, that was clearly intentional. Gillian's sister ran a tight ship.

Gillian ran into the shop, leaving Torie to watch the car, whose engine continued to idle menacingly. In moments, she was back, eyes alert, her instructions crisp and precise. "Don't worry about the upholstery. It's leather. If you spill, it won't hurt it."

"No food for you?"

"I need to concentrate," she said, then proceeded to do just that as she backed up quickly and directed the car to head out—in a hurry.

Even though they had two hours to chat, a real conversation wasn't possible. While the traffic was light for a major city, it was heavier than Torie would have expected. Gillian acted like she was playing chess, always plotting a move, trying to take a pawn to position herself to make her next gambit. Her pale eyes surveyed both lanes in front of her, taking advantage of every inattentive motorist to pass, her fingers gripping and releasing the wheel every few seconds.

To avoid distracting her, Torie surveyed the scenery. It was *nothing* like she'd expected. She'd studied the map thoroughly, and had seen that Columbus was located close to some very large cities. In her imagination, the whole area would look like she pictured New York, dense and urban and teeming with people. But minutes after leaving Columbus, they were on a highway that ran through farmland. Rich, fertile farmland, from the looks of it. Gentle, rolling hills, with cattle in some of the fields, an occasional barn, and surprisingly nice, surprisingly large homes every few miles. There were some run-down, seemingly abandoned farmhouses, too, but they were the exception. Perhaps they belonged to the people with the sprawling homes, and costs were prohibitive to demolish them. Given that nature would do that eventually, they might have been playing a waiting game.

The overall impression Torie got was that this was excellent farmland, and the people who owned it had done well for themselves. Of course, if you couldn't grow something worthwhile on land this rich, this free of impediments, you weren't much of a farmer. She hadn't seen this much arable land in all of Scotland, and they'd only been driving for a half hour.

"The landscape is beautiful," she heard herself say.

Gillian gave her a quick glance. "I guess it is. This is near where my dad grew up."

"On a farm?"

"Kind of. They lived on good farmland, but my grandfather didn't work it. He'd had enough of that when he was a kid." She met Torie's gaze again. "My grandfather found work in Akron as a salesman. He did well," she said, probably an understatement. "New Philly's the town. You'll see the sign."

Torie nodded, finding that an odd name, but no odder than Drumnadrochit, she supposed.

Gillian kept her laser-like focus for the entirety of the trip, talking little, ignoring the music Torie figured out how to play on the completely non-intuitive stereo system. She would have lost her mind if she'd had a car with so many lights and sensors and switches and toggles. But Gillian seemed very comfortable with the machine, talking to it like it was a human, directing it to call the airline, then sorting through layer after layer of computer prompts to finally confirm their flight was on time.

When the big green sign that hovered above the highway decreed that Cleveland was only twenty miles away, Gillian relaxed noticeably. She gave Torie a smile and said, "We're in good shape. We won't be able to stop and use the bathroom, but we'll make it."

"I never had a doubt," she said, finding that to be true. Gillian seemed so in control it was hard to imagine she would fail at her goal. But just a few miles later, they slowed to a crawl, then stopped. They were on a slight rise, and Gillian put the car in park, got out and stared into the distance, shielding her eyes with a hand. When she got back in, she said, "I'm going to have to change my prediction. We're in bad shape, and we're not going to make it."

Torie sat up tall, her pulse starting to race. "What does that mean?"

"Not much." She pressed a button and let her seat recline a few degrees, then put her hands behind her head and stretched out. "They'll put us on the next flight. I think there's a two o'clock."

Torie stared at her, amazed. How could someone be so focused, so intent on making a goal, then switch off that intensity in a matter of seconds? She would have thought Gillian would curse or drive on the shoulder to get past whatever the trouble was, but she was as passive as could be. Utterly calm.

"You're not upset?"

"Upset?" She raised an eyebrow. "Why would I be upset? All you can do is your best." Her relaxed grin made her look like she'd just woken up. "I gave it everything I had. After that, it's out of my hands."

That was the key. Gillian was as determined as anyone she'd ever met. She drove herself hard. But once she'd done that—she let go. It was actually probably the best way to be. Torie put her hand on Gillian's leg, finding the muscles loose and pliable. That was odd, but actually kind of nice. It would probably be utterly annoying to be with someone who lost her mind every time circumstances beyond her control messed with her plans. She patted Gillian's leg again and got a pleased smile in return.

"Want to hear my 'stuck in traffic' playlist?" she asked. "A solid hour of songs guaranteed to lower your blood pressure."

"I would love to," Torie said, perfectly happy to sit in a lovely car and listen to a stereo a hundred times better than any she'd ever owned.

❦ ❦ ❦

Gillian spoke to her phone through the stereo. "Play 'Traffic Sucks.'" She removed her seatbelt, then turned so her back was resting against the door. "Want to talk about last night?"

"I suppose we have to. Will you start?"

"Sure. I've got one thing I need to clear up first." She narrowed her eyes. "Did I see a tattoo on your arm? If so, why didn't I know you had one?"

Torie smiled at her. "Who has rendered the opinion I have only one?"

"You have more?" Her heart started to race. She wasn't a big fan of tattoos, but she didn't mind a few. What if Torie was covered—

"I only have the one." She patted herself on the upper arm. "I have on too many layers to show you now, but I might be convinced to bare my arm for you later."

"You're not going to tell me what it is?"

"I don't think I will," she said, clearly enjoying toying with Gillian. "When you see it clearly, you'll know. If you were paying attention, that is."

"Well, tomorrow's my real birthday. That would make a nice present. Seeing your arm, that is. I don't want to ask for too much."

"Consider your wish granted. About last night...?"

"Right." She forced herself to focus for a minute, then said, "I know I hurt your feelings by not introducing you around, but you hurt mine too."

"How's that?"

"Implying that I was dishonest or had poor morals was a low blow, Torie. I was up for hours trying to figure out what I'd done to make you say that."

"Pardon?" She blinked slowly, clearly confused. "What could you possibly be referring to?"

"Your question. The one you asked when we were in the car."

"My question…"

"I *have* integrity. And to have you imply I don't was—"

"Oh, God, that's not what I meant," she said, cutting her off. "I was asking how you think of yourself—your *whole* self. How you integrate all of the parts of you. Isn't that what you mean when you talk about brand integrity?"

"Jesus," she said, relief flooding her. "I was beside myself! I thought you were one of those people who fought dirty, and I was *not* looking forward to working through that."

"I don't think I fight dirty, but I do like to work things out when they bother me. I'm concerned," she said softly. "Kara says you have almost no overlap between the different segments of your life."

"That's why they're called segments, right?" She stared at Torie for a second, certain she wasn't understanding the question properly.

"I don't think so. There was no reason in the world you couldn't introduce me to your family, your friends, your co-workers. I wasn't going to grab you and kiss you in front of them. I know you like to keep your private life private."

"I know you're upset," Gillian said, carefully trying to unwind this. "But I don't want *anyone* to know about us at this point. I don't want to answer the questions, Torie. It's not worth it."

Her expression hardened. "That sounds like you're saying *I'm* not worth it."

"Not true! Not true!" she emphasized, trying to make sure Torie understood her. "The only person at that party that I'm completely open with is Kara. Everyone else has an agenda. The more I reveal, the more they can use the information against me."

"Your family uses information against you?"

"They might. If I told my sister about you to *any* degree she'd start hunting for information. Once she had it, she'd accidentally share it with one of her buddies at Channing Brothers, and it would spread like wildfire. My sister is *relentless*. She's one of those people who has to know every detail. Honestly, she acts like a private detective half of the time. Until you and I are certain we're going to be together permanently, I don't want to bring her into the discussion."

"That's what you're aiming for?" Torie asked, clearly skeptical.

"Of course!" She reached down and toggled her seat until she was fully upright. "Haven't I given you every indication that I'm completely serious about us?"

"Yes, but—"

"But nothing! I'm going to be a citizen soon. Would I do that if I wasn't serious?"

"Well, no—"

"I told you from the first that I wasn't playing around. I want a partner. A wife," she added, swallowing around her nervousness at saying the word. "If I'd just wanted someone to play around with, I could have that in a matter of minutes with a dating app. I want *more*."

"You've…used dating apps?" Torie asked, her eyes blinking slowly.

Oh, oh. "I don't actually want to talk about what we did before we met each other. I'm not interested in your past. I'm interested in your future. Your future with *me*."

"All right," she said, nodding warily. "But you'd tell me if you have some crazy, stalker ex-girlfriends, wouldn't you? I don't want some woman to come after me with a knife."

"No crazy ex-girlfriends," Gillian said, immensely glad that was the truth. "I haven't done anything I'm ashamed of. And I've tried very hard to never hurt anyone if I could possibly avoid it."

"If that's true, I think we'll be fine."

"I think so too." She slid her hand over and grasped Torie's. "Do you still have that rule about not kissing in the car?"

"I do," she said. "I feel sleazy in a car, lurking about in the shadows. I'm afraid you're going to have to wait until you get me alone." She revealed a charmingly sexy smile. "I hope we're sharing a room."

"That was my plan," Gillian said. She leaned over until her lips were just a few millimeters from Torie's. "I can't wait."

❦ ❦ ❦

As soon as they were on the plane, a surprisingly small one, Gillian pulled her computer from the stylish leather-trimmed nylon bag that fit atop her rolling suitcase. As it powered up, she said, "I didn't know I was going to have a traveling companion, so I put off doing a few things I have to finish for tomorrow. If I get them done now, I won't have to worry about them again."

"Go right ahead. I can catch up on some sleep."

"I've got a perfectly good shoulder if you'd like to use it." Her hand went into her bag again and emerged with something that looked like a scarf. "This is the best travel gadget I've ever bought." She unwrapped the scarf, then placed it against Torie's neck.

"It's rigid," she said, surprised.

"It is. Now I'll wrap it around you, and it'll keep the cold air off your neck while it's supporting your head."

Torie did her best to close her eyes and shut off her mind, but it wasn't easy. Their long, tense drive had thoroughly keyed her up. Her gaze kept drifting to Gillian's computer, but she was unable to see a thing. "Do you have x-ray vision?" she finally asked. "It's like I'm looking through some kind of murky haze."

"It's a privacy screen." She turned her computer, and when Torie looked directly at it, it was darker than it should have been, but otherwise sharp. "Industrial espionage," she whispered. "We're very paranoid about our little secrets."

"You keep the recipe for your soap right on that machine?"

She was still smiling when she said, "I have a rough idea of what's in laundry detergent, but I couldn't whip a batch of it up. I'm more worried about someone seeing the details of a new marketing campaign, or when we're going to change the label, or…" She leaned all the way over and barely whispered, "unveil our new instant-pour cap. Very hush-hush," she said, seemingly serious.

Torie patted her leg and said, "Your secrets are safe with me." It was going to take some time to get used to the corporate world. And probably even longer to train herself not to laugh at what Gillian obviously considered important elements of her job. Selling soap was clearly a very serious business.

The day was clear and bright, and as they descended to an altitude that let them break through the clouds, Torie could start to see the contours of the land. Surprised once again, she saw what looked to be a lot of golf courses. Long, undulating green stripes, then a few intersecting circles of big homes, then a little lake or a meandering stream, then another golf course. Why did these people flock to Scotland for golf? All they had to do was walk out the front door and set a ball on a tee!

Gillian was still working, her nimble fingers never stopping as they typed furiously on her laptop. She'd spread out, taking up some of Torie's space with complicated-looking spreadsheets that she'd used different colored highlighters to notate. Back and forth she'd go, grasping one report, checking something, then tossing it aside to find another.

Torie was desperate to talk to her, to share her observations, to ask questions about where they were. But Gillian was clearly very busy, and any work she got done now was work she wouldn't have to do later. And watching Gillian work when they were in New York was *not* something she was looking forward to.

With her gaze glued to the landscape, she finally saw the ocean, glittering blue and clear beneath them. It didn't often look so benign at home, with small, gentle waves rolling toward deep, sandy beaches. She couldn't imagine how many sun-worshipers you could pack onto one of those, but then they passed what looked like a massive amusement park, spilling down a long, straight boardwalk, with a roller coaster and other rides stretching toward the sky.

Minutes later, they banked, making butterflies in her stomach. Then she saw it in the far distance, a mighty, powerful, gleaming city, glass and steel surrounded by water. She couldn't help herself. Grasping Gillian's arm, she yanked on it. "Look!" she said, giddy with excitement.

"Uh-huh," she said, offering only a slight smile. "It's pretty from here." Then her eyes headed right back to her computer, where her fingers really began to fly.

The city didn't get closer. In fact, she lost sight of it completely as they continued to descend. When they landed, minutes later, the only thing in sight was a routine, boring airport.

"Welcome to Newark," the flight attendant said. "It's fifty-three degrees, sunny, and calm. We thank you for flying with us, and hope you have a wonderful day."

"New Jersey?" Torie asked. "Did you do this so we came to the same airport I have to leave from on Wednesday?"

"Not really. I almost always stay in New Jersey. I'd rather spend my travel budget on business class seats than an expensive hotel."

"You can…" She thought of how to phrase the question. "The choice is yours? I talk to a lot of business people, and they're always complaining about how their companies handcuff them. Not long ago, I spoke to a pair of fellas who'd had to share a room at my hotel," she said, laughing. "They couldn't cry about that enough."

"It depends on the company. Since I'm a VP, I can go business class if I'm going across the country. But I'm supposed to go coach for a short flight like this. Thankfully, my boss is a bigger baby than I am. He throws tens of thousands of dollars away on perks when he travels, so he lets us do what we want, so long as we don't go over budget." She smiled. "I hope you don't mind staying in Hoboken. It's not exciting, but tonight it's two hundred bucks less than the same chain in Manhattan. Economizing on the hotel will let me go business class on the way home."

"Hoboken, huh? That's not exactly what I was planning on for my first visit to the Big Apple, but I'll manage."

"Just a ferry ride away from the action," Gillian promised. "With a lot less noise."

It was still bright and clear, but the sun was starting to slip. They still had a couple of hours until dark, but Torie couldn't stop herself from wishing they had the time back they'd wasted sitting in the Cleveland airport. While seeing Gillian was paramount, seeing New York was only behind by an inch, and Torie knew she had to make the most of every minute.

She'd showered, and was now ironing the wrinkles from their clothes while Gillian washed up. She'd also thought they might head right to bed, but so far they'd had almost no sexual spark. That made sense, given they'd been fixated on the journey, but she was still a little worried about it. If they were going to make this work, it was going to be a sexual relationship. A *good* one. If she'd just wanted companionship, she could have worked harder at finding friends in Aberdeen.

The bathroom door opened, and a cloud of steam flowed out. Torie could see the mirror, and caught sight of Gillian wiping a big circle in the middle of it. The image wasn't sharp, but she saw that she'd fastened a towel around herself, which barely contained her trim, athletic body.

"I made reservations for a place I go to all the time," Gillian said. "But we can easily change. It's not hard to get into restaurants on Sunday. Especially this early in the day."

"What kind of restaurant?"

"Mmm. They have everything. It's a little bit French, but not very."

"I like a little bit French. Can we walk?"

"It's in Manhattan. I eat in the restaurant here if I'm alone, but I'm not going to have you eating hotel food." She stuck her head out the door, revealing a big grin. "You deserve something special."

"I'm very easy to please if you'd rather stay here. I'm more interested in the sights than I am in the food."

"We'll have both. After dinner, we'll walk around Greenwich Village. That's where the restaurant is."

"Ahh, the Village," Torie said. "Do poets and writers and painters still live there?"

"No idea. In Manhattan, I know some good restaurants, some good bars, and I can navigate my way around on the subway. Other than that, I get to see the inside of meeting rooms at our advertising agencies, and meeting rooms in our New York office. Exciting, huh?"

"We'll manage." Torie watched her start to dry her hair, only briefly hoping the carefully secured towel dropped to the floor. If she hadn't been so hungry, she would have tugged it off herself, but they had to get into a romantic mood, and she desperately hoped Greenwich Village could help lead them there.

They were both dressed, and Torie watched as Gillian slipped into a dark blue quilted jacket, then check herself out in the hallway mirror. After she helped Torie into her coat, Gillian stepped closer and let her hands rest upon Torie's hips. The most adorable smile always settled onto her face when she was about to come close for a kiss, and it appeared as expected.

When she drew near, Torie could feel Gillian's warm breath caress her lips right before a soft kiss brushed by. Gillian stayed so close their lips almost touched again. "I know I'm not acting like someone who's been dying to be alone with you, but I'm starting to feel like myself now." She gently caressed her cheek with her palm, letting her eyes close briefly at the sensation. "I've still got a million things running through my mind, though. I want to make sure you get a taste of the city on your first night, I want to make sure we have a great meal, I want to get you settled so you have something fun to do tomorrow while I'm gone—"

"I'm here to see you, Gillian," she interrupted. "We can order room service if you'd like."

That clearly confused her. Her body grew stiff as her eyes widened. "Do you want me to cancel our reservations? I thought it would be kind of romantic to go to the Village, but if you don't want to…"

Okay. She wasn't herself yet.

"Let's go have dinner. I make it a habit to never refuse romance."

"Great," she said, clearly feeling better when they followed her plans. "I think you'll like this place. Some of the food is really spicy."

"Can't wait," Torie said, although she would have been just as happy to start the *intensely* romantic portion of their relationship. After waiting over three months, her patience was nearing its end.

The restaurant had been more than a little French. In fact, the dishes all had a French base, but with Moroccan, Tunisian, and other Arab-inflected influences. The place had been nearly empty when they'd entered, but their server was funny, friendly and knowledgeable, and the food so spicy and flavorful that Torie could still taste hints of mint and other spices that she didn't have the background to name. But they were delicious. No one needed to explain that to her.

It was a cool night, but the chill merely rejuvenated her. Walking around the dimly lit, cobbled streets, filled with people hurrying to dinner, they moved slowly, window-shopping and chatting.

"I feel like I'm in another reality," Torie said. "Going from home to Ohio to New Jersey to New York in just two days has me thoroughly befuddled." They weren't holding hands, but Torie stayed close, enjoying the warmth Gillian's body generated. She could have pushed the point and taken her hand, but she'd decided to let her choose how close they should be. They'd have to discuss the rules about that eventually, but there was no rush.

"It's odd for me too." She revealed a warm, but teasing smile. "If I'd known you were coming..."

"I will never, ever surprise you again, Gillian Cumberland Lindsay. I brought a present for your birthday, and I'm on the verge of telling you what it is right now."

"I like *little* surprises," she said. "Very little ones."

They were in front of a store that sold T-shirts with slogans and ads on them, and she could see Gillian's alert gaze travel over each. She couldn't imagine her wearing any of them, not even for a joke, but she seemed interested.

"You know, we've been talking or writing every day," Torie said. "And I've answered more than a hundred of your questions, but I feel like we're almost strangers. I don't think it's possible to substitute for the stark reality of being in each other's presence."

"Strangers?" she said, turning to show puzzled, wide eyes.

"Maybe not strangers, but there's so much I don't know." They were on a narrow side street, one with very few other people. Torie got bold and stroked Gillian's cheek, pleased when she nuzzled against her hand. "You learn about people from seeing them in action. That's been a surprise," she admitted. "I thought we'd pick up right where we left off." She let her voice drop to a sober tone. "We haven't."

"Um, I get the impression you think I'm kidding, but I'm really not. It takes me a while to get used to changed circumstances." She took a look over her shoulder, then grasped Torie's hands and held them to her chest. "I'm trying to figure out how to have my meetings and get the things I have to do finished while making sure you're entertained..." She shrugged, clearly upset. "I'm having trouble getting my bearings. I'm not on vacation this week, Torie, but I desperately want to be."

"This is what we can't figure out over the internet," she said, gazing into Gillian's troubled eyes. "I don't know how you are when you're working. You don't really know how I am when I'm on vacation."

"But that's not..." She frowned, her forehead lined with worry. "You don't regret coming, do you?"

"Of course not." She slid her arms around Gillian's waist and hugged her tightly. "I'm just putting words to how I feel. I want you to know me, and at this point, the only way to make that happen is to tell all."

"So one day I'll just know you?"

"If we're lucky, we'll pick up on little cues. We just don't know them yet." She gripped Gillian's arm and gave it a squeeze. "Is this the West Village?"

"I think so. Why?"

"Because there's a lesbian bar in the West Village. Apparently, one of the last in the city. Want to give it a try?"

Even in the dim glow of the warm lamplight, Torie could see her swallow nervously. "I've never been to a lesbian bar."

"I think you should correct that omission before you turn forty." She took a look at her watch. "We've got four hours."

⚘ ⚘ ⚘

When she'd been in college, Gillian had friends who'd pile onto a train at the Noyes stop on the Purple Line and go to a gay bar in Chicago, but she'd never gone along. Doing that had felt like something almost guaranteed to frustrate her. She lived in a sorority house, and couldn't have considered bringing a woman home from a bar. And if you weren't going to get lucky, why bother going to a smoky, loud, stuffy club?

She'd felt the same once she'd settled in Columbus again. She could have brought a woman home then, of course, but she'd always thought the kind of woman she was looking for wouldn't be all alone in a bar.

But now that they approached the door, she was forced to admit there had been more to it. If she hadn't ever been to a gay bar just because of circumstance, why would there be a trickle of sweat cooling the small of her back? She wasn't about to bring that up, of course. Adults weren't afraid of going into a bar, and she prided herself on being a mature adult. One who could handle uncomfortable situations.

Torie pushed through the black door, clearly unafraid, with Gillian following close behind. It was dark inside, a little gloomy. Not very crowded, either. But the music playing from the jukebox was current, and lively, and the people at the bar turned and gave them somewhat encouraging smiles when they stepped inside and let the door close.

"My treat," Torie said. "What will you have?"

Gillian took a look at the wall behind the bar, where name brand alcohol was displayed. There was a lot, but it was mostly the common stuff that every bar had. "Let's have a whisky," she said. "If it's good, I'll have a splash of water. If not, add some ice."

"Spoken like an aficionado," Torie teased. "Grab a seat. I'll be back in no time."

She marched over to the bar, pulling her wallet from her back pocket as she moved. She looked awfully cute in a heavy, oatmeal-colored sweater and the insulated vest Gillian had given her for Christmas. She obviously didn't like to carry a purse unless she had to, but it was kind of cool to see her whip her phone or her charge card out of her back pocket with practiced ease. It gave her a gayer vibe than normal, and Gillian found she liked her looking more androgynous.

In a matter of seconds, Torie was chatting with the bartender and two women who were sitting at the bar. She was laughing and nodding and having a grand old time, while Gillian sat, alone. Finally, Torie carried two drinks over to the table and placed them onto cocktail napkins. "The bartender had to dig around to find it, but this is good whisky."

"You made friends."

She shrugged. "People seem to like my accent. Not that I have one," she added, grinning. "It's your lot that bends the language all out of shape."

"I can't argue with that. It would be cool if we still spoke with English accents, wouldn't it?"

"Scottish," she said, putting it on thick. "Your ancestors came from Leith and North Ronaldsay, lassie. No one in either line had an English accent." She held her glass up. "Here's to what I suppose we should call our second date. It's been an odd one so far, but it's getting better and better."

"To second dates," Gillian agreed, tapping her glass against Torie's. She took a sip. "Not bad at all. Lots of peat and…honey, I think."

"Uh-huh. It's nice and smooth." They sat across from each other at the high, narrow table, smiling gamely. They were still clearly not fully acclimated to each other yet, but they were getting there.

"I've got an idea," Gillian said. "If you'll join me, I'll take Thursday and Friday off and stay in New York." She tried to make her smile as charming as possible, but Torie's eyes narrowed.

"Of course I'd like to, but I can't change my ticket now. And missing more work would be a problem. I'm losing five days as it is."

"I know your ticket cost a lot," Gillian said soberly. "Doesn't it make sense to get the most out of that investment? It just seems crazy to only have three evenings together." She shook her head. "I can't possibly get out of anything I've got going on this week. Other than dinner," she added. "I'm cutting out of whatever they've planned for the evening."

"They plan…?"

"I'm a big client," she said, simply telling the truth. "They take me to something every time I'm here. Ball games, plays, concerts. They took me to see Adele last time I was in town."

Torie reached over and slapped at her. "She's from my island! Shouldn't I have seen her first?"

"You need better connections."

"I've none," she grumbled. Looking up with a slight smile, she said, "I want to stay. You know I do…"

"I'll pay you back for the days you miss."

"No," she moaned, dropping her head onto the table. "I don't want to take money from you. It seems so… I don't have a word for it, but it feels wrong."

"If you won't take cash, let me pay for something you usually cover. You pay some of Kirsty's rent, right?"

"Half," she admitted.

"I'll write a check for that. I won't be giving you cash, I'll just be making up for some of the money you've lost by staying longer."

"Gillian," she said, shaking her head, "her rent is *much* more than I'd make by working two more days."

"Then stay longer." Gillian leaned over and placed a soft kiss on Torie's mouth. "I'll pay her rent, your rent, anyone's rent. I just want you to stay."

She could see Torie struggle with the decision, but she finally nodded. "If I can find a substitute, I'll stay until Friday."

"Saturday," Gillian said. "Fly home on Saturday night. Then you'll have Sunday to rest up for the week."

"Saturday," she agreed, giving Gillian a reluctant grin. "Do you always get your way?"

"I sure try to." She stood and put her hand out when a slow, syrupy love song came on the jukebox. "Now I'd like to dance with you. Will I get my way?"

"You will."

Torie hopped off her stool and slid her hand into Gillian's. Then they headed to the small dance floor in the back of the room. They were the only two, and her body tingled at the prospect of dancing with a woman in public. As she slid one arm around Torie's waist, she tried hard to show some confidence, but she was pretty certain she wasn't pulling it off.

Then Torie looked up at her, a beautiful smile on her face. Like magic, some of Gillian's anxiety began to drain away as she focused only on her. It was just the two of them. The women at the bar might watch, but so what? Only Torie's opinion mattered, and she seemed really happy.

Their bodies drew closer and closer, until they were barely moving, just shuffling their feet as they hugged each other to music. Gillian could feel her smile grow, then a knot in the pit of her stomach caught her by surprise. In a second, there were tears on her cheeks and she found herself whispering, "I'm so sorry I've never done this before."

Torie tilted her chin and their eyes met. Then she placed her hand on the back of Gillian's head and pressed her forward a couple of inches. Their lips met gently, and when she stood tall again, Torie said, "You're doing it now." As her grin grew, she added, "I love that you're doing it with me."

Gillian hugged her hard, nearly overcome by the feelings that beat in her chest. She wasn't exactly sure what she was feeling, or why she was so upset, but she would have left if Torie hadn't been holding onto her.

Once again, she listened to the music, trying to let it guide her. It took a few bars, but she started to move more freely, to enjoy the pressure of Torie's body against her own as they moved together. It was a stunningly powerful feeling. Freeing in a way she hadn't for one second expected. The song ended just as she was starting to get into it, then another came on, this one faster and more upbeat.

"More," she said, reaching down to grasp the belt loops of Torie's jeans and hold on tightly.

"Let's go," Torie agreed. Her hips started to move as she placed her hands low on Gillian's back. She'd obviously been holding back before, but now she started to get into it.

Gillian was grinning like an idiot, her gaze trained on Torie's body as she moved effortlessly around the small space, pulling Gillian along with her. As the moments passed, her body loosened up too, and she started to sing along. Eyes closed, head tilted back, she let go, not caring who watched or who heard. Torie's hands slid into the back pockets of her jeans and pressed her close. Then

Gillian's leg slipped between Torie's and she felt the warmth of her body on her thigh, making her heart beat so fast she grew dizzy.

When the song ended, Torie looked up with glittering eyes. "I'm not stopping," she said, giving Gillian a glorious smile. "Too much fun."

"I'm staying here until I nail this," Gillian agreed, holding on tightly as the opening strains of the next song rang in her ears.

Torie had lost track of how many songs they'd danced to. But Gillian had lost every bit of her stiffness, which was all that mattered. Now they moved around in a lazy circle, one or the other singing along when they knew the words, or just holding each other and laughing. This was as close to her childhood self as she ever got—and to get to this place with Gillian was a fantastic treat. While it was wonderful to be with a mature woman, they both needed to stow the mature part away every once in a while to let their childish selves out. Torie was simply thrilled that they'd been able to unleash some of that unfettered joy tonight.

When the song ended, Gillian gave her a quick kiss, saying, "Don't move." Then she raced back to their table, grabbed her wallet, and went to the bar. By the time she got there, the bartender was walking down the bar to put two tall glasses of ice water and two short ones of whisky down. "Twenty bucks," she called out, having to shout to be heard over the music.

Torie walked over to stand next to her and they chugged the water, then downed the whisky.

"Whoa!" Gillian yelped. "That packed a punch!"

"Back to work," Torie said, giving her a sharp slap on the bottom.

Laughing, Gillian grabbed her and twirled her around. The room continued to spin for a few seconds, but Torie gamely started to dance again, ready for whatever Gillian could throw at her.

CHAPTER TWENTY-ONE

WOMEN HAD BEEN STRAGGLING INTO the bar for the last half hour, and now a few of the newcomers joined them on the dance floor. Gillian took a moment to check her watch. "Ten o'clock," she said, speaking into Torie's ear. "I've only got two more hours to be a woman in my thirties."

"Want to spend it upright?" She made her eyebrows waggle. "Or horizontal?"

"Horizontal," Gillian said, not taking a second to think. "Ready?"

"I love a woman who can make quick decisions."

"That's something I'm pretty good at," she admitted. Making another one, she grabbed her purse and pulled her phone out. "We're not wasting half an hour taking the PATH train, either." To read the text, she had to squint, something she was now having to do on a routine basis. Reading glasses were right around the corner. "Our car will be here in two minutes."

"You don't fool around," Torie said, speaking loudly.

"Oh, yes I do. I'm really good at it, too," she said, not as confident as she'd hoped to be, but determined to give it her best.

Torie put her coat on and headed for the door, giving a friendly wave to the bartender. Gillian followed her out and scanned the cars that crawled down the narrow street, looking for one with the glowing "U" in the windshield.

A black car slowed, and the window rolled down. "Gillian?" the guy said, using a hard "g".

"That's me," she said, holding open the back door for Torie to slide across.

"There's a twenty-dollar surcharge for tolls." The driver's eyes met hers. "Okay?"

"Is that negotiable?"

"Flat fee."

"Then it's okay," she said, laughing softly. She sat back and rolled her window down a tiny bit, just to cool off. "I'd go broke if I lived here."

"It's as bad as London," Torie agreed. "I almost cried when that woman took twenty dollars from me for the whisky."

Gillian leaned over a little, pressing her shoulder against Torie's. "But it was good, wasn't it?"

"It was," she said, smiling back. They reached the tunnel in just a few minutes, then Gillian squinted against the glare of the unflattering lights and the white tile as they flew through the span. In a minute, she pointed to a sign on the wall that flashed by, inlaid tiles spelling out New York-New Jersey on their respective sides.

"I'd like that picture," Torie said.

"We'll go into the city tomorrow, too. I'll make sure my phone's ready."

They exited the tunnel and snaked along dark streets, spotting quick glances of the enormity of Manhattan when there was a break in the buildings. "So cool," Torie whispered. "I think I like being over on this side. Hidden New York."

Their driver pulled up in front of the hotel and waited patiently while they got out. Then he pulled away in a flash, obviously heading for another pickup.

They went up in the elevator, rising quickly to the top floor, where Gillian got her key card out and placed it over the sensor, glad to have it work the first time.

She dashed over to the window, flung the drapes open, then raised the shade to reveal a stunning view of the bulk of Manhattan, white lights predominating, flecked with red, blue and purple bursts.

"It's fantastic," Torie breathed, walking over slowly as her head swiveled back and forth, taking it all in.

"I told you it'd be worth the wait. When you're in the city, all you can see are buildings right next to you. This is worth the trouble, in my book."

"Can I kiss you with that background? I don't know which is prettier, you or the skyline. But I bet your kiss could tilt the score in your favor."

"Aww, you're more romantic by the minute." Gillian's hands settled on her waist. "First you dance like a pro, and now you've got a silver tongue. What next?"

"I guess we'll find out," she said, showing her first bout of nerves when her voice shook.

"It'll be fine," Gillian said. "This is just one night in our lives together. It's not a one and done, you know. We're just going to get to know each other better now."

"Naked," Torie reminded her. "Don't forget that."

"We can leave the lights off if you want." She put her arms around her body, which was trembling. That little bit of vulnerability made Gillian's protective instincts rise, making her promise herself she'd be sensitive to every possible need Torie showed.

They held each other tenderly for a few minutes, their bodies gently swaying almost like they had on the dance floor. "Kiss?" Gillian asked.

Torie's chin tilted up and their lips touched, gently and softly. She met Gillian's pressure, then started to push further, kicking up the heat. When a short, low growl left Gillian's chest, she tightened her grasp and started to probe Torie's warm, silky mouth, with her tongue gliding everywhere in gentle exploration.

By the time she started to pull away to take a breath, Torie was shivering. There was no better feeling than knowing you were starting to rock a woman's foundations, and a sly smile settled on Gillian's face when she held her to return for more. But the shivering increased, making her realize it wasn't arousal that made Torie shake.

"What's going on in your head?" Gillian asked. She pressed Torie to her body and gently rubbed her back, trying to soothe her. "You want to… Don't you?"

"Of course." She pulled away and started for the bathroom. "I think I'd feel better if we took a shower. Would that be okay? I…" She bit at her lip, clearly beset by her emotions.

"Sure. Sure," Gillian said. "Whatever you want." She grasped her hand and pulled her to a stop. "But don't you think we should talk for a while first? You told me you were going to tell me everything that was on your mind, but I think there's something causing some trouble up there right now." She tapped at her temple, trying to make light of it.

"Just nerves," she said, not meeting Gillian's eyes. "It's taking me a minute to get comfortable."

"Then let's sit down for a minute and talk about *that*." She tugged a reluctant Torie over to the sofa and sat close. "I know you haven't had many opportunities over the last few years, but things were good back when you had a partner, right?"

Her head shook briefly. "Not good. No."

"A few more words wouldn't be out of line," Gillian said, still trying to sound light and casual. "Any words at all. Just throw some together. They don't even have to make sense."

That got a little smile out of her. "I've been with just two women, and I've yet to experience any sensual pleasures to treasure."

"Neither?" Now her own heart was starting to beat faster. If Torie didn't like sex, they were going to have bigger hurdles than their distance to overcome.

"Neither," she said glumly. "You know I came out at uni, right?"

"I do."

"Well, the woman I came out with was a classmate, who lived at home." She was quiet for a minute, then said, "Even saying we came out together is a stretch."

"How so?"

"We didn't talk about what was going on," Torie said. "We just let things… happen."

"That's not giving me much," Gillian said. "What kind of things did you do?"

"Well, Isla had a car, and we kept coming up with reasons to go somewhere in that little thing, even though it was more trouble to drive than take a bus."

"Ahh. Once you were in the car, that gave you permission to explore."

"I guess." She nodded more forcefully. "Yes, I suppose that was it. We'd park in a quiet place and do whatever we could manage. But we never did *anything* outside of that car. After a few months, she decided she liked the lads after all, and that was that."

"She liked the lads better than you? Damaged goods," Gillian said, flicking her hand.

"She was a bit," Torie agreed, chuckling. "But I let her decide what we'd do and when we'd do it, so I participated in the scheme."

"And *that's* where you developed your hatred of kissing in cars."

Torie stared at her for a few seconds, mouth agape. "I never thought of it, but that must be. Oh, my goodness," she whispered. "The mind is a funny thing, isn't it?"

"It is. So, after that you met Sheila?"

"That's right. And things were much better with her. She liked sex well enough, and after a while we moved in together. But…" She took in a deep breath and let it out slowly. "There were only a few things she liked doing. Every time I tried to move down and…" She was blushing so deeply Gillian was afraid she'd have a heart attack.

"She didn't like you to go down on her?"

"Right. And she acted like there were land-mines around my lower half. Her face never got close to the parts of me I wanted her to touch."

She was about to say something disparaging about Sheila, but Gillian stopped herself. Everyone had their quirks, and pointing them out to a former lover probably wasn't the wisest thing to do. "That was her," she said. "Lots of people like some things and don't like others."

260

"It made me feel like I was…" Implausibly, her cheeks turned even redder. "Unattractive or unappealing. Which I was," she insisted, staring into Gillian's eyes with intractable certainty.

"That's not true!"

"It *was*. That part of my body didn't appeal to her in the least."

"That was *her* issue," Gillian insisted. "Her likes and dislikes were about her, Torie. Not you. You had the bad luck of not synching up with the first couple of people you were with. It happens. I've had more than my share of women I didn't click with. I just moved on."

"I didn't have that opportunity. By the time Sheila and I were forced to split up, I had an infant in my bedroom. Since then, he's been my priority. My only priority."

"Well, you're in a different place in your life now." She tucked an arm around her and pulled her close. Sniffing the subtle, herbal scent she wore helped center Gillian as she thought. "I hope you agree with me later tonight, but over the last few years I've gotten a lot better at sex. It's partly practice," she admitted, "but it's also something else. Something important."

"I've had almost *no* practice. Even when we did what Sheila liked, sex was never the playful, joyful experience I'd hoped it would be. It was always… mannered."

She looked so defeated. Filled with empathy, Gillian said, "You have a lot of practice using the most important sex tool in your bag." Playfully, she pressed on her own chin, then lightly touched the tip of her tongue. "That's the critical part. You just have to use your tongue."

"I know! But I have no experience—"

"You use it constantly. You're using it now."

"What are you talking about?"

Torie was usually amenable to playful teasing, but today wasn't a good day for it. "All you have to do is talk. Without talking, sex isn't good for hardly anyone."

"I talk," she said, already sounding defensive.

"In bed. I thought I was pretty adept, but when I was with Grace, she changed me." She spent a moment thinking of their time together, a time that almost invariably made her smile. "When we were first together, she'd ask me what I liked, and I usually said something like, 'everything,' or something equally nonspecific."

"I'm not sure *what* I like," Torie said, her anxiety clearly growing.

"Sure you do. When I touch you or kiss you or ask you to touch me in a certain way, I want you to try to give me feedback. If it's too much or not enough, let me know. If I'm touching you for too long in one spot, tell me to knock it off. Use some sensitivity," she added, chuckling, "but tell me to knock it off."

"I don't think I've ever said a word while having sex," she admitted. "We did it, cuddled for a minute, then fell asleep."

"Let's try the method Grace taught me." When she pulled Torie over to nuzzle against her neck, she seemed much more pliant. "I won't be as doctrinaire as she was, but I'm going to check with you a lot."

"How was she doctrinaire?"

Gillian let out a laugh. "I wasn't talking enough, so one morning she spent about an hour touching me in every way possible. I had to keep telling her if I liked it a lot, a little, or not at all. She was relentless!"

"I'm not relentless," Torie said soberly.

"But you want to have good sex, don't you?"

Her eyes fluttered closed. "More than I can say."

"Then we've got to learn to talk—in bed, out of bed, wherever. We have to put in some effort to have a good sex life, Torie, but I guarantee it'll be worth the trouble."

"I'll try," she said, looking like she was not anticipating this task in the least.

"I probably make it sound like a big deal. It's not. It's just talking." She gripped her chin and made her mouth open and close. "I know you like to talk."

Torie leaned against Gillian heavily, letting out a sigh. "I'm still nervous."

"I'm nervous too." She laughed a little. "I've just told you I'm kind of awesome in bed. What if you don't agree? I'll look like an idiot!"

Torie started to laugh, breaking the tension in an instant. "Poor you," she soothed. "I promise I'll lie and tell you you're fabulous even if you're completely ham-handed."

"That works. I want you to talk, but it's fine with me if most of your words are compliments." She gave her another pat. "Still want that shower?"

"I think so. But…" Her eyes started to shift, unable to focus on Gillian.

"You'd rather go solo, right?"

"Um…" She started to nod. "Just this once. If I have a few minutes alone I might be able to—"

"You don't need to explain." Gillian got up and extended her hand, easily pulling Torie to her feet. "I didn't get my things in order yet. I'll get ready for tomorrow while you're showering."

"I'll be fast," Torie said, heading for the bathroom.

When she left, Gillian gave herself a pep talk, patiently reminding herself that this was just one night in what she hoped would be a long, long relationship. If it didn't go well, that didn't mean it never would.

She hung her suits up, then steamed the wrinkles from a blouse. When she was putting the ironing board away, she jumped when Torie's hand touched her hip. "It's all yours. My body, and perhaps my mind, have been scrubbed clean."

Gillian turned to look at her, skin pink from the hot water, her hair lying flat, or flattish. She let her hand press down on a hank of hair with a bump in it, but it popped right back up when she took her hand away. "I've never seen your hair wet. I like it lying down."

"But it doesn't lie down," she said, reaching up to grasp the bit that Gillian had noticed. "At least not all of it. I have three significant cowlicks. A few years ago, the woman who cuts my hair suggested I stop trying to make it lie down. Now I let most of it do what it wants, then urge some of it to go in a different direction so it looks planned."

"Whatever you do, I like it." Gillian kissed the independent-minded group of hairs, then said, "I'll be back in a few minutes. Don't go away."

"Not a chance," Torie said, smiling gamely.

As soon as Gillian left, Torie removed her bath sheet and rubbed her hair briskly. She'd forgotten to take a robe with her when she'd entered the bathroom, now finding two of them in the closet. After a quick knock, she opened the door and tossed one onto the sink, then put the second one on.

This wasn't going well at *all*, but she was determined to make up for all of the missteps she'd made so far. A wry laugh bubbled up as she thought of her dreams of their reconnecting. In them, Gillian had grasped her in a passionate embrace that lasted for four days, then they had a tearful goodbye at the airport, a scene somewhat resembling *Casablanca*. Maybe that had been silly. They were simply average people who had to bend and change to be able to fit together comfortably. And one of them had as much experience as most kids had clocked by the age of fifteen.

Thankfully, Gillian was being remarkably patient with her. She was sure her patience had a limit, but it was nowhere in sight—at the moment. Now Torie was determined to pull up her socks and give it her best. No more whimpering, no more shivering.

The bathroom door opened, and Gillian stood there, fluffy white robe tied at the waist. She had a silly smile on her face, and she let her gaze drift to the bed. "Hey, look! There's a place we could lie down for a while and catch a little nap." She raised both arms and stretched them out, yawning noisily. "Want to join me?"

Torie walked over to her and wrapped her in a hug. They stayed just that way for a minute, adjusting to the feel of each other's bodies. "I'm okay now," she said. "Talking helped."

"It usually does." Gillian lifted her head and their eyes met, neither blinking for a few seconds. "We'll be fine," she said quietly. "More than that, we'll have fun. And if you're not in the mood tonight, we'll see how we feel tomorrow. We've got time."

"Thanks," Torie murmured. "But I'm wide awake and ready for anything you have in mind. It's almost your birthday, you know. Surely there's a little something special I can give you."

Chuckling, Gillian put her hands on Torie's bum and pulled her close. "I can think of a few things…" She dipped her head and covered Torie's mouth with her own, giving her a possessive kiss that made her heart start to beat harder in seconds. "I've thought about this every single night since I left Scotland," she said. "*Every* night."

"I have too," Torie sighed. "I'd gotten good at convincing myself to ignore my sex drive, but thoughts of you have woken it up." She laughed. "It's *wide* awake now, but it's got the jitters."

Gillian's smile was a little feral, but Torie's anxieties had almost completely disappeared. She slipped her arms around her and tilted her head, exposing her neck. "I'm all yours."

Dipping her head, Gillian kissed and nibbled on the tender skin, continuing to caress it until her breathing started to pick up. "Your skin's flawless," she murmured. "A sculptor would drool."

Torie held her tighter, urging her on. "More," she whispered.

Given permission, Gillian increased the force of her kisses, really getting into it. Her hands joined in, cupping and squeezing Torie's bum, then sliding up to explore her back. As their mouths met again and again, Gillian started to breathe heavily, and Torie's heart beat harder in response. There was nothing more bonding, more unifying than the merging of bodies, of desire. The years of wanting this—of refusing to even consider having this—floated away without a thought. They had it now.

The tie on the robe loosened, then Gillian's warm hand slid inside and settled on her hip. The air conditioning hit Torie's exposed skin, making her shiver.

"Nervous?" Gillian asked, barely whispering.

"Cold." She pointed at the vent blowing on them.

A playful grin lit her expression. "We'd better get away from it then." She pointed directly at the bed. "How about there?"

"Good choice."

Torie grasped the heavy white comforter and tugged, loosening it from its moorings. Then Gillian grabbed the whole thing and staggered as she tried to throw it into the corner, grunting as it flew across the room. "That weighed thirty pounds," she insisted. "And there's still a lighter comforter on the bed. Where do they think we are? The arctic?"

"I'll need that one," Torie assured her. She sat, then waited for Gillian to join her. As soon as gentle arms encircled her body, she lay down, then smiled when Gillian lay next to her, their heads on the same pillow. "Our first real time in bed together," she said, grinning. "This morning didn't really count."

"It could have been sooner if you'd given me any hints when we were on our trip. I would have been very, very happy to have started this in November."

"Now's the right time," Torie said. "I know you now. I trust you now."

"That's all well and good," Gillian said, with a playful grin, "but I trusted you fifteen seconds after I met you. And by trusted, I mean I thought you were hot." She slipped her hand inside the robe again, letting it trail up and down Torie's body. "You were. You are."

Lying down somehow had given her a boost of confidence, and Torie got more assertive, moving closer to drape her arm and leg across Gillian's body as she started to kiss her in earnest.

That was the perfect way to ramp things up. Gillian was as compliant as could be, opening herself up to Torie's wandering hand, responding in moments to each caress. "More of that," she whispered, eyes closed. "I love to be touched. Every part of me."

Such an open invitation was too good to ignore, so Torie tried to satisfy her. New territory opened when she pulled on the robe, and she stared at Gillian's bare body as the cool lights of Manhattan twinkled across the river. She'd known it was going to be lovely, but it was lovelier than she could have guessed. Riding a bike long distances on most weekends did very good things to a woman's shape. Everything was firm and toned, but so warm and supple, so touchable. Lost in the sensation in moments, Torie cleared her mind completely and let her fingertips guide her. They were emboldened to dive beneath the fabric and glide along the warm softness of Gillian's skin, which pebbled as Torie explored.

A firm hand settled on the back of her neck, pulling Torie forward. When she kissed her again, Gillian let out a gentle sigh. "Perfect. I love being touched, but being kissed at the same time is *so* much better."

"I want to make you happy," Torie murmured before kissing her again and again.

"You do," Gillian sighed, clearly content.

As she continued to stroke and caress her body, Torie's confidence grew with each passing minute. Knowing Gillian would guide her was remarkably soothing, when she would have guessed just the opposite to be true. But this wasn't Gillian setting a bar and demanding Torie reach it. She was just expressing her needs, and doing it in such a casual way that it felt more like they were having a conversation. One with few words, but a conversation nonetheless.

"I love this," Torie whispered as she shifted down the bed to replace her fingers with her mouth.

"Love doesn't begin to cover it," Gillian purred. "Keep doing that until you're sick of it." She laughed at herself, but each time she said something offhand like that it encouraged Torie anew.

"That's going to be a while," she promised, sure of that. Gillian's body was a garden of delights, and in a very short time Torie found herself addicted to wringing sighs and moans from her, then causing her to suck in a quick breath in surprise or pleasure. Every sound was welcomed. Cherished.

When she let her tongue, then her mouth tease a firming nipple, a brief moment of dizziness knocked her off stride. Her brain had obviously short-circuited after touching the softest, sexiest breasts in the history of humanity. While she'd been distracted by Gillian's long, lean legs that afternoon in Aberdeen, Torie had always—since puberty—been mesmerized by breasts. Having the ability to touch and taste and kiss the most perfect ones in existence was almost too much for her to bear.

She knew she was exaggerating, but only a little. Their shape, their weight, their softness, their resiliency...all perfect. Torie's head swam with sensation, as her skin pebbled from excitement when the heated flesh reacted to her kisses.

Gillian had started to squirm on the bed, moving her hips as her breathing continued to grow faster. Every single time she twitched, the pulse between Torie's thighs grew stronger. It was like they were connected. Desire and touch. Touch and desire. Inexplicably entwined.

"I want to touch you here," Torie said, letting her hand slide down an enviably flat belly to settle between Gillian's legs. Her mouth was dry, and her hand shook slightly, but this time she was sure it was mostly from arousal.

As her legs parted, Gillian grasped her hand. "Lie next to me," she whispered.

Torie scooted up so their shoulders were at the same level, then she rolled onto her side. Gillian guided her hand, then pressed the fingers against herself, letting out a gasp as Torie's fingers brushed across her heated, slick skin. "So nice," Gillian sighed. "Just like that," she added when Torie's fingers moved of their own accord. "Nice and slow and gentle. Anywhere you want to go is good. Every part is sensitive." She bit at her bottom lip as her hips swayed in time to Torie's gliding touch. "Yessss," she sighed every time Torie hit a sensitive spot, which was nearly constantly.

Gillian's head lifted and she blinked like she'd just woken. "Do you have a free hand? If you don't…" Her hand bumped into Torie's, clearly ready to join in if needed.

"Show me what you like," she said, fairly sure she couldn't get her own hand in there without some major adjustments.

Without a pause, Gillian's feet hit the mattress and her hips tilted upward. Then her fingers slipped under Torie's as she let out a sharp gasp. "A little faster…" Her words had come out so quickly it took Torie a second to hear them. But the moment she did, her hand started to move faster, then sped up again as Gillian continued to make the most adorable sounds, almost whimpering, clearly from pleasure. "Yeah, yeah, yeah, yeah," she panted as her body shook hard for long seconds, her head thrashing back and forth, then slowly coming to a complete halt. Then both hands shot in the air, and she called out, "Touchdown!" then began to laugh, burying her face against Torie's chest. "Orgasms make me silly," she said, still chuckling while Torie held her tenderly. Then she stuck an arm out and tucked it around Torie to tumble her onto her chest. "You're very good at this," she said, singing the words in a funny tune. "We're going to have a fantastic time in bed. Tonight was just the start of something awesome."

"I'm so relieved!" Torie said, laughing. "I knew you were enjoying that, but I wasn't sure I'd be able to…finish up," she added, unsure of what term to use.

"Teamwork," Gillian said, grinning. "That was okay, wasn't it? I didn't clear that with you beforehand, but I always find it hard to get that other hand around when I'm lying next to someone."

"I'm glad you helped." Torie picked Gillian's hand up and kissed it. "Feel free to jump in anytime you wish. I like working with a partner."

"We'll figure it out. I don't *have* to have fingers inside, but it feels better if I do." Her grin increased. "And I don't see any reason not to make just about everything feel better when I can." She kissed the crown of Torie's head. "How about you? Do you like something inside?"

"Um, yes. Yes, I do." She gently patted Gillian's cheek. "We've just talked about sex more than I have in my entire life."

"Just because you started late doesn't mean you can't catch up." Her eyes grew wide. "If you want to."

"I do. This is good for me. If I'd done this when I was with Sheila, I might have saved myself a lot of worrying."

"Mmm, it sounds like Sheila wasn't really into it. But you are," she teased, poking Torie all about her body. "You're definitely into it."

"I suppose I am," she said, knowing she was blushing. "I think I'm going to have to be to keep up with you."

"Slow and steady wins the race," Gillian said. She flipped Torie onto her back with a thrust of her hips, then hovered over her. "I'm going to start slow, and keep it up until you can't take another second. We're going to have fun," she insisted. "A lot of fun."

"I already am. This is more fun than I've had with my clothes off in an awfully long time, Gillian. It's been *fantastic*."

"It's better to receive than to give," she teased. She pressed Torie's shoulders to the bed, then covered her mouth and kissed her tenderly. "I'm so happy we're together."

Torie wrapped her arms around Gillian's shoulders and held her tightly, nuzzling her face against her neck, almost overcome with emotion. "So happy," she agreed.

Then they started to kiss again, the feeling similar, but strangely different from when she was leading. Now she relaxed completely, opening herself up to Gillian's determined kisses. Soon, that delightful tongue was probing her mouth, touching tender spots that made her shiver. The anticipation started to build almost at once. It was just a tongue, but as it invaded her body she knew it was only the first wave of sensation. Soon, fingers and maybe even a tongue would touch places that hadn't been caressed in so long she could barely recall how it had felt. But she no longer had to recall. The reality was so much better than the memory. She shivered roughly at the delightful sensation of Gillian's touch when warm fingers slid inside her robe again and started to drive her crazy.

She was shaking with desire when a gentle, moist mouth settled over her nipple and bathed it with warmth, then pressure. Gillian was clearly having a fantastic time, letting out soft, pleased sounds as she made Torie quiver.

Caressing Gillian's head as she suckled and tugged at her flesh, flashes of sensation rolled down her body until she was shivering as badly as she had earlier. But Gillian didn't check with her this time. Anyone could see she was feeling pure, unadorned pleasure, with Gillian pushing the limits as fast and as far as she could.

Slowly, she moved down, with Torie's mouth turning dry as she looked down at Gillian's sly grin. "I'm going to try some things." She rested on her arms for a moment. "I don't have a script, so tell me if you don't like something." A tender, clearly sincere smile tugged the corners of her mouth up. "I'll do anything to please you."

"I know," Torie whispered, stroking her hair just to bleed off some of the anxiety.

Then Gillian was gently pressing her legs open, with her broad shoulders pinning them back, opening Torie's body to her touch. The softest thing imaginable caressed her trembling flesh, then Gillian nuzzled against her. Torie's body shook hard, the unimaginably tender touch too silky to possibly be human.

The last thing she wanted to do was talk, but Gillian clearly wanted feedback. "Perfect," Torie murmured, hoping one-word comments were sufficient.

After a few minutes of slow, gentle movements, Torie felt Gillian shift a little. Then two fingers began to tickle all around her opening, one from each side. All she could do was let out a growl, but that seemed like plenty as Gillian laughed softly. Then the fingers started to slide inside, pressing outward as they went. Torie was sure her eyes were rolling around inside her head, but she couldn't utter a single word of encouragement. Gillian was going to have to figure this out for herself. Those demonic fingers stroked deep inside, filling her to capacity, tickling and playing with her very essence.

She had no idea how long Gillian had been driving her mad, but she started to feel a thrumming in her belly, a growing need that pulsed deep inside. Her hand had been on Gillian's head, just resting there to connect with her, but when she heard a pained whimper she let go, realizing she'd been pulling her hair. That threw her off, thoroughly destroying her concentration. Gillian seemed to sense that, and she slowed down too, making her touch much gentler. For a while she kept that up, then, when Torie's world seemed to shrink to just the few inches they both focused on, she started to press herself against Gillian.

With another throaty growl, Gillian pushed back, stiffening her tongue and probing every nook it could reach. Her fingers moved in and out slowly, methodically, as the sensation once more began to build from within.

Words wouldn't come, despite trying to form them. Then it hit her, like she'd been knocked off her feet. Her climax washed over her without warning as she gripped Gillian's shoulders with her fingers, digging into the flesh as wave after wave of sensation roared through her body, leaving her shaking and wet with perspiration.

Unlike Gillian, orgasms didn't energize Torie. Instead, she felt like she'd been deboned, now just a limp mass of flesh, with occasional electric zaps tickling between her legs. "I can't move. Or think," she murmured, even those few words taking all of her strength.

Gillian lifted a limp leg and scooted under it, then crawled up the bed like a soldier, pulling herself along by placing her forearms one in front of the other, dramatically grunting as she moved. "Made it," she said, dropping onto her belly.

With effort, Torie reached over and patted her back. "You deserve a *significant* raise."

Flipping over, Gillian gave her a happy-looking grin. "I don't need payment for doing something I enjoy so much." She pulled Torie to her, giving her a long, soulful kiss. "I had a fantastic time. Best birthday present I could have ever hoped for."

Torie took a look at the clock. "Ahh! It's your birthday!"

"It's been the best birthday I can remember, and it's only been going for twenty minutes," Gillian said. Then she yawned, her fatigue obviously catching up to her. "Sleepy," she mumbled.

"Cuddle?" Torie opened her arms.

"Have to." She slid over and let herself be wrapped in a hug, nuzzling against Torie's neck for a few moments. "Who knows where we'll wind up, but I'd love to try to stay close all night."

"Me too." She placed a few soft kisses to the top of Gillian's head, while gently patting her back. "Sleep now."

"Okay," she sighed. "I've got to get up at seven thirty, but I want you to stay in bed. I want you all rested up when I get home."

"Do my best." She hugged her one last time, holding on as Gillian burrowed against her body. "Sleep well, my birthday princess."

"I'm a princess," she mumbled, then twitched a few times before falling fast asleep.

CHAPTER TWENTY-TWO

WAKING A FEW MINUTES BEFORE her alarm, Gillian reached out blindly and felt around for Torie. She turned her head, seeing she'd obviously gotten up at some point in the night and had donned a sweater. Gillian smiled at the image of her, curled up in a ball, with a bit of blue wool sticking out where her hands gripped the light comforter, now pulled up to her chin.

Quietly, Gillian got up and wrestled with the monster she'd thrown into the corner the night before, straightening it out to be able to drape it over her. With a gentle smile, Torie stretched out a moment later, already warmer. They were going to have to figure out some accommodation, since Gillian was able to sleep with just a sheet unless it was below freezing. But they'd get there. No problem would be as difficult as their physical distance. She started for the bathroom, then stopped in her tracks. Physical distance wasn't worth talking about when compared to the trouble Aiden and Kirsty could cause!

Banishing that troubling thought, she closed the bathroom door and flipped on the light, squinting while her eyes adjusted. Then she smiled, the grin growing when she saw what a wreck she was. Hair everywhere, eyes half-closed. But that messy hair had been earned the fun way, and she was truly looking forward to a birthday—a significant one at that—all because of whom she was going to spend it with.

It had taken a concerted effort, and she'd definitely disappointed the VP at the ad agency, who'd snared tickets to a very in-demand musical, but Gillian was free by six. The trip back to Hoboken was surprisingly quick, and she held her key up to the sensor at six thirty.

"Happy birthday!" Torie said as the door opened. Then her arms were around Gillian and kisses were pressed to twenty different spots on her face.

"It's like having a puppy," Gillian joked, wiping her face as she dropped her bag.

"I missed you." Torie grabbed her for another forceful hug. "I can't even let you take your coat off."

"Want me to leave it on? I assume we're going out."

"I made reservations at the place you suggested, but the earliest I could get was eight thirty. Too late?"

She shrugged and started to take her coat off. "Not really. That'll give me a chance to change and clear my mind of all of the silly stuff I had to jam into it today."

Torie grasped her shoulders and held her still. Then her gaze traveled from head to toe, assessing Gillian carefully. "I can't believe how good you look. Powerful," she decided, making a stern face. "Wealthy. Important." Tickling under her chin, she added, "And as pretty as a picture." She led Gillian over to the table in front of the windows. "I found a bakery I knew you'd like, and bought a wee cake."

Resting on the table was a lovely little chocolate number, decorated with tiny fondant cherry blossoms. "It's so pretty," Gillian said.

"It is, isn't it? And you can't celebrate with a chocolate cake if you don't have some champagne, right?"

"I won't argue with that." She pressed a finger into the cake, sliding it downward to scoop a bit out. "Ganache," she said, grinning. "I wasn't hungry before, but now I am."

"Want dessert first?"

"I think I do. Actually, I'm sure I do. Let me change clothes while you dish out a couple of pieces." As she moved away she said, "You can have some too."

"Ha! I'll fight for this, even though it's your birthday. But I'm not cutting it until you blow out your candles."

By the time Gillian had changed into jeans and a sweater, her cake was glowing brightly. "My eyes!" she said, holding her forearm over them. "That's as bright as the sun!"

"Come over here and blow," Torie teased, grasping her by the hand and tugging her close.

"That's too obvious a joke, so I'll skip it." She leaned close, sucked in a breath and extinguished the candles in one stream of air. "Nice job," she decided. "Now my wish will come true."

Gathering her into an embrace, Torie whispered into her ear, "I hope I'm part of your wish."

"You're all of it. Last year, my sole wish was for a girlfriend to share my life with, so I know birthday wishes can come true."

"Oh! Your present." She ran over to the dresser, opened a drawer, and returned with a wrapped package. There was no box, and the wrapping wasn't crisp, but Gillian was inordinately excited to hold the gift in her hand.

"You brought this from home," she said, grinning.

"How do you know that?"

"Well, you don't have scissors, or tape…and you couldn't have banged this up this badly in just an afternoon. It looks like you kicked it!"

"Travel doesn't agree with thin paper, and I'm too cheap to buy the very expensive kind." She pushed it against Gillian's chest. "Go on and open it before it falls apart."

She did, tearing the thin paper with a finger. Inside was a beautifully knit scarf, mostly bright blue, with the color fading into a spring green at both ends. "It's absolutely gorgeous. And my favorite colors."

"I made it," she said, beaming with pride. "I tried to have it ready for Christmas, but I was off by at least a month. I should have sent it then, but after spending so much time working on it, I decided to save it for your birthday." She took the scarf and wrapped it around Gillian's neck, adjusting it so the ends hung at equal lengths. "It looks wonderful on you. Just like I knew it would."

Removing it to take a better look, Gillian kept sneaking glances at Torie, who was grinning like the Cheshire Cat. "Are you serious? You made this? With your own two hands?"

She held them up and wiggled her fingers. "No loom."

"I'm…amazed. I had no idea you could knit at all, much less like a pro."

"I can sew, do needlework, cross-stitch… All kinds of things. When you're stuck inside for three days because of fog, you've read all of your library books, and you don't have a telly, you'd better have something to occupy yourself."

"You didn't have a television?"

"Sometimes we did, sometimes we didn't. It all depended on the situation. When I learned to knit, on Fair Isle, we didn't."

"You're so talented," Gillian said, still staring at the fine, perfectly formed stitches.

"I'm not bad, but my mum has me beat. My granny, who was a wizard, taught her."

Gillian gazed at her for a few seconds. "How long did this take you to make? Be honest."

She looked like she was going to attempt to slide past the question, but she shrugged and said, "I dedicated two or three hours a day to it for the entire month of December, but I was only half finished. I think I wrapped it up at the end of January." She grinned, looking a little shy. "It took a while."

Gillian tucked her arms around Torie and held her in a tender embrace. "I've never had a better present. I'm not just saying that, Torie. I mean it sincerely."

She sniffed and pulled away to wipe at her eyes. "I've never cried so much in my life!"

"You really like it? I know you're used to expensive things, but I can't afford to compete with what you can buy yourself—"

Gillian cut her off with a kiss. When she pulled away, she said, "I don't need expensive things. They don't mean anything compared to something like this." She folded the scarf and clutched it to her chest. "I'll treasure this." Slipping an arm around Torie, she pulled her close. "And you."

An hour later, they lay on the bed, both naked under the heavy comforter. Gillian's kisses tasted of chocolate and wine, an inspired pairing. When Torie turned to her left she saw the gorgeous New York skyline, to her right, the beautiful glow of Gillian's pale eyes. Both sights equally magical.

"I think I'd better cancel that dinner reservation," she said, placing a soft kiss to Gillian's cheek. "Unless you want dinner after three pieces of cake."

"And half a bottle of champagne," she added, sounding a little silly.

"Oh, I didn't forget that. Given that I can hardly focus on the screen to cancel, I definitely helped you drain that bad boy."

"I love it when you put on an American accent," Gillian said, chuckling.

"I don't do it on purpose. I just think of something I've heard and repeat it as I've heard it. I think that was a line from a movie." She finished and put her phone back on the bedside table. "Mission accomplished. Now, where were we?"

"We were doing things like this," Gillian said, slipping her hand around Torie's thigh from behind to lightly tug on her sex.

"Right. That's exactly what we were doing." She wrapped her arms around Gillian and held her tightly, kissing her face and neck and ears until she was weak with laughter. "I think we should keep doing that until we're well sick of each other."

"You can try," Gillian said, grinning up at her. "But your lips are going to wear out before I'm sick of your kisses."

"We'll just have to see, won't we. I think we should start now." She pressed her to the bed, then playfully started to work her way down. She'd wanted to do this the moment they'd gotten into bed, but an attack of nerves had put her off. Now they'd been playing for a while, and had both been satisfied once or twice. Even if she made a mess of it, it wouldn't ruin their evening.

Gillian put her hands behind her head and pulled herself up a bit, doing a crunch as she watched Torie slide down the bed. "Where ya goin'?"

"I'm changing neighborhoods. I've heard it's nice down here, so I thought I'd see for myself." Teasing helped, but she was still a ball of nerves.

"I think you'll like it, but it might be more appealing if it had a good scrub." She made her eyebrows jump a couple of times. "Urban renewal, so to speak."

"I prefer Glasgow to Edinburgh, so I'd say I like things less polished. Let's see how it goes."

Gillian's playful smile vanished, and her voice grew serious. "Let's not focus on a big finish, okay? Just get to know me."

"All right. Um, I wouldn't mind some advice from an estate agent. Someone who knows the neighborhood well."

"I know just the person." She smiled again. "This is definitely a good neighborhood, but there are all sorts of dead-end streets and alleys. I think you ought to explore all of them. Actually, the hidden alleyways deserve much more of your attention than the town center."

"Interesting." Torie opened Gillian with her fingers to gaze at the slick skin, as pink as her lips after they'd kissed for a while.

"In my experience, some people go right to the town center and park. That's not ideal."

Growing more confident, Torie took her finger and gently explored, getting a few sharp intakes of breath for her troubles. "This looks like a nice street," she said, gliding along near her opening.

"One of my favorites," Gillian sighed, her eyes now closed.

"How's this?" She leaned forward and took a tentative swipe along the sensitive skin, waiting for Gillian's response.

"Good," she said softly. "At first, I'd go slow and soft, like you'd approach a skittish kitten." She started to laugh. "I can't think of a way to stick with the neighborhood theme while telling you to use the flat of your tongue, and switching to cats isn't going to make it a bit easier."

Torie joined her, both of them chuckling at how silly the game was. "How's this?" she asked, doing as Gillian asked.

"Really good," she said, clearly happier with that technique. "Just lick all around really gently. Then, when you see where I'm more sensitive, you can point your tongue a little more. Just don't go crazy at the town center," she added, laughing again. "It's too sensitive for anything more than a perfunctory lick."

"How will I know exactly where you're too sensitive?" she asked, her anxiety rising in a heartbeat.

"I'll tell you." Gillian reached down and ruffled Torie's hair. "I talk, remember?"

"Right." Once again, she focused her attention and did exactly as Gillian had suggested. Soft, unhurried swipes of her tongue, all across the neighborhood.

Quietly, Gillian made some noises and shifted her body, directing Torie to the left, then shifting again so she could reach the right for a while. It was funny, actually, understanding exactly what Gillian wanted without her using many words at all. All Torie had to do was stay alert and follow the cues she gave, which were many.

She'd been so focused Torie hadn't really paid attention to the actual sensation, but now that she loosened up, she found it remarkably sensual. Like bathing herself in Gillian's pleasure. She kept going, leading, responding, listening, tasting. All of her senses focused on Gillian's luscious body.

Her instinct was to try to enter her, but she was using every part of her attention to get just this bit right. As they got to know each other better, she'd figure out how to add some frills. Gillian's hands were on her shoulders, the fingers pressing into her skin. While still providing some guidance, she'd gone into another level of concentration, now just panting softly and moving herself up and down, chasing Torie's tongue. Then they got perfectly in sync and Torie knew she was close. She stayed right where she was, grinning to herself as Gillian's mews and moans got higher pitched. Finally, her thighs started to shake, then she let out a gasp as she pulled away, with Torie trapped between her thighs, which quivered roughly.

"Are you sure you've never been to this neighborhood?" she demanded when she'd caught her breath.

Torie rested her cheek on her thigh, watching her flesh tremble every few seconds. "I've never been, but I'm going to return." She shifted her weight so she could rise up on her arms, letting their gazes meet. "Actually, I might relocate. How are the schools?"

Gillian grasped her arms and tugged on her, able to pull Torie up without much trouble. Then she kissed her, while holding her in a fervid embrace. "That was epic," she whispered. "So much better than you can imagine." They lay next to one another, with Gillian tracing her lips with a finger. "Having someone you care about like I do you…" She sighed heavily. "Having you work so hard to please me was truly awesome."

"Awesome," she teased, trying to imitate her accent exactly. "That's exactly how I felt when you touched me. It's so remarkably intimate when you're with someone you care for." Their lips met again, tenderly and gently. "I care for you more than I can say," Torie whispered. "I hope this has been a great day for you, Gillian. I truly do."

"It has been." She took a quick look at the clock. "And it's only nine. Want to keep going until we're faint?"

"Best idea you've had all night. If you're ready, I'm ready."

The room was a bit of a mess, with pillows, sheets and duvets having been haphazardly thrown about to allow them room to maneuver themselves into a wide variety of positions, all of which Torie was ready to try one more time. But Gillian clearly needed some time to recover. She'd been very rambunctious for the last quarter hour, and was now lying on her back, with an attractive sheen of perspiration covering her flushed chest. In all of her sexual exploits, which were, as she'd already admitted, circumspect, Torie was certain she'd never made a woman sweat.

Gillian reached for her and pulled her into her arms, cuddling against her as a quiet little sound emerged. Rather like a purr, but not quite so loud.

"I've missed this so much," Gillian whispered. "Much more than I even realized."

"Oh, I'm certain I have you beat," Torie said, chuckling. "I've even avoided watching movies that show explicit scenes. Reminding myself of what I couldn't have always depressed me."

"Are you talking about sex?"

Torie turned just enough to make eye contact. "Have I missed a change of topics?"

With a very attractive smile curling the corners of her mouth, Gillian said, "I was talking about how I've missed the emotional part of connecting with a woman. The physical part is great… Don't get me wrong." She sighed, the sound soft and delicate. "But it's this part, the part where we let down our barriers and really get close that I've longed for."

"Why?" Torie asked, tenderly starting to play with the strands of Gillian's hair that had spread out in many directions. "Why haven't you had that? You can't convince me there isn't a woman in Columbus who would have refused you."

Laughing, Gillian said, "There are a few." She was quiet for a few moments, then said, "I'm not sure why I've been so risk-averse, but I truly have been. Maybe I was still smarting from my break-up with Grace, but I also have to admit I've gotten pickier as I've gotten older. If something doesn't seem like it has the potential to be great, I don't bother."

"And no one's been even partially great?"

"No," she said, touching Torie's chin to move her so their eyes met again. "No one until you."

"Is Grace partnered?"

"She is. At least she was the last time I heard. She got a big promotion, which I knew she wanted, but...she hadn't had a baby." She shrugged slightly. "She's a few years older than I am, so she's going to have to use some sort of intervention if she still wants to give birth." Gillian rose up to grasp a pillow and tuck it behind her head. "Maybe it wasn't the baby thing that made her break up with me. Maybe I just wasn't enough for her."

"Why didn't you live together? I find it odd that you had the discussion about having a child when you couldn't even agree on where to live."

"Oh, we agreed," she said, with a grim expression. "We agreed that we couldn't figure out a way to keep our jobs and our sanity if we bought a house together."

"Because...?"

"She had a great job in Dayton, in hospital administration. Dayton isn't all that far... Maybe an hour when the traffic isn't bad. But we both worked long hours, and neither of us wanted to add a long commute at the end of our day."

Torie sat up, scooted around until they faced each other, then leaned close. "You wouldn't move halfway?"

"Neither of us ever brought it up," she said, looking puzzled by her own behavior.

"And you're sure you loved this woman?"

"I was sure I did," she said, with a sad smile. "Now?" She reached up and grasped Torie in her arms, holding her close. "If I wasn't willing to even move, how could I have loved her?"

"Well, she wasn't willing to move for you, either."

"True. I suppose it just wasn't quite right." Now the smile that covered her face was full, and very bright. "I'm so glad it wasn't right, because I *know* this is."

Torie was sound asleep, lying on her back with her arms and legs splayed out in odd positions. Gillian rolled onto her side and gazed at her for a few minutes, unwilling to disturb her by getting up, even though she hadn't brushed or flossed her teeth. Sometimes you had to prioritize, and tonight Torie's sleep was more important than Gillian's dental hygiene.

Resisting the urge to caress her face, Gillian decided that if she'd been able to plan her own birthday, it would have been an exact replica of this night. Just a few hours to laze about in bed, eating top notch chocolate cake and drinking very acceptable Champagne, along with long interludes of lovemaking. They weren't calling it that yet, but that's exactly what it was. Smiling when Torie shivered in her sleep, clearly out for the night, Gillian started to tuck the comforter up around her shoulders, but a bit of dark ink caught her eye. They'd been naked together for hours over the last two days, but she'd never been able to talk when she'd noticed it. Now looking at it carefully, she realized it was a Pictish symbol. It was well done, with crisp, thin lines. She recalled that Pict was a Roman term for "painted people," probably referring to their tattooed skin. Given how Torie identified with the ancient people of Scotland, being marked with one of their symbols seemed like a perfect choice. She tucked the comforter around her, and stealthily slid out of bed. Given how she felt about Torie, she was going to have to have her name emblazoned somewhere. *That* would be a dramatic way to come out at work.

She found her phone on the way to the bathroom, and checked her messages. There were a lot of them, from ex-lovers, biking buddies and co-workers. Kara had her kids sing happy birthday, so out of tempo and pitch that it would have gone viral if Gillian had posted it somewhere. But the last message, sent just a half hour earlier, didn't have its intended effect. She was certain her sister wanted her to feel cared for when she watched the short video of the boys waving and wishing her a happy birthday. But she felt like a shit. Amanda had called six times through the evening, finally leaving the message. Another video, sent earlier, had Amanda looking so damned sincere when she said how much she loved Gillian. She had no real reason to doubt her, but what was that love based on? They hardly knew each other, but so much of what she did know, she didn't like. Amanda could proclaim her love all she wanted, but when she voted for people who wanted to prevent Gillian from marrying… She tossed the phone aside and went to use the bathroom. She was certain her sister meant well, and just as certain she had no idea how her politics hurt the people she claimed to love. And that just sucked.

❦ ❦ ❦

On Saturday evening, they sat in the American Airlines first class lounge at Newark Airport, waiting for their respective flights. Torie had never been in an airport lounge, but it hadn't taken long to figure out why people fought for the right to enter them. It wasn't even the complimentary food and drinks that impressed her. It was the relative quiet. Sitting in a chair, sipping a glass of sparkling water, with enough open space to have a civilized conversation should have been something every traveler got to experience. But that's not how the world worked. The people who traveled often, and paid the highest prices for their tickets, got the perks.

Torie realized why she was focusing on the lounge, the businessmen who took up two chairs when they only needed one, and the new mother trying to breastfeed her infant without drawing any attention to herself. She simply couldn't look at Gillian. Every time she did, she found herself on the verge of tears, and she truly didn't want to be one of those long-distance relationship people who greeted like weans at every departure.

Gillian had been staring out the window, watching other planes load. But she turned when Torie was gazing at her, with their eyes meeting for a few seconds. A ghost of a smile curled her lips and she nodded, acknowledging all of the things they'd said to each other when they were alone. How much they'd enjoyed being together, how precious each day had seemed, how they'd never again let so many months pass without a visit. All of the things they couldn't say now. At least not without the risk of someone hearing them, or noticing the loving looks they shared, or the small intimacies they'd had to stop the moment they'd closed the door to their room. The wall that separated them wasn't just distance, and it was slowly going back up, one brick at a time.

CHAPTER TWENTY-THREE

GILLIAN HAD BEEN CLEANING HER house for the past three hours, a task her cleaning service usually handled very well. When she realized she was scratching the finish from the oven burners, she tossed the scrub pad into the sink and removed her rubber gloves.

Picking up her phone, she called Kara.

"Hey! How'd it go?"

"It went great," Gillian said. "But it's over, and now I'm like a puppy taken away from my litter mates."

"Aww… That's cute. But sad, too."

"Yeah. I…um…I don't like this sad stuff. When I wished for a girlfriend on my last birthday, I assumed I'd get one who fit right into my life. I was hoping I'd have someone who spent her whole day trying to make me happy." She let out a rueful laugh. "Isn't that what you're supposed to get?"

"Come over. The kids are in bed, and Ben's watching football. We can have a glass of wine."

"Can I crawl onto your lap and have you pet me until I fall asleep?"

There were a few moments of silence, then Kara said, "I've done that twice already tonight. Once more won't hurt. Get over here."

Gillian had, of course, been kidding. They were never very physical with their affection for one another, and she didn't want to change that dynamic. But Kara gave her a longer, more enthusiastic hug than normal when she opened the door twenty minutes later, serving only to embarrass Gillian.

"I brought wine," she said. "I'm in a white Bordeaux mood."

Kara took it from her hand and looked at the label. "Nice stuff."

"Birthday present. I got a *lot* of wine," she said, chuckling. "I guess that's what people give you when you're old."

"Hey, G," Ben called out, not getting up from his recliner.

She normally went into the den and chatted with him, but she was more focused on Kara tonight. "Hey, there. Who's winning?" she asked from the doorway.

"Browns aren't playing, so I don't care."

"Carry on," she said, following Kara to the living room. In just a few minutes the wine had been poured and they sat on opposite ends of the sofa, facing each other. They'd been sitting like that since they'd met in college, and neither of them could think of a reason to change. The only difference was that now they made sure to take their shoes off, a consideration they hadn't always exercised at their sorority house.

"So," Gillian said, "here's the problem." She took in a breath, steeling herself. "I'm falling in love with Torie."

"Kind of obvious," Kara said, poking her with a foot. "Why's that a problem?"

Slightly annoyed that Kara had to ask, Gillian ticked off the reasons. "We're from different continents, neither of us could live in the other country without some difficulty, she's got an independent streak a mile wide, which means she won't let me buy her a ticket to visit more often, and..." She sighed heavily. "I miss her, Kara. She's been gone one day, and I miss her like crazy."

"You didn't mention the two people who can really put a crimp in this," she said soberly.

Gillian gazed at her for a few moments, drawing a blank.

"Her sister and her nephew. Did you forget about them?"

"Of course not. But I'm feeling better about all of that. Her sister's been sober for over a full year now, and given that's the first time *that's* happened in thirteen years, that's a big plus, right?"

"Who are you trying to convince? Me? If so, you're going to have to work harder. I've seen my uncle fall off the wagon after twenty years, G. And my cousins have both been in rehab more times than I can count. It's hard staying sober."

"Yeah, but Kirsty's doing really well. Torie thinks she's motivated to stick to the program now. And Aiden's more able to take care of himself. He's desperate to have some independence, so Torie's going to stop going over there every afternoon to make his tea."

"The biggest problem is distance now, huh? That's not what you said at the start of this."

"Things are different. We're *really* close now. I know how much she loves Aiden, but she's starting to love me too. And while we might have to roll with the punches, my opinion's going to matter. I *know* that."

"I hope that's true. But I've got to tell you, if it ever came to the kids' welfare versus Ben's, he's going to lose out. While I chose him, they're part of me."

"I get that," she said, taking a sip of the wine, which really was delicious. "But Aiden's Torie's nephew, not her kid. I know she loves him, but I don't think that's the same as being someone's mom. I mean, I love my nephews, but if one of them needed me at the same time Torie did?" She shook her head. "I hope the kid's got other options."

🌿 🌿 🌿

On a dreary, drizzly April afternoon, Torie slipped under an awning, waiting for the light to change. She was in front of a fast food outlet, and when she turned slightly, she spotted her sister sitting at a table.

Unexpectedly seeing Kirsty in an unfamiliar setting let Torie see her as a stranger would, a sensation that struck her because it was so rare. In just seconds, a sense of relief settled on her like a warm blanket. Kirsty simply looked like a clerk stepping out from behind her cash register to have a bit of lunch. The dark green vest with the words "Fruit and Veg" stitched across the back did nothing for her style, but Torie paid little attention to her clothes. She was too taken by her affect. Kirsty's eyes were wide open, clear and alert. No more heavy-lidded, glassy-eyed stares, or worse, the furtive glances when her compulsion made her think of nothing but her next fix.

They didn't share much physically, with Kirsty taking after the Sinclairs more than the Gunns. But their coloring was similar, and now Kirsty's pale skin looked like she simply hadn't had much sun—not that she was ashen from dope sickness. She'd put on a few pounds, which made her look closer to her age. Actually, her grooming had improved in every area, with her multi-colored hair now giving her a youthful edge. If Torie had been in charge, the candy-floss blue color would go right to the bin, but Kirsty hadn't allowed her natural ginger to show in many years.

The pleasure Torie got from seeing her sister as just another young woman only lasted for a minute. Then she started to worry. It was early for lunch, and this part of town was a bit of a distance from her market. Actually, the pizza this place sold wasn't worth a special trip, so why was Kirsty here? Even after fifteen months, a period of sobriety three times greater than she'd ever been able to accomplish, Torie was still examining her sister's behavior for any variation from her usual pattern. Would that ever stop?

Even though she knew she wouldn't be welcomed, Torie was just about to go in to see what was going on when a tall, handsome man entered to sit next to Kirsty. Once again, warning bells rang in Torie's head. Her sister's taste in men went from bad to worse, with her internal compass consistently sending her into the arms of lowlifes, drug dealers, and abusers. But this guy not only looked respectable, he likely had a job—or he wore a tool belt and carried a hardhat just to appeal to the ladies.

They clearly knew each other, since he grasped the piece of pizza she'd bought for him, sliced off the end, and fed it to her, with her grinning like a besotted schoolgirl. Still tempted to go in, Torie decided to let them have their time together. But she was determined to find out who he was, and what he meant to Kirsty—and Aiden.

Later that afternoon, Torie tried to swallow the hurt that lanced her when Aiden's face fell upon seeing her in the kitchen of his flat.

"I have food," he said as he dropped his books onto the table.

"I'm happy to see you too," she said, unable to slough off the slight. Try as she might, his dismissal of her got to her more often than she'd like. "I had the time, and thought I'd make something fresh before I have to go out of town for a few days."

"What?" he asked, reluctantly walking over to stand next to her and peer at the cooktop.

"Marinara sauce. You get to choose the pasta." The child loved Italian food more than any kid in Rome.

"Linguini," he said, brightening.

"Great. I think we have enough to make two meals worth. Make a note on the chalkboard to buy more, okay?"

He walked over to the board and started to write. After wiping away the first three attempts to spell it properly, he simply wrote "big pasta."

"Are you staying?" he asked, giving her a look she couldn't interpret.

"For tea? I thought I would. Do you mind?"

"I guess not."

He started for his room, but stopped abruptly when she said, "I saw your mum at lunch today."

"Really?" He turned and gazed at her, his eyes slightly narrowed.

"I did. She was with a friend. Probably a co-worker or something."

"Nah," he said, clearly pleased to know something she didn't. "That's Pee Yot."

"Who?"

"Her boyfriend." He went over to the chalkboard and printed the name. P-i-o-t-r. "He's Polish. You kinda don't say the 'T,' and you kinda don't say the 'R,' but you say them a little. I didn't get it quite right, but he said I did better than most people."

"You've met this guy?"

"Just for a minute." He shrugged. "He wants to make me like him, I think."

"Nice guy?"

"I guess." He seemed to think for a minute. "He likes fitbaw."

"Well, I guess that's enough. Will you set the table?"

He let out a sigh heavy enough to show he carried the weight of the world on his shoulders. But he went to the cupboard and took out two plates, then opened the utensils drawer. It wasn't much, but he did it without verbal complaint, and Torie had learned to celebrate the small things.

Kirsty came directly home from her shift, giving them a few minutes before Torie had to leave for the pub.

"I didn't know you were coming today," she said, with a slight frown. It seemed like no one in the family knew how to properly greet another human being.

"I had a little time, and since I'm going to Glasgow for a few days, I thought I'd make some pasta."

"Any extra?"

Torie rolled her eyes, but what could you do? "Some, but you have to leave enough for Aiden. You know he wants to eat the minute he gets home."

"Everybody does," she said, going to the refrigerator to pull out the container. Kirsty clearly didn't care much about presentation, since she simply pried the lid off and stuck a fork into the cold pasta. It was actually kind of funny to watch a grown woman, with her jacket still on, gobbling down food like a hungry thief.

"Saw you at the pizza place today," Torie said, not wanting to waste time bringing it up in a more delicate way. "New boyfriend?"

Kirsty's eyes narrowed. "You don't need to spy on me. I couldn't be more sober if—"

"I wasn't spying, Kirsty. I was waiting for the light to change, and I saw you when I stood under the awning. I wasn't *looking* for you," she stressed. "I just saw you."

"Yeah, he's new." She put the top back on the container and replaced it, a victory for neatness. Now she took off her coat and tossed it onto the table. After pouring a large glass of fizzy juice, she walked over to the sofa and flopped down, letting out a heavy sigh. "I suppose you have a thousand questions?"

"Just one. Is he a nice guy?"

"Yeah," she said, not jumping on Torie for asking, also a rarity. "I think Aiden likes him, even though they haven't spent any time together." Her expression hardened, like she expected to be reprimanded and was getting out in front of the issue. "My sponsor said not to have him around until I was sure he was trustworthy." She let out a short laugh. "Like there's a way to know *that*."

"I think you can tell, but it takes time. What's he like?"

"Me," she said, looking proud of herself. "And his mother. She's in Krakow. And…" Her chin tilted up as she thought. "He likes football, but he only wants to watch the Polish team." She laughed a little. "He's not very Scottish, even though he's been here for six years."

"Married? I mean ever," she added when Kirsty gave her a scowl.

"No. He says he stayed away from women until he had some money saved. He watches every penny."

"So you had to pay for the pizza?"

"He's not *that* cheap. He's more like dad. He's careful."

Torie got up and put her hand on her sister's shoulder, giving it a squeeze. "If you can find a guy like dad, you'll be lucky."

"He's only like him in some ways." Their eyes met again. "But he's solid."

"He…" She paused, knowing Kirsty would be angry at the question, but she simply had to ask. "He supports your sobriety?"

"*Yes*. He doesn't even drink. At all. He said he gets a headache and his face flushes if he has even a little. There's no temptation there," she said, scowling.

"I don't mean to supervise. I hope you know I only ask because I care about you."

"You care about Aiden," she said, pouting. "But you don't have to worry. Piotr is exactly the kind of guy you'd approve of." She got up and walked over to the door as Torie was putting her jacket on. She leaned against a small wooden table and said, "Um, I haven't stayed overnight yet. If I did, would you watch Aiden?"

"Not every night," Torie warned. "But I'd be happy to stay over once in a while."

"Tomorrow?" she asked, smiling expectantly.

"Saturday. I won't get back from Glasgow until late, but I'll come here directly."

"Thanks," Kirsty said, grasping Torie's shoulder and pulling her close for a kiss to the cheek. "I promise I won't have him here until I'm sure he's all right."

"That's all I ask," Torie said. Impulsively, she gave Kirsty a firm hug, holding on for a few seconds, relishing the closeness. "I hope he makes you happy."

"I do too. It's about time I met a guy I didn't have to worry would steal my purse," she grumbled.

"I can empathize," Torie said, although her empathy didn't match exactly. "We're both due for some love in our lives."

After Torie raced home on a clear, warm Friday in May, she spent a few minutes chatting with her mother, then went into her room to strip off her clothes and get into her pajamas. Even though it was one thirty in the morning, she had some energy because she didn't have a single obligation until five o'clock that night. The prospect of fifteen and a half hours of freedom made her nearly giddy, and if she could get away with it, she was going to spend at least twelve of those hours in bed.

She and Gillian had spent more time than they should have arguing about it, but Torie had finally relented and taken herself off the weekend schedule for waitressing. That not only let her get more rest, she was now available to accompany Aiden when he had a competition for his new hobby—robotics. He'd only started recently, but he was already more engaged than he'd been about anything school-related in a long while.

Her tablet computer chirped and she clicked it open. "Where are your pajamas?" Torie demanded. Their Saturday and Sunday afternoon chats had expanded to include Friday nights, which they'd named their pajama party, but Gillian wasn't in uniform.

"After we talk, I'm going over to my sister's for an adults only dinner. I've put her off three times since my birthday, and she finally told me I had no option." She took a sip of her drink, and Torie tried to guess what she was having. It had the look of a vodka and tonic. "Tonight, I'm going to tell them I'm going to the UK next month, just in case she notices my absence."

Torie perked up at the news. "You're telling her about us?"

"No," she said, letting out a wry laugh. "I'm going to tell her I'm going to Europe on business." Her voice grew low and sexy, with a timber that always made Torie shiver a little bit. "The business of chasing you around a bedroom four or five times a day."

"Why not tell her?" she asked, sidestepping the fun part of Gillian's comment.

"Not worth it."

Torie thought for a moment, unsure if she wanted to broach this particular topic, given it might lead to a fight, but she decided to jump in. They could only make progress if they talked about things they didn't *want* to get into. "You say that a lot. About all sorts of things."

"No, I don't," she said, blinking in surprise. "I don't."

"You do, Gillian. You say it about anything you don't want to deal with. I'm starting to wonder what *is* worth a fight."

"Lots of things. Specifically, you. You know I'd gladly talk to Amanda about our relationship if there was any benefit to it. But there's not."

"Of course there is! It's been great having my mum and dad ask about you. If I hadn't told them, they'd know something was going on, but they probably wouldn't have asked." She could see that Gillian still looked puzzled. "Telling my parents has let us get closer. Wouldn't you like to have a better relationship with your sister?"

"Sure." She started to nod, then stopped. "Why am I lying? I'm perfectly fine with where things are. As long as we don't talk about any loaded topic, it's all right."

"No, it's not," Torie insisted. "It's…" She fumbled for a word. "It's sterile. You have more connection to the guy who cuts your hair."

"Isaiah is interesting," she said, clearly growing defensive. "And as far as I know, he doesn't want to destroy the foundations of our democracy. I know I shouldn't be so angry, but I can't get over having my sister not only vote, but support someone I think is profoundly evil." She stopped and closed her eyes for a second. "Here's my motto. When you can't win the game, why play? Focus on the things that have a possibility of a payoff, and spend your time there. I can't change my sister, so I'm not going to try."

"You've never tried to get closer, Gillian. You've admitted that."

"That's true." She picked up her tablet and brought it closer to her face. So close that Torie could almost count her eyelashes. "Don't expect that to change. I'm not unhappy with the way things are, and I would be very *un*happy to get into it and have her admit she's in favor of taking away what few rights gay people have. That's not even scratching the list of all of the other people this fascist administration has hurt. It's not worth it," she stressed, speaking each word crisply.

Realizing she wasn't going to win the point, Torie said, "I've gotten the message. Would you like to hear what I've got planned for us so far?"

After moving the tablet away, Gillian's expression was once again open and sunny. "I would truly love to hear every single thing you've planned." A smile grew and she added, "As long as you've scheduled plenty of time where we're completely naked."

⚜ ⚜ ⚜

The kids normally ate early, so Amanda's plan had been to get them fed and into bed before the adults had dinner. But her timing must have been off, since both boys were running around the house in their pajamas when Gillian arrived. Amanda tried to get Chapin into bed while Gillian was enlisted to read a story to Spencer, but she simply wasn't doing it right. The kid was very particular, and wanted the story about a barnyard read with accurate representations of all of the animals. Having never tried to sound like a goat or a calf, Gillian was botching it up pretty badly. Finally, Spencer called out, "Mom! Make her do it right!"

Amanda poked her head in and said, "Are you trying to sound like the animals?"

"I have no idea what a goat sounds like," Gillian said, amazed she had to even construct such a silly sentence. "Doesn't he have a book with just humans?"

Amanda didn't roll her eyes, actually showing very little frustration with her older sister's ineptitude. "Try this one," she said, coming into the room to pluck a book from the shelf.

Gillian held the book in her hands, staring at it as though she were hallucinating. She was sure both Amanda and Spencer could see she was unable to move, or speak, but she couldn't make herself even flinch. The almost pristine book bore an image of a lighthouse, brick with wide white stripes decorating it. Looking up at it was a small girl, dressed in a dark, knee-length coat, a matching hat with ribbons trailing down her back, and ankle socks with black shoes that made her look like she was going somewhere special. "The Keeper's Daughter," was embossed across the top third of the book, and that title struck her like a blow. Torie had suggested a boy from Kirkwall, or the ferry boat pilot might have impregnated Jeannie. But if there was a lighthouse on North Ronaldsay, wouldn't the lighthouse keeper have had some free time? Torie had explained how they usually had three keepers, one of whom was always off-duty. What would a man have done to keep himself occupied on an island of fewer than two hundred people that didn't even have electricity. It didn't take a leap of logic to suggest one activity.

Finally forcing her hands to move, she opened the cover and peered at the copyright page, seeing it had been published in 1950, in Edinburgh. "Was this ours?" she got out, with her voice sounding strained.

"I don't remember it, but it was in the house." Amanda slipped it away from Gillian's hands and inspected it just as carefully. "Hmm." Turning, she pulled another title from the neatly arranged shelf. As soon as Gillian saw it, it resonated with her.

"I remember that one," she said, still sounding nothing like herself.

"Right. All of the books we read, like this one, are barely hanging on by a thread. That's why I don't usually read them to the boys."

Gillian looked up at her, seeing echoes of their mother so strong she almost gasped. It must have been the light, or the setting, since Amanda usually didn't look like her at all. One good memory Gillian retained was of lying in her little bed, with her mom reading to her at night. Seeing Amanda doing the same thing must have triggered something. She tugged the book from Amanda and held it like a treasure. "I think this was mom's. From when she was a girl."

The book was whisked from her hands so quickly Gillian's blouse fluttered from the breeze. "I'll put it away so it doesn't get ruined."

Gillian ached from the loss, tempted to grab it right back. But she couldn't do that. Instead, she focused on the fact that the books existed at all. "You…kept the books we read as kids?"

"I have all of the books Mom saved. You didn't want them," she rushed to add.

Gillian examined the familiar book about a friendly giant while Spencer watched her. "You'd just graduated from high school when we had to sell the house," she said, idly thumbing through the pages. "Where did you keep everything?"

"In suitcases." Amanda settled on the bed next to Gillian. "These books, some things from school, the sash with my Girl Scout merit badges." She let out a wistful sigh. "Some of those glass figurines Mom liked, and a couple of her winter scarves." She reached over and put her hand on Gillian's knee. "I think one of them might have been her mother's. It's pretty old, and looks handmade."

"Hmm. I'll take a picture and have Torie take a look—" She swallowed, having no idea how to get out of this one. "Um, I'm probably going to see her in a couple of weeks… When I'm in the UK."

"I didn't know you were going," Amanda said, cocking her head like a puppy waiting for a treat.

"Yeah. Business," Gillian said. "But as long as I'm there, I'm adding a few days. I'm going to go take a look around the island where Mom was born."

"You are?" Amanda's eyes had gotten so wide she looked like she'd been frightened. Spencer sensed she was upset and cuddled up against her, burying his head against her belly. While gently stroking his hair, Amanda gathered herself and said, "I don't know why, but I've been fantasizing about going to Scotland with you." She looked down at her son, never meeting Gillian's gaze. "I know we've never taken a trip together, but I thought it might be nice…" She sniffled, then reached up to wipe her eyes. "I thought it would be a nice way to get closer, and to keep Mom alive…at least a little bit."

"Oh, shit," Gillian sighed, earning a sharp look from her little nephew. "Sorry," she added, patting his bony shoulder. "I shouldn't use that word, Spencer."

"Can I have *my* story now?" he asked, turning his head to gaze into Amanda's eyes.

She nodded, took the book from Gillian's hands, stood, and replaced it on the shelf. They still hadn't made eye contact when she sat back down and picked up the book Gillian had muffed. "Let's start at the beginning," she said, her patient, loving tone one Gillian couldn't ever recall hearing from their own mother. Back then she'd always been tired, and rushed, clearly wanting to get the story read so she could check the task off her list. But Amanda hadn't echoed that behavior. She'd learned to be a caring, connected parent. Maybe it had been by osmosis, but she'd done it, and should be complimented for the accomplishment. But that didn't change the fact that she supported a racist, sexist, Islamaphobe, a choice Gillian couldn't imagine forgiving.

After dinner, Gillian poured herself a drink and went into the living room. Amanda made herself a cup of tea, and sat at the far end of the sofa, paying an inordinate amount of attention to her cup. Finally, when Gillian's skin was beginning to itch, Amanda said, "How long will you be in Scotland?"

"Not very," she said quickly. "I've got a lot to do in London." That was a total lie, but she wasn't about to admit she was spending two full weeks with Torie.

"And your friend…the tour guide…is going to go to the island with you?"

"I might need a translator." She smiled, then realized Amanda didn't understand she was teasing. "Some of the people up there have pretty strong accents."

"Mom didn't," Amanda said softly.

"She was a baby when she left. I assume our grandmother had one, but…" She shrugged. "I don't know anyone who knew her. It's like she barely existed."

"I'd like to go," Amanda said. "I know I can't go with *you*, but I have this need…" Another little attack of the sniffles had her reaching for a tissue and blotting her eyes. "I don't think I'll ever get over wanting more from Mom." She batted her watery blue eyes, looking nearly as devastated as she had when their mother had died. "Do you feel like that too?"

"No," Gillian said, wincing when she realized she'd responded too quickly. "Um, I mean that she and I weren't as close as you two were. I feel like I got what she was willing to give."

"But you're going to Scotland..." Amanda was nearly issuing a written invitation for Gillian to tell her the whole truth. But she just couldn't. If she told her about Torie, and Amanda didn't take it well, they wouldn't even have the tenuous connection they currently had.

"Well, I'm going to be awfully close..." She shrugged. "I'm actually more interested in our grandmother and her family. I kind of identify with a woman forced to make it on her own when she was just seventeen. You've got to admire the guts she had to pick up her new baby and take off. She just put her troubles behind her and found a new life."

"I can see how that would resonate with you," Amanda said, her gaze having grown a little chilly. She stood and carried her cup into the kitchen, saying, "I'll take a good photo of the scarf I'm talking about. Maybe your friend has an opinion on whether it's from Scotland."

"I'll definitely ask her," Gillian said, standing when it became clear she was being dismissed. She went into the kitchen to watch her sister start to unload the dishwasher. "Can I bring you anything from our ancestral home?"

"No, thank you," Amanda said, turning her back to put some plates into the cabinet. "I hope you have a good time."

"Me too." She moved to stand behind Amanda, and placed a kiss to her cheek. "I'll poke my head into Rick's man cave to say goodbye."

"I guess we'll see you when you get back." She turned and gave Gillian a look that almost made her cry. Her feelings were right there... But Gillian wasn't sure what they were. Amanda was definitely sad, but there was more. Much more than Gillian would ever be able to discern. They just didn't have enough shared history to be able to dig deep, and it was too late to find the connection they should have formed when they were children. Whose fault was that? Given she was older, it had to be on her. But she honestly didn't know what she could have done differently.

After saying goodbye to Rick, Gillian walked to her car, tossing the keys in the air to catch them. A memory hit her, making her feel so guilty, so quickly, her breath caught in her throat. Her childhood memories were few, and she was certain she'd never recalled this one before. In fact, this was probably the earliest memory she'd ever had access to. But it was vivid. She was standing over Amanda's crib when she was a tiny baby, watching her cry. She didn't have any context for the memory other than the very strong desire to send the scrawny little screamer back where it had come from. The awful part, the part that made her a little sick to her stomach, was that she was almost certain her opinion had never really changed. Amanda had sucked up all of the love and attention their mother had to give, and Gillian was sure she'd struggled with that as a child. Now? The jury was still out thirty-six years later.

Chapter Twenty-Four

Flying business class certainly wasn't a difficult way to cross the Atlantic. Especially when you were able to lie in a pod that approximated a bed and sleep for most of the trip. Gillian had been very successful at the sleeping part, and was now trying to wake up. A pleasant man was offering her a cup of tea, and she managed to sit up and take it. "How long until we land?" she asked.

"Less than an hour. I wanted to give you time to have a bite of breakfast."

"You're too good to me," she said, tossing her hair from her eyes to sip the dark, strong brew.

She wasn't sure what time it was, but they were scheduled to land at nine. The sun was shining brightly, and she took that as a very good sign. Torie had finally relented and agreed to take two weeks off from both the restaurant and the pub, a huge win on Gillian's scorecard. Now all they had to do was spend every moment of that time together, and she'd be a very happy camper.

The only part of the trip Gillian wasn't looking forward to was the last bit to Aberdeen. Once she was in Scotland, she wanted to see Torie, not the countryside flying by. But Aberdeen wasn't very near Edinburgh, so she had to take her lumps. After being processed through immigration, and retrieving her suitcase, she started for the cab stand, hoping she could make the ten thirty train.

Just as she was scanning the overhead signs, a hand settled on her hip and she turned to find the most welcome sight she could imagine. Torie smiled at her and opened her arms. It had been almost three months, three achingly slow months that she'd been sure would never pass. But when those arms settled around her body, it was like only moments had elapsed.

"God, I've missed you," she whispered.

Torie's hug grew tighter, and Gillian could tell she was struggling not to cry. It must have looked like one of them was just back from the war, but she truly didn't care if everyone in Scotland saw them. Tilting her head back a few inches, she gazed into Torie's eyes and felt her heart start to pound. Unable to stop the urge, she kissed her, lost in the sensation to let the kiss continue longer than was polite.

"I think we're blocking traffic," Torie said, managing to pull away.

"They can go around." Gillian held her even tighter, unwilling to let go for any reason.

"If we start moving, we'll be at our hotel in a short while. Doesn't that sound better than standing in an airport?"

"We're staying in Edinburgh? I don't have to take a two-hour train ride?"

"Not until tomorrow. I didn't want you to have to keep traveling today. You've come far enough."

"But that means you've spent the last three hours on a bus."

"True." She placed a quick kiss to Gillian's lips. "You're easily worth it."

As soon as the door to their room clicked closed, Gillian's body wrapped around Torie's and held on like she expected a hurricane-force wind to separate them.

"This is how I wanted you to greet me when I showed up at your party," Torie murmured. "I was right. This is nice."

"I screwed up. Maybe the worst screw-up I've ever committed." She leaned back enough to be able to tilt her chin. "I won't ever make that mistake again." Their lips met for a long, tender kiss. Torie breathed in her scent, different than she remembered, more herbal. But her mouth was fresh and clean and sweet, making her want to stay right in the doorway for hours.

"My brain thinks it's only four in the morning," Gillian murmured when they broke apart and locked eyes. "Maybe we should lie down."

"Tired?"

"No," she said, grinning wolfishly. "I slept for almost five hours. Skipped dinner and popped a sleeping pill so I'd be alert when I got here."

"You look alert," Torie said, mesmerized by the spark in her clear, pale eyes. Taking the lead, she grasped Gillian's hand and tugged her over next to the bed. Then she slowly started to undress her, smiling as she worked.

"This is what *I* wanted the night you showed up for my party," Gillian teased. "Well, not exactly at the party, but I had pretty high hopes for the afterparty."

Torie kept unbuttoning and unfastening, smiling as fabric slid from skin. "I screwed up. Not by any means the biggest screw-up of my life, but I shouldn't have been so thin-skinned." Their eyes met again. "I was just so wounded."

"No one's wounded today. At least not yet," she added, making her eyebrows waggle. "I can't guarantee there won't be some stiff muscles or overuse injuries..."

Gillian was naked now, her fit, shapely body so attractive that Torie had to stop herself from pushing her down and devouring her. "That reminds me," she said, intentionally distracting herself to slow the pace. "I'm going to get some lotion. I've been fantasizing about giving you a massage."

"Really? I got a nice little package from the airline. Botanical something or other. Want that?"

"Sure." She sniffed at her face. "I wondered why you smelled different. I'm used to spring flowers."

Gillian went to her bag, tossed it onto the bed, and unzipped it. When she took out a stylish leather pouch, she emptied the contents atop her suitcase, then grasped a small container. "Thyme and rosemary," she said, having to extend her arm a bit to read the print. "Pretty herbal."

"After I massage you, I'll take a few bites. I bet you'll taste like lamb."

Laughing, Gillian said, "I can't imagine what I'd taste like, but I'm calling Scotland Yard if you try it. Is that right?" she asked. "Scotland Yard?"

"No. But nice try." Torie started to unbutton her gilet, but Gillian took over the second she'd put her case back onto the floor.

"Allow me," she said, starting to concentrate. "You fantasize about massaging me, and I fantasize about undressing you. I win in both fantasies."

It just took a minute, now that summer was kind enough to allow for fewer layers, then their bare bodies finally pressed together and they both let out satisfied sighs. "Exactly how I remembered," Torie breathed. "Fantastic."

Gillian stroked her flanks for a moment, then reached down to draw the covers back. She sat down and pulled Torie to stand between her legs, gazing up at her as her hands caressed her body, now covered in goose bumps. "I had PBS on a few weeks ago, and a ballet came on."

"PBS?"

"Classy TV. Anyway, I watched this woman float across the stage and it hit me. You look just like a ballerina." Her smile grew as her hands moved with more focus, grasping and holding Torie's bum, then pressing into her thighs. "You're as graceful and elegant as any woman I've ever touched. Ever *seen*," she corrected. "You're so pretty, Torie. Beautiful in every way."

"You make me feel pretty," she admitted. "Every once in a while, I'll see myself in a window as I walk by and think, 'Not bad at all.'" She laughed with embarrassment at admitting that, but knew Gillian would appreciate it. "You've boosted my confidence sky-high."

"It should have been stratospheric already," she said soberly. "But if I can make you see yourself as you are, I'm happy."

"Why don't you lie down and let me touch you? I really want to."

"The pleasure is all mine." She lay down and stretched out on her belly, with her arms up over her head. Torie climbed on, sitting astride her hips, then squeezed some of the lotion in a long line down her back.

"I didn't know I'd find a woman's back so sexy, but yours makes my pulse race," she said, feeling it start to thrum before her fingers had even brushed along the silky skin. "I love how lean and muscular it is." Her fingers moved along her scapula, clearly defined. "Is this beautiful body from riding a bike?"

"I suppose so. If you want me to I'll start lifting weights. Or learn Mandarin." Her body shook when she laughed. "I'll do anything to make you happy."

"At this point, I wouldn't change a thing about you." Tickling down her spine, she added, "One day, years from now, I'm sure I'll have a long list of improvements. But now…? You're perfect."

Gillian shifted to be able to turn her head and meet Torie's gaze. "You believe we'll be together years from now?"

"I do," she said, dead certain of that fact. "Unless you're a world-class liar, which I'd have a tough time believing."

"I'd never lie about something so important." Gillian flipped all the way over, and sat up with Torie now on her lap. Their noses were almost touching, and she spoke softly and clearly. "I've been honest from the start, and I plan on staying that way." Her eyes blinked slowly, and with their radiant blue color shining in the morning sun, she whispered, "I love you. I've been wanting to tell you that since we were in New Jersey, but I didn't want you to think I was just saying it because I should have. I love you," she repeated, tilting her chin so their lips could meet tenderly.

"I love you too," Torie said, her voice barely a whisper. "I love you *so* much."

"Make love to me," Gillian said. "Show me what's in your heart." She started to lie down, pulling Torie with her.

They were face to face, emotion arcing between them like an electric pulse. Torie lifted her hand and caressed Gillian's beautiful face. "I've never felt like this about anyone. It's…big," she said, then chuckled at her inarticulateness. "It's like I felt about Aiden the night we brought him home and I watched him sleep. Being responsible for a child at that point in time wasn't something I'd planned, but I knew I'd do anything in the world to care for him." She placed an achingly tender kiss to Gillian's lips. "That's how I feel about you. You're in my heart."

"Exactly," Gillian whispered, blinking away a few tears. "You're in my heart. That's the perfect way to put it."

Torie wrapped her in a fierce hug and nuzzled against her. "I love you," she murmured again, thrilled to simply say it. "I'm in love with you, and I'd shout that from the battlements of Edinburgh Castle if I didn't think they'd lock me up."

"That won't be a problem, since I wouldn't think of letting you leave this room. Not before I show you *exactly* how I feel about you."

Torie woke and tried to orient herself, puzzled by the crinkling noise from somewhere near the floor...

Gillian was on her knees in front of her suitcase, digging through it like a squirrel. She met Torie's eyes and gave a guilty shrug. "I just ate the tiny package of shortbread I took from the plane. Next I'm going for the toothpaste. This room has no food!"

"Do you normally have a fully-stocked kitchen in your hotel rooms?"

"Why is there no mini-bar? Don't they know they're giving up thousands of dollars of pure profit? Hungry tourists are the only people in the world who'll pay twenty-five dollars for a small jar of macadamia nuts."

Torie rolled into a sitting position and put her feet onto the floor. "I think we'd better shower first, but as soon as we're clean, I'm taking you out for a proper meal. Never let it be said that Torie Gunn let the woman she loved eat toothpaste on the day they declared their devotion to one another."

Gillian stood and flicked on the light in the bath. "I'm not sure who'd spread that story around, but I promise I won't tell a soul." She stepped into the shower and started to adjust the water. "I *am* going to suggest they sell snacks in the room, though. Leaving cash on the table is just stupid."

Gillian had a crying need to get places quickly, so Torie allowed her to pay for train tickets on Sunday morning. It saved only thirty minutes, and cost nearly twice as much, so Torie rarely splurged unless she had a pressing need to be on time. That wasn't the case on a clear, warm, Sunday morning, but she'd refused so many of Gillian's financial offers that she didn't want to seem unreasonable.

The ride was always pleasant, but having Gillian next to her made it so much lovelier that Torie hardly had words for how she felt. All she could manage was to sneak a look at her beautiful companion so frequently that her neck began to ache.

Gillian didn't look like she'd spent the previous night on an airplane. Her cheeks bore the healthy glow of skin exposed to moderate, but frequent applications of sun, along with plenty of exercise. Blue eyes were bright with interest as she surveyed the passing landscape, and she frequently made a small appreciative sound when she spotted something she liked.

Torie had dressed carefully, bringing her best casual clothes. But she still looked like someone at least one, and possibly two levels down the social ladder.

Gillian always looked nice, having a good eye for color and fabric and cut that highlighted her coloring and her body. Now that Torie had seen her in both autumn and summer, she'd begun to recognize her style. She definitely preferred patterned cotton blouses, along with very expensive, solid color sweaters, worn over stylish jeans. Today's sweater was a mint green v-neck, very soft, over a plaid blouse made up of shades of pale green and blue. Nothing she wore begged for attention, but it was all first-class and very appropriate. She'd fit right in with the high-ranking executives from the various Aberdeen oil company concerns, and stand out like a sore thumb with the Gunns. But Torie wasn't overly worried about that. Gillian didn't seem to care that they weren't on the same social strata. In fact, she didn't even seem to notice, other than her frequent offers to pay for things Torie couldn't afford.

She started when she finally noticed Gillian staring at her. "I'm sorry," she said. "Did you say something?"

"Nothing important." She tapped Torie's chin with her finger. "You're pretty when you're daydreaming."

"Just thinking. Um, do you mind stopping by my sister's flat? I want to pick Aiden up."

"For...?" A dark brown eyebrow lifted.

"To spend time with him. I've not seen him much this week, and I'll barely see him at all over the next fortnight. Given the day is so fine, I thought this would be the perfect time to do something together."

Gillian didn't look very happy, but she said the right words. "Great. What did you have in mind?"

"I'm not sure. I thought we'd let him choose. You don't mind, do you?"

Her smile was more plastic than genuine, but working with clients had made Gillian very adept at faking being amenable. "If you want to spend the first day of our vacation with your nephew, that's exactly what we'll do."

Mmm, not anywhere near excitement, but Torie could live with that. Aiden wouldn't want to be together either, so they could all share a communal sense of mild disappointment.

It was almost noon when they arrived at Kirsty's flat, with Gillian gamely carrying her heavy suitcase up the stairs. She was barely breathing hard when Torie knocked just to be polite, then slid her key in the lock.

Aiden was still in his pajamas, a tracksuit so small he'd had to remove the cuffs so they didn't cut off the circulation to his skinny shins. Torie would never understand his desire to hold on to and wear his oldest, shabbiest clothes, but she'd largely given up on the fight to convince him to change. The telly was on, as always, and he was eating a piece of pizza from a box that rested on the coffee table.

"Hello there," Torie called, raising her voice above the din.

Aiden turned around and stared. "Why are you here?"

"Since she's working all day, I told your mum we'd come by," she said, ignoring the unfriendly welcome. "I'd like you to meet my friend Gillian."

"Hullo," he said, clearly only to avoid being scolded.

"Hi, Aiden. It's good to meet you." She was in her friendly, outgoing, professional mode, but wasn't making any immediate headway.

He stood up and seemed to realize how silly he looked in his ill-fitting clothing. "I'll go get dressed."

She let him go, then said, "Give me a minute." After swinging by to turn the telly down, she followed. With a brief knock, she entered the room, knowing he hadn't had time to whip his clothing off yet. "I thought we'd do something together this afternoon. The weather is glorious," she said, sounding too enthusiastic even to herself.

"I want to watch footy." He dug through his chest of drawers, finding the jeans he wanted, along with a T-shirt. "Can I get by?" She was blocking the doorway, and had already decided she wasn't going to move until they'd reached an agreement. "You can pick what we do, but we're going to do something. Think about it while you get dressed."

"I want to watch my team," he whined. "I've been waiting all week for this match."

To her, it seemed like football was on 'round the clock, but she knew he truly loved Aberdeen F.C. "All right. We'll stay here and watch with you." Gillian wasn't going to love the idea, but she wouldn't complain.

"You'll talk," he said, clearly disgusted at the mere thought of idle conversation during a match. "You don't like it at all, so you should go do something else."

"We can go out together, or we can stay in together," she said, staring into his eyes until he reluctantly met her gaze. "Your choice."

He was mumbling to himself as he walked away, but she was well used to that. After walking back into the sitting room, Torie spotted Gillian digging through her suitcase again. "Still looking for something to eat?"

"I brought a couple of presents for Aiden," she said, pulling out two wrapped packages.

"Oh, that's so nice of you!" She gave her a hug, then a quick kiss to the cheek. "You know you didn't have to do that."

"I know," she said, nodding. "But kids like presents, and I want him to like me."

Lowering her voice, Torie said, "He's going to be in a mood for a while. His favorite team's playing this afternoon, so he doesn't want to go out. Of course, he doesn't want us to stay in to watch it with him, either. He's sure we'll ruin the entire experience."

Gillian sat down, with a puzzled look on her face. "Um, why not let him do what he wants?"

"Because he's thirteen. What he wants is to lie on this sofa, eating pizza, and playing with his game console. While I'd like him to see the sun once in a while, and eat a vegetable."

"Maybe he'll agree to eat a vegetable tomorrow if you let him watch the game today." She'd put on her most ingratiating smile, but it wasn't having its intended effect.

"It's more than that, Gillian. He'd like to live on his own, with frequent visits from some takeaway place. But that kind of isolation is awful for him. I'm trying to get him to talk, to tell me what's going on in his life, but he'll only talk after he's loosened up. That takes time."

"Why make an issue of it today? We're down to fourteen days together. Do you want to waste one of them fighting with Aiden?"

Torie walked into the kitchen to get a drink of water and collect her thoughts. While her glass filled, she reminded herself that Gillian had no experience with teenagers, and she was justifiably looking forward to being alone. After gulping down the water, she returned to the sitting room, certain her little break hadn't helped. She was still on edge when she said, "Don't fight me on this, all right? I don't want it to be two against one."

"I'm on your side," Gillian said quietly. "Really. I'm just thinking about how I felt when I was a kid. I stopped doing things with my family when I was about Aiden's age, and I don't ever recall my parents making me tag along once I'd declared my independence."

Torie gazed at her for a few moments, then tried to soften what she knew were stinging words by resting a hand on her cheek. "Your parents didn't do you any favors by letting you pull away. They should have chased you and let you know they wanted to be with you."

"I don't think they did," she said, shrugging. "When I didn't tag along, they only had to worry about one kid, and my sister had always been easier to deal with."

Aiden walked back into the room, and Torie nearly levitated as she removed her hand from Gillian's face. She knew she was blushing, and was equally sure Aiden knew he'd caught her doing something. She just wasn't sure he knew what he'd seen.

"What did you decide?" she asked, her voice breaking.

"I'll go out," he said, clearly unhappy. "I don't care where."

"Get your trunks. We're going to slap some color onto that pasty white skin."

❦ ❦ ❦

They headed south in Torie's little car, with Aiden in the backseat playing a game on a device that must have been kind of dated. It didn't make any noise, other than a soft click when he hit the buttons, and for most of the ride, that was the only sound. It felt like Aiden was fully in charge of how much fun they'd be allowed to have, and Gillian hated the experience a whole lot. She and Torie were going to spend one of their precious fourteen days not talking or touching, and Aiden clearly wasn't enjoying himself, which was ostensibly the point of taking him out.

The scenery was nice, though, especially with the sun shining so brightly. Every field was bright green, and every sheep looked fluffy and white, just like the few big clouds that hung low over the water.

They'd been through several towns, but the one they were approaching was slightly larger than the rest. While still small, it was right on the water, with a gentle hill dotted with sheep a few hundred yards from the shore.

"I think you're going to love this place," Torie said. "And I know Aiden is. We used to come here when he was a wee loon. The only argument then was trying to get him out of the water at the end of the day."

Gillian turned to see if Aiden was going to respond, but he acted like he hadn't heard a word.

Torie pulled over on the side of the road, then they all got out and carried their suits and towels to an unwelcoming wall, painted tan. There was no sign at all, but voices rang out on the other side, and the top of a slide was visible.

"An open fence would be better advertising," Gillian mused. "You want to see people having fun, right?"

"I think they need the wall as a wind break. It can get gusty."

They went around to the entrance, with Torie insisting on paying for all of them. Then they went into their respective dressing rooms to put on their suits.

Gillian had only brought one, thinking she wouldn't need it at all, but wanting to be prepared. Now she had second thoughts. As she stuffed herself into the top, Torie took a look and froze, staring. "Do you have something to wear over that? That's…" She blinked a few times. "That might be illegal in Scotland."

"I thought we might get a hotel with a hot tub or something. I didn't know we'd be at a community pool with a bunch of little kids."

"It looks fantastic on you," Torie said, pulling on her own plain blue tank suit. Her grin started to brighten. "I guess we'll figure out if Aiden's straight or not. If he doesn't try to catch a look, he's totally gay."

"Really looking forward to that," Gillian said, putting her cotton blouse on over her suit, then wrapping a towel around her waist.

They went out into the pool area, where Aiden was standing, arms crossed over his narrow chest. He'd put on the Ohio State football jersey Gillian had brought for him, so long it nearly covered his trunks. But he'd seemed vaguely pleased that she'd given him something, although it was clear he'd also been puzzled. It *was* a little odd, now that she thought of it. Since Torie hadn't told him about their relationship, he'd just thought his aunt's friend had come to visit bearing a gift. She'd kept the second, more expensive present hidden, planning on giving it to him if things went well. The jury was definitely still out on that point.

Torie went up behind the kid, grabbed the hem of his jersey and gave it a yank. "Taps aff, lad," she said, laughing as Aiden wrapped his long arms even more tightly around his bare chest as he skittered away, getting some distance.

"Taps what?" Gillian asked.

"Glasgow slang. When it's even marginally nice, the guys take their tops off. They bare their chests with alarming frequency," she added, chuckling. "You can get snow blind from seeing all of that white flesh on the first warm day of the year."

The pool was really quite nice, with places to sit in the shade, a modest water slide, and lots of floating toys for the young kids. It was big, too, as large as the one at OSU. "You say the local government keeps this up?" Gillian asked.

"Uh-huh. Plus a lot of volunteers. It's lovely, isn't it?"

"It is. I love swimming pools."

"Salt water," Torie said. "From right over there," she added, pointing toward the sea.

Gillian had stuck a hand in the ocean on her last trip. That was enough to convince her to stay far, far away from it for the rest of her life. "I think I'll just keep my tap on," she decided. "You can go torture your nephew."

"No, no, you've got to come too. You'll love it," she promised, taking her by the hand and pulling her along.

"I hate being cold." She stopped, making Torie halt along with her. "What am I saying? No one's as cold as you are!"

"See? If I can do it, you can do it. Come on now."

Gillian pulled her top over her head, then dropped her towel. When they got close to Aiden, he gave her a glance, then stopped and let his gaze travel to lock onto her chest. His eyes widened, then he swiftly turned away, his cheeks turning as pink as his aunt's often did.

Torie rescued him from his mortification by grasping his hand and pulling him into the water with her, emerging in a second to shake her head and call out, "It's perfect. Come in!"

Throwing caution to the wind, Gillian jumped, only to find the water had been thoroughly heated. "I thought I'd have to knock icicles off, but it's great!"

"It is that," Torie agreed. She grabbed Aiden and wrestled with him briefly, winding up with the boy held in her embrace. She looked over his shoulder and said, "Last time we were here, Aiden wanted me to carry him around on my back. Want to do that again?"

"You're not funny," he said, slithering out of her grip. A ball flew across the pool and hit him in the back, making him whirl around to see who'd thrown it.

A pair of boys about his age waved to him, and he winged the ball back, making it skitter across the surface. The guys clearly were inviting him to join them, and he swam over when they tossed the ball his way again.

"I was going to let him be in the sun for fifteen minutes so he could get some Vitamin D," Torie said. "Which one of us is going to pull him out to slather him with sunblock?"

"That would be you," Gillian said, absolutely thrilled that Aiden had found some playmates. She had her own, and didn't want to share.

❦ ❦ ❦

They stayed until the pool closed, and even though Aiden was quiet when it was just the three of them again, he'd clearly had fun. In the middle of the afternoon, a girl had joined the group, and Torie had enjoyed watching three goofy boys try to impress her while attempting to convey they were just being their normal cool selves.

"I'm in the market for some of Scotland's best fish and chips," Torie said. "Who's with me?"

"Given that I've only had breakfast, I'm in," Gillian said. "I used to wonder how you stayed so thin. The answer has become painfully obvious. You don't eat!"

"I eat a lot. I just forget if I'm doing something else."

"She doesn't eat much," Aiden said, actually joining in the conversation.

"Well, I'll show you my ravenous appetite in three minutes. The shop is right next to where I parked the car."

They walked along the road a very short distance, with Gillian staring at the sandy harbor. It was low tide, and all of the local boats were lying on their sides, waiting for it to rise.

"Is that…okay for those boats?" she asked, clearly puzzled.

"Why wouldn't it be?"

"I don't know. It just looks like they're…broken."

"They're not broken," Torie laughed. "Everyone knows the tides, and you just schedule your sailing around them."

"Oh, you and your local knowledge," she teased. "You wandered around New York like you'd never seen a big city. I had to explain something to you every ten minutes."

Torie steeled herself, waiting for the explosion.

"New York?" Aiden stopped and stared at her. "When were you in New York?"

"March," she said. "You knew I was gone for a few days."

"I didn't know you were in America," he said, clearly getting agitated. "Why didn't you tell me?"

"I don't know," she said, lying her ass off. "I didn't think you'd be interested."

He was still standing right where he'd stopped, glaring at her. "Why were you there?"

"To visit Gillian," she said quietly. "I'm sorry I didn't tell you, Aiden. I should have."

"Are you gay?" he demanded, cheeks flushing pink. "Tell me!"

"Yes," Torie said, sick with anger at herself for not telling him earlier. "I was waiting to make sure Gillian and I were able to commit to one another before I told you, but that was probably a mistake."

"I'm not hungry," he growled, then turned to walk away. There was a low stone wall that separated the road from the sea and he sat on it, then tossed his legs over to the other side and jumped down. He had to run down the steep slope to remain upright, but he made it, then started to walk, head down, hands in the pockets of his jeans.

"I have to go after him," Torie said, panic rising in her chest.

Gillian grabbed her arm and held it. "Give him a minute. Let him get his thoughts together."

"I can't," she said, following Aiden's path. The angle was intense, but the sand by the wall was firm, letting her run down it much as Aiden had done. She was sure he could outrun her, but he wasn't trying to, not even turning around to see if she was following. She lowered her head and ran as fast as she could, catching up to him in just a few minutes. Panting and sweating, she slowed down and tried to catch her breath.

"Wait," she demanded. "Please, Aiden. Wait a second."

He slowed down, which was something. Not quite obeying, but not ignoring her.

She'd bent over to catch her breath, holding onto her knees, sucking in air. Finally, she could talk without gasping, and she had to jog a little to catch him again. "I know you want to be alone, but I can't let you just walk away." She put her hand on his shoulder, but he shook it off. "Just tell me where you're going. If you want to walk on the beach for a while, that's perfectly fine. Just promise you won't leave."

"Where would I go?" he demanded.

The boy had a point. If he wasn't planning on walking into the sea, he couldn't get into much trouble. She reached into her pocket and pulled out all of her money, counting it quickly. Thirty-seven pounds. "Here," she said. "The arcade's still open. You can get something to eat there."

He took it, then gave her a suspicious gaze. She never gave him money to waste, and he clearly thought there was a catch of some sort. "I can have all of this?"

"You can. I just don't want you wandering around near the sea."

He nodded, then took a left, heading back up the hill toward the street. "Should we wait for you at the chippy?" she asked, knowing that sounded stupid. The chippy and the ice cream shop were the only spots still open in the evening. "I know you're mad, Aiden, and I can see you want some time alone." She took in a deep breath, trying to seem like a proper adult. "But I don't want to abandon you."

"If I had a phone, you could call me." He gave her a very insolent glare, reigniting their long-running battle.

"Take mine." She eased it from her pocket and handed it to him. "If you leave the arcade, text Gillian." She yanked the phone back, quickly went to her texts, and deleted every one. Reading those would have scarred him for life. "Her number's on my favorites page."

He still seemed very suspicious, and she worried that he'd assume he'd get cash and freedom every time he threw a major fit. But this seemed different. Being soaked in guilt was probably influencing her, but it would take a while to not feel like a shit.

The phone went into his back pocket, money in the front. Then he started to climb up the hill, notably shorter here than where they'd come down.

"We'll be at the chippy," she called out. "If you change your mind…"

He didn't alter his stride, continuing on, his oversized shirt and baggy jeans making him look so tiny, so young. But he was growing up, becoming more adult, and she'd made a grievous error in not changing the way she treated him. An error she prayed he'd let her try to fix.

Gillian was at her side a moment later. "Is he okay?"

"I don't think so." All she wanted to do was let Gillian hold her, but she didn't want to further incite Aiden on the off chance he turned around. "I said we'd go eat. If he feels better he might join us, but I think it's more likely he'll stay at the arcade until he runs out of money."

"Should I give him more?"

"He has enough. I gave him almost forty pounds."

"I don't know how much games cost," Gillian said. "Will that last long?"

"I don't know either. I suppose we'll find out."

☙ ☙ ☙

The food at the little cafe was extraordinary for a place so far from a major city. The only problem was that they posted the calorie counts for every item on the menu. The griddled haddock and mushy peas were good, but Gillian gazed longingly at the deep-fried fish and chips and battered mushrooms Torie was whipping through.

"I guess you do eat," Gillian said, snatching a chip. Good thing she didn't care for the vinegar Torie had sprinkled on them. If there had been ketchup, she'd have fought her for them despite the seven hundred calories.

"I eat more when I'm anxious." She blew on a steaming hot mushroom and popped it into her mouth. "I'm anxious," she added unnecessarily.

"What do we do?"

"I'm not sure. I know he needs some time to himself, but this isn't the best place for that. When the arcade closes, there's nothing else." She took another bite of her fish, chewing thoughtfully. "I hope I can talk to him alone before we have to get back into the car. The ride out was bad enough. It'll be worse now that he's really got something to be angry about."

"Does he have a phone? You could text him to see how he's doing."

"I gave him mine." She rolled her eyes. "He's been begging for one for well over a year, but I haven't wanted to add another expense to my monthly, nor give him another excuse to be lost to human contact." She sighed deeply. "I suppose I'll have to get one for him. Then I can at least text him and hope he's in the mood to respond."

Gillian's phone buzzed and she handed it to Torie. "For you."

"He says the arcade's closing." She typed quickly. "They didn't have any food." Grumbling to herself, she continued to type. "He will allow me to bring him some, though." She looked up. "I've no money. Will you...?"

"Fish and chips?"

"Add some coleslaw too. He likes that and it's as close to a vegetable as I'm going to get into him today."

❧ ❧ ❧

The sun was still shining brightly, although it was low in the sky. Aiden's red hair shone like a beacon as the golden glow reflected off it as he sat on the seawall, his feet dangling over the side.

Torie placed the box of food in his hands and sat next to him. He must have been starving, since he dug in immediately, not even trying to maintain his previously icy demeanor.

"Want to tell me what about today made you the angriest?" she asked. "Is it that I'm gay, or that I didn't tell you."

"That girl," he said, stuffing three fat chips into his mouth simultaneously. "The one at the pool."

"Yes," Torie said, unable to guess where this was going.

"She asked if you were. You were putting sunblock on Gillian, and she asked if she was your bird."

"And you said..."

"I said she was daft," he admitted quietly. "I should have known."

"You're right. You are one hundred percent right. I was waiting to tell you, but I should have known you were old enough now to discuss it."

"I don't *care*," he stressed. "You can do whatever you want. But I should have known."

"You're right, Aiden. I would have told you ages ago, but I didn't have anyone in my life. Now that I do, I guess I was waiting for the perfect time. Which was stupid," she added.

"Aren't you gay all the time? Do you turn it on or off when you're not with someone?"

For a moment, she thought he was asking a serious question. Then she saw the anger in his eyes and realized he was making a point. "You're right. I've been gay my whole life, and I should have told you that when you were young."

"Why didn't you?" he demanded again, his eyes narrowed.

"I don't know," she said staring down at the hearty plants that clung tenaciously to the sand. "I guess I just didn't want to bring it up if I was never going to have a girlfriend."

"You always said there was nothing wrong with being gay." This time the look he gave her had a touch of empathy in it. "Don't you believe that?"

"I believe it, but not everyone else does. I took the easy way out, which was, as I've already admitted, stupid."

"Yeah, it was stupid." He spoke quietly, not looking at her. "I don't have to tell people, do I?"

"No. You don't have to tell. Granny and Granda would prefer I kept it quiet too. You're not the only one who doesn't want his friends to know."

"They just found out?" His dark red eyebrows rose to their full height.

"They knew, but we haven't talked about it for a long time. I think they hoped I'd get over it."

"Can you?" he asked, his head cocking.

"Not that I know of. Luckily, I'm happy being gay, so I don't want to change. I just struggle with the fact that some people don't like it at all."

"Yeah. Some don't." He faced her once again, with a hint of a smile beginning to form. "I'm not a kid anymore. We'll get along better if you stop treating me like a baby."

She draped an arm around his shoulders and pulled him over to kiss his head. "I know. It's just hard to let go." He hadn't slithered out of her grip, so she took full advantage and wrapped him in a hug. "I love you more than you can imagine," she murmured.

"I love you too," he said, the first time he'd said those words in at least a year. A lovely day had turned to shit, but hearing those words gave her a burst of optimism for their relationship that she hadn't felt in quite a while.

Releasing him, she gave him a slap on the leg. "Had enough food?"

"I think so. But I wouldn't mind some pudding."

"I'll make something when we get back to your flat. How's that?"

"Good. Can I pick?"

"You can." They both stood and started back for the car. "Can I have my phone?"

He gave her a sly grin and said, "I was hoping you'd forget." He handed it over, adding, "My birthday's coming up soon."

"January isn't very soon. And half-birthdays don't count."

Gillian watched Torie and Aiden walk back toward the car. They'd obviously reconciled, even though they weren't showing any concrete signs of affection. But they both walked with a loose, casual stride, the way people who were unguarded did when they were together. Seeing this might be the right time, she went back to the car and pulled the second gift from her tote bag. Climbing over the seawall to run down the slope, she headed toward the pair. When they got close, she extended the package and said, "Your aunt told me you've joined the robotics club at school."

"Yeah," he said, regarding her warily.

"If you like robots, I thought you might like one of these."

He cast a quick glance at Torie, then accepted the gift. He had the wrapping off in a flash, then stared at the picture on the box. "A drone?" Another puzzled look to Torie, then a delighted smile covered his face, just like a child at Christmas. "This is really for me?"

"Yeah. Of course," she said, thrilled that he obviously liked it. Now Gillian spared a glance for Torie, who was clearly the one they all had to receive approval from. Thankfully, she was also smiling, but her expression had a hint of resignation to it. Turning back to Aiden, Gillian said, "The box is open because I took it out and tested it. It didn't make sense to bring you a present that didn't work."

"Can you show me how to use it?"

"I can," she said, proud of herself for watching hours of online videos to figure out how to operate the damn thing. "The sun's still up. Want to do it now?"

"Can we?" he asked, turning to Torie.

Gillian felt like a kid waiting for her friend's mom to let them do something fun, and found herself grinning when Torie said, "Of course. But you have to teach me too. I don't want to be the only person in Aberdeen who doesn't know how to fly a drone."

After making ginger biscuits for Aiden, they returned to Torie's hotel. She seemed a little stiff when they walked in, but that made sense. Gillian assumed her fellow employees only knew her as a server, not a guest. But she held her head high, making eye contact with anyone who gave her a second glance.

As soon as they entered the room, Torie fell onto the bed, face-first. "What a day," she moaned. "If you'd told me the squirming little red-faced baby I took home that cold, rainy night in January would one day thoroughly shame me for keeping secrets from him..."

Gillian started to undress, finally feeling some effects of her travel. All she wanted to do was push Torie to one side and sleep for twelve hours. "We certainly had some ups and downs," she admitted. It seemed like such a difficult task that she didn't even take her toiletries out to brush her teeth. Now naked, she peeled the bedspread away and squeezed into the small space Torie had left for her. "I didn't enjoy being with thirteen-year-olds when I was one."

"You didn't?" Torie rolled onto her side, freeing up some space.

"Adults were more fun," she said, already feeling her body start to relax. "Kids were too full of drama. Everything was the very best or the very worst. I hated all of that."

"Were you able to find adults who wanted to hang out with you? The pictures you've shown me make me think you wouldn't have had any trouble."

"No," she said, chuckling. "My friends were older, but just a couple of years. I mostly kept to myself until my peers stopped being so ridiculously dramatic. They were more tolerable by junior year of high school." She let out a laugh. "Of course, my friends had all graduated already, so maybe I only tolerated my classmates because the teachers wouldn't hang with me."

"I can see that," Torie said. "I was one of the girls who would have driven you crazy."

"I can see *that*," Gillian teased. "You still do, but I'm going to have to sleep before I've got the energy to be driven mad. Cool?"

"Sure." Torie leaned over and kissed her, whispering, "I love you."

"I love you too. I'll love you even more if you'll let me sleep until noon."

"You may sleep the entire day away." With one more kiss on the cheek, Torie got up to get ready for bed. Gillian stretched out and sighed at how wonderful it felt to be lying in bed—with no teenagers in sight.

CHAPTER TWENTY-FIVE

GILLIAN WOKE PARTIALLY, SCRATCHED UNDER her chin, then grumbled and tried to fall back to sleep. But the itch continued. Slowly, her eyes opened fully to see a smirking Torie looming over her. "I'm trying to be nice," she said. "I thought tickling you with the little feather that worked its way out of my pillow might wake you gently."

"Mmm. It did." She wrapped an arm around Torie and tumbled her onto her side, hoping to cuddle her back to sleep.

Regrettably, Torie wasn't to be dissuaded. "Don't you want to get up?" she asked gently. "The sun's supposed to make an appearance by ten. We haven't been down near the border yet. This is a good day to drive down and explore a bit."

Sighing, Gillian forced her feet to the floor and stood, then took a look at her watch. They'd slept for nearly seven hours. That was probably enough. "I'm up," she announced. "Shower?"

"You first. You're dangerous when wet, and I want to make sure we get out of here." She put her arms around Gillian and gave her a long hug. "We'll come back early tonight and play, all right?"

She looked so hopeful, Gillian couldn't refuse her. "I'll make it quick."

"I'll touch up one of your blouses while you shower. Teamwork," she added, her grin showing just how ready she was to get moving.

Fifteen minutes after rising, they were both dressed. The breeze that came in through the open window wasn't cold, but it certainly wasn't warm. Over a cotton turtleneck, Torie was wearing one of her thicker wool waistcoats, this one navy with a red ribbon down the placket, along with khaki colored jeans, and brown leather boots. She looked like she might be going on a hunt or was planning on thwacking her way through the heather on some adventurous hike.

Gillian had her hand on the doorknob, but Torie stopped her. "I haven't kissed you yet today. We don't want to let those little details go unnoticed."

Smiling, Gillian opened her arms and purred softly when Torie snuggled into her embrace. "I love holding you," she murmured. "As soon as you're in my arms, this amazing sense of peace comes over me. Every time."

"I feel it too," she whispered. "Isn't this the best part of having a girlfriend? Having someone who calms you down and makes you feel like everything is right in the world?"

Laughing softly, Gillian said, "I wouldn't go that far, but you make *my* world right."

"That's all I want. Just that, and I'll be a happy woman." She tilted her head and placed her lips upon Gillian's, exerting gentle pressure. Just a normal, sweet, good-morning kiss. As Gillian started to pull back, Torie chased her, their mouths still pressing against one another. Then a firm tongue slid across her lips, seeking entry. Given they were following Torie's schedule, Gillian happily allowed any detour she chose. Torie's tongue slid inside, warm and soft and slippery.

Unable to keep from letting out a soft moan, Gillian leaned against the door, ready for whatever came next. Hands cupped her butt as Torie's tongue started to explore, probing her delicately. She hadn't intended to return the favor, but found her hands squeezing Torie's ass, making her growl.

Then Torie's torso pressed into her, pinning her to the door, her tongue never stopping its determined journey.

Increasing the pressure, Gillian grasped her harder and pulled her close, making her heels rise, with the toes of her boots scraping across the wooden floor.

A purr of pleasure made chills go down Gillian's spine. For a woman who hadn't had much sex in her life, Torie was exquisitely responsive, letting Gillian know in a second if she liked something. This morning, she was into a little force.

Taking over, Gillian pushed away from the door and let her more aggressive side show. Holding onto Torie's hips, she guided her backwards, pressing against her until they were at the bed. Then she gave her a sizzling kiss, keeping up the pressure until Torie was hungrily sucking her tongue into her mouth. Then, with the flats of her hands, she gave her a push, smiling when Torie looked up at her, clearly ready for anything.

Gillian stood tall and started to slowly remove her belt, doubling it up and thwacking her own leg with it. When Torie's eyes widened, she tossed it aside and chuckled. "I can't guarantee you won't have welts, but they'll be from my mouth."

"What about the borderlands?" Torie asked. She'd tossed her arms over her head and let it fall back, exposing her throat. "Don't you want to see some sights?"

Gillian whipped off her shirt, then her bra. After unzipping her jeans, she climbed on top of Torie and placed her breast into her open mouth. "I do," she whimpered when her flesh was gently suckled. "The border I most want to see is this one…" She slid her hand between their bodies and ran her nails across Torie's inner thigh. "And this one." She wasn't even sure what part she was touching, but Torie moaned when her fingernails scraped along it. "The most interesting borders in Scotland are right in this bed."

The next morning, Torie sat on a bench outside of the Union Square Mall, waiting. They'd been wandering around, window shopping and planning their day when Torie had gotten a call from the office manager at Deep Dive. When she realized she'd be on the call for a while, working out logistics for a group tour, she'd let Gillian wander off on her own. Now she'd been waiting for fifteen minutes, and was beginning to get antsy.

Even though they'd communicated every single day for more than seven months, there were so many things you didn't learn about a person until you were actually with them. For all she knew, Gillian had a horrible sense of direction and had wandered away to cross the River Don, where she was now hopelessly lost. She was just taking out her phone to text when a shadow descended over her, shielding her from the sun's rays. "I was just going to call. Thought you might be lost."

"The lost have been found," she said, grinning. The sun was just behind her head, creating a halo effect when Torie looked up. "That's religious, right?"

"I'll buy it." She started to stand, but a white plastic bag was now dangling in front of her face. "What's this?"

"Presents. For you and Aiden."

"Gillian," she said, her frustration rising in moments. "You know how I feel about that."

"I shouldn't have called them presents," she said quickly. "Think of them as stress relievers. You'd like a little less stress in your life, wouldn't you?"

"I can't wait to see how my stress level will plummet when I have…" She reached into the bag to retrieve a rectangular box. "A phone? An expensive phone will help my stress?"

"It might." Gillian sat next to her and said, "I got one for each of you, and I'm going to pay the monthly charges."

Torie opened her mouth to complain, but Gillian held a finger to her lips. "Can I explain?"

"Of course." She sucked her lip between her teeth, determined to wait until Gillian was finished to resume complaining.

"Okay. These have a feature that lets you track other phones. If the other person consents, of course. Aiden gets a phone, which he really wants, but you'll still have some control. If he blocks the tracking feature, you'll get a notification. You can tell him that if he does that, he loses the phone for some time period—or forever."

Her head cocked as she thought, her need to keep refusing floating away in the breeze. "I can see where he is? In real time?"

"There's a short delay, but other than that, you can see exactly where the phone is so long as it's not out of range."

"God, that would be so helpful," she sighed. "Thank you." She leaned over and kissed her cheek. "Sorry I started to jump on you." She carefully explored the box, trying not to give into the excitement of having something new—something she *never* would have bought for herself. Her own phone had cost under a hundred pounds, used, and while it had a terrible camera and very little memory, it let her use the internet and text to her heart's content. "I just don't want Aiden to think he can have things like this on a routine basis. He's already too enamored with name brands."

"So am I," Gillian said, offering up a guilt-free shrug. "I'm the worst."

Torie ignored that comment. She was powerless to change Gillian, but she prayed Aiden didn't try to use her to get the things he wanted. He'd never known anyone who could actually buy him all of the gadgets he lusted after. These two could make a very dangerous pair.

🌱 🌱 🌱

For the two days they'd been in Aberdeen, Gillian had been tapping away on her computer every chance she got, always playfully hiding the screen. Torie would see her open it up, type for a while, then nod, clearly satisfied. No amount of questioning could get her to give up her secret, so Torie had decided to simply enjoy the pleasure Gillian was getting from whatever scheme she was cooking up. For a woman who hated to be surprised, she seemed to get a lot of satisfaction from arranging some event, or gift, or...whatever it was she was planning.

On Tuesday morning, Torie woke to Gillian organizing her things, creating two piles on the floor, then standing to gaze at them, hands on hips.

"Are you doing anything in particular? Or do you just like to talk to your clothes?"

"I'm not talking," she said, turning to smile, a lazy, sweet one that she only showed in the minutes after she woke. "I'm deciding. You'd better get up, since you've got some deciding to do, too."

Torie slipped from the comfy bed, grasping the blanket to wrap around herself to protect her body from the cool breeze that blew in through the open window. "What deciding do I need to do?"

"We're going on a trip," she said, almost absently. "I think you'll need warm clothes, but you should bring the bare minimum." A third, smaller pile was formed, this one containing Gillian's laptop, a pair of shoes, a travel guide, all of her blouses, and two sweaters. She turned and clapped her hands. "Chop chop. Gotta get going."

"What are we doing?"

"We're packing. Then we're going to your flat to drop off everything we don't need. Then we're…" She stopped and playfully held her lips closed. "You almost got me to say what we're doing."

"No more clues?"

"None," she said, her grin turning impish. "You've got to trust me."

"I have from the first," Torie said, amazingly secure in that decision.

Two hours later, a cab pulled up in front of the flat. Gillian got in first and said, "Airport, please."

"Airport?" Torie cried. "I didn't bring my passport. Will I need it?"

"You will not." She peered at Torie carefully. "You don't mind small planes, do you?"

"How small?"

"Wee," she said, holding her thumb and index finger just an inch apart.

"I guess we'll find out, won't we. Don't blame me if my stomach decides it doesn't like it."

"Who else will I blame?" Gillian reached over and grasped Torie's hand, humming a little tune to herself as they drove along the congested streets of Aberdeen, on their way to points unknown.

It didn't take Torie long to figure out where they were going. Once they were in line for the flight to Kirkwall, she was certain they'd hop on another, smaller plane to North Ronaldsay. Gillian was the kind of woman who had to see things for herself, and visiting her mother's birthplace had to be high on her list of "must do's."

After two short flights, the wheels of the seven-passenger plane touched down, and they bobbed along the runway for a minute before the engine's whine changed pitch and they came to a stop.

"North Ronaldsay," the captain announced, barely having to raise his voice for everyone in the cabin to hear him. "The weather's fine, and should remain that way for the next three days."

"How long are we staying?" Torie asked as they waited for the people in front to squeeze out the small door.

"A week," Gillian said, seemingly happy with that choice. "I hope we get some rough weather. I want to see this place in every variation."

Torie laughed at Gillian's silly wish. In recorded history, there might have been a week when an Orcadian island didn't see a drop of rain, but that was definitely not the norm.

🐝 🐝 🐝

Gillian had read everything possible about the island, which actually wasn't much, so she'd hired a local guy to drive them around and add commentary. Robby assured her he'd be at her beck and call, but when they stepped outside the small building that served as a terminal, it seemed silly to be in a car on such a nice day. "You don't mind walking, do you? Our accommodations are only a little more than a mile."

"I can handle a mile," Torie said. "Especially since my girlfriend made me leave nearly everything at home. I never would have thought the things I needed to stay just across Aberdeen would be more than I'd need all the way past the southern tip of Norway."

"It's not that far," Gillian said, chuckling at Torie's exaggeration.

"Norway's that way," she insisted, pointing. "Due east of us. We're around the same latitude as Oslo right now. Trust me."

"Huh. Learn something new every day, don't you?" She laughed. "My having no sense of direction isn't new, but…"

They started to walk, with Gillian using the time to closely observe the landscape. It wasn't hard to take in every bit. She'd thought the Mainland had been a little flat and unremarkable, but it was a lush paradise compared to North Ronaldsay. At least you could see a few moderate hills on the Mainland. Not here. The land was as flat as a pancake, without even a tall plant to break up the monotony. Granted, she hadn't traveled much, but she was quite sure she'd never been anywhere so devoid of interest. The only thing it had going for it was the green crop of…something that the sheep were munching on.

Torie hadn't spoken yet, but she finally gave voice to what Gillian had been thinking. "Some healthy-looking cows, very rocky soil, a few fields where they're growing kale and swede, and a stone fence or two. Are we heading for some fabulous attraction at the end of this road?" Her smile grew brighter when their eyes met for a moment. "I don't mind if we aren't. I'm just trying to temper my expectations."

"God, I hope there's something good. If not, we're screwed." Gillian let out a laugh. "But we'll be together, right?"

"I haven't seen another soul, so we'll have to be together. How on earth can they support an airfield?"

"They have flights three times a *day*," Gillian said, laughing. "Since the tickets only cost twenty pounds, I think your tax dollars are at work."

"Twenty pounds? Maybe they save money by not having any security. We could have been carrying machetes and they wouldn't have noticed."

"Only if they weighed a lot," she said, thinking of how strict the pilot had been about the weight restrictions. "A lightweight machete wouldn't be a problem."

They kept walking down the road, which looked like it might be the only one on the entire island. One car passed and returned several times, but that was it. There was definitely no ring road on North Ronaldsay. But the sun was shining, the wind barely moved, and Torie was by her side. Things could definitely have been worse.

About three quarters of the way to the end of the island there was a slight rise in elevation. Torie squinted and said, "Ahh… The Holy Grail lies ahead. A great big lighthouse. I assumed there'd be one, but I didn't know it would be tall." She gripped Gillian's hand. "I'm glad."

"It's the biggest land-based house in the entire UK," Gillian said, getting a little buzz just from looking at it from a distance. "The day trippers from the plane must go out there, then turn around for the return flight, which is in something like two hours. But not us," she crowed. "We're going to walk around a two-mile long, mostly barren island for a whole week!" She gripped Torie's arm and squeezed it tightly. "I think I've lost my mind! With all of the things we could be doing, I chose to drag you past the tip of Norway to look at a lighthouse. That and a bird observatory are *literally* the only things here."

"We don't need diversions," Torie soothed. "When we're together it's impossible to be bored."

"Are you sure?" she asked, her anxiety building so fast her fingers had begun to tingle.

"No," Torie admitted, laughing. "But if we're bored, we can always go to bed. There's never a dull moment when we're naked."

"You say that now," Gillian said, chuckling. "Let's see if I can hold your attention over the long run."

"You can," Torie said, smiling up at her. "That's one of my core beliefs."

As they got closer, Gillian started to blink her eyes more frequently, trying to see into the distance. The elevation rose a little bit, just enough to give her the perspective to see some detail... Her blood started to pump faster and harder in her veins, and her head got a little light. She wasn't sure she spoke, or just thought the words, but when Torie gripped her arm she realized she'd said them aloud.

"That's exactly how the lighthouse on the cover of my mother's book looked."

"Your mother's...?"

She turned and gripped her hand. "I didn't tell you this, because I wanted it to be a surprise, but my mom had a children's book, published in Edinburgh, in 1950. It was about a little girl whose father was a lighthouse keeper." She turned her head to look one more time. "The lighthouse looked just like this one."

"Are you certain?" Torie had dropped her bag to grab onto Gillian's arm, holding on so tightly she was going to leave a bruise.

"I am. *The Keeper's Daughter* pictured a very tall lighthouse, with unpainted brick broken up by wide white stripes. That's not common, is it?"

"I don't know every lighthouse," Torie said, staring into the distance with the same focus that Gillian had, "but I've not seen one like it. Do you... Do you really think it's possible that your mother's book was about this house?" She blinked a couple of times, then said, "Did the book make you think your grandmother and the lighthouse keeper...?"

"It did. I was sitting in my nephew's room, and when Amanda put the book in my hand I got this...insight, I guess. It just seemed obvious to me." She looked around the desolate island slowly. "If I'd known there was so little to do here, it would have occurred to me even sooner. A lighthouse keeper must have seemed very exotic to a girl born here."

"What can you tell me about the story?"

"Nothing! Amanda ripped it out of my hands before I could read a word. But I'm going to gobble it down the second I get home. Actually, I might have my cab drop me at Amanda's."

"Oh, Gillian, this makes me want to cry. It feels like the story's right here. But it's hidden," she said, sighing.

"It is. And it might stay that way," she said, still a little shaky. "But if anyone on this island knows the tale, we're going to dig it up."

They continued their walk in silence, both of them staring at the lighthouse as they inched closer. Nearly everyone from the plane was, as expected, taking in the structure. There was a tiny shop next to the tower, run by a friendly woman with a warm smile and an accent that knocked your socks off. Torie seemed to understand her immediately, but Gillian was still trying to decipher her greeting seconds later.

"Yes, we are," Torie said, but Gillian had no idea what the question was.

"I made reservations for one of the keeper's cottages," Gillian said, assuming that's what they were talking about.

The woman said something, and Gillian found herself nodding. Then Torie diplomatically interpreted. "Mary assumed we were the people who'd made the reservation. She's going to show us around now." She turned to Mary and added, "Her ears get very stuffed up when she flies. She's nearly deaf at the moment, but she'll be sorted soon."

Mary continued to talk while she walked them over to a surprisingly large cottage, painted white with brown detailing around the windows. It was just yards from the lighthouse, and Gillian was so excited she nearly ripped the key from Mary's hand when she was slow to get the door open.

When she walked inside, Gillian let out a contented sigh. It was just what she'd hoped for. A neat, clean cottage, with a full kitchen, a bedroom with a full-sized bed, and an updated bath. The living room was cheery and bright, and there were books on the shelves and plenty of knit throws to ward off the chill. "Perfect," she said, smiling at Mary.

She spoke again, and Gillian caught a single word. "Groceries."

"Yes, I ordered groceries. They were supposed to be on our flight."

Mary replied with words Gillian didn't catch, then a man with a full head of snow-white hair and a wide smile poked his head in. "Delivery," he said, entering bearing two cardboard boxes. "Enough to last, I'd think. You're with us the full week?"

"We are," Gillian said, thankful to be able to understand every word.

"Robby Gibbs," he said, extending his hand for a shake.

"Good to meet you. I contacted you about driving us around, but it was such a nice day we decided to walk."

"It is that. Would you like bicycles? Very reasonable rates," he added.

"Sure. Riding's my hobby."

"I'll get you sorted as soon as I get the return flight off. If you're in a hurry, go ahead and take the bikes. I know where to find you."

As he left, Gillian said, "He gets the flight off?"

"He's the air traffic controller," Mary said, her words now as clear as a bell. Why that happened was anyone's guess, but it had happened enough for Gillian to believe that your ear adjusted if you were patient. You just needed a partner to explain away your rudeness by claiming you'd gone temporarily deaf.

🌵 🌵 🌵

The second Mary closed the door, Gillian rushed over and threw her arms around Torie, hugging her so hard her feet left the ground. "You're not disappointed, are you?" She settled her back down and leaned back, letting Torie see her worried expression. "I was so fixated on seeing where my grandmother lived that I didn't let myself even consider what we'd do for a week. I would have reserved the room for just a day or two, but they have a weekly minimum…"

"Some people like tropical paradises," Torie said. "I like rugged beauty. The sea, a rocky shore, a windswept plain… This is perfect."

"Really? I saw Robby bring the groceries in and I thought, 'I've just locked Torie into a week of cooking.'"

"I like to cook. You know that." She tickled under her chin. "And I should get started, since I know you're hungry."

There was a quiet knock at the door, and Gillian went to answer. She tossed the door open wide, and Torie spied Mary's silvery hair.

"My savory pies are just out of the oven," she said. "Come over to the shop if you'd like."

"We'd like," Torie called out. "Then we can get started investigating the island."

"Oh, you'll have no trouble doing that," she said, chuckling softly. "You've a full week."

🌵 🌵 🌵

There were six small tables in the cafe, and Gillian saw that every person from their flight was there, all of them digging into their lunch. When they sat down, Mary brought over small, round pies, about the size of an American muffin, and placed them on the table. "Local mutton," she said with a proud smile on her face. "Raised almost exclusively on seaweed."

Torie looked up, brow knit together. "Seaweed? Exclusively?"

"I'm told only these sheep and one other land animal…perhaps an amphibian?" She seemed lost in her thoughts, probably trying to place that amphibian in her memory. Then she blinked a few times and finished her sentence. "Can survive on seaweed."

"But how…?"

"They've had to adapt. The ones who didn't died."

"But we saw grass," Torie said.

"Oh, yes. We have grass, but they only have access to it during lambing season, when they need the extra nutrients. They normally can't get past the sheep dyke, which has been up for…" She furrowed her brow, clearly a slow and thoughtful thinker. "A hundred and fifty years. They're a hearty group, that's for certain. Small, but hearty."

Torie just nodded politely, but Gillian could see she had more questions. Undoubtedly, she'd ask around until she was satisfied.

They each took a bite of their mutton pies, and stopped chewing at exactly the same moment. "This is…interesting," Gillian said. She took a look around, seeing that all of the other visitors were still upright, but it probably took a while to experience the effects of food poisoning.

"It doesn't taste like any mutton I've ever had," Torie said.

"What is mutton? I've never had it."

"Mature sheep," Torie whispered. "Lambs are babies. Mutton is adults."

"I've been eating babies?" Gillian said, making the people at the next table whip their heads around to stare at her. "Sheep," she said, trying to pitch her voice at the same level as before. "Baby sheep."

"You have," Torie said quietly. "You didn't know that?"

"We don't talk about things like that. You can live in America and never see a farm."

"But your grandfather grew up on one."

"The farm he grew up on was beef cattle, with a very small dairy," Gillian said. "I do know what veal are, so I guess I should have known there was a sheep equivalent." She took another bite, and it went down much better now that she realized it was simply something very different from what she was used to.

"You know, this is pretty good," Torie said. "It's remarkably tender."

"I could get used to this. I think I'm going to start eating mutton. The poor little lambs should get to have some time to play in the grass before we eat them."

"They graze on seaweed," Torie said reflectively. "What's *that* all about?"

They were the last two lingering over their lunch, and when Mary walked by to clear a table, Gillian caught her attention. "I didn't mention this when I booked the cottage, but my mother was born on the island."

"Was she then," Mary said, looking more than a little skeptical.

"She was. I was wondering if you might have known her mother. Jeannie Sinclair."

"I know the name," she said thoughtfully, "but I can't place her. How old would she be?"

"Around eighty."

"Mmm. Eight years younger. We wouldn't have been in school at the same time, but that shouldn't..." Her gaze focused more sharply. "What were her parents' names?"

"I don't know," Gillian said, ready to kick herself for not doing a little research on such a simple point.

Torie pulled her phone from her pocket and flipped her finger across the screen a few times. Finally, she said, "Alexander and Alice. Alice's maiden name was Hamilton."

"Oh, yes," Mary said, nodding forcefully, her thin, straight white hair moving with her. "There's no one left, but I knew of the family. She looked puzzled for a second, then said, "The girl, Jeannie you say..."

"Yes," Gillian said. "My grandmother."

"Is she still alive?"

"No. I'm afraid she died before I was born. My mother's gone, too, so I'm trying to find out any info I can." She shrugged, trying to get past the wave of emotion that washed over her. "My family tree has very few roots."

Clearly empathetic, Mary's hand dropped to hover right above Gillian's shoulder. But she didn't let it land. That didn't seem odd, though. The Scots she'd encountered had been a very friendly bunch, but they were a little reserved when it came to physical contact. "If I remember, there was some talk..." she said, trailing off.

"If you mean that my grandmother was a single mother, that was more than talk. She gave birth to my mom when she was only seventeen, and left the island with her new baby soon after."

"That's as I recall," Mary said, sighing. "Your mother never knew her father?"

"She didn't. But I've heard speculation that her father might have worked on the island..."

"Mmm." Mary's pleasant expression grew a little chilly. "People say cruel things when they should keep about their own business. The girl's reputation was ruined by gossip. I'll never understand the need some people have to take a bad situation and make it worse."

Given the sharp tone her voice had taken on, Mary wasn't going to be the one to spill the beans, if there were any beans to be spilled. Gillian backed off quickly. "I have no expectation of finding out who my grandfather is, but I wanted to see where my grandmother lived."

"Ahh," she said, smiling once again. "Robby can show you. A young family lives on their croft now…" She started to laugh. "Young in that they're under sixty, but just barely."

"I'd love that," Gillian said. "I don't even know why it's important to me, but I'm very interested in seeing her home."

"Then you will." She took a device from a pocket in her apron and pressed a button. "Robby, come around home when you have a chance."

A crackling voice replied, "I'm occupied, but I'll come if I must."

"There's no hurry." When she put the device back, she smiled at Gillian. "Goodness knows you have time to spare."

✿ ✿ ✿

Instead of waiting for Robby, they decided to ride their bikes over to him. Torie was certain Gillian had too much nervous energy built up to wait, and she leapt at the chance to ride when Mary indicated where Robby was.

The road was in very good shape, a straight shot up and down the island, with occasional turn offs that led to individual homes. A substantial building sat about halfway down the island, with a shiny red fire brigade truck parked in front. They slowed down, and Torie pointed to a man squatting down, rolling up a length of canvas hose. "Hello, Robby," she called out.

"Hello there." He stood, clad in the kind of coveralls emergency workers wore. "Just putting things right here. I like to take everything out and give it a test every month."

"You're on the fire department?"

"Retained," he said, his brow furrowing for a moment. "The government disbanded the regular fire service years ago."

"It's just you now?"

"Every able-bodied person helps out. We don't have many calls, but we're ready when they come."

"You're a busy man," Torie said, wondering how able-bodied a man close to ninety could be.

"Not half as busy as I used to be. I've slowed down recently," he said, looking a little puzzled by that development.

"We all do," she acknowledged. "Mary said you could direct us to Alexander and Alice Sinclair's croft. She said it was close by."

"Alex Sinclair?" He narrowed his gaze, clearly thinking. "He's been gone for some time. I wouldn't be surprised to learn it's been thirty years." He turned so the freshening wind wasn't directly in his face, then wiped at his forehead. "Could he have been at my father's wake? I think he was…"

Torie watched Gillian's expression turn from puzzled to stunned. She hoped Robby stuffed a sock in it, but he seemed unable to let it go.

"He *was* there," he said, slapping his hands together. "I remember him saying he'd be the next to go, and I think his prediction came true. Of course, the Sinclairs were always looking at the dark side. Alex, his father Gordon…" He let out a laugh, really seeming delighted by something. "My father used to say the boys in school called Gordon the grim reaper. And that's when they were just loons!"

"We weren't actually looking for any of the family members," Torie said, seeing that Gillian looked very pale. "I know they're all gone now. We simply wanted to see the croft where they used to live."

"Ahh. The McHugh's live there now, but most people still know it as the Sinclair croft. If you keep going, you'll see the first turnoff. That's the place. They're not home though."

"They're not?"

"I saw them in line for the ferry this morning, but I didn't stop to ask where they were off to."

"Not a problem," Torie said. "We'll just ride our bikes over there and take a peek."

"I'll be here if you have more questions," he said. "It takes me longer and longer to do the things I used to be able to knock out in quick order."

"We might come by when we're finished," Torie said, taking another look at Gillian, who'd gone silent, and was gazing out at the sea like she was trying to distract herself.

Torie started to pedal, and in just a few strokes Gillian was next to her.

"It's true, isn't it," she said, quietly. "My great-grandfather was alive when I was a girl."

"It is," Torie said, tearing up at the sorrow-filled look on Gillian's face. "I was going to show you all of the research when we had a bit of time to really get into it… It just wasn't something I wanted to do on the telephone."

"I get that," she said, staring straight ahead.

"Let's go over by the sea. We can talk for a while."

Nodding, Gillian turned and started to pedal hard, creating a gap between them that Torie couldn't begin to close. By the time she arrived at the expanse of large, rust-colored, flattish rocks that created the shoreline, Gillian was off her bike, perched on a dry rock like she'd been there all day, with her arms wrapped around her shins, compressing herself into a surprisingly small package.

Torie couldn't tell if she needed some time to reflect, or if she wanted information, so she took a seat on her own rock and waited for Gillian to look at her. It only took a minute.

"What kind of woman would turn her back on her own grandfather?" she asked quietly. "Clearly, I didn't know a lot about my mother's life, but I'm certain she never took off to visit Scotland. As near as I can recall, she was never gone overnight until my father died."

"I don't think we'll ever know what happened," Torie said. "Your great-grandmother died well before you were born, but you were eleven years old when your great-grandfather died."

"I don't get it," she said, staring at the calm waters slapping haphazardly at the rocks, the day as calm as it probably ever got. "Her mom was dead by then. Even if my grandmother had issues with her father, wouldn't my mother have wanted to know him?"

"I've thought about this a thousand times," Torie said, "and all I can come up with is that your grandmother completely severed her relationship with her parents when she left, and your mother didn't want to re-kindle them." She took in a breath and said, "I found a notice about your grandmother's death in your local newspaper."

"You did?" Gillian's brows shot up.

"I did. It said she was a lifelong resident of Columbus." She could hear her voice growing softer, the way it often did when she had to deliver bad news. "She must have never told anyone her full truth."

"My mother certainly knew," Gillian said, with a bitter edge to her voice. "Her birthplace was on her marriage certificate." She scrubbed at her face with her hands. "Did my grandmother put on an American accent for her whole damn life? Could you even get away with that?"

Treating it like a serious question, Torie switched over to her usual American accent and said, "I could do this if I had to. *Perhaps* for the rest of my life. But it would wear on me. I'd never be completely comfortable, I don't think."

"My mother was never completely comfortable," Gillian said, her voice having grown reflective. "I've never thought of it like that, but she wasn't."

"How do you mean…?"

"It's hard to quantify," she said, still gazing into the navy-blue depths of the water, "but I don't think I ever knew her to truly relax. She was always on the move, working on her computer, or making a list for the housekeeper, or working in her garden." She faced Torie and said, "She was a hell of a gardener. She could have won competitions if she'd cared about that kind of thing."

"I was only able to take a very brief look when I was at your home, but I noticed your garden. It was stunning, Gillian. Did your mom teach you how to —"

"Of course not," she said dismissively. "I helped my designer lay it out, but only on paper. I'm certain I never touched my mom's garden."

She scooted around so she was fully facing the sea now, staring out at it for a full minute before she spoke again. "My mom used her garden time to be alone. Amanda and I learned not to disturb her when she was working, and boy, did she work. She was tall, and strong, and could turn over her whole vegetable garden with a pitchfork. I remember one time hearing my dad say she attacked that garden like she was mad at it."

"Mmm. She didn't have your ability to relax."

"I'm more like my dad," Gillian said, then nodded decisively. "I'm like my mother only in that I learned to delegate every task I don't like to someone else. Other people did our laundry, our cooking, our housework… She just worked in the garden when the weather was good, and spent the winter in the basement, starting her vegetables from seed, with grow lights. She was fanatical," she said softly. "My dad was kind of right, but I don't think it was anger that drove my mom. I think it was shame."

"It's generational," Torie said softly. "When you grow up having to keep family secrets, you have a hard time learning how to be open."

Gillian turned to her and stared for a few seconds before saying, "I'm as open as I want to be, Torie. Any secrets I keep are for *practical* reasons."

Scooting across the rocks wasn't easy, and Torie was sure she'd have grit ground into the fabric of her jeans, but she finally managed to share Gillian's rock. "I swear I wasn't speaking about you. I was thinking about your mom, and how deep her shame must have been. To continue with the lie even after her mother was dead…"

Gillian pulled Torie close and kissed the top of her head. "I'm sorry I snapped at you. This has me…"

"Deeply, and understandably upset," she said, finishing her thought. "This would upset anyone, Gillian."

"I am upset," she admitted. "But I'm getting closer to acknowledging I'm not going to learn much more. No one but my mom can ever tell me why she kept her background to herself, and those reasons died with her."

"I'm afraid that's true," Torie said. "All we can do is try to learn from her pain."

Gillian rose effortlessly, then offered a hand to pull Torie to her feet. "They say we're only as sick as our secrets." A bitter laugh was nearly covered by the sharp slap of a single wave breaking against the rocks. "My family was terminally ill."

🌿 🌿 🌿

They only had about a quarter mile to cover, but the wind had picked up and was now in their faces, making Torie really have to push. It wasn't super easy for Gillian, either, her last encounter with a heavy, coaster-brake bike having been many, many years earlier.

From a distance, the Sinclair house was completely unremarkable, as was the farm. She wasn't great at estimating acreage, but would have been surprised if this one had been larger than twenty acres. It was flat, devoid of any trees or even a sturdy shrub. But there were a few healthy-looking cows grazing, and a portion of the farm was sectioned off for crops. Gillian wasn't able to identify many vegetables when they were in the ground, but some of the plants had big leaves, dark green and ribbed.

As they got close to the house, she stopped her bike, with Torie lumbering up beside her, nearly out of breath. For a woman who was on her feet all day, and didn't carry an extra pound, her aerobic capacity was surprisingly weak.

"This is not a place I can picture you in," Torie said, her speech interrupted by the quick breaths she had to take.

Gillian looked at the dun-colored walls, taking in the unkempt area around the house. It was a muddy mess, but that was probably because a shed for the cows was right next to the main house. The cows must have slipped about in the rain, destroying any kind of lawn the owners tried to keep.

It wasn't a wreck by any means, but it was clearly a lean operation, not possibly able to produce enough income to even pay for the satellite dish securely attached to the roof of the main house.

"How can they live?" she heard herself asking. "There aren't any calves, so they're clearly not going to send the cows to market. Is a few acres of…some kind of vegetable going to keep them going?"

"They could probably get twenty pounds for this whole crop of kale." She shrugged. "They must have retired here after having earned a pension somewhere else. I assume they grow the vegetables for their own use, but they clearly didn't go for variety."

"What must it have been like back in my grandmother's day?" Gillian asked, unable to imagine living off the tiny plot.

"Hard," Torie said simply. "Most days were hard, some were harder. They got up with the sun, and worked until dark. Then they had a very simple meal and might have read by lamplight. If you needed to be entertained, you would have gone mad."

Gillian turned to Torie. "I'm never going to know the truth, so I'm going to make up my own story." She took a breath, and delivered the tale, trying to make it sound as upbeat as possible. "My grandmother was a young, impressionable girl, who fell for a charming cad. She got pregnant before she knew how to protect herself, then went along with the program when her parents found a way to move her to America." She closed her eyes, trying to get the tone right. "She was scared at first, but whatever relative sponsored her was kind and helpful. After being in Ohio for a short while, she started to dig it. She found a job…"

"She was a clerk for the county," Torie said. "I'm not sure what that means…"

"County clerk?" Gillian shook her head. "No way. That's an important job. I bet she did something like keep those ledgers I had to pay to see. Anyway, she got a government job, raised my mom, and was able to put her feet up at the end of the day. No cows to milk, no fields to till. She had an apartment—"

"I have a copy of a deed," Torie said, grinning. "She owned her home."

"Even better. She owned a warm and cozy home, there were good schools for her daughter to attend, and she managed to send her to Ohio State, where she earned a degree. Maybe my grandmother didn't have the most exciting life, but it was a good one." She slapped her hands together, feeling like she was shaking the dust of this depressing tale from them. "I'm sticking with that until I learn otherwise."

Torie stood next to her and put an arm around her waist. "You know I love Scotland," she said quietly, "but leaving Orkney in the 1950s was a good choice. It takes a certain kind of person to revel in the isolation up here, and if your grandmother was anything like you, she needed some mental stimulation. That would have been hard to get here, but I bet she had plenty of it in Ohio."

"Thanks," Gillian said. "I'm very grateful that you're participating in my fantasy."

"I think it's closer to a reality. And if you don't learn another fact, I think you know enough to let this go."

Gillian looked at her for a few moments, seeing the sharp intelligence in her dark eyes. There was something more... "I'm not sure why you're doling information out bit by bit, but I'm not complaining." She felt herself begin to smile, with those little muscles around her mouth not having been used for a couple of hours. "I feel like you're giving me info on a 'need-to-know' basis."

Torie grasped her hand and kissed the back of it. "I've done a massive amount of research, as I said I would. There's a family story here, and no good story's satisfying if every detail is thrown at you at once." She pulled Gillian close, and gently kissed each cheek. "But I'll just hand you my phone and let you read my notes if you'd rather."

"No, no, I trust you to spin the tale. Just let me know now if I'm going to open a door and have my grandfather sitting by the fire, having a wee dram of whisky."

"I'll jump ahead and spoil the ending," Torie said, with her caring nature coming through strongly. "I've learned dates, and names, but I haven't found anyone who can confirm any of our speculation."

"But you didn't know my speculation about the lighthouse keeper."

Torie raised an eyebrow. "I'm a historian, Gillian. I did a cursory investigation of every man within thirty years of Jeannie's age, and I dug a little deeper into the ones who seemed promising." She smiled. "The lighthouse keeper was at the top of my list, especially when I discovered he was in his twenties when your mum was born."

"I should never have doubted you." Gillian picked up the bike and started to ride back to their cottage, not willing at that moment to let the tears that burned her throat escape. It had been a ridiculous thought, but she'd honestly harbored the belief that she'd meet someone...anyone...who knew exactly what had happened to her grandmother. Even silly beliefs died hard.

They'd had enough mutton for one day, so Torie decided to roast a chicken for dinner. Gillian had purchased everything she needed for a meal, including a large bag of assorted mushrooms, which she was busily cleaning and slicing.

"I think I've got our week planned out," Gillian said. She was sitting on a stool and using the kitchen counter to jot down her notes.

"Do tell."

"Well, I think you'll love the Broch of Burrian. It's Iron Age and maybe Norse. They think people used it for defensive purposes until the ninth century."

"Nice," Torie said, smiling. "I could bend your ear for hours there. Even extemporaneously."

"We'll give that a whole day," she said, making a note.

"A whole day?" Torie's brow rose.

"We've got to have breakfast, then lounge around and make love…" She shrugged. "It'll take a day."

"Okay. What next?"

"The Stone Stane. It's one of those monoliths. Maybe part of a stone circle. This one has a hole in the middle—"

"Like the Stone of Odin?"

"You're asking me?"

Torie chuckled. "The Stone of Odin was a sacred standing stone. People would put their hands through the hole and shake to seal contracts and make vows. We missed a stone circle on the Mainland if you want to go back. I'm sure there's a ferry…"

"Oh, I think we'll be plenty busy here." She made a note. "One day for the Stone Stane."

"A day," Torie said. "To see one stone."

"We'll have lunch, lounge around, make love…"

"There's a pattern here…"

"Fine," she said, blowing out a breath. "I'll load us up and schedule both the Old Kirk and the New Kirk for one day. How's that?"

"Are these ruins or existing churches?"

"The Old Kirk is a ruin and the New Kirk is a multipurpose room now."

"We'd better get up early that day. So much to do!"

"How about golf?"

"We went the length of this island, Gillian. There was no course."

"The pasture by the old church is a nine-holer. Robby's got clubs and balls to rent."

"I'll just bet he does."

"I haven't played much this year, so I'll need to practice. That'll take a day. Maybe two."

"We're running out of time! We're going to have to cram a lot into those final days."

"Well, we have to go to the bird observatory. The birds are still migrating up to Iceland and Greenland and Scandinavia. They say you can see some real rare ones, especially right after a fog." She looked down her list. "We'll squeeze in looking for seals and whales whenever we walk around. The walk outside the sheep dyke is twelve miles long, so that would be a good thing to do in the evening, since it stays light so late."

Torie wiped her hands dry and walked over to straddle one of Gillian's legs. "Have I told you I love you today?" She laced her hands behind her neck, then cocked her head in question.

"I think so, but you can tell me again. I can't hear it enough."

"I love you," she said softly, then leaned in to place soft, moist kisses all over Gillian's face. "We're going to have a lovely time, even if we don't leave this cottage."

"Oh, I think we have to leave. Robby's probably the coroner, and he'll break in to check on us if we don't."

CHAPTER TWENTY-SIX

THE NEXT EVENING, OVER A wee dram of whisky served in their living room, Gillian listened to Torie and Robby comparing lighthouse keeper stories. As expected, Robby had been the keeper of the North Ronaldsay house for nearly fifty years, and he'd taken them on a long tour earlier in the day, clearly charmed by Torie's knowledge of lighthouses in general. Now they were getting down to the nitty gritty, talking about different types of lights and why they'd been developed. It was all over Gillian's head, but she couldn't have been happier to listen. Watching her lover trade bits of info with a guy who knew just about everything was a treat, and she shivered at how attracted she was to Torie's brain. Smart girls were endlessly fascinating.

When there was a short break in the conversation, Gillian said, "Mary told me she didn't know my grandmother, but I thought you might. Do you remember Jeannie Sinclair?"

"I don't," he said, shaking his head. "We talked about her this afternoon, Mary and I, but together we couldn't pull a single memory up. Not that I was surprised…"

"Because?"

"Well," he said, his smile looking a little uncomfortable. "When you live on an island this small, you know everyone. But you don't know everyone *well*. The Sinclairs kept themselves to themselves more than most."

"You mentioned Gordon Sinclair earlier," Gillian said, unsatisfied with what was clearly a hedge. "Actually, you said something that led me to think he wasn't well liked."

"Oh, I don't think I said *that*," he said, fidgeting in his chair. "I didn't know the man at all, to be honest. It's just that my father spoke of him…"

"Because…"

"Well, he used him as an example. Let's say I had a hard time getting on with a friend." He was clearly struggling to finish, but he managed to. "He'd remind me that it was important to be friends with everyone, lest I be thought of as a Gordon Sinclair." He winced as he finished his statement, clearly embarrassed.

"My great-great-grandfather was so disliked people used him as—"

"I don't think he was exactly disliked," Robby rushed to assure her. "I think it was more that he was a very independent thinker. We've been largely self-governing for hundreds of years around here, having to work hard to reach agreement. I got the impression Gordon wasn't easy to sway…"

"So he was a contrarian on an island full of people who tried to accommodate each other."

Robby laughed. "I can't say that's exactly true, but he wasn't afraid to speak his mind and stand his ground." He narrowed his eyes for a second, adding, "You've not asked me about Alex, but I knew him a bit. He was older than I was, but we had some…interactions."

"Was he nicer than his father?" Gillian asked, shifting her gaze to see Torie looking a little ill-at-ease.

"Nicer? That's not a comparison I'd like to make. But he was also one who had firm ideas. He didn't participate much in the community, but he surprised us all when it came time to decide whether to pave the lanes to the houses. He was very much against it and I was very much for it. The fact that I owned the paving business didn't color my judgment," he added, showing a smile so impish it made Gillian laugh.

"Is there any job you didn't do?"

"I've never taught at the school, nor preached at the church—when it was a proper church, that is. I've had my say at community meetings, though. I can hold the floor longer than some would like."

"You're saying my great-grandfather was pretty argumentative."

"That's your word, not mine. But it *was* hard to change his mind. All I recall of your great-grandmother is that she was quiet." He paused, clearly drawing on whatever memories he could conjure up. "I remember that she was a very pretty woman, but she spoke less than a China doll." He looked at Gillian pointedly. "In public, that is. You can't know how a person behaves at home."

"Do you think my great-grandfather kept her from interacting with other people?"

He barked out a laugh. "Oh, no, I wouldn't think something like that. We're going back many, many years, Gillian. It was a rare woman who had much time to socialize. What with big families, every woman I knew spent a whole day just getting her washing done."

"I think my great-grandmother only had one child," Gillian said. She shot a look at Torie. "True?"

"True."

"Well, even with a small family, everyone was busy. Many people met to talk or have a cup of tea or something a little stronger, but just as many didn't."

"Clearly my great-grandparents weren't at the hub of the North Ronaldsay social scene."

"No, no, that's more than true." He took in a breath, nodding to himself. "Alex was a dour man, who didn't seem to have much interest in pleasure. He didn't even drink," he said, his eyes going wide. "Trust me on this. There are few tee-totals on North Ronaldsay."

"You're saying Jeannie had a stern, argumentative father who didn't get along well with his neighbors, and a mother who barely spoke."

"Alice must have been nearly silent for neither Mary nor I to have any specific thoughts of her."

Gillian knew she should just let it go, but she couldn't convince herself to drop the ball at this point. "I don't know if Mary said anything to you, but I hinted I'd heard the gossip about the lighthouse keeper and my grandmother."

"Mmm," he said, gazing at her without giving away his thoughts.

"Do you think that could be true?"

He held up his hands. "How can anyone know? We're down to fewer than fifty people now, but our population wasn't large even back then. There couldn't have been more than five children near your grandmother's age. You know how people are. They tick off all the possible suspects when a girl gets herself in the family way."

"That means..."

"Adrian Ross, the assistant lighthouse keeper, was an attractive young man, Gillian."

"Did you say Ross? Is that a common name?"

"It is. Very. I think we had three Ross families at one time." He cocked his head. "Why do you ask?"

"Not important," she said. "Go on with your story."

He seemed to think for a minute, then continued. "Ross had a wife, but no children. There was no reason for people to link him and your grandmother, but..."

"But what?"

He rolled his eyes. "There were very few boys or men near your grandmother's age, and the ones a little older would have been married. Back then, people picked a mate and married as soon as they finished school. Ross was a good-looking man, and more than one woman looked for him at the pub on his nights off."

"So, you're saying he was…what? That he ran around on his wife?"

"Oh, no," he said, looking agitated. "You didn't hear that from me. All I meant was that he was our version of…what's the fella's name? The good looking one that all the girls love?"

"Um…Brad Pitt?"

"No, no, the one with the dark hair… Cary Grant," he said, clearly proud of himself for remembering. "For a few years there, he was our version of Cary Grant. Tall, broad shoulders, dark hair. He could tell a tale and have the whole pub soaking up every word. The men gripped their wives' hands a little tighter when he rolled in, I'll grant you that."

"So, he was known to like the ladies, and when my grandmother got pregnant…"

"The fella who piloted the ferry that took the children to Kirkwall liked the ladies too, but he looked like the other fella. Who's the one with the face that could scare the devil himself?"

"I have no idea," Gillian said.

"Lon Chaney. He looked like Lon Chaney in *The Hunchback of Notre Dame*. Not a single person mentioned him as the father, and believe me, he would have had plenty of opportunity. He spent hours a day with those children, and he was just a few years older than they were."

"Good lord," Gillian said, catching Torie trying to cover a laugh. "Are you saying you don't think the rumor has any real validity?"

His smile was once again so charming that Gillian wondered if he hadn't had some success in convincing a few girls to abandon their morals to sneak off with him. "Back in the fifties, we didn't have electricity, or even reliable radio. We had to make our own news, and most of it revolved around who was doing what to whom. Your poor grandmother was her day's…what's the name of the pretty girl who had the baby without telling who the father was?"

"Um…" Gillian shot Torie a look. "Do you have any idea?"

"Ingrid Bergman?" she said, holding up her hands. "I think she had an affair with—"

"No, no. That was years ago. This just happened." He stroked his chin for a second, then slapped his thigh. "Minnie Driver."

"Minnie Driver!" Gillian stared at him. *What were the chances of a guy jumping from Cary Grant to Minnie Driver?*

"She's the one. Am I right? She had the baby and never said who the father was."

"I have no idea," Gillian said. "I didn't know she had a baby at all."

"Oh, sure. It was in all the papers. We have the internet now, you know. Most days," he added quietly.

"Okay," Gillian said. "So, you think my grandmother was like Minnie Driver, and while the assistant lighthouse keeper had the charm and the looks of Cary Grant, Lon Chaney was likely my grandfather."

"Oh, no," he said, laughing. "I keep up on things. I know all about chromosomes and such. There's not a bit of Lon Chaney in you, lassie. But you don't have that dimple in your chin, either. I'd say your grandfather could have been any one of a hundred men, but was probably some lad from Kirkwall. A nice young lass from North Ronaldsay probably fell for a fella from the big town, with thoughts of building a life there." He shrugged. "Why that didn't happen, I couldn't begin to say."

"Thanks for the information," Gillian said, reaching over to add a wee dram of whisky to his glass. "I wish I'd learned the Sinclairs were beloved by all, and that my grandmother's boyfriend loved her desperately, but was prevented from marrying her for some noble reason, but that was clearly not the case."

CHAPTER TWENTY-SEVEN

THEY SPENT THEIR LAST FULL day on the island doing a final, slow lap. The day was sunny and surprisingly warm, letting them roll up their jeans and wade into the water, trying to see how close they could get to the sheep who were nibbling on whatever seaweed they could find at low tide. Gillian reminded Torie of a child chasing a pigeon. She had no chance of touching one of the surprisingly small sheep, but her desire to try was nearly unquenchable.

Torie nearly exhausted her battery taking pictures of Gillian running around in the water, but she was determined to get a good one of her chasing the same type of sheep her grandmother probably ran after when she was a girl.

When she finally tired, they walked home to change out of their wet clothes and have a bite of lunch. Even though it was still bright and sunny, they could see dark clouds in the distance, ready to move in. The nice weather was clearly time-limited.

The fog rolled in at five, covering the island in a pale gray blanket. The light in the tower still swung around, trying to illuminate both land and sea, but it only served to swipe through the fog, brightening a wide stripe of it. A boat couldn't possibly have seen the light unless it was close enough to crash. The moment she had the thought, a foghorn sounded, so loud it made Torie levitate.

"Well, we've now seen and heard every single thing on this island," Gillian said, grinning like a kid. "I love it."

"You wouldn't love it if you had to be out in this."

"We *do* have to be out in this," she said, standing up and extending her hand for Torie to grasp.

"I'm not going out," she said, pushing the hand away. "You could fall into the sea!"

"No way. Not going to happen. We're going to take another peek at the lighthouse. Robby gave me permission."

"It's locked."

Gillian reached into her back pocket and withdrew a big set of keys. "Not a problem."

"When did you do this?"

"Earlier. Robby knows what a fan I am, so he said we could go up at night. This is our last night, so…"

"Are you sure?" Torie said, standing and putting her hand on Gillian's waist. "It's started to rain, and the fog is really bad."

"I know. But we can see the light. We'll just head for it."

"If you insist," Torie said, unable to refuse any of Gillian's requests.

"I'll get all of the snacks we have left. Go get our rain jackets, okay? Boots too."

"They're outside," Torie reminded her. "Where they belong. I can well see that you weren't raised in a boot-wearing land. When we live together," she said, smiling widely, "you'll have to keep them outdoors. I won't allow muck and mud in my house."

"Will you get them? I like to sit down to put mine on."

"That's because of those gorgeous calf muscles of yours," Torie said. "Since I love them, I suppose I can't complain that they make your boots a little snug."

By the time Torie returned, Gillian had two tote bags packed and ready.

"I was gone fifteen seconds," she said, staring at the neatly packed bags.

"I work fast. Ready?"

"As I'll ever be. Just promise not to let me wander off and fall into the sea."

"I don't think you're the type to wander. You'll have such a tight hold on me that if one of us goes, the other's sure to follow."

"Somehow…not reassuring," Torie said, managing to smile.

They put their coats on and zipped up tight, hoods drawn close around their faces. Gillian's new rain jacket was a bright yellow, looking just as warm as the one she'd generously left for Torie on her last trip. They started down the path, with Torie feeling a little silly for thinking the trip would be dangerous. If you stayed on the path, you'd bump right into the lighthouse.

They'd only walked fifteen or twenty feet when Gillian stopped to look up. As the light traveled over their heads, a bird would occasionally pass through it, a black dot that disappeared as the light moved on.

"Cool!" she yelled over the now driving rain and punishing wind.

Torie gripped her arm tighter, lowered her head, and fought to move forward. She didn't know what the force of the wind was, but it was awesome—in the traditional definition, not the American one. She actually felt like she was pushing against something, leaning into it with her shoulder, working for each step. Then she lifted a foot too high and the wind caught it and nearly knocked her over—even though she was holding onto Gillian with all of her might.

The bags Gillian carried beat against her legs, occasionally veering off to whack Torie as well. Finally, after what seemed like ten minutes to cover the short distance, they were at the door. Gillian struggled to get the key into the lock, but she finally succeeded and they tumbled into the dry warmth of the lighthouse.

"We could have drowned standing up!" Gillian gasped. "I don't think I've ever respected the force of nature as much as I do this minute!"

Torie slapped at her with an open hand. "How many months ago did a wind not as bad as this break your arm? Have you lost your mind?"

She unzipped her jacket and lowered her hood, with a silly grin on her face. "That already happened," she said, with logic only she could possibly understand. "I've had the wind injury, so I don't have to worry about it any more. We'll stay right here until this calms down, though. Since you haven't had the wind injury, our number might be up."

"Good lord." She pulled her own hood down and stood there for a moment, listening to the building creak. "There's no way the ferry's coming tomorrow if this doesn't calm down significantly. And if the ferry doesn't come…" She didn't finish her thought. They both knew they'd have to scramble to find a seat on the Island Land-Rover, as the locals called the wee plane.

"Mary told me she's very good at predicting the weather, and that this will pass by midnight." Gillian took her coat off and guided her flashlight up at the revolving light, always kind of spooky at night as it cast shadows all around. "Wow. The wind's really wailing. What would you do if that hit you when you were on a little boat?"

"Or a big boat. Think of your poor ancestor Hamish having to cross the sea to America. Storms like this can last for two or three days." She shivered just thinking about it. "They say people on the ships wanted to capsize just to make it stop."

"Ooo," Gillian whimpered. "Happy thoughts. Let's think happy thoughts."

"Race you to the top?"

"It's a hundred and seventy-six steps!"

"I know." Torie took off, her boots thumping against the stairs, climbing in a tight circle until she started to feel dizzy.

Gillian was, of course, right on her tail, laughing. "Not much of a race," she said, seeming to find the situation remarkably funny.

"You're faster than I am. I was going for surprise."

"Surprise!" She pushed past and kept on going, with Torie only slightly embarrassed that Gillian was still carrying both tote bags while managing to easily whip past her.

The last fifty steps had her legs quivering, but Torie forgot that in a second. Gillian had used her free time to start setting out candles, big, pillar style ones, around the lantern room. She had the first two lit, and was racing for the third, grinning like a child.

"Where did you get those?" Torie asked, amazed. "I know you didn't have them in your backpack."

"I ordered them from the same place I got the groceries. They deliver every day, you know."

"But…" She clapped her mouth shut, realizing their provenance wasn't important. The fact that Gillian had made such careful plans was. Torie walked over to her and waited until she'd blown out the long match she was using. Then she enfolded her in a hug and held on for a long while. "You're such a romantic." They kissed, an unhurried, slow one that made her knees a little weak. "Being a romantic who's good at long-term planning is a pairing I'm very unused to, and very, very fond of."

"I wanted to make our last night on the island special." She turned and gave the gray cloud a scowl. "We should have done this last night. The sunset was spectacular, and seeing it from here would have been sweet."

"We saw the sunset perfectly well. It was warm, we had a bottle of wine with us, and we got to sit on the ground and kiss until dark. How could that have been improved?"

"We could have had food," she said, chuckling. "I should have bought more snacks. I've been hoarding these," she admitted, starting to remove biscuits and cheese and some cured meats from her tote bag. A bottle of red wine appeared, along with two glasses. "Once this is gone, we've got absolutely nothing left. We'll have to go to the Bird Observatory and beg for breakfast."

"Their restaurant is open to the public," Torie reminded her. "We won't have to beg." She grasped the denim near Gillian's hip and plucked at it. "Unless you've spent every dollar you brought, and your pockets are empty. Which is entirely possible," she chided. "North Ronaldsay is going to put up a memorial to you."

"Robby's the big man around here, and he likes you best. If there's a memorial, it'll be to you." She gave Torie another delicate kiss. "I'd vote for you, too."

"So?" Torie said, taking a match and striking it to help light the candles. "Are we just going to sit up here? Or have you arranged for the locals to serenade us or put on a play?"

She snapped her fingers. "I *knew* I'd forgotten something."

"I'd faint dead away if a stream of pipers started to march up those stairs," Torie said, chuckling. "I'd rather be alone."

"My favorite way to be." She put her hands on her hips and looked around the room. "There aren't many cushions. Want me to run back and get some?"

"Let's sit on these chairs and just watch. I like the fog."

The chairs were canvas, but they were tall enough to allow for a clear view out of the windows, and pretty comfortable, even if they creaked and groaned when you moved. "Nice," Torie said when Gillian unscrewed the cap and started to pour the wine.

They clinked their glasses together, and both took a sip. "You've even managed to find a good bottle of wine," Torie said. "Don't tell me this is from the air drop."

"I bought this one in Aberdeen. I wanted something special, and I had a feeling the selection from the Tesco in Kirkwall wouldn't cut it." She held the bottle up and inspected it. "Good red wine's expensive, but it's worth a splurge every once in a while." Taking another sip, she nodded, clearly satisfied. "Our last night on my ancestral island is a special event. Remind me to take the label off and save it. I like keeping things to bring back memories of special trips."

Torie reached over and grasped her hand, sighing as she stared out at the fog, so thick even the circling light wasn't able to cut through it. "What's your wish?" she asked, not having planned that question. They were just so relaxed that words tumbled from her mouth with no warning. "For us, that is. If you could have this work out exactly as you wanted, what would happen."

"As you might have guessed," Gillian said, clearing her throat, "I've given that some thought."

"I'd be surprised if you haven't. You're a planner."

"I am." She tilted her chin as she gathered her thoughts and Torie let her gaze wander all over her face. She had such classically all-American good looks. Nothing too large, nothing too small. Just an open, friendly, well-balanced set of features that made her seem approachable. She could have been a spokesperson for some decidedly American product, like a soft drink or... Letting out a laugh, she had to admit Gillian was the perfect person to sell soap. If she told you a product would make your clothes sparkling clean, you'd believe it.

Torie had been so intent on staring at Gillian, she started when she spoke.

"If I could have what I wanted, I'd move here. We'd get our own place, of course, and you'd finish your degree. I'm not sure how easy it would be for me to find a job, but..." She shrugged. "I've got a good reputation, and I could market just about any product. I'm not limited to soap."

"But..." Torie was too stunned to respond for a minute. "We've talked about this at length. You need to stay with Channing Brothers for two more years to be eligible for your pension."

"Right. But I wouldn't get any money until I actually retired. I'd have to be sixty-seven or something like that to see a dime."

"That may be true, but you're so close, Gillian. You can't walk away from a pension. You told me yourself that not many companies even offer them any longer."

"That's true. But that's so far in the future I'm just not going to worry about it."

"But—"

"The pension's just a promise, Torie, and I don't think we should focus on it. The important issue is my stock options. I've got a wagon-load of them that I can exercise at the end of next year."

"I'm not sure what that means—practically, that is. I understand they give you stock in the company as part of your compensation, but..." She told the whole truth. "I'm entirely ignorant when it comes to corporations."

"No, you're not. It's just not your world. Essentially, I'll come into some free money if I'm still employed there eighteen months from now."

"I love free money. I think," Torie admitted, chuckling. "I've never had any, but I can't imagine not liking it."

"It's not a guarantee. I've had years where the stock price was under water. The options are worthless then."

"Are we talking a lot of money?"

Gillian nodded soberly, making Torie's imagination soar. That could be anything from a few thousand dollars, which would be huge to her, or much, much more, knowing how Gillian regarded money.

"You can't walk away from a significant amount of money," Torie said, shaking her head. "Even if you don't need it now, you can put it away for your retirement. I've seen what happens to people who weren't able to do that, and it's not pretty."

"Unless I stay until I retire, I'll always have to walk away from some options. It's just that this bunch was bigger, actually *much* bigger than usual, so it would be more painful." She met Torie's eyes, her expression sober. "You didn't ask me what made financial sense. You asked me what I wanted." She gripped Torie's hand tightly. "I want to be with you, and if I just pushed myself a tiny bit, I'd quit over the phone and stay for good."

Torie closed her eyes and let herself imagine Gillian's dream. Having a loving partner at her side, being able to finish her degree, having someone to share the burden of caring for Aiden... Her imagination swirled around, letting her picture an idyllic life, full of nothing but love and support.

"You look like you like that idea," Gillian said softly.

Torie's eyes blinked open. "Of course I do! But it's too risky. You don't have any thoughts of a job..."

"It *is* risky. But I haven't taken many risks in my life. I think it's time I start."

"Is this mostly, or even partly, a desire to run away? I know how upset you've been about the direction your country's taking."

"That's part of it. Of course it is," she admitted, nodding. "But only about ten percent. The truth is, I love you, and I love Scotland. You're in Scotland, as luck would have it, so I can have two things I'm crazy about if I just move three thousand six hundred and thirty-four miles."

"It sounds much, much easier than I think it would actually be," Torie warned. "I think we'd have a bumpy ride getting settled. Aberdeen has a vibrant economy, but we don't have any massive manufacturing concerns. You might have to find work in Edinburgh or Glasgow or even London."

"No big deal. Finding a job is just one of a series of hurdles we'll have to leap over. The big issue is...what do *you* want."

"Ideally?" She started when the wind hit the lighthouse so forcefully that it shivered. "Ideally, I'd like to live through this storm," she said, almost laughing at the fear she saw in Gillian's eyes.

"Was that...normal?"

"Unpleasantly so. When a gust hits hard, that energy has to go somewhere."

"You don't think..."

"It won't fall," Torie assured her. "This tower's been standing since the mid-nineteenth century. If the storms its been hit with haven't knocked it over yet, this little one won't."

"This one's little?"

"Uh-huh," she said, watching her eyes grow wide. "We're fine. Promise." She leaned over and gave her a kiss. "But storms like this were pretty frightening for me when I was a kid."

"I'm not a kid, and I'm ready to run!"

"We don't need to do that. We'll drink our wine and nibble on our cheese. By the time we're ready to leave, it will have calmed down. I trust Mary's prediction."

"That makes one of us," Gillian said, gulping some wine.

"Still want to hear my wish?"

"I do." She grasped Torie's hand firmly. "Take my mind off the present."

"Well, if I'm going to be completely honest, as well as completely self-involved, I'd like to live with you in America until you were eligible for your pension. Then you'd have earned your options, and also be guaranteed some money in your golden years."

"That's your motivation? You'd leave your home? The home I know you love with all your heart, just for some cash?"

"No," Torie said quietly. "I'll never leave Scotland permanently. But I'd like…a break. I've been caring for Aiden for thirteen years, but Kirsty's got things well in hand at the moment." She took a breath and expressed the fear that had begun to nag at her. "I'd like to have a year or two where I can focus on us. Before my parents start to need care."

"You think that's going to be soon?" Gillian asked, looking a little skittish.

"I fear it might. We've gotten good at keeping people alive for longer periods, but when you don't exercise or eat the right foods…bad things happen." She forced herself to look at the bright side. "But they're healthy enough now, they're both still working, and they can easily help out when Kirsty needs assistance." She took Gillian's hand and held it tenderly. "I feel like this is my chance to have an adventure. I love the promise of America, Gillian. I love the exuberance of your people. I love how you believe you can do just about anything if you put your mind to it. We're a more prudent, or maybe a more realistic people. We don't dream as big as you do in America."

"Well, I'd rather leave, but I can stick it out for a while if you really want me to."

"I think I do," Torie said. "At least that's my wish. I could have an adventure, and you could earn some money that we'll probably have to spend on my parents. Doesn't that sound like fun?"

Gillian's smile was as bright as the light that floated around above their heads, doing its best to light up the gray fog. "If that would make you happy, it honestly sounds fantastic."

"I couldn't leave Aiden for long. I honestly couldn't imagine a scenario where I could. But being gone for a year or two might be good for all involved.

Kirsty would truly be in charge, and he might mature a bit if I wasn't around to baby him as I do."

"Then we'll figure out how to get you into the US. I'll save all of the extra dough that falls into my hands, and put it into a special account. We'll use that to make sure your parents have a comfortable retirement. They won't have to worry about a thing."

"I think you're entirely serious."

"I am. If this is your wish, I'm all in."

"You make me fall more in love with you every day." Torie stood and slipped in front of Gillian's chair, pressing into her body when she laced her arms around her neck. "I love you so much," she whispered before delivering a dazzling display of kisses, each one filled with the love that grew in her heart with each passing day.

Their food was gone, demolished in a stunningly short amount of time, and Gillian carefully portioned the last of the wine between their glasses. She'd had more than Torie, but she was remarkably clear-headed. The punishing storm probably accounted for that. It was hard to let your guard down when the waves were hitting the structure so hard it sounded like an explosive charge.

They were sitting on the floor, using a couple of wool blankets as cushions. It wasn't terribly comfortable, but Gillian wouldn't have moved for anything. The fog had finally dissipated, and now she could see the rain lashing against the windows, sheeting down like someone was directing a hose at them.

"This is so cool," she murmured.

"Not frightened any longer?"

"No. Now that I can see, I'm fine. It was just not knowing what was out there that I didn't like. This? This I like."

"I think you have the soul of a lighthouse keeper," Torie said. "My dad feels the same way. But he's a lot quieter than you are. More solitary, too. Most people who have a job like yours aren't drawn to this kind of isolation."

"Oh, I'd hate it if I had to be here for weeks at a time," she admitted. "But I can't think of a better way to relax. You can let go of your thoughts and just be part of nature."

"Oh, we're part of nature," Torie said, chuckling. "Nature would knock us off our feet if we tried to get back to our cottage right now."

"I'm in no rush. Robby might wonder why I haven't returned the keys, since he kept telling me he was giving me his only set." She felt her smile grow. "He can't come get them even if he wanted to."

"Let's talk about what we'll do in O-hi-o," Torie said, her smile so filled with excitement it nearly took Gillian's breath away. The chance to make the woman she loved this happy was making her kind of giddy.

She scooted away from the wall and started to pat her pockets. "You know, there's something you could do to make moving to America a lot easier." She got to her feet and peered into the tote bag, finding what she was looking for and palming it.

"What's that?"

Gillian turned, smiled down at Torie's expectant face, and sank to one knee. As she held out a small blue velvet box, Torie's mouth dropped open. Quietly, Gillian said, "You could marry me." She blinked a few times, banishing the tears from her eyes. "Will you?"

Torie threw her arms around her so hard she almost got whiplash. Then warm tears wet her cheek as Torie's body shook in her embrace.

"Does that mean yes?"

"Yes, yes, yes, yes, and yes a thousand more times!" She pulled away and revealed her flushed face, lit with a radiant smile. "Of course I'll marry you."

"I love you more than I'd ever hoped to love a woman. You mean everything to me, Torie. Absolutely everything."

They melted into each other's arms, warm lips meeting again and again, each kiss growing in intensity. "I want to make love to you," Torie whispered, suddenly sounding drunk.

"I want you to look at your engagement ring," Gillian said. "And *then* I want you to make love to me. I spent an awful lot of time choosing this and I…"

"My God! I forgot all about it!" The box had fallen to her lap, and she started to laugh as she picked it up. "You can't say I'm only interested in you for the presents."

"I would never say that," Gillian said, finding her hands were shaking. She hadn't been nervous about asking Torie to marry her, but this was a different kind of thing. They'd never discussed it, and Torie wasn't much of a jewelry wearer. Just before she opened the box, Gillian grasped her hands. "I want you to be honest with me. If you'd rather not wear a ring, I will completely understand. If you'd like something different, I can return this. Okay?"

Torie gazed at her, and Gillian realized she was still kneeling. She sat next to her and held her hand, waiting expectantly.

"I've never considered wearing an engagement ring, but that's mostly because no one did this kind of thing when I was younger. But now?" Her smile grew. "I think I'd like for people to know I'm going to marry the most thoughtful, loving, prettiest woman in the world."

"That's not who I am, but I'm serious about the ring. If you want something different—we should get it. You're going to wear this for the rest of your life."

Torie's eyes blinked slowly. "The rest of my life. That seems like a very long time." As her smile grew, she kissed Gillian again. "That's the best part. We'll have the rest of our lives together."

"Are you going to look?" she prompted once again. "I'm on pins and needles."

Torie cracked the box open as a beatific smile covered her face. "It's so big!" she said, shaking her head. "You must have spent thousands of dollars on this!"

"I did. I want you to look down on this and think about how impermeable this stone is. That's exactly how my feelings are for you." She took the ring from the box and held it up so the candlelight played with the facets, sending a rainbow of color around the lantern room. "You're going to wear this forever, so I wanted it to be big enough to hold your interest."

"But I've never had anything so expensive," she said quietly. Then she took the ring and stared at it, clearly at a loss for words.

"Do you like it?"

Tears filled her eyes again as she nodded rapidly. "I love it. I especially love that you picked it out." Her smile grew wide. "I know you spent *hours*."

"Days," she said, chuckling. "I didn't find anything in Columbus, so I went to Cleveland, also striking out. So the last time I was in New York, I went a day early and spent the entire day looking. This one seemed right. Classic cut, elegant, not too fussy. Like you."

"But I can't afford one for you," Torie said, her lower lip starting to quiver.

"This one has a matching eternity band. Little diamonds all the way around. We'll get two so we match. Those will be our wedding rings."

"That's what you want?"

"I think so. But if I change my mind, we'll go shopping together. I'll pay, and bill you ten dollars a month until you pay it off." She started to laugh. "That's fair, right?"

"Very fair."

Gillian took the ring from her and started to slip it on her finger. It caught at the knuckle, but then slid past to firmly settle. "It looks fantastic on you," she murmured. "Your fingers are so long and elegant. They were made for a diamond."

Torie wrapped her arms around Gillian's neck and held on tight as she covered her with kisses. "I love my ring, but I'm much more excited about marrying you!"

"That's one of the biggest reasons I proposed. I knew you'd feel that way."

※ ※ ※

Gillian started to pack her tote bags up with the empty containers and wrappers from their snack. Torie had been slowly doling out the information she'd discovered, wanting to give Gillian time to assimilate and discuss each piece of the puzzle. But the time seemed right to reveal the big news. She caught Gillian as she passed by, grasping her hand and pulling her close. "I have some news."

"You're not pregnant, are you? I know we've been going at it pretty rigorously—"

"Sit down, please," Torie said, smiling at her.

Gillian moved the chair around so they'd face each other, then she sat down. "You look pretty serious. Nothing's wrong, is it?"

"Not at all. But I found some information, and I want you to know about it." She took in a breath. "I found Adrian Ross."

"You… What?"

"I found him," she said, proud of her detective work. "It took a lot of time, but I tracked him…or I should say I found out where he was born, and where his remaining family lives. Glenrothes, in Fife."

"Fife? Have we been there?"

"No. Adrian's gone now, as is his wife. They had no children."

"I think they…or rather, he did. Ross was my mother's middle name," she whispered. "She reluctantly told me it was a family name when I bugged her about it, and I never really thought about it again. I mean, Robby said the name's common, but…"

"I'll find someone, Gillian. It might be a second or third or fourth cousin, but I'll find someone who shares Adrian Ross's DNA. And if we can link you…"

"Hold on," she said, clearly troubled. "I'm not sure we should keep digging."

"What?" she said, feeling like someone had unexpectedly stepped on the brake when she'd been speeding down the motorway.

"I don't think I want to know. For sure, at least."

"But we're so close! Now that I know your mom had his last name, we're just a full stop away from finishing the story."

"What we know is enough for me," she said, looking very sure of herself. "I want this to be true, and digging deeper could possibly snatch it all away." She took Torie's hand and pressed it to her breast. "I want to believe my innate love of lighthouses was handed down from my grandfather. I want to be related to this guy."

"But we could find out…" She knew she was pushing, but it was her very nature to complete her research.

Gillian's voice had grown quiet, and she seemed very introspective. "In my mind, Adrian and Jeannie snuck up into this very tower one night to profess their love for each other. It was tender, and romantic, and wrong as hell, but I want to believe it was something both of them wanted very much. Their passions got the best of them, and they completely ignored the social mores of their day to make love."

"This is really important to you," Torie soothed, caressing Gillian's cheek, feeling her tremble slightly.

"It is. It's the happiest ending I can give my grandmother." She shivered, and her expression grew dark. "Obviously, it's much more likely that Adrian was a total creep, a guy who screwed his way around this whole island. He might not have given a second thought to destroying an innocent girl's reputation, something that meant everything back then. But I don't want to know that if it's true. I want to delude myself into thinking it was a wildly romantic love affair between two people who were desperate to be together." She wrapped her arms around Torie and nearly crushed her with the force of her embrace. "Like us," she said, with her voice quavering. "Let me believe they loved each other like we do. Let me give my grandmother a little happiness. Please," she whispered, with tears filling her eyes.

"I promise I will never ask another question about Jeannie Sinclair," Torie soothed, gently wiping the tears from Gillian's cheek. "I have her direct line nailed down back to the 1600s. Her story's complete."

"God!" Gillian gasped, pulling away to stare. "I don't need to know if I'm related to Adam or Eve!"

"I don't like to leave a stone unturned. As soon as I finish the Lindsay clan, I'm going to have your whole family tree put onto a scroll of some sort. I've been shopping," she said, grinning.

"If you hadn't already agreed to marry me…" Gillian said, pulling her close for another long kiss.

"But I have. And I'm not giving this ring back, so you have to keep me."

"Oh, I'll keep you," she said, sighing heavily. "I'll keep you by my side until the world falls into anarchy." She checked her watch. "I give it a year."

"Now, now," Torie soothed. "Try to look on the bright side. I can tell you tales of rulers who'll make your president and our prime minister look like Cincinnatus."

"I didn't pay attention in history class. Was he after Franklin Pierce?"

"A bit before," Torie said, smirking. "I have no idea who this Pierce fellow was, but I don't have time to ask for clarification, my beloved fiancée. I would toss you to the floor and make love to you right here, but once you convinced me this is where your mother was conceived, I need to return to the cottage to get back into the mood."

"Follow me," Gillian said, grasping her tote bags and starting for the stairs. "And this time, try to keep up."

CHAPTER TWENTY-EIGHT

THE RAIN HAD STOPPED EERILY close to when Mary had predicted, with morning bringing huge, fluffy clouds hanging like ornaments over a clear sky. They'd been on the ferry for nearly an hour, having to dash outside repeatedly so Gillian didn't lose her breakfast. Torie hadn't thought to ask if she was a good sailor. Apparently, she wasn't.

"Aren't you glad it's summer?" Torie asked, shouting to be heard over the waves that crashed against the bow as it dipped and shuddered.

"This isn't very summery," Gillian yelled back. "I checked the weather at home, and it's twenty degrees warmer. *That's* summer."

"Take a look at this gorgeous ring," she said, prying her hand from the railing to blind Gillian with its sparkle. "That'll take your mind off things."

"Still love it?" she said, her pale face and strained expression touching Torie's heart.

"I will love it every day of my life. Promise."

"Gonna tell your parents?"

"Of course!"

"Think I should meet them?"

Torie slapped herself in the forehead. "You haven't met my parents?"

"Nope. Nor your sister. Want to have dinner with them soon?" She paused. "If I'm ever able to eat again, that is."

"You'll be fine. This is just a little rough patch. We probably should have flown."

"If there was a way to get that flying Range Rover to swoop down low, I'd leap for it," Gillian said, seemingly completely serious.

They landed in Kirkwall in the late afternoon, with Gillian's color returning to normal as soon as they were in calmer water. Once on land, they stood on the dock for a few minutes, with Gillian grasping a sturdy piling to hold on. "The ground's still moving," she said, looking entirely puzzled.

"You don't have your sea legs yet. Just give it a minute."

"I think I need to sit down and have a bite. As usual, I didn't get lunch. Think there's somewhere close where we could have something light?"

"My new phone has the answer to just about anything," Torie said, whipping it out to check a restaurant review site. "There's a spot that looks promising not fifty metres from here."

"Again, I don't know how far that is, but I'm game."

"When's our flight back to Aberdeen?"

"Tomorrow. I've got something to take care of in the morning, then we're leaving at three."

Torie took her hand and they started to walk toward the restaurant. "Are you going to tell me what you've got up your sleeve?"

"Just one of the arms I'm looking forward to wrapping around you as soon as we reach our hotel. It's been *hours* since we've made love," she sighed.

"I'm very glad to hear your wobbly sea legs haven't hurt your libido. As soon as we get some food into you, we'll get right on that."

"And maybe some of that good dark Orkney beer. I really like that stuff."

"You're getting more Scottish every day," Torie said, clutching Gillian's hand more firmly as they crossed the street and darted into the restaurant, seeking nourishment for what Torie hoped was a long night.

⚜ ⚜ ⚜

They slept in, neither of them moving until it was almost ten o'clock. "I had no idea you could sleep so long," Gillian murmured into Torie's ear as her eyes fluttered open.

"Is it morning?"

"It's nearly lunch," Gillian said, her soft laughter such a delightful sound to wake to.

"We have until three," she sighed. "Let's stay until they come to physically throw us out."

"No, no," Gillian said, slipping out of bed to take Torie's hands and pull her into a sitting position. "I've got to handle that little matter I spoke of yesterday. And I need you to go with me."

"Shower together?"

"If we can both fit, I'm happy to." She walked over to pick up her toiletry kit. "If there was one thing I could change about Scotland, I'd make the showers bigger."

"That's not much of a wish," Torie said. "Are you sure that's all you'd change?"

"I didn't say that. I just said that was my top priority." She went into the bath and took a peek. "We'll have to squeeze, but I think we can make it. I might not be able to wash your back, but I'm sure I can get the front half nice and clean."

"You'd better go first. And alone," Torie said, knowing Gillian's tricks. "If you want to run this errand, we don't have time to get sidetracked, something you're all too good at."

When Torie emerged from the shower, Gillian was tucking a pale blue blouse into a pair of navy-blue slacks that bore a sharp crease. "Why do you look like you're going to work?" She walked over as she held her towel around her body, taking a closer look at the blouse, which was quite elegant for a weekday morning in Kirkwall.

"I have an appointment," she said, clearly trying to look sophisticated. "I assume you'll be taking my picture, and I want to look nice."

Torie cocked her head, unable to guess where this was heading. Then Gillian reached into her suitcase and removed another small box, extracting a gold signet ring. She placed it on the little finger of her right hand, then waved it under Torie's nose. "The Lindsays are back to reclaim the birthright we'd abandoned."

"You're taking your citizenship oath?" she asked, her voice rising with excitement.

"I am. Believe me," she said dramatically. "Getting all of these dates to line up was no small task. But today, the Lord Lieutenant of Orkney will welcome me and one other person into the country." She grinned widely. "I'm so excited I'm about to wag my tail."

"My phone is charged, and I promise to drain the battery taking photos of you. I'm so happy!"

When they entered the council chamber, Gillian swallowed when she saw the large portrait of the queen resting on an easel. She'd been thinking about this day for months, but now that it was here she was much more nervous than she'd thought she'd be.

That was kind of silly. It wasn't like she was renouncing her US citizenship. This was just an addition, a status she was entitled to based on her mother's birth. Still, when a guy entered the room wearing the fanciest military uniform she thought she'd ever seen, her knees were quaking.

The man strode right over to her, extending a hand. Gillian was sure her own was damp, but she gave his a firm shake. "Gillian Lindsay," she said. "It's very nice to meet you, sir."

"And it's a pleasure to meet you, as well. I'm very happy to welcome you to Scotland. I've been told that your mother was born here?"

"She was. I hope she'd be proud of me for claiming citizenship." As she said that, she could feel a few tears leak from her eyes, smiling when some tissues were pressed into her hand. "I'd like to introduce you to my fiancée. She keeps me in tissues, since I often find myself crying over the warmth of the people and the beauty of this wondrous land. Torie Gunn, this is Lord Lieutenant Alistair McGuinness."

"Very nice to meet you," he said, shaking her hand. "I think we're ready to begin." He handed her a sheet of paper. "You've chosen the affirmation, correct?"

"Correct."

"Then go right ahead when you're ready, Miss Lindsay."

Even though she'd memorized the oath, she was worried she'd forget something, so she glanced at the sheet as she cleared her throat and started to speak, catching a glimpse of Torie with her camera held high.

"I, Gillian Cumberland Lindsay, do solemnly, sincerely and truly affirm and declare that on becoming a British Citizen, I will be faithful and bear true allegiance to Her Majesty Queen Elizabeth the Second, her heirs, and successors according to law.

"I will give my loyalty to the United Kingdom, and respect its rights and freedoms. I will uphold its democratic values. I will observe its laws faithfully and fulfill my duties and obligations as a British citizen."

She nodded at the photo and said in a strong, clear voice, "God save the Queen."

Her heart was hammering in her chest as she listened to her fellow new citizen repeat the same words, with her large contingent of supporters filled with joy as they also took photos. Then everyone in the room faced the portrait of the Queen and someone played a recording of a band striking up the familiar tune. She looked over at Torie, who joined in, singing, "God save our gracious Queen, long live our noble Queen, God save the Queen. Send her victorious, happy and glorious, long to reign over us. God save the Queen."

Gillian knew she should have been looking at the photo of her new monarch. But she couldn't take her eyes off Torie. Tears were streaming down her cheeks, and Gillian couldn't wait to get her alone and kiss every one away.

⚜ ⚜ ⚜

They just had time for a quick celebratory toast in a bar near the council chamber before heading for the airport. Gillian could still tear up at the thought of the ceremony, and she'd frequently read her scroll and gazed at the commemorative medallion the Lord Lieutenant had presented her with.

"This means more to me than my American citizenship," she said quietly, tapping the piece of acrylic. "Being an American was an accident of birth. This was a choice."

"I want to make that same commitment to your home," Torie said, giving her a watery smile. "I want to be an American." She let out a quick laugh. "If we vote for independence, I wonder how we'll sort out who's a Scottish citizen?"

"You know that's beyond me," Gillian said, laughing along with her. "But whatever you are, I want that, too. As soon as I get home, I'll set the wheels in motion to have you become an American. Soon, we'll be two women with four… or more citizenships." She felt a little flutter in her stomach as she hefted her medallion in her hand. "We probably give new citizens some ugly gold thing with a massive photo of our current president emblazoned on it. I'm sure he's figured out a way to make it all about him."

"In the not too distant future, we'll move back to Scotland," Torie soothed. "You'll feel much better about your home when you get a little distance."

"That's not up for debate. I could hardly feel worse about my home." She smiled. "I'm going to have to stop saying that automatically when I refer to America. Home isn't as permanent a designation as I thought it was."

The flight to Aberdeen was so short it was more like a drive across Columbus during rush hour. They landed before four, then took a cab to Torie's flat.

When they entered, Torie's dad flipped off the TV and stood, holding onto the arm of the sofa for a moment to get his feet under himself.

He made a good attempt at a smile, but just a glance made it clear he wasn't a people person.

"Hi, Dad," Torie said, walking across the room to give him a hug. "Meet Gillian, the woman who stole my heart instead of taking a tour of Edinburgh Castle."

"We've still never done that," Gillian said, walking over to shake.

"Hugh," he said, giving her a firm handshake. "Good to have you."

Hugh was probably in his early sixties. Full head of bristly hair, cut short so it stood up, maybe to hide some treacherous cowlicks. It was still mostly red but not the fiery color Torie had said he'd had as a younger man. Now it was more of a rose gold, with some pure white in the back near the hairline.

Physically, he seemed hale and hearty, a sturdy, muscular guy with big, strong hands and arms that seemed like they could bend steel. But when he walked, he looked twenty years older. His knees were clearly shot, and the drawn expression on his face when he'd walked just a few steps made it clear they gave him fits. *How did he play golf?*

"Mum not home?" Torie asked.

"She'll be along soon." He turned and grasped the back of the sofa, using it to support himself while he pivoted around to flop down onto the seat again. He grabbed a bag of chips and tried to hide them by putting them up against the arm of the sofa, probably sick of hearing Torie's *very* mild lectures. If Gillian had been in charge of grocery shopping, she wouldn't have brought junk into the house. Period. But that wasn't Torie's style. That's probably why the Gunns all got along so well. There was nothing to argue about when everyone gave in whenever there was a dispute. Gillian noted the chips were one of the weird flavors Scots seemed to prefer. She supposed she could gag down a potato chip flavored with shrimp and cocktail sauce, but why would she?

"Your trip was good?" Hugh asked, now that he'd hidden his chips like a naughty child.

"Very good. We spent a week in North Ronaldsay," Torie said, laughing a little.

Her father's chin shot up as he stared at her with surprise. "North Ronaldsay? For a full week?"

"Uh-huh," Torie said. "We wanted to have a quiet vacation."

"Well, that's a trip I might even like." He nodded a few times, clearly serious. "Maybe we should do that."

"I think Mum might like a more lively vacation," Torie said, heading into the kitchen. She turned and met Gillian's gaze. "But it was perfect for us. I'm going to start dinner. Why don't you and Dad get to know each other," she said, disappearing before Gillian could complain.

She sat next to Hugh on the sofa, giving him a second to start things off.

"So," he said, clearing his throat as he shifted nervously in his seat. "Torie tells us you work for the Pixie washing-up soap people."

Gillian struggled to hide a laugh. "Well, the company I work for makes Pixie through our UK subsidiary. I market laundry products, sticking to our American brands."

"Ahh," he said, nodding. "That's a different thing then."

The front door opened, and a panting, pink-cheeked woman stood there, holding onto the frame as she caught her breath. "I made it."

Torie emerged to go over to the door, relieving her mother of a big tote bag, then helping her with her coat. "I missed you," Torie said, kissing her cheek. "I hate being away from home for a whole week."

"And I've missed you," the woman said, fondly stroking her cheek.

They looked alike, vaguely. But Torie's mom was shorter and rounder and much less angular than her daughter. Her hair was a bright shade of blonde, definitely not natural, but maybe reminiscent of the color it had once been. With a fairly short, flattering cut, it made her look younger than she probably was. But the thing Gillian noticed most was the pleasure in her eyes at seeing her daughter. For that alone, Gillian knew she'd like her. She was wearing maroon surgical scrubs and white clogs, reminding Gillian that she worked as a home health aide, or carer as Torie put it.

"I thought you might be working late," Torie said. "I know Mrs. Laird needs more care now."

"Och, she does. The poor woman sleeps around-the-clock most times, but she has to be turned often. Wouldn't want her getting bed sores."

Gillian stood up and Torie's mom turned toward her, smiling brightly. "And you're our Torie's Gillian."

"I am definitely Torie's Gillian," she said, liking the phrase a lot.

"My mum, Jean," Torie said.

"I couldn't be happier to meet you," she said, walking over to take both of Gillian's hands in her own and squeeze them.

Gillian's ear had a chance to recognize one of the accents that Torie used occasionally. She was a hell of a mimic, getting her mom's broad tones down perfectly. Come to think of it, Hugh's accent was the one Torie used when she really wanted to put it on thick. "Is there anything nicer than coming home after a long day to find this one having returned from a long trip?" Jean asked, putting her arm around Torie.

"I can't think of a thing," Gillian agreed.

"Sit," Torie urged, guiding her mother to a chair. "Get to know my Gillian."

"I've been looking forward to this for months," Jean said. She rested her hands on her knees and leaned forward, saying, "Torie tells us you make the Pixie washing-up soap."

"She doesn't," Hugh said. "Not at all. Her company owns the company that makes it."

"Oh." She gave Gillian a puzzled look. "Who's your company?"

"Channing Brothers. They're the number two soap and home products corporation in the US."

"Oh, my," she said. "Isn't that nice?"

"She's got a very important job," Torie called out from the kitchen. "I keep her humble by teasing her about being a soap salesman."

"Oh, you shouldn't tease," Jean said. "Not about a person's work. The world needs soap just as much as it does those computers that everyone thinks are so important."

"Listen to your mother," Gillian called back, finding it kind of odd to be yelling from room to room.

"I do. But I'll still tease you. I don't want you to get a big head."

"She's always been like this," Jean said, rolling her eyes. "She's a bit of a tease."

"I like that about her. Besides, she's right. I can start thinking I'm more important than I am. She reminds me I'm just a soap salesman."

"She teases us all, but we still love her. Don't we, Hugh?"

Hugh had clearly had enough socializing, since he'd turned the TV back on, tuned to a show with a couple of commentators playing clips of soccer matches. "We do indeed. She's a fine girl. Never given us a bit of trouble."

Torie entered the room, holding Gillian's gaze for a few seconds. "Gillian's a fine girl, too," she said softly. Both of her parents turned her way as she added, "She's going to be your daughter-in-law, so that's important for you to know."

"She's what?" Jean gasped, staring. "Is that even possible?"

"It is," Torie said, still gazing at Gillian with a charmingly sweet look on her lovely face. "We don't have any firm plans, but we're going to marry." She grasped her mother's hand, then turned it so her own was on top. "She bought me the prettiest engagement ring I could imagine."

"Oh, my goodness!" It looked like Jean's eyes might fly from her head. "Is that a diamond?"

"It is. Obviously, I can't buy a similar one for her, but Gillian claims she doesn't need one. Thankfully."

"I'd have to explain it away at work," Gillian said, catching Torie's expression, seeing her smile fade. "But I'll wear a wedding ring. Proudly," she added, glad to see that comment brighten Torie's face once again.

"But you live in America," Jean said. "Does that mean..." She stared up at Torie, with tears immediately coming to her eyes. "Are you leaving us?"

"I couldn't think of leaving Scotland for long..." She turned to Gillian and gave her a smile filled with love. "But it's better for her financially if she stays with her company for another year or two." Her gaze turned back to her mother, and she said soberly, "I can't be away from her that long, so we'll live in America until she's able to leave."

"I'd like to come back here as soon as possible," Gillian said. "I wouldn't dream of asking Torie to leave her family."

"But you'll have to leave yours," Jean said, eyes as wide as a startled kitten's.

"True. But I'm fine with that. I'm ready for a break from America." She let out a sigh. "I'm not happy with the direction the country's going in."

"Your president's mother was Scottish, you know," Jean said tentatively. "We're so sorry about that."

Gillian barked out a laugh, charmed by how sincere she seemed. "We don't blame you. But it would have been nice if she'd stayed right here and married a local Scottish guy. Anyone at *all*," she added. "The world would be a better place if that woman had never left the Outer Hebrides."

❧ ❧ ❧

It was late when they got back to the hotel. Her mum had been chattier than usual, which was saying something. Gillian seemed a little tired, but that was probably from trying so hard to be charming for nearly six hours.

Gillian used her key card to open the door, then went directly to the bed and flopped onto it, splayed out in all directions. "I'm beat," she moaned. Her head lifted slightly so their eyes met. "But I've got to stay up to make love. There won't be time in the morning."

Torie lay next to her and pulled her shoulders close so Gillian's head rested on her chest. "I'm sorry we stayed so late. But I wanted my parents to get to know you."

"Think they liked me?" she asked, a surprisingly vulnerable expression on her face.

"Of course they did. Everyone likes you."

"I'm not going to marry everyone's daughter." She pulled away and shifted around so their faces were close. "They didn't seem thrilled about that part."

"Mmm, they're not bigots, but they're..." She thought for a minute. "I guess they're confused. I'm not sure my mum knew women could be lesbians before I came out to her. And my dad went looking for a job where he had to interact with the fewest number of people possible. I'm surprised he didn't become an undertaker so he didn't have to speak to a soul."

"Do you think they'll get used to me?"

"They'll love you," she said, certain of that. "Everyone will. They're just quiet people."

"Your mum's not very quiet," Gillian teased. "She's a chatterbox."

363

"True, but you've seen she doesn't really have much to say. She just uses a lot of words to say it."

"Yeah, I can see that." She took her pillow and fluffed it up so it better supported her head, bringing their faces to the same level. "I hate to see your mum working so hard. Caring for a frail old woman's hard work, even if she only weighs seven stone, which could be two or two thousand pounds for all I know."

"Close to a hundred," Torie said. "A stone is fourteen pounds."

"Oh," she said, a smile lighting up her face. "That's an easy enough conversion. I'm good with the maths, as you say."

"You're good at a lot of things." Torie reminded her of what one of those things was when she slid her hand onto her upper thigh and gave it a squeeze. "Want to show me?"

"Yes," she agreed, chuckling. "But we have things to discuss. I need to know when you're coming to America again. I hope the answer is August."

"August!" She shouldn't have said that so loudly when her lips were right by Gillian's face. "I can't possibly get away in August. That's my busiest month for tours."

"September, then."

"That's my second busiest month. Things don't slow down for me until October."

"That's four months!" She sat upright, clearly stunned.

"I know," Torie soothed, grasping her hand and pulling her back down. "But I might be able to stay for two or even three weeks if I can get people to cover for me."

"That's another thing," Gillian said, her voice taking on the crisp, businesslike tone that usually meant she was going to try to get her way. "It's time you quit at least one of those jobs. They're not fulfilling, and they just wear you out. I want you to do things that make your life richer, Torie."

"I'm fine," she said, tired of going over this again. "I switched to the lunch shift, just like you asked me to. But I actually liked working breakfast better. That gave me a long break in the middle of the day to get things done. Now I've only got a couple of hours, just enough to start something, but not enough to finish it."

"You enjoy giving tours, right?"

"You know I do."

"Then why not dedicate yourself to that? You'd make more money per hour, and get a lot more satisfaction from it."

"We've been over this," Torie said, trying to keep her voice from taking on a sharp tone. "Deep Dive doesn't cover Aberdeen. Even in Edinburgh and Glasgow they can only keep me fully busy in the summer. In the winter I might do one tour a month."

"I'm a marketer," she said, her voice filled with her natural confidence. She sat up and took Torie's hand. "I'll hire someone to build you a website. Once we get that done, we'll do some search engine optimization to have your name pop up as soon as someone types 'Aberdeen.' Not only will you have some local clients, you'll keep *all* the money."

"I don't think that's as easy a task as you make it out to be. Deep Dive has been doing this for years, and they can only manage two full-time employees. That's covering all of Scotland, Gillian. They get half of all of the money that comes in and they're certainly not making millions."

"You're not making millions now," Gillian said, cocking her head. "You only have to replace what you're actually losing. I'd think you could do that by giving two or three local tours a week."

"You're probably right. But 'probably' is the important word. It would be speculative, and my bills are not. I can't afford the growing pains associated with a seasonal business."

Her brow furrowed as those cool, clear eyes slid across Torie's face. "Please don't think this is a rude question, but your dad works full time, your mom works over twenty hours a week, and you work nearly two full-time jobs. Your grandmother willed your flat to your parents, and I don't see any of you throwing money away. What are all of these bills?"

"You know I pay half of Kirsty's rent," she said, *really* not wanting to get into this.

"And…?"

"I have bills," she said, feeling her cheeks color. "I'm working my way out of some serious debt. And I'm trying to save so I have a cushion in case I get ill or injured."

"You have me," she said, taking both of Torie's hands and holding them to her chest. "I'm your cushion."

"I know I could rely on you if I were ill," she admitted, "but I'll not have you paying off my debts. It will take me years, but I'll be done with them eventually."

Gillian held her a little more firmly, not speaking. But her gaze was pointed, penetrating, clearly asking for more.

"If you're worried about being saddled with my bad credit, we can wait until I've sorted everything out before we marry," she said, immediately seeing the hurt on Gillian's face. "I'm sorry," she whispered, throwing her arms around her and holding on tightly. "I'm ashamed of how much I owe, and I get…irritated when you force me to talk about it."

"Then get it over with. What happened? Did you go crazy with credit cards when you were young?"

"I did a bit of that," Torie admitted. "We had so many expenses to outfit an infant while we were paying for Kirsty's first trip to rehab. But that's not the problem." She took in a deep breath and just spit it out. "I didn't keep a close eye on my statements. By the time I realized what she'd done, I was thirty thousand pounds in debt."

She watched as the information slowly settled in Gillian's head. She looked like she was about to cry when she said, "Wasn't there anything you could do? Any way to prove you hadn't run up the bills?"

"Not without having my sister arrested," she said, feeling a little sick at the thought of how *that* would have followed Kirsty for the rest of her life. "She's stolen my identity, wrecked my car, ruined my credit, and…" Snapping her mouth shut, she whispered, "I've never told anyone about any of that. I wish I hadn't told you."

"I'm on your side!"

"I know that," Torie soothed. "I just don't want you to be angry with Kirsty. When she was using, she wasn't in her right mind."

"How are you not more resentful? If I were standing on my feet for hours every night mostly to pay off debts my sister had run up…" She shivered. "I sure wouldn't be making her dinner most nights, or paying half of her rent."

"I'm angrier than I wish I were," she admitted. "I know she has a disease, and that she's worked hard to heal, but…" She shrugged. "Sometimes I want to pummel her."

"Do you truly love me?" Gillian asked, her eyes nearly burning Torie with their intensity.

"Of course!"

"Then let me help. I'll show you all of my financial statements, Torie. You can see in black and white that I can pay off your debt without harming myself." She grasped her by the shoulders and held on tightly. "I want you to be fulfilled by your jobs, not beaten down."

"I can't," she said, struggling not to cry. "I've never relied on anyone for that kind of help, and it makes me feel awful to even contemplate it."

"Why? You've got to make me understand, because that makes no sense!"

"I'm not certain," she said, telling the truth. "But I promise I'll think about it."

"We're both going to have to give things up to have a happy marriage," Gillian said soberly. "One thing you might need to give up is a little bit of independence. I swear I'm not trying to control you. I just want you to have less stress in your life."

"I understand. And I promise I'll think about why I'm so resistant." Torie leaned forward and gave her a kiss. "I swear I will."

"All right," Gillian sighed, flopping back down on her back. "You may make love to me now."

"Thanks so much," Torie said, laughing as she felt some of the tension leave her body. "Are you going to help?"

"Probably." She was giving her the cutest smile she'd ever seen. "But I want to see what you can do on your own. I have a feeling you're pretty ingenious."

"I love you," Torie sighed, bending her head to kiss her again, savoring the silkiness of her lips. "I love you to the depths of my heart, Gillian, and I can't wait until we're lying just like this again—in Columbus, O-hi-o."

CHAPTER TWENTY-NINE

GILLIAN HAD GOTTEN THROUGH HER first day back at work by dreaming of her bed—which she was now going to dive into.

To her great pleasure, Ron had been out of the office, so she'd only had to deal with the mountain of email and instant messages that had come in during her trip. But she was still so tired her body ached, with her mental powers not much better.

She'd taken her shoes off the minute she'd entered, and now searched around the house for them. It wasn't possible to lose a pair of heels in fewer than three minutes, but it seems she had...

The doorbell rang, and she went to answer, something she usually didn't do. But sometimes it was a delivery that needed a signature. Throwing the door open, she stared at her sister, who held up the missing pair of heels. "Are you throwing these away?"

"Of course not," she said, taking them from her. "They're nearly new."

"Leaving them in the driveway probably isn't the best place to store them," Amanda said, passing by to breeze into the house. She was still wearing her work clothes, a brightly colored blue and white print dress that made her look very summery. But the scent that wafted off the insulated bag she carried was what really caught Gillian's attention.

"What do you have there?"

"I came home from work to find dinner ready to eat. A platter of barbecued chicken, baked beans, coleslaw, and cornbread. Right next to it was a note saying Rick had gotten tickets to see the Indians and was taking the boys." She proceeded to the kitchen, where she set the bag on the counter and started to unzip it. "Since I assumed you'd be too tired to cook for yourself, I thought we could make a dent in this together."

"Um..." Gillian could hardly send her sister packing, but she sure did want to. "Mind if I change?"

"Go right ahead," Amanda said, pulling plates from the cabinet like it was her own house.

After putting on a T-shirt and a pair of shorts, Gillian went back downstairs bearing another set of clothing. Extending it, she said, "My yoga pants won't fall off you, and the cleaners shrunk this blouse."

"I haven't worn your clothes since I was in high school," she said, smiling warmly.

"There was an even larger disparity in our sizes then. What fit you?"

"Nothing," she said, taking the clothes and heading for the powder room. "I missed you, so I used to sleep in the T-shirts you left behind when you went to college."

Gillian just stared at her as she walked away, finding it hard to believe that Amanda had ever been so…interested in her.

❧ ❧ ❧

It was a perfect night, the kind of evening Torie would have delighted in. Amanda was sipping a white wine spritzer, daintily eating a small amount of everything, while Gillian kept stuffing pieces of cornbread slathered with butter into her mouth. Irene was one *awesome* cook.

"So?" Amanda said. "What do you have to share?"

"About…?"

"Your trip!" She was staring at Gillian like she was dense, which she actually was at the moment.

"Right," she said, nodding. "Well, it was wonderful, but also kind of sad."

Amanda grasped her hand and pulled it close. "What's this?"

"Oh. Our clan crest. I'm going full Scot," she said, unwilling to say exactly *how* Scottish she'd become. "I bought a necklace for you, but I was going to save it for your birthday." She put her hand over her mouth. "Oops."

"Thank you," Amanda said, looking a little less stiff. "I can wait. Now tell me why your trip made you sad."

Gillian shrugged. "It's hard to explain when you haven't seen the island Mom was born on. Want me to get my laptop? I've got my photos on there."

"I'd love to see them."

Gillian got up, realizing almost all of her photos were either of Torie, or of the two of them together. Many were of them kissing while trying to take a reasonable selfie, something she would *never* share with her sister, or anyone else for that matter. Dropping back down, she said, "Jet lag. I haven't downloaded them yet. I'll have to try to convey what it was like."

Amanda looked crestfallen, probably guessing that Gillian just didn't want to share. Feeling like a shit, she tried to get to the heart of the matter.

"Um, North Ronaldsay is hanging on by a thread. Only about fifty people live there, and most of them are old. They had to close the primary school last year when the only kid moved on."

"Fifty people?" Amanda said.

"Uh-huh. It's a four-hour ferry ride from Kirkwall, which is also out in the middle of nowhere, and I can't imagine the government will continue to support it the way it has. It made me sad to see an island that's on its last legs, since most of the people really want it to hang on."

"Was it more vibrant when Mom was born?"

"I wouldn't think so. It was a bit more populated back when our grandmother was a girl, but even then I think they only had around two hundred people."

"That's probably enough to support a grade school..."

"It was. But it would have been a harsh, harsh life, Amanda. No electricity, no gas heat, no indoor plumbing."

She started to laugh. "You've got your timeline mixed up, Gill. Our grandmother would only be eighty. Everyone had electricity by the thirties."

"Not on North Ronaldsay, they didn't. They didn't get electricity until the 1980s."

"That can't be right!"

"Oh, it is. It's a flat little pancake of an island, on the same latitude as Oslo. They have no natural harbor, and landing the ferry's only possible when the sea's relatively calm. If it's rough, it doesn't go. Every improvement takes a long time, and costs a lot."

"But it's pretty, isn't it?

"Pretty? No," Gillian said, trying to be honest. "It's got a stark kind of beauty, but there are no trees, no shrubs, no mammals except for cows and sheep. It's desolate now, and since our grandmother was born during the Depression, I can't even imagine how much worse it was then." She didn't actually have to imagine, since Torie had gone on a flight of fancy and made up an entire day in the life of a crofter during the Great Slump as she called it, but Amanda didn't need to know that.

"Did you find where our grandmother lived?"

"I did. Nice people live there now. We met them the day before we left. They have kids in various parts of Great Britain, and they spend months every year visiting them. They're only around during the summer, which actually feels like early spring."

"So they wouldn't have known our grandmother," Amanda said, pushing her plate away.

"I couldn't find anyone who was a friend. People knew her name, but no one recalled anything personal about her, which is just weird." She stopped for a second. "Actually, no one knew any of the women, just our great-grandfather Alex, and our great-great-grandfather Gordon." She shrugged. "He must have been the life of the party. The kids at school called him the grim reaper."

"Oh, my God!"

"Yeah. The men in the family sound like some real hard-asses. I was going to say I couldn't guess what happened to our grandmother, but I can."

"Meaning?"

"I've decided that Jeannie had an affair with the assistant lighthouse keeper. He was a married man named Adrian Ross—"

"That's mom's middle name!"

"I know," Gillian said gently. "That was the kicker for me. There was a lot of gossip about them, and the keeper and his wife left the island in the middle of his assignment, which was very uncommon. It all stacks up," she said. "So, I've convinced myself that Jeannie fell in love, but when she got pregnant, her father sent her away. When she got to America, I think she severed her relationship with her family." She gazed at Amanda for a moment, making the decision to tell nearly everything. "Our great-grandfather was alive when we were kids. But mom must not have been in contact with him."

"You're not serious," Amanda said, her voice shaking. "You can't be."

"I am. I have a copy of his obituary from the newspaper in Kirkwall. It mentioned Jeannie as having predeceased him, but there wasn't a word about our mom…or us."

"But why?" Amanda said, tears ready to spill from her pale eyes.

"Shame," Gillian said. "Anger. Disappointment. Something like that." She swallowed nervously before adding, "Mom did the same thing. I've got the obituary from when Jeannie died. It said she was born in Columbus, which we know was a lie."

"Good God," Amanda whispered. "Why did everything have to be such a secret?"

"I don't know. But that's three generations who got pretty screwed up because of being ashamed of who they were and what they'd done."

Amanda stared at her for what felt like an hour, with Gillian's skin prickling from the intensity of the gaze. But she didn't say a word. She just let the silence drag on.

Gillian had poured herself a beer, but she'd let it go warm, too muddled to lower her inhibitions at the time. Now she needed a little muddling, and she got up from the table to toss it and pour a fresh one. "Can I get you anything?" she asked as she opened the refrigerator.

"No, thanks," Amanda said.

As she poured her beer, Gillian started to talk, just trying to cut the tension. "North Ronaldsay was an odd place. If I'd been Jeannie, I would have snuck off to catch the ferry to Aberdeen when I was a child. I would have preferred to live on the streets of a big city than in a windswept village where everyone knew everything you did."

Amanda gave her a cold look. "That's not surprising. You couldn't survive in a town where people knew your business. Do you even know your neighbors?"

"By sight," she admitted, feeling a little bad about that now that Amanda brought it up.

When Gillian sat down again, Amanda grasped her wrist and gave it a squeeze. "I'm sorry the island wasn't nicer." She looked down at her plate, still half full of food. "What on earth did you do for a full week?"

Gillian wracked her brain. Had she let it slip she'd been there that long? "Um…not much. I just wandered around, trying to get a feel for the place."

"I looked at the website. The rooms looked nice, but…a week? How did you fill the time? How did you feed yourself?"

"It wasn't hard," she said, feeling worse by the minute. "I made some friends."

"Friends?" Amanda's eyebrow rose.

"Sure. Robby and Mary run the little restaurant and the cottages. They introduced me to the people who live in the Sinclair croft. And they've got a bird sanctuary with a cafe and a place where you can get a drink… Um, I went to movie night at the community center, just to see if anyone showed up who might have known Jeannie." She shrugged. "The days just passed."

"Mmm." Amanda got up and started to clear the plates. "I suppose I'll get going," she said, sounding defeated. "I'd love to see your photos…if you ever download them. I still haven't seen the ones from your first trip."

"I'll clean everything up and make an album. If I just keep the ones from when the sun's shining, you'll really want to visit."

Amanda stopped in her tracks and gazed at Gillian for a few moments. "I wanted to go with *you*. Don't act like you didn't know that."

"Next time," Gillian said, trying to keep it light. "I think I'll be returning, and I'll know enough to plan a good trip."

"I'm sure that's true," Amanda said, brushing past to deposit the plates in the sink, leaving Gillian to mentally kick herself for the clumsy way she'd handled every bit of the evening. "You're very adept at taking care of yourself."

On the last day of June, the usual Friday night pajama party was scheduled for seven, but Gillian had a tough time finding a place to speak in private. Given she was sitting in the lounge at JFK, pajamas were out, too, even though she'd seen people running around in outfits that weren't much more appropriate.

The lounge had a few carrels where you could set up your computer and work in relative privacy, and when one harried-looking guy started to pack up, Gillian jumped up and stood next to him.

"The seat's not even cold yet," he grumbled.

She didn't reply, having no interest in carrying on a conversation with a grumpy stranger. The minute he pushed past, she whipped off her jacket and draped it over the chair, then ran back to get her carryon. In the two seconds she'd been gone, a woman had arrived to gaze at the chair critically. "Mine," Gillian said, slipping in front of her. "Sorry, but I've got to make a Skype call."

"Doesn't everyone," she snapped, a definite Scottish accent tickling Gillian's ears. She set her tablet up and dialed, smiling when Torie's pretty face came into view. As always, she kept her tablet too close, but even her distorted face was cute.

"Hi," Gillian said. "I've got to be quiet. I'm stuck at the airport."

"Ooo. I was looking forward to seeing you in that skimpy vest and shorts you wore last week. Your blouse is nice, though. New?"

"No," she said, looking down to remind herself of what she had on. "You haven't seen most of my summer clothes yet. God knows I didn't need them in Scotland."

"I thought you were taking a five o'clock flight home."

"Supposed to. Big thunderstorms over the Midwest. Everywhere from Oklahoma through Illinois. Nasty, nasty weather."

"Mmm, I'm no expert, but isn't Ohio further east than Illinois?"

"Someone's been studying her US map," Gillian joked. "Yes, it is, but the storm's moving quickly." She turned her head to scan the departures board. "The east coast is still open, but only for flights going north and south."

"And east," Torie said, a sweet smile turning her lips up. "That's the best direction, since that's where the love of your life lives."

Something about the way she said that made Gillian stand up, grab her stuff, and march over to the reception desk. The tablet was shaking violently as Torie said, "What are you doing?"

"Hold on and you'll see." She smiled at a woman who sat in front of a computer and said, "Is there any availability on the nine o'clock to London?"

The ear bud vibrated with Torie's voice. "London?"

"Yes, London," Gillian said quietly. "Why should I sit here for hours when I can be on the way to you?"

"Um, your job?"

"I can take Monday off and fly back on Tuesday, since that's a holiday."

"It is?"

"Independence Day," Gillian said, chuckling. "I guess it's Dependence Day for me, since I'm so friggin' tied to you it's not funny."

"There's one seat left," the woman said, jostling Gillian's attention back to the business at hand. "It's premium economy class, Ms. Lindsay. Would you like me to book it?"

"I heard that," Torie said. "Now you're going to look like a jerk if you don't come just because you're not going to be pampered."

"Book it," she said decisively. Addressing Torie, she added, "I don't have to have a bed as long as I've got one in Scotland. With you in it."

"Pardon?" the woman asked, busily typing.

"Sorry. I'm on the phone."

"Are you blushing?" Torie asked. "I think you're blushing!"

Gillian turned around and said, "Probably. You make me do a lot of things I can't control. Now don't tell me you can't meet me in Edinburgh or Glasgow."

"Your choice," Torie said, grinning happily. "I will find a substitute for my shifts and meet you anywhere you choose. Even London."

"Really?" She thought for a minute. "That will save me some time. I'll book you a flight. Check your mail in a few minutes, then get some sleep—something I won't be able to do, of course. But I'm not complaining. I get to see my fiancée in just a few hours, and I couldn't be happier."

She cut the connection before Torie could complain, then got busy arranging for three more flights, two for Torie and a return for herself, determined to pay for business class on the way home if she couldn't use points. There was no way she could go to work on Wednesday if she didn't get some sleep on the flight back—given she was planning on staying up very late every night in London, reacquainting herself with her fiancée's magnificence. As she looked at her calendar, she saw that it had been thirteen days since she'd left Scotland. How could fewer than two weeks seem so long?

Torie lay on her side in a very comfortable bed. The weather in London was just as dreary as Aberdeen's had been, but everything was brighter when she gazed at her fiancée, sleeping so peacefully next to her.

Even though Scotland and England shared a land mass, it had been years since she'd been in London, and she'd jumped in like a typical tourist the day before, dragging Gillian to the British Museum, then the National Gallery, while barely making a dent in either. While she itched to get up and see some sights, she wasn't going to be that kind of girlfriend—the type who only cared about her own agenda. Traveling from New York took a lot out of a person, and she'd resolved to let Gillian sleep all day if she needed to.

Stealthily, she got out of bed and went to shower, managing to get clean, get her hair in order, get dressed, then pull out her phone and handle all of her email before her partner showed even the slightest sign of life.

If she'd stayed perfectly still, Gillian would undoubtedly have gone back to sleep. But that was a larger sacrifice than Torie was willing to make. Quietly, she moved over to the bed and perched on the edge, hoping to see those pretty blue eyes open.

A smile lit Gillian's face when they did just that, blinking slowly, then focusing. "My dream came true," she said, flopping onto her back and stretching. "There's nothing better than waking up and finding you close by." She rose a little. "Showered and dressed?"

"I've been up for a while. But I don't want to push you." She placed her fingertips atop Gillian's eyes and urged the lids down. "If you want to go right back to sleep, you can."

"I'll get up." Sitting all the way up, she gave Torie a kiss and swung her feet around, then stood. "What's on your list of things to do?"

"Whatever you want. I could spend a month at the British Museum, but you're the visitor. You pick."

"Is it actively raining?"

Torie went to the window and gave the street a long look. They were staying at a posh hotel right across from King's Cross, and the plaza was filled with people, none of whom had their umbrellas up. "Not at the moment. But that could change by the time we reach the street."

"I want to be outside." Gillian started for the bathroom, with Torie following her, both to continue the conversation, and watch her hips sway when she walked.

"Let's go to Green Park. You've got a raincoat, don't you?"

"I don't, but I don't mind getting wet. I should stop somewhere and buy another shirt and some jeans, though. I only have two business suits and two blouses in that suitcase, and I'm not willing to wear what I had on last night for four days."

Torie pulled her to a stop and gave her a long kiss. "I love that you just hopped onto a plane and came here. That's the most romantic thing you've ever done."

Her eyes opened wide. "More romantic than finding the isolated lighthouse where my grandmother fell in love to propose to you? Your standards are astronomical!"

"I forgot about that," she said, chuckling. "You've clearly got to keep working to please me."

"Happily." She went into the bath and turned on the shower. "I'm out of underwear, too. I guess I'll go commando today."

Torie went into Gillian's suitcase and found her dirty underthings, neatly stuffed into a bag purpose-made for them. Returning to the bath, she ran water in the sink. "I love you enough to wash your knickers."

"That's one of my favorite words," she said, laughing. "Not sure why, but I love it. I used it at work not long ago, and got some very puzzled looks."

Torie took some shower gel and agitated it until the water was sudsy. "I assume you were talking about how your soap cleans delicates, and not about your personal knickers."

"Right. No one at work knows I wear—or don't wear knickers. I'd like it to stay that way."

The finality of that comment rubbed Torie the wrong way. For just a moment she was going to let it pass, but found herself trying to make a joke of it. "I know you haven't come out to anyone at work, but have you let anyone at *all* in on your exotic affair with a mysterious woman from the east?"

The shower enclosure was glass, and Gillian pressed her face against it. "I don't know much about geography, but I don't think Scotland's technically in the east."

"Have you?" she asked, ignoring the comment.

"You know I haven't," Gillian said quietly. "Kara knows, and that's enough for now." She shut off the water, reached out and grabbed a towel, then roughly rubbed it over her head. "I get the feeling you think I've got all of these friends I share my private life with, and I'm somehow ashamed to let them in on a secret." She was scowling when she lowered the towel. "I don't, Torie. I have the people I ride with, co-workers, and family members."

"Why don't you have any lesbian friends?" An additional thought occurred to her and she spit out the question. "Without friends, where did you find women to go out with?"

"I have lesbian friends. Some," she added quietly. "But I met most of them through Grace. She…and they, live in Dayton, which isn't very close." She held the towel in front of her, still dripping. It was a cool day, and the window was cracked open, and she began to shiver. "I think her friends liked me well enough when we were together, but we didn't stay in touch. I told you that," she added. "Months ago. Grace got our mutual friends in the break-up."

"You didn't answer my second question. Not going to?"

"There wasn't one specific place I met women," she said, beginning to look irritated. "Here and there. It's not hard." She took the towel and started to pat her arms. "I'm *going* to tell people. I just don't want to say anything until I have something concrete to tell them."

She faced Gillian and gave her a long look. "We're engaged. That's not concrete to you? It certainly is to me."

Hurrying to finish drying off, she did a haphazard job, then tucked the towel around her waist. Her arms went around Torie, and she hugged her to her chest. "It's more than concrete. But if I tell people I'm engaged to a woman from another country, they'll want to know what that means. Am I moving? Are you coming to America? When's the wedding? All sorts of questions I don't have answers for yet."

Torie pulled away and continued to rinse the soap from the knickers. "Won't it be even more uncomfortable when you tell someone you're supposedly close to that you've met a woman, romanced her over a period of months, had her visit you at your home, taken a long vacation to her home country, proposed, have worked out the details, whatever they may be, and are now getting married? If someone did that to me, I'd assume we weren't very close at all."

"*That* won't be a surprise to anyone. Trust me on that. It's not worth going into it if I don't have the details nailed down."

Torie started to speak, but Gillian talked over her. "I mean it. Giving someone a rough outline of what you're proposing is never as effective as the finished product. People want to see a full-color layout, with photos and music and all of the bells and whistles."

"We're not talking about an ad campaign, Gillian. We're talking about our lives together. Your sister is going to be astounded!"

"A big surprise will be good for her. Her life is pretty routine."

She seemed entirely oblivious to the fact that Torie wanted to shake her. With a slight smile on her lips, she started to blow her hair dry. Torie went back to the bedroom to sit and stare at her in the mirror, realizing, not for the first time, that you could spend an awful lot of time with someone, yet still not know them fully. That definitely made things interesting, but not always in a good way.

On Monday evening, they stood in the far corner of a car on the London Eye, watching the city spread out around them, white lights twinkling in every direction as they slowly rose to an impressive height. Gillian stood behind Torie, with her arms draped over her shoulders. They were too similar in height for her to do that comfortably, but the urge to wrap her up in her arms and hold her was too strong to ignore.

They'd only had three full days together, but it had been enough to slake her thirst. That parched feeling would start to grow tomorrow afternoon, of course, but there was nothing they could do to prevent that—for the moment.

She dipped her head and kissed Torie's cheek, then moved delicately down her neck, making her giggle.

Quietly, Torie said, "You don't seem at all bashful about being affectionate here."

"I don't work with anyone in London who'd recognize me. Once I get a job over here, I assume I'll be my old self, but I feel free now." She kissed her cheek again, lingering with her lips hovering over the soft skin. "Even if we were in my lobby at work right now, I think I'd kiss you. I don't want to let you go," she murmured, about to cry.

"Don't cry, or I'll start," Torie warned. She turned and nuzzled against Gillian's neck, both of them ignoring the other people surrounding them. "It breaks my heart to just get a little taste of you and have you leave."

"I can't afford to come every two weeks, but I can't afford not to. It's not going to take long for my emotional needs to exceed my financial resources." She tightened her hold and added, "Maybe I'll sell my car and buy something super cheap. I could use the money on plane tickets."

"We'll go back and forth. I've got a more flexible schedule than you do, and if we plan ahead we can use your miles, right?"

"If we're lucky. So you'll come in August?"

"You know I can't. I'm doing tours every Saturday and Sunday, and I've even booked a few weekday outings. Business has picked up now that I've pushed Deep Dive to include Stirling and Dundee in their advertising."

"Your gain, my loss," Gillian sighed. "I'll figure out a way to squeeze a Friday off and come in a month or so. You're free at night, right?"

"I'll find someone to work my shift at the bar. Let me make sure which weekend works best with the tours I have scheduled, okay?"

"All right. I'll see if I can squeeze an award flight out of them at the airport tomorrow. They treat you better when they're looking at you."

"I love looking at you," Torie whispered, smiling gently. "We've got the whole of London to take in, but I haven't noticed it. You're all I see."

"Me too." She chuckled. "But that big building down there is pretty impressive. Is that parliament?"

Torie turned and nodded. "Want the history?"

Gillian tucked her arms around her, rested her chin on her shoulder, and said, "I'd love it."

🌿 🌿 🌿

Falling asleep at one thirty in the afternoon, after having just forced her body to adjust to being on London time, wasn't going to happen. Gillian had managed to get a business class seat, but the prospect of lying down didn't appeal in the least, especially since they were still sitting at the gate a good twenty minutes after boarding.

If she made her Charlotte connection, and it departed on time, she'd get home at midnight. Unfortunately, she had a status meeting with Ron and the members of her team set for eight, and she had to stop at a bakery to pick up breakfast first.

Six thirty was going to come very, very early, and a pretty woman with golden red hair wasn't going to be snuggled up next to her in bed, which made the whole prospect of going to work just not seem worth the trouble. That wasn't the best attitude to have, but it was getting to be a common one.

She hadn't told Torie about a development at work, mainly because it infuriated her, but she kept thinking about it. Channing Brothers was acquiring a British-based company that made household cleansers, and they'd just announced that one of Gillian's peers was going to be based there for at least two years while they worked on the merger. She was still so angry she could barely look at the guy, who didn't even want to go. And if she'd been alone with Ron, who'd made the decision, she might have actually strangled him. But since no one knew she was engaged to a woman from Scotland... She shook her head sharply. Telling Torie would only make her turn up the heat on her obviously strongly-held belief that Gillian had to start coming out to strangers on the street.

Torie just didn't seem to understand the whole dynamic, neither at work, nor at home. Hugh and Jean clearly weren't wild about having a gay daughter, but they weren't openly hostile—just reserved. Torie didn't get what it was like to be surrounded by people who would have been happy to throw her into a work camp for undesirables.

She nodded when the flight attendant came by with glasses of champagne, even though she knew afternoon drinking usually gave her a headache. Staring out at the gloriously warm, stunningly clear and sunny July afternoon, she groused to herself about the weather. Today was the only great day they'd had, but they'd spent the morning in bed, mostly holding each other and privately ruminating about their situation. There was nothing either of them could say to change it, and they'd both been mildly depressed. Torie had rallied a half hour before they had to leave, managing to pull Gillian from her funk enough to have some hurried, slightly out-of-sync sex. It had been nice, but not nearly as nice as usual.

Thinking back on the whole trip, she had to admit they'd been a bit off much of the time. Ever since that first morning in the shower, things had been a little strained. Not enough to ruin the weekend, but just enough to make her feel like they weren't on the same page. Probably because they weren't.

She pulled out her phone and saw that she still had a good cell signal. Grumbling again, she wrote an email to her sister, inviting her to her home for a barbecue on Saturday, with Sunday as a rain date. She might insist that she hadn't become Torie's lap dog, but that was an outright lie.

After her morning meeting, Gillian sat in the stuffy conference room, being thoroughly dressed down for the first time in her career at Channing Brothers. The Global President of Fabric Care had unexpectedly attended their meeting, and it hadn't gone well—at all.

"Were we *boring* you?" Ron thundered, pacing back and forth in front of her chair. "Jeff had to ask you about your numbers for print campaigns three times, Gillian. You were off by a whole digit!"

"I lost my place," she said, looking down like a dog being slapped on the snout with a newspaper. "I corrected myself."

"*Eventually.* You weren't sharp," he said, stopping to glare. "What's wrong with you? Are you ill?"

"I'm perfectly fine. I'm just a little off."

"Are you pregnant? My wife got forgetful when she was in her first trimester." He shook his head. "That's silly. You're too old to have a baby."

She jumped to her feet and moved across the room, just so she couldn't take a swing at him. "There is nothing wrong with me. I made a mistake, which I corrected. I'm sure Jeff is used to people practically peeing themselves when he sits in on their meetings."

"He is," Ron said, giving her a withering glare. "But you weren't nervous. You looked half-asleep, and trust me, he's not used to people acting bored."

"I wasn't bored," she called out to his departing back. Then she slumped into a chair, disgusted with herself. "I was dead tired," she said softly. "And if I know what's good for me, that will be the last time I visit Scotland for just a few days."

Gillian didn't tell Torie about her poor performance in front of the big boss. There was no sense in worrying her or making her feel guilty for encouraging her to visit for such a short time. But she didn't offer to go again, placidly accepting Torie's best offer—to visit Columbus for two weeks starting on the first of October. That wasn't nearly soon enough, but it was going to have to do. Channing Brothers wasn't paying her the big bucks to show up at work half-asleep and groggy.

Sunday morning broke hot and steamy, but the sun rose to reveal a clear day. Her bicycle gang normally drove well out of town to ride in the country, but once in a while they stayed close. Today they did the whole Alum Creek Trail, taking them all over Columbus. The sun was just starting to make her uncomfortable when they rolled through Wolfe Park, and she ignored the heat to focus on the brightness. A summer's day in Central Ohio would always remind her of how gorgeous America was, how gifted it had been in both natural resources and weather.

The trees were stunningly green, some so big their leaf canopies threw the path into deep shade. Scotland had trees, of course, but she hadn't seen any quite this impressive. If she'd been hovering above the city right now, she knew the broad shoulders of the trees and their crowns of beautiful leaves would be the only thing she'd see. You needed lots of sun, a warm spring, and a long summer to make trees like this thrive. But as much as she loved summer in Ohio, Scotland was perfect for her—it had Torie.

One thing Rick liked to do was barbecue, so Gillian had stopped at the German place her family had been going to forever to buy sausages. Adding some marinated chicken breasts to a platter, she covered everything with foil, set all of the food on the outside table, then went back into the house. By the time she reached the kitchen window to peer out, Rick was getting the grill ready, with Chapin right next to him, learning the trade.

"Hey, Spencer," she said, summoning her nephew who was running around the kitchen acting like he was an airplane. "Take these tools out to your dad, and when you get back I'll give you a present."

The kid gazed at her suspiciously, but reached his little hands out and took them, then made for the door. The men in her family were amazingly easy to manipulate. Now she just had to look around for something interesting to give the kid. He probably wouldn't be satisfied with anything in sight, so she pulled her wallet from her purse and took out a couple of bucks. *Every*one in her family loved money.

Kara had clued her in on the latest DVD that kids her nephews' age were into, and, thankfully they didn't own it yet. Once their attention was locked onto the TV in the upstairs den, she found Amanda and said, "Hey, come outside with me for a minute. I want to have some time away from the kids to talk about something."

"I want that every night, but I rarely get it."

"I bought a copy of 'Space Monkeys' for them. They're completely immobile."

"Oh, sure," she said, chuckling, "I could do that too, but they don't issue new movies every day." They started to walk out the back door, with Amanda adding, "They say we should limit their screen time to fewer than two hours a day." A wry laugh bubbled up. "Whoever said that didn't have two kids under six. Rick would happily plunk them down in front of the TV for the entire day if I didn't keep an eye on him."

"We grew up glued to the TV and we turned out all right," Gillian said, then thought maybe she'd spoken without thinking that through.

Rick was sitting at her glass-topped table, looking very content. Loading him and Amanda up with whiskey sours had been a fine idea, even if it meant she'd probably have to drive them home. They were chronically cheap drunks.

She wasn't nearly as nervous as she thought she'd be, which truly surprised her. The thought of disappointing Torie was obviously a greater motivator than losing whatever thin bonds she had with her sister. She remained standing, and cleared her throat. "I've got an…" She started to say announcement, but that was giving away the punchline way too early. Now both of them were looking at her, and her armpits got wet in an instant. It was like last year, when she'd unexpectedly had to address the shareholders at the annual meeting after Ron had lost his voice. A bunch of people staring at her, as her heart flew to her throat.

"I've…um…" They'd lost their smiles, and she knew she was bombing. Trying to amp up her enthusiasm, she said, "I spent last weekend in Scotland."

"Scotland?" Amanda gasped. "You were just there."

"I know. I went back."

"Why?" Amanda set her glass down on the table a little harder than she should have, making the glass sing out when it hit.

"I met someone special on my first trip. I went back this time…" She swallowed, trying not to sound so damned nervous. "I went back this time to propose."

"Propose?" Rick looked like he'd just seen a bear burst through the viburnum. "You proposed to a guy? I guess being the boss at work has carried over—"

He stopped on a dime, undoubtedly because Amanda had grabbed or kicked him under the table. His head swiveled in her direction, and he saw the look on her face. Grim and angry.

Gillian barreled through. "There isn't a man involved, Rick. I've fallen in love with a woman, and I've asked her to marry me. I'm gay," she added, almost choking on the word. "I have been since I was in college."

"But you didn't care enough to tell me…to tell us," Amanda said, so angry steam could have shot from her ears. "What did you think we'd do? Stop you from seeing the boys? As if you'd mind that!"

That hit her the wrong way, and Gillian found herself snapping, "I suppose that thought crossed my mind." Amanda looked so wounded Gillian softened her voice. "But that's not why I've kept this to myself. I was just so scarred from when I came out to Mom and Dad…"

"You did that?" Amanda demanded, voice rising. "When?"

"My freshman year of college. I brought one of my sorority sisters home for Thanksgiving. We…" She knew her cheeks were blazing, but she was sick of having nothing but secrets bind them together. "That was the night we both discovered we were attracted to women. We got carried away, and Mom threw open the door to my room." She swallowed again, with the lump in her throat almost choking her. "We were naked."

"Oh, wow," Rick murmured. "Awkward."

"Yeah," Gillian said, nodding. "It was awkward."

"What happened?" Rick said, giving Gillian his full attention. He actually looked interested, rather than judgmental, and that let her continue.

"It was the middle of the night, but Mom told her to get out. Dad took her to the airport and dumped her out of the car. She never spoke to me again, but I saw her on campus, so I know she got home."

"Damn," Rick murmured. "I didn't know your mom, but I've never gotten the impression she was so…"

Gillian sat heavily on an empty seat. "She was. I bet Catrina still has nightmares about that morning."

Amanda's anger appeared to have vanished in an instant. She leaned over and spoke in her patented Human Resources voice. "What can we do to help you get past that, Gillian? It's clearly made you afraid of being yourself."

"Help me? Really?" She gazed at two sets of eyes, neither of them seeming to bear even a hint of judgment. "If you really wanted to help, you could have voted for someone who didn't fill his cabinet with homophobes. *That* would have helped."

Amanda stared at her for a moment, then reclaimed her anger in even less time. "What a ridiculous thing to say! I dare you to find a politician who's been consistently supportive of gay rights for his or her whole career. They don't exist!"

"Your whole job is to offer support to *all* of your employees," Gillian yelled. "Yet you voted for a guy who slanders Latinos, blacks, Muslims…"

"That was just campaign rhetoric," Rick said. "Hillary said things just as bad."

"No, she didn't," Gillian said. "She did not!"

"It is so small-minded of you to claim that all republicans are homophobic," Amanda said, clearly furious. "The democrats have just decided they can only win if they appeal to every minority group. Believe me, if they thought they'd win by making homosexuality a crime, they'd do it in a minute."

Given that Gillian hated politics, and found most politicians to be the most self-serving people on the planet, she didn't really have a lot of motivation to defend her party. Amanda was probably right, but the democrats had decided to embrace gay rights, so she was sticking with them until they stopped. "You know what? I really don't care how pure anyone is. I'm able to marry because the Democratic party pushed for marriage equality. So forgive me for being a little hurt by my sister supporting a party that would take that away from me in a second. Once they're finished removing reproductive freedom from all women, that is."

"The world is a lot more complex than you make it out to be, Gillian. If the government was smaller, and our tax bill was lower, we'd all be much better off. That's the party platform I support, and if so many of you hadn't abandoned the Republican party over abortion, which you're never even going to *need*," she stressed, "we'd still have a strong moderate wing." She sucked in a breath and kept going. "I know a bunch of wackos have pushed us too far to the right, but I'm not going to abandon the principles I hold just because they're out of favor. If we'd had a little more support, we could have Bush or Rubio in office today, and believe me, things would be much more normal."

"We could argue about this all day," Gillian said, "but you're not going to convince me the jerk you supported isn't trying to create a totalitarian state."

"And you can't convince me that the democrats don't want to punish me for being successful!" She made her hand into a fist and hit the table sharply. "Just for the record, your homophobic sister helped craft a very explicit non-discrimination policy for our LGBT employees. We haven't had one complaint about anti-gay bias since it was enacted."

Gillian sighed. This was a huge waste of her time. "We also have an excellent anti-discrimination policy, and if I wanted to destroy my career, I'd complain about the so-called jokes I hear all too frequently. That's the reality, Amanda. Homophobia is in the culture as firmly as misogyny. We're steeped in both."

She looked a little chagrined, but not cowed. "If you wanted to help other people in your organization, wouldn't it be a good idea to call people out for insulting gay people? I mean, you might risk a little, but other, less powerful people might gain."

"Thanks for the advice," she snapped. "Can we wrap this up now? I'm getting married, and I wanted you to know."

Amanda gazed at her for a minute, her cheeks still flushed. But she was too well-school in dealing with angry employees to lose control—for long. Other than the pink in her cheeks, she now appeared calm and collected. "Do you have a picture of the woman you're going to marry? I assume she's the one who came to your party."

"That's correct. I'll be right back." She left to get her laptop, and when she returned, Amanda and Rick had their heads together, talking quietly. She plunked the laptop down and opened it. A closeup of Torie was her screensaver, and she smiled as those big, brown eyes looked right at her. In the photo, the sun was behind her, lighting up her hair to show every bit of red. "Torie Gunn," she said, "of Aberdeen, Scotland. Historian, tour guide, server, bartender. And doting aunt to thirteen-year-old Aiden."

"She's a pretty girl," Rick said, his voice soft and respectful. "And lucky, too, to have found you." He cleared his throat. "Is she moving here soon?"

This was the part she didn't want to get into. "I have no idea when we're going to be able to marry. We've got a lot of things to work out with immigration and all of that. But we'd like to do it as soon as we can. Being this far from someone you love is just awful."

Amanda turned the laptop and stared at the picture for a minute. "I can't believe she was in my house and you didn't even properly introduce us." The hurt in her voice was palpable. "What must she think of us?"

"I've been in the closet my whole life, Amanda. I'd convinced myself it was easier, but being with Torie has let me see how hard it really is." She gazed at the photo, mesmerized by Torie's gentle, loving smile. "I'm not ready to tell anyone at work, but it's time for me to be more honest." She let her gaze touch both of them. "I'm trying to be more honest with you."

"I'm so glad I'm straight," Rick said, chuckling. "I don't think we're ever going to agree on politics, but neither of us have anything against gay people. We'll do whatever we can to help you have a great wedding."

She truly wanted to say it would have been nice to have had their help in defeating a racist, sexist, Islamaphobe who kicked gay people when it was convenient, but that horse had left the barn. Instead, she nodded and said, "Thanks. I appreciate that."

With tears in her eyes, Amanda said, "Could I look at your photos of Scotland now? I'm truly interested in it…and you."

"Of course." Gillian sat next to her sister and pulled up the first bunch from her initial trip. "I met Torie when I'd only been in Edinburgh for a few hours, so she's in most of the photos. But…" She swallowed, still having a tough time talking about her with even a tenth of the feeling she held for her in her heart. "That's also because I was crazy for her as soon as we met."

Rick was even more of a lightweight than Amanda, and by late afternoon he was lying on the floor of the den, with the boys dozing against him, using his body as a pillow. It was actually such a sweet scene that Gillian almost teared up, feeling sorry for herself for not having a single memory where she'd felt so connected to her own father.

When she reached the kitchen, Amanda was pouring two more drinks, and she handed one to Gillian, then gripped her by the arm and tugged her along until they were once again seated at the outdoor dining table.

Amanda took a long drink, then set her glass down carefully. "We need to clear the air," she said, with her gaze flitting across Gillian's face. "You keep me at arm's length. You always have." She reached across the table and gripped Gillian's hand—hard. "Tell me why."

"Why?" She had no idea what to say. None at *all*.

"Yes. Why," Amanda repeated. "I feel like you want to keep me in your life, but only if I'm at a certain distance. When I make it clear I'd like to be closer, you run."

"I…I don't know why I'm like that," she said, mostly telling the truth. "I…um, maybe I was jealous of the attention mom showed you when you were a baby. That might have set the tone." She didn't add that was Torie's analysis, arrived at after such intense questioning that she felt like she'd been in the dentist's chair for a full day.

"You're saying you've resented me since I was *born*? How could I have done anything to you when I was an infant?"

"You didn't do anything. And I'm not even sure this is the problem. But…I had very little time with either of our parents, and when you came along, what little I had was cut way, way back. By the time you were a cute little thing, talking up a storm and being adorable, Mom, in particular, spent all of her spare time on you. I remember her taking you to work and showing you off to everyone." She took in a breath. "While I was a headstrong seven-year-old who'd passed my cuteness sell-by date."

"A lot of kids have some sibling rivalry, Gill, but this has been going on for thirty-six years."

She stared into Amanda's eyes, trying to recall any significant encounters between them. Something hit her, and she let herself spit it out without doing her usual tactic of burying every feeling that came up. "When Dad died, I felt like an ogre for leaving you and Mom to go to college. I knew you both needed support, but I was so damned relieved to be away. In Evanston, I could grieve in my own way and not have to support either of you." She met Amanda's gaze again. "I still feel like a horrible person for that."

"It *was* selfish. If you'd been around, Mom might not have worked herself to…death," she said quietly. She gripped Gillian's hand again, shaking it gently. "But you were a kid. You were just eighteen, Gill. It made sense that you wanted to run away from your grief. I forgive you for that. I do," she insisted.

"Then I dumped you again when Mom died. I…um…figured you'd never forgive me for that, so I just kind of…let you go when it became clear you wanted to join Rick's family."

"Oh, Gill. Why do you jump to conclusions like that? I've been chasing you my whole life, but you've always, *always* been just a little bit faster than I am."

"I don't want to be," she said, then backed off that a little bit. "I don't *want* to want to be. I'm trying to learn how to be more connected. Torie's helping so much."

"I want you to be connected," Amanda said. "To her, but also to us. We're your family, Gill. Every one of us loves you, but you've got to show us that you love us back."

"I'm trying," she said, truly determined to try harder. "I swear I'm going to keep working on this."

Amanda drained her glass, then stood and put her hand on Gillian's shoulder. "When I'm sober, we're going to have a talk about politics. We clearly don't agree on a lot of points, but my beliefs don't make me evil."

Gillian looked up at her, seeing what seemed like a loving, caring sister. So how could she support a party that either embraced or didn't distance itself from hate?

🌵 🌵 🌵

Sitting outside in a tank top and running shorts, her usual summer pajamas, Gillian sat with the last rays of the sunset visible just over her back fence. She'd started trying to video chat just ten minutes after Torie got off work, but it took almost a half hour for her to answer. Without preamble, Gillian said, "Guess what I did today?"

"Um, it's Saturday, so… A special bike ride?"

"I had a good ride, actually. Stayed close to home and rode a local trail. Only clocked about fifty miles, but we went out early and did it fast, trying to get out of the sun before it killed us."

"Oh, it's hot there?" She started to unwind the wool scarf she had around her neck, then unbuttoned her tartan plaid gilet before pulling the blanket off her bed to wrap around her shoulders.

"Clearly hotter than it is there," she said, chuckling. "But it was hot here for another reason. I had my family over for dinner and told them about us."

"What?" She jumped up so hastily she clipped the edge of the tablet and sent it clattering to the floor. Gillian got a little sick to her stomach as the tablet lurched around, then it was close to Torie's face again. "Tell me *everything*."

"Well, I don't recall the exact words I used, but I said I'd recently been in Scotland to see the person I'd met last November. They were both staring at me when I added that I'd proposed."

"Wow. You just started right at the grand finale, didn't you."

"I guess I did. Funny thing. When I said I'd gone to Scotland to propose, Rick implied that I should have let my future husband do that. He's worried that being the boss at work means I'm going to try to be the boss in my marriage, which he clearly thinks is a bad idea."

Torie started to laugh. "He's right there. You're definitely not going to be the boss in your marriage."

"Too true. I'm glad to say the afternoon went better than I thought it would. Amanda and Rick defended themselves as non-homophobic, and after I yelled at them for a while, we all let it drop."

"Good," Torie said. "See? I told you it wouldn't be that bad."

"It was kind of awful, to be honest. But it's over, and I'm very glad for that."

A big smile covered Torie's face. "I'm so proud of you. Truly, I am."

"I'm proud of myself," Gillian said. "I'm going to try to be more open. Maybe I'll even make some friends."

"You've got a very good one in Scotland. Even if I didn't love you, I'd be honored to be your friend."

⚜ ⚜ ⚜

Torie picked up her phone that afternoon, puzzled to see the words "United States" on the caller ID. "Hello?"

"Is this Torie?"

"It is. Who's calling?"

"It's Amanda, Gillian's sister."

"Oh!" Torie was sitting down, but she stood and threw her shoulders back, standing like she was in the military. "Hello, Amanda. I'm…surprised to hear from you."

"I suppose you are. I…um…I found your number myself. I assumed Gillian wouldn't give it to me."

"Oh," Torie said once again, feeling very off stride.

"I didn't ask, mainly because I didn't want her to refuse. I wanted to talk to you whether or not she wanted me to."

"All right," Torie said. "Let's talk."

"First, I wanted to apologize for not taking more time to speak with you during Gillian's party."

"You didn't know…"

"No, I didn't, but having a guest come all the way from Scotland merited my attention. Actually, if I'd spent some time talking to you, I would have known you and Gillian were together. She's very good at hiding her feelings by making everything a joke, but I have a feeling you're not like that. And if we'd been able to talk about this a few months ago... Well, I'm not sure how that would have changed things, but I wish I'd known sooner."

"I can imagine that's true. I didn't tell my nephew about us right away, and when he found out, he was furious. That taught me a lesson," she admitted.

"One that Gillian didn't pick up on," Amanda said, clearly still unhappy.

"No, she was very reticent. I think that has as much to do with her job as anything, but..."

"She thinks we're anti-gay because we vote Republican," Amanda said, sounding very puzzled. "Rick and I simply want a smaller government, less bureaucracy, and fewer taxes. I don't understand how that makes me anti-gay. I'm not," she insisted. "I'm thrilled that Gillian's found love, and it couldn't matter less that you're a woman, Torie. I swear that's true."

"I believe you, Amanda. I do. But try to look at it from her perspective. A lot of people in your party *are* anti-gay. Can't you see how that might hurt her?"

"I really can't. People in her party want to bludgeon us with taxes only because we've been successful. I wish Gillian could understand that there are many, many people in my party who are very much in favor of gay rights. But she seems to tar us all with the same brush. She's unable to feel the love I have for her, and that *destroys* me, Torie." She started to sniffle, and Torie found herself in the odd position of trying to comfort her fiancée's sister from across the sea.

"Give her some time. I know it can be hard, but it might help if you tell her how much you care. I'm not sure she knows that, Amanda."

"That's only because she doesn't want to," she said, her voice turning a little cold. "Some of my earliest memories are of chasing her as she rode away on her bike, acting like she couldn't hear me crying for her to slow down so I could catch up."

"She's a loner," Torie agreed. "But I don't think she wants to be. She's simply awful at letting herself be vulnerable, but she's trying, Amanda. I can promise you that."

"I suppose time will tell. But I want you to know that Rick and I are very pleased you'll be a part of our family, Torie. We very much look forward to spending some time with you when you come to visit. We both hope it's soon."

Torie felt herself smile. "I assume it's obvious that I hope that even more than you do. I've been able to get to know the loving, vulnerable, dedicated woman that your sister is, Amanda, and I promise I'll try my best to help you get to know her too."

Amanda let out a sigh. "It sounds like you and I will get along perfectly. You seem so much more reasonable than Gillian can be."

"I don't think that's true," Torie said. "But I have to admit my sister would probably get on much better with Gillian than she and I do. Maybe it's just tough for sisters to be open with each other."

"Then we'll be excellent sisters-in-law. I'd truly like that Torie."

"As would I. And over time, I guarantee Gillian will be easier to reach. She's determined to change, Amanda, and when she makes up her mind, I've never seen her fail to reach her goal."

CHAPTER THIRTY

ON THE FIRST OF OCTOBER, Gillian spent the evening cleaning and arranging fresh flowers in both the bath and the bedroom. She had a cleaning service in twice a month, and they'd done a thorough job just a few days earlier, but she wanted everything to be pristine for Torie.

While impatiently watching some silly home renovation show, she tracked Torie's flight with her phone, refreshing the app every fifteen minutes. She knew she was making time crawl, but she didn't do well when she had time to kill and nothing to keep her busy. Instead of driving herself nuts, she changed into sweats and her running shoes, grabbed her phone, and ran around her neighborhood. By the time she'd covered a four-block section five times, some of the tension she'd been carrying in her shoulders and back started to ease.

Once back home, she filled her tub and took a bubble bath, something she almost never did. But it helped. A lot. After shaving her legs, she rinsed out the tub again, then got dressed. She had some navy-blue chinos that she'd grown to love, finding them just a tiny bit dressier than her usual jeans, and slightly more comfortable. Her Scottish sweater and the scarf Torie had made for her had her looking a little overdressed for October, but she was sure Torie would appreciate seeing her wear it. Rolling her eyes at herself, she acknowledged she would've worn a hair shirt if Torie wanted her to. It had taken her a while to find out what love really felt like, and she had to admit she never would have guessed it meant voluntarily giving up control in nearly every area just to make sure your partner was happy. But it was such a glorious feeling that for the first time in her life, being dependent on another person didn't make her feel hemmed in. In fact, it was freeing in ways she never would have guessed.

Arriving at the airport a half hour early, she paced around the baggage claim until the arrival board showed the loveliest word, *landed*, next to the flight number. Then a much longer wait for Torie to get through customs. Eventually, some passengers came down the escalator, perhaps from Torie's flight. They definitely looked bedraggled enough to have been traveling all day. Not the prettiest girl in Scotland, though. Torie's eyes were bright and alert, her hair neatly, or rather, purposefully arranged. She wore a blue turtleneck covered by her Gunn clan tartan gilet and a pair of jeans that looked freshly pressed, with Gillian's tangerine jacket folded over her arm.

Gillian started to wave, and a smile curled Torie's lips before she set her bag down and waved back, enthusiastically. She was clearly traveling light, since she bypassed the luggage claim and walked directly into Gillian's arms.

"Can we kiss in public in Columbus, O-hi-o?" she asked, her eyes twinkling playfully.

"My sister!" Gillian said, intentionally playing it up. "It's been so long!" Then she grasped her firmly and dipped her, leaning over to place a sizzler on her lips.

Torie was laughing during the kiss, and continued when Gillian put her back onto her feet. "You've lost your mind."

"I have. Just under a year ago, to be precise. But I'm happy to be crazy about you. No checked bag?"

"You won't mind seeing me in the same thing every three days, will you? I thought it would be easier to do my laundry than to carry a lot."

"I'd be happy if you had only the clothes on your back. It's what's inside that matters." She grasped her hand and held it to her chest. "I couldn't be happier to see you."

"Then take me home. I'm going to finally have a minute to look around your house. My last visit was, to put it gently, truncated."

"Not this time. I've got you for two whole weeks, and we're going to make the most of them."

☙ ☙ ☙

It was only ten thirty when they pulled into Gillian's drive. Three thirty on Torie's body clock, but she'd been able to sleep on and off on the plane. Gillian hadn't been able to use her awards points for a business class seat for the outbound flight, but premium economy was so much nicer than regular coach that Torie felt very pampered nonetheless.

She gazed at the house, once again reflecting on how little it seemed like something Gillian would have chosen.

"I never would have taken you for the sort of woman who wraps orange lights around the railing on your porch. Did you do the decorating?"

"I did," she said, getting out and moving to the rear of the car to lift the carry-on out. "I just did it because you were coming," she said, shrugging and showing a shy grin. "Pumpkins on the porch," she added as they walked up the path. "I thought we could carve them."

"Very festive," Torie said, nodding with approval at the spooky jack-o-lantern flag that hung from a pole.

"I usually put a flag up on Memorial Day and the Fourth of July. It seemed silly to let the pole sit in the back of the closet the rest of the year, so I bought these silly flags."

She nearly cried at Gillian's obvious attempts to present herself and her home in the best possible light. It was so astounding that a woman as accomplished as she was pushed herself to add these little touches.

After she'd opened the door, Gillian held it open wide, but Torie paused on the porch for a minute.

She'd always been taken by the images of American families sitting on wide covered porches like this one, especially since such things were so uncommon in her part of Scotland. They always seemed to reflect a distinctly American vision of home and hearth, and she felt a tingling sensation climb up her spine as she reveled in the fact that she'd been plunked into the American dream.

The house smelled of cinnamon and some type of warm spice, and when Gillian touched a single button all of the lights on the first floor powered up to the point where you could walk through the house without tripping over anything. She pressed another button and the light in the hallway grew brighter. "Want to stay down here for a while? Or are you ready to crash?"

"Let's sit and talk. I have to wind down."

"Great," she said, bringing the hallway light down while increasing the ones for the living area. Now that she had a chance to look around carefully, Torie decided the house might have been from the Victorian era, Edwardian at the latest, but it had been improved significantly. Torie wasn't an expert in home renovation, but she knew that square rooms, sharp edges, level floors, and pristine ceilings were a rarity in homes over a hundred years old.

They went into the front room, and Gillian flipped a switch that made the fire in the grate come to life, burning like it had been stoked twenty minutes earlier. "What's this?" Torie asked, walking over to it. It was covered with glass, but seemed like a proper fire.

"Gas logs. If you look closely, you'll see they're not real wood. Some kind of ceramic, I think."

Torie stared at her. "Why not use real logs?"

"This is easier," she said, then sat at one end of a large, comfortable-looking sofa, covered in chocolate-colored leather. "I like being able to flip a switch. It's more energy efficient too, not to mention the fact that I'm not adding any sooty air to the environment."

"Really?" Torie said, sitting next to her and leaning close. "All of those reasons?"

"No," she admitted, chuckling. "I just like being able to flip a switch." She tucked an arm around Torie and gave her a soft kiss on the cheek. "Want a drink? I can make just about anything you'd like."

"I don't think so, but you go ahead."

"I don't need one. I'm just being a good host."

"You're a very good host." She sighed heavily. "I feel at home here. It's such a warm and welcoming space you've created for yourself."

"Thanks."

Torie could feel her body start to relax as she settled more comfortably into the supple leather.

"I was tempted to rent an apartment," Gillian said, "but I wanted to live in this neighborhood, and the rental situation wasn't ideal."

"We're in the actual city, correct?"

"Uh-huh. This neighborhood's called Victorian Village. There are trendier places, but I like it here. It's quiet."

"I thought your home was from that era."

"Just after, really. 1906. It was a mess when I bought it, but I've got it just where I want it now. I had the hardscaping done when I was in Scotland the first time, and that was my last big project."

"It's a big house, isn't it?"

"Not really. Around twenty-five hundred square feet." She gave Torie a squeeze. "I can't tell you what that is in metres, so don't even ask."

She laughed. "I can easily understand imperial measurements. One day I'll understand your temperature calculations, then I'll be set. So…what all did you do to your home? Other than very much?"

"That's accurate. It had four bedrooms, but just one bath. I changed it around to three bedrooms and two baths, then I added a half-bath under the stairs near the kitchen. Other than that, it's about the same."

Chuckling, Torie said, "Except for the fact that you ripped out all the walls and the ceilings, replaced all of the wiring, moved quite a few walls and…"

"A few more things," Gillian admitted, grinning. "I've been here almost nine years, and, like I said, I just finished. Instead of taking exotic vacations, I've spent my money on upgrades."

"And bicycles," Torie said, eyeing the very sleek one in the hallway. "Do most Americans keep a bicycle right by the main door?"

"Probably not." She leaned over and kissed her again. "You're right. I spent a lot of money on that bike. It's not entirely custom, but it's close. There's no way I'd leave it in the garage, since I haven't wanted to spend the money to install an alarm out there. They can have the junk I've got stored, but they'd better not touch my baby."

"Do you have an old bike I could ride? I'd love to go out with you."

"I do," she said, her grin brightening. "Our legs are close to the same length, so my spare would probably fit you just fine."

"I'm not doing a hundred miles, so we don't have to get too precise. We'll go when you want to stretch your legs, not destroy mine."

Gillian's expression turned serious, and she said, "I'm planning on being home most of the time, but I've got to go into the office tomorrow, bright and early. The big boss is stopping by, and I've got to meet with him. Is that okay?"

Torie patted her leg. "You do what you have to do." She stood, moved over to the wall, then flipped off the fireplace. Like magic, the flame flickered for a moment, then turned off with a soft "whoosh." "All you have to do right now is take me to bed. I feel like I've traveled across the globe to be here."

"You have," Gillian said, draping an arm across her shoulders. "Let's get you to bed."

They went upstairs together, with Gillian carrying the suitcase.

"You're very gallant," Torie observed. "You always carry things, and open doors, and let me go first. Do I seem frail?"

"Uh-huh," Gillian said, chuckling. "Very."

They went into Gillian's large bedroom, and when they were near the bed Torie grabbed her by the shoulders and yanked her off her feet, with both of them tumbling onto the surface. "Still think I'm frail?"

"I never did," she admitted, starting to laugh. "From that first day at Buchan Ness, when I saw you wielding a massive wrench, I knew you were tough." Her eyes took on a sparkle. "You were lying on the floor, putting so much pressure on whatever you were trying to free up that your feet kept lifting off the ground. I was hooked," she said, her voice taking on a dreamy quality. She closed her eyes, and Torie pinned her to the bed with her body, then started kissing her with deadly intent.

"You're such a pretty woman," Torie whispered, sliding her hand down to slip under Gillian's waistband. "I feel so centered when I touch you. Just having my hand here," she murmured, caressing her belly through her knickers, "grounds me to the planet in ways I can't begin to understand."

"I love you," Gillian whispered. "And I'm so happy to have you here."

"I'm so happy to be here." She shifted to loom over Gillian as her fingers slipped further in. "And here."

"Every part of me has missed every part of you." A smile started to grow as Torie began to explore, letting her fingers become slowly reacquainted with the mysteries of Gillian's body. "Especially this part."

Early in the morning, Gillian's bladder nudged her out of a dream. She put her hand down to push herself up, but it landed on something soft and warm. It took her a second to recall that Torie was in her bed, and she began to smile as she slipped away and went to pee. Returning to bed, she quietly got in, careful not to shake the surface, having learned Torie was a pretty light sleeper. She'd been missed, and she smiled when Torie rolled onto her side, stuck her hand out behind herself, then put it on Gillian's hip when she snuggled into her body. That simple act, an unconscious desire for closeness, made her smile grow. Being in love was as good as it got.

Torie lay in bed for hours after Gillian had crept out, almost silently, at six thirty. She wasn't sleeping soundly, but it felt so nice to simply have a significant lie-in that she remained in bed until her back ached.

At ten, she finally roused herself and sat up, looking around to acclimate herself. Her gaze caught sight of the teddy bear Gillian had bought on her first trip to Scotland, and her heart swelled with love for her hopelessly romantic lover. The bear's Gunn tartan kilt looked very smart as he leaned against the bedside lamp, keeping an eye on Gillian when Torie couldn't be there.

As she went into the bath, Torie smiled at the notes plastered all over, telling her little details about the room and inviting her to pick which sink she'd like to claim. That made her laugh. She'd been sharing a single sink with three or four people for most of her life. She was not possessive about porcelain.

After showering and blowing her hair dry, she got dressed and went downstairs. More notes, each one with a tiny hand-drawn heart, pointed her toward the toaster, and gave her a list of the available breakfast fare. Torie was certain Gillian had filled an entire trolley with food she didn't normally eat, but that was good for her. If they were to live together, they'd both have to learn how to put the other first—something Gillian hadn't done for a very long time. Given what she'd seen so far, she was a quick study.

After making tea, she wandered out to the garden. It was a magnificent day, dry, warm, slightly breezy. There wasn't a single cloud in the sky, and the strong, angled sunlight warmed her thoroughly. Even in October, she might not need a gilet in America.

There was a deck made out of some narrow boards, probably teak, but it was more of a wide landing than the traditional deck she'd seen on home renovation shows, as this one had no railing around it. But it did have a wrought-iron cafe table, sporting several bright red begonias in a nesting of attractive ceramic vases, along with two chairs. Another landing was one step lower, then you were in the garden itself, which was absolutely lovely. Wide flagstones led you along a curving path to a patch of brick upon which a large, rectangular dining table sat, with spring chairs clustered around it. The chairs were clearly meant to have cushions, which were tucked away somewhere for the winter, but Torie could imagine having dinner there on a lazy summer evening, under the canopy of a very large tree whose branches spread across half of the space. It obviously prevented grass from growing well, since the entire area was dotted with shade-loving plants. A patch of grass was small, but well-tended, and it carried all the way back to a tall redwood fence. Climbing vines decorated each of four trellises, each one slightly different from the next. By the garage, tiered plantings had clearly been picked for autumn. With blazing red shrubs taking up the top position, followed by shorter green plants with red berries, then clusters of yellow and purple hearty mums. Someone had planned this very carefully, and had spent a fortune bringing it to life.

Something swaying in the low branch of the tree caught her eye, and Torie walked over to see a bird feeder, decked out as a red and white striped lighthouse. Her heart caught in her throat when she saw that the house was several years old, with the red paint faded from the sun. The lighthouse obsession had clearly been genuine. The seed in the feeder was running a little low, and she walked around the garden, looking for more. As she investigated, she found three other feeders, each one a different style of lighthouse. When she came upon a large quantity of birdseed in a metal container in the garage, she filled each of the feeders, happy to offer a small contribution to Gillian's perfect garden.

Torie stood there, letting the sun bake her until she was almost too warm. A tinkling sound caught her attention and she followed it to the far edge of the decking, where a small pond had some sort of bubbler installed that made water drip from one large stone to the next. It wasn't very large, and it was clearly man-made, but that didn't make it any less attractive, or tranquilizing. She sat on a wooden bench that faced the water, drew her knees up, then wrapped her arms around them and let herself relax completely. Gillian wouldn't be home for hours, but there was every chance she'd find her right here, letting her mind flit about with no destination. Holidays were very, very good things, especially when spent at the home of the woman you loved.

Gillian didn't blow in until seven, worry covering her expression, her body rigid with anxiety. "I'm so sorry," she said, stopping to let her head drop forward. "I haven't stopped from the moment I walked into my office until I ran to my car, twenty minutes ago."

"Come here," Torie said, meeting her halfway to take her in her arms and hold her tenderly. "Did they work you very, very hard today?"

"They did," she sighed as she rested her head upon Torie's shoulder. "But I suddenly feel perfectly fine. I wonder why?" She lifted her head and gazed at Torie with a warm smile. "I know. It's because you're here."

"Let me take a look at you." She put her hands on Gillian's hips and pushed her back a few inches. "I don't know how anyone thinks about soap when you're in a room." She clucked her tongue while shaking her head. "You're a remarkably pretty woman."

"No one at work ever says that," she teased. Her hair had gotten a little longer, but it still curled under in a perfect long bob, glossy and gleaming chestnut strands, thick and straight. Her dark green dress fit like a glove, tailored and simple, sleeveless to show off her toned arms. A burnt orange boucle knit jacket was slung over one arm, and tasteful gold earrings, necklace and a single bracelet gave her an elegant polish. Gillian dropped her briefcase, then tossed her jacket onto the counter and extended her arms. "I need a hug to clear my mind. I was on a hamster wheel from hell today."

"Do you have to go in tomorrow?"

"I should," she sighed. "But I'm not going to. I'll have to take a bunch of calls, but I'm sick of giving up vacation days. I'm supposed to get thirty, and I've taken seventeen."

"Let me make you some dinner. I saw that the refrigerator is stuffed, but I wasn't sure what your plans were."

"Let's have something simple. A sandwich or a salad would be perfect." She went to a corner of the kitchen and opened a tall cabinet to reveal bottles of all shapes and sizes. "But I need a dose of Penicillin to start my vacation."

"Penicillin?"

"Uh-huh," she said, taking out a bottle of Laphroaig, and another of Johnnie Walker. "Blended scotch, fresh lemon juice, honey syrup, and muddled ginger, shaken, then a bit of Laphroaig floated on top."

"Which one of us is the bartender?" Torie demanded. "I've never heard of this drink."

"You'll thank me soon. Let's get moving on those sandwiches. Chop-chop," she insisted, playfully clapping her hands together. "You do the food, I'll handle the drinks."

"You're very purposeful when you've got your business-clothes on," Torie said. "Once we have one or two of those cocktails, I'm going to remove every stitch of your clothing so I can be in charge again."

"I'm happy to let you take over. I've been the queen of the castle all day long. Now I'd love to follow along like a compliant serf."

CHAPTER THIRTY-ONE

ON GILLIAN'S FIRST REAL VACATION day, they spent a good part of the afternoon speaking with an immigration attorney. He'd laid things out quite clearly, but they were both oddly quiet after leaving his office, both reflecting on the information on their own.

They made dinner together, with Gillian being a very good prep cook. She took her time chopping vegetables, but when each variety had been scraped into small glass bowls, they were models of uniformity. Gillian should have been an engineer or an architect. Her precision had to be wasted on the business of soap sales.

Late that night, they were on their second after-dinner drink, both of them having changed into pajamas. After having made sure Gillian had several sets, Torie chose to use her limited packing space for other things, and she now sat on the sofa in Gillian's flannel pajamas. The silly girl hadn't realized they were Royal Stewart plaid, but now that she knew, Torie assumed she'd throw them away and find some with the Lindsay colors.

"So, what do you think of everything we learned today," Gillian said, finally broaching the subject.

"What do I think?" She ran her finger down the lines of the plaid to be able to ignore the piercing blue eyes that were locked onto her. "I was pleased to learn the process wasn't as arduous as I feared it would be." She turned to meet Gillian's eyes. "I have friends who've tried to do graduate work here, and they were unsuccessful."

"You know that's not my real question. I want to know if you're willing to make the move."

"Willing?" She saw the hope-filled look in those eyes and leaned over to kiss Gillian soundly. "I'm much more than willing. If I didn't have obligations, I'd have been here months ago." She took Gillian's hand and held it tenderly while she traced the barely visible veins with her finger. "I hope you know that."

"I do," she said quietly. "But you do have obligations. What are you willing to do about them?"

Sighing heavily, Torie said, "Things are going well enough right now. Aiden loves the robotics club he's joined, but he's at school late every night, and usually doesn't get home until I've had to leave for work. So, I don't get to check up on him like I've been doing."

"You could quit…"

Torie patted her leg and nodded. "I know that. I've been making dinner for five. I eat with my mother, leave a portion for Dad to have before he leaves for his shift the next day, then drop off two portions for Aiden and Kirsty on my way to work." She clapped her hands together. "The timing has to be precise."

"Does she not know *how* to cook…?"

"She's chosen not to learn, and I make it easy for her to get away with it." She let out a frustrated breath, with her lips making a funny noise. "I know I'm enabling her to remain a child, but I've got to make sure Aiden has something besides fried chicken, pizza, curry, chips, and crisps."

"You seem a little resentful," Gillian said, wincing as she spoke.

"I am." She leaned heavily to her side, until most of her weight was pressed against Gillian's shoulder. "I don't want to be, but I am. With both of them. I'm not certain Aiden needs to be at school so late. I worry he's intentionally coming home when he knows I'll be gone."

"Ooo, that must hurt you to the core," Gillian soothed. "Ungrateful little jerk."

Surprisingly, that made Torie laugh. "I'm afraid he is that. But I think that's true for many boys his age."

"But other boys aren't hurting the feelings of the woman I love." Gillian wrapped her arms around Torie's body and cuddled her for a few minutes. It felt so good to be touched when she was feeling down, something she craved so badly when they were apart. "My offer still stands to quit my job and move to Scotland. If I were there, you could have Aiden come to our flat after school. And since you wouldn't have to work at night, you'd have time to help him with his homework."

"I'd still have to take dinner to my parents, but that would make things easier."

"Is there a reason you have to…?" She stopped abruptly.

"It's the same reason I cook for Aiden. My dad will compliantly eat a well-balanced meal, but he'd never cook one for himself. And my Mum's far too tired to shop and cook when she gets home."

"Um, I don't want to point out the obvious, but she could easily cook something in the morning. Or just toss something into a slow cooker on the way out the door. Then they'd both have a hot meal."

"She should," Torie agreed. "But she doesn't. The older she gets, the less careful she is about her health. I don't understand it, but I can't convince her to change."

"I could pay their rent so she didn't have to work—"

"No," Torie said sharply. "I know you have good intentions, and I'm not saying my parents aren't lovely people. Truly they are. But it's better for my mother to have to work. She'd sit in front of the telly all day if she didn't have to get up and get out. My father's the same. He's harming himself gravely by sitting for his entire shift at the office tower he guards, then sitting on the sofa the rest of the time, but I can't make any headway."

"I still think things might be easier for you if I were there."

"I'm certain they would be. But does that make sense for us?"

"I think it might," Gillian said. "But I'd rather you moved here."

"You do? But every time we've talked, you've made it clear you're ready to leave."

"I am, but I want you to get a break. I understand that you'll have to care for your parents at some point, but that point isn't now. They've gotten used to your feeding them, but it won't kill them to fend for themselves while they can."

Torie looked into her eyes, seeing the certainty they held.

"I'd also like you here because we need some time alone to get to know one another. Living together will require some adjustment. I think," she said, chuckling. "I've never lived with anyone, but everyone I know who moves in together complains a lot."

"I think I'm ready to move, but I'm very worried about throwing all of my chicks from the nest."

"You shouldn't be. Your family can take care of themselves. I'm sure of it."

She let her gaze slip to the floor, feeling more than a little ashamed of her family. "They're rather lazy. I'm certain none of them, well, I'm certain my parents don't think they're taking advantage of me—"

"They are," Gillian stressed. "You're paying most of the bills, and doing most of the work."

"My mum does her share of cleaning. And she does their laundry…"

"I assume she doesn't make much as a carer, right?"

"Not much, no. But she could walk to a fish processing plant and earn more than she currently does. It's hard, boring work, but the pay's not bad. There have also been some government programs she could have used to get herself trained in something where she'd make more." She let out a weary sigh. "She's not interested. She likes caring for people, so she's never tried to maximize her income."

"It will never stop," Gillian said softly. "It will just get worse as they get older."

"That's been my worry for years," she admitted. "Lying in bed and thinking of what it will be like in twenty years, with both of them in their eighties, and me almost sixty. I'll have to work four jobs then, since Mum won't be able to carry her load." She met Gillian's gaze. "At least that's what I used to do. Now I think about being with you. Somehow, I've convinced myself everything will work out if we're together."

"It will," Gillian said, her voice full of its usual conviction. "I promise you things will be better."

"I'm just afraid they'll innocently take me down with them," Torie whispered, her body starting to shake as tears streamed down her cheeks. "I know they won't intend that, but I'm afraid it will happen."

"No, it won't," Gillian said, wrapping her in a tender hug.

"And you'll start to resent me if I continue to dote on them once we move to Scotland."

"I won't," she said, then corrected herself. "I'll try not to. I promise. But I do think that you deserve to put yourself on equal footing with your family. You've given them nearly fifteen years of your life. That's more than enough."

She looked at Gillian for a long minute, feeling a spark of hope. "But what would I do if I were here? I couldn't just sit around and wait for you to come home."

"We need a long-term plan. If we're going to move to Scotland once I vest in my pension plan, it makes sense for you to finish your degree there. So…" She was clearly running through ideas in her head. "I think it would help for you to take some graduate level classes at OSU, just to get back up to speed with being a student."

"I would love to do that," she said, a strange bit of euphoria coming over her at the mere thought of taking a class for fun. "Is that possible?"

"I'll find out. Before this vacation's over, we'll have talked to at *least* the history department head. I've got contacts," she said, revealing the haughty smile that Torie was thoroughly besotted by.

"All right. So let's say that I can take classes. That will keep me somewhat busy. What else?"

"I'd be happy to have you at home," Gillian said. "But I think you need more. How about helping Americans plan their ancestry trips to Scotland? Don't a lot of tourists come to search for their family ties?"

"Many do, yes."

"We'll figure out how to get you some clients. It might cost a little to get started, but I can cover that. I'll *happily* cover it," she added.

"Gillian, it's never been in doubt that you're excessively generous with your money." She reached over and took the warm hand in her own. "Let's do a little work to investigate. I don't know what the competition is."

"I do," Gillian said, with her cheeks taking on a little added color. "I've been doing market research for weeks. There are people who do what I'm proposing, but they're very amateurish. We'll knock them out of the water," she insisted, her pale eyes bright with certainty. "I found a guy from our IT group who's a wizard at making good websites. He'll do one for just a few thousand dollars—"

"Thousand! You can do a website for free!"

"Not a good one," Gillian said patiently. "Yours has to be slick. You want people to think they're buying the best—which they will be."

"Och! My head hurts," Torie said, leaning back against the sofa. "Let's put that aside for the moment and focus on the bigger issue. When should I move?" Her heart was beating quickly, with the promise of a new start with Gillian making her light-headed.

"Now. I want you to stay right here."

"Realistically," Torie insisted. "I have to go back home. The lawyer made it clear I have to go through an immigration interview in Britain."

"Fine. Then the day after your immigration interview."

"How about the first of the year?"

"Too late," Gillian said, not budging.

"Let's work our way back into the right date. When do you want to get married?"

She shrugged, trying to act like she hadn't given it any thought. As if *that* were possible. "A lot of people do it on Valentine's Day. It would make our anniversary easy to remember." She looked up, with her feelings so clear they were almost tangible.

Torie leaned into her and placed a soft kiss to her lips. "Have we made love on this sofa?"

"Don't think so," she said, the hazy mist that clouded her eyes every time they started to make love appearing.

"Then tonight will be a first. As soon as we make this life-altering decision, I'm going to show you just how much I love you."

"Valentine's Day," Gillian said firmly.

"Agreed. That means I can come any time after November the fourteenth and meet the requirement that we marry within ninety days of my entering the country. Why don't I come right after Christmas? Let's make it January the first. Then we'll have six weeks to plan."

"Not soon enough," she said, her love-addled expression darkening.

"But I'll miss Christmas. I think I should be there for one more Christmas with Aiden."

Gillian took her hand and placed it over her heart. "Shouldn't you want to have your first Christmas with me?"

"Yes," Torie said, one second after looking into those sweet eyes. "That's exactly what I want. I'll come two months from now."

"You forgot something," Gillian said, a small frown crossing her forehead.

"Not surprisingly! There's a cyclone roaring through my brain at the moment."

"You said we'd make love the moment we made the decision." She looked at her expensive watch, with the diamonds sparkling in the firelight. "A moment's up."

Laughing, Torie grasped her firmly and tumbled her onto her side. "I'm so glad I have you to remind me of the most important things in my life."

"That's the second job I'm taking on. I've been a slacker only having one."

On Saturday morning, Gillian jerked awake when Torie climbed onto her hips, staring down at her with narrowed eyes. "When did you have time to send meals to my family?"

She blinked to clear her eyes, then nodded. "Um, when did we talk about your moving here?"

"Tuesday night."

She smiled up at her. "Wednesday, obviously. Did they like them?"

"Of course!" She slid off her body and fell onto her back, then planted one foot on the bed with the other crossed over her knee. "They're going to get a box on their doorstep every day, with all of the goods, along with precise recipes, to make lunch and dinner. All without having to put up with my supervision."

"Um, it was just dinner for Kirsty and Aiden, since he gets lunch at school."

"Ahh. I spoke with my mum, and she said Kirsty got a box as well. I assumed you'd spoiled them both."

"I like your parents more than your sister, if I'm going to be honest. If not for Aiden, Kirsty would get zip."

"Zip?" She reached over to press the sides of Gillian's mouth together, making her lips purse out like a fish's. "What's a zip?"

"Nada. Do you speak Spanish?"

"A wee bit. My family is very happy with los regalos."

"I don't speak that much," Gillian said, chuckling.

"Well, they're happy, and I'm happy that you're so thoughtful. They assumed I sent the meals, even though that only shows how little they know me. I can't imagine what you paid for that!"

"Not much at all. My colleague in London looked into it for me. I assume he's wondering who I'm feeding in Scotland, but he was polite enough not to ask. Given we've never met in person, he might think I have four Scottish children living in Aberdeen."

Torie rolled onto her side and planted a long, sweet kiss to Gillian's lips. When she broke away, she moved just an inch or two, staying so close their breath warmed the other's mouth. "It's eight. Is there time for me to thank you properly? I've got something special in mind."

Gillian gave her a swat on the seat. "Save that thought. We've got to get cracking if we're going to serve brunch to four people."

"Six. We're going to eat too."

"Then we've really got to get cracking." She set her feet on the floor, then started for the bath, already making a to-do list in her head.

⚜ ⚜ ⚜

Her sister was due soon, having been warned that brunch would be on the table at ten on the dot. Gillian looked at her watch and nodded. "These pancakes will be ready in five minutes. They'll keep in the oven, right?"

"You have a warming drawer," Torie reminded her. "It works well." Standing behind her, she put her hands on Gillian's shoulders. "You seem a little tight here. Nervous?"

"Yeah," she admitted. "Very."

"It'll be all right," Torie soothed, slipping her hands around Gillian's waist. "If they don't like me this time, I'm sure I can win them over eventually. I'm the number one rated guide in Edinburgh, you know," she added, chuckling.

Gillian turned and stared at her. "I'm not worried about them liking you!"

"You aren't?"

"Of course not," she scoffed, turning to check the edge of a pancake. "I'm just trying to be more connected to my family. It's not easy to stick my neck out, but I know you want me to."

Torie put a hand to her chest, a move that always calmed Gillian down. "You're honestly doing this for me?"

She gazed at her for a minute, always surprised when she didn't know everything automatically. "Just about everything I do is for you."

"I don't know what benevolent goddess brought you to me, but I'd build a shrine to her if I did." She lightly touched the tip of Gillian's nose. "You're the perfect woman. I'm so glad I was the first person to discover that."

"Aww." She slipped the last pancake from the pan and stooped to put the platter in the warming drawer. "We've got a full day planned here. Are you excited about seeing your first football game?"

"I most certainly am. You're going to have to explain every element to me, but I'm very much looking forward to this."

Gillian just grinned at her, not having any desire to reveal how much she'd had to pay for good seats to watch OSU as they would, no doubt, destroy Maryland that afternoon.

The boys should have been playing outside, but they were only interested in watching cartoons on the big TV Gillian had in her upstairs den. Torie was determined to win over each member of the family, deciding to start with the smallest ones first.

Gillian had, as usual, prepared for the day, returning home one afternoon with boxes of toys. Torie hoped she'd learn to relax and just talk to the little fellas, but at this point she was better at giving them presents than time. Maybe she'd learn.

Torie pulled out a big box of Legos and sat on the floor to open it. In a second, Spencer scooted across the floor and sat on his heels, gazing at her intently. "What's that?"

"It's a mobile police unit." She gave him a puzzled look. "I'm not sure how to set it up. Do you have any advice?"

Chapin was in the mix in a matter of moments. "I know how," he said, squeezing between his younger brother and Torie. "My friend Hunter has this."

"I wanna!" Spencer yelped.

Gillian had been right. Torie got up and grabbed the second set. "I've got a firetruck too. Want to help me with the firetruck, Spencer?"

"I want the police," he said, pouting.

Chapin held his hands out. "I want the firetruck. I don't have that one."

Torie looked up as Gillian walked in. "I see Columbus is going to be well protected in a matter of minutes." She folded her legs under herself and sat down gracefully. "Who can I play with?"

"You're gonna play?" Chapin asked, eyeing her suspiciously.

"Sure. I know how to build things."

He shrugged, then took the firetruck from Torie. "You can help. But don't tell me how to do it. I can read."

"You can?" she asked, blinking in surprise.

"Yeah." He got the box open, then took the instructions out. Torie watched him look at the pictures carefully, just like his aunt would have. There were very few words, but they didn't stop him. "Here," he said, handing Gillian a bunch of gray pieces that she could use to build a garage for the truck. "You do this."

"Okay," she said, looking over his head to grin at Torie. "Will you help me if I get stuck?"

"You won't. You're a grown-up."

"Is that what I am?" she said, chuckling. "I've been wondering about that."

"Nuh-uh," Spencer said. "You're a lesbenese." He giggled when he spit the word out. "My mom said."

"You're not supposed to say that," Chapin whispered loudly. "It hurts her feelings."

"No, it doesn't," Gillian said, clearly surprised. "Do you know what a lesbian is?"

"It's…" Chapin pursed his lips for a moment. "You and her," he decided, pointing at Torie.

"That's exactly what it is. Me and her. I love Torie just like your dad loves your mom. We're going to get married."

"Will you have cake?" Spencer asked, eyes bright.

"We will definitely have cake."

"Can I come?" He looked up at her with such hope Torie had to stop herself from crying.

"Absolutely. We'll have cake and balloons and—"

"Face painting?" Spencer asked.

"Sure. Why not?" She met Torie's eyes, the love she held in her heart so easily conveyed with just a look. "If you want face painting, we'll have face painting. Don't you think we should get married soon?"

"Do it now," Chapin decided.

"I don't think we can get it together for today. But I think people who love each other should get married as fast as they can." She rolled her eyes and added, "Given the dictates of a bunch of bureaucrats who should be catching bad guys rather than stopping a sweet Scottish girl from living here."

The boys had lost interest once the cake and face painting had been decided, but Gillian was still *very* interested. The lovesick look in her eyes would have been obvious to just about anyone—except young boys who had building projects to complete.

After the boys were actually cooperating to a good extent, Gillian took Torie's hand and led her downstairs. "I told you they needed toys. I've got this being a better aunt thing all figured out."

They stopped at the foot of the stairs, and Torie put her hands on Gillian's hips. "Talking to them was the thing that impressed them. Getting down on their level and letting them set the agenda is all you need to do."

"Toys help," she said, her impish smile impossible to resist. After kissing for a minute, they started for the backyard. Amanda and Rick sat at the table drinking warm apple cider that packed a punch. Gillian had warned that she and Torie would probably have to drive them home, but the alcohol had relieved some of the tension that had been obvious at the beginning. Gillian stood at the threshold for a moment, whispering, "I'd much rather be riding my bike."

"And I'd rather be watching your bum while you ride in front of me, but no one said being an adult was going to be easy."

Rick looked up and caught sight of them. "I snuck upstairs a while ago to see you playing. I hope you weren't planning on keeping those Legos here. They'll lose it if they can't take them home."

"I might not know a lot about kids," Gillian said, walking into the yard, then taking a chair out and holding it for Torie to sit, "but I know that much."

Amanda took a sip of her cider, looking very attractive as the sun caressed her face. The Lindsay women had both been gifted in the looks department. "Have you two talked about your wedding?"

"We don't talk about much else," Gillian said. Again, she took Torie's hand, likely trying to get everyone used to mild displays of affection. "We're talking about Valentine's Day."

"Ooo. That's so romantic," Amanda said. "Will you have a big wedding? One of my co-workers had over three hundred people at his. He claims he invited every gay person in Columbus." She blinked her pale eyes slowly. "Were you there, Gillian?"

Oh, they were definitely going to have to drive them home. Amanda had the capacity of a child!

"I don't think I've ever been to a same-sex wedding. And your co-worker can keep the record for the biggest one in the history of Columbus. We'll keep it small. Just family and a few friends."

"Won't it be hard to leave your family?" Amanda asked, turning to Torie.

Torie nodded. "Very. But you have to make sacrifices for love. It won't be easy to lie around the house all day and become a woman of leisure, but I'm willing to give it my best."

Gillian had a funny look in her eye when she tapped her sister on the shoulder and said, "After Torie moves here, she's going to need to go back to visit her family. Why don't you and I go with her on that first trip?"

Amanda's jaw dropped open, but Gillian kept going. "I know it's hard for you to get away, but it would be tough to get up to North Ronaldsay with the boys, besides their being bored to tears. What do you say? Torie will stay with her family, and you and I can go explore."

"Do you mean that?" Amanda asked, still looking completely stunned.

"I do. I'm actually ready to calendar a trip. How's June?"

Amanda reached for her purse, knocking every item in it onto the ground. She finally found her phone, leaving the rest of her things lying right where they'd landed. "Name the date, and I'll make it happen," she said, her finger hovering over the calendar. Torie noticed Amanda hadn't even looked to Rick for permission. Clearly one of the Lindsay sisters was the dominant one in her relationship. That number wasn't going to change.

The last Saturday of their vacation was spent with Kara's family. The afternoon was warm and sunny, with the tall, young trees that suggested a barrier around the garden showing a profusion of colored leaves, ranging from brilliant red to the softest yellow.

The day had been so iconically American that Torie felt like she was in one of those movies about a plucky football team and the trials and tribulations of their beautiful small town.

They sat on the ground with the baby, who was now technically a toddler, watching him try to climb atop his older brother's scooter. It was a stretch, but if Torie held it still he could stand on it. The grass was long enough and lush enough to prevent him from actually going anywhere even if he'd had the motor skills, which he didn't. But he was having fun imagining he could travel as quickly as his big brothers did. He'd grown so much since she'd met him in

March that she was still adjusting to his burgeoning talents, but that was part of the fun of being around kids. They were new people each time you saw them.

Ben, Kara's husband, walked over with three bottles of beer in his hands. "You're going to like this one," he said, extending a bottle toward Gillian. "It's a brown ale that's a whopping nine percent alcohol."

Gillian took it and read the label. "Almost local," she said, nodding. "Cleveland's got some good breweries."

"Torie?" he said, holding out a bottle.

"I think I'm going to stick to the hot apple cider. Gillian can drink, and I can drive." She let out a laugh. "Although it would probably be safer for her to drive impaired than for me to drive sober. I've never driven a car that can lurch away from a stop sign like hers can. Especially when I'll have to sit on the wrong side of the car and stay on the wrong side of the road."

"She loves her cars," he said, giving Gillian a fond smile. "How many have you had since I've known you?"

"Mmm." She shook her head. "I'm not sure. Too many. I'm keeping this one until the repair bills are greater than the monthly on a new one, though. I'll never be able to afford faster or prettier, so I'm retiring from the car buying game."

"It is nice," he said, sounding wistful. "When Eli's out of college I'm going to buy myself something I really want."

"Cars will be self-driving by then," Gillian joked. "I can't imagine they'll be as much fun."

"Fine. Ruin my fantasy," he said, his smile making him look like he could have still been in college. But he would have had to wear a cap to pull that off. He'd lost too much hair for a twenty-year-old.

Eli turned to look up at him, distracting himself enough that he fell. His head glanced off Gillian's bottle, and he got a face full of brown ale before tumbling to the ground. Even though his father was right in front of him, the child thrashed about, searching for his mom, waiting to scream in pain until he saw her.

Ben rolled his eyes and bent over to pick him up to take him to Kara. "Kid acts like I'm the mail man," he grumbled as they walked away.

"I wonder if I did that?" Gillian asked, leaning back on a hand as she took a long sip of her very sudsy beer.

"What? Cry when you hurt yourself?"

"No. I wonder if I looked to my mom to fix things," she said, her voice soft and reflective.

That cut Torie like a knife, and she closed her eyes for a second, unable to look at the sweet, innocent expression on Gillian's face.

"I don't remember ever feeling that way," she continued, "but I must have. Right?" She turned her gaze to Torie for confirmation.

"All kids need someone to reassure them, but..." She trailed off. "I don't know if it was your mom. Probably," she added a little weakly, assuming Gillian's dad wouldn't have been much more reliable.

"We had a babysitter I was crazy about. Beverly was with us from my earliest memories until Amanda went to school, so that was..." She seemed to be counting up the years. "Gosh. She was probably with us for ten years. No wonder I was close to her."

"She minded you during the day?"

"She lived with us. My dad's business took off like a shot, and we moved to the house we grew up in when I was just a year old. There was a bedroom with a bath next to the kitchen." She leaned her head back and took a long sip of her beer, with the light breeze making the ends of her shiny, dark hair sway. "I wonder what they paid her? Besides as little as possible. She was a great person," she added, smiling. "Patient, friendly. She was pretty old, much older than my parents, and much more interested in my sister and me. Great cook, too." She looked like she was going to cry when she said, "People bring a woman like that in, then just throw her away when they're done with her. We got to say goodbye, but I remember not knowing about it ahead of time. It was like 'Say goodbye to Beverly,' when she already had her coat on."

"Maybe you went to Beverly when you hurt yourself," Torie said softly.

"I assume I did, given she was with us from the time we woke until after dinner, when she went to her room. One of our parents usually put us to bed, but there were many days we didn't see either of them. They seemed like overseers, just breezing in to check on things." She laughed again, but the sound was tinged with regret. "Well, my mom was like a live-in gardener, who had ancillary responsibilities for child care."

Torie didn't comment on that. She didn't want to cry, and knew she couldn't speak without letting her voice betray her. Gillian wasn't exactly a motherless child, but she wasn't too far away to be able to identify, and that broke Torie's heart.

🌵🌵🌵

Gillian, Ben, and Skip were throwing a football around. Despite pleas to join them, Torie wasn't about to break her nose giving it a try. Americans seemed fixated with being able to throw balls of all sorts, while Europeans concentrated on footwork. She was certain she'd represent herself honorably if they were kicking a ball around, but she couldn't throw to save her life.

Skip, whom she assumed had a regular name too, was eight, and had enough strength and coordination to throw the ball with some accuracy. But Gillian still had to chase it down frequently, given how expansive the garden was. She'd had more to drink than normal, but she was still in control. Torie had never seen her lose that, and wasn't sure she wanted to.

Kara walked over to plunk Eli down on Torie's lap. "Will you keep an eye on him while he takes his bottle?" She tapped the child on the nose, smiling down at him. "I know he's too old to be taking one, but it's his security blanket." She lowered her voice. "I started watering down the milk, just so he doesn't have too many calories, but he doesn't seem to notice." Eli yanked the bottle from his mother's hands and started to lustily suck.

"It's almost his nap time, so he'll fall asleep. I hate to have liquid dribbling into his mouth when he's not alert."

"Sure. I love having a baby in my arms again," she said, looking down at the angelic face that blinked up at her, blue eyes getting a little hazy.

Kara pulled up a chair and stuck her legs out, stretching for a moment. "What have you two been up to this week? I know Gillian had a million things on her list."

"We've done a few things, but we both wanted a low-key vacation. Lunch somewhere different every day. Bike riding. Then we met with an immigration attorney," she added, rolling her eyes, "and we talked to a very helpful professor at Ohio State after Gillian managed an introduction."

"From me," she said, chuckling. "One of the partners at my firm's on the board of governors. He made the call to hook you up."

"The rat!" Torie yelped. "Gillian said she was so important she could call anyone in Columbus and get them to drop everything to meet with us."

"Did you believe her?"

Torie laughed as she shook her head. "My sweet little soap salesman loves to tease, but I have some awareness of her real place in society."

Kara reached over and adjusted Eli's bottle, then gripped Torie's arm for a second. "I love hearing you talk about her that way. No one ever has."

"Which…?"

"She's had girlfriends, and…" She trailed off. "She's told me about most of the women she was interested in. But none of them ever seemed truly crazy about her. Do you know what I mean?"

"I'm certainly crazy about her, so I suppose I do, but I can't imagine why the others weren't. She's so far beyond anyone I could have put on my wish list that I'm always on the lookout for someone wanting to fight me for her."

"That," Kara said, pointing at her. "That recognition of how special she is. That's what I'm talking about. But I suppose it makes sense. She didn't let the others see her like you do. She was always guarded."

"Sometimes she's so open it astounds me," Torie said softly. "Granted, that's often hard for her, but she's really trying."

"I'm not sure if you're just the right woman, or if she's finally at a place in her life where she's ready, but I can stop worrying about her," Kara said, playfully wiping her brow.

"Even when we move to Scotland? That's our current plan, you know. As soon as Gillian's vested in her pension…"

"Oh, sure," she said, not pausing a beat. "She'll be fine in Europe. And given that we mostly talk on the phone, I'll just call her when she's going home instead of going into the office. As long as my needs are met, I give my blessing," she said, grinning.

"You mean a lot to her," Torie said soberly. "She's going to have a hard time not seeing you as often as she does now."

"Really? I mean, we're obviously close, but…"

"She thinks of you as her family. You're the person she spends her holidays with, and losing that will make her sad."

"I don't see her sad very often. Actually, we're not very serious with each other. I talk to other people when I need a shoulder to cry on. Maybe… Maybe I should try going a little deeper."

"She's getting better at that," Torie said. "Actually, I think she relishes being able to cry."

Kara gave her arm another squeeze. "She trusts you." She leaned over and placed gentle kisses on her and Eli's foreheads. "So do I, and since you'll never meet anyone who has her back like I do, that's a real compliment."

❧ ❧ ❧

On Sunday morning, the last day of their vacation, they got up early and rode their bikes around the neighborhood. Nothing too strenuous. Just giving them a chance to be outside for a while, since long flights loomed ahead for Torie, and a shorter one for Gillian, who'd arranged for meetings in New York just so they could have a few more hours together.

They'd wasted the rest of the day doing their favorite things, lying in bed together, talking little, touching constantly. Torie didn't think it ideal that they both got quiet when they were sad, but that wasn't something easily changed.

At the airport, they were allowed to board first, with Gillian greeting the flight attendant by name. "Hi there, Jackson," she said, flashing their boarding passes. "Last row, starboard."

"Feebo," he said, walking with them to check that they had everything they needed. "You know the drill."

"More than I wish I did."

Gillian insisted Torie sit by the window, and when Jackson walked away she said, "Feebo?"

"Front even, back odd. That's how they serve meals. I like to sit in the last seat, and odd numbered flights are served back to front, so I always check the flight number before I make my reservation." She chuckled. "I don't want to miss out on my cheese plate."

"This looks like the plane I took from Edinburgh to London to meet you. No frills."

"None," Gillian agreed. "It's silly to pay for first class on this type of plane, but Channing Brothers doesn't mind, so I'm taking full advantage." She was dressed casually, with her dark blue chinos, a print cotton blouse and a light sweater thrown over her shoulders, but she still looked like she might have owned the airline.

"So?" she said, after shifting around in her seat to face Torie. "Now that you've really seen America, what's your impression?"

"Mmm, so much," she sighed. "What will linger is how large everything is. Houses, gardens, cars, stores, food. Does anyone truly need a grocery store as big as the one we went to near Kara's home? I understand that Americans love peanut butter, but two or three types should be enough for anyone. And not just peanut butter. Cashew, almond… It was dizzying!"

"America is the land of plenty, and we want to make a point of that. We can't use up all of the resources on the planet if we don't go big." She smiled, wanly. "I've got to get over my disaffection with my country. It's not making my life better in any way."

"I like your country. I really do. I felt like I could breathe deeper with all of that open space. Not to mention the weather! So many days without a drop of rain."

"We're having a bit of a drought," Gillian said. "We get a lot of rain."

"More than we do."

"I still don't believe that. Not possible."

"It's true! Several more inches a year. Ours just comes in dribs and drabs. You must get some fierce storms."

"No worse than the one we had at the lighthouse!"

"That was one to remember," she admitted. "But I'm serious about my interest in America. I'd love to explore it. I'm really curious about those big, wide open spaces in the west. Could we go there some day?"

"We'll visit every state if that would make you happy. One at a time. You pick where we start."

"Well, I've always wanted to go to Washington, and Philadelphia, and Boston. I can dig into American history there. But what calls to me is the place where they have those sandstone arches," she said, feeling a burst of excitement at the prospect. "I have this image of golden light and massive arches above my head that I'd love to experience. I see people on bicycles in every photo, so you'd love it too."

"I'll start researching where it is. Sounds like a great place for a honeymoon, doesn't it?"

"It does."

"Then that's the place. I'll check it out and find the best place to stay," she said, confident as usual. "Um." For just a second, she looked slightly terrified. Then she lowered her voice and said, "I've given this an amazing amount of thought, and after serious reflection, I think I'd be fine with you having a baby."

"A baby!" Thankfully, the engines had started up and were whining loudly enough that only the person right in front of them heard her shriek. "What in the world brought that up?" She gripped Gillian's arm, digging her fingers into the flesh. "Please tell me you don't want one. I don't think I could—"

"No, no, not me," she said, clearly relieved. "I've never wanted one. But I see you with Kara's kids and my nephews and you seem so into them—"

"I love kids, but I have *no* desire to give birth. I've raised one child, and that's been more than enough." She grasped Gillian's arm and squeezed it tightly. "I nearly fainted. Taking you on is going to keep me busy enough, thank you very much. The last thing I need or want is a baby." She shivered at the thought. "A baby," she whispered, making Gillian laugh. "You've gone mad."

Chapter Thirty-Two

On Monday evening, Gillian sat in her hotel room, waiting for the sluggish wi-fi to connect to Torie. Finally, her face appeared on the screen, with a sweet, but tired, smile curling the corners of her mouth.

"I miss America," she said. Then she pursed her lips and blew a kiss. "And you. In reverse order."

"Me too. So much. This is the worst part of our visits. Getting back into our routines makes it so clear we're apart."

"It really does." She sighed heavily. "I arrived this morning to gray skies and just enough rain to annoy me. After I got settled, I walked to the market. Everything was gray. Buildings, streets, peoples' faces." She laughed softly. "I miss your beautiful house, the tranquilizing garden, that fantastic front porch with your adorable decorations, all of the big trees on your street…" Sighing again, she said, "It was like being in one of those homes you see on American TV shows, with your gorgeous self included."

"I feel like this room," Gillian admitted. "Bland and uninspired. I sat in a bunch of meetings today, but I'm sure I didn't add any value. I've got to snap out of this, since my boss watches me like a hawk."

"Does he?" Torie asked, her smile disappearing. "What do you mean by that?"

"Nothing. I'm just saying he's the kind of guy who notices if you're not sharp."

"Gillian," she said, in the tone of voice she probably used with Aiden when he didn't do his homework. "I love that you prioritize me, but those people pay your salary. You need to keep your focus."

"I know," she said quietly. "But the next two months are going to be hard."

"I'll be there soon. We can put up with anything for two months, can't we?"

"That remains to be seen," she said glumly. "I sure do hope so."

It took several days to have both of her parents in the same room at the same time, but that was their usual. When Aiden had been born, they'd worked out a plan to always have one of them at home. They hadn't needed to stick to that schedule for quite a few years now, but she supposed they were all creatures

of habit. Now she was going to let them know her habits were about to change
—dramatically.

It had been a while since she'd made a traditional Sunday roast, but it was
one of her father's favorites. She'd watched him sitting happily in the living room
all afternoon, smiling as the scent of roasting meat permeated the space.

Her mum had helped a bit, whipping up the batter for the Yorkshire
pudding, while Torie roasted parsnips and carrots to add just a hint of vitamins
to the feast.

Both of her parents had praised the dishes, with her admitting she'd done a
great job of having everything hot and ready at the same time. Now it was time
for pudding, but she lingered at the table, feeling her nerves build until her
hands were shaking.

"When I was in Ohio," she said, having to clear her throat. "Gillian and I
made some decisions."

"You're leaving, aren't you?" her mother said, already on the verge of tears.

Torie nodded, fighting the lump in her throat. "I am, Mum, but not
permanently."

"For how long?" her dad asked.

"Well, Gillian would prefer to move here right away, but she'll get a pension
if she stays for a little more than a year."

"A pension? How old is she?" her mother asked.

"Oh, she won't get it now. She'll just be entitled to it when she retires. That
will be around twenty-five years from now. But it's a significant amount of
money. More than I make at all of my jobs combined."

"Oh, my," her mother said, her words so soft they barely registered.

"If she doesn't stay for another fourteen months, she'll get nothing. She's
willing to do that, but I just can't let her." She reached out and grasped each of
her parents' hands. "Do you understand? I need to be with her soon, but I want
to secure our futures, too."

"You'd be daft to throw away that kind of money," her father said. "You've
got to do what makes sense."

"What makes sense for me is to be with Gillian," Torie said, with her heart
beating a little faster at the thought. "I plan on leaving in the middle of
December, and we'll marry on Valentine's Day."

"Here?" her mother asked, looking hopeful.

"In Ohio," Torie said, wincing when her mother's face fell. "But I guarantee
Gillian's already bought tickets for all of you to help us celebrate."

"I think we're finally going to America, Hugh," her mum said, dabbing at her eyes.

❦ ❦ ❦

A week after she returned, Torie called Gillian for their normal Friday night pajama party. When the image of her smiling face lit up the screen, Torie sighed. "I love looking at you. You're almost as pretty on a screen as you are in person."

"You may compliment me all night," Gillian said. "I've become addicted to praise."

"Oh! You made me forget the news. Guess who's getting married next week?"

"Me? I hope it's me," she said, grinning widely.

"It's not you, silly. My sister's getting married." She shook her head. "Well, she's having a civil service here. At some point, they're going to Poland to have what Piotr calls a real wedding at his family's church. I can't see my sister convincing a priest she's ready to convert, but that's a bridge they'll have to cross on their own."

"That's very cool! Both Gunn girls married in a short time. Is she excited?"

"She seems to be. I'm not sure what the rush is, but Piotr wants to do it right away. They're not even having guests. He says they'll have a big wedding in Poland that will count, whatever that means. I'm actually looking forward to that one. We'll be able to go, won't we?"

"We can go anywhere you want," Gillian said. "Anywhere at all. Any time, too. If you want to go to Poland right now…"

"I can wait," Torie said, chuckling. "I love having such a compliant fiancée, by the way."

"That's my middle name. Gillian 'C' for Compliant Lindsay."

❦ ❦ ❦

On the last Saturday in November, a cool, breezy, but sunny day, Torie carried two bags full of supplies up the stairs to Kirsty's flat. Her mother was behind her, laboring up the steps, and they reached the top at roughly the same time.

After knocking, Kirsty threw open the door, smiling like a kid. "Come in, come in," she urged.

Torie put her bags down and watched her sister hug their mother. She honestly looked like a different woman, having made a few changes in anticipation of her wedding. Her hair was all one color, a deep wine tone, and longer than she'd worn it in years. Her clothes were now those of a regular

423

woman in her late twenties, rather than a groupie for a punk band, and she seemed more…polite, or maybe polished was the right word.

"Piotr has a batch of biscuits already in the oven," she said. "Let's make sure he doesn't get too big a head start."

Torie wasn't even sure how it had come to pass that they were going to make Christmas treats together, but here they were. She'd met Piotr several times, but they'd never done more than make polite small talk. So this was a test in some ways, but she had to admit the bar was set low. So long as he didn't abuse her sister in any way, he was tops in her book.

They went into the small kitchen, where he'd set up his baking operation. Clearly a neat guy, he had everything lined up perfectly. When he turned and gave them a big smile, Torie could see what had attracted her sister. Besides being ruggedly handsome, he gave off the aura of someone who had things under control. That was a wonderful quality for Kirsty to crave, and Torie was certain she'd stay on the straight and narrow if she could just stick with that.

"Hello," he said, his voice big and deep and booming. "I don't know how we will share this space, but we will find a way."

"We could set up in the dining room," Torie said. "I brought a big piece of oilcloth just in case."

"Excellent idea," he said, walking into the dining area to help. "May I have the cloth?"

Torie handed it to him and watched him adjust it so it covered every inch. It was actually quite nice to have someone take over. God knew she was tired of being the only adult in the room.

Piotr went back into the kitchen when his timer went off, then emerged with a baking sheet filled with star-shaped biscuits. He smiled and stated the name, but Torie just stared at him. Her ears clearly didn't know how to adjust to Polish words. After putting the sheet down, he took out a notebook and wrote down the words, gwiazdki z nieba. "Heavenly stars," he said. "I'll dip them in chocolate when they cool."

"Do you like to cook?" Torie asked.

Kirsty answered for him. "He does. He had a room in a house before, but the owners were twats. They wouldn't let him use the kitchen once they got home, which meant he couldn't even make himself a meal. He's making up for that now," she said, clearly pleased. "He makes tea every night."

"It was fine there," he said, then his voice lowered and he added, "I think that is not a nice name to call people, Kirsty."

"You're right," she said, moving over to put her hand on his shoulder. A little of her normal feistiness showed through when she winked at their mum and said, "But they were. Massive twats."

"She keeps me, how do you say? On my toes?" Piotr said, clearly charmed by her, much to Torie's relief.

"There's no doubt about that," Torie said. "She's had us on our toes since the day she was born."

☙ ☙ ☙

Torie walked her mum to the door at one thirty, leaning over to kiss her cheek. "I hate to have you work on your normal day off."

"Oh, you know how it is. I do someone a favor, then she'll do one for me. I like this new patient, though. She's much more interactive than Mrs. Laird was." She smiled, looking a little impish. "Of course, she was on death's door for two years."

"I'm glad you're working with someone who talks to you. I'll see you tonight if you're still up."

"Don't take any of those biscuits home to your father. He'll eat them all before I get there. You know what a sweet tooth he has."

"You'll beat me home. I'm going straight to work." Her weaning plan wasn't popular, but she'd started to make a large casserole every couple of days, rather than a fresh meal every afternoon. It was clear her parents were a little puzzled about the change in her habits, but they hadn't said anything.

"Oh." Her mum blinked a few times, looking like she wanted to ask a question. Then she smiled and offered a hug. "We'll see you tonight. Don't work too hard."

"Same to you, Mum." She heard footsteps rising as her mother's were falling, then Aiden's intermittently deepening voice pricked her ears. He kicked the stairs as he journeyed the rest of the way, smiling when he saw Torie.

"I smell biscuits," he said.

"You certainly do. Want to help make a few more batches?"

"Why so many?" he said, dropping his backpack right at the door.

"Piotr is sending most of them home to his family, but I'll give some to my co-workers and Mum's going to take some."

Piotr and Kirsty came into the room, with Piotr gently saying, "I think you make the mistake of thinking your room is at the door, Aiden. It's there," he said, pointing to the hallway.

With a relatively benign eye-roll, Aiden picked up his backpack and took it into his room.

"Children are like dogs," Piotr said. "They want to run wild in the streets, but they fit into a family better if they have rules."

Torie couldn't disagree with that, but she had a feeling the antipathy she could sense from Aiden focused on exactly those rules.

The biscuits covered most horizontal surfaces, with many of them now cool enough to pack. Piotr had bought large tins, each decorated with some Christmas theme, and he set them on the dining table. "Aiden," he called out, "help, please?"

He came out and met his mother's eyes. "What do I have to do?"

"Help us pack up the tins, will you?"

"Can I eat some?"

"Of course. We're keeping that pile there."

He went over and jammed two into his mouth, then came back to the table.

"Wasn't your robots work over at one?" Piotr asked. He didn't sound accusatory, just interested.

"Went late."

"Pick up the phone and text when that happens. Your mother worries."

"She knows where I am," Aiden grumbled. "I'm at lab."

"Torie," Piotr said, giving her a pleasant smile. "Shouldn't a boy this age do something besides watch another child make a robot move?"

"Um…" She caught Aiden's look, which was instantly annoyed. "I think the robotics team has been great for him."

"Sure. Sure. It's fine. But a boy needs to use his body to make it strong." He pulled his hands up near his ears in a bodybuilder's pose. "I didn't get strong by watching something else move. *I* moved."

"Aiden has to move a lot. He's in charge of having everything at hand to fix the robots when they're not working properly."

"I know. I know. But he's never tried sport. How can he know he wouldn't be good if he doesn't try?" He looked at Aiden for a moment. "I just ask him… Try one. Only one. Any kind he likes."

"I have lab every afternoon and all day on Saturday," Aiden said, clearly sick of the topic. "That's what I like."

"You like football," Piotr said. "I could teach you so much. I played every minute. It's fun!"

"I don't want to," Aiden said, slowly and forcefully. He went into the kitchen to wash his hands, probably a requirement under the new regime, then came back and started to drop cookies into a tin.

426

"It wouldn't hurt to try sport," Kirsty said. "You could do it when your new term starts."

"I played last year, and I didn't like it." Aiden glared at her, then snapped, "You don't need my help. You've got three adults to fill a bunch of tins." Then he turned and headed for his room.

Torie was immensely thankful that Piotr didn't force the issue. He shrugged amiably and said, "I will have to work harder to convince him."

"He's never been good at sport," Torie said. "And if he's not good at something, he loses interest very quickly."

"It's too much of the television. My family didn't own one, so we had to be outside. That was better."

"Probably true, but he'd just watch his phone if he didn't have a proper television."

Kirsty started to work, doing a pretty nice job of arranging things. "I was telling Piotr about your immigration interview," she said. "When is it again?"

"Next week. I'm terrified, but I suppose that's normal."

"I'm very happy I could come to Scotland without getting permission," Piotr said. "The US is very hard. I have cousins who tried for years to get in. They gave up and are in Ireland now."

"They say this is pretty perfunctory," Torie said, "but it's *so* important."

Piotr gave her a puzzled glance, then she realized Kirsty probably hadn't understood the word either. "Routine," she said, correcting herself.

"So, you will do this interview, and then you will move?" Piotr said.

"My ticket is for December the fifteenth," she said, still quaking with fear over the date approaching so swiftly.

"And then you're a citizen," Kirsty said.

"Oh, no, it's not that easy. Gillian has to petition to adjust my status from nonimmigrant to conditional resident. That requires a longer interview, and I'll have to take a physical."

"They don't want you if you're sick?"

"I'm not sure," she said, having never thought of the reasoning behind the rule. "I can be a conditional resident for two years, then I petition to change to resident status. That's when they really take a look and try to make sure we don't have a fake marriage."

"And *then* you're a citizen," Kirsty said.

"It's not automatic even then, but that's the process. We'll probably be back here before it's all finished, but we've decided to follow through with it no matter where we live. I want to be able to enter the US without having the immigration guys breathing down my neck."

"We will visit you in America," Piotr said. "I've always wanted to go."

"Me too," Kirsty agreed. "Disney World!"

❧ ❧ ❧

On the first of December, Torie raced home from the bar, changed into her pajamas, then got her tablet set up. By the time she'd dialed, she'd managed to control her breathing, but her heart was still racing. Then Gillian came into view and she let out a sigh. "It's so nice to see you," she murmured.

"Bad day?"

"A whirlwind. I had my immigration interview in London at nine this morning, but it didn't actually happen until eleven thirty. The whole time I was waiting I was trying to get a signal to check on the next available flight back home. Luckily, I made the two o'clock, but I didn't have a lot of time to spare."

"All of that rushing to get back for your shift?"

"Everyone I normally use as a replacement is on holiday. That's what comes from having people take over for you constantly. I've been repaying everyone ever since I told them I'm leaving."

"Why are we wasting time talking about your job? Tell me how the interview went!"

"Well, I think. I talked to someone who seemed very young and quite inexperienced. She had a cheat sheet in front of her, and she had a hard time making eye contact because she had to keep referring to it." She laughed. "If you'd watched us, you'd have been sure *she* was the person trying to get into the country. She was a nervous wreck!"

"When will they notify us?"

"She wasn't sure, but I think you'll get the notification, since you're the one who filed the petition. Soon, I hope."

❧ ❧ ❧

Piotr had some surprising, but admirable attributes. One of them had been to never stay overnight at the flat before he and Kirsty married. So when he moved in after the wedding there was a much steeper acclimation curve than he and Aiden might have had if he'd been around more.

Three weeks into the new arrangement, Aiden was doing whatever possible to be away from home, but he'd gone out of his way to spend time with Torie, even inviting her to watch his meet on Saturday. She had to switch with a co-worker to take the breakfast shift at the hotel, but she arrived at eleven to watch him and at least a hundred other kids standing around a large gymnasium, trying to get their simple robots to pick up a yellow cone and place it atop another. There were also red cones, and Aiden had assured her those were worth more points.

He wasn't even in the pit, as they called the place where the robots performed their tasks. He was the newest member of the team, and hadn't any experience in programming or robot repair. It seemed like he was charged with making sure the more experienced kids had the right tools and supplies to keep the very temperamental machines running. He did, however, look cute in his polo shirt. The company that sponsored the team had provided very sharp-looking shirts, as nice as any he owned. Aiden was clearly thrilled by it, since he took it off the moment he got home, folded it neatly, and put it away, not wanting to ruin it with pasta sauce.

While she was very glad for his interest in such a wholesome endeavor, it didn't take long to be stupefyingly bored, and her thought turned to Gillian, and her dangling the possibility of a baby in front of her. Utter nonsense! The people who had kids fifteen years apart were clearly under some form of temporary amnesia. They'd simply forgotten that cute little babies turned into surly teenagers who wanted nothing more than to not spend their time with you. Luckily, she'd brought her knitting, and she gave one half of her focus to Aiden, and the other to the lightweight scarf she was making that would match Gillian's raincoat.

Once the meet had finished, with Aiden's team having come in ninth out of twelve teams, they dropped his new friend Clive off at his home and went out for a quick meal. Aiden chose hamburgers, and, now that Torie had so little input concerning his diet, she went along without a word of complaint. She'd never guessed that not being in charge could feel so utterly wonderful.

CHAPTER THIRTY-THREE

THREE DAYS BEFORE SHE WAS to leave Scotland, Torie picked Aiden up to head to the mall to purchase some Christmas presents for the family. Oddly, now that she was on the verge of being unemployed, she felt free to loosen her purse strings and give Aiden a hundred pounds to spend. He was pleased, and being in a good mood made him a little more talkative than normal. Or maybe he liked being with her more since she wasn't riding him as hard.

She kept feeling like she might cry, knowing this was the last time they'd do something like this for quite a while. Leave it to Aiden to snap out of his funk just when she was about to leave. If he'd been this way for the last year… That was a ridiculous wish. Growing up was hard for kids, especially once their hormones took over. All in all, Aiden was doing just fine, and once he got used to Piotr, there was every chance he'd prosper.

They walked around the large mall, looking at the very expensive things in the windows. Aiden didn't seem to have a firm idea about what he wanted to buy, but Torie wasn't going to argue if he wanted to purchase robots for everyone. She'd *given* him the money, and his choices were his own.

They stood in front of an expensive women's clothing store, with him eyeing the mannequins critically. "Do you think Mum would like jeans? She just has the one pair, I think."

Historically, Kirsty had worn leggings, black ones, usually paired with a couple of T-shirts that were ripped or had the sleeves removed. But since Piotr now saw her every day she'd begun to dress more conservatively. Torie wasn't sure if that was her choice, or if Piotr had asked her to change, but she looked more like a responsible adult now. "I'm sure she'd love some. She normally wears one size larger than I do. Do you want me to try some on?"

"I guess," he said, still staring with narrowed eyes. "But if I buy those I'll only have forty pounds left. I've got to get something for Piotr, I guess, but I want to spend most of it on Granny and Granda."

"It's tough to make decisions like this, isn't it?"

"Uh-huh. Did you know Mum's quitting her job?" he asked, just dropping that like it was of no importance.

"She's *what?*"

"I heard her tell Piotr she was giving notice today. Two weeks."

"Why in the world would she quit the job I…?" She shut her mouth firmly. Aiden didn't need to know how hard Torie had worked to get her the position as a cashier at the local grocery superstore. If Torie hadn't gone to school with the hiring manager, or personally guaranteed she'd pay for monthly drug testing…

"I think Piotr doesn't want her to work at all. Like it looks bad for him if she's got to. At least at such a shit job."

"That's not a shit job," Torie said, scowling at him. "There's no such thing as a shit job. And stop saying 'shit.' It doesn't make you sound older to curse, Aiden. It honestly makes you seem younger."

He raised his chin in a defiant look, then stared back at the display window. She knew this was just a phase, and that he'd eventually mature enough to be a delight to be around, just like he'd been for the first twelve years of his life. But that didn't make these long, awkward silences any easier to take.

They left without purchasing a thing, which Torie was actually pleased by. Seeing Aiden be thoughtful with his hundred pounds was a massive relief. He might delay his shopping until Christmas Eve, he might not spend the money at all, or he might spend it all on himself in the end. But at least he didn't rush to spend it the moment it had hit his hands. That was a promising sign.

It was getting late, and she was tempted to just drop Aiden off, but she did her usual and found a place to park to walk him all the way up to the flat. She trusted him to go in, but she was using every opportunity to stay close, beginning to feel an emptiness in her soul at the prospect of leaving. Even leaving for a situation she knew would be best for all of them in the end didn't lessen the sting of loss.

Piotr was in the kitchen, cooking up something that smelled of spices she wasn't familiar with. Torie poked her head in and said, "I brought Aiden home. Have a good night!"

"Wait. Please," he said, wiping his hands clean. "Why don't you stay? Kirsty will be home in a while. We can talk then."

"I've got to leave for work at four thirty. Doesn't she get home after six today?"

"Yes, yes," he said, with a frown crossing over his features. "Maybe it is better to talk now."

"Talk about…?"

"Aiden?" he called out. "Will you come, please?"

It took him longer than was polite, but he reappeared. "Yeah?"

"Sit. Please," he said, pointing to the dining table. They both did, and Piotr stood at the head of the table and put on what looked like a forced smile. "Kirsty and I decide it is better for us to move home."

"Home?" Aiden said, looking up, eyes wide. "This is home."

"*My* home. My mother is old now and cannot move so fast," he said. "It's hard for her now. Kirsty can help."

"Kirsty's going to care for your mother?" Torie's mouth dropped open. "She's agreed to this?"

"Yes. Yes. Of course. We have big house. Plenty of room. They will love each other."

"They haven't met?"

"They speak on telephone. Everyone will get along."

Aiden jumped to his feet, his cheeks so pink he looked like he'd been lying in the sun for a full day. "I'm not going to Poland!" He whirled around to stared at Torie. "I'm not!"

"Maybe we'd better talk about this some more," Torie said, addressing Piotr. "How could Aiden even go to school? He doesn't speak Polish."

"He will learn. I didn't know English when I came here." He reached over and slapped him on the back. "He's a smart boy. There is school for language. He goes for some months, then is fine."

"Does your mother speak English?"

He shook his head. "We will all teach her. All will be well."

"I'm not going!" Aiden raced out the door, without even stopping to put his coat on. Torie leapt up to go after him, but Piotr put a restraining hand on her arm.

"Let him go and be mad for a while. He'll get over it."

"Piotr, I didn't say this when he was here, but he's not like you. You were obviously a hard-working guy who wanted to live here. I can't tell you how impressed I am with your English skills, but it had to have taken you more than a few months to get them."

"Young minds learn faster," he said blithely.

"Not when they don't try."

He made a face, then said, "I don't want to offend, but you and Kirsty treat him like a baby. You don't make him try hard."

She opened her mouth to complain, then realized she couldn't honestly do that. "Let's say you're right. You can't expect a kid to change in a matter of weeks! When are you planning on moving?"

"Soon. I have a job to finish, then we go."

"I'm leaving for America in three days!"

"This is why I tell you now," he said patiently. "There is no worry. Aiden will come. He must."

"I don't know that's true," she said, grabbing her coat and heading out to find her nephew, who was undoubtedly somewhere close by, shivering in the cold.

✤ ✤ ✤

Once a quarter, Gillian and Ron went to New York, accompanied by all of the other marketing VPs. It was a chance for all of them to sit in a room with their primary advertising agency and make sure they were working synergistically. She'd been preparing for the meeting all week, and they'd been at it for two hours when her phone buzzed. She'd gotten into the habit of turning it off during meetings, but she had it set so texts from Torie came through no matter what. The device was lying face-down on the table, and she waited until one of the creatives started a PowerPoint presentation, having to dim the lights, to flip it over and take a look.

Just three words, but they made her heart start to race. "CALL ME NOW!"

There was no possible way to step out. Her boss and all of her peers surrounded her, and Ron had very little patience for people who interrupted meetings to take phone calls. She was forced to sit there, her anxiety building with every second, mind racing with what could possibly be such an emergency for Torie to make that kind of demand. For fifteen minutes she fidgeted and rocked in her chair, probably looking like a child who had to pee.

Finally, the guy who was running the meeting took a look at his watch and said, "I don't know about all of you, but I'd love some coffee." The door opened, and two very attractive young women brought in trays of bagels and croissants and donuts that looked about as good as a donut had ever hoped to look. But Gillian couldn't have been less interested in food. She jumped to her feet and said, "Be right back," then raced for a window, where she might have a better signal.

She was panting with worry when Torie picked up.

"What's wrong?"

"We've got a crisis. Last night, Piotr announced that the whole family is moving to Krakow so Kirsty can take care of his aged mother."

"What? *Kirsty's* going to do that?"

"That part's going to be interesting, isn't it? But that's not what I'm worried about. Aiden has announced that he will not go. Not that I blame him. Piotr's plan is to send him to some immersion program for a few months, then plunk him into a Polish-language high school next autumn."

"What do you mean he won't go? He's not even fourteen. He's got to go."

"I didn't say he didn't *want* to go, Gillian. When he says he won't go, he means it. They'll have to tranquilize him to get him on a plane."

"Have you talked—"

"Of course I talked to him! I brought him here after I found him wandering the streets in his shirtsleeves. He stayed overnight, even though my sister was upset with me for keeping him. My mother tried to talk some sense into him while I went to the market, but she didn't make any progress."

"What does he plan on doing?"

"He wants to stay here. My mother did me no favors by telling him that he could. I'm still so angry with her I can barely see straight…"

"That's out of the question. Even I can see they wouldn't be able to handle him."

"That's why I'm calling. We've got to figure out an alternative. One he'll agree to."

"I'm locked in a meeting right now. An important one. I'll have a few minutes after lunch. Can I call you then?"

"I've got a million things to do today. I'll call you at seven your time." She let out a heavy sigh. "Please work with me on this, Gillian. We have *got* to come up with a solution."

❧ ❧ ❧

She'd only had an hour to herself, but Gillian had used it well. Her peers were on their way to a private dining room at a very trendy restaurant, but instead of changing into something more appropriate for dinner, her stated reason for peeling off from the group, she'd snuck off to a conference room to do some research. Her mind was whirling with details when her phone rang. "Hi," she said, her heart going out to Torie as she gazed at her strained expression.

"What an awful day," she moaned. "I spent the morning arguing with my mother, the early evening arguing with my sister, and the rest of the evening with Aiden, trying to convince him to listen to reason. Now I want to inject him with something, stick him into a steamer trunk, and ship him off to Poland, no return address."

"That seems a little harsh," Gillian said, forcing herself to joke. "I think I've got a more humane idea."

"You do?" Torie looked at her with such trust, like she'd been sure Gillian would figure this out.

"I think so. There's a British school in Krakow. He'll be able to speak English for all of his classes, and at least some of the kids will be native English speakers."

"That's not what I was hoping for," Torie said, staring into the camera, unblinking.

"Okay. If he really doesn't want to leave home, there's an excellent boarding school not too far from you. People from the royal family have gone there, so it must be good. It costs a ton, but I'll dig into my savings to pay for his tuition."

"I was hoping you'd come up with the obvious solutions," Torie interrupted, "but since you haven't mentioned them, I will. There are only two. Either I stay here, or he comes to America with me."

"What?" Gillian stared at the camera. "You can't be serious."

"I've never been more serious."

"But…" She swallowed, feeling like she might throw up. "We're going to be newlyweds, Torie. The whole point of your moving here was to spend time alone. We need that to get our marriage off on a good foot. You're the one who insisted on that."

Torie continued to stare into the camera. Then she said, very quietly, "Whether I'm married or single, I'm responsible for Aiden. My sister should have primary responsibility, of course, but when she drops the ball I have to pick it up."

"But she hasn't dropped the ball—"

"She's planning on uprooting him to go to a place he's never been. To live with a woman he's never met. And to speak a difficult language that he doesn't know. All of that so she can screw up at some point—probably soon—and wind up right back in Scotland. Jobless."

"You don't know that," Gillian soothed.

"No, I don't. But Kirsty isn't a caretaker. She'll open a can of soup for the old woman, then spend the day watching TV. If Piotr doesn't get tired of her within a year, I don't know much about human nature. Either he'll divorce her, or she'll leave him when he starts demanding more of her. Uprooting Aiden will have been a totally unnecessary waste."

"Give her a chance! Come on, Torie. She's been clean and sober for longer than I've known you. She's made so much progress!"

"You can't change your personality. You know I love her, but she's lazy. And when Piotr sees just how lazy she is, he'll dump her."

"I still think we have to stand back and let her try. Aiden's her son."

"I am not going to let her experiment with him." She was so angry she was seething. "Shouldn't you get busy?"

"With what?"

"Cancelling my plane ticket, then calling off the wedding. I can't come to America."

"But—"

"We'll get married in Scotland." Even from over three thousand miles away, Gillian could see her throat constrict as she swallowed. "If you're willing to move here and live with me and Aiden, that is. If not..." She leaned close to the camera and stared into it, unblinking. "I will miss you every moment until the day I die." Then she cut the connection, leaving Gillian to stare at the screen, as stunned as if she'd been hit in the face with a brick.

☙ ☙ ☙

At midnight, Gillian paced across her tiny hotel room floor, imposing on Kara, who'd kindly agreed to stay up and talk after Gillian's interminable dinner.

"I've never seen her so angry," she said quietly.

"Do you think you could reason with me if Ben wanted to take the kids to a new country they didn't want to go to?"

"Bad analogy," Gillian said, annoyed. "This is like your sister and her husband taking little what's her name to a country she didn't want to go to. You'd be upset, and you'd feel bad for the kid, but you wouldn't try to kidnap her."

"Madison," she said, clearly equally annoyed. "My sister's daughter is named Madison."

"I knew that," Gillian said, even though she would have believed any name Kara had thrown out. "What would you do if Madison was being taken to... Sweden?"

"Bad analogy," Kara said, lobbing her argument right back at her. "I didn't raise Madison. My sister's not in a new relationship with a guy she doesn't know all that well, nor has she signed on to nurse a stranger who doesn't speak English. But if all of those situations were true—you're darned right I'd get involved. And if Madison was at the point where she was threatening to run away rather than go, I'd take her in. Even if my sister fought me tooth and nail."

"That's you," Gillian grumbled. "Madison knows you're a soft touch. One more wouldn't hurt around there, anyway. Three kids or four...same difference."

Kara didn't respond for a very long time. So long Gillian started to itch. But she was the kind of person who thought things through before she spoke. Very lawyerly. "I'm sympathetic," she said quietly. "I know this isn't what you want. I wouldn't want it either. But it's what you've got. If you mean that 'for better or worse' vow you're planning on taking, you might want to look at this from Torie's perspective."

"I am!"

"No, you're not. Her sister's got a bad track record, Gillian. That's simply the truth. And while I hope she's got it together and has picked a great guy, it's just as likely that Torie's right. Uprooting Aiden and dragging him to Poland against his will, only to send him right back when things go badly isn't a great plan. Especially for a kid who's had a hard time fitting in. It sounds like he's just started to get his feet under him."

"Why can't we just get married like other people? Haven't I waited long enough?"

"You have. But you can't guarantee your plans will come true. You can only make them and hope."

❧ ❧ ❧

Gillian stayed up as late as she could, trying to hold off calling until morning in Scotland. But she'd fallen asleep sitting up in bed, and now had to race to get downstairs for her breakfast meeting with Ron. They had a lot to do to prepare for a meeting with an EVP of the largest big-box retailer in the country. The guy's home office was in Arkansas, but he was always eager to schedule meetings in New York, even in December. He was a big theater fan, and always made it a point to catch the latest shows.

They had a full day planned, meetings in the morning, lunch at a place theater people frequented, more meetings, then dinner at a *very* fancy restaurant before taking in the most popular show on Broadway.

She rolled her suitcase behind her, and walked up to Ron's table. As his head tilted back so their eyes met, he stood up, startled. "Why do you have your suitcase? What's wrong? Are you sick?"

He should have been a doctor. She'd never met anyone so attuned to your physical well-being while simultaneously able to completely ignore the most obvious signs of emotional distress. She'd once watched him chide a guy for coming into work when he had a cold, oblivious that the guy was crying because he'd just learned his mother had died.

"I'm fine. But I have a family emergency, and I've got to leave."

"Leave?" He looked like he wasn't sure what that word even meant. "You don't mean now. You can't."

"Right now. I can catch a ten o'clock flight if I rush."

"There's no ten o'clock nonstop." They'd both memorized the schedule for every plane that made the trip between any New York City airport and Columbus.

"My mistake," she said, not wanting to reveal where she was heading. "I meant the eleven o'clock."

He took a look at her bag, then started to shake his head. "I can let you leave after lunch. You'll make the three thirty if traffic's not bad." Shrugging, he said, "That's the best I can do." He paused for a second, then said, "You don't have to donate blood or anything, right?"

Since he'd been at her birthday party, he now knew she had a sister. She'd hated that at the time, but at least that might have let him know she was a human being, with connections and ties that she needed to honor.

"No, that's not it. But I've still got to go." She clapped him on the arm and tried to smile. "You don't need me. You know my products as well as I do."

"That's not the point, Gillian," he said, his gaze becoming more focused. She'd often thought he had eyes like a snake, but when you stood close to him the comparison was even more chilling. "You're the one with the good relationship with Harley."

That was true. She'd made over ten trips to Arkansas to develop a strong tie with the guy who contributed almost twenty percent to her bottom line. She was sure he bought her products because his customers wanted them, not because he was fond of her, but he *was* fond of her, and Ron knew it. They both also knew that Harley thought Ron was a pain in the butt. A lot of clients loved him, but a few avoided him whenever possible, and Harley was the leader of that group.

She flashed on Torie telling her that being so closeted at work could hurt as much as it could protect her. At that moment, it all made sense. She couldn't explain her situation without letting him know her human side. The side she'd tried to protect since the day she'd started to work for Channing Brothers. Without taking the time to let herself bail, she closed her eyes and said, "I'm getting married."

His mouth opened and stayed that way for a few moments. "You're what?" He started to laugh. "Unbelievable! We'd all decided you were..." He trailed off, unwilling to reveal whatever demeaning characterization he and his clique had labeled her with. "Jesus! Who's the lucky guy?"

This was it. Pull the trigger or admit she didn't truly hold a single morsel of pride in her heart. She pulled the trigger. "The lucky guy is actually a lucky woman." As his eyes grew to comical proportions, she nodded.

"You're...?" He was still staring, and he'd turned slightly pale.

"I am," she nodded, sweat sliding down her back to gather at her waistband.

"Oh, shit!" He started to babble, stumbling over his words. "When I make jokes about…gay things…those are just jokes. You know that, right? I don't mean anything I say. That's just how guys fool around." He slammed his mouth shut and choked a little. "I don't mean that we fool around with each other. That's not…" His eyes closed as he tried to compose himself. "We're just having fun. You get that, right?"

She was so close to unloading on him. To telling him that he'd deeply insulted her and every other even vaguely gay person on the staff. But he'd done the same thing to every woman, every religious minority, and every Michigan football fan. The only groups he didn't "joke" about were racial minorities, and that was only because Kenny, one of her senior directors, was black. Ron was simply a jerk. A jerk she had to get along with for at least another year. In a nanosecond, she had to do the calculation; either tell him what she thought of him and get a moment's pleasure, or keep her mouth shut and protect her job. If she'd been single, she would have unloaded on him. No question. She'd put up with him for far too long, and he deserved to have a fastball thrown right into his beady little eyes. But she wasn't single. She'd promised Torie she'd stay long enough to vest in that pension plan, and she was going to do it no matter what.

"We both know you say a lot of things that could land you in some very hot water," she said, purposefully keeping her tone mild. "But I understand you're just joking. It's not like you'd ever do anything to violate the corporate non-discrimination policy."

"No! Jesus! I'd never do that!" He was the color of milk at this point, and Gillian let herself feel a tiny burst of pleasure at his discomfort.

"Of course you wouldn't. We're all buddies, right?"

"We are. We are!" he insisted, almost whimpering.

"You're not going to change how you think of me because of this, right?"

"Right!" He stuck his hand out and they shook. "Congratulations on your wedding. It's…" he trailed off, clearly confused. "This afternoon?"

"No, Ron. It's not this afternoon. My fiancée lives in Scotland, and she's scheduled to move here on Friday. We just found out she might have to bring her nephew with her. I've got to get over there and see how that's going to work. It's complicated," she said, "but I truly have to be there. Today."

"All right," he said. "I'll tell Harley you're sick."

"Good idea. He's taking steroids for a bad attack of arthritis. He'll appreciate that I'm staying away if I have anything infectious."

"Okay. I'll say you came down with the flu overnight."

"I appreciate that," she said, smiling at him. "Want anything from Scotland?"

He was still standing, seemingly unable to move. But his head tilted again and he said, "Are other people from work going to your wedding?"

"Um, no," she said, nearly laughing in his face. "Just family. I don't want to make a big deal out of it at work, so I haven't told anyone. I like to keep my private life private."

"Oh, good idea," he said, clearly relieved. "That's a really good idea. I won't say anything."

"You can if you want, but I'm not going to. Work is for work, not socializing. We do *that* with our clients." She clapped him on the back. "Thanks for handling Harley. Word of advice about him. Talk less. Listen more. And whatever you do, let him say whether he liked the play, then agree with him, even if your ears are bleeding."

Gillian not only had to sit in coach, she had a six-hour layover in Boston, and would face another, shorter one in Amsterdam. Twenty-three hours elapsed time, and halfway around the world to negotiate with a thirteen-year-old.

By the time she got to Aberdeen, Aiden's school was letting out. She could have kicked herself for not telling Torie she was coming, but she hadn't wanted to get her hopes up. If she and Aiden couldn't reach an agreement… She wasn't going to let herself even think about that. They simply *had* to.

Feeling like a predator, she stood near the entrance of the building and watched carefully. She'd always had the notion that a lot of Scottish people had red hair, and meeting the Gunns had just confirmed that belief. But it took ten minutes of staring to find one copper-haired boy emerge. Aiden wore a huge backpack that was clearly too heavy for him. He had to lean forward just to keep his balance, but the friend he walked next to was carrying a load too. She hadn't planned on what she'd say, so she walked right over to him and said, "Hey. Got a minute?"

His head jerked up and he stared at her. "What are you doing here?"

"I need to talk to you. Can you leave?"

His friend was giving her a look that suggested he was going to call the police.

"Um…" Aiden gestured to his friend with his head. "Go on ahead. I might have to skip lab."

"Sure?" the kid said, still studying her. "You should tell Mr. Lockwell if you're gonna skip."

"Tell him my aunt showed up and I had to go home."

"Your aunt?"

"Yeah," he said. "My aunt. She's American."

"Really?" The kid's eyes lit up.

"I've been there so long I've lost my accent," she said, lying through her teeth.

"Okay," the kid said. "See you." Then he hoisted his pack and continued on his way, looking just as awkward and gawky as Aiden.

"I guess it's tough to explain who I really am," Gillian said, having a burst of empathy for the kid.

"Yeah." He nodded, not meeting her eyes. "I haven't told anyone."

She let out a laugh. "I haven't told hardly anyone, and I'm the one getting married. Want to go for a bite to eat?"

"Don't you have a hotel or something? A lot of kids from school go to the places close by…"

"Fine," she said. "I just got off the plane, so I don't have a room. Is there a hotel near here?"

"There's one on my way home. Is that okay?"

"It will have to be, since you don't want to be seen in public with me." He just shrugged, not seeming to have a lick of shame about being such a little jerk. They started to walk, with Gillian pulling her carryon behind her.

"What are you doing here?" he asked again. "And why do you want to see me?"

"Take a guess." She put an arm around his shoulders, and he didn't shrug it off, his lack of rejection seeming like a good sign. "With you refusing to move, you've upset your aunt. I thought I'd come see if I can help you decide what to do."

He was shaking his head before she finished her sentence. "I'm not going. I don't like Piotr, I don't want to learn Polish, and I don't want to live with some strange lady."

"Well, when you put it that way, it doesn't sound too appealing to me either," she said, giving him a smile.

"Are you going to try to talk me into it? 'Cause you can't. I'm staying with my grandparents. Just like before."

He stopped in front of a hotel, one that might have been nice when it had been built—a hundred and fifty years ago. She raised an eyebrow, but she was so tired she hardly cared. They had plenty of rooms, probably because there were other hotels in Aberdeen, and they were soon taking a creaky, tiny elevator up to the third floor.

The room was small, and dark, but there were two upholstered chairs, and that's all they needed for their clandestine confab. Oddly, there was a mini-bar, the first she'd encountered, and she opened it up to take out a bottle of water. "Want anything?"

He was on his knees, his head almost inside the little refrigerator, in the blink of an eye. "I can have stuff?" he asked, swiveling his head to meet her eyes.

His voracious appetite might cost her as much as the room would, but she couldn't look into those big dark eyes, so like his aunt's, and refuse such a simple request. It dawned on her that he might have never stayed in a hotel.

"Why not. Just don't eat so much that you don't have an appetite for dinner."

"I always have an appetite," he said, looking over the offerings that didn't need refrigeration. He took two little bags of crisps, two candy bars and an Irn-Bru. She still recalled her astonishment when Torie had told her the bright orange soda outsold Coke products in Scotland, a fact she found even harder to believe than Aberdeen getting less rain than Columbus.

While Aiden tore into the first bag, Gillian tried to get her thoughts together. Going over the scenario during the entire flight hadn't made this any easier. So she acted like she did when she had to do something scary at work. She stopped thinking, and started talking. "I did some research, and I think there are three viable alternatives for you. One is to stay in Scotland and transfer to a boarding school. There's a good one not too far from Aberdeen."

His head shook as he stuffed chips into his mouth. "My grandparents can take me. They're happy to. Granny said."

"I'm sure they would. But they're getting older and having a kid is a lot of work. I think they'd struggle."

"What else?" he asked, clearly losing the euphoria of having found a treasure trove of junk food.

"There's a school in Krakow that's made for kids who don't speak Polish. It's a small school, and you'd be able to go home at night."

"No way. I'm not going to Poland at all."

"All of your classes would be in English. It's a new school. Top-notch facilities…"

"No," he said again, his expression darkening.

"Okay. Have you ever considered living in America?"

"What?" he asked, clearly stunned.

"Would you be interested in moving to America…" She checked her watch, so jet-lagged she wasn't sure of the day. "Tomorrow?"

"Yes!" he yelped, a tentative smile settling onto his face. "You're joking, right?"

"I'm really not in the mood to joke." She took another breath. "Here's the problem. I don't know anything about kids."

"I'm not a kid," he grumbled.

"You are. I'm good with adults, but I haven't spent much time with kids. If you come to live with us, you'd have to give me time to get used to you."

"What's that mean? I'm not any trouble." He narrowed his eyes for a moment. "Do they have robotics where you live?"

"How do I know? I didn't know robotics existed until Torie told me about them." She gathered herself and tried again. "You'd have to step your game up, Aiden. You'd have to listen to us. To *me*. Even though I've admitted I don't know what I'm doing. You'd have to actively try to fit into our brand new family."

"It wouldn't be *my* family," he said, now a little unsure. "My mum and my grandparents are my family. And my aunt," he added softly.

"Hey, I understand you don't think of me as family. I'm in the same boat as you are in that regard. But I love your aunt very much, and I'd do anything to make her happy."

"Yeah, I can see that."

"Torie says she can't be happy if you're not happy." Shrugging, she added, "I don't see any other options."

"Do you like me?" he asked, clearly tentative.

"I don't *dis*like you, but I honestly haven't formed my own opinion yet. Your aunt is crazy about you, though, and that's good enough for me." She looked him in the eye. "Do you like me?"

"I don't *dis*like you either," he said, nodding. "You like to have fun, and you're nice to my aunt. She's a lot happier since she met you." He pulled his phone from his pocket. "I love the phone you got me. And my drone. Once Clive saw I had one, he invited me to join the robotics team. We use it all the time."

"I'm glad. But I'm serious about how little I know about kids. I promise I'll screw some things up. I'm sure I'll hurt your feelings, or ask you to do things you're not ready for. I'll probably treat you like an adult, even though you're not."

"I think that's okay." He tossed an empty bag onto the small table between them, then opened the next. "Does my aunt want me to come to America? She seems awfully sick of me."

"She's not sick of you. But she is worried." She moved the big menu for room service that blocked her view of the kid. "She worries about you a lot. I hope you know that's because she loves you so much."

"I guess," he admitted, not meeting her eyes. "She's just on me all the time. She watches me more now than she did when I was a baby."

"You couldn't leave the house on your own when you were a baby. You can get into more trouble now."

"Why does everybody think I'm going to get into trouble?" he demanded, his voice rising. "I'm not my mum!"

"I don't think anyone thinks you are," she soothed, realizing as she said it that Torie wasn't far from doing that. "Every good parent worries about their kid. Especially when a kid's your age. They haven't figured you out yet."

"What's that mean?"

"Well," she said, not even sure what she'd meant. But it became clear as she considered her comment. "You're not a kid any more, but you're not an adult, either. You're in that middle phase. The place where you stop doing what you're told to do and start making your own decisions. At this point, the adults in your life don't know what those decisions will be." She laughed softly. "If you're like I was at your age, you're in the dark, too."

He was concentrating on getting the potato chip shards from the bag, and acted like he hadn't heard a thing she'd said. But he had to have been listening, so she kept going.

"There's one big thing I'm worried about," she said, waiting for him to respond.

He didn't, not in words, at least. But he turned his head and gave her a quick look from the corner of his eye.

"I live in a big city, with a bunch of high schools, but if you came to live with us you'd probably go to one close to my house." She had his attention now, with those big, dark eyes watching her warily. "People in the neighborhood are going to know your aunt and I are married."

He looked away, sullen again.

"If my neighbors know, their kids will know. So the kids in your school will figure out you live with your aunt and her wife. I know that's not…" She fought for the right word. "I know you'd probably rather people didn't know that."

"Why can't you just be people who live together? A lot of my friends have relatives living with them. Be like that."

She shook her head slowly. "I promise we're not going to go out of our way to announce that we're gay. We won't ever sit in the car and kiss when we come pick you up." She took a breath and continued, "But we're not ashamed of loving each other, Aiden. We're not going to hide."

"I don't like it," he said, his voice cracking when he tried to lower it. "I liked her better when she was normal." He must have heard himself, for he tried to rephrase. "Like everybody else."

"She's not like everybody else," Gillian said. "She's not like *any*one else. Everyone's kind of unique once you really get to know people. But Torie loves you more than anything in the world."

"Except you," he said, roughly ripping open a candy bar.

"We have a different kind of love. But I can guarantee you that she hasn't lost one ounce of the love she had for you before she met me. In fact, she's going to call off the wedding if you won't come with us."

"She will not," he scoffed. "It's all she talks about."

"I know that. But she said it, and I'm sure she meant it. If you won't come to America, I'm going to quit my job and move here." She shrugged. "I don't know anything about oil, so I'll probably have to work out of Glasgow or Edinburgh. That means we'd live there. All three of us."

He let his head tilt back to rest on the back of the chair. The sigh he let out made him sound like an old man. "Either way, I have to leave Aberdeen."

"I think so. Neither your mom nor your aunt want you to stay with your grandparents."

"I want to stay with my mum," he said, with his voice breaking. "Why do I have to move to do that?"

"Because your mom's moving, and she wants you with her. Why don't you at least think about giving Poland a try. Do you want to see the website of the British school I found?"

"I guess," he said, that small concession feeling like a huge win.

She took her laptop out of her travel tote and opened it. "I want to make sure you understand that I think you'd like America. Even though I'm not great with kids, I promise I'll try to make things as good as I can for you."

"Maybe. But you're not my mom, and neither is my aunt."

"I know that." Her computer was almost ready, and as she typed in her name and room number she said, "It means a lot to you to live with your mom, doesn't it."

He nodded, slowly, then wiped at his eyes with the back of a hand, clearly trying to hide his tears. "She's my mum," he said, putting a profound statement into very few words.

"Yeah, she is. And I'm sure it means an awful lot to her to have you go to Poland with her and Piotr." She smiled at him, touched by how emotionally fragile he seemed. He'd gone from a sullen teenager to a child in a matter of moments. The change made her a little dizzy, but it also made him much more human. More three-dimensional than the stereotype of a difficult teen.

"Everything was fine before Piotr and..." He took a breath, trying that one over. "Before Piotr showed up."

"Yeah." She found the website and passed him the laptop, watching as he carefully paged through, looking at the photos of kids in the brightly-colored classrooms, laden with impressive technology. "Change can be pretty awful. But your mom seems happy, don't you think?"

"I guess." He continued to look, lingering on a page with a group of girls about his age, most of them pretty darned cute if they were in your preferred demographic. "Everybody speaks English here?"

"All classes are in English. But some of the kids are from different countries, so they won't have great English skills yet. You'd be pretty far ahead of a lot of them."

"That'd be a first," he said, smirking.

"I'm being serious, Aiden. I didn't speak to anyone at the school, but my friend called and had a long talk with the headmaster while I was on my flight. Since many of the kids are from Poland, they're struggling to learn English. You'd probably be at the top of the heap."

He looked at her sharply, resembling his aunt so much in that moment that Gillian's heart skipped a beat. The kid might not be a star at school, but he was bright. There was no doubt about that. "You really mean that? You think I might not be at the bottom of the class?"

"Being able to speak the language would give you a huge advantage. I'm sure of that."

"And I could live with my mum? You're sure I wouldn't have to stay over?"

"Positive. You'd live at home." She felt a little guilty about offering what was, in essence, a bribe, but she had to get the kid to make a decision. "I know you'd be fine during the school year, but you might be bored during holidays. If you wanted to, you could come to America during your school breaks. Your aunt's not going to be working, so she'd have plenty of time to spend with you."

He stared at her for a minute, with her nearly able to see the competing urges tumbling around in his head. "Okay," he said, thoughtfully enlarging one of the photos of some students to look at it more carefully. "I'll give it a try."

"Be back in a moment," she said, desperate to use the bathroom. Seconds later, she almost levitated when someone banged on the door so hard they might have snapped the hardware. "The housekeepers around here are a little aggressive," Gillian called out. "Will you tell them we don't need anything?"

She finished up, and washed her hands, then spent a moment taking a look at herself in the harshly lit bathroom. She looked about as she felt, tired, anxious, and pale, with dark smudges under her eyes.

"Aiden?" she said when she was certain she heard voices.

She flung the door open to see Torie holding the boy in a loose embrace, stroking his flushed cheek with her hand as they spoke quietly.

"I'm so sorry I didn't let you know I was coming," Gillian said, stopping short when Torie looked up with such a love-filled expression it nearly stopped her heart.

"I thought he'd been kidnapped," she said. "I've never been so glad to have Aiden disobey my very clear orders to never wander off." She started to let him go, then gripped his cheek and tugged on it. "Today I'm happy you snuck away." She pointed her phone at Gillian. "The ability of this phone to track my boy kept me from losing my mind."

As Aiden stepped back, Gillian's breath was squeezed from her body when Torie flung herself at her. She grasped Gillian's face and held it tenderly for a few seconds, then pressed their lips together, with the same nourishing sensation settling upon her like it always did the first time they kissed.

After a few seconds, Gillian pulled away and murmured, "We're embarrassing your nephew."

"He's going to have to get used to it." She squeezed Gillian just as hard as she had before. "Aiden tells me you're the first person in his life to not treat him like a baby."

Aiden's dark eyes went wide. "I didn't say that! I just said that—"

"He said you offered to pack both of us onto a plane tomorrow, but you didn't *order* him to come with us. You gave him the facts and the time to make up his mind."

Once again, she was rendered breathless by a desperate hug. Torie was right in her face, murmuring, "I love you more at this minute than I ever have."

Aiden's head was practically on the table, but he was going to have to get used to this. His aunt was going to be hugged and kissed and cuddled far more than he would ever be comfortable with. But that's just how things were done in Columbus, O-hi-o, when the prettiest girl in Scotland and the luckiest soap salesman in the world settled down to live happily ever after.

EPILOGUE

ON FEBRUARY THE FIFTEENTH, GILLIAN stood in the warm Florida sun and adjusted her sunglasses. As her hand dropped away, the sun caught her brand new ring, and she studied it for a moment.

She'd never envisioned herself wearing diamonds, even tiny, round ones. But she was inordinately fond of the band, with each little bit of carbon reminding her of the strength and permanence of her bond with her wife.

It was going to take a while to feel comfortable referring to Torie that way, but she was going to try to make a point of it. Well, not at work, but definitely in their private life. Who knew? Maybe some day she'd talk about Torie at work as easily as she discussed the cleaning power of Bam!, the detergent that blasts soil from your family's clothes with twenty-three powerful enzymes.

"Pink or black?" Torie asked, holding up two different styles of mouse-eared caps.

"Black. Looks better with your hair."

"I thought so too," she said, grinning. "We agree on everything, don't we?"

"So far, but it's only been a day."

Torie rolled her eyes and got back to shopping.

Aiden had so far refused the offer of a hat, T-shirts, and pins. Fourteen was a tough age for a boy who'd not grown up surrounded by rodent goodies to find something that appealed to him. But he'd been a good sport, not actively complaining about a thing. Gillian had been studying the dizzying variety of other options he could partake in, and she approached him. "You like video games, right?"

"A lot. Why?"

"Hold on." She found Piotr over in the T-shirt section, deciding which style looked best on Kirsty. "Hey," she said quietly. "Aiden's bored. Would you be willing to take him over to play video games for a while? It's not too far from here."

He raised his eyebrows, but took a look across the store, seeing Aiden leaning against a post near the entry. "This is too young for him," he agreed. "He doesn't know you can be adult and like it."

"Right. Like our wives," she said, chuckling.

"They like it very much. Too much for my wallet." He kissed Kirsty on the cheek, spoke to her quietly, then went with Gillian as they threaded through the crowd to return to Aiden.

Gillian wasn't sure which of them had convinced Piotr he could reach Aiden better if he used a lighter hand, but they seemed much more fond of each other than they'd been just a few weeks earlier. A small part of her believed Aiden was actually looking forward to moving to Poland at the end of his term, although that was probably pushing it. All she was certain of was that he was going to give it a try.

"We are going to play video games," Piotr announced when they stood in front of Aiden. "No more baby stuff for us."

"All right," Aiden said, breaking into a smile for the first time in hours.

Gillian surreptitiously slipped Piotr two hundred-dollar-bills. She wasn't sure if he truly believed the American custom that the newly married couple had to pay for everything on their family honeymoon, but he hadn't put up a fuss.

"Text us when you're coming back," Gillian said. "There's a lot to do over there, so feel free to stay all day."

"We will," Piotr said, leaning in to kiss her cheek. This was a new development, and she liked it. Anything that made them closer as a family made Torie happy, and Torie's happiness was her number one goal.

After Aiden and Piotr walked away, Torie reappeared, sliding her arm around Gillian's waist. "Now that my sister's busy shopping, and my parents are sitting in the shade eating ice cream, and my nephew and brother-in-law have just taken off, I'm beginning to believe you want to be alone with me. Or are you trying to get rid of all of us so you can finally have a minute to yourself?"

Gillian slid her arms around her new wife and smiled like a contented puppy lying in the sun. "I don't need a single thing. The temperature's perfect, the sun's shining, my sister and her family are entertaining themselves until dinner, and my wife seems very content. All is right in my world."

Torie gave her a robust hug, squeezing her hard. "Even though we're about as far from our preferred Utah honeymoon as you can be and still be in America?"

"Absolutely."

"Even though both of our families are with us?"

"Absolutely. Every one of my honeymoons is going to include our families."

"Really?" she asked, blinking slowly as she studied Gillian. "You're spending every minute making sure everyone else is happy."

"Truly. I'm having a wonderful day. And it's going to get better and better."

Smirking, Torie put on her remarkably good Texas accent and said, "You seem pretty sure of yourself, cowgirl."

"I sure am." After one more discreet kiss to the cheek, Gillian whispered, "Your parents will want to turn in by nine. We'll get our sisters and brothers-in-law and their kids tucked away by midnight. Then, once we're alone, I'll be in my happy place."

"And just where is that?" Torie asked, always receptive to Gillian pouring her heart out.

"In your arms," she said, with her heart swelling with love as the smile on Torie's face grew. "My own private happiest place on earth."

They started for the door, passing the crystal display. The sun was about to set, and it poured into the store as it began its descent. A prism appeared at the corner of Gillian's vision, and she turned her head to see the golden light hit a perfectly detailed crystal lighthouse. It was large, about twelve inches tall, and given the mouse markup, it probably cost a fortune. But she was drawn to it as sure as if it had been a magnet, and she'd been wearing armor. As she reached for it, Torie's hand settled upon her own. Those warm brown eyes twinkled in the setting sun when she said, "Don't you dare buy that—without having it engraved."

THE END

By Susan X Meagher

Novels

Arbor Vitae
All That Matters
Cherry Grove
Girl Meets Girl
The Lies That Bind
The Legacy
Doublecrossed
Smooth Sailing
How To Wrangle a Woman
Almost Heaven
The Crush
The Reunion
Inside Out
Out of Whack
Homecoming
The Right Time
Summer of Love
Chef's Special
Fame
Vacationland
Wait For Me
The Keeper's Daughter

Serial Novel

I Found My Heart In San Francisco

Awakenings: Book One
Beginnings: Book Two
Coalescence: Book Three
Disclosures: Book Four
Entwined: Book Five
Fidelity: Book Six
Getaway: Book Seven
Honesty: Book Eight
Intentions: Book Nine
Journeys: Book Ten
Karma: Book Eleven
Lifeline: Book Twelve
Monogamy: Book Thirteen
Nurture: Book Fourteen
Osmosis: Book Fifteen
Paradigm: Book Sixteen
Quandary: Book Seventeen
Renewal: Book Eighteen
Synchronicity: Book Nineteen
Trust: Book Twenty
United: Book Twenty-One
Vengeance: Book Twenty-Two

Anthologies

Undercover Tales
Outsiders

You can contact Susan at Susan@briskpress.com

Information about all of Susan's books can be found at
www.susanxmeagher.com or www.briskpress.com

To receive notification of new titles, send an email to
newsletters@briskpress.com

facebook.com/susanxmeagher

twitter.com/susanx